DEBT
OF
HONOR

Tom Clancy

DEBT OF HONOR

Thorndike Press • Chivers Press
Thorndike, Maine USA   Bath, Avon, England

This Large Print edition is published by Thorndike Press, USA and by Chivers Press, England.

Published in 1994 in the U.S. by arrangement with G. P. Putnam's Sons.

Published in 1995 in the U.K. by arrangement with HarperCollins Publishers Ltd.

U.S. Hardcover 0-7862-0335-8 (Basic Series Edition)
U.K. Hardcover 0-7451-7783-2 (Windsor Large Print)

The text of this Large Print edition is unabridged.
Other aspects of the book may vary from the original edition.

Set in 16 pt. News Plantin.

Printed in the United States on acid-free paper.

British Library Cataloguing in Publication Data available

Library of Congress Cataloging in Publication Data

Clancy, Tom, 1947–
    Debt of honor / Tom Clancy.
        p.   cm.
    ISBN 0-7862-0335-8 (lg. print : alk. paper)
    1. Large type books. 2. Ryan, Jack (Fictitious character) — Fiction. 3. Intelligence service — United States — Fiction. I. Title.
    [PS3553.L245D43   1994b]
    813'.54—dc20   94-34297

For Mom and Dad

A man's character is his fate
— *Heraclitus*

Prologue

Sunset, Sunrise

In retrospect, it would seem an odd way to start a war. Only one of the participants knew what was really happening, and even that was a coincidence. The property settlement had been moved up on the calendar due to a death in the attorney's family, and so the attorney was scheduled for a red-eye flight, two hours from now, to Hawaii.

It was Mr. Yamata's first property closing on American soil. Though he owned many properties in the continental United States, the actual title transfer had always been handled by other attorneys, invariably American citizens, who had done precisely what they had been paid to do, generally with oversight by one of Mr. Yamata's employees. But not this time. There were several reasons for it. One was that the purchase was personal and not corporate. Another was that it was close, only two hours by private jet from his home. Mr. Yamata had told the settlement attorney that the property would be used for a weekend getaway house. With the astronomical price of real estate in Tokyo, he could buy several hundred acres for the price of a modestly large penthouse apartment in his city of residence. The view from the house he planned to build on the promontory would be breathtaking, a vista of the blue Pacific, other islands

9

of the Marianas Archipelago in the distance, air as clean as any on the face of the earth. For all those reasons Mr. Yamata had offered a princely fee, and done so with a charming smile.

And for one reason more.

The various documents slid clockwise around the circular table, stopping at each chair so that signatures could be affixed at the proper place, marked with yellow Post-It notes, and then it was time for Mr. Yamata to reach into his coat pocket and withdraw an envelope. He took out the check and handed it to the attorney.

"Thank you, sir," the lawyer said in a respectful voice, as Americans always did when money was on the table. It was remarkable how money made them do anything. Until three years before, the purchase of land here by a Japanese citizen would have been illegal, but the right lawyer, and the right case, and the right amount of money had fixed that, too. "The title transfer will be recorded this afternoon."

Yamata looked at the seller with a polite smile and a nod, then he rose and left the building. A car was waiting outside. Yamata got in the front passenger seat and motioned peremptorily for the driver to head off. The settlement was complete, and with it the need for charm.

Like most Pacific islands, Saipan is of volcanic origin. Immediately to the east is the Marianas Trench, a chasm fully seven miles deep where one geological plate dives under another. The result is a collection of towering cone-shaped mountains, of which the islands themselves are merely the tips. The Toyota Land Cruiser followed a moderately smooth road north, winding around Mount Achugao and the Mariana Country Club toward Marpi Point. There it stopped.

Yamata alighted from the vehicle, his gaze resting on some farm structures that would soon be erased, but instead of walking to the building site for his new house, he headed toward the rocky edge of the cliff. Though a man in his early sixties, his stride was strong and purposeful as he moved across the uneven field. If it had been a farm, then it had been a poor one, he saw, inhospitable to life. As this place had been, more than once, and from more than one cause.

His face was impassive as he reached the edge of what the locals called Banzai Cliff. An onshore wind was blowing, and he could see and hear the waves marching in their endless ranks to smash against the rocks at the base of the cliff — the same rocks that had smashed the bodies of his parents and siblings after they, and so many others, had jumped off to evade capture by the advancing U.S. Marines. The sight had horrified the Marines, but Mr. Yamata would never appreciate or acknowledge that.

The businessman clapped his hands once and bowed his head, both to call the attention of the lingering spirits to his presence and to show proper obeisance to their influence over his destiny. It was fitting, he thought, that his purchase of this parcel of land now meant that 50.016% of the real estate on Saipan was again in Japanese hands, more than fifty years since his family's death at American hands.

He felt a sudden chill, and ascribed it to the emotion of the moment, or perhaps the nearness of his ancestors' spirits. Though their bodies had been swept away in the endless surf, surely their *kami* had never left this place, and awaited his return. He shuddered, and buttoned his coat. Yes, he'd build here, but only after he'd done what was necessary first.

First, he had to destroy.

It was one of those perfect moments, half a world away. The driver came smoothly back, away from the ball, in a perfect arc, stopped for the briefest of

11

moments, then accelerated back along the same path, downward now, gaining speed as it fell. The man holding the club shifted his weight from one leg to the other. At the proper moment, his hands turned over as they should, which caused the club head to rotate around the vertical axis, so that when the head hit the ball it was exactly perpendicular to the intended flight path. The sound told the tale — a perfect *tink* (it was a metal-headed driver). That, and the tactile impulse transmitted through the graphite shaft told the golfer everything he needed to know. He didn't even have to look. The club finished its follow-through path before the man's head turned to track the flight of the ball.

Unfortunately, Ryan wasn't the one holding the club.

Jack shook his head with a rueful grin as he bent to tee up his ball. "Nice hit, Robby."

Rear Admiral (lower half) Robert Jefferson Jackson, USN, held his pose, his aviator's eyes watching the ball start its descent, then bounce on the fairway about two hundred fifty yards away. The bounces carried it another thirty or so. He didn't speak until it stopped, dead center. "I meant to draw it a little."

"Life's a bitch, ain't it?" Ryan observed, as he went through his setup ritual. Knees bent, back fairly straight, head down but not too much, the grip, yes, that's about right. He did everything the club pro had told him the previous week, and the week before that, and the week . . . bringing the club back . . . and down . . .

. . . and it wasn't too bad, just off the fairway to the right, a hundred eighty yards, the best first-tee drive he'd hit in . . . forever. And approximately the same distance with his driver that Robby would have gotten with a firm seven-iron. About the only good news was that it was only 7:45 A.M., and there was nobody around to share his embarrassment.

12

At least you cleared the water.

"Been playing how long, Jack?"

"Two whole months."

Jackson grinned as he headed down to where the cart was parked. "I started in my second year at Annapolis. I have a head start, boy. Hell, enjoy the day."

There was that. The Greenbrier is set among the mountains of West Virginia. A retreat that dates back to the late eighteenth century, on this October morning the white mass of the main hotel building was framed with yellows and scarlets as the hardwood trees entered their yearly cycle of autumn fire.

"Well, I don't expect to beat you," Ryan allowed as he sat down in the cart.

A turn, a grin. "You won't. Just thank God you're not working today, Jack. I am."

Neither man was in the vacation business, as much as each needed it, nor was either man currently satisfied with success. For Robby it meant a flag desk in the Pentagon. For Ryan, much to his surprise even now, it had been a return to the business world instead of to the academic slot that he'd wanted — or at least thought he'd wanted — standing there in Saudi Arabia, two and a half years before. Perhaps it was the action, he thought — had he become addicted to it? Jack asked himself, selecting a three-iron. It wouldn't be enough club to make the green, but he hadn't learned fairway woods yet. Yeah, it was the action he craved even more than his occasional escape from it.

"Take your time, and don't try to kill it. The ball's already dead, okay?"

"Yes, sir, Admiral, sir," Jack replied.

"Keep your head down. I'll do the watching."

"All *right*, Robbie." The knowledge that Robbie would not laugh at him, no matter how bad the shot, was somehow worse than the suspicion that he might.

13

On last reflection, he stood a little straighter before swinging. His reward was a welcome sound:

Swat. The ball was thirty yards away before his head came up to see it, still heading left . . . but already showing a fade back to the right.

"Jack?"

"Yeah," Ryan answered without turning his head.

"Your three-iron," Jackson said chuckling, his eyes computing the flight path. "Don't change anything. Do it just like that, every time."

Somehow Jack managed to put his iron back in the bag without trying to wrap the shaft around his friend's head. He started laughing when the cart moved again, up the right-side rough toward Robby's ball, the single white spot on the green, even carpet.

"Miss flying?" he asked gently.

Robby looked at him. "You play dirty, too," he observed. But that was just the way things went. He'd finished his last flying job, screened for flag, then been considered for the post of commander of the Naval Aviation Test Center at Naval Air Station, Patuxent River, Maryland, where his real title would have been Chief Test Pilot, U.S. Navy. But instead Jackson was working in J-3, the operations directorate for the Joint Chiefs of Staff. War Plans, an odd slot for a warrior in a world where war was becoming a thing of the past. It was more career-enhancing, but far less satisfying than the flying billet he'd really wanted. Jackson tried to shrug it off. He'd done his flying, after all. He'd started in Phantoms and graduated to Tomcats, commanded his squadron, and a carrier air wing, then screened early for flag rank on the basis of a solid and distinguished career during which he'd never put a foot wrong. His next job, if he got it, would be as commander of a carrier battle group, something that had once seemed to him a goal beyond the grasp of Fortune itself. Now that he was there, he wondered where all the time had gone, and what lay ahead. "What happens when we get old?"

"Some of us take up golf, Rob."

"Or go back to stocks and bonds," Jackson countered. *An eight-iron*, he thought, *a soft one*. Ryan followed him to his ball.

"Merchant banking," Jack proffered. "It's worked out for you, hasn't it?"

That made the aviator — active or not, Robby would always be a pilot to himself and his friends — look up and grin. "Well, you turned my hundred thou' into something special, Sir John." With that, he took his shot. It was one way to get even. The ball landed, bounced, and finally stopped about twenty feet from the pin.

"Enough to buy me lessons?"

"You sure as hell need 'em." Robby paused and allowed his face to change. "A lot of years, Jack. We changed the world." And that was a good thing, wasn't it?

"After a fashion," Jack conceded with a tight smile. Some people called it an end to history, but Ryan's doctorate was in that field, and he had trouble with the thought.

"You really like it, what you're doing now?"

"I'm home every night, usually before six. I get to see all the Little League games in the summer, and most of the soccer games in the fall. And when Sally's ready for her first date, I won't be in some goddamned VC-20B halfway to nowhere for a meeting that doesn't mean much of anything anyway." Jack smiled in a most comfortable way. "And I think I prefer that even to playing good golf."

"Well, that's a good thing, 'cuz I don't even think Arnold Palmer can fix your swing. But I'll try," Robby added, "just because Cathy asked me to."

Jack's pitch was too strong, forcing him to chip back onto the green — badly — where three putts carded him a seven to Robby's par four.

15

"A golfer who plays like you should swear more," Jackson said on the way to the second tee. Ryan didn't have a chance for a rejoinder.

He had a beeper on his belt, of course. It was a satellite beeper, the kind that could get you almost anywhere. Tunnels under mountains or bodies of water offered some protection, but not much. Jack plucked it off his belt. It was probably the Silicon Alchemy deal, he thought, even though he'd left instructions. Maybe someone had run out of paper clips. He looked at the number on the LCD display.

"I thought your home office was New York," Robby noted. The area code on the display was 202, not the 212 Jack had expected to see.

"It is. I can teleconference most of my work out of Baltimore, but at least once a week I have to catch the Metroliner up there." Ryan frowned. 757-5000. The White House Signals Office. He checked his watch. It was 7:55 in the morning, and the time announced the urgency of the call more clearly than anything else could. It wasn't exactly a surprise, though, was it? he asked himself. Not with what he'd been reading in the papers every day. The only thing unexpected was the timing. He'd expected the call much sooner. He walked to the cart and the golf bag, where he kept his cellular phone. It was the one thing in the bag, actually, that he knew how to use.

It took only three minutes, as an amused Robby waited in the cart. Yes, he was at The Greenbrier. Yes, he knew that there was an airport not too far from there. Four hours? Less than an hour out and back, no more than an hour at his destination. Back in time for dinner. He'd even have time to finish his round of golf, shower, and change before he left, Jack told himself, folding the phone back up and dropping it in the pocket of the golf bag. That was one advantage of the world's best chauffeur service. The problem was that once they had you, they never

16

liked to let go. The convenience of it was designed only to make it a more comfortable mode of confinement. Jack shook his head as he stood at the tee, and his distraction had a strange effect. The drive up the second fairway landed on the short grass, two hundred ten yards downrange, and Ryan walked back to the cart without a single word, wondering what he'd tell Cathy.

The facility was brand-new and spotless, but there was something obscene about it, the engineer thought. His countrymen hated fire, but they positively loathed the class of object that this room was designed to fabricate. He couldn't shake it off. It was like the buzz of an insect in the room — unlikely, since every molecule of the air in this clean-room had gone through the best filtration system his country could devise. His colleagues' engineering excellence was a source of pride to this man, especially since he was among the best of them. It would be that pride that sustained him, he knew, dismissing the imaginary buzz as he inspected the fabrication machinery. After all, if the Americans could do it, and the Russians, and the English, and the French, and the Chinese, and even the Indians and Pakistanis, then why not them? There was a symmetry to it, after all.

In another part of the building, the special material was being roughly shaped even now. Purchasing agents had spent quite some time acquiring the unique components. There were precious few. Most had been made elsewhere, but some had been made in his country for use abroad. They had been invented for one purpose, then adapted for others, but the possibility had always existed — distant but real — that the original application beckoned. It had become an institutional joke for the production people in the various corporations, something not to take seriously.

But they'd take it seriously now, the engineer

thought. He switched off the lights and pulled the door shut behind him. He had a deadline to meet, and he would start today, after only a few hours of sleep.

Even as often as he'd been here, Ryan had never lost his mystical appreciation for the place, and today's manner of arrival hadn't been contrived to make him look for the ordinary. A discreet call to his hotel had arranged for the drive to the airport. The aircraft had been waiting, of course, a twin-prop business bird sitting at the far end of the ramp, ordinary except for the USAF markings and the fact that the flight crew had been dressed in olive-green nomex. Friendly smiles, again of course, deferential. A sergeant to make sure he knew how to use the seat belt, and the perfunctory discussion of safety and emergency procedures. The look-back from the pilot who had a schedule to meet, and off they went, with Ryan wondering where the briefing papers were, and sipping a U.S. Air Force Coca-Cola. Wishing he'd changed into his good suit, and remembering that he had deliberately decided not to do so. Stupid, beneath himself. Flight time of forty-seven minutes, and a direct approach into Andrews. The only thing they left out was the helicopter ride in from Andrews, but that would only have attracted attention. Met by a deferential Air Force major who'd walked him over to a cheap official car and a quiet driver, Ryan settled back in his seat and closed his eyes while the major took the front seat. He tried to nap. He'd seen Suitland Parkway before, and knew the route by heart. Suitland Parkway to I-295, immediately off that and onto I-395, take the Maine Avenue Exit. The time of day, just after lunch, guaranteed rapid progress, and sure enough, the car stopped at the guard shack on West Executive Drive, where the guard, most unusually, just waved them through. The canopied entrance to

18

the White House basement level beckoned, as did a familiar face.

"Hi, Arnie." Jack held his hand out to the President's chief of staff. Arnold van Damm was just too good, and Roger Durling had needed him to help with the transition. Soon enough President Durling had measured his senior staffer against Arnie, and found his own man wanting. He hadn't changed much, Ryan saw. The same L. L. Bean shirts, and the same rough honesty on his face, but Arnie was older and tireder than before. Well, who wasn't? "The last time we talked here, you were kicking me loose," Jack said next, to get a quick read on the situation.

"We all make mistakes, Jack."

Uh-oh. Ryan went instantly on guard, but the handshake pulled him through the door anyway. The Secret Service agents on post had a pass all ready for him, and things went smoothly until he set off the metal detector. Ryan handed over his hotel room key and tried again, hearing yet another ping. The only other metal on his body except for his watch turned out to be his divot tool.

"When did you take up golf?" van Damm asked with a chuckle that matched the expression of the nearest agent.

"Nice to know you haven't been following me around. Two months, and I haven't broken one-ten yet."

The chief of staff waved Ryan to the hidden stairs to the left. "You know why they call it 'golf'?"

"Yeah, because 'shit' was already taken." Ryan stopped on the landing. "What gives, Arnie?"

"I think you know," was all the answer he got.

"Hello, Dr. Ryan!" Special Agent Helen D'Agustino was as pretty as ever, and still part of the Presidential Detail. "Please come with me."

The presidency is not a job calculated to bring youth to a man. Roger Durling had once been a paratrooper

19

who'd climbed hills in the Central Highlands of Vietnam, he was still a jogger, and reportedly liked to play squash to keep fit, but for all that he looked a weary man this afternoon. More to the point, Jack reflected quickly, he'd come straight in to see the President, no waiting in one of the many anterooms, and the smiles on the faces he'd seen on the way in carried a message of their own. Durling rose with a speed intended to show his pleasure at seeing his guest. Or maybe something else.

"How's the brokerage business, Jack?" The handshake that accompanied the question was dry and hard, but with an urgency to it.

"It keeps me busy, Mr. President."

"Not too busy. Golf in West Virginia?" Durling asked, waving Ryan to a seat by the fireplace. "That'll be all," he told the two Secret Service agents who'd followed Ryan in. "Thank you."

"My newest vice, sir," Ryan said, hearing the door close behind him. It was unusual to be so close to the Chief Executive without the protective presence of Secret Service guards, especially since he had been so long out of government service.

Durling took his seat, and leaned back into it. His body language showed vigor, the kind that emanated from the mind rather than the body. It was time to talk business. "I could say I'm sorry to interrupt your vacation, but I won't," the President of the United States told him. "You've had a two-year vacation, Dr. Ryan. It's over now."

Two years. For the first two months of it, he'd done exactly nothing, pondered a few teaching posts in the sanctity of his study, watched his wife leave early every morning for her medical practice at Johns Hopkins, fixed the kids' school lunches and told himself how wonderful it was to relax. It had taken those two months before he'd admitted to himself that the absence of activity was more stressful than anything

20

he'd ever done. Only three interviews had landed him a job back in the investment business, enabled him to race his wife out of the house each morning, and bitch about the pace — and just maybe prevent himself from going insane. Along the way he'd made some money, but even that, he admitted to himself, had begun to pall. He still hadn't found his place, and wondered if he ever really would.

"Mr. President, the draft ended a lot of years ago," Jack offered with a smile. It was a flippant observation, and one he was ashamed of even as he said it.

"You've said 'no' to your country once." The rebuke put an end to the smiles. Was Durling that stressed-out? Well, he had every right to be, and with the stress had come impatience, which was surprising in a man whose main function for the public was being pleasant and reassuring. But Ryan was not part of the public, was he?

"Sir, I was burned out then. I don't think I would have been — "

"Fine. I've seen your file, all of it," Durling added. "I even know that I might not be here now except for what you did down in Colombia a few years ago. You've served your country well, Dr. Ryan, and now you've had your time off, and you've played the money game some more — rather well, it would seem — and now it's time to come back."

"What post, sir?" Jack asked.

"Down the hall and around the corner. The last few residents haven't distinguished themselves there," Durling noted. Cutter and Elliot had been bad enough. Durling's own National Security Advisor had simply not been up to the task. His name was Tom Loch, and he was on the way out, the morning paper had told Ryan. It would seem that the press had it right for once. "I'm not going to beat around the bush. We need you. I need you."

21

"Mr. President, that's a very flattering statement, but the truth of the matter is — "

"The truth of the matter is that I have too much of a domestic agenda, and the day only has twenty-four hours, and my administration has fumbled the ball too many times. In the process we have not served the country as well as we should have. I can't say that anywhere but inside this room, but I can and must say it here. State is weak. Defense is weak."

"Fiedler in Treasury is excellent," Ryan allowed. "And if you want advice about State, move Scott Adler up. He's young, but he's very good on process and pretty good on vision."

"Not without good oversight from this building, and I don't have the time for that. I will pass your approbation on to Buzz Fiedler," Durling added with a smile.

"He's a brilliant technician, and that's what you need across the street. If you're going to catch the inflation, for God's sake, do it now — "

"And take the political heat," Durling said. "That's exactly what his orders are. Protect the dollar and hammer inflation down to zero. I think he can do it. The initial signs are promising."

Ryan nodded. "I think you're right." *Okay, get on with it.*

Durling handed over the briefing book. "Read."

"Yes, sir." Jack flipped open the binder's cover, and kept flipping past the usual stiff pages that warned of all manner of legal sanctions for revealing what he was about to read. As usual, the information United States Code protected wasn't all that different from what any citizen could get in *Time*, but it wasn't as well written. His right hand reached out for a coffee cup, annoyingly not the handleless mug he preferred. The White House china was long on elegance but short on practicality. Coming here was always like visiting a particularly rich boss. So many of the appointments were just a little too —

"I know about some of this, but I didn't know it was this . . . interesting," Jack murmured.

" 'Interesting'?" Durling replied with an unseen smile. "That's a nice choice of words."

"Mary Pat's the Deputy Director of Operations now?" Ryan looked up to see the curt nod.

"She was in here a month ago to plead her case for upgrading her side of the house. She was very persuasive. Al Trent just got the authorization through committee yesterday."

Jack chuckled. "Agriculture or Interior this time?" That part of CIA's budget was almost never in the open. The Directorate of Operations always got part of its funding through legerdemain.

"Health and Human Services, I think."

"But it'll still be two or three years before — "

"I know." Durling fidgeted in his seat. "Look, Jack, if it mattered to you that much, then why — "

"Sir, if you've read through my file, you know why." *Dear God,* Jack wanted to say, *how much am I expected to —* But he couldn't, not here, not to this man, and so he didn't. Instead he went back into the briefing book, flipping pages, and read as rapidly as comprehension permitted.

"I know, it was a mistake to downplay the human-intelligence side of the house. Trent and Fellows said so. Mrs. Foley said so. You can get overloaded in this office, Jack."

Ryan looked up and almost smiled until he saw the President's face. There was a tiredness around the eyes that Durling was unable to conceal. But then Durling saw the expression on Jack's own face.

"When can you start?" the President of the United States asked.

The engineer was back, flipping on the lights and looking at his machine tools. His supervisory office was almost all glass, and elevated slightly so that he could see all the activity in the shop with no more effort than a raised head. In a few minutes his staff would start arriving, and his presence in the office earlier than any of the team — in a country where showing up two hours early was the norm — would set the proper tone. The first man arrived only ten minutes later, hung up his coat, and headed to the far corner to start the coffee. Not tea, both men thought at the same time. Surprisingly Western. The others arrived in a bunch, both resentful and envious of their colleague, because they all noticed that the chief's office was lit and occupied. A few exercised at their worktables, both to loosen themselves up and to show their devotion. At start-time minus two hours, the chief walked out of his office and called for his team to gather around for the first morning's talk about what they were doing. They all knew, of course, but they had to be told anyway. It took ten minutes, and with that done, they all went to work. And this was not at all a strange way for a war to begin.

Dinner was elegant, served in the enormous high-ceilinged dining room to the sound of piano, violin, and the occasional *ting* of crystal. The table chatter was ordinary, or so it seemed to Jack as he sipped his dinner wine and worked his way through the main course. Sally and little Jack were doing well at school, and Kathleen would turn two in another month, as she toddled around the house at Peregrine Cliff, the dominating and assertive apple of her father's eye, and the terror of her day-care center. Robby and Sissy, childless despite all their efforts, were surrogate aunt and uncle to the Ryan trio, and took as much pride in the brood as Jack and Cathy did. There was a sadness to it, Jack thought, but those were the breaks, and he wondered if Sissy still cried about it

24

when alone in bed, Robby off on a job somewhere. Jack had never had a brother. Robby was closer than a brother could ever have been, and his friend deserved better luck. And Sissy, well, she was just an angel.

"I wonder how the office is doing."

"Probably conjuring up a plan for the invasion of Bangladesh," Jack said, looking up and reentering the conversation.

"That was last week," Jackson said with a grin.

"How do they manage without us?" Cathy wondered aloud, probably worrying about a patient.

"Well, concert season doesn't start for me until next month," Sissy observed.

"Mmmm," Ryan noted, looking back down at his plate, wondering how he was going to break the news.

"Jack, I know," Cathy finally said. "You're not good at hiding it."

"Who — "

"She asked where you were," Robby said from across the table. "A naval officer can't lie."

"Did you think I'd be mad?" Cathy asked her husband.

"Yes."

"You don't know what he's like," Cathy told the others. "Every morning, gets his paper and grumbles. Every night, catches the news and grumbles. Every Sunday, watches the interview shows and grumbles. Jack," she said quietly, "do you think I could ever stop doing surgery?"

"Probably not, but it's not the same — "

"No, it's not, but it's the same for you. When do you start?" Caroline Ryan asked.

1

Alumni

There was a university somewhere in the Midwest, Jack had once heard on the radio, which had an instrument package designed to go inside a tornado. Each spring, graduate students and a professor or two staked out a likely swath of land, and on spotting a tornado, tried to set the instrument package, called "Toto" — what else? — directly in the path of the onrushing storm. So far they had been unsuccessful. Perhaps they'd just picked the wrong place, Ryan thought, looking out the window to the leafless trees in Lafayette Park. The office of the President's National Security Advisor was surely cyclonic enough for anyone's taste, and, unfortunately, much easier for people to enter.

"You know," Ryan said, leaning back in his chair, "it was supposed to be a lot simpler than this." *And I thought it would be,* he didn't add.

"The world had rules before," Scott Adler pointed out. "Now it doesn't."

"How's the President been doing, Scott?"

"You really want the truth?" Adler asked, meaning, *We are in the White House, remember?* and wondering if there really were tape machines covering this room. "We screwed up the Korean situation, but we lucked out. Thank God we didn't screw up Yugoslavia that

26

badly, because there just isn't any luck to be had in that place. We haven't been handling Russia very well. The whole continent of Africa's a dog's breakfast. About the only thing we've done right lately was the trade treaty — "

"And that doesn't include Japan and China," Ryan finished for him.

"Hey, you and I fixed the Middle East, remember? That's working out fairly nicely."

"Hottest spot right now?" Ryan didn't want praise for that. The "success" had developed some very adverse consequences, and was the prime reason he had left government service.

"Take your pick," Adler suggested. Ryan grunted agreement.

"SecState?"

"Hanson? Politician," replied the career foreign-service officer. And a proud one at that, Jack reminded himself. Adler had started off at State right after graduating number one in his Fletcher School class, then worked his way up the career ladder through all the drudgery and internal politics that had together claimed his first wife's love and a good deal of his hair. It had to be love of country that kept him going, Jack knew. The son of an Auschwitz survivor, Adler cared about America in a way that few could duplicate. Better still, his love was not blind, even now that his current position was political and not a career rank. Like Ryan, he served at the pleasure of the President, and still he'd had the character to answer Jack's questions honestly.

"Worse than that," Ryan went on for him. "He's a lawyer. They always get in the way."

"The usual prejudice," Adler observed with a smile, then applied some of his own analytical ability. "You have something running, don't you?"

Ryan nodded. "A score to settle. I have two good guys on it now."

The task combined oil-drilling and mining, to be followed by exquisitely fine finishing work, and it had to be performed on time. The rough holes were almost complete. It had not been easy drilling straight down into the basaltic living rock on the valley even one time, much less ten, each one of the holes fully forty meters deep and ten across. A crew of nine hundred men working in three rotating shifts had actually beaten the official schedule by two weeks, despite the precautions. Six kilometers of rail had been laid from the nearest *Shin-Kansen* line, and for every inch of it the catenary towers normally erected to carry the overhead electrical lines instead were the supports for four linear miles of camouflage netting.

The geological history of this Japanese valley must have been interesting, the construction superintendent thought. You didn't see the sun until an hour or more after it rose, the slope was so steep to the east. No wonder that previous railway engineers had looked at the valley and decided to build elsewhere. The narrow gorge — in places not even ten meters across at its base — had been cut by a river, long since dammed, and what remained was essentially a rock trench, like something left over from a war. *Or in preparation for one*, he thought. It was pretty obvious, after all, despite the fact that he'd never been told anything but to keep his mouth shut about the whole project. The only way out of this place was straight up or sideways. A helicopter could do the former, and a train could do the latter, but to accomplish anything else required tampering with the laws of ballistics, which was a very difficult task indeed.

As he watched, a huge Kowa scoop-loader dumped another bucketload of crushed rock into a hopper car. It was the last car in the train's "consist," and soon the diesel switch engine would haul its collection of cars out to the mainline, where a standard-gauge electric locomotive would take over.

"Finished," the man told him, pointing down into the hole. At the bottom, a man held the end of a long tape measure. Forty meters exactly. The hole had been measured by laser already, of course, but tradition required that such measurements be tested by the human hand of a skilled worker, and there at the bottom was a middle-aged hard-rock miner whose face beamed with pride. And who had no idea what this project was all about.

"*Hai,*" the superintendent said with a pleased nod, and then a more formal, gracious bow to the man at the bottom, which was dutifully and proudly returned. The next train in would carry an oversized cement mixer. The pre-assembled sets of rebar were already stacked around this hole — and, indeed, all the others, ready to be lowered. In finishing the first hole, this team had beaten its nearest competitor by perhaps six hours, and its furthest by no more than two days — irregularities in the subsurface rock had been a problem for Hole Number 6, and in truth they'd done well to catch up as closely as they were now. He'd have to speak to them, congratulate them for their Herculean effort, so as to mitigate their shame at being last. Team 6 was his best crew, and it was a pity that they'd been unlucky.

"Three more months, we will make the deadline," the site foreman said confidently.

"When Six is also finished, we will have a party for the men. They have earned it."

"This isn't much fun," Chavez observed.

"Warm, too," Clark agreed. The air-conditioning system on their Range Rover was broken, or perhaps it had died of despair. Fortunately, they had lots of bottled water.

"But it's a dry heat," Ding replied, as though it

mattered at a hundred fourteen degrees. One could think in Celsius, instead, but that offered relief only as long as it took to take in another breath. Then you were reminded of the abuse that the superheated air had to be doing to your lungs, no matter how you kept score. He unscrewed the top from a plastic bottle of spring water, which was probably a frigid ninety-five, he estimated. Amazing how cool it tasted under the circumstances.

"Chilldown tonight, all the way to eighty, maybe."

"Good thing I brought my sweater, Mr. C." Chavez paused to wipe off some sweat before looking through the binoculars again. They were good ones, but they didn't help much, except to give a better view of the shimmering air that roiled like the surface of a stormy, invisible sea. Nothing lived out here except for the occasional vulture, and surely by now they had cleaned off the carcasses of everything that had once made the mistake of being born out here. And he'd once thought the Mojave Desert was bleak, Chavez told himself. At least coyotes lived there.

It never changed, Clark thought. He'd been doing jobs like this one for . . . thirty years? Not quite but close. Jesus, thirty years. He still hadn't had the chance to do it in a place where he could really fit in, but that didn't seem terribly important right now. Their cover was wearing thin. The back of the Rover was jammed with surveying equipment and boxes of rock samples, enough to persuade the local illiterates that there might be an enormous molybdenum deposit out there in that solitary mountain. The locals knew what gold looked like — who didn't? — but the mineral known affectionately to miners as Molly-be-damned was a mystery to the uninitiated in all but its market value, which was considerable. Clark had used the ploy often enough. A geological discovery offered people just the perfect sort of luck to appeal to their invariable greed. They just loved the idea

30

of having something valuable sitting under their feet, and John Clark looked the part of a mining engineer, with his rough and honest face to deliver the good and very confidential news.

He checked his watch. The appointment was in ninety minutes, around sunset, and he'd shown up early, the better to check out the area. It was hot and empty, neither of which came as much of a surprise, and was located twenty miles from the mountain they would be talking about, briefly. There was a crossroads here, two tracks of beaten dirt, one mainly north-south, the other mainly east-west, both of which somehow remained visible despite the blowing sand and grit that ought to have covered up all traces of human presence. Clark didn't understand it. The years-long drought couldn't have helped, but even with occasional rain he had to wonder how the hell anyone had lived here. Yet some people had, and for all he knew, still did, when there was grass for their goats to eat . . . and no men with guns to steal the goats and kill the herdsmen. Mainly the two CIA field officers sat in their car, with the windows open, drank their bottled water, and sweated after they ran out of words to exchange.

The trucks showed up close to dusk. They saw the dust plumes first, like the roostertails of motorboats, yellow in the diminishing light. In such an empty, desperate country, how was it possible that they knew how to make trucks run? Somebody knew how to keep them running, and that seemed very remarkable. Perversely, it meant that all was not lost for this desolate place. If bad men could do it, then good men could do it as well. And that was the reason for Clark and Chavez to be there, wasn't it?

The first truck was well in advance of the others. It was old, probably a military truck originally, though with all the body damage, the country of origin and the name of the manufacturer were matters of speculation. It circled their Rover at a radius of about a hundred meters, while the eyes of the crew checked them out at a discreet, careful distance, including one man on what looked like a Russian 12.7mm machine gun mounted in the back. "Policemen," their boss called them — once it was "technicals." After a while, they stopped, got out and just stood there, watching the Rover, holding their old, dirty, but probably functional G3 rifles. The men would soon be less important. It was evening, after all, and the caq was out. Chavez watched a man sitting in the shade of his truck a hundred meters away, chewing on the weed.

"Can't the dumb sunzabitches at least smoke it?" the exasperated field officer asked the burning air in the car.

"Bad for the lungs, Ding. You know that." Their appointment for the evening made quite a living for himself by flying it in. In fact, roughly two fifths of the country's gross domestic product went into that trade, supporting a small fleet of aircraft that flew it in from Somalia. The fact offended both Clark and Chavez, but their mission wasn't about personal offense. It was about a long-standing debt. General Mohammed Abdul Corp — his rank had largely been awarded by reporters who didn't know what else to call him — had, once upon a time, been responsible for the deaths of twenty American soldiers. Two years ago, to be exact, far beyond the memory horizon of the media, because after he'd killed the American soldiers, he'd gone back to his main business of killing his own countrymen. It was for the latter cause that Clark and Chavez were nominally in the field, but justice had many shapes and many colors, and it pleased Clark to pursue a parallel agenda. That Corp was also a dealer in narcotics seemed a special gift from a good-humored God.

"Wash up before he gets here?" Ding asked, tenser

now, and showing it just a little bit. All four men by the truck just sat there, chewing their caq and staring, their rifles lying across their legs, the heavy machine gun on the back of their truck forgotten now. They were the forward security element, such as it was, for their General.

Clark shook his head. "Waste of time."

"Shit, we've been here *six* weeks." All for one appointment. Well, that was how it worked, wasn't it?

"I needed to sweat off the five pounds," Clark replied with a tense smile of his own. Probably more than five, he figured. "These things take time to do right."

"I wonder how Patsy is doing in college?" Ding murmured as the next collection of dust plumes grew closer.

Clark didn't respond. It was distantly unseemly that his daughter found his field partner exotic and interesting . . . and charming, Clark admitted to himself. Though Ding was actually shorter than his daughter — Patsy took after her tall and rangy mom — and possessed of a decidedly checkered background, John had to allow for the fact that Chavez had worked as hard as any man he'd ever known to make himself into something that fate had tried very hard to deny him. The lad was thirty-one now. *Lad?* Clark asked himself. Ten years older than his little girl, Patricia Doris Clark. He could have said something about how they lived a rather crummy life in the field, but Ding would have replied that it was not his decision to make, and it wasn't. Sandy hadn't thought so either.

What Clark couldn't shake was the idea that his Patricia, his baby, might be sexually active with — Ding? The father part of him found the idea disturbing, but the rest of him had to admit that he'd had his own youth once. Daughters, he told himself, were God's revenge on you for being a man: you lived in mortal fear that they might accidentally encounter somebody like — yourself at that age. In Patsy's case, the similarity in question was just too striking to accept easily.

"Concentrate on the mission, Ding."

"Roger that, Mr. C." Clark didn't have to turn his head. He could see the smile that had to be poised on his partner's face. He could almost feel it evaporate, too, as more dust plumes appeared through the shimmering air.

"We're gonna get you, motherfucker," Ding breathed, back to business and wearing his mission face again. It wasn't just the dead American soldiers. People like Corp destroyed everything they touched, and this part of the world needed a chance at a future. That chance might have come two years earlier, if the President had listened to his field commanders instead of the U.N. Well, at least he seemed to be learning, which wasn't bad for a President.

The sun was lower, almost gone now, and the temperature was abating. More trucks. Not too many more, they both hoped. Chavez shifted his eyes to the four men a hundred yards away. They were talking back and forth with a little animation, mellow from the caq. Ordinarily it would be dangerous to be around drug-sotted men carrying military weapons, but tonight danger was inverting itself, as it sometimes did. The second truck was clearly visible now, and it came up close. Both CIA officers got out of their vehicle to stretch, then to greet the new visitors, cautiously, of course.

The General's personal guard force of elite "policemen" was no better than the ones who had arrived before, though some of this group did wear unbuttoned shirts. The first one to come up to them smelled of whiskey, probably pilfered from the General's private stock. That was an affront to Islam, but then so was trafficking in drugs. One of the things Clark admired about the Saudis was their direct and pe-

34

remptory method for processing that category of criminal.

"Hi." Clark smiled at the man. "I'm John Clark. This is Mr. Chavez. We've been waiting for the General, like you told us."

"What you carry?" the "policeman" asked, surprising Clark with his knowledge of English. John held up his bag of rock samples, while Ding showed his pair of electronic instruments. After a cursory inspection of the vehicle, they were spared even a serious frisking — a pleasant surprise.

Corp arrived next, with his most reliable security force, if you could call it that. They rode in a Russian ZIL-type jeep. The "General" was actually in a Mercedes that had once belonged to a government bureaucrat, before the government of this country had disintegrated. It had seen better times, but was still the best automobile in the country, probably. Corp wore his Sunday best, a khaki shirt outside the whipcord trousers, with something supposed to be rank insignia on the epaulets, and boots that had been polished sometime in the last week. The sun was just under the horizon now. Darkness would fall quickly, and the thin atmosphere of the high desert made for lots of visible stars even now.

The General was a gracious man, at least by his own lights. He walked over briskly, extending his hand. As he took it, Clark wondered what had become of the owner of the Mercedes. Most likely murdered along with the other members of the government. They'd died partly of incompetence, but mostly of barbarism, probably at the hands of the man whose firm and friendly hand he was now shaking.

"Have you completed your survey?" Corp asked, surprising Clark again with his grammar.

"Yes, sir, we have. May I show you?"

"Certainly." Corp followed him to the back of the Rover. Chavez pulled out a survey map and some

35

satellite photos obtained from commercial sources.

"This may be the biggest deposit since the one in Colorado, and the purity is surprising. Right here." Clark extended a steel pointer and tapped it on the map.

"Thirty kilometers from where we are sitting . . ."

Clark smiled. "You know, as long as I've been in this business, it still surprises me how this happens. A couple of billion years ago, a huge bubble of the stuff must have just perked up from the center of the earth." His lecture was lyrical. He'd had lots of practice, and it helped that Clark read books on geology for recreation, borrowing the nicer phrases for his "pitch."

"Anyway," Ding, said, taking his cue a few minutes later, "the overburden is no problem at all, and we have the location fixed perfectly."

"How can you do that?" Corp asked. His country's maps were products of another and far more casual age.

"With this, sir." Ding handed it over.

"What is it?" the General asked.

"A GPS locator," Chavez explained. "It's how we find our way around, sir. You just push that button there, the rubber one."

Corp did just that, then held the large, thin green-plastic box up and watched the readout. First it gave him the exact time, then started to make its fix, showing that it had lock with one, then three, and finally four orbiting Global Positioning System satellites. "Such an amazing device," he said, though that wasn't the half of it. By pushing the button he had also sent out a radio signal. It was so easy to forget that they were scarcely a hundred miles from the Indian Ocean, and that beyond the visible horizon might be a ship with a flat deck. A largely empty deck at the moment, because the helicopters that lived there had lifted off an hour earlier and were now sitting at a secure site thirty-five miles to the south.

Corp took one more look at the GPS locator before handing it back. "What is the rattle?" he asked as Ding took it.

"Battery pack is loose, sir," Chavez explained with a smile. It was their only handgun, and not a large one. The General ignored the irrelevancy and turned back to Clark.

"How much?" he asked simply.

"Well, determining the exact size of the deposit will require — "

"*Money*, Mr. Clark."

"Anaconda is prepared to offer you fifty million dollars, sir. We'll pay that in four payments of twelve and a half million dollars, plus ten percent of the gross profit from the mining operations. The advance fee and the continuing income will be paid in U.S. dollars."

"More than that. I know what molybdenum is worth." He'd checked a copy of *The Financial Times* on the way in.

"But it will take two years, closer to three, probably, to commence operations. Then we have to determine the best way to get the ore to the coast. Probably truck, maybe a rail line if the deposit is as big as I think it is. Our up-front costs to develop the operation will be on the order of three hundred million." Even with the labor costs here, Clark didn't have to add.

"I need more money to keep my people happy. You must understand that," Corp said reasonably. Had he been an honorable man, Clark thought, this could have been an interesting negotiation. Corp wanted the additional up-front money to buy arms in order to reconquer the country that he had once almost owned. The U.N. had displaced him, but not quite thoroughly enough. Relegated to dangerous obscurity in the bush, he had survived the last year by running caq into the cities, such as they were, and he'd made enough from the trade that some thought him to be a danger to the state again, such as it was. With new arms, of course, and control over the country, he would then renegotiate the continuing royalty for the molybdenum. It was a clever ploy, Clark thought, but obvious, having dreamed it up himself to draw the bastard out of his hole.

"Well, yes, we are concerned with the political stability of the region," John allowed, with an insider's smile to show that he knew the score. Americans were known for doing business all over the world, after all, or so Corp and others believed.

Chavez was fiddling with the GPS device, watching the LCD display. At the upper-right corner, a block went from clear to black. Ding coughed from the dust in the air and scratched his nose.

"Okay," Clark said. "You're a serious man, and we understand that. The fifty million can be paid up-front. Swiss account?"

"That is somewhat better," Corp allowed, taking his time. He walked around to the back of the Rover and pointed into the open cargo area. "These are your rock samples?"

"Yes, sir," Clark replied with a nod. He handed over a three-pound piece of stone with very high-grade Molly-be-damned ore, though it was from Colorado, not Africa. "Want to show it to your people?"

"What is this?" Corp pointed at two objects in the Rover.

"Our lights, sir." Clark smiled as he took one out. Ding did the same.

"You have a gun in there," Corp saw with amusement, pointing to a bolt-action rifle. Two of his bodyguards drew closer.

"This *is* Africa, sir. I was worried about — "

"Lions?" Corp thought that one pretty good. He

turned and spoke to his "policemen," who started laughing amiably at the stupidity of the Americans. "We kill the lions," Corp told them after the laughter settled down. "Nothing lives out here."

Clark, the General thought, took it like a man, standing there, holding his light. It seemed a big light. "What is that for?"

"Well, I don't like the dark very much, and when we camp out, I like to take pictures at night."

"Yeah," Ding confirmed. "These things are really great." He turned and scanned the positions of the General's security detail. There were two groups, one of four, the other of six, plus the two nearby and Corp himself.

"Want me to take pictures of your people for you?" Clark asked without reaching for his camera.

On cue, Chavez flipped his light on and played it toward the larger of the two distant groups. Clark handled the three men close to the Rover. The "lights" worked like a charm. It took only about three seconds before both CIA officers could turn them off and go to work securing the men's hands.

"Did you think we forgot?" the CIA field officer asked Corp as the roar of rotary-wing aircraft became audible fifteen minutes later. By this time all twelve of Corp's security people were facedown in the dust, their hands bound behind them with the sort of plastic ties policemen use when they run out of cuffs. All the General could do was moan and writhe on the ground in pain. Ding cracked a handful of chemical lights and tossed them around in a circle downwind of the Rover. The first UH-60 Blackhawk helicopter circled carefully, illuminating the ground with lights.

"BIRD-DOG ONE, this is BAG MAN."

"Good evening, BAG MAN, BIRD-DOG ONE has the situation under control. Come on *down!*" Clark chuckled into the radio.

The first chopper down was well outside the lighted

area. The Rangers appeared out of the shadows like ghosts, spaced out five meters apart, weapons low and ready.

"Clark?" a loud, very tense voice called.

"Yo!" John called back with a wave. "We got 'im."

A captain of Rangers came in. A young Latino face, smeared with camouflage paint and dressed in desert cammies. He'd been a lieutenant the last time he'd been on the African mainland, and remembered the memorial service for those he'd lost from his platoon. Bringing the Rangers back had been Clark's idea, and it had been easy to arrange. Four more men came in behind Captain Diego Checa. The rest of the squad dispersed to check out the "policemen."

"What about these two?" one asked, pointing to Corp's two personal bodyguards.

"Leave 'em," Ding replied.

"You got it, sir," a spec-4 replied, taking out steel cuffs and securing both pairs of wrists in addition to the plastic ties. Captain Checa cuffed Corp himself. He and a sergeant lifted the man off the ground while Clark and Chavez retrieved their personal gear from the Rover and followed the soldiers to the Blackhawk. One of the Rangers handed Chavez a canteen.

"Oso sends his regards," the staff sergeant said. Ding's head came around.

"What's he doing now?"

"First Sergeants' school. He's pissed that he missed this one. I'm Gomez, Foxtrot, Second of the One-Seventy-Fifth. I was here back then, too."

"You made that look pretty easy," Checa was telling Clark, a few feet away.

"Six weeks," the senior field officer replied in a studiously casual voice. The rules required such a demeanor. "Four weeks to bum around in the boonies, two weeks to set the meet up, six hours waiting for it to happen, and about ten seconds to take him down."

"Just the way it's supposed to be," Checa observed. He handed over a canteen filled with Gatorade. The Captain's eyes locked on the senior man. Whoever he was, Checa thought at first, he was far too old to play games in the boonies with the gomers. Then he gave Clark's eyes a closer look.

"How the fuck you do this, man?" Gomez demanded of Chavez at the door to the chopper. The other Rangers leaned in close to get the reply.

Ding glanced over at his gear and laughed. "Magic!"

Gomez was annoyed that his question hadn't been answered. "Leaving all these guys out here?"

"Yeah, they're just gomers." Chavez turned to look one last time. Sooner or later one would get his hands free — probably — retrieve a knife, and cut his fellow "policemen" free; then they could worry about the two with steel bracelets. "It's the boss we were after."

Gomez turned to scan the horizon. "Any lions or hyenas out here?" Ding shook his head. *Too bad,* the sergeant thought.

The Rangers were shaking their heads as they strapped into their seats on the helicopter. As soon as they were airborne, Clark donned a headset and waited for the crew chief to set up the radio patch.

"CAPSTONE, this is BIRD DOG," he began.

The eight-hour time difference made it early afternoon in Washington. The UHF radio from the helicopter went to USS *Tripoli*, and then it was uplinked to a satellite. The Signals Office routed the call right into Ryan's desk phone.

"Yes, BIRD DOG, this is CAPSTONE."

Ryan couldn't quite recognize Clark's voice, but the words were readable through the static: "In the bag, no friendlies hurt. Repeat, the duck is in the bag and there are zero friendly casualties."

41

"I understand, BIRD DOG. Make your delivery as planned."

It was an outrage, really, Jack told himself as he set the phone back. Such operations were better left in the field, but the President had insisted this time. He rose from his desk and headed toward the Oval Office.

"Get'm?" D'Agustino asked as Jack hustled down the corridor.

"You weren't supposed to know."

"The Boss was worried about it," Helen explained quietly.

"Well, he doesn't have to worry anymore."

"That's one score that needed settling. Welcome back, Dr. Ryan."

The past would haunt one other man that day.

"Go on," the psychologist said.

"It was awful," the woman said, staring down at the floor. "It was the only time in my life it ever happened, and . . ." Though her voice droned on in a level, emotionless monotone, it was her appearance that disturbed the elderly woman most of all. Her patient was thirty-five, and should have been slim, petite, and blonde, but instead her face showed the puffiness of compulsive eating and drinking, and her hair was barely presentable. What ought to have been fair skin was merely pale, and reflected light like chalk, in a flat grainy way that even makeup would not have helped very much. Only her diction indicated what the patient once had been, and her voice recounted the events of three years before as though her mind was operating on two levels, one the victim, and the other an observer, wondering in a distant intellectual way if she had participated at all.

"I mean, he's who he is, and I worked for him, and I *liked him* . . ." The voice broke again. The

42

woman swallowed hard and paused a moment before going on. "I mean, I *admire* him, all the things he does, all the things he stands for." She looked up, and it seemed so odd that her eyes were as dry as cellophane, reflecting light from a flat surface devoid of tears. "He's so charming, and caring, and — "

"It's okay, Barbara." As she often did, the psychologist fought the urge to reach out to her patient, but she knew she had to stay aloof, had to hide her own rage at what had happened to this bright and capable woman. It had happened at the hands of a man who used his status and power to draw women toward him as a light drew moths, ever circling his brilliance, spiraling in closer and closer until they were destroyed by it. The pattern was so like life in this city. Since then, Barbara had broken off from two men, each of whom might have been fine partners for what should have been a fine life. This was an intelligent woman, a graduate of the University of Pennsylvania, with a master's degree in political science and a doctorate in public administration. She was not a wide-eyed secretary or summer intern, and perhaps had been all the more vulnerable because of it, able to become part of the policy team, knowing that she was good enough, if only she would do the one more thing to get her over the top or across the line, or whatever the current euphemism was on the Hill. The problem was, that line could be crossed only in one direction, and what lay beyond it was not so easily seen from the other side.

"You know, I would have done it anyway," Barbara said in a moment of brutal honesty. "He didn't have to — "

"Do you feel guilty because of that?" Dr. Clarice Golden asked. Barbara Linders nodded. Golden stifled a sigh and spoke gently. "And you think you gave him the — "

"Signals." A nod. "That's what he said, 'You gave

43

me all the signals.' Maybe I did."

"No, you didn't, Barbara. You have to go on now," Clarice ordered gently.

"I just wasn't in the mood. It's not that I wouldn't have done it, another time, another day, maybe, but I wasn't feeling well. I came into the office feeling fine that day, but I was coming down with the flu or something, and after lunch my stomach was queasy, and I thought about going home early, but it was the day we were doing the amendment on the civil-rights legislation that he sponsored, so I took a couple Tylenol for the fever, and about nine we were the only ones left in the office. Civil rights was my area of specialty," Linders explained. "I was sitting on the couch in his office, and he was walking around like he always does when he's formulating his ideas, and he was behind me. I remember his voice got soft and friendly, like, and he said, 'You have the nicest hair, Barbara' out of the blue, like, and I said, 'Thank you.' He asked how I was feeling, and I *told* him I was coming down with something, and he said he'd give me something he used — brandy," she said, talking more quickly now, as though she was hoping to get through this part as rapidly as possible, like a person fast-forwarding a videotape through the commercials. "I didn't see him put anything in the drink. He kept a bottle of Rémy in the credenza behind his desk, and something else, too, I guess. I drank it right down.

"He just stood there, watching me, not even talking, just watching me, like he knew it would happen fast. It was like . . . I don't know. I knew something wasn't right, like you get drunk right away, out of control." Then her voice stopped for fifteen seconds or so, and Dr. Golden watched her — like he had done, she thought. The irony shamed her, but this was business; it was clinical, and it was supposed to help, not hurt. Her patient *was* seeing it now. You could tell from the eyes, you always could. As though the mind really were a VCR, the scene paraded before her, and Barbara Linders was merely giving commentary on what she saw, not truly relating the dreadful personal experience she herself had undergone. For ten minutes, she described it, without leaving out a single clinical detail, her trained professional mind clicking in as it had to do. It was only at the end that her emotions came back.

"He didn't have to rape me. He could have . . . asked. I would have . . . I mean, another day, the weekend . . . I knew he was married, but I *liked* him, and . . ."

"But he did rape you, Barbara. He drugged you and raped you." This time Dr. Golden reached out and took her hand, because now it was all out in the open. Barbara Linders had articulated the whole awful story, probably for the first time since it had happened. In the intervening period she'd relived bits and pieces, especially the worst part, but this was the first time she'd gone through the event in chronological order, from beginning to end, and the impact of the telling was every bit as traumatic and cathartic as it had to be.

"There has to be more," Golden said after the sobbing stopped.

"There is," Barbara said immediately, hardly surprised that her psychologist could tell. "At least one other woman in the office, Lisa Beringer. She . . . killed herself the next year, drove her car into a bridge support-thing, looked like an accident, she'd been drinking, but in her desk she left a note. I cleaned her desk out . . . and I found it." Then, to Dr. Golden's stunned reaction, Barbara Linders reached into her purse and pulled it out. The "note" was in a blue envelope, six pages of personalized letter paper covered with the tight, neat handwriting of a woman who had made the decision to end her life, but who

45

wanted someone to know why.

Clarice Golden, Ph.D., had seen such notes before, and it was a source of melancholy amazement that people could do such a thing. They always spoke of pain too great to bear, but depressingly often they showed the despairing mind of someone who could have been saved and cured and sent back into a successful life if only she'd had the wit to make a single telephone call or speak to a single close friend. It took only two paragraphs for Golden to see that Lisa Beringer had been just one more needless victim, a woman who had felt alone, fatally so, in an office full of people who would have leaped to her aid.

Mental-health professionals are skilled at hiding their emotions, a talent necessary for obvious reasons. Clarice Golden had been doing this job for just under thirty years, and to her God-given talent had been added a lifetime of professional experience. Especially good at helping the victims of sexual abuse, she displayed compassion, understanding, and support in great quantity and outstanding quality, but while real, it was all a disguise for her true feelings. She loathed sexual predators as much as any police officer, maybe even more. A cop saw the victim's body, saw her bruises and her tears, heard her cries. The psychologist was there longer, probing into the mind for the malignant memories, trying to find a way to expunge them. Rape was a crime against the mind, not the body, and as dreadful as the things were that the policeman saw, worse still were the hidden injuries whose cure was Clarice Golden's life's work. A gentle, caring person who could never have avenged the crimes physically, she hated these creatures nonetheless.

But this one was a special problem. She maintained a regular working relationship with the sexual-crime units of every police department in a fifty-mile radius, but this crime had happened on federal property, and she'd have to check to see who had jurisdiction. For that she'd talk to her neighbor, Dan Murray of the FBI. And there was one other complication. The criminal in question had been a U.S. senator at the time, and indeed he still had an office in the Capitol Building. But this criminal had changed jobs. No longer a senator from New England, he was now Vice President of the United States.

ComSubPac had once been as grand a goal as any man might have, but that was one more thing of history. The first great commander had been Vice Admiral Charles Lockwood, and of all the men who'd defeated Japan, only Chester Nimitz and maybe Charles Layton had been more important. It was Lockwood, sitting in this very office on the heights overlooking Pearl Harbor, who had sent out Mush Morton and Dick O'Kane and Gene Fluckey, and the rest of the legends to do battle in their fleet boats. The same office, the same door, and even the same title on the door — Commander, Submarine Force, United States Pacific Fleet — but the rank required for it was lower now. Rear Admiral Bart Mancuso, USN, knew that he'd been lucky to make it this far. That was the good news.

The bad news was that he was essentially the receiver of a dying business. Lockwood had commanded a genuine fleet of submarines and tenders. More recently, Austin Smith had sent his forty or so around the world's largest ocean, but Mancuso was down to nineteen fast-attack boats and six boomers — and all of the latter were alongside, awaiting dismantlement at Bremerton. None would be kept, not even as a museum exhibit of a bygone age, which didn't trouble Mancuso as much as it might have. He'd never liked the missile submarines, never liked their ugly purpose, never liked their boring patrol pattern, never liked the mind-set of their commanders. Raised in fast-attack, Mancuso had always preferred to be where the action is — was, he corrected himself.

Was. It was all over now, or nearly so. The mission of the nuclear-powered fast-attack submarine had changed since Lockwood. Once the hunters of surface ships, whether merchants or men-of-war, they'd become specialists in the elimination of enemy subs, like fighter aircraft dedicated to the extermination of their foreign cousins. That specialization had narrowed their purpose, focusing their equipment and their training until they'd become supreme at it. Nothing could excel an SSN in the hunting of another.

What nobody had ever expected was that the other side's SSNs would go away. Mancuso had spent his professional life practicing for something he'd hoped would never come, detecting, localizing, closing on, and killing Soviet subs, whether missile boats or other fast-attacks. In fact, he'd achieved something that no other sub skipper had ever dreamed of doing. He'd assisted in the capture of a Russian sub, a feat of arms still among his country's most secret accomplishments — and a capture was better than a kill, wasn't it? — but then the world had changed. He'd played his role in it, and was proud of that. The Soviet Union was no more.

Unfortunately — as he thought of it — so was the Soviet Navy, and without enemy submarines to worry about, his country, as it had done many times in the past, had rewarded its warriors by forgetting them. There was little mission for his boats to do now. The once large and formidable Soviet Navy was essentially a memory. Only the previous week he'd seen satellite photos of the bases at Petropavlovsk and Vladivostok. Every boat the Soviets — Russians! — were known to have had been tied alongside, and on some of the overheads he'd been able to see the orange streaks of rust on the hulls where the

48

black paint had eroded off.

The other possible missions? Hunting merchant traffic was largely a joke — worse, the Orion drivers, with their own huge collection of P-3C aircraft, also designed for submarine hunting, had long since modified their aircraft to carry air-to-surface missiles, and had ten times the speed of any sub, and in the unlikely event that someone wanted to clobber a merchant ship, they could do it better and faster.

The same was true of surface warships — what there were of them. The sad truth, if you could call it that, was that the U.S. Navy, even gutted and downsized as it was, could handle any three other navies in the world in less time than it would take the enemies to assemble their forces and send out a press release of their malicious intent.

And so now what? Even if you won the Super Bowl, there were still teams to play against next season. But in this most serious of human games, victory meant exactly that. There were no enemies left at sea, and few enough on land, and in the way of the new world, the submarine force was the first of many uniformed groups to be without work. The only reason there was a ComSubPac at all was bureaucratic inertia. There was a Com-everything-else-Pac, and the submarine force had to have its senior officer as the social and military equal of the other communities, Air, Surface, and Service.

Of his nineteen fast-attack boats, only seven were currently at sea. Four were in overhaul status, and the yards were stretching out their work as much as possible to justify their own infrastructure. The rest were alongside their tenders or their piers while the ship-service people found new and interesting things to do, protecting *their* infrastructure and military/civilian identity. Of the seven boats at sea, one was tracking a Chinese nuclear fast-attack boat; those submarines were so noisy that Mancuso hoped the sonarmen's ears weren't being seriously hurt. Stalking them was about as demanding as watching a blind man on an empty parking lot in broad daylight. Two others were doing environmental research, actually tracking midocean whale populations — not for whalers, but for the environmental community. In so doing, his boats had achieved a real march on the tree-huggers. There were more whales out there than expected. Extinction wasn't nearly the threat everyone had once believed it to be, and the various environmental groups were having their own funding problems as a result. All of which was fine with Mancuso. He'd never wanted to kill a whale.

The other four boats were doing workups, mainly practicing against one another. But the environmentalists were taking their own revenge on Submarine Force, United States Pacific Fleet. Having protested the construction and operation of the boats for thirty years, they were now protesting their dismantlement, and more than half of Mancuso's working time was relegated to filing all manner of reports, answers to questions, and detailed explanations of his answers. "Ungrateful bastards," Mancuso grumbled. He was helping out with the whales, wasn't he? The Admiral growled into his coffee mug and flipped open a new folder.

"Good news, Skipper," a voice called without warning.

"Who the hell let you in?"

"I have an understanding with your chief," Ron Jones replied. "He says you're buried by paperwork."

"He ought to know." Mancuso stood to greet his guest. Dr. Jones had problems of his own. The end of the Cold War had hurt defense contractors, too, and Jones had specialized in sonar systems used by submarines. The difference was that Jones had made himself a pile of money first. "So what's the good news?"

50

"Our new processing software is optimized for listening to our warm-blooded oppressed fellow mammals. *Chicago* just phoned in. They have identified another twenty humpbacks in the Gulf of Alaska. I think I'll get the contract from NOAA. I can afford to buy you lunch now," Jones concluded, settling into a leather chair. He liked Hawaii, and was dressed for it, in casual shirt and no socks to clutter up his formal Reeboks.

"You ever miss the good old days?" Bart asked with a wry look.

"You mean chasing around the ocean, four hundred feet down, stuck inside a steel pipe two months at a time, smelling like the inside of an oilcan, with a touch of locker room for ambience, eating the same food every week, watching old movies and TV shows on tape, on a TV the size of a sheet of paper, working six on and twelve off, getting maybe five decent hours of sleep a night, and concentrating like a brain surgeon all the time? Yeah, Bart, those were the days." Jones paused and thought for a second. "I miss being young enough to think it was fun. We were pretty good, weren't we?"

"Better 'n average," Mancuso allowed. "What's the deal with the whales?"

"The new software my guys put together is good at picking out their breathing and heartbeats. It turns out to be a nice clear hertz line. When those guys are swimming — well, if you put a stethoscope up against them, your eardrums would probably meet in the middle of your head."

"What was the software really for?"

"Tracking Kilo-class boats, of course." Jones grinned as he looked out the windows at the largely empty naval base. "But I can't say that anymore. We changed a few hundred lines of code and ginned up a new wrapper for the box, and talked to NOAA about it."

Mancuso might have said something about taking that software into the Persian Gulf to track the Kilo-class boats the Iranians owned, but intelligence reported that one of them was missing. The submarine had probably gotten in the way of a supertanker and been squashed, simply crushed against the bottom of that shallow body of water by a tanker whose crew had never even noticed the rumble. In any case, the other Kilos were securely tied to their piers. Or maybe the Iranians had finally heard the old seaman's moniker for submarines and decided not to touch their new naval vessels again — they'd once been known as "pigboats," after all.

"Sure looks empty out there." Jones pointed to what had once been one of the greatest naval facilities ever made. Not a single carrier in view, only two cruisers, half a squadron of destroyers, roughly the same number of frigates, five fleet-support ships. "Who commands Pac Fleet now, a chief?"

"Christ, Ron, let's not give anybody ideas, okay?"

2

Fraternity

"You got him?" President Durling asked.

"Less than half an hour ago," Ryan confirmed, taking his seat.

"Nobody hurt?" That was important to the President. It was important to Ryan, too, but not morbidly so.

"Clark reports no friendly casualties."

"What about the other side?" This question came from Brett Hanson, the current Secretary of State. Choate School and Yale. The government was having a run on Yalies, Ryan thought, but Hanson wasn't as good as the last Eli he'd worked with. Short, thin, and hyper, Hanson was an in-and-out guy whose career had oscillated between government service, consulting, a sideline as a talking head on PBS — where you could exercise real influence — and a lucrative practice in one of the city's pricier firms. He was a specialist in corporate and international law, an area of expertise he'd once used to negotiate multinational business deals. He'd been good at that, Jack knew. Unfortunately he'd come into his cabinet post thinking that the same niceties ought to — worse, did — apply to the business of nation-states.

Ryan took a second or two before replying. "I didn't ask."

"Why?"

Jack could have said any one of several things, but he decided that it was time to establish his position. Therefore, a goad: "Because it wasn't important. The objective, Mr. Secretary, was to apprehend Corp. That was done. In about thirty minutes he will be handed over to the legal authorities, such as they are, in his country, for trial in accordance with their law, before a jury of his peers, or however they do it over there." Ryan hadn't troubled himself to find out.

"That's tantamount to murder."

"It's not my fault his peers don't like him, Mr. Secretary. He's also responsible for the deaths of American soldiers. Had we decided to eliminate him ourselves, even that would not be murder. It would have been a straightforward national-security exercise. Well, in another age it would have been," Ryan allowed. Times *had* changed, and Ryan had to adapt himself to a new reality as well. "Instead, we are acting as good world-citizens by apprehending a dangerous international criminal and turning him over to the government of his country, which will put him on trial for drug-running, which is a felony in every legal jurisdiction of which I am aware. What happens next is up to the criminal-justice system of his country. That is a country with which we have diplomatic relations and other informal agreements of assistance, and whose laws, therefore, we must respect."

Hanson didn't like it. That was clear from the way he leaned back in his chair. But he would support it in public because he had no choice. The State Department had announced official American support for that government half a dozen times in the previous year. What stung worse for Hanson was being outmaneuvered by this young upstart in front of him.

"They might even have a chance to make it now, Brett," Durling observed gently, putting his own seal of approval on Operation WALKMAN. "And it never happened."

"Yes, Mr. President."

"Jack, you were evidently right about this Clark fellow. What do we do about him?"

"I'll leave that to the DCI, sir. Maybe another Intelligence Star for him," Ryan suggested, hoping that Durling would forward it to Langley. If not, maybe a discreet call of his own to Mary Pat. Then it was time for fence-mending, a new skill for Ryan. "Mr. Secretary, in case you didn't know, our people were under orders to use nonlethal force if possible. Beyond that, my only concern is the lives of our people."

"I wish you'd cleared it through my people first," Hanson grumped.

Deep breath, Ryan commanded himself. The mess was of State's making, along with that of Ryan's predecessor. Having entered the country to restore order after it had been destroyed by local warlords — another term used by the media to give a label to common thugs — the powers-that-be had later decided, after the entire mission had gone to hell, that the "warlords" in question had to be part of the "political solution" to the problem. That the problem had been created by the warlords in the first place was conveniently forgotten. It was the circularity of the logic that offended Ryan most of all, who wondered if they taught a logic course at Yale. Probably an elective, he decided. At Boston College it had been mandatory.

"It's done, Brett," Durling said quietly, "and nobody will mourn the passing of Mr. Corp. What's next?" the President asked Ryan.

"The Indians are getting rather frisky. They've increased the operating tempo of their navy, and they're conducting operations around Sri Lanka — "

"They've done that before," SecState cut in.

"Not in this strength, and I don't like the way they've continued their talks with the 'Tamil Tigers,' or whatever the hell those maniacs call themselves now. Conducting extended negotiations with a guerrilla group operating on the soil of a neighbor is not an act of friendship."

This was a new concern for the U.S. government. The two former British colonies had lived as friendly neighbors for a long time, but for years the Tamil people on the island of Sri Lanka had maintained a nasty little insurgency. The Sri Lankans, with relatives on the Indian mainland, had asked for foreign troops to maintain a peace-keeping presence. India had obliged, but what had started in an honorable fashion was now changing. There were rumbles that the Sri Lankan government would soon ask for the Indian soldiers to leave. There were also rumbles that there would be some "technical difficulties" in effecting their removal. Concurrent with that had come word of a conversation between the Indian Foreign Minister and the U.S. Ambassador at a reception in Delhi.

"You know," the Minister had said after a few too many, but probably purposeful drinks, "that body of water to our south is called the *Indian* Ocean, and we have a navy to guard it. With the demise of the former Soviet threat, we wonder why the U.S. Navy seems so determined to maintain a force there."

The U.S. Ambassador was a political appointee — for some reason India had turned into a prestige post, despite the climate — but was also a striking exception to Scott Adler's professional snobbery. The former governor of Pennsylvania had smiled and mumbled something about freedom of the seas, then fired off an encrypted report to Foggy Bottom before going to bed that night. Adler needed to learn that they weren't all dumb.

"We see no indication of an aggressive act in that direction," Hanson said after a moment's reflection.

"The ethnic element is troubling. India can't go north, with the mountains in the way. West is out. The Pakis have nukes, too. East is Bangladesh —

56

why buy trouble? Sri Lanka has real strategic possibilities for them, maybe as a stepping-stone."

"To where?" the President asked.

"Australia. Space and resources, not many people in the way, and not much of a military to stop them."

"I just don't see that happening," SecState announced.

"If the Tigers pull something off, I *can* see India increasing its peace-keeping presence. The next step could be annexation, given the right preconditions, and then all of a sudden we have an imperial power playing games a long way from here, and making life somewhat nervous for one of our historical allies." And helping the Tigers to get something going was both easy and a time-honored tactic. Surrogates could be so useful, couldn't they? "In historical terms such ambitions are most inexpensively stopped early."

"That's why the Navy's in the Indian Ocean," Hanson observed confidently.

"True," Ryan conceded.

"Are we strong enough to deter them from stepping over the line?"

"Yes, Mr. President, at the moment, but I don't like the way our Navy is being stretched. Every carrier we have right now, except for the two in overhaul status, is either deployed or conducting workups preparatory for deployment. We have no strategic reserve worthy of the name." Ryan paused before going on, knowing that he was about to go too far, but doing so anyway: "We've cut back too much, sir. Our people are strung out very thin."

"They are simply not as capable as we think they are. That is a thing of the past," Raizo Yamata said. He was dressed in an elegant silk kimono, and sat on the floor at a traditional low table.

The others around the table looked discreetly at their watches. It was approaching three in the morning, and though this was one of the nicest geisha houses in the city, the hour *was* late. Raizo Yamata was a captivating host, however. A man of great wealth and sagacity, the others thought. Or most of them.

"They've protected us for generations," one man suggested.

"From what? Ourselves?" Yamata demanded coarsely. That was permitted now. Though all around the table were men of the most exquisite good manners, they were all close acquaintances, if not all actually close friends, and all had consumed their personal limit of alcohol. Under these circumstances, the rules of social intercourse altered somewhat. They could all speak bluntly. Words that would ordinarily be deadly insults would now be accepted calmly, then rebutted harshly, and there would be no lingering rancor about it. That, too, was a rule, but as with most rules, it was largely theoretical. Though friendships and relationships would not end because of words here, neither would they be completely forgotten. "How many of us," Yamata went on, "have been victims of these people?"

Yamata hadn't said "barbarians," the other Japanese citizens at the table noted. The reason was the presence of the two other men. One of them, Vice Admiral V. K. Chandraskatta, was a fleet commander of the Indian Navy, currently on leave. The other, Zhang Han San — the name meant "Cold Mountain" and had not been given by his parents — was a senior Chinese diplomat, part of a trade mission to Tokyo. The latter individual was more easily accepted than the former. With his swarthy skin and sharp features, Chandraskatta was regarded by the others with polite contempt. Though an educated and very bright potential ally, he was even more *gaijin* than the Chinese guest, and the eight *zaibatsu* around the table each imagined that he could smell the man, despite their previous intake of saké, which usually deadened the senses. For this reason, Chandraskatta occupied the place of honor, at Yamata's right hand, and the zaibatsu wondered if the Indian grasped that this supposed honor was merely a sophisticated mark of contempt. Probably not. He was a barbarian, after all, though perhaps a useful one.

"They are not as formidable as they once were, I admit, Yamata-*san,* but I assure you," Chandraskatta said in his best Dartmouth English, "their navy remains quite formidable. Their two carriers in my ocean are enough to give my navy pause."

Yamata turned his head. "You could not defeat them, even with your submarines?"

"No," the Admiral answered honestly, largely unaffected by the evening's drink, and wondering where all this talk was leading. "You must understand that this question is largely a technical exercise — a science experiment, shall we say?" Chandraskatta adjusted the kimono Yamata had given him, to make him a real member of this group, he'd said. "To defeat an enemy fleet, you must get close enough for your weapons to reach his ships. With their surveillance assets, they can monitor our presence and our movements from long distance. Thus they can maintain a covering presence on us from a range of, oh, something like six hundred kilometers. Since we are unable to maintain a corresponding coverage of their location and course, we cannot maneuver them out of place very easily."

"And that's why you haven't moved on Sri Lanka yet?" Tanzan Itagake asked.

"It is one of the considerations." The Admiral nodded.

"How many carriers do they now have?" Itagake went on.

"In their Pacific Fleet? Four. Two in our ocean, two based in Hawaii."

"What of the other two?" Yamata inquired.

"*Kitty Hawk* and *Ranger* are in extended overhaul status, and will not be back at sea for one and three years, respectively. Seventh Fleet currently has all the carriers. First Fleet has none. The U.S. Navy has five other carriers in commission. These are assigned to the Second and Sixth fleets, with one entering overhaul status in six weeks." Chandraskatta smiled. His information was completely up to date, and he wanted his hosts to know that. "I must tell you that as depleted as the U.S. Navy may appear to be, compared to only — what? five years ago? Compared to five years ago, then, they are quite weak, but compared to any other navy in the world, they are still immensely strong. One of their carriers is the equal of every other aircraft carrier in the world."

"You agree, then, that their aircraft carriers are their most potent weapon?" Yamata asked.

"Of course." Chandraskatta rearranged the things on the table. In the center he put an empty saké bottle. "Imagine that this is the carrier. Draw a thousand-kilometer circle around it. Nothing exists in that circle without the permission of the carrier air group. In fact, by increasing their operating tempo, that radius extends to fifteen hundred kilometers. They can strike somewhat farther than that if they need to, but even at the minimum distance I demonstrated, they can control a vast area of ocean. Take those carriers away, and they are just another frigate navy. The difficult part of the exercise is taking them away," the Admiral concluded, using simple language for the industrialists.

Chandraskatta was correct in assuming that these merchants knew little about military affairs. However, he had underestimated their ability to learn. The Admiral came from a country with a warrior tradition little known outside its own borders. Indians had stopped Alexander the Great, blunted his army,

60

wounded the Macedonian conqueror, perhaps fatally, and put an end to his expansion, an accomplishment the Persians and Egyptians had singularly failed to do. Indian troops had fought alongside Montgomery in the defeat of Rommel — and had crushed the Japanese Army at Imphal, a fact that he had no intention of bringing up, since one of the people at the table had been a private in that army. He wondered what they had in mind, but for the moment was content to enjoy their hospitality and answer their questions, elementary as they were. The tall, handsome flag officer leaned back, wishing for a proper chair and a proper drink. This saké these prissy little merchants served was closer to water than gin, his usual drink of choice.

"But if you can?" Itagake asked.

"As I said," the Admiral replied patiently, "then they are a frigate navy. I grant you, with superb surface ships, but the 'bubble' each ship controls is far smaller. You can protect with a frigate, you cannot *project* power with one." His choice of words, he saw, stopped the conversation for a moment.

One of the others handled the linguistic niceties, and Itagake leaned back with a long "Ahhhh," as though he'd just learned something profound. Chandraskatta regarded the point as exceedingly simple — forgetting for a moment that the profound often was. However, he recognized that something important had just taken place.

What are you thinking about? He would have shed blood, even his own, to know the answer to that question. Whatever it was, with proper warning, it might even be useful. He would have been surprised to learn that the others around the table were churning over exactly the same thought.

"Sure are burning a lot of oil," the group-operations officer noted as he began his morning brief.

61

USS *Dwight D. Eisenhower* was on a course of zero-nine-eight degrees, east by south, two hundred nautical miles southeast of Felidu Atoll. Fleet speed was eighteen knots, and would increase for the commencement of flight operations. The main tactical display in flag plot had been updated forty minutes earlier from the radar of an E-3C Hawkeye surveillance aircraft, and, indeed, the Indian Navy was burning a good deal of Bunker-Charlie, or whatever they used now to drive their ships through the water.

The display before him could easily have been that of a U.S. Navy Carrier Battle Group. The two Indian carriers, *Viraat* and *Vikrant,* were in the center of a circular formation, the pattern for which had been invented by an American named Nimitz almost eighty years earlier. Close-in escorts were *Delhi* and *Mysore,* home-built missile destroyers armed with a SAM system about which information was thin — always a worry to aviators. The second ring was composed of the Indian version of the old Russian Kashin-class destroyers, also SAM-equipped. Most interesting, however, were two other factors.

"Replenishment ships *Rajaba Gan Palan* and *Shakti* have rejoined the battle group after a brief stay in Trivandrum — "

"How long were they in port?" Jackson asked.

"Less than twenty-four hours," Commander Ed Harrison, the group-operations officer, replied. "They cycled them pretty fast, sir."

"So they just went in for a quick fill-up. How much gas do they carry?"

"Bunker fuel, about thirteen thousand tons each, another fifteen hundred each of JP. Sister ship *Deepak* has detached from the battle group and is heading northwest, probably for Trivandrum as well, after conducting un-rep operations yesterday."

"So they're working extra hard to keep their bunkers topped off. Interesting. Go on," Jackson ordered.

"Four submarines are believed to be accompanying the group. We have rough positions on one, and we've lost two roughly here." Harrison's hand drew a rough circle on the display. "The location of number four is unknown, sir. We'll be working on that today."

"Our subs out there?" Jackson asked the group commander.

"*Santa Fe* in close and *Greeneville* holding between us and them. *Cheyenne* is in closer to the battle group as gatekeeper," Rear Admiral Mike Dubro replied, sipping his morning coffee.

"Plan for the day, sir," Harrison went on, "is to launch four F/A-18 Echoes with tankers to head east to this point, designated POINT BAUXITE, from which they will turn northwest, approach to within thirty miles of the Indian battle group, loiter for thirty minutes, then return to BAUXITE to tank again and recover after a flight time of four hours, forty-five minutes." For the four aircraft to do this, eight were needed to provide midair refueling support. One each on the way out and the return leg as well. That accounted for most of *Ike*'s tanker assets.

"So we want them to think we're still over that way." Jackson nodded and smiled, without commenting on the wear-and-tear on the air crews that such a mission profile made necessary. "Still tricky, I see, Mike."

"They haven't gotten a line on us yet. We're going to keep it that way, too," Dubro added.

"How are the Bugs loaded?" Robby asked, using the service nickname for the F/A-18 Hornet, "Plastic Bug."

"Four Harpoons each. White ones," Dubro added. In the Navy, exercise missiles were color-coded blue. Warshots were generally painted white. The Harpoons were air-to-surface missiles. Jackson didn't have to ask about the Sidewinder and AMRAAM air-to-air missiles that were part of the Hornet's basic load. "What I want to know is, what the hell are they up to?" the battle-group commander observed quietly.

That was what everyone wanted to know. The Indian battle group — that was what they called it, because that's exactly what it was — had been at sea for eight days now, cruising off the south coast of Sri Lanka. The putative mission for the group was support for the Indian Army's peace-keeping team, whose job was to ameliorate the problem with the Tamil Tigers. Except for one thing: the Tamil Tigers were cosseted on the *northern* part of the island nation, and the Indian fleet was to the south. The Indian two-carrier force was maneuvering constantly to avoid merchant traffic, beyond sight of land, but within air range. Staying clear of the Sri Lankan Navy was an easy task. The largest vessel that country owned might have made a nice motor yacht for a nouveau-riche private citizen, but was no more formidable than that. In short, the Indian Navy was conducting a covert-presence operation far from where it was supposed to be. The presence of fleet-replenishment ships meant that they planned to be there for a while, and also that the Indians were gaining considerable at-sea time to conduct workups. The plain truth was that the Indian Navy was operating exactly as the U.S. Navy had done for generations. Except that the United States didn't have any ambitions with Sri Lanka.

"Exercising every day?" Robby asked.

"They're being right diligent, sir," Harrison confirmed. "You can expect a pair of Harriers to form up with our Hornets, real friendly, like."

"I don't like it," Dubro observed. "Tell him about last week."

"That was a fun one to watch." Harrison called up the computerized records, which ran at faster-than-normal speed. "Start time for the exercise is about now, sir."

On the playback, Robby watched a destroyer squadron break off the main formation and head southwest, which had happened to be directly toward the *Lincoln* group at the time, causing a lot of attention in the group-operations department. On cue, the Indian destroyers had started moving randomly, then commenced a high-speed run due north. Their radars and radios blacked out, the team had then headed east, moving quickly.

"The DesRon commander knows his stuff. The carrier group evidently expected him to head east and duck under this stationary front. As you can see, their air assets headed that way." That miscue had allowed the destroyers to dart within missile-launch range before the Indian Harriers had leaped from their decks to attack the closing surface group.

In the ten minutes required to watch the computerized playback, Robby knew that he'd just seen a simulated attack on an enemy carrier group, launched by a destroyer team whose willingness to sacrifice their ships and their lives for this hazardous mission had been demonstrated to perfection. More disturbingly, the attack had been successfully carried out. Though the tin cans would probably have been sunk, their missiles, some of them anyway, would have penetrated the carriers' point defenses and crippled their targets. Large, robust ships though aircraft carriers were, it didn't require all that much damage to prevent them from carrying out flight operations. And that was as good as a kill. The Indians had the only carriers in this ocean, except for the Americans, whose presence, Robby knew, was a source of annoyance for them. The purpose of the exercise wasn't to take out their own carriers.

"Get the feeling they don't want us here?" Dubro asked with a wry smile.

"I get the feeling we need better intelligence information on their intentions. We don't have dick at the moment, Mike."

"Why doesn't that surprise me," Dubro observed. "What about their intentions toward Ceylon?" The older name for the nation was more easily remembered.

"Nothing that I know about." As deputy J-3, the planning directorate for the Joint Chiefs of Staff, Robby had access to literally everything generated by the U.S. intelligence community. "But what you just showed me says a lot."

All you had to do was look at the display, where the water was, where the land was, where the ships were. The Indian Navy was cruising in such a way as to position itself between Sri Lanka and anyone who might approach from the south to come to Sri Lanka. Like the U.S. Navy, for example. It had practiced an attack on such a force. To that end, it was clearly prepared to remain at sea for a long time. If it was an exercise, it was an expensive one. If not? Well, you just couldn't tell, could you?

"Where are their amphibs?"

"Not close," Dubro answered. "Aside from that, I don't know. I don't have the assets to check, and I don't have any intel on them. They have a total of sixteen LSTs, and I figure twelve of them can probably operate as a group. Figure they can move a heavy brigade with them, combat-loaded and ready to hit a beach somewhere. There's a few choice sites on the north coast of that island. We can't reach them from here, at least not very well. I need more assets, Robby."

"There aren't more assets to give, Mike."

"Two subs. I'm not being greedy. You can see that." The two SSNs would move to cover the Gulf of Mannar, and that was the most likely invasion area. "I need more intelligence support, too, Rob. You can see why."

"Yep." Jackson nodded. "I'll do what I can. When do I leave?"

"Two hours." He'd be flying off on an S-3 Viking antisubmarine aircraft. The "Hoover," as it was known, had good range. That was important. He'd be flying to Singapore, the better to give the impression that Dubro's battle group was southeast of Sri Lanka, not southwest. Jackson reflected that he would have flown twenty-four thousand miles for what was essentially a half hour's worth of briefing and the look in the eyes of an experienced carrier aviator. Jackson slid his chair back on the tiled floor as Harrison keyed the display to a smaller scale. It now showed *Abraham Lincoln* heading northeast from Diego Garcia, adding an additional air wing to Dubro's command. He'd need it. The operational tempo required to cover the Indians — especially to do so deceptively — was putting an incredible strain on men and aircraft. There was just too much ocean in the world for eight working aircraft carriers to handle, and nobody back in Washington understood that. *Enterprise* and *Stennis* were working up to relieve *Ike* and *Abe* in a few months, and even that meant there would be a time when U.S. presence in this area would be short. The Indians would know that, too. You just couldn't conceal the return time of the battle groups from the families. The word would get out, and the Indians would hear it, and what would they be doing then?

"Hi, Clarice." Murray stood up for his luncheon guest. He thought of her as his own Dr. Ruth. Short, a tiny bit overweight, Dr. Golden was in her middle fifties, with twinkling blue eyes and a face that always seemed on the edge of delivering the punch line of a particularly good joke. It was that similarity between them that had fostered their bond. Both were bright, serious professionals, and both had elegant intellectual disguises. Hearty-fellow and hearty-lady-well-met, the life of whatever party they might attend, but under the smiles and the chuckles were keen minds that missed little and collected much. Murray thought of Golden as one hell of a potential cop. Golden had much the same professional evaluation of Murray.

"To what do I owe this honor, ma'am?" Dan asked in his usual courtly voice. The waiter delivered the menus, and she waited pleasantly for him to depart. It was Murray's first clue, and though the smile remained fixed on his face, his eyes focused in a little more sharply on his diminutive lunch guest.

"I need some advice, Mr. Murray," Golden replied, giving another signal. "Who has jurisdiction over a crime committed on federal property?"

"The Bureau, always," Dan answered, leaning back in his seat and checking his service pistol. Business to Murray was enforcing the law, and feeling his handgun in its accustomed place acted as a sort of personal touchstone, a reminder that, elevated and important as the sign on his office door said he was today, he had started out doing bank robberies in the Philadelphia Field Division, and his badge and gun still made him a sworn member of his country's finest police agency.

"Even on Capitol Hill?" Clarice asked.

"Even on Capitol Hill," Murray repeated. Her subsequent silence surprised him. Golden was never reticent about much. You always knew what she was thinking — well, Murray amended, you knew what she wanted you to know. She played her little games, just as he did. "Talk to me, Dr. Golden."

"Rape."

Murray nodded, setting the menu down. "Okay, first of all, please tell me about your patient."

"Female, age thirty-five, single, never married. She was referred to me by her gynecologist, an old friend. She came to me clinically depressed. I've had three sessions with her."

Only three, Murray thought. Clarice was a witch at this stuff, so perceptive. Jesus, what an interrogator she would have made with her gentle smile and quiet motherly voice.

"When did it happen?" Names could wait for the moment. Murray would start with the barest facts of the case.

"Three years ago."

The FBI agent — he still preferred "Special Agent" to his official title of Deputy Assistant Director — frowned immediately. "Long time, Clarice. No forensics, I suppose."

"No, it's her word against his — except for one thing." Golden reached into her purse and pulled out photocopies of the Beringer letter, blown up in the copying process. Murray read through the pages slowly while Dr. Golden watched his face for reaction.

"Holy shit," Dan breathed while the waiter hovered twenty feet away, thinking his guests were a reporter and a source, as was hardly uncommon in Washington. "Where's the original?"

"In my office. I was very careful handling it," Golden told him.

That made Murray smile. The monogrammed paper was an immediate help. In addition, paper was especially good at holding fingerprints, especially if kept tucked away in a cool, dry place, as such letters usually were. The Senate aide in question would have been fingerprinted as part of her security-clearance process, which meant the likely author of this document could be positively identified. The papers gave time, place, events, and also announced her desire to die. Sad as it was, it made this document something akin to a dying declaration, therefore, arguably, admissible in federal district court as evidentiary material in a criminal case. The defense attorney would object — they always did — and the objection would be overruled — it always was — and the jury members would hear every word, leaning forward as they always did to catch the voice from the grave. Except in this case it wouldn't be a jury, at least not at first.

Murray didn't like anything about rape cases. As a man and a cop, he viewed that class of criminal with special contempt. It was a smudge on his own manhood that someone could commit such a cowardly, foul act. More professionally disturbing was the troublesome fact that rape cases so often came down to one person's word against another's. Like most investigative cops, Murray distrusted all manner of eyewitness testimony. People were poor observers — it was that simple — and rape victims, crushed by the experience, often made poor witnesses, their testimony further attacked by the defense counsel. Forensic evidence, on the other hand, was something you could prove, it was incontrovertible. Murray loved that sort of evidence.

"Is it enough to begin a criminal investigation?"

Murray looked up and spoke quietly: "Yes, ma'am."

"And who he is — "

"My current job — well, I'm sort of the street-version of the executive assistant to Bill Shaw. You don't know Bill, do you?"

"Only by reputation."

"It's all true," Murray assured her. "We were classmates at Quantico, and we broke in the same way, in the same place, doing the same thing. A crime is a crime, and we're cops, and that's the name of the song, Clarice."

But even as his mouth proclaimed the creed of his agency, his mind was saying, *Holy shit*. There was a great big political dimension to this one. The President didn't need the trouble. Well, who ever needed this sort of thing? For goddamned sure, Barbara Linders and Lisa Beringer didn't need to be raped by someone they'd trusted. But the real bottom line was simple: thirty years earlier, Daniel E. Murray had graduated from the FBI Academy at Quantico, Virginia, had raised his right hand to the sky and sworn an oath to God. There were gray areas. There always would be. A good agent had to use his judgment, know which laws could be bent, and how far. But not this far, and not this law. Bill Shaw was of the same cut. Blessed by fate to occupy a position as apolitical as an office in Washington, D.C., could be, Shaw had built his reputation on integrity, and was too old to change. A case like this would start in his seventh-floor office.

"I have to ask, is this for-real?"

"My best professional judgment is that my patient is telling the truth in every detail."

"Will she testify?"

"Yes."

"Your evaluation of the letter?"

"Also quite genuine, psychologically speaking." Murray already knew that from his own experience, but someone — first he, then other agents, and ultimately a jury — needed to hear it from a pro.

"Now what?" the psychologist asked.

Murray stood, to the surprised disappointment of the hovering waiter. "Now we drive down to headquarters and meet with Bill. We'll get case agents in to set up a file. Bill and I and the case agent will walk across the street to the Department and meet with the Attorney General. After that, I don't know exactly. We've never had one like this — not since the early seventies, anyway — and I'm not sure of procedure just yet. The usual stuff with your patient. Long, tough interviews. We'll talk to Ms. Beringer's family, friends, look for papers, diaries. But that's the technical side. The political side will be touchy."

And for that reason, Dan knew, he'd be the man running the case. Another *Holy shit!* crossed his mind, as he remembered the part in the Constitution that would govern the whole procedure. Dr. Golden saw the wavering in his eyes and, rare for her, misread what it meant.

"My patient needs — "

Murray blinked. *So what?* he asked himself. *It's still a crime.*

"I know, Clarice. She needs justice. So does Lisa Beringer. You know what? So does the government of the United States of America."

He didn't look like a computer-software engineer. He wasn't at all scruffy. He wore a pinstriped suit, carried a briefcase. He might have said that it was a disguise required by his clientele and the professional atmosphere of the area, but the simple truth was that he preferred to look neat.

The procedure was just as straightforward as it could be. The client used Stratus mainframes, compact, powerful machines that were easily networked — in fact they were the platform of choice for many bulletin-board services because of their reasonable price and high electronic reliability. There were three of them in the room. "Alpha" and "Beta" — so labeled with white letters on blue plastic boards — were the primaries, and took on the front-line duties on alternate days, with one always backing up the other. The third machine, "Zulu," was the emergency backup, and whenever Zulu was operating, you knew that a service team was either already there or on the way. Another facility, identical in every way except for the number of people around, was across the East River, with a different physical location, different power source, different phone lines, different satellite uplinks. Each building was a high-rise fire-resistant structure with an automatic sprinkler system around the computer room, and a DuPont 1301 system inside of it, the better to eliminate a fire in seconds. Each system-trio had battery backups sufficient to run the hardware for twelve hours. New York safety and environmental codes perversely did not allow the presence of emergency generators in the buildings, an annoyance to the systems engineers who were paid to worry about such things. And worry they did, despite the fact that the duplication, the exquisite redundancies that in a military context were called "defense in depth," would protect against anything and everything that could be imagined.

Well, nearly everything.

On the front service panel of each of the mainframes was an SCSI port. This was an innovation for the new models, an implicit bow to the fact that desktop computers were so powerful that they could upload important information far more easily than the old method of hanging a tape reel.

In this case, the upload terminal was a permanent fixture of the system. Attached to the overall system control panel which controlled Alpha, Beta, and Zulu was a third-generation Power PC, and attached to it in turn was a Bernoulli removable-disk drive. Colloquially known as a "toaster" because its disk was about the size of a piece of bread, this machine had a gigabyte of storage, far more than was needed for this program.

"Okay?" the engineer asked.

The system controller moved his mouse and selected Zulu from his screen of options. A senior operator behind him confirmed that he'd made the right selection. Alpha and Beta were doing their normal work, and could not be disturbed.

"You're up on Zulu, Chuck."

"Roger that," Chuck replied with a smile. The pinstriped engineer slid the cartridge into the slot and waited for the proper icon to appear on the screen. He clicked on it, opening a new window to reveal the contents of PORTA-1, his name for the cartridge.

The new window had only two items in it: IN-

STALLER and ELECTRA-CLERK-2.4.0. An automatic antivirus program immediately swept through the new files, and after five seconds pronounced them clean.

"Looking good, Chuck," the sys-con told him. His supervisor nodded concurrence.

"Well, gee, Rick, can I deliver the baby now?"

"Hit it."

Chuck Searls selected the INSTALL icon and double-clicked it.

ARE YOU SURE YOU WANT TO REPLACE "ELECTRA-CLERK 2.3.1" WITH NEW PROGRAM "ELECTRA-CLERK 2.4.0"?

a box asked him. Searls clicked the "Yes" box.

ARE YOU REALLY SURE????

another box asked immediately.

"Who put that in?"

"I did," the sys-con answered with a grin.

"Funny." Searls clicked YES again.

The toaster drive started humming. Searls liked systems that you could hear as they ran, the *whip-whip* sounds of the moving heads added to the whir of the rotating disk. The program was only fifty megabytes. The transfer took fewer seconds than were needed for him to open his bottle of spring water and take a sip.

"Well," Searls asked as he slid his chair back from the console, "you want to see if it works?"

He turned to look out. The computer room was walled in with glass panels, but beyond them he could see New York Harbor. A cruise liner was heading out; medium size, painted white. Heading where? he wondered. Someplace warm, with white sand and blue skies and a nice bright sun all the time. Someplace a hell of a lot different from New York City, he was sure of that. Nobody took a cruise to a place like the Big Apple. How nice to be on that ship, heading away from the blustery winds of fall. How much nicer still not to return on it, Searls thought with a wistful smile. Well, airplanes were faster, and you didn't have to ride them back either.

The sys-con, working on his control console, brought Zulu on-line. At 16:10:00 EST, the backup machine started duplicating the jobs being done by Alpha, and simultaneously backed up by Beta. With one difference. The throughput monitor showed that Zulu was running slightly faster. On a day like this, Zulu normally tended to fall behind, but now it was running so fast that the machine was actually "resting" for a few seconds each minute.

"Smokin', Chuck!" the sys-con observed. Searls drained his water bottle, dropped it in the nearest trash bucket, and walked over.

"Yeah, I cut out about ten thousand lines of code. It wasn't the machines, it was the program. It just took us a while to figure the right paths through the boards. I think we have it now."

"What's different?" the senior controller asked. He knew quite a bit about software design.

"I changed the hierarchy system, how it hands things off from one parallel board to another. Still needs a little work on synchronicity, tally isn't as fast as posting. I think I can beat that in another month or two, cut some fat out of the front end."

The sys-con punched a command for the first benchmark test. It came up at once. "Six percent faster than two-point-three-point-one. Not too shabby."

"We needed that six percent," the supervisor said, meaning that he needed more. Trades just ran too heavy sometimes, and like everyone in the Depository Trust Company, he lived in fear of falling behind.

"Send me some data at the end of the week and maybe I can deliver a few more points to you," Searls promised.

"Good job, Chuck."

"Thanks, Bud."

"Who else uses this?"

"This version? Nobody. A custom variation runs the machines over at CHIPS."

"Well, you're the man," the supervisor noted generously. He would have been less generous had he thought it through. The supervisor had helped design the entire system. All the redundancies, all the safety systems, the way that tapes were pulled off the machines every night and driven upstate. He'd worked with a committee to establish every safeguard that was necessary to the business he was in. But the quest for efficiency — and perversely, the quest for security — had created a vulnerability to which he was predictably blind. All the computers used the same software. They had to. Different software in the different computers, like different languages in an office, would have prevented, or at the very least impeded, crosstalk among the individual systems; and that would have been self-defeating. As a result, despite all the safeguards there was a single common point of vulnerability for all six of his machines. They all spoke the same language. They had to. They were the most important, if the least known, link in the American trading business.

Even here, DTC was not blind to the potential hazard. ELECTRA-CLERK 2.4.0 would not be uploaded to Alpha and Beta until it had run for a week on Zulu, and then another week would pass before they were loaded onto the backup site, whose machines were labeled "Charlie," "Delta," and "Tango." That was to ensure that 2.4.0 was both efficient and "crash-worthy," an engineering term that had come into the software field a year earlier. Soon, people would get

76

used to the new software, marvel at its faster speed. All the Stratus machines would speak exactly the same programming language, trade information back and forth in an electronic conversation of ones and zeros, like friends around a card table talking business.

Soon they would all know the same joke. Some would think it a good one, but not anyone at DTC.

3

Collegium

"So, we're agreed?" the Chairman of the Federal Reserve Board asked. Those around the table nodded. It wasn't that hard a call. For the second time in the past three months, President Durling had made it known, quietly, through the Secretary of the Treasury, that he would not object to another half-point rise in the Discount Rate. That was the interest rate which the Federal Reserve charged to banks that borrowed money — where else would they borrow such sums, except from the Fed? Any rise in that rate, of course, was passed immediately on to the consumer.

It was a constant balancing act, for the men and women around the polished oak table. They controlled the quantity of money in the American economy. As though by turning the valve that opened or closed the floodgate on an irrigation dam, they could regulate the amount of currency that existed, trying always not to provide too much or too little.

It was more complex than that, of course. Money had little physical reality. The Bureau of Engraving and Printing, located less than a mile away, had neither the paper nor the ink to make enough one-dollar bills for what the Fed parceled out every day. "Money" was mainly an electronic expression, a matter of sending a message: *You, First National Bank of Podunk, now have an additional three million dollars which you may lend to Joe's Hardware, or Jeff Brown's Gas-and-Go, or for new homeowners to borrow as mortgage loans to pay back for the next twenty years.* Few of these people were paid in cash — with credit cards there was less for a robber to steal, an employee to embezzle, or most inconveniently of all, a clerk to count, recount, and walk to the local branch of the bank. As a result, what appeared by the magic of computer E-mail or teleprinter message was lent out by written draft, to be repaid later by yet another theoretical expression, usually a check written on a small slip of special paper, often decorated with the picture of a flying eagle or a fishing boat on some lake that didn't exist, because the banks competed for customers and people liked such things.

The power of the people in this room was so stunning that even they rarely thought about it. By a simple decision, the people around the table had just made everything in America cost more. Every adjustable-rate mortgage for every home, every auto loan, every credit card revolving line, would become more expensive every month. Because of that decision, every business and household in America would have less disposable income to spend on employee benefits or Christmas toys. What began as a press release would reach into every wallet in the nation. Prices would increase on every consumer item from home computers to bubble gum, thus reducing further still everyone's real buying power.

And this was good, the Fed thought. All the statistical indicators said the economy was running a little too hot. There was a real danger of increasing inflation. In fact, there was always inflation to one degree or another, but the interest raise would limit it to tolerable levels. Prices would still go up somewhat, and the increase in the discount rate would make them go up further still.

It was an example of fighting fire with fire. Raising interest rates meant that, at the margin, people would borrow less, which would actually reduce the amount of money in circulation, which would lessen the buying pressure, which would cause prices to stabilize, more or less, and prevent something that all knew to be more harmful than a momentary blip in interest rates.

Like ripples expanding from a stone tossed into a lake, there would be other effects still. The interest on Treasury bills would increase. These were debt instruments of the government itself. People — actually institutions for the most part, like banks and pension funds and investment firms that had to park their clients' money somewhere while waiting for a good opportunity on the stock market — would give money, electronically, to the government for a term varying from three months to thirty years, and in return for the use of that money, the government itself had to pay interest (much of it recouped in taxes, of course). The marginal increase in the Federal-funds rate would raise the interest rate the government had to pay — determined at an auction. Thus the cost of the federal deficit would also increase, forcing the government to pull in more of the domestic money supply, reducing the pool of money available to personal and business loans and further increasing interest rates for the public through market forces over and above what the Fed enforced itself.

Finally, the mere fact that bank and T-Bill rates would increase made the stock market less attractive to investors because the government-guaranteed return was "safer" than the more speculative rate of return anticipated by a company whose products and/or services had to compete in the marketplace.

On Wall Street, individual investors and professional managers who monitored economic indicators took the evening news (increases in the Fed rate were usually timed for release after the close of the markets) phlegmatically and made the proper notes to "go short on" (sell) their positions in some issues. This would reduce the posted values of numerous stocks, causing the Dow Jones Industrial Average to sink. Actually, it was not an average at all, but the sum of the current market value of thirty blue-chip stocks, with Allied Signal on one end of the alphabet, Woolworth's on the other, and Merck in the middle. It was an indicator whose utility today was mainly that of giving the news media something to report to the public, which for the most part didn't know what it represented anyway. The dip in "the Dow" would make some people nervous, causing more selling, and more decline in the market until others saw opportunity in stock issues that had been depressed farther than they deserved to be. Sensing that the true value of those issues was higher than the market price indicated, they would buy in measured quantities, allowing the Dow (and other market indicators) to increase again until a point of equilibrium was reached, and confidence restored. And all these multifaceted changes were imposed on everyone's individual lives by a handful of people in an ornate boardroom in Washington, D.C., whose names few investment professionals even knew, much less the general public.

The remarkable thing was that everyone accepted the entire process, seemingly as normal as physical laws of nature, despite the fact that it was really as ethereal as a rainbow. The money did not physically exist. Even "real" money was only specially made paper printed with black ink on the front and green on the back. What backed the money was not gold or something of intrinsic value, but rather the collective belief that money *had* value because it *had to have* such value. Thus it was that the monetary system of the United States and every other country in the world was entirely an exercise in psychology, a thing of the mind, and as a result, so was every other aspect of the American economy. If money was simply a matter of communal faith, then so was everything else. What the Federal Reserve had done that afternoon was a measured exercise in first shaking that faith and then allowing it to reestablish itself of its own accord through the minds of those who held it. Holders of that faith included the governors of the Fed, because they truly understood it all — or thought that they did. Individually they might joke that nobody really understood how it all worked, any more than any of them could explain the nature of God, but like theologians constantly trying to determine and communicate the nature of a deity, it was their job to keep things moving, to make the belief-structure real and tangible, never quite acknowledging that it all rested on nothing even as real as the paper currency they carried with them for the times when the use of a plastic credit card was inconvenient.

They were trusted, in the distant way that people trusted their clergy, to maintain the structure on which worldly faith always depended, proclaiming the reality of something that could not be seen, an edifice whose physical manifestations were found only in buildings of stone and the sober looks of those who worked there. And, they told themselves, it all worked. Didn't it?

In many ways Wall Street was the one part of America in which Japanese citizens, especially those from Tokyo itself, felt most at home. The buildings were so tall as to deny one a look at the sky, the streets so packed that a visitor from another planet might think that yellow cabs and black limousines were the primary form of life here. People moved along the crowded, dirty sidewalks in bustling anonymity, eyes rigidly fixed forward both to show purpose and to avoid even visual contact with others who might be competitors or, more likely, were just in the way. The whole city of New York had taken its demeanor from this place, brusque, rapid, impersonal, tough in form, but not in substance. Its inhabitants told themselves that they were where the action was, and were so fixed on their individual and collective goals that they resented all the others who felt precisely the same way. In that sense it was a perfect world. Everyone felt exactly the same. Nobody gave much of a damn about anyone else. At least, that's the way it appeared. In truth, the people who worked here had spouses and children, interests and hobbies, desires and dreams, just like anybody else, but between the hours of eight in the morning and six in the evening all that was subordinated to the rules of their business. The business, of course, was money, a class of product that knew no place or loyalty. And so it was that on the fifty-eighth floor of Six Columbus Lane, the new headquarters building of the Columbus Group, a changeover was taking place.

The room was breathtaking in every possible aspect. The walls were solid walnut, not veneer, and lovingly maintained by a well-paid team of craftsmen. Two of the walls were polished glass that ran from the carpet to the Celotex ceiling panels, and offered a view of New York Harbor and beyond. The carpet was thick enough to swallow up shoes — and to deliver a nasty static shock, which the people here had learned to tolerate. The conference table was forty feet of red granite, and the chairs around it priced out at nearly two thousand dollars each.

The Columbus Group, founded only eleven years before, had gone from being just one more upstart, to *enfant terrible,* to bright rising light, to serious player, to among the best in its field, to its current position as a cornerstone of the mutual-funds community. Founded by George Winston, the company now controlled a virtual fleet of fund-management teams. The three primary teams were fittingly called Niña, Pinta, and Santa Maria, because when Winston had founded the company, at the age of twenty-nine, he'd just read and been captivated by Samuel Eliot Morison's *The European Discovery of the New World*, and, marveling at the courage, vision, and sheer *chutzpah* of the restless navigators from Prince Henry's school, he'd decided to chart his own course by their example. Now forty, and rich beyond the dreams of avarice, it was time to leave, to smell the roses, to take his ninety-foot sailing yacht on some extended cruises. In fact, his precise plans were to spend the next few months learning how to sail *Cristobol* as expertly as he did everything else in his life, and then to duplicate the voyages of discovery, one every summer, until he ran out of examples to follow, and then maybe write his own book about it.

He was a man of modest size that his personality seemed to make larger. A fitness fanatic — stress was the prime killer on the Street — Winston positively glowed with the confidence imparted by his superb conditioning. He walked into the already-full conference room with the air of a President-elect entering his headquarters after the conclusion of a successful campaign, his stride fast and sure, his smile courtly and guileless. Pleased with this culmination of his professional life on this day, he even nodded his head to his principal guest.

"Yamata-san, so good to see you again," George Winston said with an extended hand. "You came a long way for this."

"For an event of this importance," the Japanese industrialist replied, "how could I not?"

Winston escorted the smaller man to his seat at the far end of the table before returning toward his own at the head. There were teams of lawyers and investment executives in between — rather like football squads at the line of scrimmage, Winston thought, as he walked the length of the table, guarding his own feelings as he did so.

It was the only way out, damn it, Winston told himself. Nothing else would have worked. The first six years running this place had been the greatest exhilaration of his life. Starting with less than twenty clients, building their money and his reputation at the same time. Working at home, he remembered, his brain racing to outstrip his paces across the room, one computer and one dedicated phone line, worried about feeding his family, blessed by the support of his loving wife despite the fact that she'd been pregnant the first time — with twins, no less, and *still* she'd never missed a chance to express her love and confidence — parlaying his skill and instinct into success. By thirty-five it had all been done, really. Two floors of a downtown office tower, his own plush office, a team of bright young "rocket scientists" to do the detail work. That was when he'd first thought about getting out.

In building up the funds of his clients, he'd bet his own money, too, of course, until his personal fortune, after taxes, was six hundred fifty-seven million dollars. Basic conservatism would not allow him to leave his money behind, and besides, he was concerned about where the market was heading, and so he was taking it all out, cashing in and switching over to a more conservative manager. It seemed a strange course of action even to himself, but he just didn't want to be *bothered* with this business anymore. Going "conservative" was dull, and would necessarily cast away enormous future opportunities, but, he'd asked himself for years, what was the point? He owned six palatial homes, two personal automobiles at each, a helicopter, he leased a personal jet, *Cristobol* was his principal toy. He had everything he'd ever wanted, and even with conservative portfolio management, his personal wealth would continue to rise faster than the inflation rate because he didn't have the ego to spend even as much as the annualized return would generate. And so he'd parcel it out in fifty-million-dollar blocks, covering every segment of the market through investment colleagues who had not achieved his personal success, but whose integrity and acumen he trusted. The switchover had been under way for three years, very quietly, as he'd searched for a worthy successor for the Columbus Group. Unfortunately, the only one who'd stepped forward was this little bastard.

"Ownership" was the wrong term, of course. The true owners of the group were the individual investors who gave their money to his custody, and that was a trust which Winston never forgot. Even with his decision made, his conscience clawed at him. Those people relied on him and his people, but him most of all, because his was the name on the most important door. The trust of so many people was a heavy burden which he'd borne with skill and pride, but enough was enough. It was time to attend to the needs of his own family, five kids and a faithful wife who were tired of "understanding" why Daddy had to be away so much. The needs of the many. The needs of the few. But the few were closer, weren't they?

Raizo Yamata was putting in much of his personal fortune and quite a bit of the corporate funds of his many industrial operations in order to make good the funds that Winston was taking out. Quiet though Winston might wish it to be, and understandable as his action surely was to anyone with a feel for the business, it would still become cause for comment. Therefore it was necessary that the man replacing him be willing to put his own money back in. That sort of move would restore any wavering confidence. It would also cement the marriage between the Japanese and American financial systems. While Winston watched, instruments were signed that "enabled" the funds transfer for which international-bank executives had stayed late at their offices in six countries. A man of great personal substance, Raizo Yamata.

Well, Winston corrected himself, great personal liquidity. Since leaving the Wharton School, he'd known a lot of bright, sharp operators, all of them cagey, intelligent people who'd tried to hide their predatory nature behind façades of humor and bonhomie. You soon developed an instinct for them. It was that simple. Perhaps Yamata thought that his heritage made him more unreadable, just as he doubtless thought himself to be smarter than the average bear — or bull in this case, Winston smiled to himself. Maybe, maybe not, he thought, looking down the forty-foot table. Why was there no excitement in the man? The Japanese had emotions, too. Those with whom he'd done business had been affable enough, pleased as any other man to make a big hit on the Street. Get a few drinks into them and they were no different from Americans, really. Oh, a little more reserved, a little shy, perhaps, but always polite, that's what he liked best about them, their fine manners, something that would have been welcome in New Yorkers. That was it, Winston thought. Yamata *was* polite, but it wasn't genuine. It was pro forma with him, and shyness had nothing to do with it. Like a little robot. . . .

No, that wasn't true either, Winston thought, as the papers slid down the table toward him. Yamata's wall was just thicker than the average, the better to conceal what he felt. Why had he built such a wall? It wasn't necessary here, was it? In this room he was among equals; more than that, he was now among partners. He had just signed over his money, placed his personal well-being in the same boat as so many

87

others. By transferring nearly two hundred million dollars, he now owned over one percent of the funds managed by Columbus, which made him the institution's largest single investor. With that status came control of every dollar, share, and option the fund had. It wasn't the largest fleet on the Street by any means, but the Columbus Group was one of the leaders. People looked to Columbus for ideas and trends. Yamata had bought more than a trading house. He now had a real position in the hierarchy of America's money-managers. His name, largely unknown in America until recently, would now be spoken with respect, which was something that ought to have put a smile on his face, Winston thought. But it didn't.

The final sheet of paper got to his chair, slid across by one of his principal subordinates, and, with his signature, about to become Yamata's. It was just so easy. One signature, a minute quantity of blue ink arranged in a certain way, and with it went eleven years of his life. One signature gave his business over to a man he didn't understand.

Well, I don't have to, do I? He'll try to make money for himself and others, just like I did. Winston took out his pen and signed without looking up. *Why didn't you look first?*

He heard a cork pop out of a champagne bottle and looked up to see the smiles on the faces of his former employees. In consummating the deal he'd become a symbol for them. Forty years old, rich, successful, retired, able to go after the fun dreams now, without having to stick around forever. That was the personal goal of everyone who worked in a place like this. Bright as these people were, few had the guts to give it a try. Even then, most of them failed, Winston reminded himself, but he was the living proof that it could happen. Tough-minded and cynical as these investment professionals were — or pretended

88

to be — at heart they had the same dream, to make the pile and leave, get away from the incredible stress of finding opportunities in reams of paper reports and analyses, make a rep, draw people and their money in, do good things for them and yourself — and *leave.* The pot of gold was *in* the rainbow, and at the end was an exit. A sailboat, a house in Florida, another in the Virgins, another in Aspen . . . sleeping until eight sometimes; playing golf. It was a vision of the future which beckoned strongly.

But why not now?

Dear God, what had he done? Tomorrow morning he'd wake up and not know what to do. Was it possible to turn it off just like that?

A little late for that, George, he told himself, reaching for the offered glass of Moët, taking the obligatory sip. He raised his glass to toast Yamata, for that, too, was obligatory. Then he saw the smile, expected but surprising. It was the smile of a victorious man. Why that? Winston asked himself. He'd paid top dollar. It wasn't the sort of deal in which anyone had "won" or "lost." Winston was taking his money out, Yamata was putting his money in. And yet that smile. It was a jarring note, all the more so because he didn't understand it. His mind raced even as the bubbly wine slid down his throat. If only the smile had been friendly and gracious, but it wasn't. Their eyes met, forty feet apart, in a look that no one else caught, and despite the fact that there had been no battle fought and no victors identified, it was as though a war was being fought.

Why? Instincts. Winston immediately turned his loose. There was just something — what? A nastiness in Yamata. Was he one of those who viewed everything as combat? Winston had been that way once, but grown out of it. Competition was always tough, but civilized. On the Street everyone competed with everyone else, too, for security, advice, consensus, and competition, which was tough but friendly so long as everyone obeyed the same rules.

You're not in that game, are you? he wanted to ask, too late.

Winston tried a new ploy, interested in the game that had started so unexpectedly. He lifted his glass, and silently toasted his successor while the other people in the room chattered across the table. Yamata reciprocated the gesture, and his mien actually became more arrogant, radiating contempt at the stupidity of the man who had just sold out to him.

You were so good at concealing your feelings before, why not now? You really think you're the cat's ass, that you've done something . . . bigger than I know. What?

Winston looked away, out the windows to the mirror-calm water of the harbor. He was suddenly bored with the game, uninterested in whatever competition that little bastard thought himself to have won. *Hell,* he told himself, *I'm out of here. I've lost nothing. I've gained my freedom. I've got my money. I've got everything. Okay, fine, you can run the house and make your money, and have a seat in any club or restaurant in town, whenever you're here, and tell yourself how important you are, and if you think that's a victory, then it is. But it's not a victory* over *anyone,* Winston concluded.

It was too bad. Winston had caught everything, as he usually did, identified all the right elements. But for the first time in years, he'd failed to assemble them into the proper scenario. It wasn't his fault. He understood his own game completely, and had merely assumed, wrongly, that it was the only game in town.

Chet Nomuri worked very hard not to be an American citizen. His was the fourth generation of his family in the U.S. — the first of his ancestors had arrived right after the turn of the century and before the

"Gentlemen's Agreement" between Japan and America restricting further immigration. It would have insulted him had he thought about it more. Of greater insult was what had happened to his grandparents and great-grandparents despite full U.S. citizenship. His grandfather had leaped at the chance to prove his loyalty to his country, and served in the 442nd Regimental Combat Team, returning home with two Purple Hearts and master-sergeant stripes only to find that the family business — office supplies — had been sold off for a song and his family sent to an intern camp. With stoic patience, he had started over, built it up with a new and unequivocal name, Veteran's Office Furniture, and made enough money to send his three sons through college and beyond. Chet's own father was a vascular surgeon, a small, jolly man who'd been born in government captivity, and whose parents, for that reason — and to please *his* grandfather — had maintained some of the traditions, such as language.

Done it pretty well, too, Nomuri thought. He'd overcome his accent problems in a matter of weeks, and now, sitting in the Tokyo bathhouse, everyone around him wondered which prefecture he had come from. Nomuri had identification papers for several. He was a field officer of the Central Intelligence Agency, perversely on assignment for the U.S. Department of Justice, and completely without the knowledge of the U.S. Department of State. One of the things he had learned from his surgeon father was to fix his eyes forward to the things he could do, not back at things he couldn't change. In this the Nomuri family had bought into America, quietly, undramatically, and successfully, Chet told himself, sitting up to his neck in hot water.

The rules of the bath were perfectly straightforward. You could talk about everything but business, and you could even talk about that, but only the gossip, not the substantive aspects of how you made your money and your deals. Within those loose constraints, seemingly everything was open for discussion in a surprisingly casual forum in this most structured of societies. Nomuri got there at about the same time every day, and had been doing so long enough that the people he met were on a similar schedule, knew him, and were comfortable with him. He already knew everything there was to know about their wives and families, as they did about his — or rather, about the fictional "legend" that he'd built himself and which was now as real to him as the Los Angeles neighborhood in which he'd come to manhood.

"I need a mistress," Kazuo Taoka said, hardly for the first time. "My wife, all she wants to do is watch television since our son is born."

"All they ever do is complain," another salaryman agreed. There was a concurring series of grunts from the other men in the pool.

"A mistress is expensive," Nomuri noted from his corner of the bath, wondering what the wives complained about in their bathing pools. "In money and time."

Of the two, time was the more important. Each of the young executives — well, not really that, but the borderline between what in America would seem a clerkship and a real decision-making post was hazy in Japan — made a good living, but the price for it was to be bound as tightly to his corporation as one of Tennessee Ernie Ford's coal miners. Frequently up before dawn, commuting to work mainly by train from outlying suburbs, they worked in crowded offices, worked hard and late, and went home most often to find wives and children asleep. Despite what he'd learned from TV and research before coming over here, it still came as a shock to Nomuri that the pressures of business might actually be destroying the social fabric of the country, that

92

the structure of the family itself was damaged. It was all the more surprising because the strength of the Japanese family unit was the only thing that had enabled his own ancestors to succeed in an America where racism had been a seemingly insurmountable obstacle.

"Expensive, yes," Taoka agreed morosely, "but where else can a man get what he needs?"

"That is true," another said on the other side of the pool. Well, not really a pool, but too big for a tub. "It costs too much, but what is it worth to be a man?"

"Easier for the bosses," Nomuri said next, wondering where this would lead. He was still early in his assignment, still building the foundation for embarking on his real mission, taking his time, as he'd been ordered to do by Ed and Mary Pat.

"You should see what Yamata-san has going for him," another salaryman observed with a dark chuckle.

"Oh?" Taoka asked.

"He is friendly with Goto," the man went on with a conspiratorial look.

"The politician — ah, yes, of course!"

Nomuri leaned back and closed his eyes, letting the hundred-plus-degree water of the bath envelop him, not wanting to appear interested as his brain turned on its internal tape-recorder. "Politician," he murmured sleepily. "Hmph."

"I had to run some papers to Yamata-san last month, a quiet place not far from here. Papers about the deal he just made today, in fact. Goto was entertaining him. They let me in, I suppose Yamata-san wanted me to have a look. The girl with them . . ." His voice became slightly awed. "Tall and blonde, such fine bosoms."

"Where does one buy an American mistress?" another interjected coarsely.

"And she knew her place," the storyteller went on. "She sat there while Yamata-san went over the papers, waiting patiently. No shame in her at all. Such lovely bosoms," the man concluded.

So the stories about Goto are true, Nomuri thought. *How the hell do people like that make it so far in politics?* the field officer asked himself. Only a second later he reproved himself for the stupidity of the question. Such behavior in politicians dated back to the Trojan War and beyond.

"You cannot stop there," Taoka insisted humorously. The man didn't, elaborating on the scene and earning the rapt attention of the others, who already knew all the relevant information on the wives of all present, and were excited to hear the description of a "new" girl in every clinical detail.

"Who cares about them?" Nomuri asked crossly, with closed eyes. "They're too tall, their feet are too big, their manners are poor, and — "

"Let him tell the story," an excited voice insisted. Nomuri shrugged his submission to the collegial will while his mind recorded every word. The salaryman had an eye for detail, and in less than a minute Nomuri had a full physical description. The report would go through the Station Chief to Langley, because the CIA kept a file on the personal habits of politicians all over the world. There was no such thing as a useless fact, though he was hoping to get information of more immediate use than Goto's sexual proclivities.

The debriefing was held at the Farm, officially known as Camp Peary, a CIA training facility located off of Interstate 64 between Williamsburg and Yorktown, Virginia. Cold drinks were gunned down as rapidly as the cans could be popped open, as both men went over maps and explained the six weeks in-country that had ended so well. Corp, CNN said, was going to begin his trial in the following week.

94

There wasn't much doubt about the outcome. Somewhere back in that equatorial country, somebody had already purchased about fifteen feet of three-quarter-inch manila rope, though both officers wondered where the lumber for the gallows would come from. Probably have to ship it in, Clark thought. They hadn't seen much in the way of trees.

"Well," Mary Patricia Foley said after hearing the final version. "Sounds like a good clean one, guys."

"Thank you, ma'am," Ding replied gallantly. "John sure shovels out a nice line of BS for people."

"That's experience for you," Clark noted with a chuckle. "How's Ed doing?"

"Learning his place," the Deputy Director for Operations replied with an impish grin. Both she and her husband had gone through the Farm together, and Clark had been one of their instructors. Once the best husband-wife team the Agency had, the truth of the matter was that Mary Pat had better instincts for working the field, and Ed was better at planning things out. Under those circumstances, Ed really should have had the senior position, but Mary Pat's appointment had just been too attractive, politically speaking, and in any case they still worked together, effectively co–Deputy Directors, though Ed's actual title was somewhat nebulous. "You two are due some time off, and by the way, you have an official attaboy from the other side of the river." That was not a first for either officer. "John, you know, it's really time for you to come back inside." By which she meant a permanent return to a training slot here in the Virginia Tidewater. The Agency was upsizing its human-intelligence assets — the bureaucratic term for increasing the number of case officers (known as spies to America's enemies) to be deployed into the field. Mrs. Foley wanted Clark to help train them. After all, he'd done a good job with her and her husband, twenty years before.

"Not unless you want to retire me. I like it out there."

"He's dumb that way, ma'am," Chavez said with a sly grin. "I guess it comes with old age."

Mrs. Foley didn't argue the point. These two were among her best field teams, and she wasn't in that much of a hurry to break up a successful operation. "Fair enough, guys. You're released from the debrief. Oklahoma and Nebraska are on this afternoon."

"How are the kids, MP?" That was her service nickname, though not everybody had the rank to use it.

"Just fine, John. Thanks for asking." Mrs. Foley stood and walked to the door. A helicopter would whisk her back to Langley. She wanted to catch the game, too.

Clark and Chavez traded the look that comes with the conclusion of a job. Operation WALKMAN was now in the books, officially blessed by the Agency, and, in this case, by the White House.

"Miller time, Mr. C."

"I guess you want a ride, eh?"

"If you would be so kind, sir," Ding replied.

John Clark looked his partner over. Yes, he had cleaned himself up. The black hair was cut short and neat, the dark, heavy beard that had blurred his face in Africa was gone. He was even wearing a tie and white shirt under his suit jacket. Clark thought of the outfit as courting clothes, though on further reflection he might have recalled that Ding had once been a soldier, and that soldiers returning from the field liked to scrape off the physical reminders of the rougher aspects of their profession. Well, he could hardly complain that the lad was trying to look presentable, could he? Whatever faults Ding might have, John told himself, he always showed proper respect.

"Come on." Clark's Ford station wagon was parked in its usual place, and after fifteen minutes they pulled into the driveway of his house. Set outside the grounds of Camp Peary, it was an ordinary split-level rancher, emptier now than it had been. Margaret Pamela Clark, his elder daughter, was away at college, Marquette University in her case. Patricia Doris Clark had chosen a school closer to home, William and Mary in nearby Williamsburg, where she was majoring in pre-med. Patsy was at the door, already alerted for the arrival.

"Daddy!" A hug, a kiss, followed by something which had become somewhat more important. "Ding!" Just a hug in this case, Clark saw, not fooled for a moment.

"Hi, Pats." Ding didn't let go of her hand as he came into the house.

4

Activity

"Our requirements are different," the negotiator insisted.

"How is that?" his counterpart asked patiently.

"The steel, the design of the tank, these are unique. I am not an engineer myself, but the people who do the design work tell me this is so, and that their product will be damaged by the substitution of other parts. Now," he went on patiently, "there is also the issue of commonality of the parts. As you know, many of the cars assembled in Kentucky are shipped back to Japan for sale, and in the event of damage or the need for replacement, then the local supply will immediately be available for use. If we were to substitute the American components which you suggest, this would not be the case."

"Seiji, we are talking about a gasoline tank. It is made of — what? Five pieces of galvanized steel, bent and welded together, with a total internal capacity of nineteen gallons. There are no moving parts," the official of the State Department pointed out, interjecting himself into the process and playing his part as he was paid to do. He'd even done a good job of feigning exasperation when he'd used his counterpart's given name.

"Ah, but the steel itself, the formula, the proportions of different materials in the finished alloy, these have been optimized to the precise specifications required by the manufacturer — ”

“Which are standardized all over the world.”

“Sadly, this is not the case. Our specifications are most exacting, far more so than those of others, and, I regret to say, more exacting than those of the Deerfield Auto Parts Company. For that reason, we must sadly decline your request.” Which put an end to this phase of the negotiations. The Japanese negotiator leaned back in his chair, resplendent in his Brooks Brothers suit and Pierre Cardin tie, trying not to gloat too obviously. He had a lot of practice in doing so, and was good at it: it was his deck of cards. Besides, the game was just getting easier, not harder.

“That is most disappointing,” the representative of the U.S. Department of Commerce said. He hadn’t expected otherwise, of course, and flipped the page to go on to the next item on the agenda of the Domestic Content Negotiations. It was like a Greek play, he told himself, some cross between a Sophoclean tragedy and a comedy by Aristophanes. You knew exactly what was going to happen before you even started. In this he was right, but in a way he couldn’t know.

The meat of the play had been determined months earlier, long before the negotiations had stumbled upon the issue, and in retrospect sober minds would certainly have called it an accident, just one more of the odd coincidences that shape the fate of nations and their leaders. As with most such events, it had begun with a simple error that had occurred despite the most careful of precautions. A bad electrical wire, of all things, had reduced the available current into a dip tank, thus reducing the charge in the hot liquid into which the steel sheets were dipped. That in turn had reduced the galvanizing process, and the steel sheets were in fact given merely a thin patina, while they appeared to be fully coated. The *non*-galvanized sheets were piled up on pallets, wrapped with steel bands for stability, and covered with plastic. The error would be further compounded in the finishing and assembly process.

The plant where it had happened was not part of the assembler. As with American firms, the big auto-assembly companies — which designed the cars and put their trademarks on them — bought most of the components from smaller parts-supply companies. In Japan the relationship between the bigger fish and the smaller ones was both stable and cutthroat: stable insofar as the business between the two sets of companies was generally one of long standing; cutthroat insofar as the demands of the assemblers were dictatorial, for there was always the threat that they would move their business to someone else, though this possibility was rarely raised openly. Only oblique references, usually a kindly comment on the state of affairs at another, smaller firm, a reference to the bright children of the owner of such a firm, or how the representative of the assembler had seen him at a ball game or bathhouse the previous week. The nature of the reference was less important than the content of the message, and that content always came through loud and clear. As a result, the little parts-companies were not the showcases of Japanese heavy industry that other nationalities had come to see and respect on worldwide television. The workers didn't wear company coveralls, didn't eat alongside management in plush cafeterias, didn't work in spotless, superbly organized assembly plants. The pay for these workers was also something other than the highly adequate wage structure of the assembly workers, and though the lifelong employment covenant was becoming fiction even for the elite workers, it had never existed at all for the others.

At one of the nondescript metal-working shops, the bundles of not-quite-galvanized steel were unwrapped, and the individual sheets fed by hand to cutting machines. There the square sheets were mechanically sliced, and the edges trimmed — the surplus material was gathered and returned to the steel mill for recycling — so that each piece matched the size determined by the design, invariably to tolerances less than a millimeter, even for this fairly crude component which the owner's eyes would probably never behold. The larger cut pieces moved on to another machine for heating and bending, then were welded into an oval cylinder. Immediately thereafter the oval-cut end pieces were matched up and welded into place as well, by a machine process that required only one workman to supervise. Pre-cut holes in one side were matched up with the pipe that would terminate at the filler cap — there was another in the bottom for the line leading to the engine. Before leaving the jobber, the tanks were spray-coated with a wax-and-epoxy-based formula that would protect the steel against rust. The formula was supposed to bond with the steel, creating a firm union of disparate materials that would forever protect the gas tank against corrosion and resultant fuel leakage. An elegant and fairly typical piece of superb Japanese engineering, only in this case it didn't work because of the bad electrical cable at the steel plant. The coating never really attached itself to the steel, though it had sufficient internal stiffness to hold its shape long enough for visual inspection to be performed, and immediately afterwards the gas tanks proceeded by roller-conveyor to the boxing shop at the end of the small-parts plant. There the tanks were tucked into cardboard boxes fabricated by yet another jobber and sent by truck to a warehouse where half of the tanks were placed aboard other trucks for delivery to the assembly plant, and the other half went into identically sized cargo containers which were loaded aboard a ship for transport to the United States. There the tanks would be attached to a nearly identical automobile at a plant owned by the same international conglomerate, though this plant was located in the hills of Kentucky, not the Kwanto Plain outside of Tokyo.

All this had taken place months before the item had come onto the agenda of the Domestic Content Negotiations. Thousands of automobiles had been assembled and shipped with defective fuel tanks, and all had slipped through the usually excellent quality-assurance procedures at the assembly plants separated by six thousand miles of land and sea. In the case of those assembled in Japan, the cars had been loaded aboard some of the ugliest ships ever made, slab-sided auto-carriers which had the riding characteristics of barges as they plodded through the autumnal storms of the North Pacific Ocean. The sea-salt in the air reached through the ships' ventilation systems to the autos. That wasn't too bad until one of the ships drove through a front, and cold air changed rapidly to warm, and the instant change in relative humidity interacted with that of the air within various fuel tanks, causing salt-heavy moisture to form on the exterior of the steel, inside the defective coating. There the salt immediately started working on the unprotected mild steel of the tank, rusting and weakening the thin metal that contained 92-octane gasoline.

Whatever his other faults, Corp met his death with dignity, Ryan saw. He had just finished watching a tape segment that CNN had judged unsuitable for its regular news broadcast. After a speech whose translation Ryan had on two sheets of paper in his lap, the noose was placed over his head and the trap was sprung. The CNN camera crew focused in on the body as it jerked to a stop, closing an entry on his country's ledger. Mohammed Abdul Corp. Bully,

102

killer, drug-runner. Dead.

"I just hope we haven't created a martyr," Brett Hanson said, breaking the silence in Ryan's office.

"Mr. Secretary," Ryan said, turning his head to see his guest reading through a translation of Corp's last words. "Martyrs all share a single characteristic."

"What's that, Ryan?"

"They're all dead." Jack paused for effect. "This guy didn't die for God or his country. He died for committing crimes. They didn't hang him for killing Americans. They hanged him for killing his own people and for selling narcotics. That's not the stuff martyrs are made of. Case closed," Jack concluded, sticking the unread sheets of paper in his out basket. "Now, what have we learned about India?"

"Diplomatically speaking, nothing."

"Mary Pat?" Jack asked the CIA representative.

"There's a heavy mechanized brigade doing intensive training down south. We have overheads from two days ago. They seem to be exercising as a unit."

"Humint?"

"No assets in place," Mrs. Foley admitted, delivering what had become a CIA mantra. "Sorry, Jack. It'll be years before we can field people everywhere we want."

Ryan grumbled silently. Satellite photos were fine for what they were, but they were merely photographs. Photos only gave you shapes, not thoughts. Ryan needed thoughts. Mary Pat was doing her best to fix that, he remembered.

"According to the Navy, their fleet is very busy, and their pattern of operations suggests a barrier mission." The satellites *did* show that the Indian Navy's collection of amphibious-warfare ships was assembled in two squadrons. One was at sea, roughly two hundred miles from its base, exercising together as a group. The other was alongside at the same naval base undergoing maintenance, also as a group. The base was distant from the brigade undergoing its own exercises, but there was a rail line from the army base to the naval one. Analysts were now checking the rail yards at both facilities on a daily basis. The satellites were good for that, at least.

"Nothing at all, Brett? We have a pretty good ambassador over there as I recall."

"I don't want him to press too hard. It could damage what influence and access we have," SecState announced. Mrs. Foley tried not to roll her eyes.

"Mr. Secretary," Ryan said patiently, "in view of the fact that we have neither information nor influence at the moment, anything he might develop will be useful. Do you want me to make the call or will you?"

"He works for me, Ryan." Jack waited a few beats before responding to the prod. He hated territorial fights, though they were seemingly the favorite sport in the executive branch of the government.

"He works for the United States of America. Ultimately he works for the President. My job is to tell the President what's going on over there, and I need information. Please turn him loose. He's got a CIA chief working for him. He has three uniformed attachés. I want them all turned loose. The object of the exercise is to classify what looks to the Navy and to me like preparations for a possible invasion of a sovereign country. We want to prevent that."

"I can't believe that India would really do such a thing," Brett Hanson said somewhat archly. "I've had dinner with their Foreign Minister several times, and he never gave me the slightest indication — "

"Okay." Ryan interrupted quietly to ease the pain he was about to inflict. "Fine, Brett. But intentions change, and they did give us the indicator that they want our fleet to go away. I want the information. I am requesting that you turn Ambassador Williams loose to rattle a few bushes. He's smart and I trust his judgment. That's a request on my part. I can ask

104

the President to make it an order. Your call, Mr. Secretary."

Hanson weighed his options, and nodded agreement with as much dignity as he could summon. Ryan had just cleared up a situation in Africa that had gnawed at Roger Durling for two years, and so was the prettiest kid on the block, for the moment. It wasn't every day that a government employee increased the chances for a President to get himself reelected. The suspicion that CIA had apprehended Corp had already made its way in the media, and was being only mildly denied in the White House pressroom. It was no way to conduct foreign policy, but that issue would be fought on another battlefield.

"Russia," Ryan said next, ending one discussion and beginning another.

The engineer at the Yoshinobu space-launch complex knew he was not the first man to remark on the beauty of evil. Certainly not in his country, where the national mania for craftsmanship had probably begun with the loving attention given to swords, the meter-long *katana* of the samurai. There, the steel was hammered, bent over, hammered again, and bent over again twenty times in a lamination process that resulted in over a million layers of steel made from a single original casting. Such a process required an immense amount of patience from the prospective owner, who would wait patiently even so, displaying a degree of downward-manners for which that period of his country was not famous. Yet so it had been, for the samurai needed his sword, and only a master craftsman could fabricate it.

But not today. Today's samurai — if you could call him that — used the telephone and demanded instant results. Well, he would still have to wait, the engineer thought, as he gazed at the object before him.

In fact, the thing before his eyes was an elaborate lie, but it was the cleverness of the lie, and its sheer engineering beauty that excited his self-admiration. The plug connections on the side of it were fake, but only six people here knew that, and the engineer was the last of them as he headed down the ladder from the top portion of the gantry tower to the next-lower level. From there, they would ride the elevator to the concrete pad, where a bus waited to carry them to the control bunker. Inside the bus, the engineer removed his white-plastic hard-hat and started to relax. Ten minutes later, he was in a comfortable swivel chair, sipping tea. His presence here and on the pad hadn't been necessary, but when you built something, you wanted to see it all the way through, and besides, Yamata-san would have insisted.

The H-11 booster was new. This was only the second test-firing. It was actually based on Soviet technology, one of the last major ICBM designs the Russians had built before their country had come apart, and Yamata-san had purchased the rights to the design for a song (albeit written in hard currency), then turned all the drawings and data over to his own people for modification and improvement. It hadn't been hard. Improved steel for the casing and better electronics for the guidance system had saved fully 1,200 kilograms of weight, and further improvements in the liquid fuels had taken the performance of the rocket forward by a theoretical 17 percent. It had been a bravura performance by the design team, enough to attract the interest of NASA engineers from America, three of whom were in the bunker to observe. And wasn't *that* a fine joke?

The countdown proceeded according to plan. The gantry came back on its rails. Floodlights bathed the rocket, which sat atop the pad like a monument — but not the kind of monument the Americans thought.

"Hell of a heavy instrument package," a NASA observer noted.

"We want to certify our ability to orbit a heavy payload," one of the missile engineers replied simply.

"Well, here we go. . . ."

The rocket-motor ignition caused the TV screens to flare briefly, until they compensated electronically for the brilliant power of the white flame. The H-11 booster positively leaped upward atop a column of flame and a trail of smoke.

"What did you do with the fuel?" the NASA man asked quietly.

"Better chemistry," his Japanese counterpart replied, watching not the screen but a bank of instruments. "Better quality control, purity of the oxidizer, mainly."

"They never were very good at that," the American agreed.

He just doesn't see what he sees, both engineers told themselves. Yamata-san was correct. It was amazing.

Radar-guided cameras followed the rocket upward into the clear sky. The H-11 climbed vertically for the first thousand feet or so, then curved over in a slow, graceful way, its visual signature diminishing to a white-yellow disk. The flight path became more and more horizontal until the accelerating rocket body was heading almost directly away from the tracking cameras.

"BECO," the NASA man breathed, just at the proper moment. BECO meant booster-engine cutoff, because he was thinking in terms of a space launcher. "And separation . . . and second-stage ignition . . ." He got those terms right. One camera tracked the falling first stage, still glowing from residual fuel burnoff as it fell into the sea.

"Going to recover it?" the American asked.

"No."

All heads shifted to telemetric readouts when visual contact was lost. The rocket was still accelerating, exactly on its nominal performance curve, heading southeast. Various electronic displays showed the H-11's progress both numerically and graphically.

"Trajectory's a little high, isn't it?"

"We want a high-low orbit," the project manager explained. "Once we establish that we can orbit the weight, and we can certify the accuracy of the insertion, the payload will deorbit in a few weeks. We don't wish to add more junk up there."

"Good for you. All the stuff up there, it's becoming a concern for our manned missions." The NASA man paused, then decided to ask a sensitive question. "What's your max payload?"

"Five metric tons, ultimately."

He whistled. "You think you can get that much performance off this bird?" Ten thousand pounds was the magic number. If you could put that much into low-earth-orbit, you could then orbit geosynchronous communications satellites. Ten thousand pounds would allow for the satellite itself and the additional rocket motor required to attain the higher altitude. "Your trans-stage must be pretty hot."

The reply was, at first, a smile. "That is a trade secret."

"Well, I guess we'll see in about ninety seconds." The American turned in his chair to watch the digital telemetry. Was it possible they knew something he and his people didn't? He didn't think so, but just to make sure, NASA had an observation camera watching the H-11. The Japanese didn't know that, of course. NASA had tracking facilities all over the world to monitor U.S. space activity, and since they often had nothing to do, they kept track of all manner of things. The ones on Johnston Island and Kwajalein Atoll had originally been set up for SDI testing, and the tracking of Soviet missile launches.

★ ★ ★

The tracking camera on Johnston Island was called *Amber Ball*, and its crew of six picked up the H-11, having been cued on the launch by a Defense Support Program satellite, which had also been designed and orbited to give notice of Soviet launches. Something from another age, they all told themselves.

"Sure looks like a -19," the senior technician observed to general agreement.

"So does the trajectory," another said after a check of range and flight path.

"Second stage cutoff and separation, trans-stage and payload are loose now . . . getting a small adjustment burn — whoa!"

The screen went white.

"Signal lost, telemetry signal lost!" a voice called in launch control.

The senior Japanese engineer growled something that sounded like a curse to the NASA representative, whose eyes tracked down to the graphic-display screen. Signal lost just a few seconds after the trans-stage ignition. That could mean only one thing.

"That's happened to us more than once," the American said sympathetically. The problem was that rocket fuels, especially the liquid fuels always used for the final stage of a space launch, were essentially high explosives. What could go wrong? NASA and the U.S. military had spent over forty years discovering every possible mishap.

The weapons engineer didn't lose his temper as the flight-control officer had, and the American sitting close to him put it down to professionalism, which it was. And the American didn't know that he was a weapons engineer, anyway. In fact, to this point everything had gone exactly according to plan. The trans-stage fuel containers had been loaded with high explosives and had detonated immediately after the separation of the payload package.

The payload was a conical object, one hundred eighty centimeters wide at the base and two hundred six in length. It was made of uranium-238, which would have been surprising and unsettling to the NASA representative. A dense and very hard metal, it also had excellent refractory qualities, meaning that it resisted heat quite well. The same material was used in the payloads of many American space vehicles, but none of them was owned by the National Aeronautics and Space Administration. Rather, objects of very similar shapes and sizes sat atop the few remaining nuclear-tipped strategic weapons which the United States was dismantling in accordance with a treaty with Russia. More than thirty years earlier, an engineer at AVCO had pointed out that since U238 was both an excellent material for withstanding the heat of a ballistic reentry and made up the third stage of a thermonuclear device, why not make the body of the RV part of the bomb? That sort of thing had always appealed to an engineer, and the idea had been tested, certified, and since the 1960s become a standard part of the U.S. strategic arsenal.

The payload so recently part of the H-11 booster was an exact engineering mockup of a nuclear warhead, and while *Amber Ball* and other tracking devices were watching the remains of the trans-stage, this cone of uranium fell back to earth. It was not a matter of interest to American cameras, since it was, after all, just an orbit-test payload that had failed to achieve the velocity necessary to circle the earth.

Nor did the Americans know that MV *Takuyo*, sitting halfway between Easter Island and the coast of Peru, was not doing the fishery-research work it was supposed to be doing. Two kilometers to the east of *Takuyo* was a rubber raft, on which sat a GPS locator and a radio. The ship was not equipped with a radar capable of tracking an inbound ballistic target, but the descending RV gave its own announcement in the pre-dawn darkness; glowing white-hot from its reentry friction, it came down like a meteor, trailing a path of fire right on time and startling the extra lookouts on the flying bridge, who'd been told what to expect but were impressed nonetheless. Heads turned rapidly to follow it down, and the splash was a mere two hundred meters from the raft. Calculations would later determine that the impact point had been exactly two hundred sixty meters from the programmed impact point. It wasn't perfect, and, to the disappointment of some, was fully an order of magnitude worse than that of the Americans' newest missiles, but for the purposes of the test, it was quite sufficient. And better yet, the test had been carried out in front of the whole world and still not been seen. Moments later, the warhead released an inflated balloon to keep it close to the surface. A boat launched from *Takuyo* was already on the way to snag the line so that the RV could be recovered and its instrumented data analyzed.

"It's going to be very hard, isn't it?" Barbara Linders asked.

"Yes, it will." Murray wouldn't lie to her. Over the past two weeks they'd become very close indeed, closer, in fact, than Ms. Linders was with her therapist. In that time, they had discussed every aspect of the assault more than ten times, with tape recordings made of every word, printed transcripts made of the recordings, and every fact cross-checked, even to the extent that photographs of the former senator's office had been checked for the color of the furniture and carpeting. Everything had checked out. Oh, there had been a few discrepancies, but only a few, and all of them minor. The substance of the case was unaffected. But all of that would not change the fact that, yes, it would be very hard.

Murray ran the case, acting as the personal representative of Director Bill Shaw. Under Murray were twenty-eight agents, two of them headquarters-division inspectors, and almost all the rest experienced men in their forties, chosen for their expertise (there were also a half dozen young agents to do legwork errands). The next step would be to meet with a United States Attorney. They'd already chosen the one they wanted, Anne Cooper, twenty-nine, a J.D. from the University of Indiana, who specialized in sexual-assault cases. An elegant woman, tall, black, and ferociously feminist, she had sufficient fervor for such cases that the name of the defendant wouldn't matter to her more than the time of day. That was the easy part.

Then came the hard part. The "defendant" in question was the Vice President of the United States, and the Constitution said that he could not be treated like a normal citizen. In his case, the "grand jury" would be the United States House of Representatives' Committee on the Judiciary. Anne Cooper would work technically *in cooperation with* the chairman and staffers of the committee, though as a practical matter she'd actually run the case herself, with the committee people "helping" by grandstanding and leaking things to the press.

The firestorm would start, Murray explained slowly and quietly, when the chairman of the committee was informed of what was coming. Then the accusations would become public; the political dimension made it unavoidable. Vice President Edward J. Kealty would indignantly deny all accusations, and his defense team would launch its own investigation of Barbara Linders. They would discover the things that Murray had already heard from her own lips, many of them damaging, and the public would not be told, at first, that rape victims, especially those who did not report their crimes, suffered crushing loss of self-esteem, often manifested by abnormal sexual behavior. (Having learned that sexual activity was the only thing that men wanted of them, they often sought more of it in a futile search for the self-worth ripped away from them by the first attacker.) Barbara Linders had done that, had taken antidepression medications, had skipped through half a dozen jobs and two abortions. That this was a result of her victimization, and not an indication of her unreliability, would have to be established before the committee, because once the matter became public information, she would be unable to defend herself, not allowed to speak openly, while lawyers and investigators on the other side would have every chance to attack her as thoroughly and viciously as, but far more publicly than, Ed Kealty ever had. The media would see to that.

"It's not fair," she said, finally.

"Barbara, it *is* fair. It's necessary," Murray said as gently as he could. "You know why? Because when we impeach that son of a bitch, there won't be any doubts. The trial in the U.S. Senate will be a formality. *Then* we can put him in front of a real federal district-court jury, and then he will be convicted like the criminal he is. It's going to be hard on you, but when he goes to prison, it'll be a lot harder on him. It's the way the system works. It isn't perfect, but it's the best we have. And when it's all over, Barbara, you will have your dignity back, and nobody, ever, will take it away from you again."

"I'm not going to run away anymore, Mr. Murray." She'd come a long way in two weeks. There was metal in her backbone now. Maybe not steel, but it grew stronger every day. He wondered if it would be strong enough. The odds, he figured, were 6–5 and pick 'em.

"Please call me Dan. My friends do."

"What is it you didn't want to say in front of Brett?"

"We have a guy in Japan . . ." Mrs. Foley began, without giving Chet Nomuri's name. She went on for several minutes.

Her account wasn't exactly a surprise. Ryan had made the suggestion himself several years earlier, right here in the White House to then-President Fowler. Too many American public officials left government service and immediately became lobbyists or consultants to Japanese business groups, or even to the Japanese government itself, invariably for much higher pay than what the American taxpayer provided. The fact was troubling to Ryan. Though not illegal per se, it was, at the least, unseemly. But there was more to it than that. One didn't just change office location for a tenfold increase in income. There had to be a recruitment process, and that process had to have some substance to it. As with every other form of espionage, an agent-recruit needed to provide up-front proof that he could deliver something of value. The only way for that to happen was for those officials who yearned for higher income to give over sensitive information while they were still in government employment. And that *was* espionage, a felony under Title 18 of U.S. Code. A joint CIA/FBI operation was working quietly to see what it could see. It was called Operation SANDALWOOD, and that's where Nomuri came in.

"So what have we got so far?"

"Nothing on point yet," Mary Pat replied. "But we have learned some interesting things about Hiroshi Goto. He has a few bad habits." She elaborated.

"He doesn't like us very much, does he?"

"He likes female Americans just fine, if you want to call it that."

"It's not something we can use very easily." Ryan leaned back in his chair. It was distasteful, especially for a man whose elder daughter would soon start dating, something that came hard to fathers under the

114

best of circumstances. "There's a lot of lost souls out there, MP, and we can't save them all," Jack said without much conviction in his voice.

"Something smells about this, Jack."

"Why do you say that?"

"I don't know. Maybe it's the recklessness of it. This guy could be their Prime Minister in another couple of weeks. He's got a lot of support from the zaibatsu. The present government is shaky. He ought to be playing statesman, not cocksman, and putting a young girl on display like that . . ."

"Different culture, different rules." Ryan made the mistake of closing tired eyes for a moment, and as he did so his imagination conjured up an image to match Mrs. Foley's words. *She's an American citizen, Jack. They're the people who pay your salary.* The eyes opened back up. "How good's your officer?"

"He's very sharp. He's been in-country for six months."

"Has he recruited anybody yet?"

"No, he's under orders to go slow. You have to over there. Their society has different rules. He's identified a couple unhappy campers, and he's taking his time."

"Yamata and Goto . . . but that doesn't make sense, does it? Yamata just took a management interest on the Street, the Columbus Group. George Winston's outfit. I know George."

"The mutual-funds bunch?"

"That's right. He just hung 'em up, and Yamata stepped up to take his place. We're talking big bucks, MP. Hundred-million minimum for the price of admission. So you're telling me that a politician who professes not to like the United States hangs out with an industrialist who just married himself to our financial system. Hell, maybe Yamata is trying to explain the facts of life to the guy."

"What do you know about Mr. Yamata?" she asked.

115

The question caught Jack short. "Me? Not much, just a name. He runs a big conglomerate. Is he one of your targets?"

"That's right."

Ryan grinned somewhat crookedly. "MP, you sure this is complicated enough? Maybe toss in another element?"

In Nevada, people waited for the sun to set over the mountains before beginning what had been planned as a routine exercise, albeit with some last-minute modifications. The Army warrant officers were all experienced men, and they remained bemused by their first official visit to "Dreamland," as the Air Force people still called their secret facility at Groom Lake. This was the place where you tested stealthy aircraft, and the area was littered with radar and other systems to determine just how stealthy such things really were. With the sun finally gone and the clear sky dark, they manned their aircraft and lifted off for a night's testing. The mission for tonight was to approach the Nellis flight line, to deliver some administrative ordnance, and to return to Groom Lake, all undetected. That would be hard enough.

Jackson, wearing his J-3 hat, was observing the newest entry in the stealth business. The Comanche had some interesting implications in that arena, and more still in special operations, fast becoming the most fashionable part of the Pentagon. The Army said they had a real magic show worth watching, and he was here to watch. . . .

"Guns, guns, guns!" the warrant officer said over the guard channel ninety minutes later. Then on intercom, "God, what a beautiful sight!"

The ramp at Nellis Air Force Base was home to the Air Force's largest fighter wing, today augmented further still with two visiting squadrons for the on-

116

going Red Flag operation. That gave his Comanche over a hundred targets for its 20-millimeter cannon, and he walked his fire among the even rows of aircraft before turning and exiting the area to the south. The casinos of Las Vegas were in sight as he looped around, making room for the other two Comanches, then it was back down to fifty feet over the uneven sand and a northeasterly heading.

"Getting hit again. Some Eagle jockey keeps sweeping us," the backseater reported.

"Locking up?"

"Sure as hell trying to, and — Jesus — "

An F-15C screeched overhead close enough that the wake turbulence made the Comanche rock a little. Then a voice came up on guard.

"If this was an Echo, I'd have your ass."

"I just knew you Air Force guys were like that. See you at the barn."

"Roger. Out." In the distance at twelve o'clock, the fighter lit off its afterburners in salute.

"Good news, bad news, Sandy," the backseater observed.

Stealthy, but not quite stealthy enough. The low-observable technology built into the Comanche was good enough to defeat a missile-targeting radar, but those damned airborne early-warning birds with their big antennas and signal-processor chips kept getting hits, probably off the rotor disc, the pilot thought. They had to do a little more work on that. The good news was that the F-15C, with a superb missile-tracking radar, couldn't get lockup for his AMRAAMs, and a heat-seeker was a waste of time for all involved, even over a cold desert floor. But the F-15*E*, with its see-in-the-dark gear, could have blown him away with a 20mm cannon. Something to remember. So, the world was not yet perfect, but Comanche was still the baddest helicopter ever made.

CWO4 Sandy Richter looked up. In the dry, cold

desert air he could see the strobe lights of the orbiting E-3A AWACS. Not all that far away. Thirty thousand feet or so, he estimated. Then he had an interesting thought. That Navy guy looked smart enough, and maybe if he presented his idea in the right way, he'd get a chance to try it out. . . .

"I'm getting tired of this," President Durling was saying in his office, diagonally across the West Wing from Ryan's. There had been a couple of good years, but they'd come to a screeching halt in the past few months. "What was it today?"

"Gas tanks," Marty Caplan replied. "Deerfield Auto Parts up in Massachusetts just came up with a way to fabricate them into nearly any shape and capacity from standard steel sheets. It's a robotic process, efficient as hell. They refused to license it to the Japanese — "

"Al Trent's district?" the President cut in.

"That's right."

"Excuse me. Please go on." Durling reached for some tea. He was having trouble with afternoon coffee now. "Why won't they license it?"

"It's one of the companies that almost got destroyed by overseas competition. This one held on to the old management team. They smartened up, hired a few bright young design engineers, and pulled their socks up. They've come up with half a dozen important innovations. It just so happens that this is the one that delivers the greatest cost-efficiency. They claim they can make the tanks, box 'em, and ship them to Japan cheaper than the Japanese can make them at home, and that the tanks are also stronger. But we couldn't even make the other side budge on using them in the plants they have over here. It's computer chips all over again," Caplan concluded.

"How is it they can even ship the things over — "

"The ships, Mr. President." It was Caplan's turn

118

to interrupt. "Their car carriers come over here full and mainly return completely empty. Loading the things on wouldn't cost anything at all, and they end up getting delivered right to the company docks. Deerfield even designed a load-unload system that eliminates any possible time penalty."

"Why didn't you push on it?"

"I'm surprised he didn't push," Christopher Cook observed.

They were in an upscale private home just off Kalorama Road. An expensive area of the District of Columbia, it housed quite a few members of the diplomatic community, along with the rank-and-file members of the Washington community, lobbyists, lawyers, and all the rest who wanted to be close, but not too close, to where the action was, downtown.

"If Deerfield would only license their patent." Seiji sighed. "We offered them a very fair price."

"True," Cook agreed, pouring himself another glass of white wine. He could have said, *But, Seiji, it's their invention and they want to cash in on it,* but he didn't. "Why don't your people — "

It was Seiji Nagumo's turn to sigh. "Your people were clever. They hired a particularly bright attorney in Japan and got their patent recognized in record time." He might have added that it offended him that a citizen of his country could be so mercenary, but that would have been unseemly under the circumstances. "Well, perhaps they will come to see the light of reason."

"It could be a good point to concede, Seiji. At the very least, sweeten your offer on the licensing agreement."

"Why, Chris?"

"The President is interested in this one." Cook paused, seeing that Nagumo didn't get it yet. He was still new at this. He knew the industrial side, but not the politics yet. "Deerfield is in Al Trent's congressional district. Trent has a lot of clout on the Hill. He's chairman of the Intelligence Committee."

"And?"

"And Trent is a good guy to keep happy."

Nagumo considered that for a minute or so, sipping his wine and staring out the window. Had he known that fact earlier in the day, he might have sought permission to give in on the point, but he hadn't and he didn't. To change now would be an admission of error, and Nagumo didn't like to do that any more than anyone else in the world. He decided that he'd suggest an improved offer for licensing rights, instead — not knowing that by failing to accept a personal loss of face, he'd bring closer something that he would have tried anything to avoid.

5

Complexity Theory

Things rarely happen for a single reason. Even the cleverest and most skillful manipulators recognize that their real art lies in making use of that which they cannot predict. For Raizo Yamata the knowledge was usually a comfort. He usually knew what to do when the unexpected took place — but not always.

"It has been a troublesome time, that is true, but not the worst we have experienced," one of his guests pronounced. "And we are having our way again, are we not?"

"We've made them back off on computer chips," another pointed out. Heads nodded around the low table.

They just didn't see, Yamata told himself. His country's needs coincided exactly with a new opportunity. There was a new world, and despite America's repeated pronouncements of a new order for that new world, only disorder had replaced what had been three generations of — if not stability, then at least predictability. The symmetry of East and West was now so far back in the history of contemporary minds that it seemed like a distant and unpleasant dream. The Russians were still reeling from their misguided experiment, and so were the Americans, though most of their pain was self-inflicted and had come after the event, the fools. Instead of merely maintaining their power, the Americans had cast it aside at the moment of its ascendancy, as they had so often in their history, and in the dimming of two formerly great powers lay the opportunity for a country that *deserved* to be great.

"These are small things, my friends," Yamata said, graciously leaning across the table to refill cups. "Our national weakness is structural and has not changed in real terms in our lifetime."

"Please explain, Raizo-chan," one of his friendlier peers suggested.

"So long as we lack direct access to resources, so long as we cannot control that access ourselves, so long as we exist as the shopkeeper of other nations, we are vulnerable."

"Ah!" Across the table a man waved a dismissive hand. "I disagree. We are strong in the things that matter."

"And what are those things?" Yamata inquired gently.

"First and most importantly, the diligence of our workers, the skill of our designers . . ." The litany went on while Yamata and his other guests listened politely.

"And how long will those things matter if we no longer have resources to use, oil to burn?" one of Yamata's allies inquired with a litany of his own.

"Nineteen forty-one all over again?"

"No, it will not be that way . . . exactly," Yamata said, rejoining the conversation. "Then it was possible for them to cut off our oil because we bought almost all of it from them. Today it is more subtle. Back then they had to freeze our assets to prevent us from spending them elsewhere, yes? Today they devalue the dollar relative to the yen, and our assets are trapped there, are they not? Today they trick us into investing our money there, they complain when we do, they cheat us at every turn, they keep what we give to them for their property, and then they steal back what we've bought!"

This tack caused heads first to turn and then to nod. Every man in the room had lived through that experience. That one, Yamata saw, had bought Rockefeller Center in New York, had paid double what it was really worth, even in that artificially inflated real-estate market, been tricked and cheated by the American owners. Then the yen had risen relative to the dollar, which meant that the dollar had lost value relative to the yen. If he tried to sell now, everyone knew, it would be a disaster. First, the real-estate market in New York City had dropped of its own accord; second, and as a result, the buildings were worth only half of the dollars that had already been paid; third, the dollars were worth only half the value in yen that they had been in the beginning. He'd be lucky to get back a quarter of what he'd put into the deal. In fact, the rent he was earning barely paid the interest payments on the outstanding debt.

That one there, Yamata thought, had bought a major motion-picture studio, and across the table a rival had done the same. It was all Raizo could do not to laugh at the fools. What had each bought? That was simple. In each case, for a price of billions of dollars, they had purchased three hundred or so hectares of real estate in Los Angeles and a piece of paper that said they now had the ability to make movies. In both cases the previous owners had taken the money and quite openly laughed, and in both cases the previous owners had recently made a quiet offer to buy the property back for a quarter, or less, of what the Japanese businessman had paid — enough to retire the outstanding debt and not a single yen more.

It went on and on. Every time a Japanese company

had taken its profits from America and tried to re-invest them back in America, the Americans screamed about how Japan was stealing their country. Then they overcharged for everything. Then their government policy made sure that the Japanese lost money on everything, *so that* Americans could then buy it all back at cut-rate prices, all the while complaining that those prices were too high. America would rejoice at recovering control of its culture, such as it was, when in reality what had happened was the largest and best concealed robbery in world history.

"Don't you see? They're trying to cripple us, and they are succeeding," Yamata told them in a quiet, reasonable voice.

It was the classic business paradox which all know but all forget. There was even a simple aphorism for it: borrow one dollar and the bank owns you; borrow a million dollars and you own the bank. Japan had bought into the American auto market, for example, at a time when the U.S. auto industry, fat from its huge exclusive clientele, was driving up prices and allowing quality to stagnate while its unionized workers complained about the dehumanizing aspects of their work — the highest-paid jobs in blue-collar America. The Japanese had started in that market at an even lower status than Volkswagen, with small, ugly cars that were not all that well made and contained unimpressive safety features, but that were superior to American designs in one way: they were fuel-efficient.

Three historical accidents had then come to Japan's aid. The American Congress, upset with the "greed" of oil companies who wanted to charge world price for their products, had placed a cap on the wellhead price of domestic crude oil. That had frozen American gasoline prices at the lowest level in the industrial world, discouraged new oil exploration, and encouraged Detroit to make large, heavy, fuel-*in*efficient

124

cars. Then the 1973 war between Israel and the Arab states had placed American drivers in gasoline lines for the first time in thirty years, and the trauma had stunned a country that had deemed itself above such things. Then they'd realized that Detroit only made automobiles that drank gasoline as though through the floodgates of a dam. The "compact" cars that the American manufacturers had started making in the previous decade had almost immediately grown to midsize, were no more fuel-efficient than their larger cousins, and weren't all that well made in any case. Worst of all, the American manufacturers, to a man, had all recently invested money in large-car plants, a fact that had almost been the undoing of Chrysler. This oil shock had not lasted long, but long enough for America to rethink its buying habits, and the domestic companies had not possessed the capital or the engineering flexibility to change rapidly to what unaccustomedly nervous American citizens wanted.

Those citizens had immediately increased purchases of Japanese automobiles, especially in the crucial, trend-setting West Coast markets, which had had the effect of funding research and development for the Japanese firms, which in turn had hired American styling engineers to make their products more attractive to their growing market and utilized its own engineers to improve such things as safety. Thus, by the second great oil shock of 1979, Toyota, Honda, Datsun (later Nissan), and Subaru were in the right place with the right product. Those were the salad days. The low yen and high dollar had meant that even relatively low prices guaranteed a handsome profit, that their local dealers could add a surcharge of a thousand dollars or more for *allowing* people to purchase these marvelous automobiles — and *that* had given them a large, eager sales force of American citizens.

What had never occurred to any of the men at the

table, Yamata knew, was the same thing that had never occurred to the executives of General Motors and the United Auto Workers union. Both had assumed that a happy state of affairs would extend into blissful eternity. Both had forgotten that there was no Divine Right of Businessmen any more than there was a Divine Right of Kings. Japan had learned to exploit a weakness of the American auto industry. In due course, America had learned from its own mistakes, and just as Japanese companies had capitalized on American arrogance, in the same way they almost immediately built — or bought — monuments to their own. Meanwhile the American companies had ruthlessly downsized everything from their automobile designs to their payrolls because they had relearned the economic facts of life even as the Japanese had allowed themselves to forget them. The process went mainly unseen, especially by the players, who were not assisted by the media "analysts" who were too busy looking at trees to discern the shape of the cyclical forest.

To normalize things further, the exchange rate changed — as it had to change with so much money flowing in one direction — but the Japanese industrialists hadn't seen it coming any more clearly than Detroit had noted the approach of its own troubles. The relative value of the yen had gone up, and that of the dollar down, despite the best efforts of Japanese central bankers to keep their own currency weak. With that change went much of the profit margin of the Japanese firms — including the values of properties bought in America that had crashed enough in value to be seen as net losses. And you couldn't transport Rockefeller Center to Tokyo in any case.

It had to be this way. Yamata saw that even if these men did not. Business was a cycle, like riding a wave up and down, and no one had as yet found a way to make the cycle smooth out. Japan was all the more vulnerable to it, since, in serving America, Japanese industry was really part of the American economy and subject to all of its vagaries. The Americans would not remain more foolish than the Japanese indefinitely, and with their return to sanity, they would have their advantages of power and resources yet again, and his chance would be gone forever. His country's chance, too, Yamata told himself. That was also important, but it was not the thing that made his eyes burn.

His country could not be great so long as its leaders — not in the government, but here around this table — failed to understand what greatness was. Manufacturing capacity was nothing. The simple act of cutting the shipping lanes to the sources of raw materials could idle every factory in the country, and then the skill and diligence of the Japanese worker would have no greater meaning in the great scheme of things than a Buson haiku. A nation was great because of power, and his country's power was just as artificial as a poem. More to the point, national greatness was not something awarded, but something won; it had to be acknowledged by another great nation that had been taught humility . . . or more than one. Greatness came not from a single national asset. It came from many. It came from self-sufficiency in all things — well, in as many things as possible. His companions around the table had to see that before he could act on their behalf and his nation's. It was his mission to raise up his nation and to humble others. It was his destiny and his duty to make these things happen, to be the catalyst for all the energy of others.

But the time was not yet right. He could see that. His allies were many, but there were not enough of them, and those who opposed him were too fixed in their thinking to be persuaded. They saw his point, but not as clearly as he did, and until they changed their way of thinking, he could do no more than what he was doing now, offering counsel, setting the stage. A man of surpassing patience, Yamata-san smiled politely and ground his teeth, with the frustration of the moment.

"You know, I think I'm starting to get the hang of this place," Ryan said as he took his place in the leather chair to the President's left.

"I said that once," Durling announced. "It cost me three tenths of a point of unemployment, a fight with House Ways and Means, and ten real points of approval rating." Though his voice was grave, he smiled when he said it. "So what's so hot that you're interrupting my lunch?"

Jack didn't make him wait, though his news was important enough to merit a dramatic reply: "We have our agreement with the Russians and Ukrainians on the last of the birds."

"Starting when?" Durling asked, leaning forward over his desk and ignoring his salad.

"How does next Monday grab you?" Ryan asked with a grin. "They went for what Scott said. There've been so many of these START procedures that they want just to kill the last ones quietly and announce that they're gone, once and for all. Our inspectors are already over there, and theirs are over here, and they'll just go and do it."

"I like it," Durling replied.

"Exactly forty years, boss," Ryan said with some passion, "practically my whole life since they deployed the SS-6 and we deployed Atlas, ugly damned things with an ugly damned purpose, and helping to make them go away — well, Mr. President, now I owe you one. It's going to be your mark, sir, but I can tell my grandchildren that I was around when it happened." That Adler's proposal to the Russians and Ukrainians had been Ryan's initiative might end up as a footnote, but probably not.

"Our grandchildren either won't care or they'll ask what the big deal was," Arnie van Damm observed, deadpan.

"True," Ryan conceded. Trust Arnie to put a neutral spin on things.

"Now tell me the bad news," Durling ordered.

"Five billion," Jack said, unsurprised by the hurt expression he got in return. "It's worth it, sir. It really is."

"Tell me why."

"Mr. President, since I was in grammar school our country has lived with the threat of nuclear weapons on ballistic launchers aimed at the United States. Inside of six weeks, the last of them could be gone."

"They're already aimed — "

"Yes, sir, we have ours aimed at the Sargasso Sea, and so do they, an error that you can fix by opening an inspection port and changing a printed-circuit card in the guidance system. To do that takes ten minutes from the moment you open the access door into the missile silo and requires a screwdriver and a flashlight." Actually, that was true only for the Soviet — *Russian!* Ryan corrected himself for the thousandth time — missiles. The remaining American birds took longer to retarget due to their greater sophistication. Such were the vagaries of engineering science.

"All gone, sir, gone forever," Ryan said. "I'm the hard-nosed hawk here, remember? We can sell this to the Hill. It's worth the price and more."

"You make a good case, as always," van Damm announced from his chair.

"Where will OMB find the money, Arnie?" President Durling asked. Now it was Ryan's turn to cringe.

"Defense, where else?"

"Before we get too enthusiastic about that, we've gone too far already."

"What will we save by eliminating our last mis-

129

siles?" van Damm asked.

"It'll cost us money," Jack replied. "We're already paying an arm and a leg to dismantle the missile subs, and the environmentalists — "

"Those wonderful people," Durling observed.

" — but it's a one-time expense."

Eyes turned to the chief of staff. His political judgment was impeccable. The weathered face weighed the factors and turned to Ryan. "It's worth the hassle. There *will* be a hassle on the Hill, boss," he told the President, "but a year from now you'll be telling the American people how you put an end to the sword of — "

"Damocles," Ryan said.

"Catholic schools." Arnie chuckled. "The sword that's hung over America for a generation. The papers'll like it, and you just know that CNN will make a big deal about it, one of their hour-long special-report gigs, with lots of good pictures and inaccurate commentary."

"Don't like that, Jack?" Durling asked, smiling broadly now.

"Mr. President, I'm not a politician, okay? Isn't it sufficient to the moment that we're dismantling the last two hundred ICBMs in the world?" Well, that wasn't exactly true, was it? *Let's not wax too poetic, Jack. There are still the Chinese, Brits, and French.* But the latter two would fall into line, wouldn't they? And the Chinese could be made to see the light through trade negotiations, and besides, what enemies did they have left to worry about?

"Only if people see and understand, Jack." Durling turned to van Damm. Both of them ignored Jack's not-quite-spoken additional concerns. "Get the media office working on this. We do the formal announcement in Moscow, Jack?"

Ryan nodded. "That was the deal, sir." There would be more to it, careful leaks, unconfirmed at first. Congressional briefings to generate more. Quiet calls to various TV networks and trusted reporters who would be in exactly the right places at exactly the right times — difficult because of the ten-hour difference between Moscow and the last American ICBM fields — to record for history the end of the nightmare. The actual elimination process was rather messy, which was why American tree-huggers had such a problem with it. In the case of the Russian birds, the warheads were removed for dismantlement, the missiles drained of their liquid fuels and stripped of valuable and/or classified electronic components, and then one hundred kilograms of high explosives were used to blast open the top of the silo, which in due course would be filled with dirt and leveled off. The American procedure was different because all the U.S. missiles used solid fuels. In their case, the missile bodies were transported to Utah, where they were opened at both ends; then the rocket motors were ignited and allowed to burn out like the world's largest highway flares, creating clouds of toxic exhaust that might snuff out the lives of some wild birds. In America the silos would also be blasted open — a United States Circuit Court of Appeals had ruled that the national-security implications of the international arms-control treaty superseded four environmental-protection statutes, despite many legal briefs and protests to the contrary. The final blast would be highly dramatic, all the more so because its force would be about one ten-millionth of what the silo had once represented. Some numbers, and some concepts, Jack reflected, were simply too vast to be appreciated — even by people like himself.

The legend of Damocles had to do with a courtier in the circle of King Dionysius of Sicily, who had waxed eloquent on the good fortune of his king. To make a point in the cruel and heavy-handed way of "great" men, Dionysius had invited his courtier,

131

Damocles, to a sumptuous banquet and sat him in a comfortable place directly under a sword, which in turn was suspended from the ceiling by a thread. The purpose was to demonstrate that the King's own good fortune was as tenuous as the safety of his guest.

It was the same with America. Everything it had was still under the nuclear sword, a fact made graphically clear to Ryan in Denver not too long before, and for that reason his personal mission since returning to government service had been to put the end to the tale, once and for all.

"You want to handle the press briefings?"

"Yes, Mr. President," Jack replied, surprised and grateful for Durling's stunning generosity.

" 'Northern Resource Area'?" the Chinese Defense Minister asked. He added dryly, "Interesting way of putting it."

"So what do you think?" Zhang Han San asked from his side of the table. He was fresh from another meeting with Yamata.

"In the abstract, it's strategically possible. I leave the economic estimates to others," the Marshal replied, ever the cautious one despite the quantity of mao-tai he'd consumed this evening.

"The Russians have been employing three Japanese survey firms. Amazing, isn't it? Eastern Siberia has hardly even been explored. Oh, yes, the gold deposits at Kolyma, but the interior itself?" A dismissive wave of the hand. "Such fools, and now they must ask others to do the job for them . . ." The Minister's voice trailed off, and his gaze returned to Zhang Han San. "And so, what have they found?"

"Our Japanese friends? More oil for starters, they think as big a find as Prudhoe Bay." He slid a sheet of paper across the table. "Here are the minerals they've located in the last nine months."

"All this?"

"The area is almost as large as all of Western Europe, and all the Soviets ever cared about was a strip around their damned railroads. The fools." Zhang snorted. "All their economic problems, the solution for them lay right under their feet from the moment they assumed power from the czar. In essence it's rather like South Africa, a treasure house, but including oil, which the South Africans lack. As you see, nearly all of the strategic minerals, and in such quantities. . . ."

"Do the Russians know?"

"Some of it." Zhang Han San nodded. "Such a secret is too vast to conceal entirely, but only about half — the items on the list marked with stars are those Moscow knows about."

"But not these others?"

Zhang smiled. "No."

Even in a culture where men and women learn to control their feelings, the Minister could not conceal his amazement at the paper in his hands. They didn't shake, but he used them to place the page flat on the polished table, smoothing it out as though it were a piece of fine silk.

"This could double the wealth of our country."

"That is conservative," observed the senior field officer of his country's intelligence service. Zhang, covered as a diplomat, actually conducted more diplomacy than most of his country's senior foreign-service officers. It was more of an embarrassment to them than to him. "You need to remember that this is the estimate the Japanese have given us, Comrade Minister. They fully expect access to half of what they discover, and since they will perforce spend most of the development money . . ."

A smile. "Yes, while we take most of the strategic risks. Offensive little people," the Minister added. Like those with whom Zhang had negotiated in Tokyo, the Minister and the Marshal, who continued

133

to keep his peace, were veterans of the 8th Route Army. They too had memories of war — but not of war with America. He shrugged. "Well, we need them, don't we?"

"Their weapons are formidable," the Marshal noted. "But not their numbers."

"They know that," Zhang Han San told his hosts. "It is, as my main contact says, a convenient marriage of needs and requirements, but he hopes that it will develop, in his words, into a true and cordial relationship between peoples with a true — "

"Who will be on top?" the Marshal asked, smiling coarsely.

"They will, of course. He thinks," Zhang Han San added.

"In that case, since they are courting us, it is they who need to make the first overt moves," the Minister said, defining his country's policy in a way that would not offend his own superior, a small man with elfin eyes and the sort of determination to make a lion pause. He looked over at the Marshal, who nodded soberly. The man's capacity for alcohol, both of the others thought, was remarkable.

"As I expected," Zhang announced with a smile. "Indeed, as they expect, since they anticipate the greatest profit."

"They are entitled to their illusions."

"I admire your confidence," the NASA engineer observed from the viewers' gallery over the shop floor. He also admired their funding. The government had fronted the money for this industrial conglomerate to acquire the Soviet design and build it. Private industry sure had a lot of muscle here, didn't it?

"We think we have the trans-stage problem figured out. A faulty valve," the Japanese designer explained. "We used a Soviet design."

"What do you mean?"

"I mean that we used their valve design for the trans-stage fuel tanks. It wasn't a good one. They tried to do everything there with extremely light weight, but — "

The NASA representative blinked hard. "You mean to tell me that their whole production run of the missile was — "

A knowing look cut the American off. "Yes. At least a third of them would have failed. My people believe that the test missiles were specially engineered, but that the production models were, well, typically Russian."

"Hmph." The American's bags were already packed, and a car was waiting to take him to Narita International for the interminable flight to Chicago. He looked at the production floor of the plant. It was probably what General Dynamics had looked like back in the 1960s, at the height of the Cold War. The boosters were lined up like sausages, fifteen of them in various stages of assembly, side by side, one after the other, while white-coated technicians performed their complicated tasks. "These ten look about done."

"They are," the factory manager assured him.

"When's your next test shot?"

"Next month. We've got our first three payloads ready," the designer replied.

"When you guys get into something, you don't fool around, do you?"

"It's simply more efficient to do it this way."

"So they're going to go out of here fully assembled?"

A nod. "That's right. We'll pressurize the fuel tanks with inert gas, of course, but one of the nice things about using this design is that they're designed to be moved as intact units. That way you save final-assembly time at the launch point."

"Move them out by truck?"

135

"No." The Japanese engineer shook his head. "By rail."

"What about the payloads?"

"They're being assembled elsewhere. That's proprietary, I'm afraid."

The other production line did not have foreign visitors. In fact it had few visitors at all despite the fact that it was located in the suburbs of Tokyo. The sign outside the building proclaimed it to be a research-and-development center for a major corporation, and those who lived nearby guessed that it was for computer chips or something similar. The power lines that went into it were not remarkable, since the most power-hungry units were the heating and air-conditioning units that sat in a small enclosure in the back. Traffic in and out was unremarkable as well. There was a modest parking lot with space for perhaps eighty automobiles, and the lot was almost always at least half full. There was a discreet security fence, pretty much like what would have been around any other light-industry facility anywhere in the world, and a security shack at both entrances. Cars and trucks came and went, and that was pretty much that for the casual observer.

Inside was something else. Although the two external security points were staffed by smiling men who politely gave directions to disoriented motorists, inside the building it was something else entirely. Each security desk featured hidden attachments which held German-made P-38 pistols, and the guards here didn't smile much. They didn't know what they were guarding, of course. Some things were just too unusual to be recognized. No one had ever produced a TV documentary on the fabrication of nuclear devices.

The shop floor was fifty meters long by fifteen wide, and there were two evenly spaced rows of machine tools, each of them enclosed with Plexiglas. Each en-

136

closure was individually climate-controlled by a separate ventilation system, as was the room as a whole. The technicians and scientists wore white coveralls and gloves not unlike those required of workers in a computer-chip plant, and indeed when some of them stepped outside for a smoke, passersby took them for exactly that.

In the clean room, roughly shaped plutonium hemispheres came in at one end, were machined into their final shapes at several stages, and emerged from the other end so polished they looked like glass. Each was then placed in a plastic holder and hand-carried out of the machine shop to the storage room, where each was set on an individual shelf made of steel covered with plastic. Metal contact could not be allowed, because plutonium, in addition to being radioactive, and warm due to its alpha-radiation decay, was a reactive metal, quick to spark on contact with another metal, and actually flammable. Like magnesium and titanium, the metal would burn with gusto, and, once ignited, was the very devil to extinguish. For all that, handling the hemispheres — there were twenty of them — became just one more routine for the engineers. That task had long since been completed.

The harder part was the RV bodies. These were large, hollow, inverted cones, 120 centimeters in height and 50 across at the base, made of uranium-238, a darkly reddish and very hard metal. At just over four hundred kilograms each, the bulky cones had to be precisely machined for absolute dynamic symmetry. Intended to "fly" after a fashion, both through vacuum and, briefly, through air, they had to be perfectly balanced, lest they become unstable in flight. Ensuring that had to everyone's surprise turned out to be the most difficult production task of all. The casting process had been reordered twice, and even now the RV bodies were periodically rotated, similar to the procedure for balancing an automobile tire, but with far more stringent tolerances. The exterior of each of the ten was not as finely machined as the parts that went inside, though they were smooth to the ungloved touch. Inside was something else. Slight but symmetrical irregularities would allow the "physics package" — an American term — to fit in snugly, and, if the moment came — which everyone hoped it would not, of course — the enormous flux of high-energy "fast" neutrons would attack the RV bodies, causing a "fast-fission" reaction, and doubling the energy released by the plutonium, tritium, and lithium deuteride within.

That was the elegant part, the engineers thought, especially those unfamiliar with nuclear physics who had learned the process along the way. The U-238, so dense and hard and difficult to work, was a highly refractory metal. The Americans even used it to make armor for their tanks, it resisted external energy so well. Screeching through the atmosphere at 27,000 kilometers per hour, air friction would have destroyed most materials, but not this one, at least not in the few seconds it took, and at the end of the process, the material would form part of the bomb itself. Elegant, the engineers thought, using that most favored of words in their profession, and that made it worth the time and the trouble. When each body was complete, each was loaded onto a dolly and rolled off to the storage room. Only three remained to be worked on. This part of the project was two weeks behind schedule, much to everyone's chagrin.

RV Body #8 began the first machining process. If the bomb was detonated, the uranium-238 from which it was made would also create most of the fallout. Well, that was physics.

It was just another accident, perhaps occasioned by the early hour. Ryan arrived at the White House just after seven, about twenty minutes earlier than usual because traffic on U.S. Route 50 happened to be uncommonly smooth all the way in. As a result, he hadn't had time to read through all his early briefing documents, which he bundled under his arm at the west entrance. National Security Advisor or not, Jack still had to pass through the metal detector, and it was there that he bumped into somebody's back. The somebody in question was handing his service pistol to a uniformed Secret Service agent.

"You guys still don't trust the Bureau, eh?" a familiar voice asked the plainclothes supervisory agent.

"*Especially* the Bureau!" was the good-humored retort.

"And I don't blame them a bit," Ryan added. "Check his ankle, too, Mike."

Murray turned after passing through the magnetic portal. "I don't need the backup piece anymore." The Deputy Assistant Director pointed to the papers under Jack's arm. "Is that any way to treat classified documents?"

Murray's humor was automatic. It was just the man's nature to needle an old friend. Then Ryan saw that the Attorney General had just passed through as well, and was looking back in some annoyance. Why was a cabinet member here so early? If it were a national-security matter, Ryan would have known, and criminal affairs were rarely so important as to get the President into his office before the accustomed eight o'clock. And why was Murray accompanying him? Helen D'Agustino was waiting beyond to provide personal escort through the upstairs corridors. Everything about the accidental confrontation lit off Ryan's curiosity.

"The Boss is waiting," Murray said guardedly, reading the look in Jack's eyes.

"Could you stop by on the way out? I've been meaning to call you about something."

139

"Sure." And Murray walked off without even a friendly inquiry about Cathy and the kids.

Ryan passed through the detector, turned left, and headed up the stairs to his corner office for his morning briefs. They went quickly, and Ryan was settling into his morning routine when his secretary admitted Murray to his office. There was no point in beating around the bush.

"A little early for the A.G. to show up, Dan. Anything I need to know?"

Murray shook his head. "Not yet, sorry."

"Okay," Ryan replied, shifting gears smoothly. "Is it something I *ought* to know?"

"Probably, but the Boss wants it on close-hold, and it doesn't have national-security implications. What did you want to see me about?"

Ryan took a second or two before answering, his mind going at its accustomed speed in such a case. Then he set it aside. He knew that he could trust Murray's word. Most of the time.

"This is code-word stuff," Jack began, then elaborated on what he'd learned from Mary Pat the day before. The FBI agent nodded and listened with a neutral expression.

"It's not exactly new, Jack. Last few years we've been taking a quiet look at indications that young ladies have been — enticed? Hard to phrase this properly. Modeling contracts, that sort of thing. Whoever does the recruiting is very careful. Young women head over there to model, do commercials, that sort of thing, goes on all the time. Some got their American careers started over there. None of the checks we've run have turned up anything, but there are indications that some girls have disappeared. One in particular, as a matter of fact, she fits your man's description. Kimberly something, I don't recall the last name. Her father is a captain in the Seattle police department, and his next-door neighbor is SAC of our Seattle of-

140

fice. We've gone through our contacts in the Japanese police agencies, quietly. No luck."

"What does your gut tell you?" Ryan asked.

"Look, Jack, people disappear all the time. Lots of young girls just pack up and leave home to make their way in the world. Call it part feminism, part just wanting to become an independent human being. It happens all the time. This Kimberly-something is twenty, wasn't doing well at school, and just disappeared. There's no evidence to suggest kidnapping, and at twenty you're a free citizen, okay? We have no *right* to launch a criminal investigation. All right, so her dad's a cop, and his neighbor is Bureau, and so we've sniffed around a little. But we haven't turned up anything at all, and that's as far as we can take it without something to indicate that a statute may have been violated. There are no such indicators."

"You mean, a girl over eighteen disappears and you can't — "

"Without evidence of a crime, no, we can't. We don't have the manpower to track down every person who decides to make his or her own future without telling Mom and Dad about it."

"You didn't answer my initial question, Dan," Jack observed to his guest's discomfort.

"There are people over there who like their women with fair hair and round eyes. There's a disproportionate number of missing girls who're blonde. We had trouble figuring that out at first until an agent started asking their friends if they maybe had their hair color changed recently. Sure enough, the answer was yes, and then she started asking the question regularly. A 'yes' happened in enough cases that it's just unusual. So, yes, I think something may be happening, but we don't have enough to move on," Murray concluded. After a moment he added, "If this case in question has national-security implications . . . well . . ."

"What?" Jack asked.

"Let the Agency check around?"

That was a first for Ryan, hearing from an FBI official that the CIA could investigate something. The Bureau guarded its turf as ferociously as a momma grizzly bear defended her cubs. "Keep going, Dan," Ryan ordered.

"There's a lively sex industry over there. If you look at the porn they like to watch, it's largely American. The nude photos you see in their magazines are mainly of Caucasian females. The nearest country with a supply of such females happens to be us. Our suspicion is that some of these girls aren't just models, but, again, we haven't been able to turn anything solid enough to pursue it." And the other problem, Murray didn't add, was twofold. If something really were going on, he wasn't sure how much cooperation he'd receive from local authorities, meaning that the girls might disappear forever. If it were not, the nature of the investigation would be leaked and the entire episode would appear in the press as another racist piece of Japan-bashing. "Anyway, it sounds to me like the Agency has an op running over there. My best advice: expand it some. If you want, I can brief some people in on what we know. It isn't much, but we do have some photographs."

"How come you know so much?"

"SAC Seattle is Chuck O'Keefe. I worked under him once. He had me talk to Bill Shaw about it, and Bill okayed a quiet look, but it didn't lead anywhere, and Chuck has enough to keep his division busy as it is."

"I'll talk to Mary Pat. And the other thing?"

"Sorry, pal, but you have to talk to the Boss about that."

Goddamn it! Ryan thought as Murray walked out. Are there always secrets?

142

6

Looking In, Looking Out

In many ways operating in Japan was highly difficult. There was the racial part of it, of course. Japan was not strictly speaking a homogeneous society; the Ainu people were the original inhabitants of the islands but they mainly lived on Hokkaido, the northernmost of the Home Islands. Still called an aboriginal people, they were also quite isolated from mainstream Japanese society in an explicitly racist way. Similarly Japan had an ethnic-Korean minority whose antecedents had been imported at the turn of the century as cheap labor, much as America had brought in immigrants on both the Atlantic and Pacific coasts. But unlike America, Japan denied citizenship rights to its immigrants unless they adopted a fully Japanese identity, a fact made all the more odd in that the Japanese people were themselves a mere offshoot of the Korean, a fact proven by DNA research but which was conveniently and somewhat indignantly denied by the better sections of Japanese society. All foreigners were *gaijin*, a word which like most words in the local language had many flavors. Usually translated benignly as meaning just "foreigners," the word had other connotations — like "barbarian," Chet Nomuri thought, with all of the implicit invective that the word had carried when first coined by the Greeks. The irony was that as an American citizen he was *gaijin* himself, despite 100 percent Japanese ethnicity, and while he had grown up quietly resenting the racist policies of the U.S. government that had once caused genuine harm to his family, it had required only a week in the land of his ancestors for him to yearn for a return to Southern California, where the living was smooth and easy.

It was for Chester Nomuri a strange experience, living and "working" here. He'd been carefully screened and interviewed before being assigned to Operation SANDALWOOD. Having joined the Agency soon after graduating UCLA, not quite remembering why he'd done so except for a vague desire for adventure mixed with a family tradition of government service, he'd found somewhat to his surprise that he enjoyed the life. It was remarkably like police work, and Nomuri was a fan of police TV and novels. More than that, it was so damned *interesting*. He learned new things every day. It was like being in a living history classroom. Perhaps the most important lesson he'd learned, however, was that his great-grandfather had been a wise and insightful man. Nomuri wasn't blind to America's faults, but he preferred life there to life in any of the countries he'd visited, and with that knowledge had come pride in what he was doing, even though he still wasn't quite sure what the hell he was really up to. Of course, neither did his Agency, but Nomuri had never quite understood that, even when they'd told him so at the Farm. How could it be possible, after all? It must have been an inside-the-institution joke.

At the same time, in a dualism he was too young and inexperienced to appreciate fully, Japan could be an easy place in which to operate. That was especially true on the commuter train.

The degree of crowding here was enough to make his skin crawl. He had not been prepared for a country in which population density compelled close contact

144

with all manner of strangers, and, indeed, he'd soon realized that the cultural mania with fastidious personal hygiene and mannerly behavior was simply a by-product of it. People so often rubbed, bumped, or otherwise crushed into contact with others that the absence of politeness would have resulted in street killings to shame the most violent neighborhood in America. A combination of smiling embarrassment at the touches and icy personal isolation made it tolerable to the local citizens, though it was something that still gave Nomuri trouble. "Give the guy some space" had been a catch-phrase at UCLA. Clearly it wasn't here, because there simply wasn't the space to give.

Then there was the way they treated women. Here, on the crowded trains, the standing and sitting salarymen read comic books, called *manga*, the local versions of novels, which were genuinely disturbing. Recently, a favorite of the eighties had been revived, called *Rin-Tin-Tin*. Not the friendly dog from 1950s American television, but a dog with a female mistress, to whom he talked, and with whom he had . . . sexual relations. It was not an idea that appealed to him, but there, sitting on his bench seat, was a middle-aged executive, eyes locked on the pages with rapt attention, while a Japanese woman stood right next to him and stared out the train's windows, maybe noticing, maybe not. The war between the sexes in this country certainly had rules different from the ones with which he'd been raised, Nomuri thought. He set it aside. It was not part of his mission, after all — an idea he would soon find to be wrong.

He never saw the cutout. As he stood there in the third car of the train, close to the rear door, hanging on to an overhead bar and reading a paper, he didn't even notice the insertion of the envelope into the pocket of his overcoat. It was always that way — at the usual place the coat got just a touch heavier.

145

He'd turned once to look and seen nothing. Damn, he'd joined the right outfit.

Eighteen minutes later the train entered the terminal, and the people emerged from it like a horizontal avalanche, exploding outward into the capacious station. The salaryman ten feet away tucked his "illustrated novel" into his briefcase and walked off to his job, wearing his customarily impassive mien, doubtless concealing thoughts of his own. Nomuri headed his own way, buttoning his coat and wondering what his new instructions were.

"Does the President know?"

Ryan shook his head. "Not yet."

"You think maybe he ought to?" Mary Pat Foley asked.

"At the proper time."

"I don't like putting officers at risk for — "

"At risk?" Jack asked. "I want him to develop information, not to make a contact, and not to expose himself. I gather from the case notes I've seen so far that all he has to do is make a follow-up question, and unless their locker rooms are different from ours, it shouldn't expose him at all."

"You know what I mean," the Deputy Director (Operations) observed, rubbing her eyes. It had been a long day, and she worried about her field officers. Every good DDO did, and she was a mother who'd once been picked up by the KGB's Second Chief Directorate herself.

Operation SANDALWOOD had started innocently enough, if an intelligence operation on foreign soil could ever be called innocent. The preceding operation had been a joint FBI/CIA show, and had gone very badly indeed: an American citizen had been apprehended by the Japanese police with burglar tools in his possession — along with a diplomatic passport, which in this particular case had been more of a hindrance than a help. It had made the papers in a small way. Fortunately the media hadn't quite grasped what the story was all about. People were buying information. People were selling information. It was often information with "secret" or higher classifications scrawled across the folders, and the net effect was to hurt American interests, such as they were.

"How good is he?" Jack asked.

Mary Pat's face relaxed at little. "Very. The kid's a natural. He's learning to fit in, developing a base of people he can hit for background information. We've set him up with his own office. He's even turning us a nice profit. His orders are to be very careful," Mrs. Foley pointed out yet again.

"I hear you, MP," Ryan said tiredly. "But if this is for-real — "

"I know, Jack. I didn't like what Murray sent over either."

"You believe it?" Ryan asked, wondering about the reaction he'd get.

"Yes, I do, and so does Murray." She paused. "If we develop information on this, then what?"

"Then I go to the President, and probably we extract anyone who wants to be extracted."

"I will *not* risk Nomuri that way!" the DDO insisted, a little too loudly.

"Jesus, Mary Pat, I never expected that you would. Hey, I'm tired, too, okay?"

"So you want me to send in another team, let him just bird-dog it for them?" she asked.

"It's your operation to run, okay? I'll tell you *what* to do, but not *how*. Lighten up, MP." That statement earned the National Security Advisor a crooked smile and a semiapology.

"Sorry, Jack. I keep forgetting you're the new guy on this block."

"The chemicals have various industrial uses," the

147

Russian colonel explained to the American colonel.

"Good for you. All we can do is burn ours, and the smoke'll kill you." The rocket exhaust from the liquid propellants wasn't exactly the Breath of Spring either, of course, but when you got down to it, they *were* industrial chemicals with a variety of other uses.

As they watched, technicians snaked a hose from the standpipe next to the missile *puskatel,* the Russian word for "silo," to a truck that would transport the last of the nitrogen tetroxide to a chemical plant. Below, another fitting on the missile body took another hose that pumped pressurized gas into the top of the oxidizer tank, the better to drive the corrosive chemical out. The top of the missile was blunt. The Americans could see where the warhead "bus" had been attached, but it had already been removed, and was now on another truck, preceded by a pair of BTR-70 infantry fighting vehicles and trailed by three more, on its way to a place where the warheads could be disarmed preparatory to complete disassembly. America was buying the plutonium. The tritium in the warheads would stay in Russia, probably to be sold eventually on the open market to end up on watch and instrument faces. Tritium had a market value of about $50,000 per gram, and the sale of it would turn a tidy profit for the Russians. Perhaps, the American thought, that was the reason that his Russian colleagues were moving so expeditiously.

This was the first SS-19 silo to be deactivated for the 53rd Strategic Rocket Regiment. It was both like and unlike the American silos being deactivated under Russian inspection. The same mass of reinforced concrete for both, though this one was sited in woods, and the American silos were all on open ground, reflecting different ideas about site security. The climate wasn't all that different. Windier in North Dakota, because of the open spaces. The base temperature was marginally colder in Russia, which balanced out the wind-chill factor on the prairie. In due course the valve wheel on the pipe was turned, the hose removed, and the truck started up.

"Mind if I look?" the USAF colonel asked.

"Please." The Russian colonel of Strategic Rocket Forces waved to the open hole. He even handed over a large flashlight. Then it was his turn to laugh.

You son of a bitch, Colonel Andrew Malcolm wanted to exclaim. There was a pool of icy water at the bottom of the puskatel. The intelligence estimate had been wrong again. Who would have believed it?

"Backup?" Ding asked.

"You might end up just doing sightseeing," Mrs. Foley told them, almost believing it.

"Fill us in on the mission?" John Clark asked, getting down to business. It was his own fault, after all, since he and Ding had turned into one of the Agency's best field teams. He looked over at Chavez. The kid had come a long way in five years. He had his college degree, and was close to his master's, in international relations no less. Ding's job would probably have put his instructors into cardiac arrest, since their idea of transnational intercourse didn't involve fucking other nations — a joke Domingo Chavez himself had coined on the dusty plains of Africa while reading a history book for one of his seminar groups. He still needed to learn about concealing his emotions. Chavez still retained some of the fiery nature of his background, though Clark wondered how much of it was for show around the Farm and elsewhere. In every organization the individual practitioners had to have a "service reputation." John had his. People spoke about him in whispers, thinking, stupidly, that the nicknames and rumors would never get back to him. And Ding wanted one, too. Well, that was normal.

"Photos?" Chavez asked calmly, then took them from Mrs. Foley's hand. There were six of them.

Ding examined each, handing them over one by one to his senior. The junior officer kept his voice even but allowed his face to show his distaste.

"So if Nomuri turns up a face and a location, then what?" Ding asked.

"You two make contact with her and ask if she would like a free plane ticket home," the DDO replied without adding that there would be an extensive debriefing process. The CIA didn't give out free anythings, really.

"Cover?" John asked.

"We haven't decided yet. Before you head over, we need to work on your language skills."

"Monterey?" Chavez smiled. It was about the most pleasant piece of country in America, especially this time of year.

"Two weeks, total immersion. You fly out this evening. Your teacher will be a guy named Lyalin, Oleg Yurievich. KGB major who came over a while back. He actually ran a network over there, called THISTLE. He's the guy who turned the information that you and Ding used to bug the airliner — "

"Whoa!" Chavez observed. "Without him . . ."

Mrs. Foley nodded, pleased that Ding had made the complete connection that rapidly. "That's right. He's got a very nice house overlooking the water. It turns out he's one hell of a good language teacher, I guess because he had to learn it himself." It had turned into a fine bargain for CIA. After the debriefing process, he'd taken a productive job at the Armed Forces Language School, where his salary was paid by DOD. "Anyway, by the time you're able to order lunch and find the bathroom in the native tongue, we'll have your cover IDs figured out."

Clark smiled and rose, taking the signal that it was time to leave. "Back to work, then."

"Defending America," Ding observed with a smile, leaving the photos on Mrs. Foley's desk and sure that actually having to defend his country was a thing of the past. Clark heard the remark and thought it a joke too, until memories came back that erased the look from his face.

It wasn't their fault. It was just a matter of objective conditions. With four times the population of the United States, and only one third the living space, they had to do something. The people needed jobs, products, a chance to have what everyone else in the world wanted. They could see it on the television sets that seemed to exist even in places where there were no jobs, and, seeing it, demanded a chance to have it. It was that simple. You couldn't say "no" to nine hundred million people.

Certainly not if you were one of them. Vice Admiral V. K. Chandraskatta sat on his leather chair on the flag bridge of the carrier *Viraat*. His obligation, as expressed in his oath of office, was to carry out the orders of his government, but more than that, his duty was to his people. He had to look no further than his own flag bridge to see that: staff officers and ratings, especially the latter, the best his country could produce. They were mainly signalmen and yeomen who'd left whatever life they'd had on the subcontinent to take on this new one, and tried hard to be good at it, because as meager as the pay was, it was preferable to the economic chances they took in a country whose unemployment rate hovered between 20 and 25 percent. Just for his country to be self-sufficient in food had taken — how long? Twenty-five years. And *that* had come only as charity of sorts, the result of Western agroscience whose success still grated on many minds, as though his country, ancient and learned, couldn't make its own destiny. Even successful charity could be a burden on the national soul.

And now what? His country's economy was bouncing back, finally, but it was also hitting limits. India needed additional resources, but most of all needed space, of which there was little to be had. To his country's north was the world's most forbidding mountain range. East was Bangladesh, which had even more problems than India did. West was Pakistan, also overcrowded, and an ancient religious enemy, war with whom could well have the unwanted effect of cutting off his country's oil supply to the Muslim states of the Persian Gulf.

Such bad luck, the Admiral thought, picking up his glasses and surveying his fleet because he had nothing else to do at the moment. If they did nothing, the best his country might hope for was something little better than stagnation. If they turned outward, actively seeking room . . . But the "new world order" said that his country could not. India was denied entry into the race to greatness by those very nations that had run the race and then shut it down lest others catch up.

The proof was right here. His navy was one of the world's most powerful, built and manned and trained at ruinous expense, sailing on one of the world's seven oceans, the only one named for a country, and even here it was second-best, subordinate to a fraction of the United States Navy. That grated even more. America was the one telling his country what it could and could not do. America, with a history of — what? — scarcely two hundred years. Upstarts. Had they fought Alexander of Macedon or the great Khan? The European "discovery" voyages had been aimed at reaching *his* country, and that land mass discovered by *accident* was now denying greatness and power and justice to the Admiral's ancient land. It was, all in all, a lot to hide behind a face of professional detachment while the rest of his flag staff bustled about.

"Radar contact, bearing one-three-five, range two

hundred kilometers," a talker announced. "Inbound course, speed five hundred knots."

The Admiral turned to his fleet-operations officer and nodded. Captain Mehta lifted a phone and spoke. His fleet was off the normal commercial sea and air routes, and the timing told him what the inbound track would be. Four American fighters, F-18E Hornet attack fighters off one of the American carriers to his southeast. Every day they came, morning and afternoon, and sometimes in the middle of the night to show that they could do that, too, to let him know that the Americans knew his location, and to remind him that he didn't, couldn't know theirs.

A moment later he heard the start-up noise from two of his Harriers. Good aircraft, expensive aircraft, but not a match for the inbound Americans. He'd put four up today, two from *Viraat* and two from *Vikrant*, to intercept the four, probably four, American Hornets, and the pilots would wave and nod in a show of good humor, but it would be a bilateral lie.

"We could light off our SAM systems, show them that we tire of this game," Captain Mehta suggested quietly. The Admiral shook his head.

"No. They know little about our SAM systems, and we will volunteer them nothing." The Indians' precise radar frequencies, pulse width, and repetition rates were not open information, and the American intelligence services had probably never troubled itself to find them out. That meant that the Americans might not be able to jam or spoof his systems — probably they could, but they wouldn't be certain of it, and it was the lack of certainty that would worry them. It wasn't much of a card, but it was the best in Chandraskatta's current hand. The Admiral sipped at his tea, making a show of his imperturbable nature. "No, we will take notice of their approach, meet them in a friendly manner, and let them go on their way."

Mehta nodded and went off without a word to express his building rage. It was to be expected. He was the fleet-operations officer, and his was the task of divining a plan to defeat the American fleet, should that necessity present itself. That such a task was virtually impossible did not relieve Mehta of the duty to carry it out, and it was hardly surprising that the man was showing the strain of his position. Chandraskatta set his cup down, watching the Harriers leap off the ski-jump deck and into the air.

"How are the pilots bearing up?" the Admiral asked his air officer.

"They grow frustrated, but performance thus far is excellent." The answer was delivered with pride, as well it might be. His pilots were superb. The Admiral ate with them often, drawing courage from the proud faces in the ready rooms. They were fine young men, the equal, man for man, of any fighter pilots in all the world. More to the point, they were eager to show it.

But the entire Indian Navy had only forty-three Harrier FRS 51 fighters. He had but thirty at sea on both *Viraat* and *Vikrant*, and that did not equal the numbers or capability aboard a single American carrier. All because they had entered the race first, won it, and then declared the games closed, Chandraskatta told himself, listening to the chatter of his airmen over an open-voice channel. It simply wasn't fair.

"So, what are you telling me?" Jack asked.

"It was a scam," Robby answered. "Those birds were maintenance-intensive. Guess what? The maintenance hasn't been done in the past couple of years. Andy Malcolm called in on his satellite brick this evening. There was water at the bottom of the hole he looked at today."

"And?"

"I keep forgetting you're a city boy." Robby grinned sheepishly, or rather like the wolf under a fleece coat. "You make a hole in the ground, sooner or later it fills with water, okay? If you have something valuable in the hole, you better keep it pumped out. Water in the bottom of the silo means that they weren't always doing that. It means water vapor, humidity in the hole. And corrosion."

The light bulb went off. "You telling me the birds — "

"Probably wouldn't fly even if they wanted them to. Corrosion is like that. Probably dead birds, because fixing them once they're broke is a very iffy proposition. Anyway" — Jackson tossed the thin file folder at Ryan's desk — "that's the J-3 assessment."

"What about J-2?" Jack asked, referring to the intelligence directorate of the Joint Chiefs of Staff.

"They never believed it, but I expect they will now if we open enough holes and see the same thing. Me?" Admiral Jackson shrugged. "I figure if Ivan let us see it in number one, we'll find pretty much the same thing everywhere else. They just don't give a good fuck anymore."

Intelligence information comes from many sources, and an "operator" like Jackson was often the best source of all. Unlike intelligence officers whose job it was to evaluate the capabilities of the other side, almost always in a theoretical sense, Jackson was a man whose interest in weapons was making them work, and he'd learned from hard experience that using them was far more demanding than looking at them.

"Remember when we thought they were ten feet tall?"

"I never did, but a little bastard with a gun can still ruin your whole day," Robby reminded his friend. "So how much money have they hustled out of us?"

"Five big ones."

"Good deal, our federal tax money at work. We just paid the Russkies five thousand million dollars to 'deactivate' missiles that couldn't leave the silos unless they set the nukes off *first*. Fabulous call, Dr. Ryan."

"They need the money, Rob."

"So do I, man. Hey, boy, I'm scratching the bottom to get enough JP to keep our planes in the air." It was not often understood that every ship in the fleet and every battalion of tanks in the Army had to live on a budget. Though the commanding officers didn't keep a checkbook per se, each drew on a fixed supply of consumable stores — fuel, weapons, spare parts, even food in the case of warships — that had to last a whole year. It was by no means unknown for a man-of-war to sit several weeks alongside her pier at the end of the fiscal year because there was nothing left to make her run. Such an event meant that somewhere a job was not getting done, a crew was not being trained. The Pentagon was fairly unique as a federal agency, in that it was expected to live on a fixed, often diminishing budget.

"How much thinner do you expect us to be spread?"

"I tell him, Rob, okay? The Chairman — "

"Just between you and me, the Chairman thinks operations are something that surgeons do in hospitals. And if you quote me on that, no more golf lessons."

"What is it worth to have the Russians out of the game?" Jack asked, wondering if Robby would calm down a little.

"Not as much as we've lost in cuts. In case you haven't noticed, my Navy is still stretched from hell to breakfast, and we're doing business with forty percent less ships. The ocean didn't get any smaller, okay? The Army's better off, I grant that, but the Air Force isn't, and the Marines are still sucking hind tit, and *they're* still our primary response team for the next time the boys and girls at Foggy Bottom fuck up."

"Preaching to the choir, Rob."

"More to it than just that, Jack. We're stretching the people, too. The fewer the ships, the longer they have to stay out. The longer they stay out, the worse the maintenance bills. It's like the bad old days in the late seventies. We're starting to lose people. Hard to make a man stay away from his wife and kids that long. In flying, we call it the coffin corner. When you lose experienced people, your training bills go up. You lose combat effectiveness no matter which way you go," Robby went on, talking like an admiral now.

"Look, Rob, I gave the same speech a while back on the other side of the building. I'm doing my best for you," Jack replied, talking like a senior government official. At that point both old friends shared a look.

"We're both old farts."

"It's a long time since we were on the faculty of Canoe U," Ryan allowed. His voice went on almost in a whisper. "Me teaching history, and you prostrating yourself to God every night to heal your leg."

"I should've done more of that. Arthritis in the knee," Robby said. "I have a flight physical in nine months. Guess what?"

"Down-check?"

"The big one." Jackson nodded matter-of-factly. Ryan knew what it really meant. To a man who'd flown fighter planes off carriers for over twenty years, it was the hard realization that age had come. He couldn't play with the boys anymore. You could explain away gray in the hair by citing adverse genes, but a down-check would mean taking off the flight suit, hanging up the helmet, and admitting that he was no longer good enough to do the one thing he'd yearned for since the age of ten, and at which he'd excelled for nearly all of his adult life. The bitterest part would be the memories of the things he'd said as a lieutenant, j.g., about the older pilots of his youth, the hidden smirks, the knowing looks shared with his fellow youngsters, none of whom had ever expected it would come to them.

"Rob, a lot of good guys never get the chance to screen for command of a squadron. They take the twenty-year out at commander's rank and end up flying the night shift for Federal Express."

"And make good money at it, too."

"Have you picked out the casket yet?" That broke the mood. Jackson looked up and grinned.

"Shit. If I can't dance, I can still watch. I'm telling you, pal, you want us to run all these pretty operations we plan in my cubicle, we need help from this side of the river. Mike Dubro is doing a great job hanging paper with one hand, but he and his troops have limits, y'dig?"

"Well, Admiral, I promise you this: when the time comes for you to get your battle group, there will be one for you to drive." It wasn't much of a pledge, but both men knew it was the best he could offer.

She was number five. The remarkable part was — hell, Murray thought in the office six blocks from the White House, it was all remarkable. It was the profile of the investigation that was the most disquieting. He and his team had interviewed several women who had admitted, some shamefacedly, some without overt emotional involvement, and some with pride and humor, at having bedded Ed Kealty, but there were five for whom the act had not been entirely voluntary. With this woman, the latest, drugs had been an additional factor, and she felt the lonely personal shame, the sense that she alone had fallen into the trap.

"So?" Bill Shaw asked after what had been a long day for him, too.

"So it's a solid case. We now have five known victims, four of whom are living. Two would stand up as rapes in any courtroom I've ever been in. That does not count Lisa Beringer. The other two demonstrate the use of drugs on federal property. Those two are virtually word-for-word, they identify the label on the brandy bottle, the effects, everything."

"Good witnesses?" the FBI Director asked.

"As good as can be expected in this sort of case. It's time to move with it," Murray added. Shaw nodded in understanding. Word would soon begin to leak out. You simply couldn't run a covert investigation for very long, even under the best of circumstances. Some of the people you interviewed would be loyal to the target of the inquiry, and no matter how carefully you phrased the opening questions, they would make the not overly great leap of imagination required to discern the nature of the probe, often because they suspected it themselves. Then those non-witnesses would worry about getting back to the target to warn him, whether from conviction in his innocence or hope of deriving a personal profit. Criminal or not, the Vice President was a man with considerable political power, still able to dole out large and powerful tokens to those who won his favor. In another age, the Bureau might not have gotten this far. The President himself, or even the Attorney General, would have conveyed a quiet warning, and senior staff members would themselves have sought out the victims and offered to make amends of one sort or another, and in many cases it would have worked. The only reason they'd gotten this far, after all, was that the FBI had the permission of the President, the cooperation of the AG, and a different legal and moral climate in which to work.

"As soon as you go to talk to the Chairman . . ."

Murray nodded. "Yeah, might as well have a press conference and lay out our evidence in an organized way." But they couldn't do that, of course. Once the substance of their evidence was given over to political figures — in this case the chairman and ranking minority member of the House Committee on the Judiciary — it would leak immediately. The only real control Murray and his team would possess would be in selecting the time of day. Late enough, and the news would miss the morning papers, incurring the wrath of the editors of *The Washington Post* and *The New York Times*. The Bureau had to play strictly by the rules. It couldn't leak anything because this was a criminal proceeding and the rights of the target had to be guarded as closely as — actually even closer than — those of the victims, lest the eventual trial be tainted.

"We'll do it here, Dan," Shaw said, reaching his decision. "I'll have the A.G. make the phone call and set the meet. Maybe that'll put the information on close-hold for a little while. What exactly did the President say the other day?"

"He's a standup guy," the Deputy Assistant Director reported, using a form of praise popular in the FBI. "He said, 'A crime's a crime.' " The President had also said to handle the affair in as "black" a way as possible, but that was to be expected.

"Fair enough. I'll let him know what we're doing personally."

Typically, Nomuri went right to work. It was his regular night at this bathhouse with this group of salarymen — he probably had the cleanest job in the Agency. It was also one of the slickest ways of getting information he'd ever stumbled across, and he made it slicker still by standing for a large bottle of saké that now sat, half empty, on the edge of the wooden tub.

160

"I wish you hadn't told me about that round-eye," Nomuri said with his own eyes closed, sitting in his usual corner and allowing his body to take in the enveloping heat of the water. At one hundred eight degrees, it was hot enough to lower blood pressure and induce euphoria. Added to it was the effect of the alcohol. Many Japanese have a genetic abnormality called "Oriental Flush" in the West, or with greater ethnic sensitivity, "pathological intoxication." It is actually an enzyme disorder, and means that for a relatively low quantity of alcoholic intake, there is a high degree of result. It was, fortunately, a trait which Nomuri's family did not share.

"Why is that?" Kazuo Taoka asked from the opposite corner.

"Because now I cannot get the gaijin witch out of my mind!" Nomuri replied good-naturedly. One of the other effects of the bathhouse was an intimate bonhomie. The man next to the CIA officer rubbed his head roughly and laughed, as did the rest of the group.

"Ah, and now you want to hear more, is it?" Nomuri didn't have to look. The man whose body rubbed on his leaned forward. Surely the rest would do it as well. "You were right, you know. Their feet are too big, and their bosoms also, but their manners . . . well, that they can learn after a fashion."

"You make us wait?" another member of the group asked, feigning a blustery anger.

"Do you not appreciate drama?" There was a merry chorus of laughs. "Well, yes, it is true that her bosoms are too big for real beauty, but there are sacrifices we all must make in life, and truly I have seen worse deformities . . ."

Such a good raconteur, Nomuri thought. He did have a gift for it. In a moment he heard the sound of a cork being pulled, as another man refilled the little cups. Drink was actually prohibited in the bathhouse for health reasons, but, rarely for this country, it was a rule largely ignored. Nomuri reached for his cup, his eyes still closed, and made a great show of forming a mental picture masked by a blissful smile, as additional details slid across the steaming surface of the water. The description became more specific, fitting ever closer to the photograph and to other details he'd been passed on his early-morning train. It was hardly conclusive yet. Any of thousands of girls could fit the description, and Nomuri wasn't particularly outraged by the event. She'd taken her chances one way or another, but she was an American citizen, and if it were possible to help her, then he would. It seemed a trivial sidebar to his overall assignment, but if nothing else it had caused him to ask a question that would make him appear even more a member of this group of men. It made it more likely, therefore, to get important information out of them at a later date.

"We have no choice," a man said in another, similar bathhouse, not so far away. "We need your help."

It wasn't unexpected, the other five men thought. It was just a matter of who would hit the wall first. Fate had made it this man and his company. That did not lessen his personal disgrace at being forced to ask for help, and the other men felt his pain while outwardly displaying only dispassionate good manners. Indeed, those men who listened felt something else as well: fear. Now that it had happened once, it would be far easier for it to happen again. Who would be next?

Generally there could be no safer form of investment than real estate, real fixed property with physical reality, something you could touch and feel, build, and live on, that others could see and measure. Although there were continuing efforts in Japan to make new fill land, to build new airports, for example, the general rule was as true here as it was elsewhere: it made sense to buy land because the supply of real land was fixed, and because of that the price was not going to drop.

But in Japan that truth had been distorted by unique local conditions. Land-use policy in the country was skewed by the inordinate power of the small holders of farmland, and it was not unusual to see a small patch of land in the midst of a suburban setting allocated to the growing of a quarter hectare of vegetables. Small already — the entire nation was about the size of California, and populated with roughly half the people of the United States — their country was further crowded by the fact that little of the land was arable, and since arable land also tended to be land on which people could more easily live, the major part of the population was further concentrated into a handful of large, dense cities, where real-estate prices became more precious still. The remarkable result of these seemingly ordinary facts was that the commercial real estate in the city of Tokyo alone had a higher "book" value than that of all the land in America's forty-eight contiguous states. More remarkably still, this absurd fiction was accepted by everyone as though it made sense, when in fact it was every bit as madly artificial as the Dutch Tulip Mania of the seventeenth century.

But as with America, what was a national economy, after all, but a collective belief? Or so everyone had thought for a generation. The frugal Japanese citizens saved a high proportion of their earnings. Those savings went into banks, in such vast quantities that the supply of capital for lending was similarly huge, as a result of which the interest rates for those loans were correspondingly low, which allowed businesses to purchase land and build on it despite prices that anywhere else in the world would have been somewhere between ruinous and impossible. As with any

163

artificial boom, the process had dangerous corollaries. The inflated book value of owned real estate was used as collateral for other loans, and as security for stock portfolios bought on margin, and in the process supposedly intelligent and far-seeing businessmen had in fact constructed an elaborate house of cards whose foundation was the belief that metropolitan Tokyo had more intrinsic value than all of America between Bangor and San Diego. (An additional consequence of this was a view of real-estate value that more than any other factor had persuaded Japanese businessmen that American real-estate, which, after all, looked pretty much the same as that in their own country, *had to be* worth more than what the foolish Americans charged for it.) By the early 1990s had come disquieting thoughts. The precipitous decline of the Japanese stock market had threatened to put calls on the large margin accounts, and made some businessmen think about selling their land holdings to cover their exposures. With that had come the stunning but unsurprising realization that nobody wanted to pay book value for a parcel of land; that although everyone accepted book value in the abstract, actually paying the assumed price was, well, not terribly realistic. The result was that the single card supporting the rest of the house had been quietly removed from the bottom of the structure and awaited only a puff of breeze to cause the entire edifice to collapse — a possibility studiously ignored in the discourse between senior executives.

Until now.

The men sitting in the tub were friends and associates of many years' standing, and with Kozo Matsuda's quiet and dignified announcement of his company's current cash-flow difficulties, all of them saw collective disaster on a horizon that was suddenly far closer than they had expected only two hours earlier. The bankers present could offer loans, but interest rates were higher now. The industrialists could offer favors, but those would affect the bottom-line profits of their operations, with adverse effects on already-staggering stock prices. Yes, they could save their friend from ruin, along with which, in their society, came personal disgrace that would forever remove him from this intimate group. If they didn't, he would have to take his "best" chance, to put some of his office buildings, quietly, on the market, hoping, quietly, that someone would purchase them at something akin to the assumed value. But that was most unlikely — this they knew; they themselves would not be willing to do it — and if it became known that "book value" was as fictional as the writings of Jules Verne, then they would suffer, too. The bankers would have to admit that the security of their loans, and consequently the security of their depositors' money, was also a hollow fiction. A quantity of "real" money so massive as to be comprehended only as a number would be seen to have vanished as though by some sort of evil magic. For all these reasons, they would do what had to be done, they would help Matsuda and his company, receiving concessions in return, of course, but fronting the money he and his operations needed.

The problem was that although they could do it once, probably twice, and maybe even a third time, events would soon cascade, finding their own precipitous momentum, and there would soon come a time when they could not do what was necessary to support the house of cards. The consequences were not easily contemplated.

All six of the men looked down at the water, unable to meet the eyes of the others, because their society did not easily allow men to communicate fear, and fear is what they all felt. They were responsible, after all. Their corporations were in their own hands, ruled as autocratically as the holdings of a J. P. Morgan.

With their control came a lavish lifestyle, immense personal power, and, ultimately, total personal accountability. All the decisions had been theirs, after all, and if those decisions had been faulty, then the responsibility was theirs in a society where public failure was as painful as death.

"Yamata-san is right," one of the bankers said quietly, without moving his body. "I was in error to dispute his view."

Marveling at his courage, and as though in one voice, the others nodded and whispered, *"Hai."*

Then another man spoke. "We need to seek his counsel on this matter."

The factory worked two hectic shifts, so popular was what it turned out. Set in the hills of Kentucky, the single building occupied over a hundred acres and was surrounded in turn by a parking lot for its workers and another for its products, with an area for loading trucks, and another for loading trains, run into the facility by CSX.

The premier new car on American and Japanese markets, the Cresta was named for the toboggan run at St. Moritz, in Switzerland, where a senior Japanese auto executive, somewhat in his cups, had taken up a challenge to try his luck on one of the deceptively simple sleds. He'd rocketed down the track, only to lose control at the treacherous Shuttlecock curve, turned himself into a ballistic object and dislocated his hip in the process. To honor the course that had given him a needed lesson in humility, he'd decided in the local casualty hospital to enshrine his experience in a new car, at that time merely a set of drawings and specifications.

As with nearly everything generated by the Japanese auto industry, the Cresta was a masterpiece of engineering. Popularly priced, its front-wheel drive attached to a sporty and fuel-efficient four-cylinder,

166

sixteen-valve engine, it sat two adults in the front and two or three children quite comfortably in the back, and had become overnight both the *Motor Trend* Car of the Year and the savior of a Japanese manufacturer that had suffered three straight years of declining sales because of Detroit's rebounding efforts to take back the American market. The single most popular car for young adults with families, it came "loaded" with options and was manufactured on both sides of the Pacific to meet a global demand.

This plant, set thirty miles outside Lexington, Kentucky, was state-of-the-art in all respects. The employees earned union wages without having had to join the UAW, and on both attempts to create a union shop, supervised by the National Labor Relations Board, the powerful organization had failed to get even as much as 40 percent of the vote and gone away grumbling at the unaccustomed stupidity of the workers.

As with any such operation, there was an element of unreality to it. Auto parts entered the building at one end, and finished automobiles exited at the other. Some of the parts were even American made, though not as many as the U.S. government would have wished. Indeed, the factory manager would have preferred more domestic content as well, especially in the winter, when adverse weather on the Pacific could interfere with the delivery of parts — even a one-day delay in arrival time of a single ship could bring some inventories dangerously low, since the plant ran on minimal overhead — and the demand for his Crestas was greater than his ability to manufacture them. The parts arrived mostly by train-loaded containers from ports on both American coasts, were separated by type, and stored in stockrooms adjacent to the portion of the assembly line at which they would be joined with the automobiles. Much of the work was done by robots, but there was no substitute for the skilled

167

hands of a worker with eyes and a brain, and in truth the automated functions were mainly things that people didn't enjoy anyway. The very efficiency of the plant made for the affordable cost of the Cresta, and the busy schedule, with plenty of overtime, made for workers who, with this region's first taste of really well-paying manufacturing jobs, applied themselves as diligently as their Japanese counterparts, and, their Japanese supervisors admitted quietly both to themselves and in internal company memoranda, rather more creatively. Fully a dozen major innovations suggested by workers on this line, just in this year, had been adopted at once in similar factories six thousand miles away. The supervisory personnel themselves greatly enjoyed living in Middle America. The price of their homes and the expanse of land that came with them both came as startling revelations, and after the initial discomfort of being in an alien land, they all began the process of succumbing to local hospitality, joining the local lawyers on the golf links, stopping off at McDonald's for a burger, watching their children play T-Ball with the local kids, often amazed at their welcome after what they'd expected. (The local TV cable system had even added NHK to its service, for the two hundred families who wanted the flavor of something from home.) In the process they also generated a tidy profit for their parent corporation, which, unfortunately, was now trapped into barely breaking even on the Crestas produced in Japan due to the unexpectedly high productivity of the Kentucky plant and the continuing decline of the dollar against the yen. For that reason, additional land was being bought this very week to increase the capacity of the plant by 60 percent. A third shift, while a possibility, would have reduced line maintenance, with a consequent adverse effect on quality control, which was a risk the company was unwilling to run, considering the renewed competition from Detroit.

168

Early in the line, two workers attached the gasoline tanks to the frames. One, off the line, removed the tank from its shipping carton and set it on a moving track that carried it to the second worker, whose job was to manhandle the light but bulky artifact into place. Plastic hangers held the tank briefly until the worker made the attachment permanent, and the plastic hangers were then removed before the chassis moved on to the next station.

The cardboard was soggy, the woman in the storage room noted. She held her hand to her nose and smelled sea salt. The container that had held this shipment of gas tanks had been improperly closed, and a stormy sea had invaded it. A good thing, she thought, that the tanks were all weather-sealed and galvanized. Perhaps fifteen or twenty of the tanks had been exposed to seawater. She considered mentioning it to the supervisor, but on looking around she couldn't see him. She had the authority on her own to stop the line — traditionally a very rare power for an auto-assembly worker — until the question of the gas tanks was cleared up. Every worker in the plant had that theoretical power, but she was new here, and really needed her supervisor to make the call. Looking around more, she almost stopped the line by her inaction, which caused an abrupt whistle from the line worker. Well, it couldn't be that big a deal, could it? She slid the tank on the track, and, opening the next box, forgot about it. She would never know that she was part of a chain of events that would soon kill one family and wound two others.

Two minutes later the tank was attached to a Cresta chassis, and the not-yet-a-car moved on down the seemingly endless line toward an open door that could not even be seen from this station. In due course the rest of the automobile would be assembled on the steel frame, finally rolling out of the plant as a candy-apple-red car already ordered by a family in Greeneville, Tennessee. The color had been chosen in honor of the wife, Candace Denton, who had just given her husband, Pierce, his first son after two twin daughters three years earlier. It would be the first new car the young couple had ever owned, and was his way of showing her how pleased he was with her love. They really couldn't afford it, but it was about love, not money, and he knew that somehow he'd find a way to make it work. The following day the car was driven onto a semitrailer transporter for the short drive to the dealer in Knoxville. A telex from the assembly plant told the salesman that it was on the way, and he wasted no time calling Mr. Denton to let him know the good news.

They'd need a day for dealer prep, but the car would be delivered, a week late due to the demand for the Cresta, fully inspected, with temporary tags and insurance. And a full tank of gas, sealing a fate already decided by a multiplicity of factors.

7

Catalyst

It didn't help to do it at night. Even the glare of lights — dozens of them — didn't replicate what the sun gave for free. Artificial light made for odd shadows that always seemed to be in the wrong places, and if that weren't bad enough, the men moving around made shadows of their own, pulling the eyes away from their important work.

Each of the SS-19/H-11 "boosters" was encapsulated. The construction plans for the capsule — called a cocoon here — had accompanied the plans for the missiles themselves, more or less as an afterthought; after all, the Japanese corporation had paid for all the plans, and they were in the same drawer, and so they went along. That was fortunate, the supervising engineer thought, because it had not seemed to have occurred to anyone to ask for them.

The SS-19 had been designed as an intercontinental ballistic missile, a weapon of war, and since it had been designed by Russians, it had also been engineered for rough handling by poorly trained conscript soldiers. In this, the engineer admitted, the Russians had showed true genius worthy of emulation. His own countrymen had a tendency to overengineer everything, which often made for a delicacy that had no place in such brutish applications as this. Forced to construct a weapon that could survive adverse human and environmental factors, the Russians had built a transport/loading container for their "birds" that protected them against everything. In this way the assembly workers could fit all the plugs and fittings at the factory, insert the missile body into its capsule, and ship it off to the field, where all the soldiers had to do was elevate it and then lower it into the silo. Once there, a better-trained crew of three men would attach the external power and telemetry plugs. Though not as simple as loading a cartridge into a rifle, it was by far the most efficient way of installing an ICBM that anyone had ever developed — efficient enough, indeed, that the Americans had copied it for their MX "Peacekeeper" missiles, all of which were now destroyed. The cocoon allowed the missile to be handled without fear, because all the stress points had hard contact with the inside of the structure. It was rather like the exoskeleton of an insect, and was necessary because, as forbidding as the missile might appear, it was in fact as delicate as the flimsiest tissue. Fittings within the silo accepted the base of the capsule, which allowed it to be rotated to the vertical and then lowered fully into place. The entire operation, bad lighting and all, required ninety minutes — exactly what the Soviet manual had demanded of its people, remarkably enough.

In this case, the silo crew consisted of five men. They attached three power cables along with four hoses that would maintain the gas pressure in the fuel and oxidizer tanks — the bird was not yet fueled, and the internal tanks needed pressure to maintain structural integrity. In the control bunker located six hundred meters away, within the valley's northeastern wall, the control crew of three men noted that the missile's internal systems "spun up" just as they were supposed to. It wasn't the least bit unexpected, but was gratifying even so. With that knowledge, they made a call to the phone located adjacent to the top of the silo, and the work crew waved the train off. The diesel switch engine would deposit the flatcar back on a siding and retrieve the next missile. Two would be emplaced that night, and on each of the four succeeding nights, filling all ten of the silos. The senior personnel marveled at how smoothly it had all gone, though each wondered why it should be so surprising. It was perfectly straightforward work, after all. And strictly speaking, it was, but each also knew that the world would soon be a very different place because of what they had done, and somehow they'd expected the sky to change color or the earth to move at every moment of the project. Neither had happened, and now the question was whether to be disappointed or elated by that turn of events.

"It is our opinion that you should take a harder line with them," Goto said in the sanctity of his host's office.

"But why?" the Prime Minister asked, knowing the answer even so.

"They seek to crush us. They seek to punish us for being efficient, for doing better work, for achieving higher standards than what their own lazy workers are willing to attain." The Leader of the Opposition saved his assertive speaking voice for public utterances. In private with the leader of his country's government, he was unfailingly polite in manner even as he plotted to replace this weak, indecisive man.

"That is not necessarily the case, Goto-san. You know as well as I do that we have of late reasserted our position on rice and automobiles and computer chips. It is we who have won concessions from them, and not the reverse." The Prime Minister wondered what Goto was up to. Part of it he knew, naturally enough. Goto was maneuvering with his usual crude skill to realign the various factions in the Diet. The

Prime Minister had a tenuous majority there, and the reason his government had taken a hard line on trade issues had been to assuage those on the margins of his voting bloc, ordinarily minor players and parties whose alliance of convenience with the government had magnified their power to the point where the tail really could wag the dog, because the tail knew that it held the balance of power. In this the PM had played a dangerous game on the high-wire and without a net. On the one hand he'd have to keep his own diverse political allies happy, and on the other he couldn't offend his nation's most important trading partner. Worst of all, it was a tiring game, especially with people like Goto watching from below and howling at him, hoping that their noise would make him fall.

As though you could do better, the Prime Minister thought, politely refilling Goto's cup with green tea, getting a gracious nod for the gesture.

The more basic problem he understood better than the leader of his parliamentary opposition. Japan was not a democracy in any real sense. Rather like America in the late Nineteenth Century, the government was in fact, if not in law, a kind of official shield for the nation's business. The country was really run by a relative handful of businessmen — the number was under thirty, or even under twenty, depending on how you reckoned it — and despite the fact that those executives and their corporations appeared to be cutthroat competitors, in reality they were all associates, allied in every possible way, co-directorships, banking partnerships, all manner of inter-corporate cooperation agreements. Rare was the parliamentarian who would not listen with the greatest care to a representative of one of the zaibatsu. Rarer still was the Diet member who was graced with a personal audience with one of these men, and in every such case, the elected government official came away exhilarated

174

at his good fortune, for those men were quite effective at providing what every politician needed: funds. Consequently, their word was law. The result was a parliament as thoroughly corrupted as any on earth. Or perhaps "corrupt" was the wrong term, the PM told himself. Subservient, perhaps. The ordinary citizens of the country were often enraged by what they saw, by what a few courageous journalists proclaimed, mostly in terms that, despite appearing to Westerners to be rather weak and fawning, in local context were as damning as anything Emile Zola had ever broadsheeted across Paris. But the ordinary citizens didn't have the effective power that the zaibatsu did, and every attempt to reform the political system had fallen short. As a result, the government of one of the world's most powerful economies had become little more than the official arm of businessmen elected by no one, scarcely even beholden to their own stockholders. They had arranged his own accession to the Prime Ministership, he knew now . . . perhaps a bone thrown to the common people? he wondered. Had he been *supposed* to fail? Was that the destiny that had been constructed for him? To fail so that a return to normal could then be accepted by the citizens who'd placed their hopes in his hands?

That fear had pushed him into taking positions with America that he knew to be dangerous. And now even that was not enough, was it?

"Many would say that," Goto allowed with the most perfect manners. "And I salute you for your courage. Alas, objective conditions have hurt our country. For example, the relative change of dollar and yen has had devastating effects on our investments abroad, and these could only have been the result of deliberate policy on the part of our esteemed trading partners."

There was something about his delivery, the Prime Minister thought. His words sounded scripted. Scripted by whom? Well, that was obvious enough.

The PM wondered if Goto knew that he was in even a poorer position than the man he sought to replace. *Probably not,* but that was scant consolation. If Goto achieved his post, he would be even more in the pawn of his masters, pushed into implementing policies that might or might not be well considered. And unlike himself, Goto might be fool enough to believe that he was actually pursuing policies that were both wise and his own. How long would that illusion last?

It was dangerous to do this so often, Christopher Cook knew. Often? Well, every month or so. Was that often? Cook was a Deputy Assistant Secretary of State, not an intelligence officer, and hadn't read that manual, assuming there was one.

The hospitality was as impressive as ever, the good food and wine and the exquisite setting, the slow procession through topics of conversation, beginning with the polite and entirely pro forma inquiries as to the state of his family, and his golf game, and his opinion on this or that current social topic. Yes, the weather was unusually pleasant for this time of year — a perennial remark on Seiji's part; fairly enough, since fall and spring in Washington were tolerably pleasant, but the summers were hot and muggy and the winters wet and dank. It was tedious, even to the professional diplomat well versed in meaningless chitchat. Nagumo had been in Washington long enough to run out of original observations to make, and over the past few months had grown repetitive. *Well, why should he be different from any other diplomat in the world?* Cook asked himself, about to be surprised.

"I understand that you have reached an important agreement with the Russians," Seiji Nagumo observed as the dinner dishes were cleared away.

"What do you mean?" Cook asked, thinking it a continuation of the chitchat.

"We've heard that you are accelerating the elimination of ICBMs," the man went on, sipping his wine.

"You are well informed," Cook observed, impressed, so much so that he missed a signal he'd never received before. "That's a rather sensitive subject."

"Undoubtedly so, but also a wonderful development, is it not?" He raised his glass in a friendly toast. Cook, pleased, did the same.

"It most certainly is," the State Department official agreed. "As you know, it has been a goal of American foreign policy since the late 1940s — back to Bernard Baruch, if memory serves — to eliminate weapons of mass destruction and their attendant danger to the human race. As you well know — "

Nagumo, surprisingly, cut him off. "I know better than you might imagine, Christopher. My grandfather lived in Nagasaki. He was a machinist for the naval base that was once there. He survived the bomb — his wife did not, I regret to tell you — but he was badly burned in the ensuing fire, and I can well remember his scars. The experience hastened his death, I am sorry to say." It was a card skillfully played, all the more so that it was a lie.

"I didn't know, Seiji. I'm sorry," Cook added, meaning it. The purpose of diplomacy, after all, was to prevent war whenever possible, or, failing that, to conclude them as bloodlessly as possible.

"So, as you might imagine, I am quite interested in the final elimination of those horrible things." Nagumo topped off Cook's glass. It was an excellent chardonnay that had gone well with the main course.

"Well, your information is pretty accurate. I'm not briefed in on that stuff, you understand, but I've caught a few things at the lunch room," Cook added, to let his friend know that he dined on the seventh floor of the State Department building, not in the more plebeian cafeteria.

"My interest, I admit, is personal. On the day the last one is destroyed, I plan to have a personal celebration, and to offer prayers to grandfather's spirit, to assure him that he didn't die in vain. Do you have any idea when that day will be, Christopher?"

"Not exactly, no. It's being kept quiet."

"Why is that?" Nagumo asked. "I don't understand."

"Well, I suppose the President wants to make a big deal about it. Every so often Roger likes to spring one on the media, especially with the election year on the horizon."

Seiji nodded. "Ah, yes, I can see that. So it is not really a matter of national security, is it?" he inquired offhandedly.

Cook thought about it for a second before replying. "Well, no, I don't suppose it is, really. True, it makes us more secure, but the manner in which that takes place is . . . well, pretty benign, I guess."

"In that case, could I ask a favor?"

"What's that?" Cook asked, lubricated by the wine and the company and the fact that he'd been feeding trade information to Nagumo for months.

"Just as a personal favor, could you find out for me the exact date on which the last missile will be destroyed? You see," he explained, "the ceremony I will undertake will be quite special, and it requires preparation."

Cook almost said, *Sorry, Seiji, but that* is *technically speaking a national-security matter, and I never agreed to give anyone* that *sort of information.* The hesitation on his face, and the surprise that caused it, overpowered his normal diplomat's poker face. His mind raced, or tried to in the presence of his friend. Okay, sure, for three and a half years he'd talked over trade issues with Nagumo, occasionally getting information that was useful, stuff he'd used, earning him a promotion to DASS rank, and occasionally, he'd given over information, because . . . because why? Because part of him was bored with the State Department

178

grind and federal salary caps, and once upon a time a former colleague had remarked to him that with all the skills he'd acquired in fifteen years of government service, he really could escape into private industry, become a consultant or lobbyist, and hell, it wasn't as though he were *spying* on his country or anything, was it? Hell, no, it was just *business,* man.

Was this spying? Cook asked himself. Was it really? The missiles weren't aimed at Japan and never had been. In fact, if the papers were right, they weren't aimed at anything except the middle of the Atlantic Ocean, and the net effect of their destruction was exactly zero on everyone. Nobody hurt. Nobody really helped, except in budgetary terms, and that was pretty marginal for all concerned. So, no, there wasn't a national-security element to this, was there? No. So, he could pass that information along, couldn't he?

"Okay, Seiji. I guess this once, yeah, I can see what I can find out."

"Thank you, Christopher." Nagumo smiled. "My ancestors will thank you. It will be a great day for the entire world, my friend, and it deserves proper celebration." In many sports it was called follow-through. There was no term for it in espionage.

"You know, I think it does, too," Cook said after a further moment's contemplation. It never occurred to him to be amazed that the first step over the invisible line that he had himself constructed was as easy as this.

"I am honored," Yamata said with a great show of humility. "It is a fortunate man who has such wise and thoughtful friends."

"It is you who honor us," one of the bankers insisted politely.

"Are we not colleagues? Do we not all serve our country, our people, our culture, with equal devotion? You, Ichiki-san, the temples you've restored. Ah!"

179

He waved his hand around the low polished table. "We've all done it, asking nothing in return but the chance to help our country, making it great again, and then actually doing it," Yamata added. "So how may I be of service to my friends this evening?" His face took on a quiet, passive mien, waiting to be told that which he already knew. His closest allies around the table, whose identity was not really known to the other nineteen, were studies of curious anticipation, skilled, as he was, in concealment. But for all that there was tension in the room, an atmosphere so real that you could smell it, like the odor of a foreigner.

Eyes turned almost imperceptibly to Matsuda-san, and many actually thought that his difficulties would come as a surprise to Yamata, even though the request for the meeting must have ignited his curiosity enough to turn loose his formidable investigative assets. The head of one of the world's largest conglomerates spoke with quiet, if sad, dignity, taking his time, as he had to, explaining that the conditions that had brought about his cash-flow problem had not, of course, been the fault of his management. It was a business that had begun with shipbuilding, branched out into construction, then delved into consumer electronics. Matsuda had ridden to its chairmanship in the mid-1980s and delivered for his stockholders such return as many only dreamed of. Matsuda-san gave the history himself, and Yamata did not show the least impatience. After all, it worked in his favor that all should hear in his words their own corporate success stories, because in seeing the similarity of success, they would also fear a similarity of personal catastrophe. That the cretin had decided to become a major player in Hollywood, pissing away an immense quantity of cash for eighty acres on Melrose Boulevard and a piece of paper that said he could make movies, well, that was his misfortune, was it not?

180

"The corruption and dishonor of those people is truly astounding," Matsuda went on in a voice that a Catholic priest might hear in a confessional, causing him to wonder if the sinner was recanting his sins or merely bemoaning his bad luck. In the case at hand, two billion dollars were as thoroughly gone as if burned to cook sausages.

Yamata could have said, "I warned you," except that he hadn't, even after his own investment counselors, Americans in this particular instance, had examined the very same deal and warned him off in the strongest terms. Instead he nodded thoughtfully.

"Clearly you could not have anticipated that, especially after all the assurances you were given, and the wonderfully fair terms you gave in return. It would appear, my friends, that proper business ethics are lost on them." He looked around the table to collect the nods his observation had earned. "Matsuda-san, what reasonable man could say that you were in any way at fault?"

"Many would," he answered, rather courageously, all thought.

"Not I, my friend. Who among us is more honorable, more sagacious? Who among us has served his corporation more diligently?" Raizo Yamata shook his head sorrowfully.

"Of greater concern, my friends, is that a similar fate could await us all," a banker announced quietly, meaning that his bank held the paper on Matsuda's real-estate holdings both in Japan and America, and that the failure of that conglomerate would reduce his reserves to dangerous levels. The problem was that even though he could survive the corporate failure in both real and theoretical terms, it required only the perception that his reserves were weaker than they actually were to bring his institution down, and *that* idea could appear in a newspaper merely through the misunderstanding of a single reporter. The con-

181

sequences of such a misguided report, or rumor, could begin a run on the bank, and make real what was not. Certainly the money withdrawn would then be deposited elsewhere — there was too much to go under mattresses, after all — in which case it would be lent back by a fellow corporate banker to safeguard his colleague's position, but a second-order crisis, which was quite possible, could bring everything crashing down.

What went unsaid, and for that matter largely unthought, was that the men in this room had brought the crisis upon themselves through ill-considered dealings. It was a crucial blindspot that all shared — or nearly all, Yamata told himself.

"The basic problem is that our country's economic foundation rests not on rock, but on sand," Yamata began, speaking rather like a philosopher. "As weak and foolish as the Americans are, fortune has given them things which we lack. As a result, however clever our people are, we are always at a disadvantage." He had said all of this before, but now, for the first time, they were listening, and it required all of his self-control not to gloat. Rather he dialed back his level of rhetoric even more than he had in previous discourses. He looked over to one of them, who had always disagreed with him before.

"Remember what you said, that our real strengths are the diligence of our workers and the skill of our designers? That was true, my friend. These are strengths, and more than that, they are strengths that the Americans do not have in the abundance which we enjoy, but because fortune has for reasons of her own smiled on the gaijin, they can checkmate our advantages because they have converted their good fortune into real power, and power is something we lack." Yamata paused, reading his audience once more, watching their eyes and gauging the impassivity there. Even for one born of this culture and reared

182

in its rules, he had to take his gamble now. This was the moment. He was sure of it. "But, really, that is not entirely the case either. They *chose* to take that path, while we have *chosen* not to. And so, now, we must pay the price for that misjudgment. Except for one thing."

"And what is that?" one asked for all the others.

"Now, my friends, fortune smiles on us, and the path to real national greatness is open to us. In our adversity we may, if we choose, find opportunities."

Yamata told himself that he had waited fifteen years for this moment. Then he considered the thought, watching and waiting for a response, and realized that he'd really waited a lifetime for it, since the age of ten, when in February 1944, he alone of his family had boarded the ship that would take him from Saipan to the Home Islands. He could still remember standing at the rail, seeing his mother and father and younger siblings standing there on the dock, Raizo being very brave and managing to hold back his tears, knowing as a child knows that he would see them again, but also knowing that he would not.

They'd killed them all, the Americans, erased his family from the face of the earth, encouraged them to cast their lives away, off the cliffs and into the greedy sea, because Japanese citizens, in uniform or out, were just animals to the Americans. Yamata could remember listening to the radio accounts of the battle, how the "Wild Eagles" of the *Kido Butai* had smashed the American fleet, how the Emperor's invincible soldiers had cast the hated American Marines back into the sea, how they had later slaughtered them in vast numbers in the mountains of the island claimed from the Germans after the First World War, and even then he'd known the futility of having to pretend to believe lies, for lies they had to be, despite the comforting words of his uncle. And soon the radio reports had gone on to other things, the victorious

183

battles over the Americans that crept ever closer to home, the uncomprehending rage he'd known when his vast and powerful country had found herself unable to stop the barbarians, the terror of the bombing, first by day and then by night, burning his country to the ground one city at a time. The orange glow in the night sky, sometimes near, sometimes far, and the lies of his uncle, trying to explain it, and last of all the relief he'd seen on the man's face when all was over. Except that it had never been relief for Raizo Yamata, not with his family gone, vanished from the face of the earth, and even when he'd seen his first American, a hugely tall figure with red hair and freckles on his milky skin who'd clipped him on the head in the friendly way one might do for a dog, even then he'd known what the enemy looked like.

It wasn't Matsuda who spoke in reply. It couldn't be. It had to be another, one whose corporation was still immensely strong, or apparently so. It also had to be one who had never agreed with him. The rule was as important as it was unspoken, and though eyes didn't turn, thoughts did. The man looked down at his half-empty cup of tea — this was not a night for alcohol — and pondered his own fate. He spoke without looking up, because he was afraid to see the identical look in the eyes arrayed around the black lacquer table.

"How, Yamata-san, would we achieve that which you propose?"

"No shit?" Chavez asked. He spoke in Russian, for you were not supposed to speak English here at Monterey, and he hadn't learned that colloquialism in Japanese yet.

"Fourteen agents," Major Oleg Yurievich Lyalin, KGB (retired), replied, as matter-of-factly as his ego allowed.

"And they never reactivated your net?" Clark asked, wanting to roll his eyes.

"They couldn't." Lyalin smiled and tapped the side of his head. "THISTLE was my creation. It turned out to be my life insurance."

No shit, Clark almost said. That Ryan had gotten him out alive was somewhere to the right of a miracle. Lyalin had been tried for treason with the normal KGB attention to a speedy trial, had been in a death cell, and known the routine as exactly as any man could. Told that his execution date was a week hence, he'd been marched to the prison commandant's office, informed of his right as a Soviet citizen to appeal directly to the President for executive clemency, and invited to draft a handwritten letter to that end. The less sophisticated might have thought the gesture to be genuine. Lyalin had known otherwise. Designed to make the execution easier, after the letter was sealed, he would be led back to his cell, and the executioner would leap from an open door to his right, place a pistol right next to his head and fire. As a result it was not overly surprising that his hand had shaken while holding the ballpoint pen, and that his legs were rubbery as he was led out. The entire ritual had been carried out, and Oleg Yurievich remembered his amazement on actually reaching his basement cell again, there to be told to gather up what belongings he had and to follow a guard, even more amazingly back to the commandant's office, there to meet someone who could only have been an American citizen, with his smile and his tailored clothes, unaware of KGB's wry valedictory to its traitorous officer.

"I would've pissed my pants," Ding observed, shuddering at the end of the story.

"I was lucky there," Lyalin admitted with a smile. "I'd urinated right before they took me up. My family was waiting for me at Sheremetyevo. It was one of the last PanAm flights."

185

"Hit the booze pretty hard on the way over?" Clark asked with a smile.

"Oh, yes," Oleg assured him, not adding how he'd shaken and then vomited on the lengthy flight to New York's JFK International Airport, and had insisted on a taxi ride through New York to be sure that the impossible vision of freedom was real.

Chavez refilled his mentor's glass. Lyalin was trying to work his way off hard liquor, and contented himself with Coors Light. "I've been in a few tight places, *tovarich*, but that one must have been really uncomfortable."

"I have retired, as you see. Domingo Estebanovich, where did you learn Russian so well?"

"The kid's got a gift for it, doesn't he?" Clark noted. "Especially the slang."

"Hey, I like to read, okay? And whenever I can I catch Russian TV at the home office and stuff. What's the big deal?" The last sentence slipped out in English. Russian didn't quite have that euphemism.

"The big deal is that you're truly gifted, my young friend," Major Lyalin said, saluting with his glass.

Chavez acknowledged the compliment. He hadn't even had a high-school diploma when he'd sneaked into the U.S. Army, mainly by promising to be a grunt, not a missile technician, but it pleased him that he had indeed raced through George Mason University for his subsequent undergraduate degree, and was now within a dissertation of his master's. He marveled at his luck and wondered how many others from his barrio could have done as well, given an equal smile from Chance.

"So does Mrs. Foley know that you left a network behind?"

"Yes, but all her Japanese speakers must be elsewhere. I don't think they would have tried to reactivate without letting me know. Besides, they will

186

only activate if they are told the right thing."

"Jesus," Clark whispered, also in English, since one only swears in his native tongue. That was a natural consequence of the Agency's deemphasis of human intelligence in favor of electronic bullshit, which was useful but not the be-all and end-all that the paper-pushers thought it to be. Of CIA's total of over *fifteen thousand* employees, somewhere around *four hundred fifty* of them were field officers, actually out on the street or in the weeds, talking to real people and trying to learn what their thoughts were instead of counting beans from overheads and reading newspaper articles for the rest. "You know, sometimes I wonder how we ever won the fuckin' war."

"America tried very hard not to, but the Soviet Union tried harder." Lyalin paused. "THISTLE was mainly concerned with gathering commercial information. We stole many industrial designs and processes from Japan, and your country's policy is not to use intelligence services for that purpose." Another pause. "Except for one thing."

"What's that, Oleg?" Chavez asked, popping another Coors open.

"There's no real difference, Domingo. Your people — I tried for several months to explain that to them. Business *is* the government over there. Their parliament and ministries, they are the 'legend,' the *maskirovka* for the business empires."

"In that case there's one government in the world that knows how to make a decent car." Chavez chuckled. He'd given up on buying the Corvette of his dreams — the damned things just cost too much — and settled on a "Z" that was almost as sporty for half the price. And now he'd have to get rid of it, Ding told himself. He had to be more respectable and settled if he were going to marry, didn't he?

"*Nyet.* You should understand this: the opposition is not what your country thinks it is. Why do you

187

suppose you have such problems negotiating with them? I discovered this fact early on, and KGB understood it readily."

As they had to, Clark told himself, nodding. Communist theory predicted that very "fact," didn't it? Damn, wasn't that a hoot! "How were the pickings?" he asked.

"Excellent," Lyalin assured him. "Their culture, it's so easy for them to take insults, but so hard for them to respond. They conceal much anger. Then, all you need do is show sympathy."

Clark nodded again, this time thinking, *This guy is a real pro*. Fourteen well-placed agents, he still had the names and addresses and phone numbers in his head, and, unsurprisingly, nobody at Langley had followed up on it because of those damned-fool ethics laws foisted on the Agency by lawyers — a breed of government servant that sprouted up like crabgrass everywhere you looked, as though *anything* the Agency did was, strictly speaking, ethical at all. Hell, he and Ding had *kidnapped* Corp, hadn't they? In the interests of justice, to be sure, but if they had brought him to America for trial, instead of leaving him with his own countrymen, some high-priced and highly ethical defense attorney, perhaps even acting pro bono — obstructing justice for free, Clark told himself — would have ranted and raved first before cameras and later before twelve good men (and women) about how this *patriot* had resisted an invasion of his country, et cetera, et cetera.

"An interesting weakness," Chavez noted judiciously. "People really are the same all over the world, aren't they?"

"Different masks, but the same flesh underneath," Lyalin pronounced, feeling ever more the teacher. The offhand remark was his best lesson of the day.

Of all human lamentations, without doubt the most

common is, *If only I had known.* But we can't know, and so days of death and fire so often begin no differently from those of love and warmth. Pierce Denton packed the car for the trip to Nashville. It was not a trivial exercise. Both twin girls had safety seats installed in the back of the Cresta, and in between went the smaller seat for their brand-new brother, Matthew. The twin girls, Jessica and Jeanine, were three and a half years old, having survived the "terrible twos" (or rather, their parents had) and the parallel adventures of learning to walk and talk. Now, dressed in identical short purple dresses and white tights, they allowed Mom and Dad to load them into their seats. Matthew went in after them, restless and whining, but the girls knew that the vibration of the car would soon put him back to sleep, which is what he mostly did anyway, except when nursing from his mother's breasts. It was a big day, off for a weekend at Grandmother's house.

Pierce Denton, twenty-seven, was a police officer in Greeneville, Tennessee's, small municipal department, still attending night school to finish up his college degree, but with no further ambition other than to raise his family and live a comfortable life in the tree-covered mountains, where a man could hunt and fish with friends, attend a friendly community church, and generally live as good a life as any person might desire. His profession was far less stressful than that of colleagues in other places, and he didn't regret that a bit. Greeneville had its share of trouble, as did any American town, but far less than he saw on TV or read about in the professional journals that lay on tables in the station. At quarter after eight in the morning, he backed onto the quiet street and headed off, first toward U.S. Route 11E. He was rested and alert, with his usual two cups of morning coffee already at work, chasing away the cobwebs of a restful night, or as restful as one could be with

189

an infant sleeping in the same bedroom with him and his wife, Candace. Within fifteen minutes he pulled onto Interstate Highway 81, heading south with the morning sun behind him.

Traffic was fairly light this Saturday morning, and unlike most police officers Denton didn't speed, at least not with his family in the car. Rather, he cruised evenly at just under seventy miles per hour, just enough over the posted limit of sixty-five for the slight thrill of breaking the law just a little. Interstate 81 was typical of the American interstates, wide and smooth even as it snaked southwest through the mountain range that had contained the first westward expansion of European settlers. At New Market, 81 merged with I-40, and Denton merged in with westbound traffic from North Carolina. Soon he would be in Knoxville. Checking his rearview mirror, he saw that both daughters were already lulled into a semiconscious state, and his ears told him that Matthew was the same. To his right, Candy Denton was dozing as well. Their infant son had not yet mastered the skill of sleeping through the night, and that fact took its toll on his wife, who hadn't had as much as six straight hours of sleep since . . . well, since before Matt's birth, actually, the driver told himself. His wife was petite, and her small frame had suffered from the latter stages of pregnancy. Candy's head rested on the right-side window, grabbing what sleep she could before Matthew woke up and announced his renewed hunger, though with a little luck, that might just last until they got to Nashville.

The only hard part of the drive, if you could call it that, was in Knoxville, a medium-sized city mostly on the north side of the Tennessee River. It was large enough to have an inner ring highway, I-640, which Denton avoided, preferring the direct path west.

The weather was warm for a change. The previous six weeks had been one damned snow-and-ice storm after another, and Greeneville had already exhausted its budget for road salt and overtime for the crews. He'd responded to at least fifty minor traffic accidents and two major ones, but mainly he regretted not having gotten the new Cresta to the car wash the previous night. The bright paint was streaked with salt, and he was glad the car came with underbody coating as a "standard option," because his venerable old pickup truck didn't have that, and it was corroding down to junk even as it sat still in their driveway. Beyond that, it seemed a competent little car. A few inches more leg room would have been nice, but it was her car, not his, and she didn't really need the room. The automobile was lighter than his police radio car, and had only half the engine power. That made for somewhat increased vibration, largely dampened out by the rubberized engine mounts but still there. Well, he told himself, that helped the kids to clonk out.

They must have had even more snow here, he saw. Rock salt had accumulated in the center of his lane like a path of sand or something. Shame they had to use so much. Really tore up the cars. But not his, Denton was sure, having read through all the specifications before deciding to surprise Candy with her red Cresta.

The mountains that cut diagonally across this part of America are called the Great Smokies, a name applied, according to local lore, by Dan'l Boone himself. Actually part of a single range that ran from Georgia to Maine and beyond, changing local names almost as often as it changed states, in this area humidity from the numerous lakes and streams combined with atmospheric conditions to generate fog that occurred on a year-round basis.

Will Snyder of Pilot Lines was on overtime, a profitable situation for the union driver. The Fruehauf trailer attached to his Kenworth diesel tractor was filled with rolls of carpeting from a North Carolina mill en route to a distributorship in Memphis for a major sale. An experienced driver, Snyder was perfectly happy to be out on a Saturday, since the pay was better, and besides, football season was over and the grass wasn't growing yet. He fully expected to be home for dinner in any case. Best of all, the roads were fairly clear during this winter weekend, and he was making good time, the driver told himself, negotiating a sweeping turn to the right and down into a valley.

"Uh-oh," he murmured to himself. It was not unusual to see fog here, close to the State Route 95 North exit, the one that headed off to the bomb people at Oak Ridge. There were a couple of trouble spots on I-40, and this was one. "Damned fog."

There were two ways to deal with this. Some braked down slowly for fuel economy, or maybe just because they didn't like going slow. Not Snyder. A professional driver who saw major wrecks on the side of the highway every week, he slowed down immediately, even before visibility dropped below a hundred yards. His big rig took its time stopping, and he knew a driver who'd converted some little Japanese roller-skate into tinfoil, along with its elderly driver, and his time wasn't worth the risk, not at time-and-a-half it wasn't. Smoothly downshifting, he did what he knew to be the smartest thing, and just to be sure, flipped on his running lights.

Pierce Denton turned his head in annoyance. It was another Cresta, the sporty C99 version that they made only in Japan so far, this one black with a red stripe down the side that whizzed past, at eighty or a little over, his trained eye estimated. In Greeneville that would have been a hundred-dollar ticket and a stern lecture from Judge Tom Anders. Where had those two kids come from? He hadn't even noticed their approach in his mirror. Temporary tag. Two young girls, probably one had just got her license and her new car from Daddy to go with it and was taking her friend out to demonstrate what real freedom was in America, Officer Denton thought, freedom to be a damned fool and get a ticket your first day on the road. But this wasn't his jurisdiction, and that was a job for the state boys. Typical, he thought with a shake of the head. Chattering away, hardly watching the road, but it was better to have them in front than behind.

"Lord," Snyder breathed. Locals, he'd heard in a truck stop once, blamed it on the "crazy people" at Oak Ridge. Whatever the reason, visibility had dropped almost instantly to a mere thirty feet. Not good. He flipped his running lights to the emergency-blinker setting and slowed down more. He'd never done the calculation, but at this weight his tractor-trailer rig needed over sixty feet to stop from thirty miles per hour, and that was on a dry road, which this one was not. On the other hand . . . no, he decided, no chances. He lowered his speed to twenty. So it cost him half an hour. Pilots knew about this stretch of I-40, and they always said it was better to pay the time than to pay off the insurance deductible. With everything in hand, the driver keyed his CB radio to broadcast a warning to his fellow truckers.

It was like being inside a Ping-Pong ball, he told them over Channel 19, and his senses were fully alert, staring ahead into a white mass of water vapor when the hazard was approaching from the rear.

The fog caught them entirely by surprise. Denton's guess had been a correct one. Nora Dunn was exactly eight days past her sixteenth birthday, three days past

193

getting her temporary permit, and forty-nine miles into her sporty new C99. First of all she'd selected a wide, nice piece of road to see how fast it would go, because she was young and her friend Amy Rice had asked. With the compact-disc player going full blast, and trading observations on various male school chums, Nora was hardly watching the road at all, because, after all, it wasn't all that hard to keep a car between the solid line to the right and the dashy one to the left, was it, and besides, there wasn't anybody in the mirror to worry about, and having a car was far better than a date with a new boy, because they always had to drive anyway, for some reason or other, as though a grown woman couldn't handle a car herself.

The look on her face was somewhat startled when visibility went down to not very much — Nora couldn't estimate the exact distance — and she took her foot off the accelerator pedal, allowing the car to slow down from the previous cruising speed of eighty-four. The road behind was clear, and surely the road ahead would be, too. Her driving teachers had told her everything she needed to know, but as with the lessons of all her other teachers, some she'd heard and some she had not. The important ones would come with experience. Experience, however, was a teacher with whom she was not yet fully acquainted, and whose grading curve was far too steep for the moment at hand.

She did see the running lights on the Fruehauf trailer, but she was new to the road, and the amber spots might have been streetlights, except that most interstate highways didn't have them, a fact she hadn't been driving long enough to learn. It was scarcely a second's additional warning in any case. By the time she saw the gray, square shadow, it was simply too late, and her speed was only down to sixty-five. With the tractor-trailer's speed at twenty, it was roughly the equivalent of hitting a thirty-ton stationary object at forty-five miles per hour.

It was always a sickening sound. Will Snyder had heard it before, and it reminded him of a truckload of aluminum beer cans being crunched in a compressor, the decidedly unmusical *crump* of a car body's being crushed by speed and mass and laws of physics that he'd learned not in high school but rather by experience.

The jolt to the left-rear corner of the trailer slewed the front end of the forty-foot van body to the right, but fortunately, his low speed allowed him to maintain control enough to get his rig stopped quickly. Looking back and to his left, he saw the remains of that cute new Jap car that his brother wanted to get, and Snyder's first ill-considered thought was that they were just too damned small to be safe, as though it would have mattered under the circumstances. The center- and right-front were shredded, and the frame was clearly bent. A blink and further inspection showed red where clear glass was supposed to be . . .

"Oh, my God."

Amy Rice was already dead, despite the flawless performance of her passenger-side air bag. The speed of the collision had driven her side of the car under the trailer, where the sturdy rear fender, designed to prevent damage to loading docks, had ripped through the coachwork like a chain saw. Nora Dunn was still alive but unconscious. Her new Cresta C99 was already a total loss, its aluminum engine block split, frame bent sixteen inches out of true, and worst of all, the fuel tank, already damaged by corrosion, was crushed between frame members and leaking.

Snyder saw the leaking gasoline. His engine still running, he quickly maneuvered his truck to the shoulder and jumped out, bringing his light red CO$_2$ extinguisher. That he didn't quite get there in time saved his life.

"What's the matter, Jeanine?"

"Jessica!" the little girl insisted, wondering why people couldn't tell the difference, not even her father.

"What's the matter, *Jessica*," her father said with a patient smile.

"He's stinky!" She giggled.

"Okay," Pierce Denton sighed. He looked over to shake his wife's shoulder. That's when he saw the fog, and took his foot off the gas.

"What's the matter, honey?"

"Matt did a job."

"Okay . . ." Candace unclipped her seat belt and turned to look in the back.

"I wish you wouldn't do that, Candy." He turned too, just at the wrong time. As he did, the car drifted over to the right somewhat, and his eyes tried to observe the highway and the affairs within his wife's new car.

"Shit!" His instinct was to maneuver to the left, but he was too far over to the other side to do that, a fact he knew even before his left hand had turned the wheel all the way. Hitting the brakes didn't help either. The rear wheels locked on the slick road, causing the car to skid sideways into, he saw, another Cresta. His last coherent thought was, *Is it the same one that . . . ?*

Despite the red color, Snyder didn't see it until the collision was inevitable. The trucker was still twenty feet away, jogging in, holding the extinguisher in his arms like a football.

Jesus! Denton didn't have time to say. The first

196

thought was that the collision wasn't all that bad. He'd seen worse. His wife was rammed by inertia into the crumpling right side, and that wasn't good, but the kids in the back were in safety seats, thank God for that, and —

The final deciding factor in the end of five lives was chemical corrosion. The gas tank, like that in the C99, never properly galvanized, had been exposed to salt on its trans-Pacific voyage, then even more on the steep roads of eastern Tennessee. The weld points on the tank were particularly vulnerable and came loose on impact. Distortion of the frame made the tank drag on the rough concrete surface; the underbody protection, never fully affixed, simply flaked off immediately, and another weak spot in the metal tank sprang open, and the body of the tank itself, made of steel, provided the spark, igniting the gasoline that spread forward, for the moment.

The searing heat of the fireball actually cleared the fog somewhat, creating a flash so bright that oncoming traffic panic-stopped on both sides of the highway. That caused a three-car accident a hundred yards away in the eastbound lanes, but not a serious one, and people leaped from their vehicles to approach. It also caught the fuel leaking from Nora Dunn's car, enveloping her with flames, and killing the girl who, mercifully, would never regain consciousness despite the blazing death that took her to his bosom.

Will Snyder was close enough that he'd seen all five faces in the oncoming red Cresta. A mother and a baby were the two he'd remember for the rest of his life, the way she was perched between the front seats, holding the little one, her face suddenly turned to see oncoming death, staring right at the truck driver. The instant fire was a horrid surprise, but

Snyder, though he stopped jogging, did not halt his approach. The left-rear door of the red Cresta had popped open, and that gave him a chance, for the flames were mostly, if temporarily, on the left side of the wrecked automobile. He darted in with the extinguisher held up like a weapon as the flames came back toward the gas tank under the red Cresta. The damning moment gave him but one brief instant to act, to pick the one child among three who alone might live in the inferno that was already igniting his clothes and burning his face while the driving gloves protected the hands that blasted fire-retarding gas into the rear-seat area. The cooling CO_2 would save his life and one other. He looked amid the yellow sheets and expanding white vapor for the infant, but it was nowhere to be found, and the little girl in the left seat was screaming with fear and pain, right there, right in front of him. His gloved hands found and released the chrome buckle, and he yanked her clear of the child-safety seat, breaking her arm in the process, then jerking his legs to fling himself clear of the enveloping fire. There was a lingering snowbank just by the guardrail, and he dove into it, putting out his own burning clothing, then he covered the child with the salt-heavy slush to do the same for her, his face stinging with pain that was the barest warning of what would soon follow. He forced himself not to turn. He could hear the screaming behind his back, but to return to the burning car would be suicide, and looking might only force him into it. Instead he looked down at Jessica Denton, her face blackened, her breathing ragged, and prayed that a cop would appear quickly, and with him an ambulance. By the time that happened, fifteen minutes later, both he and the child were deep in shock.

8

Fast-Forwarding

The slow news day and the proximity to a city guaranteed media coverage of some kind, and the number and ages of the victims guaranteed more still. One of the local Knoxville TV stations had an arrangement with CNN, and by noon the story was the lead item on CNN News Hour. A satellite truck gave a young local reporter the opportunity for a global-coverage entry in his portfolio — he didn't want to stay in Knoxville forever — and the clearing fog gave the cameras a full view of the scene.

"Damn," Ryan breathed in his kitchen at home. Jack was taking a rare Saturday off, eating lunch with his family, looking forward to taking them to evening mass at St. Mary's so that he could also enjoy a Sunday morning at home. His eyes took in the scene, and his hands set the sandwich down on the plate.

Three fire trucks had responded, and four ambulances, two of which, ominously, were still there, their crews just standing around. The truck in the background was largely intact, though its bumper was clearly distorted. It was the foreground that told the story, however. Two piles of metal, blackened and distorted by fire. Open doors into a dark, empty interior. A dozen or so state police officers standing around, their posture stiff, their lips tight, not talking, not trading the jokes that ordinarily went with their perspective on auto accidents. Then Jack saw one of them trade a remark with another. Both heads shook and looked down at the pavement, thirty feet behind the reporter who was droning on the way that they always did, saying the same things for the hundredth time in his short career. Fog. High speed. Both gas tanks. Six people dead, four of them kids. This is Bob Wright, reporting from Interstate 40, outside Oak Ridge, Tennessee. Commercial.

Jack returned to his lunch, stifling another comment on the inequity of daily life. There was no reason yet why he should know or do more.

The cars were dripping water now, three hundred air miles away from the Chesapeake Bay, because the arriving volunteer firemen had felt the need to wet everything down, knowing even then that it was an exercise wasted on the occupants. The forensic photographer shot his three rolls of 200-speed color, catching the open mouths of the victims to prove that they'd died screaming. The senior police officer responding to the scene was Sergeant Thad Nicholson. An experienced highway cop with twenty years of auto accidents behind him, he arrived in time to see the bodies removed. Pierce Denton's service revolver had fallen to the pavement, and that more than anything had identified him as a fellow police officer even before the routine computer check of the tags had made the fact official. Four kids, two little ones and two teens, and two adults. You just never got used to that. It was a personal horror for Sergeant Nicholson. Death was bad enough, but a death such as this, how could God let it happen? Two little children . . . well . . . He did, and that was that. Then it was time to go to work.

Hollywood to the contrary, it was a highly unusual accident. Automobiles did not routinely turn into fire-

200

balls under any circumstances, and this one, his trained eyes saw at once, should not have been all that serious. Okay, there was one unavoidable fatality from the crash itself, the girl in the death seat of the first Cresta, who'd been nearly decapitated. But not the rest, there was no obvious reason for them. The first Cresta had rear-ended the truck at . . . forty or fifty miles of differential speed. Both air bags had deployed, and one of them ought to have saved the driver of the first car, he saw. The second car had hit at about a thirty-degree angle to the first. Damned fool of a cop to make a mistake like that, Nicholson thought. But the wife hadn't been belted in . . . maybe she'd been attending to the kids in the back and distracted her husband. Such things happened, and nobody could undo it now.

Of the six victims, one had been killed by collision, and the other five by fire. That wasn't supposed to happen. Cars were not supposed to burn, and so Nicholson had his people reactivate a crossover half a mile back on the Interstate so that the three accident vehicles could remain in place for a while. He got on his car radio to order up additional accident investigators from Nashville, and to recommend notifying the local office of the National Transportation Safety Board. As it happened, one of the local employees of that federal agency lived close to Oak Ridge. The engineer, Rebecca Upton, was on the scene thirty minutes after receiving her call. A mechanical engineer and graduate of the nearby University of Tennessee, who'd been studying this morning for her PE exam, she donned her brand-new official coveralls and started crawling around the wreckage while the tow-truck operators waited impatiently, even before the backup police team arrived from Nashville. Twenty-four, petite, and red-haired, she came out from under the once-red Cresta with her freckled skin smudged, and her green eyes teary from the lingering

201

gasoline fumes. Sergeant Nicholson handed over a Styrofoam cup of coffee that he'd gotten from a fireman.

"What do you think, ma'am?" Nicholson asked, wondering if she knew anything. She looked like she did, he thought, and she wasn't afraid to get her clothes dirty, a hopeful sign.

"Both gas tanks." She pointed. "That one was sheared clean off. The other one was crumpled by the impact and failed. How fast was it?"

"The collision, you mean?" Nicholson shook his head. "Not that fast. Ballpark guess, forty to fifty."

"I think you're right. The gas tanks have structural-integrity standards, and this crash shouldn't have exceeded them." She took the proffered handkerchief and wiped her face. "Thanks, Sergeant." She sipped her coffee and looked back at the wrecks, wondering.

"What are you thinking?"

Ms. Upton turned back. "I'm thinking that six people — "

"Five," Nicholson corrected. "The trucker got one kid out."

"Oh — I didn't know. Shouldn't have happened. No good reason for it. It was an under-sixty impact, nothing really unusual about the physical factors. Smart money is there's something wrong with the car design. Where are you taking them?" she asked, feeling very professional now.

"The cars? Nashville. I can hold them at headquarters if you want, ma'am."

She nodded. "Okay, I'll call my boss. We're probably going to make this a federal investigation. Will your people have any problem with that?" She'd never done that before, but knew from her manual that she had the authority to initiate a full NTSB inquiry. Most often known for handling the analysis of aircraft accidents, the National Transportation Safety Board also looked into unusual train and vehicle mishaps and had the authority to require cooperation of every federal agency in the pursuit of hard data.

Nicholson had participated in one similar investigation. He shook his head. "Ma'am, my captain will give you all the cooperation you can handle."

"Thank you." Rebecca Upton almost smiled, but this wasn't the place for it. "Where are the survivors? We'll have to interview them."

"Ambulance took them back to Knoxville. Just a guess, but they probably air-lifted them to Shriners'." That hospital, he knew, had a superb burn unit. "You need anything else, ma'am? We have a highway to clear."

"Please be careful with the cars, we — "

"We'll treat it like criminal evidence, ma'am," Sergeant Nicholson assured the bright little girl, with a fatherly smile.

All in all, Ms. Upton thought, not a bad day. Tough luck for the occupants of the cars — that went without saying, and the reality and horror of their deaths were not lost on her — but this was her job, and her first really worthwhile assignment since joining the Department of Transportation. She walked back to her car, a Nissan hatchback, and stripped off her coveralls, donning in their place her NTSB windbreaker. It wasn't especially warm, but for the first time in her government career, she felt as though she were really part of an important team, doing an important job, and she wanted the whole world to know who she was and what she was doing.

"Hi." Upton turned to see the smiling face of a TV reporter.

"What do you want?" she asked briskly, having decided to act very businesslike and official.

"Anything you can tell us?" He held the microphone low, and his cameraman, while nearby, wasn't turning tape at the moment.

"Only off the record," Becky Upton said after

a second's reflection.

"Fair enough."

"Both gas tanks failed. That's what killed those people."

"Is that unusual?"

"Very." She paused. "There's going to be an NTSB investigation. There's no good reason for this to have happened. Okay?"

"You bet." Wright checked his watch. In another ten minutes he'd be live on satellite again, and this time he'd have something new to say, which was always good. The reporter walked away, head down, composing his new remarks for his global audience. What a great development: the National Transportation Safety Board was going to investigate the *Motor Trend* Car of the Year for a potentially lethal safety defect. No good reason for these people to have died. He wondered if his cameraman could get close enough now to see the charred, empty child seats in the back of the other car. Good stuff.

Ed and Mary Patricia Foley were in their top-floor office at CIA headquarters. Their unusual status had made for some architectural and organizational problems at the Agency. Mary Pat was the one with the title of Deputy Director (Operations), the first female to make that rank in America's lead spy agency. An experienced field officer who had worked her country's best and longest-lived agent-in-place, she was the cowboy half of the best husband-wife team CIA had ever fielded. Her husband, Ed, was less flashy but more careful as a planner. Their respective talents in tactics and strategy were highly complementary, and though Mary Pat had won the top job, she'd immediately done away with her need for an executive assistant, putting Ed in that office and making him her equal in real terms, if not bureaucratic ones. A new doorway had been cut in the wall so that he could stroll in without passing the executive secretary in the anteroom, and together they managed CIA's diminished collection of case officers. The working relationship was as close as their marriage, with all the compromises that attended the latter, and the result was the smoothest leadership of the Directorate of Operations in years.

"We need to pick a name, honey."

"How about FIREMAN?"

"Not FIRE*FIGHTER*?"

A smile. "They're both men."

"Well, Lyalin says they're doing fine on linguistics."

"Good enough to order lunch and find the bathroom." Mastering the Japanese language was not a trivial intellectual challenge. "How much you want to bet they're speaking it with a Russian accent?"

A light bulb went off in both their minds at about the same time. "Cover identities?"

"Yeah . . ." Mary Pat almost laughed. "Do you suppose anyone will mind?"

It was illegal for CIA officers to adopt the cover identity of journalists. American journalists, that is. The rule had recently been redrafted, at Ed's urging, to point out that quite a few of the agents his officers recruited were third-world journalists. Since both the officers assigned to the operation spoke excellent Russian, they could easily be covered as Russian journalists, couldn't they? It was a violation of the spirit of the rule, but not the letter; Ed Foley had his cowboy moments too.

"Oh, yeah," said Mary Pat. "Clark wants to know if we would like him to take a swing at reactivating THISTLE."

"We need to talk to Ryan or the President about that," Ed pointed out, turning conservative again.

But not his wife. "No, we don't. We need to get approval to make use of the network, not to see if

205

it's still there." Her ice-blue eyes twinkled, as they usually did when she was being clever.

"Honey, that's calling it a little close," Ed warned. But that was one of the reasons he loved her. "But I like it. Okay, as long as we're just seeing that the network still exists."

"I was afraid I was going to have to pull rank on you, dear." For which transgressions her husband exacted a wonderful toll.

"Just so you have dinner ready on time, Mary. The orders'll go out Monday."

"Have to stop at the Giant on the way home. We're out of bread."

Congressman Alan Trent of Massachusetts was in Hartford, Connecticut, taking a Saturday off to catch a basketball game between U-Mass and U-Conn, both of whom looked like contenders for the regional championship this year. That didn't absolve him from the need to work, however, and so two staffers were with him, while a third was due in with work. It was more comfortable in the Sheraton hotel adjacent to the Hartford Civic Arena than in his office, and he was lying on the bed with the papers spread around him — rather like Winston Churchill, he thought, but without the champagne nearby. The phone next to his bed rang. He didn't reach for it. He had a staffer for that, and Trent had taught himself to ignore the sound of a ringing phone.

"Al, it's George Wylie, from Deerfield Auto." Wylie was a major contributor to Trent's political campaigns, and the owner of a large business in his district. For both of those reasons, he was able to demand Trent's attention whenever he desired it.

"How the hell did he track me down here?" Trent asked the ceiling as he reached for the phone. "Hey, George, how are you today?"

Trent's two aides watched their boss set his soda

down and reach for a pad. The congressman always had a pen in his hand, and a nearby pad of Post-It notes. Seeing him scribble a note to himself wasn't unusual, though the angry look on his face was. Their boss pointed to the TV and said, "CNN!"

The timing turned out to be almost perfect. After the top-of-the-hour commercial and a brief intro, Trent was the next player to see the face of Bob Wright. This time he was on tape, which had been edited. It now showed Rebecca Upton in her NTSB windbreaker and the two crumbled Crestas being hauled aboard the wreckers.

"Shit," Trent's senior staffer observed.

"The gas tanks, eh?" Trent asked over the phone, then listened for a minute or so. "Those mother-fuckers," the congressman snarled next. "Thanks for the heads-up, George. I'm on it." He set the phone receiver back in the cradle and sat up straighter in the bed. His right hand pointed to his senior aide.

"Get in touch with the NTSB watch team in Washington. I want to talk to that girl right away. Name, phone, where she is, track her down fast! Next, get the Sec-Trans on the phone." His head went back down to his working correspondence while his staffers got on the phones. Like most members of Congress, Trent essentially time-shared his brain, and he'd long since learned to compartmentalize his time and his passion. He was soon grumbling about an amendment to the Department of the Interior's authorization for the National Forest Service, and making a few marginal notes with a green pen. That was his second-highest expression of outrage, though his staff saw his red pen poised near a fresh page on a legal pad. The combination of foolscap and a red pen meant that Trent was really exercised about something.

Rebecca Upton was in her Nissan, following the wreckers to Nashville, where she would first supervise the initial storage of the burned-out Crestas and then meet with the head of the local office to begin the procedures for a formal investigation — lots of paperwork, she was sure, and the engineer found it odd that she was not upset at her wrecked weekend. Along with her job came a cellular phone, which she assiduously used only for official business and only when absolutely necessary — she'd been in federal employ for just ten months — which meant in her case that she'd never even reached the basic monthly fee which the company charged the government. The phone had never rung in her car before, and she was startled by the sound when it started warbling next to her.

"Hello?" she said, picking it up, wondering if it were a wrong number.

"Rebecca Upton?"

"That's right. Who is this?"

"Please hold for Congressman Trent," a male voice told her.

"Huh? Who?"

"Hello?" a new voice said.

"Who's this?"

"Are you Rebecca Upton?"

"Yes, I am. Who are you?"

"I'm Alan Trent, Member of Congress from the Commonwealth of Massachusetts." Massachusetts, as any elected official from that state would announce at the drop of a hat, was not a mere "state." "I tracked you down through the NTSB watch center. Your supervisor is Michael Zimmer, and his number in Nashville is — "

"Okay, I believe you, sir. What can I do for you?"

"You're investigating a crash on I-40, correct?"

"Yes, sir."

"I want you to fill me in on what you know."

"Sir," Upton said, slowing her car down so that she could think, "we haven't even really started it yet, and I'm not really in a position to — "

"Young lady, I'm not asking you for conclusions, just for the reason why you are initiating an investigation. I am in a position to help. If you cooperate, I promise you that the Secretary of Transportation will know what a fine young engineer you are. She's a friend of mine, you see. We worked together in Congress for ten or twelve years."

Oh, Rebecca Upton thought. It was improper, unethical, probably against the rules, and maybe even fattening to reveal information from an ongoing NTSB accident investigation. On the other hand, the investigation hadn't started yet, had it? And Upton wanted to be noticed and promoted as much as the next person. She didn't know that her brief silence was as good as mind-reading to the other person on the cellular circuit, and couldn't see the smile in the Hartford hotel room in any case.

"Sir, it appears to me and to the police who responded to the accident that both gas tanks on both cars failed, causing a fatal fire. There appears on first inspection to be no obvious mechanical reason for the tanks to have done so. Therefore I am going to recommend to my supervisor that we initiate an investigation to determine the cause of the incident."

"*Both* gas tanks leaked?" the voice asked.

"Yes, sir, but it was worse than a leak. Both failed rather badly."

"Anything else you can tell me?"

"Not really at this time, no." Upton paused. Would this guy really mention her name to the Secretary? If so . . . "Something is not right about this, Mr. Trent. Look, I have a degree in engineering, and I minored in materials science. The speed of the impact does not justify two catastrophic structural failures. There are federal safety standards for the structural integrity of automobiles and their components, and those parameters far exceed the conditions I saw at the accident scene. The police officers I spoke with agree. We need to do some tests to be sure, but that's my gut-call for the moment. I'm sorry, I can't tell you any more for a while."

This kid is going far, Trent told himself in his room at the Hartford Sheraton. "Thank you, Miss Upton. I left my number with your office in Nashville. Please call me when you get in." Trent hung up the phone and thought for a minute or so. To his junior staffer: "Call Sec-Trans and tell her that this Upton kid is very good — no, get her for me, and I'll tell her. Paul, how good is the NTSB lab for doing scientific testing?" he asked, looking and feeling more and more like Churchill, planning the invasion of Europe. Well, Trent told himself, not quite that.

"Not bad at all, but the varsity — "

"Right." Trent selected a free button on his phone and made another call from memory.

"Good afternoon, Congressman," Bill Shaw said to his speakerphone, looking up at Dan Murray. "By the way, we need to see you next week and — "

"I need some help, Bill."

"What kind of help is that, sir?" Elected officials were always "sir" or "ma'am" on official business, even for the Director of the FBI. That was especially true if the congressman in question chaired the Intelligence Committee, along with holding a seat on the Judiciary Committee, and another on Ways and Means. Besides which, for all his personal . . . eccentricities . . . Trent had always been a good friend and fair critic of the Bureau. But the bottom line was simpler: all three of his committee jobs had impact on the FBI. Shaw listened and took some notes. "The Nashville S-A-C is Bruce Cleary, but we require a formal request for assistance from D-O-T before we can — okay, sure, I'll await her call. Glad to help.

Yes, sir. 'Bye." Shaw looked up from his desk. "Why the hell is Al Trent worked up over a car wreck in Tennessee?"

"Why are *we* interested?" Murray asked, more to the point.

"He wants the Lab Division to back up NTSB on forensics. You want to call Bruce and tell him to get his best tech guy on deck? The friggin' accident just happened this morning and Trent wants results yesterday."

"Has he ever jerked us around on something before?"

Shaw shook his head. "Never. I suppose we want to be on his good side. He'll have to sit in on the meeting with the chairman. We're going to have to discuss Kealty's security clearance, remember?"

Shaw's phone buzzed. "Secretary of Transportation on three, Director."

"That boy," Murray observed, "is really kicking some serious ass for a Saturday afternoon." He got out of his chair and headed for a phone on the other side of the room while Director Shaw took the call from the cabinet secretary. "Get me the Nashville office."

The police impound yard, where wrecked or stolen vehicles were stored, was part of the same facility that serviced State Police cars. Rebecca Upton had never been there before, but the wrecker drivers had, and following them was easy enough. The officer in the gatehouse shouted instructions to the first driver, and the second followed, trailed by the NTSB engineer. They ended up heading to an empty area — or almost empty. There were six cars there — two marked and four unmarked police radio cars — plus ten or so people, all of them senior by the look of them. One was Upton's boss, and for the first time she was really aware of how serious this affair was becoming.

The service building had three hydraulic lifts. Both Crestas were unloaded outside it, then manhandled inside and onto the steel tracks. Both were hoisted simultaneously, allowing the growing mob of people to walk underneath. Upton was by far the shortest person there, and had to jostle her way in. It was her case after all, or she thought it was. A photographer started shooting film, and she noticed that the man's camera case had "FBI" printed on it in yellow lettering. What the hell?

"Definite structural failure," noted a captain of the State Police, the department's chief of accident investigation. Other heads nodded sagely.

"Who has the best science lab around here?" someone in casual clothing asked.

"Vanderbilt University would be a good place to start," Rebecca announced. "Better yet, Oak Ridge National Laboratory."

"Are you Miss Upton?" the man asked. "I'm Bruce Cleary, FBI."

"Why are you — "

"Ma'am, I just go where they send me." He smiled and went on. "D-O-T has requested our help on the investigation. We have a senior tech from our Laboratory Division flying down from Washington right now." On a D-O-T aircraft, no less, he didn't say. Neither he nor anyone else in his office had ever investigated an auto accident, but the orders came from the Director himself, and that was really all he needed to know.

Ms. Upton suddenly felt herself to be a sapling in a forest of giants, but she, too, had a job to do, and she was the only real expert on the scene. Taking a flashlight from her pocket, she started a detailed examination of the gas tank. Rebecca was surprised when people gave her room. It had already been decided that her name would go on the cover of the report. The involvement of the FBI would be down-played — an entirely routine case in interagency co-operation, backing up an inquiry initiated by a young, dedicated, bright, *female* NTSB engineer. She would take the lead on the case. Rebecca Upton would get all the credit for the work of the others, because it could not appear that this was a concerted effort to-ward a predetermined goal, even though that's pre-cisely what it was. She'd also begun this thing, and for delivering political plums this large there had to be a few seeds tossed out for the little people. All the men standing around either knew or had begun to suspect it, though not all of them had begun to grasp what the real issues were. They merely knew that a congressman had gotten the immediate atten-tion of a cabinet secretary and the director of the government's most powerful independent agency, and that he wanted fast action. It appeared that he'd get it, too. As they looked up at the underside of what only a few hours before had been a family car on the way to Grandma's house, the cause of the disaster seemed as straightforward as a punch in the nose. All that was really needed, the senior FBI represen-tative thought, was scientific analysis of the crumpled gas tank. For that, they'd go to Oak Ridge, whose lab facilities often backed up the FBI. That would require the cooperation of the Department of Energy, but if Al Trent could shake two large trees in less than an hour, how hard would it be for him to shake another?

Goto was not a hard man to follow, though it could be tiring, Nomuri thought. At sixty, he was a man of commendable vigor and a desire to appear youthful. And he always kept coming here, at least three times per week. This was the tea house that Kazuo had identified — not by name, but closely enough that Nomuri had been able to identify, then confirm it. He'd seen both Goto and Yamata enter here, never together, but never more than a few minutes apart, because it would be unseemly for the latter to make the former wait too much. Yamata always left first, and the other always lingered for at least an hour, but never more than two. Supposition, he told himself: a business meeting followed by R&R, and on the other nights, just the R&R part. As though in some cinematic farce, Goto always came out with a blissful swagger to his stride as he made his way toward the waiting car. Certainly his driver knew — the open door, a bow, then the mischievous grin on his face as he came around to his own door. On every other occasion, Nomuri had followed Goto's car, discreetly and very carefully, twice losing him in the traffic, but on the last two occasions and three others he'd tracked the man all the way to his home, and felt certain that his destination after his trysts was always the same. Okay. Now he would think about the other part of the mission, as he sat in his car and sipped his tea. It took forty minutes.

It was Kimberly Norton. Nomuri had good eyes, and the streetlights were bright enough for him to manage a few quick frames from his camera before exiting the car. He tracked her from the other side of the street, careful not to look directly at her, instead allowing his peripheral vision to keep her in sight. Surveillance and countersurveillance were part of the syllabus at the Farm. It wasn't too hard, and this subject made it easy. Even though she wasn't overly tall by American standards, she did stand out here, as did her fair hair. In Los Angeles she would have been unremarkable, Nomuri thought, a pretty girl in a sea of pretty girls. There was nothing unusual about her walk — the girl was adapting to local norms, slightly demure, giving way to men, whereas in America the reverse was both true and expected. And though her Western clothing was somewhat distinctive, many people on the street dressed the same way — in fact, traditional garb was in the minority here, he realized with a slight surprise. She turned right, down another street, and Nomuri followed, sixty or seventy yards behind, like he was a goddamned private detective or something. What the hell was this assignment all about? the CIA officer wondered.

"Russians?" Ding asked.

"Free-lance journalists, no less. How's your shorthand?" Clark asked, reading over the telex. Mary Pat was having another attack of the clevers, but truth be told, she was very good at it. He'd long suspected that the Agency had a guy inside the Interfax News Agency in Moscow. Maybe CIA had played a role in setting the outfit up, as it was often the first and best source of political information from Moscow. But this was the first time, so far as he knew, that the Agency had used it for a cover legend. The second page of the op-order got even more interesting. Clark handed it over to Lyalin without comment.

"Bloody about time," the former Russian chuckled. "You will want names, addresses, and phone numbers, yes?"

"That would help, Oleg Yurievich."

"You mean we're going to be in the real spy business?" Chavez asked. It would be his first time ever. Most of the time he and Clark had been paramilitary operators, doing jobs either too dangerous or too unusual for regular field officers.

"It's been a while for me too, Ding. Oleg, I never asked what language you used working your people."

"Always English," Lyalin answered. "I never let on my abilities in Japanese. I often picked up information that way. They thought they could chat right past me."

Cute, Clark thought, *you just stood there with the*

215

open-mouth-dog look on your face and people never seemed to catch on. Except that in his case, and Ding's, it would be quite real. Well, the real mission wasn't to play spymaster, was it, and they were prepared enough for what they were supposed to do, John told himself. They would leave on Tuesday for Korea.

In yet another case of interagency cooperation, a UH-1H helicopter of the Tennessee National Guard lifted Rebecca Upton, three other men, and the gasoline tanks to Oak Ridge National Laboratory. The tanks were wrapped in clear plastic and were strapped into place as though they were passengers themselves.

Oak Ridge's history went back to the early 1940s, when it had been part of the original Manhattan Engineering Project, the cover name for the first atomic-bomb effort. Huge buildings housed the still-operating uranium-separation machinery, though much else had changed including the addition of a helipad.

The Huey circled once to get a read on the wind, then settled in. An armed guard shepherded the party inside, where they found a senior scientist and two lab techs waiting — the Secretary of Energy himself had called them in this Saturday evening.

The scientific side of the case was decided in less than an hour. More time would be required for additional testing. The entire NTSB report would address such issues as the seat belts, the efficacy of the child-safety seats in the Denton car, how the air bags had performed, and so forth, but everyone knew that the important part, the cause of five American deaths, was that the Cresta gas tanks had been made of improperly treated steel that had corroded down to a third of its expected structural strength. The rough draft of that finding was typed up — badly — on a nearby word processor, printed, and faxed to DOT headquarters, adjacent to the Smithsonian Air and

Space Museum in Washington. Though PRELIMI-NARY FINDING was the header on the two-page memo, the information would be treated as Holy Writ. Most remarkably of all, Rebecca Upton thought, it had all been accomplished in less than sixteen hours. She'd never seen the government move so fast on anything. What a shame that it didn't always do that, she thought as she dozed off in the back of the helicopter during the return flight to Nashville.

Later that night, the University of Massachusetts lost to the University of Connecticut 108–103 in overtime. Though a fanatic follower of basketball, and a graduate of U-Mass, Trent smiled serenely as he walked out into the shopping concourse outside the Hartford Civic Arena. He'd scored in a far bigger game today, he thought — though the game was not what he thought it was.

Arnie van Damm didn't like being awakened early on a Sunday morning, especially on one that he had designated as a day of rest — a day for sleeping till eight or so, reading his papers at the kitchen table like a normal citizen, napping in front of the TV in the afternoon, and generally pretending that he was back in Columbus, Ohio, where the pace of life was a lot easier. His first thought was that there had to be a major national emergency. President Durling wasn't one to abuse his chief of staff, and few had his private number. The voice on the other end caused his eyes to open wide and glare at the far wall of his bedroom.

"Al, this better be good," he growled at quarter of seven. Then he listened for a few minutes. "Okay, wait a minute, okay?" A minute later he was lighting up his computer — even he had to use one in these advanced times — which was linked to the White

House. A phone was next to it.

"Okay, Al, I can squeeze you in tomorrow morning at eight-fifteen. Are you sure about all this?" He listened for another couple of minutes, annoyed that Trent had suborned three agencies of the Executive Branch, but he was a Member of Congress, and a powerful one at that, and the exercise of power came as easily to him as swimming did to a duck.

"My question is, will the President back me up?"

"If your information is solid, yes, I expect that he will, Al."

"This is the one, Arnie. I've talked and talked and talked, but this time the bastards have killed people."

"Can you fax me the report?"

"I'm running to catch a plane. I'll have it to you as soon as I get to my office."

So why did you have to call me now? van Damm didn't snarl. "I'll be waiting for it," was what he said. His next considered move was to retrieve the Sunday papers from his front porch. Remarkable, he thought, scanning the front pages. The biggest story of the day, maybe of the year, and nobody had picked up on it yet.

Typical.

Remarkably, except for the normal activity on the fax machine, the remainder of the day went largely according to plan, which allowed the Presidential chief of staff to act like a normal citizen, and not even wonder what the following day might bring. It would keep, he told himself, dozing off on his living-room sofa and missing the Lakers and the Celts from Boston Garden.

9

Power Plays

There were more chits to be called in that Monday, but Trent had quite a few of them out there. The United States House of Representatives would open for business per usual at noon. The chaplain intoned his prayer, surprised to see that the Speaker of the House himself was in his seat instead of someone else, that there were over a hundred members to listen to him instead of the usual six or eight queued to make brief statements for the benefit of the C-SPAN cameras, and that the press gallery was almost half full instead of entirely empty. About the only normal factor was the public gallery, with the customary number of tourists and school kids. The chaplain, unexpectedly intimidated, stumbled through his prayer of the day and departed — or started to. He decided to linger at the door to see what was going on.

"Mr. Speaker!" a voice announced, to the surprise of no one on the floor of the chamber.

The Speaker of the House was already looking that way, having been prepped by a call from the White House. "The Chair recognizes the gentleman from Massachusetts."

Al Trent walked briskly down to the lectern. Once there, he took his time, setting his notes on the tilted wooden platform while three aides set up an easel, making his audience wait, and establishing the dramatic tone of his speech with eloquent silence. Looking down, he began with the required litany:

"Mr. Speaker, I request permission to revise and extend."

"Without objection," the Speaker of the House replied, but not as automatically as usual. The atmosphere was just *different,* a fact clear to everyone but the tourists, and their tour guides found themselves sitting down, which they never did. Fully eighty members of Trent's party were in their seats, along with twenty or so on the other side of the aisle, including every member of the minority leadership who happened to be in Washington that day. And though some of the latter were studies in disinterested posture, the fact that they were here at all was worthy of comment among the reporters, who had also been tipped that something big was happening.

"Mr. Speaker, on Saturday morning, on Interstate Highway 40 between Knoxville and Nashville, Tennessee, five American citizens were condemned to a fiery death by the Japanese auto industry." Trent read off the names and ages of the accident victims, and his aide on the floor uncovered the first graphic, a black-and-white photo of the scene. He took his time, allowing people to absorb the image, to imagine what it must have been like for the occupants of the two cars. In the press gallery, copies of his prepared remarks and the photos were now being passed out, and he didn't want to go too fast.

"Mr. Speaker, we must now ask, first, why did these people die, and second, why their deaths are a matter of concern to this house.

"A bright young federal-government engineer, Miss Rebecca Upton, was called to the scene by the local police authorities and immediately determined that the accident was caused by a major safety defect in both of these automobiles, that the lethal fire was

220

in fact caused by the faulty design of the fuel tanks on both cars.

"Mr. Speaker, only a short time ago those very gasoline tanks were the subject of the domestic-content negotiations between the United States and Japan. A superior product, made coincidentally in my own district, was proposed to the Japanese trade representative. The American component is both superior in design and less expensive in manufacture, due to the diligence and intelligence of American workers, but that component was *rejected* by the Japanese trade mission because it failed to meet the supposed *high and demanding* standards of their auto industry!

"Mr. Speaker, those *high* and *demanding* standards burned five American citizens to death in an auto accident which, according to the Tennessee State Police and the National Transportation Safety Board, did not in any way exceed the safety parameters set in America by law for more than fifteen years. This should have been a survivable accident, but one family is nearly wiped out — but for the courage of a union trucker, would be entirely gone — and two other families today weep over the bodies of their young daughters *because* American workers were not *allowed* to supply a *superior* component *even* to the versions of this automobile made right here in America! One of those faulty tanks was transported six thousand miles so that it could be in one of those burned-out cars — so that it could kill a husband and a wife and a three-year-old child, and a newborn infant riding in that automobile!

"Enough is enough, Mr. Speaker! The preliminary finding of the NTSB, confirmed by the scientific staff at Oak Ridge National Laboratory, is that the auto gas tanks on both these cars, one manufactured in Japan and the other assembled right here in Kentucky, failed to meet long-standing D-O-T standards for automotive safety. As a result, first, the U.S. Department of Transportation has issued an immediate recall notice for all Cresta-type private passenger automobiles . . ." Trent paused, looking around. The players in the room knew that there would be more, and they knew it would be a big one.

"Second, I have advised the President of this tragic incident and its larger ramifications. It has been also determined by the Department of Transportation that the same fuel tank for this particular brand of automobile is used in nearly every Japanese private-passenger auto imported into the United States. Accordingly, I am today introducing a bill, HR-12313, which will authorize the President to direct the Departments of Commerce, Justice and of the Treasury to . . ."

"By executive order," the White House press spokesman was saying in the White House Press Room, "and in the interest of public safety, the President has directed the Bureau of Customs, Department of the Treasury, to inspect all imported Japanese cars at their respective ports of entry for a major safety defect which two days ago resulted in the deaths of five American citizens. Enabling legislation to formalize the President's statutory authority is being introduced today by the Honorable Alan Trent, Congressman from Massachusetts. The bill will have the full support of the President, and we hope for rapid action, again, in the interest of public safety.

"The technical term for this measure is 'sectoral reciprocity,' " she went on. "That means that our legislation will mirror-image Japanese trade practices in every detail." She looked up for questions. Oddly, there were none at the moment.

"Moving on, the President's trip to Moscow has been scheduled for — "

"Wait a minute," a reporter asked, looking up, having had a few seconds to digest the opening statement. *"What was that you said?"*

"What gives, boss?" Ryan asked, going over the briefing documents.

"Second page, Jack."

"Okay." Jack flipped the page and scanned. "Damn, I saw that on TV the other day." He looked up. "This is not going to make them happy."

"Tough cookies," President Durling replied coldly. "We actually had a good year or two closing the trade gap, but this new guy over there is so beholden to the big shots that we just can't do business with his people. Enough's enough. They stop our cars right on the dock and practically take them apart to make sure they're 'safe,' and then pass on the 'inspection' bill to their consumers."

"I know that, sir, but — "

"But enough's enough." And besides, it would soon be an election year, and the President needed help with his union voters, and with this single stroke he'd set that in granite. It wasn't Jack's bailiwick, and the National Security Advisor knew better than to make an issue of this. "Tell me about Russia and the missiles," Roger Durling said next.

He was saving the real bombshell for last. The FBI was having its meeting with the people from Judiciary the following afternoon. No, Durling thought after a moment's contemplation, he'd have to call Bill Shaw and tell him to hold off. He didn't want two big stories competing on the front pages. Kealty would have to wait for a while. He'd let Ryan know, but the sexual-harassment case would stay black for another week or so.

The timing guaranteed confusion. From a time zone fourteen hours ahead of the United States' EST, phones rang in the darkness of what in Washington was the early morning of the next day.

The irregular nature of the American action, which had bypassed the normal channels within the American government, and therefore had also bypassed the people who gathered information for their country, caught everyone completely unaware. The Japanese ambassador in Washington was in a fashionable restaurant, having lunch with a close friend, and the hour guaranteed that the same was true of the senior staffers at the embassy on Massachusetts Avenue, NW. In the embassy cafeteria, and all over the city, beepers went off commanding an immediate call to their offices, but it was too late. The word was already out on various satellite TV channels, and those people in Japan who kept watch on such things had called their supervisors, and so on up the information chain until various zaibatsu were awakened at an hour certain to draw sharp comments. These men in turn called senior staff members, who were already awake in any case, and told them to call their lobbyists at once. Many of the lobbyists were already at work. For the most part, they had caught the C-SPAN coverage of Al Trent and gone to work on their own initiative, attempting damage control even before they received marching orders from their employers. The reception they got in every office was cool, even from members to whose campaign funds they made regular contributions. But not always.

"Look," said one senator, contemplating the commencement of his own reelection bid, and needing funds, as his visitor well knew, "I'm not going to the voters and saying that this action is unfair when eight people just burned to death. You have to give it time and let it play out. Be smart about it, okay?"

It was only five people who'd burned to death, the lobbyist thought, but the advice of his current mendicant was sound, or would have been under normal circumstances. The lobbyist was paid over three hun-

224

dred thousand dollars per year for his expertise — he'd been a senior Senate staffer for ten years before seeing the light — and to be an honest broker of information. He was also paid to purvey campaign funds not-so-honestly on one hand, and to advise his employers what was possible on the other.

"Okay, Senator," he said in an understanding tone. "Please remember, though, that this legislation could cause a trade war, and that would be bad for everyone."

"Events like this have a natural life, and they don't last forever," the Senator replied. That was the general opinion reported back to the various offices by five that afternoon, which translated to seven the following morning in Japan. The error was in overlooking the fact that there had never been an event quite "like this."

Already the phones were ringing in the offices of nearly every member of both houses of Congress. Most expressed outrage at the event on I-40, which was to be expected. There were a few hundred thousand people in America, spread through every state and all four hundred thirty-five congressional districts, who never missed the chance to call their representatives in Washington to express their opinions on everything. Junior staffers took the calls and made note of the time and date, the name and address of every caller — it was often unnecessary to ask, as some callers were identifiable by voice alone. The calls would be cataloged for topic and opinion, become part of every member's morning briefing information, and in most cases just as quickly forgotten.

Other calls went to more senior staff members, and in many cases to the members themselves. These came from local businessmen, mostly manufacturers whose products either competed directly in the marketplace with those from overseas, or, in a smaller number of cases, who had tried to do business in Japan and found the going difficult. These calls were not always heeded, but they were rarely ignored.

It was now a top story again on every news service, having briefly faded into the normal old-news obscurity. For today's newscasts family photographs were shown of the police officer, and his wife, and their three children, and also of Nora Dunn and Amy Rice, followed by a brief taped interview of the heroic truck driver, and distant views of Jessica Denton, orphan, writhing in pain from her burns inside a laminar room, being treated by nurses who wept as they debrided her charred face and arms. Now lawyers were sitting with all of the involved families, coaching them on what to tell the cameras and preparing dangerously modest statements of their own while visions of contingency fees danced in their heads. News crews asked for the reaction of family members, friends, and neighbors, and in the angry grief of people who had suffered a sudden and bitter loss, others saw either common anger or an opportunity to take advantage of the situation.

But most telling of all was the story of the fuel tank itself. The preliminary NTSB finding had been leaked moments after its existence had been announced on the floor of the House. It was just too good to pass up. The American auto companies supplied their own engineers to explain the scientific side of the matter, each of them noting with barely concealed glee that it was a simple example of poor quality-control on a very simple automobile component, that the Japanese weren't as sharp as everyone thought after all: "Look, Tom, people have been galvanizing steel for over a century," a midlevel Ford engineer explained to NBC "Nightly News." "Garbage cans are made out of this stuff."

"Garbage cans?" the anchor inquired with a blank look, since his were made from plastic.

"They've hammered us on quality control for years,

told us that we're not good enough, not safe enough, not careful enough to enter their auto market — and now we see that they're not so smart after all. That's the bottom line, Tom," the engineer went on, feeling his oats. "The gas tanks on those two Crestas had less structural integrity than a garbage can made with 1890s technology. And that's why those five people burned to death."

That incidental remark proved the label for the entire event. The next morning five galvanized steel trash cans were found stacked at the entrance to the Cresta Plant in Kentucky, along with a sign that read, WHY DON'T YOU TRY THESE? A CNN crew picked it up, having been tipped off beforehand, and by noon *that* was their headline story. It was all a matter of perception. It would take weeks to determine what had really gone wrong, but by that time perception and the reactions to it would have long since overtaken reality.

The Master of MV *Nissan Courier* hadn't received any notice at all. His was a surpassingly ugly ship that looked for all the world as though she had begun life as a solid rectangular block of steel, then had its bow scooped out with a large spoon for conversion into something that could move at sea. Top-heavy and cursed with a huge sail area that often made her the plaything of even the gentlest winds, she required four Moran tugboats to dock at the Dundalk Marine Terminal in the Port of Baltimore. Once the city's first airport, the large, flat expanse was a natural receiving point for automobiles. The ship's captain controlled the complex and tricky evolution of coming alongside, only then to notice that the enormous carpark was unusually full. That was odd, he thought. The last Nissan ship had come in the previous Thursday, and ordinarily the lot should have been half empty by now, making room for his cargo. Looking farther, he saw only three car-trailers waiting to load their own cargo for transport to the nearest distributor; normally they were lined up like taxis at a train station.

"I guess they weren't kidding," the Chesapeake Bay pilot observed. He'd boarded the *Courier* at the Virginia Capes and had caught the TV news on the pilot ship that anchored there. He shook his head and made his way to the accommodation ladder. He'd let the shipping agent give the word to the Master.

The shipping agent did just that, climbing up the ladder, then to the bridge. The storage lot had room for about two hundred additional cars, certainly not more than that, and as yet he had no instructions from the line's management on what to tell the captain to do. Ordinarily the ship would be in port for no more than twenty-four hours, the time required to unload the cars, refuel and revictual the ship for her return journey most of the way across the world, where the same routine would be followed in reverse, this time loading cars into the empty ship for yet another voyage to America. The ships of this fleet were on a boring but remorseless schedule whose dates were as fixed as the stars of the night sky.

"What do you mean?" the Master asked.

"Every car has to be safety inspected." The shipping agent waved toward the terminal. "See for yourself."

The Master did just that, lifting his Nikon binoculars to see agents from the Bureau of Customs, six of them, using a hydraulic jack to lift up a new car so that one of their number could crawl under it for some reason or other while others made notations on various official forms on their clipboards. Certainly they didn't seem to be in much of a hurry. Through the glasses he could see their bodies rock back in forth in what had to be mirth, instead of working as diligently as government employees ought.

That was the reason he didn't make the connection with the odd instances on which he'd seen Japanese customs inspectors doing similar but much more stringent inspections of American, German, or Swedish cars on the docks of his home port of Yokohama.

"But we could be here for days!" the Master blurted out.

"Maybe a week," the agent said optimistically.

"But there's only space for one ship here! *Nissan Voyager* is due here in seventy hours."

"I can't help that."

"But my schedule — " There was genuine horror in the Master's voice.

"I can't help that either," the shipping agent observed patiently to a man whose predictable world had just disintegrated.

"How can we help?" Seiji Nagumo asked.

"What do you mean?" the Commerce Department official replied.

"This terrible incident." And Nagumo was genuinely horrified. Japan's historical construction of wood-and-paper had long since been replaced by more substantial buildings, but its legacy was a deep cultural dread of fire. A citizen who allowed a fire to start on his property and then to spread to the property of another still faced criminal sanctions, not mere civil liability. He felt a very real sense of shame that a product manufactured in his country had caused such a horrid end. "I have not yet had an official communiqué from my government, but I tell you for myself, this is terrible beyond words. I assure you that we will launch our own investigation."

"It's a little late for that, Seiji. As you will recall, we discussed this very issue — "

"Yes, that is true, I admit it, but you must understand that even if we had reached an agreement, the materials in question would still have been in the

229

pipeline — it would not have made a difference to these people."

It was an altogether pleasant moment for the American trade-negotiator. The deaths in Tennessee, well, that was too bad, but he'd been putting up with this bastard's arrogance for three years now, and the current situation, for all its tragedy, was a sweet one.

"Seiji-san, as I said, it's a little late for that. I suppose we will be happy to have some degree of co-operation from your people, but we have our own job to do. After all, I'm sure you'll understand that the duty to protect the lives and safety of American citizens is properly the job of the American government. Clearly we have been remiss in that duty, and we must make up for our own unfortunate failings."

"What we can do, Robert, is to subsidize the operation. I have been told that our auto manufacturers will themselves hire safety inspectors to clear the vehicles in your ports, and — "

"Seiji, you know that's unacceptable. We can't have government functions carried out by industry representatives." That wasn't true, and the bureaucrat knew it. It happened all the time.

"In the interest of maintaining our friendly trade relationship, we offer to undertake any unusual expense incurred by your government. We — " Nagumo was stopped by a raised hand.

"Seiji, I have to tell you to stop there. Please — you must understand that what you propose could well be seen as an inducement to corruption under our government-ethics laws." The conversation stopped cold for several seconds.

"Look, Seiji, when the new statute is passed, this will settle out rapidly." And that wouldn't take long. A flood of mail and telegrams from rapidly organized "grass-roots" groups — the United Auto Workers, for one, smelling blood in the water as sharply as any shark — had directed every one of its members to dial up Western Union for precisely that purpose. The Trent Bill was already first in line for hearings on the Hill, and insiders gave the new statute two weeks before it appeared on the President's desk for signature.

"But Trent's bill — "

The Commerce Department official leaned forward on his desk. "Seiji, what's the problem? The Trent Bill will allow the President, with the advice of lawyers here at Commerce, to duplicate your own trade laws. In other words, what we will do is to mirror-image your own laws over here. Now, how can it *possibly* be unfair for America to use your own, fair, trade laws on your products the same way that you use them on ours?"

Nagumo hadn't quite got it until that moment. "But you don't understand. Our laws are designed to fit our culture. Yours is different, and — "

"Yes, Seiji, I know. Your laws are designed to protect your industries against unfair competition. What we will soon be doing is the same thing. Now, that's the bad news. The good news is that whenever you open markets to us, we will automatically do the same for you. The bad news, Seiji, is that we will apply your own law to your own products, and then, my friend, we will see how fair your laws are, by your own standards. Why are you upset? You've been telling me for years how your laws are not a real boundary at all, that it's the fault of American industry that we can't trade with Japan as effectively as you trade with us." He leaned back and smiled. "Okay, now we'll see how accurate your observations were. You're not telling me now that you . . . misled me on things, are you?"

Nagumo would have thought *My God*, had he been a Christian, but his religion was animistic, and his internal reactions were different, though of exactly the same significance. He'd just been called a liar, and the worst part was that the accusation was . . . true.

The Trent Bill, now officially called the Trade Reform Act, was explained to America that very evening, now that the talking heads had used the time to analyze it. Its philosophical simplicity was elegant. Administration spokesmen, and Trent himself on "MacNeil/Lehrer," explained that the law established a small committee of lawyers and technical-trade experts from the Commerce Department, assisted by international-law authorities from the Department of Justice, who would be empowered to analyze foreign trade laws, to draft American trade regulations that matched their provisions as exactly as possible, and then to recommend them to the Secretary of Commerce, who would advise the President. The President in turn had the authority to activate those regulations by executive order. The order could be voided by a simple majority of both houses of Congress, whose authority on such matters was set in the Constitution — that provision would avoid legal challenge on the grounds of separation of powers. The Trade Reform Act further had a "sunset" provision. In four years from enactment, it would automatically cease to exist unless reenacted by Congress and reapproved by the sitting President — that provision made the TRA appear to be a temporary provision whose sole objective was to establish free international trade once and for all. It was manifestly a lie, but a plausible one, even for those who knew it.

"Now what could be more fair than that?" Trent asked rhetorically on PBS. "All we're doing is to duplicate the laws of other countries. If their laws are fair for American business, then those same laws must also be fair for the industries of other countries. Our Japanese friends" — he smiled — "have been telling us for years that their laws are not discriminatory. Fine. We will use their laws as fairly as they do."

The entertaining part for Trent was in watching the man on the other side of the table squirm. The former Assistant Secretary of State, now earning over a million dollars a year as senior lobbyist for Sony and Mitsubishi, just sat there, his mind racing for something to say that would make sense, and Trent could see it in his face. He didn't have a thing.

"This could be the start of a real trade war — " he began, only to be cut off at the ankles.

"Look, Sam, the Geneva Convention didn't *cause* any wars, did it? It simply applied the same rules of conduct to all sides in a conflict. If you're saying that the use of Japanese regulations in American ports will cause a war, then there already is a war and you've been working for the other side, haven't you?" His rapid-fire retort was met with five seconds of very awkward silence. There just wasn't an answer to that question.

"Whoa!" Ryan observed, sitting in the family room of his house, at a decent hour for once.

"He's got real killer instinct," Cathy observed, looking up from some medical notes.

"He does," her husband agreed. "Talk about fast. I just got briefed in on this the other day."

"Well, I think they're right. Don't you?" his wife asked.

"I think it's going a little fast." Jack paused. "How good are their docs?"

"Japanese doctors? Not very, by our standards."

"Really?" The Japanese public-health system had been held up for emulation. Everything over there was "free," after all. "How come?"

"They salute too much," Cathy replied, her head back down in her notes. "The professor's always right, that sort of thing. The young ones never learn

233

to do it on their own, and by the time they're old enough to become professors themselves, for the most part they forget how."

"How often are you wrong, O Associate Professor of Ophthalmic Surgery, ma'am?" Jack chuckled.

"Practically never," Cathy replied, looking up, "but I never tell my residents to stop asking why, either. We have three Japanese fellows at Wilmer now. Good clinicians, good technical docs, but not very flexible. I guess it's a cultural thing. We're trying to train them out of it. It's not easy."

"The boss is always right . . ."

"Not always, he isn't." Cathy made a notation for a medication change.

Ryan's head turned, wondering if he'd just learned something important. "How good are they in developing new treatments?"

"Jack, why do you think they come here to train? Why do you suppose we have so many in the university up on Charles Street? Why do you suppose so many of them stay here?"

It was nine in the morning in Tokyo, and a satellite feed brought the American evening news shows into executive offices all over the city. Skilled translators were rendering the conversation into their native tongue. VCRs were making a permanent record for a more thorough analysis later, but what the executives heard was clear enough.

Kozo Matsuda trembled at his desk. He kept his hands in his lap and out of view so that the others in his office could not see them shake. What he heard in two languages — his English was excellent — was bad enough. What he saw was worse. His corporation was already losing money due to . . . irregularities in the world market. Fully a third of his company's products went to the United States, and if that segment of his business were in any way interrupted . . .

234

The interview was followed by a "focus segment" that showed *Nissan Courier*, still tied up in Baltimore, with her sister ship, *Nissan Voyager*, swinging at anchor in the Chesapeake Bay. Yet another car carrier had just cleared the Virginia Capes, and the first of the trio was not even halfway unloaded yet. The only reason they'd shown those particular ships was Baltimore's convenient proximity to Washington. The same was happening in the Port of Los Angeles, Seattle, and Jacksonville. *As though the cars were being used to transport* drugs, Matsuda thought. Part of his mind was outraged, but more of it was approaching panic. If the Americans were serious, then . . .

No, they couldn't be.

"But what about the possibility of a trade war?" Jim Lehrer asked that Trent person.

"Jim, I've been saying for years that we've been in a trade war with Japan for a generation. What we've just done is to level the playing field for everyone."

"But if this situation goes further, won't American interests be hurt?"

"Jim, what are those interests? Are American business interests worth burning up little children?" Trent shot back at once.

Matsuda cringed when he heard that. The image was just too striking for a man whose earliest childhood memory was of the early morning of March 10, 1945. Not even three years old, his mother carrying him from his house looking back and seeing the towering flames caused by Curtis LeMay's 21st Bomber Command. For years he'd awakened screaming in the night, and for all his adult life he'd been a committed pacifist. He'd studied history, learned how and why the war had begun, how America had pushed his antecedents into a corner from which there had been only a single escape — and that a false one. Perhaps Yamata was right, he thought, perhaps the entire affair had been of America's making. First,

235

force Japan into a war, then crush them in an effort to forestall the natural ascendancy of a nation destined to challenge American power. For all that, he had never been able to understand how the zaibatsu of the time, members of the Black Dragon Society, had not been able to find a clever way out, for wasn't war just too dreadful an option? Wasn't peace, however humiliating, to be preferred to the awful destruction that came with war?

It was different now. Now he was one of them, and now he saw what lay in the abyss of not going to war. Were they so wrong then, he asked himself, no longer hearing the TV or his translator. They'd sought real economic stability for their country: the Greater East Asia Co-Prosperity Sphere.

The history books of his youth had called it all a lie, but was it?

For his country's economy to function, it needed resources, raw materials, but Japan had virtually none except coal, and that polluted the air. Japan needed iron, bauxite, petroleum, needed almost everything to be shipped in, in order to be transformed into finished goods that could be shipped out. They needed cash to pay for the raw materials, and that cash came from the buyers of the finished products. If America, his country's largest and most important trading partner, suddenly stopped trading, that cash flow would stop. Almost sixty *billion* dollars.

There would be various adjustments, of course. Today on the international money markets, the yen would plummet against the dollar and every other hard currency in the world. That would make Japanese products less expensive everywhere —

But Europe would follow suit. He was sure of that. Trade regulations already stiffer than the Americans' would become tougher still, and that trading surplus would also decline, and at the same time the value of the yen would fall all the more. It would take more cash to buy the resources without which his country would enter total collapse. Like falling from a precipice, the downward acceleration would merely grow faster and faster, and the only consolation of the moment was that he would not be there to see the end of it, for long before that happened, this office would no longer be his. He'd be disgraced, with all the rest of his colleagues. Some would choose death, perhaps, but not so many. That was something for TV now, the ancient traditions that had grown from a culture rich in pride but poor in everything else. Life was too comfortable to give it up so easily — or was it? What lay ten years in his country's future? A return to poverty . . . or . . . something else?

The decision would partly be his, Matsuda told himself, because the government of his country was really an extension of the collective will of himself and his peers. He looked down at the shaking hands in his lap. He thanked his two employees, and sent them on their way with a gracious nod before he was able to lift his hands to the surface of his desk and reach for a telephone.

Clark thought of it as a "forever flight," and even though KAL had upgraded them to first-class, it really hadn't helped much; not even the charming Korean flight attendants in lovely traditional dress could make the process much better than it was. He'd seen two of the three movies — on other flights — and the third wasn't all that interesting. The sky-news radio channel had held his interest for the forty minutes required to update him on the happenings of the world, but after that it became repetitive, and his memory was too finely trained to need that. The KAL magazine was only good for thirty minutes — even that was a stretch — and he was current on the American news journals. What remained was crushing boredom. At least Ding had his course material to divert him. He was currently reading through the Masseys' classic *Dreadnought*, about how international relations had broken down a century earlier because the various European nations — more properly their leaders — had failed to make the leap of imagination required to keep the peace. Clark remembered having read it soon after publication.

"They just can't make it, can they?" he asked his partner after an hour of reading over his shoulder. Ding read slowly, taking in every word one at a time. Well, it was study material, wasn't it?

"Not real smart, John." Chavez looked up from his pages of notes and stretched, which was easier for his small frame than it was for Clark's. "Professor Alpher wants me to identify three or four crucial fault-points for my thesis, bad decisions, that sort of thing. More to it than that, y'know? What they had to do was, well, like step outside themselves and look back and see what it was all about, but the dumb fucks didn't know how to do that. They couldn't be objective. The other part is, they didn't think anything all the way through. They had all those great tactical ideas, but they never really looked at where things were leading them. You know, I can identify the goofs for the doc, wrap it up real nice just like she wants, but it's gonna be bullshit, John. The problem wasn't the decisions. The problem was the people making them. They just weren't big enough for what they were doing. They just didn't see far enough, and that's what the *peons* were paying them to do, y'know?" Chavez rubbed his eyes, grateful for the distraction. He'd been reading and studying for eleven hours, with only brief breaks for meals and head calls. "I need to run a few miles," he grumped, also weary from the flight.

John checked his watch. "Forty minutes out. We've already started our descent."

"You suppose the big shots are any different

today?" Ding asked tiredly.

Clark laughed. "My boy, what's the one thing in life that never changes?"

The young officer smiled. "Yeah, and the other one is, people like us are always caught in the open when they blow it." He rose and walked to the head to wash his face. Looking in the mirror, he was glad that they'd spend a day at an Agency safe house. He'd need to wash up and shave and unwind before putting on his mission identity. And maybe make some start notes for his thesis.

Clark looked out the window and saw a Korean landscape lit up with the pink, feathery light of a breaking dawn. The lad was turning intellectual on him. That was enough for a weary, eyes-closed grin with his face turned to the plastic window. The kid was smart enough, but what would happen when Ding wrote *the dumb fucks didn't know how* into his master's thesis? He was talking about Gladstone and Bismarck, after all. That got him laughing so hard that he started coughing in the airliner-dry air. He opened his eyes to see his partner emerge from the first-class head. Ding almost bumped into one of the flight attendants, and though he smiled politely at her and stepped aside to let her pass, he didn't track her with his eyes, Clark noticed, didn't do what men usually did with someone so young and attractive. Clearly his mind was set on another female form.

Damn, this is getting serious.

Murray nearly exploded: "We can't do that now! God *damn* it, Bill, we've got everything lined up, the information's going to leak sure as hell, and that's not even fair to Kealty, much less our witnesses."

"We do work for the President, Dan," Shaw pointed out. "And the order came directly from him, not even through the AG. Since when did you care about Kealty, anyway?" It was, in fact, the same line

Shaw had used on President Durling. Bastard or not, rapist or not, he was entitled to due process of law and a fair crack at defending himself. The FBI was somewhat maniacal on that, but the real reason for their veneration of judicial fair-play was that when you convicted a guy after following all the rules, you knew that you'd nailed the right bastard. It also made the appeals process a lot easier to swallow.

"This accident thing, right?"

"Yeah. He doesn't want two big stories jockeying on the front page. This trade flap is a pretty big deal, and he says Kealty can wait a week or two. Dan, our Ms. Linders has waited several years, will another couple of weeks — "

"Yes, and you know it," Murray snapped back. Then he paused. "Sorry, Bill. You know what I mean." What he meant was simple: he had a case ready to go, and it was time to run with it. On the other hand, you didn't say no to the President.

"He's already talked to the people on the Hill. They'll sit on it."

"But their staffers won't."

10

Seduction

"I agree it's not good," Chris Cook said.

Nagumo was looking down at the rug in the sitting room. He was too stunned at the events of the previous few days even to be angry. It was like discovering that the world was about to end, and that there was nothing he could do about it. Supposedly, he was a middle-level foreign-ministry official who didn't "play" in the high-level negotiations. But that was window-dressing. His task was to set the framework for his country's negotiating positions and, moreover, to gather intelligence information on what America really thought, so that his titular seniors would know exactly what opening positions to take and how far they could press. Nagumo was an intelligence officer in fact if not in name. In that role, his interest in the process was personal and surprisingly emotional. Seiji saw himself as a defender and protector of his country and its people, and also as an honest bridge between his country and America. He wanted Americans to appreciate his people and his culture. He wanted them to partake of its products. He wanted America to see Japan as an equal, a good and wise friend from whom to learn. Americans were a passionate people, so often ignorant of their real needs — as the overly proud and pampered often

241

are. The current American stance on trade, if that was what it seemed to be, was like being slapped by one's own child. Didn't they know they needed Japan and its products? Hadn't he personally trained American trade officials for years?

Cook squirmed in his seat. He, too, was an experienced foreign-service officer, and he could read faces as well as anyone. They were friends, after all, and, more than that, Seiji was his personal passport to a remunerative life *after* government service.

"If it makes you feel any better, it's the thirteenth."

"Hmph?" Nagumo looked up.

"That's the day they blow up the last missiles. The thing you asked about? Remember?"

Nagumo blinked, slow to recall the question he'd posed earlier. "Why then?"

"The President will be in Moscow. They're down to a handful of missiles now. I don't know the exact number, but it's less than twenty on each side. They're saving the last one for next Friday. Kind of an odd coincidence, but that's how the scheduling worked out. The TV boys have been prepped, but they're keeping it quiet. There'll be cameras at both places, and they're going to simulcast the last two — blowing them up, I mean." Cook paused. "So that ceremony you talked about, the one for your grandfather, that's the day."

"Thank you, Chris." Nagumo stood and walked to the bar to pour himself another drink. He didn't know why the Ministry wanted that information, but it was an order, and he'd pass it along. "Now, my friend, what can we do about this?"

"Not much, Seiji, at least not right away. I told you about the damned gas tanks, remember? I told you Trent was not a guy to tangle with. He's been waiting for an opportunity like this for years. Look, I was on the Hill this afternoon, talking to people. You've never seen mail and telegrams like this one, and goddamned CNN won't let the story go."

"I know." Nagumo nodded. It was like some sort of horror movie. Today's lead story was Jessica Denton. The whole country — along with a lot of the world — was following her recovery. She'd just come off the "grave" list, with her medical condition upgraded to "critical." There were enough flowers outside her laminar room to give the impression of a lavish personal garden. But the second story of the day had been the burial of her parents and siblings, delayed by medical and legal necessities. Hundreds had attended, including every member of Congress from Tennessee. The chairman of the auto company had wanted to attend as well, to pay personal respects and apologize in person to the family, but been warned off for security reasons. He'd offered a sincere apology on behalf of his corporation on TV instead and promised to cover all medical expenses and provide for Jessica's continuing education, pointing out that he also had daughters. Somehow it just hadn't worked. A sincere apology went a long way in Japan, a fact that Boeing had cashed in on when one of their 747s had killed several hundred Japanese citizens, but it wasn't the same in America, a fact Nagumo had vainly communicated to his government. The attorney for the Denton family, a famous and effective litigator, had thanked the chairman for his apology, and noted dryly that responsibility for the deaths was now on the public record, simplifying his case preparation. It was only a question of amount now. It was already whispered that he'd demand a billion dollars.

Deerfield Auto Parts was in negotiation with every Japanese auto assembler, and Nagumo knew that the terms to be offered the Massachusetts company would be generous in the extreme, but he'd also told the Foreign Ministry the American adage about closing the barn door after the horse had escaped. It would not be damage control at all, but merely a further admission of fault, which was the wrong thing to do in the American legal environment.

The news had taken a while to sink in at home. As horrid as the auto accident had been, it seemed a small thing, and TV commentators on NHK had used the 747 incident to illustrate that accidents did happen, and that America had once inflicted something similar in type but far more ghastly in magnitude on the citizens of that country. But to American eyes the Japanese story had appeared to be justification rather than comparison, and the American citizens who'd backed it up were people known to be on the Japanese payroll. It was all coming apart. Newspapers were printing lists of former government officials who had entered such employment, noting their job experience and former salaries and comparing them with what they were doing now, and for how much. "Mercenary" was the kindest term applied to them. "Traitor" was one more commonly used epithet, especially by organized labor and every member of Congress who faced election.

There was no reasoning with these people.

"What will happen, Chris?"

Cook set his drink down on the table, evaluating his own position and lamenting his remarkably bad timing. He had already begun cutting his strings. Waiting the extra few years for full retirement benefits — he'd done the calculations a few months earlier. Seiji had made it known to him the previous summer that his actual net income would quadruple to start with, and that his employers were great believers in pension planning, and that he wouldn't *lose* his federal retirement investments, would he? And so Cook had started the process. Speaking sharply to the next-higher career official to whom he reported, letting others know that he thought his country's trade policy was being formulated by idiots, in the knowledge that his views would work their way upward. A series of internal memoranda that said the same thing in measured bureaucratese. He had to set things up so that his departure would not be a surprise, and would seem to be based on principle rather than crass lucre. The problem was, in doing so he'd effectively ended his career. He would never be promoted again, and if he remained at State, at best he might find himself posted to an ambassadorship to . . . maybe Sierra Leone, unless they could find a bleaker spot. Equatorial Guinea, perhaps. More bugs.

You're committed, Cook told himself, and so he took a deep breath, and, on reflection, another sip of his drink.

"Seiji, we're going to have to take the long view on this one. TRA" — he couldn't call it the Trade *Reform* Act, not here — "is going to pass in less than two weeks, and the President's going to sign it. The working groups at Commerce and Justice are already forming up. State will participate also, of course. Cables have gone out to several embassies to get copies of various trade laws around the world — "

"Not just ours?" Nagumo was surprised.

"They're going to compare yours with others from countries with whom our trade relationships are . . . less controversial right now." Cook had to watch his language, after all. He needed this man. "The idea is to give them something to, well, to contrast your country's laws with. Anyway, getting this thing fixed, it's going to take some time, Seiji." Which wasn't an altogether bad thing, Cook reasoned. After all, it made for job security — if and when he crossed over from one employer to another.

"Will you be part of the working group?"

"Probably, yes."

"Your help will be invaluable, Chris," Nagumo said quietly, thinking more rapidly now. "I can help you with interpreting our laws — quietly, of course," he

245

added, seizing at that particular straw.

"I wasn't really planning to stay at Foggy Bottom much longer, Seiji," Cook observed. "We've got our hearts set on a new house, and — "

"Chris, we need you where you are. We need — *I* need your help to mitigate this unfortunate set of circumstances. We have a genuine emergency on our hands, one with serious consequences for both our countries."

"I understand that, but — "

Money, Nagumo thought, *with these people it's always* money!

"I can make the proper arrangements," he said, more on annoyed impulse than as a considered thought. Only after he'd spoken did he grasp what he'd done — but then he was interested to see how Cook would react to it.

The Deputy Assistant Secretary of State just sat there for a moment. He too was so caught up in the events that the real implications of the offer nearly slipped past him. Cook simply nodded without even looking up into Nagumo's eyes.

In retrospect, the first step — the turning over of national-security information — had been a harder one, and the second was so easy that Cook didn't even reflect on the fact that now he was in clear violation of a federal statute. He had just agreed to provide information to a foreign government for money. It seemed such a logical thing to do under the circumstances. They really wanted that house in Potomac, and it wouldn't be long before they'd have to start shopping for colleges.

That morning on the Nikkei Dow would long be remembered. It had taken that long for people to grasp what Seiji Nagumo now knew — that they weren't kidding this time. It wasn't rice all over again, it wasn't computer chips all over again, it wasn't automobiles or their parts, not telecommunications gear or construction contracts or cellular phones. It was, in fact, all of the above, twenty years of pent-up resentment and anger, some justified, some not, but all real and exploding to the surface at a single time. At first the editors in Tokyo just hadn't believed what they'd been told by their people in Washington and New York, and had redrafted the stories to fit their own conclusions until they themselves had thought the information through and come to the stunning realization on their own. The Trade Reform Act, the papers had pontificated only two days earlier, was just one more blip, a joke, *an expression of a few misguided people with a long history of antipathy to our country that will soon run its course.* It was now something else. Today it was *a most unfortunate development whose possibility of enactment into Federal Law cannot now be totally discounted.*

The Japanese language conveys information every bit as well as any other, once you break the code. In America the headlines are far more explicit, but that is merely an indelicate directness of expression typical of the *gaijin.* In Japan one talked more elliptically, but the meaning was there even so, just as clear, just as plain. The millions of Japanese citizens who owned stock read the same papers, saw the same morning news, and reached the same conclusions. On reaching their workplaces, they lifted phones and made their calls.

The Nikkei Dow had once ridden beyond thirty thousand yen of benchmark value. By the early 1990s, it had fallen to half of that, and the aggregate cash cost of the "write-down" was a number larger than the entire U.S. government debt at the time, a fact which had gone virtually unnoticed in the United States — but not by those who had taken their money from banks and placed it in stocks in an attempt to get something more than a 2 percent compounded

247

annualized return. Those people had lost sizable fractions of their life savings and not known whom to blame for it.

Not this time, they all thought. It was time to cash in and put the money back into banks — big, safe, financial institutions that knew how to protect their depositors' funds. Even if they were niggardly in paying interest, you didn't *lose* anything, did you?

Western reporters would use terms like "avalanche" and "meltdown" to describe what began when the trading computers went on-line. The process appeared to be orderly. The large commercial banks, married as they were to the large corporations, sent the same depositors' money that came in the front door right out the back door to protect the value of corporate stocks. There was no choice, really. They had to buy up huge portfolios in what turned out to be a vain stand against a racing tide. The Nikkei Dow lost fully a sixth of its net value in one trading day, and though analysts proclaimed confidently that the market was now grossly undervalued and a huge technical adjustment upward was inevitable, people thought in their own homes that if the American legislation really became law, the market for the goods their country made would vanish like the morning fog. The process would not stop, and though none said it, everyone knew it. This was especially clear to the bankers.

On Wall Street, things were different. Various sages bemoaned the interference of government in the marketplace; then they thought about it a little bit. It was plain to see, after all, that if Japanese automobiles had trouble clearing customs, that if the popular Cresta was now cursed with a visual event that few would soon put behind them, then American cars would sell more, and that was good. It was good for Detroit, where the cars were assembled, and for Pittsburgh, where much of the steel was still forged; it was good for all the cities in America (and Canada, and Mexico), where the thousands of components were made. It was good, further, for all the workers who made the parts and assembled the cars, who would have more money to spend in their communities for other things. How good? Well, the majority of the trade imbalance with Japan was accounted for in automobiles. The sunny side of thirty *billion* dollars could well be dumped into the American economy in the next twelve months, and *that,* quite a few market technicians thought after perhaps as much as five seconds' reflection, was just good as hell, wasn't it? Conservatively, thirty billion dollars going into the coffers of various companies, and all of it, one way or another, would show up as profits for American corporations. Even the additional taxes paid would help in lowering the federal deficit, thus lowering demands on the money pool, and lowering the cost of government bonds. The American economy would be twice blessed. Toss in a little *schadenfreude* for their Japanese colleagues, and even before the Street opened for business, people were primed for a big trading day.

They would not be disappointed. The Columbus Group turned out to be especially well set, having a few days earlier purchased options for a huge quantity of auto-related issues, and thus able to take advantage of a hundred-twelve-point upward jolt in the Dow.

In Washington, at the Federal Reserve, there was concern. They were closer to the seat of government power, and had insider information from the Treasury Department on how the mechanics of the Trade Reform Act would run, and it was clear that there would be a temporary shortage of automobiles until Detroit geared up its lines somewhat. Until the American companies could take up the slack, there would be the classic situation of too much money chasing too few cars. That meant an inflationary blip, and so later in the day the Fed would announce a quarter-point increase in the discount rate — just a temporary one, they told people, off the record and not for attribution. The Board of Governors of the Federal Reserve, however, viewed the entire development as good in the long term. It would be myopic on their part, but then that condition was worldwide at the moment.

Even before that decision was made, other men were discussing the long term as well. It required the largest hot tub in the bathhouse, which was then closed for the evening to its other well-heeled customers. The regular staff was dismissed. The clients would be served by personal assistants who, it turned out, kept their distance as well. In fact, even the normal ablutions were dispensed with. After the most cursory of greetings, the men removed their jackets and ties and sat around on the floor, unwilling to waste time with the usual preliminaries.

"It will be even worse tomorrow," a banker noted. That was all he had to say.

Yamata looked around the room. It was all he could do not to laugh. The signs had been clear as much as five years before, when the first major auto company had quietly discontinued its lifetime-employment policy. The free ride of Japanese business had actually ended then, for those who had the wit to pay attention. The rest of them had thought all the reverses to be merely temporary "irregularities," their favorite term for it, but their myopia had worked entirely in Yamata's favor. The shock value of what was happening now was his best friend. Disappointingly, but not surprisingly, only a handful of those in the room had seen it for what it was. In the main, those were Yamata-san's closest allies.

Which was not to say that he or they had been immune to the adversity that had taken the national unemployment rate to almost 5 percent, merely that they had mitigated their damage by carefully considered measures. Those measures were enough, however, to make their originators appear to be models of perspicacity.

"There is an adage from the American Revolution," one of their number noted dryly. He had a reputation as something of an intellectual. "From their Benjamin Franklin, I believe. We can either hang together or we will surely hang separately. If we do not stand together now, my friends, we will all be destroyed. One at a time or all at once, it will not matter."

"And our country with us," the banker added, earning Yamata's gratitude.

"Remember when they needed us?" Yamata asked. "They needed our bases to checkmate the Russians, to support the Koreans, to service their ships. Well, my friends, what do they need us for now?"

"Yes, and we need them," Matsuda noted.

"Very good, Kozo," Yamata responded acidly. "We need them so much that we will ruin our national economy, destroy our people and our culture, and reduce our nation to being their vassal — *again!*"

"Yamata-san, there is no time for that," another corporate chairman chided gently. "What you proposed in our last meeting, it was very bold and very dangerous."

"It was I who requested this meeting," Matsuda pointed out with dignity.

"Your pardon, Kozo." Yamata inclined his head by way of apology.

"These are difficult times, Raizo," Matsuda replied, accepting it graciously. Then he added, "I find myself leaning toward your direction."

Yamata took a very deep breath, angry at himself for misreading the man's intent. *Kozo is right. These* are *difficult times.* "Please, my friend, share your thoughts with us."

"We need the Americans . . . or we need something else." Every head in the room except for one looked down. Yamata read their faces, and taking a moment to control his excitement, he realized that he saw what he wished to see. It wasn't a wish or an illusion. It was really there. "It is a grave thing which we must consider now, a great gamble. And yet it is a gamble which I fear we must undertake."

"Can we really do it?" a very desperate banker asked.

"Yes," Yamata said. "We can do it. There is an element of risk, of course. I do not discount that, but there is much in our favor." He outlined the facts briefly. Surprisingly, there was no opposition to his views this time. There were questions, numerous ones, endless ones, all of which he was prepared to answer, but no one really objected this time. Some had to be concerned, even terrified, but the simple fact, he realized, was that they were more terrified by what they knew would happen in the morning, and the next, and the next. They saw the end of their way of life, their perks, their personal prestige, and that frightened them worse than anything else. Their country *owed* them for all they had done, for the long climb up the corporate ladders, for all their work and diligence, for all the good decisions they had made. And so the decision was made — not with enthusiasm — but made even so.

Mancuso's first job of the morning was to look over the op-orders. *Asheville* and *Charlotte* would have to discontinue their wonderfully useful work, tracking whales in the Gulf of Alaska, to join up for Exercise DATELINE PARTNERS, along with *John Stennis, Enterprise,* and the usual cast of thousands. The exercise had been planned months in advance, of course. It

252

was a fortunate accident that the script for the event was not entirely divorced from what this half of PacFleet was working up for. On the twenty-seventh, two weeks after the conclusion of PARTNERS, *Stennis* and *Big-E* would deploy southwest for the IO, with a single courtesy stop in Singapore, to relieve *Ike* and *Abe*.

"You know, they have us outnumbered now," Commander (Captain selectee) Wally Chambers observed. A few months earlier he'd relinquished command of USS *Key West*, and Mancuso had asked for him to be his operations officer. The transfer from Groton, where Chambers had expected another staff job, to Honolulu had not exactly been a crushing blow to the officer's ego. Ten years earlier, Wally would have been up for a boomer command, or maybe a tender, or maybe a squadron. But the boomers were all gone, there were only three tenders operating, and the squadron billets were filled. That put Chambers in a holding pattern until his "major command" ticket could be punched, and until then Mancuso wanted him back. It was not an uncommon failing of naval officers to dip into their own former wardrooms.

Admiral Mancuso looked up, not so much in surprise as in realization. Wally was right. The Japanese Navy had twenty-eight submarines, conventionally powered boats called SSKs, and he only had nineteen.

"How many are up and running?" Bart asked, wondering what their overhaul/availability cycle was like.

"Twenty-two, according to what I saw yesterday. Hell, Admiral, they're committing *ten* to the exercise, including all the Harushios. From what I gather from Fleet Intel, they're working up real hard for us, too." Chambers leaned back and stroked his mustache. It was new, because Chambers had a baby face and he thought a commanding officer should look older than twelve. The problem was, it itched.

"Everybody tells me they're pretty good," Com-SubPac noted.

"You haven't had a ride yet?" Sub-Ops asked. The Admiral shook his head.

"Scheduled for next summer."

"Well, they better be pretty good," Chambers thought. Five of Mancuso's subs were tasked to the exercise. Three would be in close to the carrier battle group, with *Asheville* and *Charlotte* conducting independent operations, which weren't really independent at all. They'd be playing a game with four Japanese subs five hundred miles northwest of Kure Atoll, pretending to do hunter-killer operations against a submarine-barrier patrol.

The exercise was fairly similar to what they expected to do in the Indian Ocean. The Japanese Navy, essentially a defensive collection of destroyers and frigates and diesel subs, would try to withstand an advance of a two-carrier battle group. Their job was to die gloriously — something the Japanese were historically good at, Mancuso told himself with a wispy smile — but also to try to make a good show of it. They'd be as clever as they could, trying to sneak their tin cans in close enough to launch their Harpoon surface-to-surface missiles, and surely their newer destroyers had a fair chance of surviving. The Kongos especially were fine platforms, the Japanese counterpart to the American Arleigh Burke class, with the Aegis radar/missile system. Expensive ships, they all had battleship names from World War II. The original *Kongo* had fallen prey to an American submarine, *Sealion II*, if Mancuso remembered properly. That was also the name of one of the few new American submarines assigned to Atlantic Fleet. Mancuso didn't have a Seawolf-class under his command yet. In any case, the aviators would have to find a way to deal with an Aegis ship, and that wasn't something they relished, was it?

All in all, it would be a good workup for Seventh Fleet. They'd need it. The Indians were indeed getting frisky. He now had seven of his boats operating with Mike Dubro, and between those and what he had assigned to DATELINE PARTNERS, that was the whole active collection. How the mighty had fallen, ComSubPac told himself. Well, that's what the mighty usually did.

The meet procedure was not unlike the courtship ritual between swans. You showed up at a precise place at a precise time, in this case carrying a newspaper — folded, not rolled — in your left hand, and looked in a shop window at a huge collection of cameras and consumer electronics, just as a Russian would automatically do on his first trip to Japan, to marvel at the plethora of products available to those who had hard currency to spend. If he were being trailed — possible but most unlikely — it would appear normal. In due course, exactly on time, a person bumped into him.

"Excuse me," the voice said in English, which was also normal, for the person he'd inadvertently nudged was clearly gaijin.

"Quite all right," Clark replied in an accented voice, without looking.

"First time in Japan?"

"No, but my first time in Tokyo."

"Okay, it's all clear." The person bumped him again on the way down the street. Clark waited the requisite four or five minutes before following. It was always so tedious, but necessary. Japan wasn't enemy soil. It wasn't like the jobs he'd done in Leningrad (in Clark's mind that city's name would never change; besides, his Russian accent was from that region) or Moscow, but the safest course of action was to pretend that it was. Just as well that it wasn't, though. There

255

were so many foreigners in this city that the Japanese security service, such as it was, would have gone crazy trying to track them all.

In fact it *was* Clark's first time here, aside from plane changes and stopovers, and that didn't count. The crowding on the street was like nothing he'd ever seen; not even New York was this tight. It also made him uneasy to stand out so much. There is nothing worse for an intelligence officer than *not* to be able to blend in, but his six-one height marked him as someone who didn't belong, visible from a block away to anyone who bothered to look. And so many people looked at him, Clark noted. More surprisingly, people made way for him, especially women, and children positively shrank from his presence as though Godzilla had returned to crush their city. So it was true. He'd heard the stories but never quite believed them. Hairy barbarian. *Funny, I never thought of myself that way,* John told himself, walking into a Mc-Donald's. It was crowded at lunch hour, and after turning his head he had to take a seat with another man. *Mary Pat was right,* he thought. *Nomuri is pretty good.*

"So what's the story?" Clark asked amid the din of the fast-food place.

"Well, I've ID'd her and I've got the building she lives in."

"That's fast work."

"Not very hard. Our friend's security detail doesn't know shit about countersurveillance."

Besides, Clark didn't say, *you look like you belong, right down to the harried and tense look of a salaryman bolting down his lunch so that he can race back to his desk.* Well, that never came hard to a field spook, did it? It wasn't hard to be tense on a field assignment. The difficult part, which they emphasized at the Farm, was to appear at ease.

"Okay, then all I have to do is get permission for

the pickup." Among other things. Nomuri wasn't authorized to know about his work with THISTLE. John wondered if that would change.

"*Sayonara.*" And Nomuri made his exit while Clark attacked his rice ball. *Not bad. The kid's all business,* he thought. His next thought was, *Rice ball at Mc-Donald's?*

The briefing documents on his desk had nothing at all to do with his being the President, but everything to do with his remaining in the office, and for that reason they were always at the top of the pile. The upward move in the approval ratings was . . . very edifying, Durling thought. Of likely voters — and they were the ones who really counted — fully 10 percent more approved of his policies than had done so last week, a numerical improvement that covered both his foreign and domestic performance. All in all, it was about what a fourth-grader might feel on bringing home a particularly good report card to doubtful parents. And that 10 percent was only the beginning, his chief pollster thought, since the implications of the policy changes were taking a little time to sink in. Already the Big Three were speculating publicly about hiring back some of the seven hundred thousand workers laid off in the previous decades, and that was just the assembly workers. Then you had to consider the people in independent parts companies, the tire companies, the glass companies, the battery companies . . . That could start to revitalize the Rust Belt, and the Rust Belt accounted for a lot of electoral votes.

What was obvious, or should have been, was that it wouldn't stop with cars. It couldn't. The United Auto Workers (cars and related parts) looked forward to the restoration of thousands of paying members. The International Brotherhood of Electrical Workers (TVs, even VCRs?) could not be far behind, and there were additional unions that had just begun to consider how large a piece of the pie they might receive. Though simple in concept, the Trade Reform Act represented, like many simple concepts, a wide-ranging alteration in how the United States of America did business. President Durling had thought he'd understood that concept, but soon the phone on his desk would ring. Looking at it, he already knew the voices that he would hear, and it wasn't too great a stretch to imagine what words they would speak, what arguments they would put forth, and what promises they would make. And he would be amenable to accepting the promises.

He'd never really planned to be President of the United States, not as Bob Fowler had planned his entire life toward that goal, not even allowing the death of his first wife to turn him from that path. Durling's last goal had been the governorship of California, and when he'd been offered the chance for the second place on the Fowler ticket he'd taken it more out of patriotism than anything else. That was not something he'd say even to his closest advisers, because patriotism was passé in the modern political world, but Roger Durling had felt it even so, had remembered that the average citizen had a name and a face, remembered having some of them die under his command in Vietnam, and, in remembering, thought that he had to do his best for them.

But what was the best? he asked himself again, as he had done on uncounted occasions. The Oval Office was a lonely place. It was often filled with all manner of visitors, from a foreign chief of state to a schoolchild who'd won an essay contest, but in due course they all left, and the President was alone again with his duty. The oath he'd taken was so simple as to be devoid of meaning. "Faithfully execute the office of . . . to the best of my ability, preserve, protect, and defend . . ." Fine words, but what did they *mean?*

Perhaps Madison and the others had figured that he'd know. Perhaps in 1789 everyone had — it was just understood — but that was more than two hundred years in the past, and somehow they'd neglected to write it down for the guidance of future generations.

Worse still, there were plenty of people ever ready to tell you what they thought the words meant, and when you added up all the advice, 2 plus 2 ended up as 7. Labor and management, consumer and producer, taxpayer and transfer recipient. They all had their needs. They all had their agendas. They all had arguments, and fine lobbyists to make them, and the scary part was that each one made sense in one way or another, enough that many believed that $2 + 2$ really did $= 7$. Until you announced the sum, that is, and then *everybody* said it was too much, that the country couldn't afford the *other* groups' *special* interests.

On top of all of that, if you wanted to accomplish anything at all, you had to *get* here, and having gotten here, to *stay* here, and that meant making promises you had to keep. At least some of them. And somewhere in the process, the country just got lost, and the Constitution with it, and at the end of the day you were preserving, protecting, and defending — *what?*

No wonder I never really wanted this job, Durling told himself, sitting alone, looking down at yet another position paper. It was all an accident, really. Bob had needed to carry California, and Durling had been the key, a young, popular governor of the right party affiliation. But now he was the President of the United States, and the fear was that the job was simply beyond him. The sad truth was that no single man had the intellectual capacity even to understand all the affairs the President was expected to manage. Economics, for example, perhaps his most important contemporary duty now that the Soviet Union was gone, was a field where its own practitioners couldn't agree on a set of rules that a reasonably intelligent man could comprehend.

Well, at least he understood jobs. It was better for people to have them than not to have them. It was, generally speaking, better for a country to manufacture most of its own goods than to let its money go overseas to pay the workers in another country to make them. That was a principle that he could understand, and better yet, a principle that he could explain to others, and since the people to whom he spoke would be Americans themselves, they would probably agree. It would make organized labor happy. It would also make management happy — and wasn't a policy that made *both* of them happy necessarily a good policy? It had to be, didn't it? Wouldn't it make the economists happy? Moreover, he was convinced that the American worker was as good as any in the world, more than ready to enter into a fair contest with any other, and that was all his policy was really aimed at doing . . . wasn't it?

Durling turned in his expensive swivel chair and peered out the thick windows toward the Washington Monument. It must have been a lot easier for George. Okay, so, yeah, he was the first, and he did have to deal with the Whiskey Rebellion, which in the history books didn't look to have been all that grave, and he had to set the pattern for follow-on presidents. The only taxes collected back then were of the tariff and excise sort — nasty and regressive by current standards, but aimed only at discouraging imports and punishing people for drinking too much. Durling was not really trying to stop foreign trade, just to make it *fair*. All the way back to Nixon, the U.S. government had caved in to those people, first because we'd needed their bases (as though Japan would really have struck an alliance with their ancient enemies!), later because . . . why? Because it had become expedient? Did anyone really know? Well, it would change now, and everyone would know why.

Or rather, Durling corrected himself, they'd think that they knew. Perhaps the more cynical would guess the real reason, and everyone would be partially right.

The Prime Minister's office in Japan's Diet Building — a particularly ugly structure in a city not known for the beauty of its architecture — overlooked a green space, but the man sitting in his own expensive swivel chair didn't care to look out at the moment. Soon enough he would be out there, looking in.

Thirty years, he thought. It could easily have been different. In his late twenties he'd been offered, more than once, a comfortable place in the then-ruling Liberal Democratic Party, with guaranteed upward mobility because even then his intelligence had been manifest, especially to his political enemies. And so they had approached him in the friendliest possible way, appealing to his patriotism and his vision for the future of his country, using that vision, holding it out before his young and idealistic eyes. It would take time, they'd told him, but someday he'd have his chance for this very seat in this very room. Guaranteed. All he had to do was to play ball, become part of the team, join up. . . .

He could still remember his reply, the same every time, delivered in the same tone, with the same words, until finally they'd understood that he wasn't holding out for more and left for the final time, shaking their heads and wondering why.

All he'd really wanted was for Japan to be a democracy in the true sense of the word, not a place run by a single party beholden in turn to a small number of powerful men. Even thirty years earlier the signs of corruption had been clear to anyone with open eyes, but the voters, the ordinary people, conditioned to two thousand years or more of acceptance,

261

had just gone along with it because the roots of real democracy hadn't taken here any more than the roots of a rice plant in the pliable alluvium of a paddy. That was the grandest of all lies, so grand that it was believed by everyone within his country as well as without. The culture of his country hadn't really changed. Oh, yes, there were the cosmetic changes. Women could vote now, but like women in every other country they voted their pocketbooks, just as their men did, and they, like their men, were part of a culture that demanded obeisance of everyone in one way or another. What came down from on high was to be accepted, and because of that his countrymen were easily manipulated.

The bitterest thing of all for the Prime Minister was that he had actually thought he'd be able to change that. His true vision, admitted to none but himself, was to change his country in a real and fundamental way. Somehow it hadn't seemed grandiose at all, back then. In exposing and crushing official corruption he'd wanted to make the people see that those on high were not worthy of what they demanded, that ordinary citizens had the honor and decency and intelligence to choose both their own path for life and a government that responded more directly to their needs.

You actually believed that, fool, he told himself, staring at the telephone. The dreams and idealism of youth died pretty hard after all, didn't they? He'd seen it all then, and it hadn't changed. Only now he knew that it wasn't possible for one man and one generation. Now he knew that to make change happen he needed economic stability at home, and that stability depended on using the old order, and the old system was corrupt. The real irony was that he'd come into office because of the failings of the old system, but at the same time needed to restore it so that he could then sweep it away. That was what he hadn't

262

quite understood. The old system had pressed the Americans too hard, reaping economic benefits for his country such as the Black Dragons hadn't dreamed of, and when the Americans had reacted, in some ways fairly and well and in others unfairly and mean-spirited, the conditions had been created for his own ascendancy. But the voters who'd made it possible for him to put his coalition together expected him to make things better for them, and quickly, and to do that he couldn't easily give more concessions to America that would worsen his own country's economic difficulties, and so he'd tried to stonewall on one hand while dealing on the other, and now he knew that it wasn't possible to do both at the same time. It required the sort of skill which no man had.

And his enemies knew that. They'd known it three years ago when he'd put his coalition together, waiting patiently for him to fail, and his ideals with him. The American actions merely affected the timing, not the ultimate outcome.

Could he fix it even now? By lifting the phone he could place a call through to Roger Durling and make a personal plea to head off the new American law, to undertake rapid negotiations. But that wouldn't work, would it? Durling would lose great face were he to do that, and though America deemed it a uniquely Japanese concept, it was as true for them as it was for him. Even worse, Durling would not believe his sincerity. The well was so poisoned by a generation of previous bad-faith negotiations that there was no reason for the Americans to suppose that things were different now — and, truth be known, he probably could not really deliver in any case. His parliamentary coalition would not survive the concessions he would have to make, because jobs were at stake, and with his national unemployment rate at an all-time high of over 5 percent, he did not have the political strength to risk increasing it further. And so, because he could not survive the political effects of such an offer, something even worse would happen, and he would not survive that either. It was only a question, really, of whether he would destroy his own political career or let someone else do it for him. Which was the greater disgrace? He didn't know.

He did know that he could not bring himself to make the telephone call to his American counterpart. It would have been an exercise in futility, just like his entire career, he now realized. The book was already written. Let someone else provide the final chapter.

11

Sea Change

The Trade Reform Act by now had two hundred bipartisan cosponsors. Committee hearings had been unusually brief, largely because few had the courage to testify against it. Remarkably, a major Washington public-relations firm terminated its contract with a Japanese conglomerate, and since it was a PR firm, put out a press release to that effect announcing the end of a fourteen-year relationship. The combination of the event at Oak Ridge and Al Trent's often-quoted barb at a senior lobbyist had made life most uncomfortable for those in foreign employ who stalked the halls of Congress. Lobbyists didn't impede the bill at all. As a man, they reported back to their employers that the bill simply could not fail passage, that any disabling changes in the bill were quite impossible, and the only possible reaction to it would be to take the long view and ride it out. In time, their friends in Congress would be able to support them again, just not now.

Just not now? The cynical definition of a good politician was the same in Japan as it was in America: a public servant who, once bought, *stayed* bought. The employers thought of all the money contributed to so many campaign funds, the thousand-dollar dinner-plates covered with mediocre food bought by (actually for) American employees of their multi-national corporations, the trips to golf courses, the entertainment on fact-finding trips to Japan and elsewhere, the personal contact — and realized that all of it mattered not a bit the one time that it really mattered. America just wasn't like Japan at all. Its legislators didn't feel the obligation to pay back, and the lobbyists, also bought and paid for, told them that it had to be this way. What, then, had they spent all that money *for?*

Take the long view? The long view was all well and good, so long as the immediate prospect was pleasant and uncluttered. Circumstances had permitted Japan the long view for nearly forty years. But today it no longer applied. On Wednesday, the Fourth, the day the Trade Reform Act cleared committee, the Nikkei Dow fell to 12,841 yen, roughly a third of what it had been in recent memory, and the panic in the country was quite real now.

" 'Plum blossoms bloom, and pleasure-women buy new scarves in a brothel room.' "

The words might have been poetic in Japanese — it was a famous haiku — but it didn't make a hell of a lot of sense in English, Clark thought. At least not to him, but the effect on the man in front of him was noteworthy. "Oleg Yurievich sends his greetings."

"It has been a long time," the man stammered after perhaps five seconds of well-concealed panic.

"Things have been difficult at home," Clark explained, a slight accent in his voice.

Isamu Kimura was a senior official in the Ministry for International Trade and Industry, MITI, the centerpiece of an enterprise once called "Japan, Inc." As such he often met with foreigners, especially foreign reporters, and so he had accepted the invitation of Ivan Sergeyevich Klerk, newly arrived in Japan

266

from Moscow, complete with a photographer who was elsewhere shooting pictures.

"It would seem to be a difficult time for your country as well," Klerk added, wondering what sort of reaction it would get. He had to be a little tough with the guy. It was possible that he'd resist the idea of being reactivated after more than two years of no contacts. If so, KGB policy was to make it clear that once they had their hooks into you, those hooks never went away. It was also CIA policy, of course.

"It's a nightmare," Kimura said after a few seconds' reflection and a deep draft of the saké on the table.

"If you think the Americans are difficult, you should be a Russian. The country in which I grew up, which nurtured and trained me — is no more. Do you realize that I must actually support myself with my Interfax work? I can't even perform my duties on a full-time basis." Clark shook his head ruefully and emptied his own cup.

"Your English is excellent."

The "Russian" nodded politely, taking the remark as surrender on the part of the man across the table. "Thank you. I worked for years in New York, covering the U.N. for *Pravda.* Among other things," he added.

"Really?" Kimura asked. "What do you know of American business and politics?"

"I specialized in commercial work. The new world's circumstances allow me to pursue it with even more vigor, and your services are highly valued by my country. We will be able to reward you even more in the future, my friend."

Kimura shook his head. "I have no time for that now. My office is in a very confused state, for obvious reasons."

"I understand. This meeting is in the manner of a get-acquainted session. We have no immediate demands."

"And how is Oleg?" the MITI official asked.

"He has a good life now, a very comfortable position because of the fine work you did for him." Which wasn't a lie at all. Lyalin was alive, and that beat the hell out of a bullet to the head in the basement of KGB Headquarters. This man was the agent who'd given Lyalin the information which had placed them in Mexico. It seemed a shame to Clark that he couldn't thank the man personally for his part in averting a nuclear war. "So tell me, in my reporter identity: how bad is the situation with America? I have a story to file, you see." The answer would surprise him almost as much as the vehemence of its tone.

Isamu Kimura looked down. "It could bring ruin to us."

"Is it really that bad?" "Klerk" asked in surprise, taking out his pad to make notes like a good reporter.

"It will mean a trade war." It was all the man could do to speak that one sentence.

"Well, such a war will do harm to both countries, yes?" Clark had heard that one often enough that he actually believed it.

"We've been saying that for years, but it's a lie. It's really very simple," Kimura went on, assuming that this Russian needed an education in the capitalist facts of life, not knowing that he was an American who did. "We need their market to sell our manufactured goods. Do you know what a trade war means? It means that they stop buying our manufactured goods, and that they keep their money. That money will go into their own industries, which we have trained, after a fashion, to be more efficient. Those industries will grow and prosper by following our example, and in doing so they will regain market share in areas which we have dominated for twenty years. If we lose our market position, we may never get it all back."

"And why is that?" Clark asked, scribbling furiously and finding himself actually quite interested.

"When we entered the American market, the yen had only about a third of the value it has today. That enabled us to be highly competitive in our pricing. Then as we established a place within the American market, achieved brand-name recognition, and so forth, we were able to increase our prices while retaining our market share, even expanding it in many areas despite the increasing value of the yen. To accomplish the same thing today would be far more difficult."

Fabulous news, Clark thought behind a studiously passive face. "But will they be able to replace all the things you make for them?"

"Through their own workers? All of them? Probably not, but they don't have to. Last year automobiles and related products accounted for sixty-one percent of our trade with America. The Americans know how to make cars — what they did not know we have taught them," Kimura said, leaning forward. "In other areas, cameras for example, they are now made elsewhere, Singapore, Korea, Malaysia. The same is true of consumer electronics. Klerk-san, nobody really understands what is happening yet."

"The Americans can really do this much damage to you? Is it possible?" *Damn,* Clark thought, maybe it was.

"It is very possible. My country has not faced such a possibility since 1941." The statement was accidental, but Kimura noted the accuracy of it the instant it escaped his lips.

"I can't put *that* in a news story. It's too alarmist."

Kimura looked up. "That was not meant for a news story. I know your agency has contacts with the Americans. It has to. They are not listening to us now. Perhaps they will listen to you. They push us too far. The zaibatsu are truly desperate. It's happened too fast and gone too far. How would *your* country respond to such an attack on your economy?"

Clark leaned back, tilting his head and narrowing his eyes as a Russian would. The initial contact with Kimura wasn't supposed to have been a substantive intelligence-gathering session, but it had suddenly turned into one. Unprepared for this eventuality, he decided to run with it anyway. The man before him seemed like a prime source, and made more so by his desperation. Moreover, he seemed like a good and dedicated public servant, and if that was somewhat sad, it was also the way the intelligence business worked.

"They did do it to us, in the 1980s. Their arms buildup, their insane plan to put defense systems in space, the reckless brinksmanship game their President Reagan played — did you know that when I was working in New York, I was part of Project RYAN? We thought he planned to strike us. I spent a year looking for such plans." Colonel I. S. Klerk of the Russian Foreign Intelligence Service was fully in his cover identity now, speaking as a Russian would, calmly, quietly, almost pedagogically. "But we looked in the wrong place — no, that wasn't it. It was right in front of us all the time and we failed to see it. They forced us to spend more, and they broke our economy in the process. Marshal Ogarkov gave his speech, demanding more of the economy in order to keep up with the Americans, but there was no more to give. To answer your question briefly, Isamu, we had the choice of surrender or war. War was too terrible to contemplate . . . and so, here I am in Japan, representing a new country."

Kimura's next statement was as startling as it was accurate: "But you had less to lose. The Americans don't seem to understand that." He stood, leaving sufficient money on the table to cover the bill. He knew that a Russian could scarcely afford to

270

pay for a meal in Tokyo.

Holy shit, Clark thought, watching the man leave. The meeting had been an open one, and so did not require covert procedures. That meant he could just get up and leave. But he didn't. Isamu Kimura was a very senior gent, the CIA officer told himself, sipping the last of the saké. He had only one layer of career officials over him, and beyond that was a political appointee, who was really a mouthpiece for the career bureaucrats. Like an assistant secretary of state, Kimura had access to everything. He'd proved that once, by helping them in Mexico, where John and Ding had apprehended Ismael Qati and Ibrahim Ghosn. For that reason alone, America owed this man a considerable debt of honor. More to the point, it made him a primo source of high-grade intelligence. CIA could believe almost anything he said. There could have been no planned script for this meeting. His thoughts and fears had to be genuine, and Clark knew at once that they had to get to Langley in a hurry.

It came as no surprise to anyone who really knew him that Goto was a weak man. Though that was a curse of his country's political leadership, it worked now in Yamata's favor.

"I will not become Prime Minister of my country," Hiroshi Goto announced in a manner worthy of a stage actor, "in order to become executor of its economic ruin." His language was that of the Kabuki stage, stylized and poetic. He was a literate man, the industrialist knew. He had long studied history and the arts, and like many politicians he placed a great deal of value in show and rather less in substance. Like many weak men, he made a great ceremony of personal strength and power. That was why he often had this girl Kimberly Norton in the room with him. She was learning, after a fashion, to perform the duties of an important man's mistress. She sat quietly, refilling cups with saké or tea, and waiting patiently for Yamata-san to leave, after which, it was clear, Goto would bed the girl. He doubtless thought this made him more impressive to his guest. He was such a fool, thinking from his testicles rather than his brain. Well, that was all right. Yamata would become his brain.

"That is precisely what we face," Yamata replied bluntly. His eyes traced over the girl, partly in curiosity, partly to let Goto think that he was envious of the man's young mistress. Her eyes showed no comprehension at all. Was she as stupid as he'd been led to believe? She'd certainly been lured over here easily enough. It was a lucrative activity for the Yakuza, and one in which some of his colleagues partook. Setting Goto up with her — indirectly; Yamata didn't view himself as a pimp, and had merely seen to it that the right person had made the right suggestion to this senior political figure — had been a clever move, though Goto's personal weaknesses had been known to many and easily identified. What was that American euphemism? "Led around by the nose"? It had to mean the same thing that Yamata had done, and a rare case of delicacy of expression for the *gaijin*.

"What can we do about it?" the Leader of the Opposition — for the moment — asked.

"We have two choices." Yamata paused, looking again at the girl, wishing that Goto would dismiss her. This was a highly sensitive matter, after all. Instead, Goto stroked her fair hair, and she smiled. Well, at least Goto hadn't stripped the girl before he'd arrived, Yamata thought, as he had a few weeks ago. Yamata had seen breasts before, even large Caucasian breasts, and it wasn't as though the zaibatsu was in the dark about what Goto did with her.

272

"She doesn't understand a word," the politician said, laughing.

Kimba-chan smiled, and the expression caught Yamata's eye. There followed a disturbing thought: was she merely reacting politely to her master's laugh or was it something else? How old was this girl? Twenties, probably, but he was not skilled in estimating the age of foreigners. Then he remembered something else: his country occasionally provided female companionship to visiting foreign dignitaries, as Yamata did for businessmen. It was a practice that went far back in history, both to make potential deals more easily struck — a man sated by a skilled courtesan would not often be unpleasant to his companions — and because men frequently loosed their tongues along with their belts. What did Goto talk about with this girl? Whom might she be telling? Suddenly the fact that Yamata had set up the relationship didn't seem so clever at all.

"Please, Hiroshi, indulge me this one time," Yamata said reasonably.

"Oh, very well." He continued in English: "Kimba-chan, my friend and I need to speak in private for a few minutes."

She had the good manners not to object verbally, Yamata saw, but the disappointment in her face was not hidden. Did that mean she was trained not to react, or trained to react as a mindless girl would? And did her dismissal matter? Would Goto relate everything to her? Was he that much under her spell? Yamata didn't know, and not knowing, at this moment, struck him as dangerous.

"I love fucking Americans," Goto said coarsely after the door slid shut behind her. It was strange. For all his cultured language, in this one area he spoke like someone of the streets. It was clearly a great weakness, and for that reason, a worrisome one.

"I am glad to hear that, my friend, for soon you

273

will have the chance to do it some more," Yamata replied, making a few mental notes.

An hour later, Chet Nomuri looked up from his *pachinko* machine to see Yamata emerge. As usual, he had both a driver and another man, this one far more serious-looking, doubtless a bodyguard or security guy of some sort. Nomuri didn't know his name, but the type was pretty obvious. The zaibatsu talked to him, a short remark, and there was no telling what it was. Then all three men got into the car and drove off. Goto emerged ninety minutes later, refreshed as always. At that point Nomuri stopped playing the vertical pinball game and changed location to a place down the block. Thirty minutes more and the Norton girl came out. This time Nomuri was ahead of her, walking, taking the turn, then waiting for her to catch up. *Okay,* he thought five minutes later. He was now certain he knew what building she lived in. She'd purchased something to eat and carried it in. Good.

"Morning, MP." Ryan was just back from his daily briefing to the President. Every morning he sat through thirty or forty minutes of reports from the government's various security agencies, and then presented the data in the Oval Office. This morning he'd told his boss, again, that there was nothing all that troubling on the horizon.

"SANDALWOOD," she said for his opening.

"What about it?" Jack asked, leaning back in his chair.

"I had an idea and ran with it."

"What's that?" the National Security Advisor asked.

"I told Clark and Chavez to reactivate THISTLE, Lyalin's old net in Japan."

Ryan blinked. "You're telling me that nobody ever — "

274

"He was doing mainly commercial stuff, and we have that Executive Order, remember?"

Jack suppressed a grumble. THISTLE had served America once, and not through commercial espionage. "Okay, so what's happening?"

"This." Mrs. Foley handed over a single printed page, about five hundred single-spaced words once you got past the cover sheet.

Ryan looked up from the first paragraph. " 'Genuine panic in MITI'?"

"That's what the man says. Keep going." Jack picked up a pen, chewing on it.

"Okay, what else?"

"Their government's going to fall, sure as hell. While Clark was talking to this guy, Chavez was talking to another. State ought to pick up on this in another day or so, but it looks like we got it first for a change."

Jack sat forward at that point. It wasn't that much of a surprise. Brett Hanson had warned about this possibility. The State Department was, in fact, the only government agency that was leery of the TRA, though its concerns had stayed within the family, as it were.

"There's more?"

"Well, yeah, there is. We've turned up the missing girl, all right. It appears to be Kimberly Norton, and sure enough, she's the one involved with Goto, and *he's* going to be the next PM," she concluded with a smile.

It wasn't really very funny, of course, though that depended on your perspective, didn't it? America now had something to use on Goto, and Goto looked to be the next Prime Minister. It wasn't an entirely bad thing. . . .

"Keep talking," Ryan ordered.

"We have the choice of offering her a freebie home, or we could — "

275

"MP, the answer to that is no." Ryan closed his eyes. He'd been thinking about this one. Before, he'd been the one to take the detached view, but he had seen a photograph of the girl, and though he'd tried briefly to retain his detachment, it had lasted only as long as it took to return home and look at his own children. Perhaps it was a weakness, his inability to contemplate the use of people's lives in the furtherance of his country's goals. If so, it was a weakness that his conscience would allow him. Besides: "Does anybody think she can act like a trained spook? Christ's sake, she's a messed-up girl who skipped away from home because she was getting crummy grades at her school."

"Jack, it's my job to float options, remember?" Every government in the world did it, of course, even America, even in these advanced feminist times. They were nice girls, everyone said, usually bright ones, government secretaries, many of them, who were managed through the Secret Service of all places, and made good money serving their government. Ryan had no official knowledge whatever of the operation, and wanted to keep it that way. Had he acquired official knowledge and not spoken out against it, then what sort of man would he be? So many people assumed that high government officials were just moral robots who did the things they had to do for their country without self-doubts, untroubled by conscience. Perhaps it had been true once — possibly it still was for many — but this was a different world, and Jack Ryan was the son of a police officer.

"You're the one who said it first, remember? That girl is an American citizen who probably needs a little help. Let's not turn into something we are not, okay? It's Clark and Chavez on this one?"

"Correct."

"I think we should be careful about it, but to offer the girl a ticket home. If she says no, then *maybe* we can consider something else, but no screwing around on this one. She gets a fair offer of a ride home." Ryan looked down at Clark's brief report and read it more carefully. Had it come from someone else, he would not have taken it so seriously, but he knew John Clark, had taken the time to learn everything about him. It would someday make for an enjoyable conversation.

"I'm going to keep this. I think maybe the President needs to read it, too."

"Concur," the DDO replied.

"Anything else like this comes in . . ."

"You'll know," Mary Pat promised.

"Good idea on THISTLE."

"I want Clark to — well, to press maybe a little harder, and see if we develop similar opinions."

"Approved," Ryan said at once. "Push as hard as you want."

Yamata's personal jet was an old Gulfstream G-IV. Though fitted with auxiliary fuel tanks, it could not ordinarily nonstop the 6,740-mile hop from Tokyo to New York. Today was different, his pilot told him. The jet stream over the North Pacific was fully one hundred ninety knots, and they'd have it for several hours. That boosted their ground speed to 782 miles per hour. It would knock two full hours off the normal flight time.

Yamata was glad. The time was important. None of what he had in his mind was written down, so there were no plans to go over. Though weary from long days that had of late stretched into longer weeks, he found that his body was unable to rest. A voracious reader, he could not get interested in any of the material that he kept on his aircraft. He was alone; there was no one with whom to speak. There was nothing at all to do, and it seemed strange to Yamata. His G-IV cruised at forty-one thousand feet, and it was a clear morning below him. He could see the surface of the North Pacific clearly, the endless ranks of waves, some of their crests decorated with white, driven by high surface winds. The immortal sea. For almost all of his life, it had been an American lake, dominated by their navy. Did the sea know that? Did the sea know that it would change?

Change. Yamata grunted to himself. It would start within hours of his arrival in New York.

"This is Bud on final. I have the ball with eight thousand pounds of fuel," Captain Sanchez announced over his radio circuit. As commander of the air wing for USS *John Stennis* (CVN-74), his F/A-18F would be the first aboard. Strangely, though the most senior aviator aboard, he was new to the Hornet, having spent all of his career in the F-14 Tomcat. Lighter and more agile, and finally with enough fuel capacity to do more than take off, circle the deck once, and return (so it often seemed), he found himself liking the chance to fly alone for a change, after a whole career spent in two-seat aircraft. *Maybe the Air Force pukes had a good idea after all. . . .*

Ahead of him, on the huge flight deck of the new carrier, enlisted men made the proper tension adjustments on the arrestor wires, took the empty weight of his attack fighter, and added the fuel amount he'd called in. It had to be done every time. *Huge flight deck,* he thought, half a mile out. For those standing on the deck it looked huge enough, but for Sanchez it increasingly looked like a matchbook. He cleared his mind of the thought, concentrating on his task. The Hornet buffeted a little coming through the burble of disturbed air caused by the carrier's massive "island" structure, but the pilot's eyes were locked on the "meatball," a red light reflected off a mirror, keeping it nicely centered. Some called Sanchez "Mister Machine," for of his sixteen hundred—

odd carrier landings — you logged every one — less than fifty had failed to catch the optimum number-three wire.

Gently, gently, he told himself, easing the stick back with his right hand while the left worked the throttles, watching his sink rate, and . . . yes. He could feel the fighter jerk from catching the wire — number three, he was sure — and slow itself, even though the rush to the edge of the angled deck seemed sure to dump him over the side. The aircraft stopped, seemingly inches from the line where black-topped steel fell off to blue water. Really, it was closer to a hundred feet. Sanchez disengaged his tail hook, and allowed the wire to snake back to its proper place. A deck crewman started waving at him, telling him how to get to where he was supposed to go, and the expensive jet aircraft turned into a particularly ungainly land vehicle on the world's most expensive parking lot. Five minutes later, the engines shut down and, tie-down chains in place, Sanchez popped the canopy and climbed down the steel ladder that his brown-jerseyed plane-captain had set in place.

"Welcome aboard, Skipper. Any problems?"

"Nary a one." Sanchez handed over his flight helmet and trotted off to the island. Three minutes after that he was observing the remainder of the landings.

Johnnie Reb was already her semiofficial nickname, since she was named for a long-term U.S. Senator from Mississippi, also a faithful friend of the Navy. The ship even smelled new, Sanchez thought, not so long out of the yards of Newport News Shipbuilding and Drydock. She'd done her trials off the East Coast and sailed around the Horn to Pearl Harbor. Her newest sister, *United States*, would be ready for trials in another year, and yet another was beginning construction. It was good to know that at least one branch of the Navy was still in business — more or less.

The aircraft of his wing came in about ninety seconds apart. Two squadrons, each of twelve F-14 Tomcats, two more with an identical number of F/A-18 Hornets. One medium-attack squadron of ten A-6E Intruders, then the special birds, three E-3C Hawkeye early-warning aircraft, two C-2 CODs, four EA-6B Prowlers . . . and that was all, Sanchez thought, not as pleased as he ought to be.

Johnnie Reb could easily accommodate another twenty aircraft, but a carrier air wing wasn't what it used to be, Sanchez thought, remembering how crowded a carrier had once been. The good news was that it was easier to move aircraft around the deck now. The bad news was that the actual striking power of his wing was barely two-thirds of what it had once been. Worse, naval aviation had fallen on hard times as an institution. The Tomcat design had begun in the 1960s — Sanchez had been contemplating high school then, and wondering when he'd be able to drive a car. The Hornet had first flown as the YF-17 in the early 1970s. The Intruder had started life in the 1950s, about the time Bud had gotten his first two-wheeler. There was not a single new naval aircraft in the pipeline. The Navy had twice flubbed its chance to buy into Stealth technology, first by not buying into the Air Force's F-117 project, then by fielding the A-12 Avenger, which had turned out to be stealthy enough, just unable to fly worth a damn. And so now this fighter pilot, after twenty years of carrier operations, a "comer" being fast-tracked for an early flag — now with the last and best flying command of his career, Sanchez had less power to wield than anyone before him. The same was true of *Enterprise*, fifty miles to the east.

But the carrier was still queen of the sea. Even in her diminished capacity, *Johnnie Reb* had more striking power than both Indian carriers combined, and Sanchez judged that keeping India from getting too aggressive ought not to be overly taxing. A damned good thing that was the only problem on the horizon, too.

"That's it," the Air Boss observed as the last EA-6B caught the number-two wire. "Recovery complete. Your people look pretty good, Bud."

"We have been working at it, Todd." Sanchez rose from his seat and headed below toward his stateroom, where he'd freshen up before meeting first with his squadron commanders, and then with the ops staff to plan the operations for DATELINE PARTNERS. It ought to be a good workup, Sanchez thought. An Atlantic Fleet sailor for most of his career, it would be his first chance to look at the Japanese Navy, and he wondered what his grandfather would have thought of this. Henry Gabriel "Mike" Sanchez had been the CAG on USS *Wasp* in 1942, taking on the Japanese in the Guadalcanal campaign. He wondered what Big Mike would have thought of the upcoming exercise.

"Come on, you have to give me something," the lobbyist said. It was a mark of just how grim things were that his employers had told him it was possible they might have to cut back on their expenditures in D.C. That was very unwelcome news. It wasn't just me, the former Congressman from Ohio told himself. He had an office of twenty people to take care of, and they were Americans, too, weren't they? And so he had chosen his target with care. This Senator had problems, a real contender in his primary, and another, equally real opponent in the general election. He needed a larger war chest. That made him amenable to reason, perhaps.

"Roy, I know we've worked together for ten years, but if I vote against TRA, I'm dead, okay? Dead. In the ground, with a wood stake through my heart, back in Chicago teaching bullshit seminars in

281

government operations and selling influence to the highest bidder." *Maybe even ending up like you,* the Senator didn't say. He didn't have to. The message carried quite clearly. It was not a pleasant thought. Almost twelve years on the Hill, and he *liked* it here. He liked the staff, and the life, and the parking privileges, and the free plane rides back to Illinois, and being treated like he was *somebody* everywhere he went. Already he was a member of the "Tuesday-Thursday Club," flying back home every Thursday evening for a very long weekend of speeches to the local Elks and Rotary clubs, to be seen at PTA meetings, cutting ribbons for every new post office building he'd managed to scrounge money for, campaigning already, just as hard as he'd done to get this goddamned job in the first place. It was not pleasant to have to go through *that* again. It would be less pleasant still to do it in the knowledge that it was all a waste of his time. He *had* to vote for TRA. Didn't Roy know that?

"I know that, Ernie. But I need something," the lobbyist persisted. It wasn't like working on the Hill. He had a staff of the same size, but this time it wasn't paid for by taxes. Now he actually had to work for it. "I've always been your friend, right?"

The question wasn't really a question. It was a statement, and it was both an implied threat and a promise. If Senator Greening didn't come over with *something,* then, maybe, Roy would, quietly at first, have a meeting with one of his opponents. More likely both. Roy, the Senator knew, was quite at ease working both sides of any street. He might well write off Ernest Greening as a lost cause and start currying favor with one or both possible replacements. Seed money, in a manner of speaking, something that would pay off in the long run because the Japs were good at thinking long-term. Everyone knew that. On the other hand, if he coughed up something now . . .

"Look, I can't possibly change my vote," Senator Greening said again.

"What about an amendment? I have an idea that might — "

"No chance, Roy. You've seen how the committees are working on this. Hell, the chairmen are sitting down right now at Bullfeathers, working out the last details. You have to make it clear to your friends that we've been well and truly rolled on this one."

"Anything else?" Roy Newton asked, his personal misery not quite showing. *My God, to have to go back to Cincinnati, practice* law *again?*

"Well, nothing on point," Greening said, "but there are a few interesting things going on, on the other side."

"What's that?" Newton asked. *Just what I need,* he thought. *Some of the usual damned gossip.* It had been fun while he'd served his six terms, but not —

"Possible impeachment hearings against Ed Kealty."

"You're kidding," the lobbyist breathed, his thoughts stopped dead in their tracks. "Don't tell me, he got caught with his zipper down again?"

"Rape," Greening replied. "No shit, rape. The FBI's been working the case for some time now. You know Dan Murray?"

"Shaw's lapdog?"

The Senator nodded. "That's the one. He briefed House Judiciary, but then this trade flap blew up and the President put it on hold. Kealty himself doesn't know yet, at least not as of last Friday — that's how tight this one is — but my senior legislative aide is engaged to Sam Fellows' chief of staff, and it really is too good to keep quiet, isn't it?"

The old Washington story, Newton thought with a smirk. *If two people know it, it's not a secret.*

"How serious?"

"From what I hear, Ed Kealty's in very deep shit. Murray made his position very clear. He wants to put Eddie-boy behind bars. There's a death involved."

"Lisa Beringer!" If there was anything a politician was good at, it was remembering names.

Greening nodded. "I see your memory hasn't failed you."

Newton almost whistled, but as a former Member, he was supposed to take such things phlegmatically. "No wonder he wants this one under wraps. The front page isn't big enough, is it?"

"That is the problem. It wouldn't affect passage of the bill — well, probably not — but who needs the complications? TRA, the Moscow trip, too. So — smart money, it's announced when he gets back from Russia."

"He's hanging Kealty out."

"Roger never has liked him. He brought Ed on board for his legislative savvy, remember? The President needed somebody who knew the system. Well, what good will he be now, even if he's cleared? Also, a major liability for the campaign. It makes good political sense," Greening pointed out, "to toss him overboard right now, doesn't it? At least, as soon as the other stuff is taken care of."

That's interesting, Newton thought, quiet for a few seconds. *We can't stop TRA. On the other hand, what if we can curse Durling's presidency? That could give us a new Administration in one big hurry, and with the right sort of guidance, a new Administration . . .*

"Okay, Ernie, that's something."

12

Formalities

There had to be speeches. Worse, there had to be a *lot* of speeches. For something of this magnitude, each of the 435 members from each of the 435 districts had to have his or her time in front of the cameras.

A representative from North Carolina had brought in Will Snyder, his hands still bandaged, and made sure he had a front-row seat in the gallery. That gave her the ability to point to her constituent, praise his courage to the heavens, laud organized labor for the nobility of its unionized members, and introduce a resolution to give Snyder official congressional recognition for his heroic act.

Next, a member from eastern Tennessee rendered a similar panegyric to his state's highway police and the scientific resources of Oak Ridge National Laboratory — there would be many favors handed out as a result of this legislation, and ORNL would get a few more million. The Congressional Budget Office was already estimating the tax revenue to be realized from increased American auto production, and members were salivating over that like Pavlov's dogs for their bell.

A member from Kentucky went to great pains to make it clear that the Cresta was largely an *American*-made automobile, would be even more so with the additional U.S. parts to be included in the design (that had already been settled in a desperate but necessarily unsuccessful accommodation effort by the corporate management), and that he hoped none would blame the workers of his district for the tragedy caused, after all, by non-American parts. The Kentucky Cresta plant, he reminded them, was the most efficient car factory in the world, and a model, he rhapsodized, of the way America and Japan *could* and *should* cooperate! And he would support this bill only because it was a way to make that cooperation more likely. That straddled the fence rather admirably, his fellow members thought.

And so it went. The people who edited *Roll Call*, the local journal that covered the Hill, were wondering if *anyone* would dare to vote against TRA.

"Look," Roy Newton told his main client. "You're going to take a beating, okay? Nobody can change that. Call it bad luck if you want, but shit happens."

It was his tone that surprised the other man. Newton was almost being insolent. He wasn't apologizing at all for his gross failure to change things, as he was paid to do, as he had promised that he could do when he'd first been hired to lobby for Japan, Inc. It was unseemly for a hireling to speak in this way to his benefactor, but there was no understanding Americans, you gave them money to do a job, and they —

"But there are other things going on, and if you have the patience to take a longer view — " *long view* had already been tried, and Newton was grateful for the fact that his client had good-enough language skills to catch the difference — "there are other options to be considered."

"And what might those be?" Binichi Murakami asked acidly. He was upset enough to allow his anger to show for once. It was just too much. He'd come

286

to Washington in the hope that he could personally speak out against this disastrous bill, but instead had found himself besieged with reporters whose questions had only made clear the futility of his mission. And for that reason he'd been away from home for weeks, despite all sorts of entreaties to return to Japan for some urgent meetings with his friend Kozo Matsuda.

"Governments change," Newton replied, explaining on for a minute or so.

"Such a trivial thing as that?"

"You know, someday it's going to happen in your country. You're kidding yourself if you think otherwise." Newton didn't understand how they could fail to grasp something so obvious. Surely their marketing people told them how many cars were bought in America by women. Not to mention the best lady's shaver in the world. Hell, one of Murakami's subsidiaries made it. So much of their marketing effort was aimed at attracting women customers, and yet they pretended that the same factors would never come to be in their own country. It was, Newton thought, a particularly strange blind spot.

"It really could ruin Durling?" The President was clearly getting all sorts of political capital from TRA.

"Sure, if it's managed properly. He's holding up a major criminal investigation, isn't he?"

"No, from what you said, he's asked to delay it for — "

"For political reasons, Binichi." Newton did not often first-name his client. The guy didn't like it. Stuffed shirt. But he paid very well, didn't he? "Binichi, you don't want to get caught playing with a criminal matter, especially for political reasons. *Especially* where the abuse of women is involved. It's an eccentricity of the American political system," he explained patiently.

"We can't meddle with that, can we?" It was an

ill-considered question. He'd never quite meddled at this level before, that was all.

"What do you think you pay me for?"

Murakami leaned back and lit up a cigarette. He was the only person allowed to smoke in this office. "How would we go about it?"

"Give me a few days to work on that? For the moment, take the next flight home. You're just hurting yourself by being here, okay?" Newton paused. "You also need to understand, this is the most complicated project I've ever done for you. Dangerous, too," the lobbyist added.

Mercenary! Murakami raged behind eyes that were again impassive and thoughtful. Well, at least he was effective at it.

"One of my colleagues is in New York. I plan to see him and then fly home from New York."

"Fine. Just keep a real low profile, okay?"

Murakami stood and walked to the outer office, where an aide and a bodyguard waited. He was a physically imposing man, tall for a Japanese at five-ten, with jet-black hair and a youthful face that belied his fifty-seven years. He also had a better-than-average track record for doing business in America, which made the current situation all the more offensive to him. He had never purchased less than a hundred million dollars' worth of American products in any year for the past decade, and he had occasionally spoken out, quietly, for allowing America greater access to his country's food market. The son and grandson of farmers, it appalled him that so many of his countrymen would want to do that sort of work. It was so damnably inefficient, after all, and the Americans, for all their laziness, were genuine artists at growing things. What a pity they didn't know how to plant a decent garden, which was Murakami's other passion in life.

The office building was on Sixteenth Street, only

a few blocks from the White House, and, stepping out on the sidewalk he could look down and see the imposing building. Not Osaka Castle, but it radiated power.

"You Jap cocksucker!"

Murakami turned to see the face, angry and white, a working-class man by the look of him, and was so startled that he didn't have time to take offense. His bodyguard moved quickly to interpose himself between his boss and the American.

"You're gonna get yours, asshole!" the American said. He started to walk away.

"Wait. What have I done to harm you?" Murakami asked, still too surprised to be angry.

Had he known America better, the industrialist might have recognized that the man was one of Washington's homeless, and like most of them, a man with a problem. In this case, he was an alcoholic who had lost both his job and his family to drink, and his only contact with reality came from disjointed conversations with people similarly afflicted. Because of that, whatever outrages he held were artificially magnified. His plastic cup was full of an inexpensive beer, and because he remembered once working in the Chrysler assembly plant in Newark, Delaware, he decided that he didn't need the beer as much as he needed to be angry about losing his job, whenever that had been. . . . And so, forgetting that his own difficulties had brought him to this low station in life, he turned and tossed the beer all over the three men in front of him, then moved on without a word, feeling so good about what he'd done that he didn't mind losing his drink.

The bodyguard started to move after him. In Japan he would have been able to hammer the *bakayaro* to the ground. A policeman would be summoned, and this fool would be detained, but the bodyguard knew he was on unfamiliar ground, and held back, then turned to see if perhaps this had been a setup to distract him from a more serious attack. He saw his employer standing erect, his face first frozen in shock, then outrage, as his expensive English-made coat dripped with half a liter of cheap, tasteless American beer. Without a word, Murakami got into the waiting car, which headed off to Washington National Airport. The bodyguard, similarly humiliated, took his seat in the front of the car.

A man who had won everything in his life on merit, who remembered life on a postage-stamp of a vegetable farm, who had studied harder than anyone else to get ahead, to win a place at Tokyo University, who had started at the bottom and worked his way to the top, Murakami had often had his doubts and criticisms of America, but he had deemed himself a fair and rational actor on trade issues. As so often happens in life, however, it was an irrelevancy that would change his mind.

They are *barbarians,* he told himself, boarding his chartered jet for the flight to New York.

"The Prime Minister is going to fall," Ryan told the President about the same time, a few blocks away.

"How sure are we of that?"

"Sure as we can be," Jack replied, taking his seat. "We have a couple of field officers working on something over there, and that's what they're hearing from people."

"State hasn't said that yet," Durling objected somewhat innocently.

"Mr. President, come on now," Ryan said, holding a folder in his lap. "You know this is going to have some serious ramifications. You know Koga is sitting on a coalition made up of six different factions, and it won't take much to blow that apart on him." *And us,* Jack didn't add.

"Okay. So what?" Durling observed, having had

his polling data updated again this very day.

"So the guy most likely to replace him is Hiroshi Goto. He doesn't like us very much. Never has."

"He talks big and tough," the President said, "but the one time I met him he looked like a typical blusterer. Weak, vain, not much substance to him."

"And something else." Ryan filled the President in on one of the spinoffs of Operation SANDALWOOD.

Under other circumstances Roger Durling might have smiled, but he had Ed Kealty sitting less than a hundred feet from him.

"Jack, how hard is it for a guy *not* to fuck around behind his wife's back?"

"Pretty easy in my case," Jack answered. "I'm married to a surgeon, remember?" The President laughed, then turned serious.

"It's something we can use on the son of a bitch, isn't it?"

"Yes, sir." Ryan didn't have to add, but only with the greatest possible care, that on top of the Oak Ridge incident, it could well ignite a firestorm of public indignation. Niccolò Machiavelli himself had warned against this sort of thing.

"What are we planning to do about this Norton girl?" Durling asked.

"Clark and Chavez — "

"The guys who bagged Corp, right?"

"Yes, sir. They're over there right now. I want them to meet the girl and offer her a free ride home."

"Debrief once she gets back?"

Ryan nodded. "Yes, sir."

Durling smiled. "I like it. Good work."

"Mr. President, we're getting what we want, probably even a little more than what we really wanted," Jack cautioned. "The Chinese general Sun Tzu once wrote that you always leave your enemy a way out — you don't press a beaten enemy too hard."

"In the One-Oh-One, they told us to kill them all

and count the bodies." The President grinned. It actually pleased him that Ryan was now secure enough in his position to feel free to offer gratuitous advice. "This is out of your field, Jack. This isn't a national-security matter."

"Yes, sir. I know that. Look, I was in the money business a few months ago. I do have a little knowledge about international business."

Durling conceded the point with a nod. "Okay, go on. It's not like I've been getting any contrarian advice, and I suppose I ought to hear a little of it."

"We don't want Koga to go down, sir. He's a hell of a lot easier to deal with than Goto will be. Maybe a quiet statement from the Ambassador, something about how TRA gives you authority to act, but — "

The President cut him off. "But I'm not really going to do it?" He shook his head. "You know I can't do that. It would have the effect of cutting Al Trent off at the ankles, and I can't do that. It would look like I was double-dealing the unions, and I can't do *that* either."

"Do you really plan to implement TRA fully?"

"Yes, I do. Only for a few months. I have to shock the bastards, Jack. We *will* have a fair-trade deal, after twenty years of screwing around, but they have to understand that we're serious for once. It's going to be hard on them, but in a few months they're going to be believers, and then they can change their laws a little, and we'll do the same, and things will settle down to a trading system that's completely fair for all parties."

"You really want my opinion?"

Durling nodded again. "That's what I pay you for. You think we're pushing too hard."

"Yes, sir. We don't want Koga to go down, and we have to offer him something juicy if we want to save him. If you want to think long-term on this, you have to consider who you want to do business with."

Durling lifted a memo from his desk. "Brett Hanson told me the same thing, but he's not quite as worried about Koga as you are."

"By this time tomorrow," Ryan promised, "he will be."

"You can't even walk the streets here," Murakami snarled.

Yamata had a whole floor of the Plaza Atheneé reserved for himself and his senior staff. The industrialists were alone in a sitting room, coats and ties off, a bottle of whiskey on the table.

"One never could, Binichi," Yamata replied. "Here *we* are the *gaijin*. You never seem to remember that."

"Do you know how much business I do here, how much I *buy* here?" the younger man demanded. He could still smell the beer. It had gotten on his shirt, but he was too angry to change clothes. He wanted the reminder of the lesson he'd learned only a few hours earlier.

"And what of myself?" Yamata asked. "Over the last few years I've put six *billion* yen into a trading company here. I finished that only a short time ago, as you will recall. Now I wonder if I'll ever get it back."

"They wouldn't do *that*."

"Your confidence in these people is touching, and does you credit," his host observed. "When the economy of our country falls into ruin, do you suppose they will let me move here to manage my American interests? In 1941 they froze our assets here."

"This is not 1941."

"No, it is not, Murakami-san. It is far worse today. We had not so far to fall then."

"Please," Chavez said, draining the last of his beer. "In 1941 my grandfather was fighting Fascists outside St. Petersburg — "

"Leningrad, you young pup!" Clark snarled, sitting next to him. "These young ones, they lose all their respect for the past," he explained to their two hosts.

One was a senior public-relations official from Mitsubishi Heavy Industries, the other a director of their aircraft division.

"Yes," Seigo Ishii agreed. "You know, members of my family helped design the fighters our Navy used. I once met Saburo Sakai and Minoru Genda."

Ding opened another round of bottles and poured like the good underling he was, dutifully serving his master, Ivan Sergeyevich Klerk. The beer was really pretty good here, especially since their hosts were picking up the tab, Chavez thought, keeping his peace and watching a master at work.

"I know these names," Clark said. "Great warriors, but" — he held up a finger — "they fought against my countrymen. I remember that, too."

"Fifty years," the PR man pointed out. "And your country was also different then."

"That is true, my friends, that is true," Clark admitted, his head lolling to one side. Chavez thought he was overdoing the alcohol stuff.

"Your first time here, yes?"

"Correct."

"Your impressions?" Ishii asked.

"I love your poetry. It is very different from ours. I could write a book on Pushkin, you know. Perhaps someday I will, but a few years ago I started learning about yours. You see, our poetry is intended to convey a whole series of thoughts — often tell a complex story — but yours is far more subtle and delicate, like — how do I say this? Like a flash picture, yes? Perhaps there is one you could explain to me. I can see the picture, but not understand the significance. How does it go?" Clark asked himself drunkenly. "Ah, yes: 'Plum blossoms bloom, and pleasure-

294

women buy new scarves in a brothel room.' Now," he asked the PR guy, "what is the meaning of that?"

Ding handled the eye contact with Ishii. It was amusing in a way. Confusion at first, then you could just about hear the eyeballs click when the code phrase sliced through his mind like the killing stroke of a rapier. Sasaki's eyes zeroed in on Clark, then noticed that it was Ding who was maintaining eye contact.

That's right. You're back on the payroll, buddy.

"Well, you see, it's the contrast," the PR official explained. "You have the pleasant image of attractive women doing something — oh, feminine, is that the word? Then the end, you see that they are prostitutes, trapped in a — "

"Prison," Ishii said, suddenly sober. "They are trapped into doing something. And suddenly the setting and the picture are not as pleasant as they seem at all."

"Ah, yes," Clark said with a smile. "That is entirely sensible. Thank you." A friendly nod to acknowledge the important lesson.

Goddamn, but Mr. C was smooth, Chavez thought. This spy stuff had its moments. Ding almost felt sorry for Ishii, but if the dumb son of a bitch had betrayed his country before, well, no sense in shedding any tears for him now. The axiom in CIA was simple, if somewhat cruel: once a traitor, always a traitor. The corresponding aphorism in the FBI was even crueler, which was odd. The FBI boys were usually so upright and clean-cut. *Once a cocksucker, always a cocksucker.*

"Is it possible?" Murakami asked.

"Possible? It's child's play."

"But the effects . . ." Yamata's idea had obvious panache, but . . .

"The effects are simple. The damage to their econ-

295

omy will prevent them from building up the industries they need to replace our products. Their consumers will recover from the initial shock and, needing products which their own corporations cannot manufacture, they will again buy them from us." If Binichi thought he was going to get the whole story, that was his problem.

"I think not. You underestimate the Americans' anger at this unfortunate incident. You must also factor in the political dimension — "

"Koga is finished. That is decided," Yamata interrupted coldly.

"Goto?" Murakami asked. It wasn't much of a question. He followed his country's political scene as much as any man.

"Of course."

An angry gesture. "Goto is a fool. Everywhere he walks he's following his penis. I wouldn't trust him to run my father's farm."

"You could say that of any of them. Who really manages our country's affairs? What more could we want in a prime minister, Binichi?" Raizo asked with a jolly laugh.

"They have one like that in their government, too," Murakami noted darkly, pouring himself another generous jolt of Chivas and wondering what Yamata was really talking about. "I've never met the man, but he sounds like a swine."

"Who is that?"

"Kealty, their Vice President. You know, this upstanding President of theirs is covering it up, too."

Yamata leaned back in his chair. "I don't understand."

Murakami filled him in. The whiskey didn't impede his memory a jot, his host noted. Well, though a cautious man, and often an overly generous one in his dealings with foreigners, he was one of Yamata's true peers, and though they often disagreed on things, there was genuine respect between them.

"That is interesting. What will your people do about it?"

"They are *thinking* about it," Binichi replied with an eloquent arch of the eyebrows.

"You trust Americans on something like this? The best of them are *ronin,* and you know what the worst are . . ." Then Yamata-san paused and took a few seconds to consider this information more fully. "My friend, if the Americans can take down Koga . . ."

Murakami lowered his head for a moment. The smell of the thrown beer was stronger than ever. The insolence of that street creature! For that matter, what of the insolence of the President? He could cripple an entire country with his vanity and his clearly feigned anger. Over what? An accident, that was all. Had the company not honorably assumed responsibility? Had it not promised to look after the survivors?

"It is a large and dangerous thing you propose, my friend."

"It is an even more dangerous thing not to do anything."

Murakami thought about it for a moment.

"What would you have me do?"

"The specifics about Kealty and Durling would be welcome."

That required only a few minutes. Murakami made a call, and the information was sent to the secure fax machine in Yamata's suite. Perhaps Raizo would be able to put it to good use, he thought. An hour later his car took him to Kennedy International, where he boarded a JAL flight to Tokyo.

Yamata's other corporate jet was another G-IV. It would be busy. The first flight was to New Delhi. It was only on the ground for two hours before taking off on an easterly heading.

★ ★ ★

"Looks like a course change," Fleet-Ops said. "At first we thought they were just doing some extended flight operations, but they've got all their birds up already and — "

Admiral Dubro nodded agreement as he looked down at the Link-11 display in the carrier's Combat Information Center. It was relayed in from an E-2C Hawkeye surveillance aircraft. The circular formation was heading due south at a speed of eighteen knots. The carriers were surrounded by their goalkeeper force of missile-armed destroyers and cruisers, and there was also a screen of picket destroyers well in advance. All their radars were on, which was something new. The Indian ships were both advertising their presence and creating a "bubble" through which no one could pass without their knowledge.

"Looking for us, you suppose?" the Admiral asked.

"If nothing else, they can make us commit to one ops-area or another. We can be southwest of them or southeast, but if they keep coming this way, they split the difference pretty clean, sir."

Maybe they were just tired of being shadowed, Dubro thought. Understandable. They had a respectable fleet, manned with people who had to be well drilled in their duties after the last few months. They'd just topped off their bunkers again, and would have all the fuel they needed to do . . . what?

"Intel?"

"Nothing on their intentions," Commander Harrison replied. "Their amphibs are still tied up. We don't have anything on that brigade J-2 was worried about. Bad weather for overheads the last few days."

"Damn those intel pukes," Dubro growled. CIA depended so much on satellite coverage that everyone pretended the cameras could see through clouds. All they had to do was put a few assets on the ground . . . was he the only one who realized that?

The computer-generated display was on a flat glass plate, a new model just installed on the ship the previous year. Far more detailed than the earlier systems, it gave superb map and chart data on which ship and aircraft locations were electronically overlaid. The beauty of the system was that it showed what you knew in exquisite detail. The problem was that it didn't show anything else, and Dubro needed better data to make his decision.

"They've had a minimum of four aircraft up for the past eight hours, sweeping south. By their operating radius I would estimate that they're carrying air-to-air missiles and aux fuel tanks for max endurance. So call it a strong effort at forward reconnaissance. Their Harriers have that new Black Fox look-down radar, and the Hummers caught some sniffs of it. They're looking as far as they can, sir. I want permission to pull the Hummer south another hundred miles or so right now, and to have them go a little covert." By which he meant the surveillance aircraft would keep its radar on only some of the time, and would instead track the progress of the Indian fleet passively, from the Indians' own radar emissions.

"No." Admiral Dubro shook his head. "Let's play dumb and complacent for a while." He turned to check the status of his aircraft. He had ample combat power to deal with the threat, but that wasn't the issue. His mission was not to defeat the Indian Navy in battle. It was to intimidate them from doing something which America found displeasing. For that matter, his adversary's mission could not have been to fight the United States Navy — could it? No, that was too crazy. It was barely within the realm of possibility that a very good and very lucky Indian fleet commander could best a very unlucky and very dumb American counterpart, but Dubro had no intention of letting that happen. More likely, just as his mission

299

was mainly bluff, so was theirs. If they could force the American fleet south, then . . . they weren't so dumb after all, were they? The question was how to play the cards he had.

"They're forcing us to commit, Ed. Trying to, anyway." Dubro leaned forward, resting one hand on the map display and tracing around with the other. "They probably think we're southeast. If so, by moving south they can block us better, and they know we'll probably maintain our distance just to keep out of their strike range. On the other hand, if they suspect we are where we really are right now, they can accomplish the same thing, or face us with the option of looping around to the northwest to cover the Gulf of Mannar. But that means coming within range of their land-based air, with their fleet to our south, and our only exit due west. Not bad for an operational concept," the battle-group commander acknowledged. "The group commander still Chandraskatta?"

Fleet-Ops nodded. "That's right, sir. He's back after a little time on the beach. The Brits have the book on the guy. They say he's no dummy."

"I think I'd go along with that for the moment. What sort of intel you suppose they have on us?"

Harrison shrugged. "They know how long we've been here. They have to know how tired we are." Fleet-Ops meant the ships as much as the men. Every ship in the Task Force had matériel problems now. They all carried spare parts, but ships could remain at sea only so long before refit was needed. Corrosion from salt air, the constant movement and pounding of wind and wave, and heavy equipment use meant that ships' systems couldn't last forever. Then there were the human factors. His men and women were tired now, too long at sea. Increased maintenance duties made them tireder still. The current catchphrase in the military for these combined problems was "leadership challenge," a polite expression meaning

300

that the officers commanding both the ships and the men sometimes didn't know what the hell they were supposed to do.

"You know, Ed, at least the Russians were predictable." Dubro stood erect, looking down and wishing he still smoked his pipe. "Okay, let's call this one in. Tell Washington it looks like they might just be making a move."

"So we meet for the first time."

"It's my pleasure, sir." Chuck Searls, the computer engineer, knew that his three-piece suit and neat haircut had surprised the man. He held out his hand and bobbed his head in what he supposed was a proper greeting for his benefactor.

"My people tell me that you are very skilled."

"You're very kind. I've worked at it for some years, and I suppose I have a few small talents." Searls had read up on Japan.

And very greedy, Yamata thought, *but well-mannered.* He would settle for that. It was, all in all, a fortunate accident. He'd purchased the man's business four years earlier, left current management in place, as was his custom, then discovered that the real brains of the outfit were in this man. Searls was the nearest thing to a wizard that his executive had ever seen, the man had reported to Yamata-san, and though the American's title hadn't changed, his salary had. And then, a few years ago, Searls had remarked that he was tiring of his job . . .

"Everything is prepared?"

"Yes, sir. The initial software upgrade went in months ago. They love it."

"And the — "

"Easter egg, Mr. Yamata. That's what we call it."

Raizo had never encountered the expression. He asked for an explanation and got it — but it meant nothing to him.

301

"How difficult to implement it?"

"That's the clever part," Searls said. "It keys on two stocks. If General Motors and Merck go through the system at values which I built in, twice and in the same minute, the egg hatches, but only on a Friday, like you said, and only if the five-minute period falls in the proper time-range."

"You mean this thing could happen by accident?" Yamata asked in some surprise.

"Theoretically, yes, but the trigger values for the stocks are well outside the current trading range, and the odds of having that happen all together by accident are about thirty million to one. That's why I picked this method for hatching the egg. I ran a computer-search of trading patterns and . . ."

Another problem with mercenaries was that they could never stop themselves from telling you how brilliant they were. Even though it was probably true in this case, Yamata found it difficult to sit through the dissertation. He did it anyway. Good manners required it.

"And your personal arrangements?"

Searls merely nodded. The flight to Miami. The connecting flights to Antigua, via Dominica and Grenada, all with different names on the tickets, paid for by different credit cards. He had his new passport, his new identity. On the Caribbean island, there was a certain piece of property. It would take an entire day, but then he'd be there, and he had no plans to leave it, ever.

For his part, Yamata neither knew nor wanted to know what Searls would do. Had this been a screen drama, he would have arranged for the man's life to end, but it would have been dangerous. There was always the chance that there might be more than one egg in the nest, wasn't there? Yes, there had to be. Besides, there was honor to be considered. This entire venture was about honor.

"The second third of the funds will be transferred in the morning. When that happens, I would suggest that you execute your plans." *Ronin,* Yamata thought, but even some of them were faithful after a fashion.

"Members," the Speaker of the House said after Al Trent had concluded his final wrap-up speech, "will cast their votes by electronic device."

On C-SPAN the drone of repeated words was replaced by classical music, Bach's Italian Concerto in this case. Each member had a plastic card — it was like an automatic teller machine, really. The votes were tallied by a simple computer displayed on TV screens all over the world. Two hundred eighteen votes were needed for passage. That number was reached in just under ten minutes. Then came the final rush of additional "aye" votes as members rushed from committee hearings and constituent meetings to enter the chamber, record their votes, and return to whatever they'd been doing.

Through it all, Al Trent stayed on the floor, mainly chatting amiably with a member of the minority leadership, his friend Sam Fellows. It was remarkable how much they agreed on, both thought. They could scarcely have been more different, a gay New England liberal and a Mormon Arizonan conservative.

"This'll teach the little bastards a lesson," Al observed.

"You sure ramrodded the bill through," Sam agreed. Both men wondered what the long-term effects on employment would be in their districts.

Less pleased were the officials of the Japanese Embassy, who called the results in to their Foreign Ministry the moment the music stopped and the Speaker announced, "HR-12313, the Trade Reform Act, is approved."

The bill would go to the Senate next, which, they reported, was a formality. The only people likely to vote against it were those furthest away from re-election. The Foreign Minister got the news from his staff at about nine local time in Tokyo and informed Prime Minister Koga. The latter had already drafted his letter of resignation for the Emperor. Another man might have wept at the destruction of his dreams. The Prime Minister did not. In retrospect, he'd had more real influence as a member of the opposition than in this office. Looking at the morning sun on the well-kept grounds outside his window, he realized that it would be a more pleasant life, after all.

Let Goto deal with this.

"You know, the Japanese make some awfully good stuff that we use at Wilmer," Cathy Ryan observed over dinner. It was time for her to comment on the law, now that it was halfway passed.

"Oh?"

"The diode laser system we use on cataracts, for one. They bought the American company that invented it. Their engineers really know how to support their stuff, too. They're in practically every month with a software upgrade."

"Where's the company located?" Jack asked.

"Someplace in California."

"Then it's an American product, Cathy."

"But not all the parts are," his wife pointed out.

"Look, the law allows for special exceptions to be made for uniquely valuable things that — "

"The government's going to make the rules, right?"

"True," Jack conceded. "Wait a minute. You told me their docs — "

"I never said they were dumb, just that they need to think more creatively. You know," she added, "just like the government does."

"I *told* the President this wasn't all that great an idea. He says the law will be in full force just a few months."

"I'll believe that when I see it."

13

Winds and Tides

"I've never seen anything like this."

"But your country made thousands of them," the PR director objected.

"That is true," Klerk agreed, "but the factories were not open to the public, and not even to Soviet journalists."

Chavez was doing the photography work, and was putting on quite a show, John Clark noted without a smile, dancing around the workers in their white coveralls and hard hats, turning, twisting, squatting, his Nikon pressed against his face, changing rolls every few minutes, and along the way getting a few hundred frames of the missile production line. They were SS-19 missile bodies, sure as hell. Clark knew the specifications, and had seen enough photos at Langley to know what they looked like — and enough to spot some local modifications. On the Russian models the exterior was usually green. Everything the Soviet Union had built for military use had to be camouflaged, even missiles inside of transport containers sitting in the bottom of concrete silos were the same pea-soup green that they liked to paint on tanks. But not these. The paint had weight, and there was no point in expending fuel to drive the few kilograms of paint to suborbital speed, and so these missile bodies were bright, shiny steel. The fittings and joints looked far more refined than he would have expected on a Russian production line.

"You've modified our original design, haven't you?"

"Correct." The PR guy smiled. "The basic design was excellent. Our engineers were very impressed, but we have different standards, and better materials. You have a good eye, Mr. Klerk. Not too long ago an American NASA engineer made the same observation." The man paused. "What sort of Russian name is Klerk?"

"It's not Russian," Clark said, continuing to scribble his notes. "My grandfather was English, a Communist. His name was Clark. In the 1920s he came to Russia to be part of the new experiment." An embarrassed grin. "I suppose he's disappointed, wherever he is."

"And your colleague?"

"Chekov? He's from the Crimea. The Tartar blood really shows, doesn't it? So how many of these will you build?"

Chavez was at the top end of the missile body at the end of the line. A few of the assembly workers were casting annoyed glances his way, and he took that to mean that he was doing his job of imitating an intrusive, pain-in-the-ass journalist right. Aside from that the job was pretty easy. The assembly bay of the factory was brightly lit to assist the workers in their tasks, and though he'd used his light meter for show, the camera's own monitoring chip told him that he had all the illumination he needed. This Nikon F-20 was one badass camera. Ding switched rolls. He was using ASA-64 color slide film — Fuji film, of course — because it had better color saturation, whatever that meant.

In due course, Mr. C shook hands with the factory representative and they all headed toward the door.

307

Chavez — Chekov — twisted the lens off the camera body and stowed everything away in his bag. Friendly smiles and bows sent them on their way. Ding slid a CD into the player and turned the sound way up. It made conversation difficult, but John was always a stickler for the rules. And he was right. There was no knowing if someone might have bugged their rental car. Chavez leaned his head over to the right so that he wouldn't have to scream his question.

"John, is it always this easy?"

Clark wanted to smile, but didn't. He'd reactivated yet another member of THISTLE a few hours earlier, who had insisted that he and Ding look at the assembly floor.

"You know, I used to go into Russia, back when you needed more than a passport and American Express."

"Doing what?"

"Mainly getting people out. Sometimes recovering data packs. Couple of times I emplaced cute little gadgets. Talk about lonely, talk about scary." Clark shook his head. Only his wife knew that he colored his hair, just a little, because he didn't like gray there. "You have any idea what we would have paid to get into . . . Plesetsk, I think, is where they made those things, the Chelomei Design Bureau."

"They really wanted us to see that stuff."

"Sure as hell," Clark agreed.

"What do I do with the photos?"

John almost said to toss them, but it *was* data, and they were working on company time. He had to draft and send a story to Interfax to maintain his cover — he wondered if anyone would print it. *Wouldn't that be a gas,* he thought with a shake of the head. All they were doing, really, was circling in a holding pattern, waiting for the word and the opportunity to meet Kimberly Norton. The film and a copy of his story, he decided, would find their way into the diplomatic bag. If nothing else, it was good practice for Ding — and for himself, Clark admitted.

"Turn that damned noise down," he said, and they switched to Russian. Good language practice.

"I miss the winters at home," Chekov observed.

"I don't," Klerk answered. "Where did you ever acquire the taste for that awful American music?" he asked with a growl.

"Voice of America," came the reply. Then the voice laughed.

"Yevgeniy Pavlovich, you have no respect. My ears can't tolerate that damned noise. Don't you have something else to play?"

"Anything would be an improvement," the technician observed to himself, as he adjusted his headphones and shook his head to clear them of the damned *gaijin* noise. Worse still, his own son listened to the same trash.

Despite all the denials that had gone back and forth over the past few weeks, the reality of it was finally plain for all to see. The huge, ugly car-carriers swinging at anchor in several different harbors were silent witnesses on every TV news broadcast on NHK. The Japanese car companies owned a total of a hundred nineteen of them, not counting foreign-flag ships operating under charter that were now heading back to their own home ports. Ships that never stayed still any longer than it took to load another cargo of autos now sat like icebergs, clogging anchorages. There was no sense in loading and dispatching them. Those awaiting pier space in American ports would take weeks to unload. The crews took the opportunity to do programmed maintenance, but they knew that when those make-work tasks were done, they would truly be out of business.

The effect snowballed rapidly. There was little

point in manufacturing automobiles that could not be shipped. There was literally no place to keep them. As soon as the huge holding lots at the ports were filled, and the train-cars on their sidetracks, and the lots at the assembly plants, there was simply no choice. Fully a half-dozen TV crews were on hand when the line supervisor at the Nissan plant reached up and pressed a button. That button rang bells all up and down the line. Ordinarily used because of a problem in the assembly process, this time it meant that the line was *stopped*. From the beginning, where the frames were placed on the moving chain-belt, to the end, where a navy-blue car sat with its door open, awaiting a driver to take it out of the building, workers stood still, looking at one another. They'd told themselves that this could never happen. Reality to them was showing up for work, performing their functions, attaching parts, testing, checking off — very rarely finding a problem — and repeating the processes for endless numbing but well-compensated hours, and at this moment it was as if the world had ceased to rotate. They'd known, after a fashion. The newspapers and TV broadcasts, the rumors that had raced up and down the line far more quickly than the cars ever had, the bulletins from management. Despite all that, they now stood around as if stunned by a hard blow to the face.

On the floor of their national stock exchange, the traders were holding small portable televisions, a new kind from Sony that folded up and fit in the hip pocket. They saw the man ring the bell, saw the workers stop their activities. Worst of all, they saw the looks on their faces. And this was just the beginning, the traders knew. Parts suppliers would stop because the assemblers would cease buying their products. Primary-metals industries would slow down drastically because their main customers were shut down. Electronics companies would slow, with the loss of

310

both domestic and foreign markets. Their country depended absolutely on foreign trade, and America was their primary trading partner, one hundred seventy *billion* dollars of exports to a single country, more than they sold to all of Asia, more than they sold to all of Europe. They imported ninety billion or so from America, but the surplus, the profit side of the ledger, was just over seventy billion American dollars, and that was money their economy needed to function; money that their national economy was designed to use; production capacity that it was designed to meet.

For the blue-collar workers on the television, the world had merely stopped. For the traders, the world had, perhaps, ended, and the look on their faces was not shock but black despair. The period of silence lasted no more than thirty seconds. The whole country had watched the same scene on TV with the same morbid fascination tempered by obstinate disbelief. Then the phone began ringing again. Some of the hands that reached for them shook. The Nikkei Dow would fall again that day, down to a closing value of 6,540 yen, about a fifth of what it had been only a few years before.

The same tape was played as the lead segment on every network news broadcast in the U.S., and in Detroit, even UAW workers who had themselves seen plants close down saw the looks, heard the noise, and remembered their own feelings. Though their sympathy was tempered with the promise of their own renewed employment, it wasn't all that hard to know what their Japanese counterparts felt right now. It was far easier to dislike them when they were working and taking American jobs. Now they too were victims of forces that few of them really understood.

The reaction on Wall Street was surprising to the unsophisticated. For all its theoretical benefits to the

311

American economy, the Trade Reform Act was now a short-term problem. American corporations too numerous to list depended on Japanese products to some greater or lesser degree, and while American workers and companies could theoretically step in to take up the slack, everyone wondered how serious the TRA provisions were. If they were permanent, that was one thing, and it would make very good sense for investors to put their money in those firms that were well placed to make up the shortfall of needed products. But what if the government was merely using it as a tool to open Japanese markets and the Japanese acted quickly to concede a few points to mitigate the overall damage? In that case, different companies, poised to place their products on Japanese shelves, were a better investment opportunity. The trick was to identify which corporations were in a position to do both, because one or the other could be a big loser, especially with the initial jump the stock market had taken. Certainly, the dollar would appreciate with respect to the yen, but the technicians on the bond market noted that overseas banks had jumped very fast indeed, buying up U.S. Government securities, paying for them with their yen accounts, and clearly betting on a major shift in values from which a short-term profit was certain to take place.

American stock values actually fell on the uncertainty, which surprised many of those who had their money on "the Street." Those holdings were mainly in mutual-funds accounts, because it was difficult, if not impossible, to keep track of things if you were a small-time holder. It was far safer to let "professionals" manage your money. The result was that there were now more mutual-funds companies than stock issues traded on the New York Stock Exchange, and they were all managed by technicians whose job it was to understand what went on in the most boisterous and least predictable economic marketplace in the world.

The initial slide was just under fifty points before stabilizing, stopped there by public statements from the Big Three auto companies that they were self-sufficient enough, thank you, in most categories of parts to maintain, and even boost, domestic auto production. Despite that, the technicians at the big trading houses scratched their heads and talked things over in their coffee rooms. *Do you have any idea how to deal with this?* The only reason only half the people asked the question was that it was the job of the other half to listen, shake its collective head, and reply, *Hell, no.*

At the Washington headquarters of the Fed, there were other questions, but just as few hard answers. The troublesome specter of inflation was not yet gone, and the current situation was unlikely to banish it further. The most immediate and obvious problem was that there would be — hell, one of the board noted, *already was!* — more purchasing power than there were products to buy. That meant yet another inflationary surge, and though the dollar would undoubtedly climb against the yen, what that really meant was that the yen would free-fall for a while and the dollar would actually fall as well with respect to other world currencies. And they couldn't have that. Another quarter point in the discount rate, they decided, effective immediately on the close of the Exchange. It would confuse the trading markets somewhat, but that was okay because the Fed knew what it was doing.

About the only good news on that score was the sudden surge in the purchase of Treasury notes. Probably Japanese banks, they knew without asking, hedging like hell to protect themselves. A smart move, they all noted. Their respect for their Japanese colleagues was genuine and not affected by the current irregularities which, they all hoped, would soon pass.

"Are we agreed?" Yamata asked.

"We can't stop now," a banker said. He could have gone on to say that they and their entire country were poised on the edge of an abyss so deep that the bottom could not be seen. He didn't have to. They all stood on the same edge, and looking down, they saw not the lacquered table around which they sat, but only an infinity with economic death at the bottom of it.

Heads nodded around the table. There was a long moment of silence, and then Matsuda spoke.

"How did this ever come to pass?"

"It has always been inevitable, my friends," Yamata-san said, a fine edge of sadness in his voice. "Our country is like . . . like a city with no surrounding countryside, like a strong arm without a heart to send it blood. We've told ourselves for years that this is a normal state of affairs — but it is not, and we must remedy the situation or perish."

"It is a great gamble we undertake."

"*Hai.*" It was hard for him not to smile.

It was not yet dawn, and they would sail on the tide. The proceedings went on without much fanfare. A few families came down to the docks, mainly to drop the crewmen off at their ships from a last night spent ashore.

The names were traditional, as they were with most navies of the world — at least those who'd been around long enough to have tradition. The new Aegis destroyers, *Kongo* and her sisters, bore traditional battleship names, mainly ancient appellations for regions of the nation that built them. That was a recent departure. It would have struck Westerners as an odd nomenclature for ships-of-war, but in keeping with their country's poetic traditions, most names for the combat ships had lyrical meanings, and were largely

314

grouped by class. Destroyers traditionally had names ending in -*kaze*, denoting a kind of wind; *Hatukaze*, for example, meant "Morning Breeze." Submarine names were somewhat more logical. All of those ended in -*ushio*, meaning "tide."

They were in the main handsome ships, spotlessly clean so as not to detract from their workmanlike profiles. One by one they lit off their jet-turbine engines and eased their way off the quays and into the channels. The captains and navigators looked at the shipping that was piling up in Tokyo Bay, but whatever they were thinking, for the moment the merchantmen were merely a hazard to navigation, swinging at their anchors as they were. Below, those sailors not on sea-and-anchor detail mainly stowed gear and saw to their duty stations. Radars were lit up to assist in the departure — hardly necessary since visibility conditions this morning were excellent, but good practice for the crewmen in the various Combat Information Centers. At the direction of combat-systems officers, data links were tested to swap tactical information between ships. In engine-control rooms the "snipes" — an ancient term of disparagement for the traditionally filthy enginemen — sat in comfortable swivel chairs and monitored computer readouts while sipping tea.

The flagship was the new destroyer *Mutsu*. The fishing port of Tateyame was in sight, the last town they would pass before turning sharply to port and heading east.

The submarines were already out there, Rear Admiral Yusuo Sato knew, but the commanders had been briefed in. His was a family with a long tradition of service — better still, a tradition of the sea. His father had commanded a destroyer under Raizo Tanaka, one of the greatest destroyermen who'd ever lived, and his uncle had been one of Yamamoto's "wild eagles," a carrier pilot killed at the Battle of Santa Cruz. The succeeding generation had continued in those footsteps. Yusuo's brother, Torajiro Sato, had flown F-86 fighters for the Air Self-Defense Force, then quit in disgust at the demeaning status of the air arm, and now flew as a senior captain for Japan Air Lines. The man's son, Shiro, had followed in his father's footsteps and was now a very proud young major, flying fighters on a more permanent basis. Not too bad, Admiral Sato thought, for a family that had no samurai roots. Yusuo's other brother was a banker. Sato was fully briefed on what was to come.

The Admiral stood, opened the watertight door on *Mutsu's* bridge and passed out to the starboard wing. The sailors at work there took a second to acknowledge his presence with dutiful nods, then went back to taking shoresights to update the ship's position. Sato looked aft and noted that the sixteen ships in the column were in a nearly perfect line, separated by a uniform five hundred meters, just becoming visible to the unaided eye in the pink-orange glow of the rising sun toward which they sailed. Surely that was a good omen, the Admiral thought. At the truck of every ship flew the same flag under which his father had served; it had been denied his country's warships for so many years but was restored now, the proud red-on-white sunburst.

"Secure the sea-and-anchor detail," the Captain's voice announced on the speaker system. Already their home port was under the visible horizon, and soon the same would be true of the headlands now on the port quarter.

Sixteen ships, Sato thought. The largest force his country had put to sea as a coherent unit in — fifty years? He had to think about it. Certainly the most powerful, not one vessel more than ten years old, proud, expensive ships with proud, established names. But the one name he'd wanted with him this morning, *Kurushio,* "Black Tide," that of his father's destroyer, which had sunk an American cruiser at the Battle of Tassafaronga, unfortunately belonged to a new submarine, already at sea. The Admiral lowered his binoculars and grunted in mild displeasure. Black Tide. It was a poetically perfect name for a warship, too. A pity it had been wasted on a submarine.

Kurushio and her sisters had left thirty-six hours earlier. The lead ship of a new class, she was running at fifteen knots for her high-speed transit to the exercise area, powered by her large, efficient diesels which now drew air through the snorkel mast. Her crew of ten officers and sixty enlisted men was on a routine watch cycle. An officer of the deck and his junior kept the watch in the sub's control room. An engineering officer was at his post, along with twenty-four ratings. The entire torpedo department was at work in their midships station, doing electronic tests on the fourteen Type 89-Mod C torpedoes and six Harpoon missiles. Otherwise the watch bill was normal, and no one remarked on the single change. The captain, Commander Tamaki Ugaki, was known as a stickler for readiness, and though he drilled his men hard, his was a happy ship because she was always a smart ship. He was locked in his cabin, and the crew hardly knew he was aboard, the only signs of his presence the thin crack of light under the door and the cigarette smoke that came out the exhaust vent. An intense man, their skipper, the crewmen thought, doubtless working up plans and drills for the upcoming exercise against the American submarines. They'd done well the last time, scoring three first-kills in ten practice encounters. That was as good as anyone might expect. Except for Ugaki, the men joked at their lunch tables. He thought like a true samurai, and didn't want to know about being second best.

317

* * *

Ryan had established a routine in his first month back of spending one day per week at the Pentagon. He'd explained to journalists that his office wasn't supposed to be a cell, after all, and it was just a more efficient use of everyone's time. It hadn't even resulted in a story, as it might have done a few years earlier. The very title of National Security Advisor, everyone knew, was a thing of the past. Though the reporters deemed Ryan a worthy successor to the corner office in the White House, he was such a colorless guy. He was known to avoid the Washington "scene" as though he feared catching leprosy, he showed up for work every day at the same time, did his job in as few hours as circumstances allowed — to his good fortune, it was rarely more than a ten-hour day — and returned to his family as though he were a normal person or something. His background at CIA was still very sketchy, and though his public acts as a private citizen and a government functionary were well known, that was old news. As a result Ryan was able to drive around in the back of his official car and few took great note of it. Everything with the man was just so routine, and Jack worked hard to keep it that way. Reporters rarely took note of a dog that didn't bark. Perhaps they just didn't read enough to know better.

"They're up to something," Robby said as soon as Ryan took his seat in the flag briefing room in the National Military Command Center. The map display made that clear.

"Coming south?"

"Two hundred miles' worth. The fleet commander is V. K. Chandraskatta, graduated Dartmouth Royal Naval College, third in his class, worked his way up. Took the senior course at Newport a few years ago. He was number one in that class," Admiral Jackson went on. "Very nice political connections. He's spent

318

a surprising amount of time away from his fleet lately, commuting back and forth — "

"Where to?" Ryan asked.

"We assume back and forth to New Delhi, but the truth of the matter is that we don't really know. It's the old story, Jack."

Ryan managed not to groan. It was partly an old story, and partly a very new one. No military officer ever thought himself possessed of enough intelligence information, and never fully trusted the quality of what he did have. In this case, the complaint was true enough: CIA still didn't have any assets on the ground in India. Ryan made a mental note to speak to Brett Hanson about the Ambassador. Again. Psychiatrists called his form of action "passive-aggressive," meaning that he didn't resist but didn't cooperate either. It was a source of constant surprise to Ryan that important grown-ups so often acted like five-year-olds.

"Correlation between his trips ashore and his movements?"

"Nothing obvious," Robby answered with a shake of the head.

"Sigint, comint?" Jack asked, wondering if the National Security Agency, yet another shadow of its former self, had attempted to listen in on the Indian fleet's radio traffic.

"We're getting some stuff via Alice Springs and Diego Garcia, but it's just routine. Ship-movement orders, mostly, nothing with real operational significance."

Jack was tempted to grumble that his country's intelligence services never had what he wanted at the moment, but the real reason for that was simple: the intelligence he did have usually enabled America to prepare, to obviate problems before they became problems. It was the things that got overlooked that developed into crises, and they were overlooked because other things were more important — until the little ones blew up.

"So all we have is what we can infer from their operational patterns."

"And here it is," Robby said, walking to the chart. "Pushing us off . . ."

"Making Admiral Dubro commit. It's pretty clever, really. The ocean is mighty big, but it can get a lot smaller when there's two fleets moving around it. He hasn't asked for an ROE update yet but it's something we need to start thinking about."

"If they load that brigade onto their amphibs, then what?"

An Army colonel, one of Robby's staff, answered. "Sir, if I were running this, it's real easy. They have troops on the ground already, playing games with the Tamils. That secures the beachhead pretty slick, and the landing is just administrative. Getting ashore as a cohesive unit is the hard part of any invasion, but it looks to me like that's already knocked. Their Third Armored Brigade is a very robust formation. Short version is, the Sri Lankans don't have anything with a prayer of slowing it down, much less stopping it. Next item on the agenda, you gobble up a few airfields and just fly your infantry forces in. They have a lot of people under arms. Sparing fifty thousand infantrymen for this operation would not be much of a stretch for them.

"I suppose the country could degenerate into a long-term insurgency situation," the Colonel went on, "but the first few months would go to the Indians almost by default, and with their ability to isolate the island with their navy, well, whatever insurgents have a yen to fight things out wouldn't have a source of resupply. Smart money, India wins."

"The hard part's political," Ryan mused. "The U.N. will get pretty excited. . . ."

"But projecting power into that area is a bitch,"

Robby pointed out. "Sri Lanka doesn't have any traditional allies, unless you count India. They have no religious or ethnic card to play. No resources for us to get hot and bothered about."

Ryan continued the thought: "Front-page news for a few days, but if the Indians are smart about it, they make Ceylon their fifty-first state — "

"More likely their *twenty-sixth* state, sir," the Colonel suggested, "or an adjunct to Tamil Nadu, for ethnic reasons. It might even help the Indians defuse their own difficulties with the Tamils. I'd guess there have been some contacts."

"Thank you." Ryan nodded to the Colonel, who had done his homework. "But the idea is, they integrate the place into their country politically, full civil rights and everything, and all of a sudden it's no story at all anymore. Slick," Ryan observed. "But they need a political excuse before they can move. That excuse has to be a resurgence of the Tamil rebels — which of course they are in a position to foment."

"That'll be our indicator," Jackson agreed. "Before that happens, we need to tell Mike Dubro what he's going to be able to do about it."

And that would not be an easy call, Ryan thought, looking at the chart. Task Group 77.1 was heading southwest, keeping its distance from the Indian fleet, but though there was an ocean in which to maneuver, not far to Dubro's west was a long collection of atolls. At the end of it was the American base at Diego Garcia: a matter of some comfort, but not much.

The problem with a bluff was that the other guy might guess it for what it was, and this game was a lot less random than a poker hand. Combat power favored the Americans, but only if they had the will to use it. Geography favored India. America really had no vital interests in the area. The U.S. fleet in the Indian Ocean was basically there to keep an eye on the Persian Gulf, after all, but instability in any region was contagious, and when people got nervous about such things, a destructive synergy took place. The proverbial stitch-in-time was as useful in this arena as any other. That meant making a decision on how far the bluff could be pressed.

"Gets tricky, doesn't it, Rob?" Jack asked with a smile that showed more amusement than he felt.

"It would be helpful if we knew what they were thinking."

"Duly noted, Admiral. I will get people cracking on that."

"And the ROE?"

"The Roles of Engagement remain the same, Robby, until the President says otherwise. If Dubro thinks he's got an inbound attack, he can deal with it. I suppose he's got armed aircraft on the deck."

"On the deck, hell! In the air, Dr. Ryan, sir."

"I'll see if I can get him to let out another foot of lead on the leash," Jack promised.

A phone rang just then. A junior staff officer — a Marine newly promoted to major's rank — grabbed it, and called Ryan over.

"Yeah, what is it?"

"White House Signals, sir," a watch officer replied. "Prime Minister Koga just submitted his resignation. The Ambassador estimates that Goto will be asked to form the new government."

"That was fast. Have the State Department's Japan desk send me what I need. I'll be back in less than two hours." Ryan replaced the phone.

"Koga's gone?" Jackson asked.

"Somebody give you a smart pill this morning, Rob?"

"No, but I can listen in on phone conversations. I hear we're getting unpopular over there."

"It has gone a little fast."

The photos arrived by diplomatic courier. In the

old days, the bag would have been opened at the port of entry, but in these kinder and gentler times the long-service government employee got in the official car at Dulles and rode all the way to Foggy Bottom. There the bag was opened in a secure room, and the various articles in the canvas sack were sorted by category and priority and hand-carried to their various destinations. The padded envelope with seven film cassettes was handed over to a CIA employee, who simply walked outside to his car and drove off toward the Fourteenth Street Bridge. Forty minutes later, the cassettes were opened in a photolab designed for microfilm and various other sophisticated systems but readily adapted to items as pedestrian as this.

The technician rather liked "real" film — since it was commercial, it was far easier to work with, and fit standard and user-friendly processing equipment — and had long since stopped looking at the images except to make sure that he'd done his job right. In this case the color saturation told him everything. Fuji film, he thought. Who'd ever said it was better than Kodak? The slide film was cut, and the individual segments fitted into cardboard holders whose only difference from those any set of parents got to commemorate a toddler's first meeting with Mickey Mouse was that they bore the legend *Top Secret*. These were numbered, bundled together, and put into a box. The box was slid into an envelope and set in the lab's out-bin. Thirty minutes later a secretary came down to collect it.

She walked to the elevator and rode to the fifth floor of the Old Headquarters Building, now almost forty years of age and showing it. The corridors were dingy, and the paint on the drywall panels faded to a neutral, offensive yellow. Here, too, the mighty had fallen, and that was especially true of the Office of Strategic Weapons Research. Once one of CIA's most important subagencies, OSWR was now scratching for a living.

It was staffed with rocket scientists whose job descriptions were actually genuine. Their job was to look at the specifications of foreign-made missiles and decide what their real capabilities were. That meant a lot of theoretical work, and also trips to various government contractors to compare what they had with what our own people knew. Unfortunately, if you could call it that, ICBMs and SLBMs, the bread-and-butter of OSWR, were almost extinct, and the photos on the walls of every office in the section were almost nostalgic in their lack of significance. Now people educated in various areas of physics were having to learn about chemical and biological agents, the mass-destruction weapons of poorer nations. But not today.

Chris Scott, thirty-four, had started in OSWR when it had really meant something. A graduate of Rensselaer Polytechnic Institute, he'd distinguished himself by deducing the performance of the *Soviet* SS-24 two weeks before a highly placed agent had spirited out a copy of the manual for the solid-fueled bird, which had earned for him a pat on the head from the then-Director, William Webster. But the -24s were all gone now, and, his morning briefing material had told him, they were down to *one* SS-19, matched by a single Minuteman-III outside of Minot, North Dakota, both of them awaiting destruction; and he didn't like studying chemistry. As a result, the slides from Japan were something of a blessing.

Scott took his time. He had lots of it. Opening the box, he set the slides in the tray of his viewer and cycled them through, making notes with every one. That took two hours, taking him to lunchtime. The slides were repackaged and locked away when he went to the cafeteria on the first floor. There the topic of discussion was the latest fall from grace of the

Washington Redskins and the prospects of the new owner for changing things. People were lingering at lunch now, Scott noticed, and none of the supervisory personnel were making much of a big deal about it. The main cross-building corridor that opened to the building's courtyard was always fuller than it had been in the old days, and people never stopped looking at the big segment of Berlin Wall that had been on display for years. Especially the old hands, it seemed to Scott, who felt himself to be one of those. Well, at least *he* had work to do this day, and that was a welcome change.

Back in his office, Chris Scott closed his drapes and loaded the slides into a projector. He could have selected only those he'd made special notes on, but this was his work for the day — perhaps the whole week if he played his cards right — and he would conduct himself with the usual thoroughness, comparing what he saw with the report from that NASA guy.

"Mind if I join you?" Betsy Fleming stuck her head in the door. She was one of the old hands, soon to be a grandmother, who'd actually started as a secretary at DIA. Self-taught in the fields of photoanalysis and rocket engineering, her experience dated back to the Cuban Missile Crisis. Lacking a formal degree, her expertise in this field of work was formidable.

"Sure." Scott didn't mind the intrusion. Betsy was also the office's designated mom.

"Our old friend the SS-19," she observed, taking her seat. "Wow, I like what they did with it."

"Ain't it the truth?" Scott observed, stretching to shake off his postlunch drowsiness.

What had once been quite ugly was now rather beautiful. The missile bodies were polished stainless steel, which allowed a better view of the structure. In the old Russian green, it had looked brutish. Now it looked more like the space launcher it was supposed to be, sleeker somehow, even more impressive in its purposeful bulk.

"NASA says they've saved a whole lot of weight on the body, better materials, that sort of thing," Scott observed. "I really believe it now."

"Shame they couldn't do that with their g'ddamn' gas tanks," Mrs. Fleming observed. Scott grunted agreement. He owned a Cresta, and now his wife refused to drive in it until the tank was replaced. Which would be a couple of weeks, his dealer had informed him. The company was actually renting a car for him in their vain effort to curry public goodwill. That had meant getting a new parking sticker, which he would have to scrape off before returning the rental to Avis.

"Do we know who got the shots?" Betsy asked.

"One of ours, all I know." Scott flipped to another slide. "A lot of changes. They almost look cosmetic," he observed.

"How much weight are they supposed to have saved?" He was right, Mrs. Fleming thought. The steel skin showed the circular patterns of the polishing rushes, almost like jeweling on a rifle bolt . . .

"According to NASA, over twelve hundred pounds on the missile body . . ." Another click of the remote.

"Hmph, but not there," Betsy noted.

"That's funny."

The top end of the missile was where the warheads went. The SS-19 was designed to carry a bunch of them. Relatively small and heavy, they were dense objects, and the missile's structure had to account for it. Any intercontinental missile accelerated from the moment its flight began to the moment the engines finally stopped, but the period of greatest acceleration came just before burnout. At that point, with most of the fuel burned off, the rate at which speed increased reached its maximum, in this case about ten gees. At the same time, the structural rigidity lent to the missile body by the quantity of fuel inside its tanks was minimal, and as a result, the structure holding the warheads had to be both sturdy and massive so as to evenly distribute the vastly increased inertial weight of the payloads.

"No, they didn't change that, did they?" Scott looked over at his colleague.

"I wonder why? This bird's supposed to orbit satellites now . . ."

"Heavy ones, they say, communications birds . . ."

"Yeah, but look at that part . . ."

The foundation for the warhead "bus" had to be strong across its entire area. The corresponding foundation for a communications satellite was essentially a thin steel annulus, a flat, sturdy donut that invariably looked too light for its job. This one was more like an unusually heavy wagon wheel. Scott unlocked a file drawer and removed a recent photo of an SS-19 taken by an American officer on the verification team in Russia. He handed it over to Mrs. Fleming without comment.

"Look here. That's the standard structure, just what the Russians designed in, maybe with better steel, better finish. They changed almost everything else, didn't they?" Fleming asked. "Why not this?"

"Looked that way to me. Keeping that must have cost them — what? A hundred pounds, maybe more?"

"That doesn't make sense, Chris. This is the first place you want to save weight. Every kilo you save here is worth four or five on the first stage." Both stood and walked to the screen. "Wait a minute . . ."

"Yeah, this fits the bus. They didn't change it. No mating collar for a satellite. They didn't change it at all." Scott shook his head.

"You suppose they just kept the bus design for their trans-stage?"

"Even if they did, they don't need all this mass

327

at the top end, do they?"

"It's almost like they wanted it to stay the way it was."

"Yeah. I wonder why."

14

Reflections

"Thirty seconds," the assistant director said as the final commercial rolled for the Sunday-morning audience. The entire show had centered on Russia and Europe, which suited Ryan just fine.

"The one question I can't ask." Bob Holtzman chuckled before the tape started rolling again. "What's it like to be the National Security Advisor in a country with no threat to its national security?"

"Relaxing," Ryan answered with a wary look at the three cameras. None had their telltale red lights burning.

"So why the long hours?" Kris Hunter asked in a voice less sharp than her look.

"If I don't show up for work," Jack lied, "people might notice how unimportant I am." Bad news. *They still don't know about India, but they know something's up. Damn.* He wanted to keep it quiet. It was one of those things that public pressure would hurt, not help.

"Four! Three! Two! One!" The assistant director jerked his finger at the moderator, a television journalist named Edward Johnson.

"Dr. Ryan, what does the Administration make of changes in the Japanese cabinet?"

"Well, of course, that's a result of the current difficulties in trade, which is not really in my purview. Basically what we see there is an internal political situation which the Japanese people can quite easily handle without our advice," Jack announced in his earnest-statesman's voice, the one that had taken a few elocution lessons to perfect. Mainly he'd had to learn to speak more slowly.

Kris Hunter leaned forward. "But the leading candidate to take the prime ministership is a long-standing enemy of the United States — "

"That's a *little* strong," Ryan interrupted with a good-natured smile.

"His speeches, his writings, his books are not exactly friendly."

"I suppose," Ryan said with a dismissive wave and a crooked smile. "The difference between discourse among friendly nations and unfriendly ones, oddly enough, is that the former can often be more acrimonious than the latter." *Not bad, Jack* . . .

"You are not concerned?"

"No," Ryan said with a gentle shake of the head. Short answers on a show like this tended to intimidate reporters, he thought.

"Thank you for coming in this morning, Dr. Ryan."

"A pleasure as always."

Ryan continued to smile until the camera lights blinked off. Then he counted slowly to ten. Then he waited until the other reporters removed their microphones. Then he removed his microphone and stood up and moved away from the working part of the set. And then it was safe to speak. Bob Holtzman followed Jack into the makeup room. The cosmeticians were off drinking coffee, and Ryan took a fistful of HandiWipes and passed the container to Holtzman. Over the mirror was a large slab of wood engraved on which was, IN HERE EVERYTHING IS OFF THE RECORD.

"You know the real reason behind equal rights for women?" Holtzman asked. "It wasn't equal pay, or bras, or any of that crap."

"Right," Jack agreed. "It was forcing them to wear makeup. We deserved everything we got. God, I hate this shit!" he added, wiping the pancake off his forehead. "Makes me feel like a cheap whore."

"That isn't too unusual for a political figure, is it?" Kristyn Hunter asked, taking wipes to do the same.

Jack laughed. "No, but it's kind of impolite for you to say so, ma'am." *Am I a political figure now?* Ryan asked himself. *I suppose I am. How the hell did that happen?*

"Why the fancy footwork on my last question, Jack?" Holtzman asked.

"Bob, if you know it *was* fancy footwork, then you know why." Ryan motioned to the sign over the mirror, then decided to tap it to make sure everyone caught the message.

"I know that when the last government fell, it was us who developed the information on the bribery scandal," Holtzman said. Jack gave him a look but nothing else. Even *no comment* would have been a substantive comment under these circumstances.

"That killed Goto's first chance to become Prime Minister. He was next in line, remember?"

"Well, now he's got another. His patience is rewarded," Ryan observed. "If he can get a coalition together."

"Don't give me that," Hunter leaned toward the mirror to finish cleaning her nose off. "You've read the stuff he's been telling their papers, same as I have. He will get a cabinet formed, and you know what arguments he's been using."

"Talk is cheap, especially for somebody in that business," Jack said. He still hadn't quite made the leap of imagination to include himself "in that business." "Probably just a blip, one more politician with

331

a few too many drinks under his belt who had a bad day at the office or the track — "

"Or the geisha house," Kris Hunter suggested. She finished removing the makeup, then sat on the edge of the counter and lit a cigarette. Kristyn Hunter was an old-fashioned reporter. Though still on the sunny side of fifty, she was a graduate of Columbia's School of Journalism and had just been appointed chief foreign correspondent for the *Chicago Tribune*. Her voice was as dry as dust. "Two years ago that bastard put a move on me. His language would shock a Marine, and his suggestions were . . . shall we say, eccentric. I presume you have information on his personal habits, Dr. Ryan?"

"Kris, never, ever, not even once will I discuss what personal stuff, if any, we have on foreign officials." Jack paused. "Wait. He doesn't speak English, does he?" Ryan closed his eyes, trying to remember what his briefing documents had said on that point.

"You didn't know? He can when it pleases him, but he doesn't when it doesn't. That day, it didn't. And his translator that day was a female, about twenty-seven. She didn't even blush." Hunter chuckled darkly. "I sure as hell did. What does that tell you, Dr. Ryan?"

Ryan had few doubts about the information that had come out of Operation SANDALWOOD. Despite that, it was very nice to hear this from a completely independent source. "I guess he likes blondes," Jack said lightly.

"So they say. They also say that he has a new one now."

"This is getting serious," Holtzman noted. "Lots of people like to fool around, Kris."

"Goto loves to show people how tough he is. Some of the rumors about Goto are downright ugly." Kris Hunter paused. "I believe them, too."

"Really?" Ryan asked with the utmost innocence.

"Woman's intuition?"

"Don't be sexist," Hunter warned, too seriously for the mood of the moment.

Ryan's voice turned earnest. "I'm not. My wife has better instincts for judging people than I do. I guess it helps that she's a doc. Fair enough?"

"Dr. Ryan, I know *you* know. I know the FBI has been looking very discreetly at a few things out in the Seattle area."

"Is that so?"

Kris Hunter wasn't buying. "You don't keep secrets about this sort of thing, not if you have friends in the Bureau like I do, and not if one of the missing girls is the daughter of a police captain whose next-door neighbor is S-A-C of the FBI's Seattle Field Division. Do I need to go on?"

"Then why are you sitting on it?"

Kris Hunter's green eyes blazed at the National Security Advisor. "I'll tell you why, Dr. Ryan. I was raped in college. I thought the bastard was going to kill me. I looked at death. You don't forget that. If this story comes out the wrong way, that girl and maybe others like her could end up dead. You can recover from rape: I did. You can't recover from death."

"Thanks," Ryan said quietly. His eyes and his nod said even more. *Yes, I understand. And you know that I understand.*

"And he's the next head of that country's government." Kris Hunter's eyes were even more intense now. "He hates us, Dr. Ryan. I've interviewed him. He didn't want me because he found me attractive. He wanted me because he saw me as a blond-and-blue symbol. He's a rapist. He enjoys hurting people. You don't forget the look in the eyes once you've seen it. He's got that look. We need to watch out for this guy. You tell the President that."

"I will," Ryan said as he headed out the door.

The White House car was waiting just outside. Jack had something to think about as it headed for the Beltway.

"Softball," the Secret Service agent commented. "Except for after."

"How long you been doing this, Paul?"

"Fourteen fascinating years," Paul Robberton said, keeping an eye on things from the front seat. The driver was just a guy from the General Services Administration, but Jack rated a Secret Service bodyguard now.

"Fieldwork?"

"Counterfeiters. Never drew my weapon," Robberton added. "Had a few fair-sized cases."

"You can read people?"

Robberton laughed. "In this job, you'd better hope so, Dr. Ryan."

"Tell me about Kris Hunter."

"Smart and tough as nails. She's right: she was sexually assaulted in college, a serial rapist. She testified against the mutt. It was back when lawyers were a little . . . free with how they treated rape victims. You know — did you encourage the rat, stuff like that. It got ugly, but she rode it out and they convicted the bum. He bit the big one in prison, evidently said the wrong thing to an armed robber. Pity," Robberton concluded dryly.

"Pay attention to what she thinks, you're telling me."

"Yes, sir. She would have been a good cop. I know she's a pretty fair reporter."

"She's gathered in a lot of information," Ryan murmured. Not all of it good, not yet pulled together properly, and colored by her own life experiences, but sure as hell, she had sources. Jack looked at the passing scenery and tried to assemble the incomplete puzzle.

"Where to?" the driver asked.

"The house," Ryan said, drawing a surprised look from Robberton. In this case, "the house" didn't mean "home." "No, wait a minute." Ryan lifted his carphone. Fortunately he knew the number from memory.

"Hello?"

"Ed? Jack Ryan. You guys busy?"

"We are allowed Sunday off, Jack. The Caps play the Bruins this afternoon."

"Ten minutes."

"Fair enough." Ed Foley set the phone back in its place on the wall. "Ryan's coming over," he told his wife. *Damn it.*

Sunday was the one day they allowed themselves to sleep. Mary Pat was still in her housecoat, looking unusually frowzy. Without a word she left the morning paper and walked off toward the bathroom to fix her hair. There was a knock at the door fifteen minutes later.

"Overtime?" Ed asked at the door. Robberton came in with his guest.

"I had to do one of the morning shows." Jack checked his watch. "I'll be on in another twenty minutes or so."

"What gives?" Mary Pat entered the room, looking about normal for an American female on a Sunday morning.

"Business, honey," Ed answered. He led everyone to the basement recreation room.

"SANDALWOOD," Jack said when they got there. He could speak freely here. The house was swept for bugs every week. "Do Clark and Chavez have orders to get the girl out yet?"

"Nobody gave us the execute order," Ed Foley reminded him. "It's just about set up, but — "

"The order is given. Get the girl out now."

"Anything we need to know?" Mary Pat asked.

"I haven't been comfortable with this from the beginning. I think maybe we deliver a little message to her sugar daddy — and we do it early enough to get his attention."

"Yeah," Mr. Foley said. "I read the paper this morning, too. He isn't saying friendly stuff, but we are laying it on them pretty hard, y'know?"

"Sit down, Jack," Mary Pat said. "Can I get you coffee or anything?"

"No, thanks, MP." He looked up after taking a place on a worn couch. "A light just went off. Our friend Goto seems to be an odd duck."

"He does have his quirks," Ed agreed. "Not terribly bright, a lot of bombast once you get through the local brand of rhetoric, but not all that many ideas. I'm surprised he's getting the chance."

"Why?" Jack asked. The State Department material on Goto had been typically respectful of the foreign statesman.

"Like I said, he's no threat to win the Nobel in physics, okay? He's an *apparatchik*. Worked his way up the way politicos do. I'm sure he's kissed his share of asses along the way — "

"And to make up for that, he has some bad habits with women," MP added. "There's a lot of that over there. Our boy Nomuri sent in a lengthy dispatch on what he's seen." It was the youth and inexperience, the DDO knew. So many field officers on their first major assignment reported everything, as though writing a book or something. It was mainly the product of boredom.

"Over here he couldn't get elected dogcatcher," Ed noted with a chuckle.

Think so? Ryan thought, remembering Edward Kealty. On the other hand, it might just turn out to be something America could use in the right forum and under the right circumstances. Maybe the first time they met, if things went badly, President Durling could make a quiet reference to his former girlfriend, and the implications of his bad habits on Japanese-American relations . . .

"How's THISTLE doing?"

Mary Pat smiled as she rearranged the Sega games on the basement TV. This was where the kids told Mario and all the others what to do. "Two of the old members are gone, one retired and one on overseas assignment, in Malaysia, as I recall. The rest of them are contacted. If we ever want to — "

"Okay, let's think about what we want them to do for us."

"Why?" MP asked. "I don't mind, but why?"

"We're pushing them too hard. I've told the President that, but he's got political reasons for pushing, and he isn't going to stop. What we're doing is going to hurt their economy pretty bad, and now it turns out that their new PM has a real antipathy to us. If they decide to push back, I want to know before it happens."

"What *can* they do?" Ed Foley sat on his son's favorite Nintendo chair.

"I don't know that, either, but I want to find out. Give me a few days to figure out what our priorities are. Damn, I don't have a few days," Jack said next. "I have to prep for the Moscow trip."

"It takes time to set up anyway. We can get our boys the comm gear and stuff."

"Do it," Jack ordered. "Tell 'em they're in the spy business for-real."

"We need presidential authorization for that," Ed warned. Activating a spy network in a friendly country was not a trivial undertaking.

"I can deliver it for you." Ryan was sure that Durling wouldn't object. "And get the girl out, earliest opportunity."

"Debrief her where?" MP asked. "For that matter, what if she says no? You're not telling us to

337

kidnap her, are you?"

Ouch, Jack thought. "No, I don't suppose that's a good idea. They know how to be careful, don't they?"

"Clark does." Mary Pat knew from what he'd taught her and her husband at the Farm, all those years ago: *No matter where you are, it's enemy territory.* It was a good axiom for field spooks, but she'd always wondered where he'd picked it up.

Most of these people should have been at work, Clark thought — but so did they, and that was the problem, wasn't it? He'd seen his share of demonstrations, most of them expressing displeasure with his country. The ones in Iran had been especially unpleasant, knowing that there were Americans in the hands of people who thought "Death to America!" was a perfectly reasonable expression of concern with the foreign policy of his country. He'd been in the field, part of the rescue mission that had failed — the lowest point, Clark told himself, in a lengthy career. Being there to see it all fail, having to scramble out of the country, they were not good memories. This scene brought some of it back.

The American Embassy wasn't taking it too seriously. Business as usual, after a fashion, the Ambassador had all his people inside the embassy building, another example of Frank-Lloyd-Wright-Meets-the-Siegfried-Line design, this one located across from the Ocura Hotel. After all, this was a civilized country, wasn't it? The local police had an adequate guard force outside the fence, and as vociferous as the demonstrators were, they didn't seem the sort to attack the severe-looking cops arrayed around the building. But the people in the street were not kids, not students taking a day off from class — remarkably, the media never reported that so many of those student demonstrations coincided with semester finals, a worldwide phenomenon. In the main, these were people in their thirties and forties, and for that reason the chants weren't quite right. There was a remarkably soft edge on the expressions. Embarrassed to be here, somewhat confused by the event, more hurt than angry, he thought as Chavez snapped his pictures. But there were a lot of them. And there was a lot of hurt. They wanted to blame someone — the inevitable *them,* the *someone else* who always made the bad things happen. That perspective was not uniquely Japanese, was it?

As with everything in Japan, it was a highly organized affair. People, already formed into groups with leaders, had arrived mostly by crowded commuter trains, boarded buses at the stations, and been dropped off only a few blocks away. *Who chartered the buses?* Clark wondered. *Who printed the signs?* The wording on them was literate, which was odd, he was slow to realize. Though often well schooled in English, Japanese citizens messed up the foreign tongue as much as one might expect, especially on slogans. He'd seen one young man earlier in the day wearing a T-shirt with the legend "Inspire in Paradise," probably an exact representation of something in Japanese, and yet another example of the fact that no language translated precisely into another. But not these signs. The syntax was perfect in every case he saw, better, in fact, than he might have seen in an American demonstration. Wasn't that interesting?

Well, what the hell, he thought. *I'm a journalist, right?*

"Excuse me," John said, touching a middle-aged man on the arm.

"Yes?" The man turned in surprise. He was nicely turned out, wore a dark suit, and his tie was neatly knotted in the collar of his white shirt. There wasn't even much anger on his face, nor any emotion that might have built up from the spirit of the moment. "Who are you?"

"I am a Russian journalist, for the Interfax News Agency," Clark said, showing an ID card marked in Cyrillic.

"Ah." The man smiled and bowed politely. Clark returned the gesture correctly, drawing an approving look for his good manners.

"May I please ask you some questions?"

"Certainly." The man almost seemed relieved to be able to stop shouting. A few questions established that he was thirty-seven, married with one child, a salaryman for an auto company, currently laid off, and very upset with America at the moment — though not at all unhappy with Russia, he added quickly.

He's embarrassed by all this, John thought, thanking the man for his opinion.

"What was that all about?" Chavez asked quietly from behind his camera.

"*Russkiy,*" "Klerk" replied sharply.

"*Da, tovarisch.*"

"Follow me," "Ivan Sergeyevich" said next, entering the crowd. There was something else odd, he thought, something he wasn't quite getting. Ten meters into the crowd, it was clear. The people at the periphery of the mob were supervisory. The inside was composed of blue-collar workers, more casually dressed, people with less dignity to lose. Here the mood was different. The looks he got were angrier, and though they became more polite when he identified himself as a non-American, the suspicion was real, and the answers to his questions, when he got answers, were less circumspect than he'd received before.

In due course the people moved off, guided by their senior leadership and shepherded by police to another place, one that had a stage prepared. That was where things changed.

Hiroshi Goto took his time, making them wait a long time even for an environment in which patience was a thoroughly inculcated virtue. He walked to the podium with dignity, noting the presence of his official entourage, arrayed in seats on the back of the stage. The TV cameras were already in place, and it was just a matter of waiting for the crowd to pack in tight. But he waited longer than that, standing there, staring at them, with his inaction forcing them to pack in tighter, and the additional time merely added to the tension.

Clark could feel it now. Perhaps the strangeness of the event was inevitable. These were highly civilized people, members of a society so ordered as to seem alien, whose gentle manners and generous hospitality contrasted starkly with their suspicion of foreigners. Clark's fear started as a distant whisper, a warning that something was changing, though his trained powers of observation caught nothing at all beyond the usual bullshit of politicians all over the world. A man who'd faced combat in Vietnam and even more danger all over the world, he was again a stranger in a strange land, but his age and experience worked against him. Even the angry ones in the middle of the crowd hadn't been all that nasty — and, hell, did you expect a man to be happy when he's been laid off? So it wasn't all that big a deal — was it?

But the whispers grew louder as Goto took a sip of water, still making them wait, waving with his arms to draw his audience in closer, though this portion of the park was already jammed with people. How many? John wondered. Ten thousand? Fifteen? The crowd grew quiet of its own accord now, hardly making any noise at all. A few looks explained it. Those on the periphery were wearing armbands on their suit coats — damn, John swore at himself, that was their uniform of the day. The ordinary workers would automatically defer to those who dressed and acted like supervisors, and the armbands were herding them in closer. Perhaps there was some other sign that hushed them down, but if so Clark missed it.

Goto began talking quietly, which stilled the crowd completely. Heads automatically leaned forward a few inches in an instinctive effort to catch his words.

Damn, I wish we'd had more time to learn the language, both CIA officers thought. Ding was catching on, his superior saw, changing lenses and locking in on individual faces.

"They're getting tense," Chavez noted quietly in Russian as he read the expressions.

Clark could see it from their posture as Goto spoke on. He could catch only a few words, perhaps the odd phrase or two, basically the meaningless things that all languages had, the rhetorical devices a politician used to express humility and respect for his audience. The first roar of approval from the crowd came as a surprise, and the spectators were so tightly packed that they had to jostle one another to applaud. His gaze shifted to Goto. It was too far. Clark reached into Ding's tote bag, and selected a camera body to which he attached a long lens, the better to read the speaker's face as he accepted the approval of the people, waiting for their applause to subside before he moved on.

Really working the crowd, aren't we?

He tried to hide it, Clark saw, but he was a politician and though they had good acting skills, they fed off their audience even more hungrily than those who worked before cameras for a living. Goto's hand gestures picked up in intensity, and so did his voice.

Only ten or fifteen thousand people here. It's a test, isn't it? He's experimenting. Never had Clark felt more a foreigner than now. In so much of the world his features were ordinary, nondescript, seen and forgotten. In Iran, in the Soviet Union, in Berlin, he could fit in. Not here. Not now. Even worse, he wasn't getting it, not all of it, and that worried him.

Goto's voice grew louder. For the first time his fist slammed down on the podium, and the crowd responded with a roar. His diction became more rapid. The crowd was moving inward, and Clark watched the speaker's eyes notice it, welcome it. He wasn't smiling now, but his eyes swept the sea of faces, left and right, fixing occasionally in a single place, probably catching an individual, reading him for reactions, then passing to another to see if he was having the same effect on everyone. He had to be satisfied by what he saw. There was confidence in the voice now. He had them, had them all. By adjusting his speaking pace he could see their breathing change, see their eyes go wide. Clark lowered the camera to scan the crowd and saw the collective movement, the responses to the speaker's words.

Playing with them.

John brought the camera back up, using it like a gunsight. He focused in on the suit-clad bosses on the edges. Their faces were different now, not so much concerned with their duties as the speech. Again he cursed his inadequate language skills, not quite realizing that what he saw was even more important than what he might have understood. The next demonstration from the crowd was more than just loud. It was angry. Faces were . . . illuminated. Goto owned them now as he took them further and further down the path he had selected.

John touched Ding's arm. "Let's back off."

"Why?"

"Because it's getting dangerous here," Clark replied. He got a curious look.

"Nan ja?" Chavez replied in Japanese, smiling behind his camera.

"Turn around and look at the cops," "Klerk" ordered.

Ding did, and caught on instantly. The local police were ordinarily impressive in their demeanor. Perhaps samurai warriors had once had the same confidence. Though polite and professional, there was usually an underlying swagger to the way they moved. They *were* the law here, and knew it. Their uniforms were as severely clean and pressed as any Embassy Marine's, and the handguns that hung on the Sam Browne belts were just a status symbol, never necessary to use. But now these tough cops looked nervous. They shifted on their feet, exchanged looks among themselves. Hands rubbed against blue trousers to wipe off sweat. They sensed it, too, so clearly that nothing needed to be spoken. Some were even listening intently to Goto, but even those men looked worried. Whatever was happening, if it troubled the people who customarily kept the peace on these streets, then it was serious enough.

"Follow me." Clark scanned the area and selected a storefront. It turned out to be a small tailor shop. The CIA officers took their place close to the entrance. The sidewalk was otherwise deserted. Casual strollers had joined the crowd, and the police were drawing in also, spacing themselves evenly in a blue line. The two officers were essentially alone with open space around them, a very unusual state of affairs.

"You reading this the same way I am?" John asked. That he said it in English surprised Chavez.

"He's really working them up, isn't he?" A thoughtful pause. "You're right, Mr. C. It is getting a little tense."

Goto's voice carried clearly over the speaker system. The pitch was high now, almost shrill, and the crowd answered back in the way that crowds do.

"Ever see anything like this before?" It wasn't like the job they'd done in Romania.

A curt nod. "Teheran, 1979."

"I was in fifth grade."

"I was scared shitless," Clark said, remembering. Goto's hands were flying around now. Clark re-aimed the camera, and through the lens the man seemed transformed. He wasn't the same person who'd begun the speech. Only thirty minutes before he'd been tentative. Not now. If this had begun as an experiment, then it was a successful one. The final flourishes seemed stylized, but that was to be expected. His hands went up together, like a football official announcing a touchdown, but the fists, Clark saw, were clenched tight. Twenty yards away, a cop turned and looked at the two *gaijin*. There was concern on his face.

"Let's look at some coats for a while."

"I'm a thirty-six regular," Chavez replied lightly as he stowed his camera gear.

It turned out to be a nice shop, and it did have coats in Ding's size. It gave them a good excuse to browse. The clerk was attentive and polite, and at John's insistence Chavez ended up purchasing a business suit that fit so well it might have been made for him, dark gray and ordinary, overpriced and identical to what so many salarymen wore. They emerged to see the small park empty. A work crew was dismantling the stage. The TV crews were packing up their lights. All was normal except for a small knot of police officers who surrounded three people sitting on a curb. They were an American TV news crew, one of whom held a handkerchief to his face. Clark decided not to approach. He noted instead that the streets were not terribly littered — then he saw why. A cleanup crew was at work. Everything had been exquisitely planned. The demonstration had been about as spontaneous as the Super Bowl — but the game had gone even better than planned.

"Tell me what you think," Clark ordered as they walked along streets that were turning back to normal.

"You know this stuff better than I do — "

"Look, master's candidate, when I ask a fucking question I expect a fucking answer." Chavez almost stopped at the rebuke, not from insult, but from surprise. He'd never seen his partner rattled before. As a result, his reply was measured and reasoned.

"I think we just saw something important. I think he was playing with them. Last year for one of my courses we saw a Nazi film, a classic study in how demagogues do their thing. A woman directed it, and it reminded me — "

"*Triumph of the Will*, Leni Riefenstahl," Clark said. "Yeah, it's a classic, all right. By the way, you need a haircut."

"Huh?"

The training was really paying off, Major Sato knew without looking. On command, all four of the F-15 Eagles tripped their brakes and surged forward along the runway at Misawa. They'd flown more than three hundred hours in the past twelve months, a third of that in the past two alone, and now the pilots could risk a formation takeoff that would do an aerial-demonstration team proud. Except his flight of four was not the local version of the Blue Angels. They were members of the Third Air Wing. Sato had to concentrate, of course, to watch the airspeed indicator in his heads-up display before rotating the aircraft off the concrete. Gear came up on his command, and he knew without looking that his wingman was no more than four meters off his tip. It was dangerous to do it this way, but it was also good for morale. It thrilled the ground crew as much as it impressed the curious driving by on the highway. A thousand feet off the ground, wheels and flaps up, accelerating through four hundred knots, he allowed himself a turn of the head both ways. Sure enough. It was a clear day, the cold air devoid of humidity, still lit by the late-afternoon sun. Sato could see the southernmost Kuriles to his north, once part of his country, stolen by the Russians at the end of the Second World War, and ruggedly mountainous, like Hokkaido, the northernmost of the Home Islands . . . One thing at a time, the Major told himself.

"Come right," he ordered over the radio circuit, bringing the flight to a new course of zero-five-five. They were still climbing, gradually, to save fuel for the exercise.

It was hard to believe that this aircraft design was almost thirty years old. But that was just the shape and the concept. Since the American engineers at McDonnell-Douglas had dreamed it all up, the improvements had been such as to transform everything but the silhouette. Almost everything on Sato's personal bird was Japanese-made, even the engines. Especially the electronics.

There was a steady stream of aircraft in both directions, nearly all of them commercial wide-bodies carrying businessmen to or from Japan, from or to North America, on a well-defined commercial routing that traced down the Kurile chain, past the Kamchatka Peninsula, then on to the Aleutians. If anyone wondered how important his country was, Sato thought in the privacy of his cockpit, this was it. The low-angle sun reflected off the aluminum tail fins of numerous aircraft, and from his current altitude of thirty-seven thousand feet he could see them lined up — like cars on a highway, it seemed, yellow dots preceding white trails of vapor that stretched off into infinity. Then it was time to go to work.

The flight of four split into separated pairs left and right of the airliner track. The training mission for the evening was not complex, but vital nonetheless. Behind them, over a hundred miles to the southwest, an airborne early-warning aircraft was assuming its station just off the northeastern tip of Honshu. That was an E-767. Based on the twin-engine Boeing airliner (as the American E-3A was based on the far older 707 airframe), a rotating dome sat atop the converted wide-body. Just as his F-15J was an improved local version of an American fighter plane, so the E-767 was a vastly improved Japanese interpretation of another American invention. They'd never learn, Sato thought, his eyes scanning the horizon every few seconds before returning to the forward visual display. They'd invented so much, then given the unfulfilled rights to his countrymen for further perfection. In fact the Americans had played the same game with the Russians, improving every military weapon the latter had ever made, but in their arrogance ignoring the possibility that someone could do the same with their own magical systems. The radar on the E-767 was like nothing aloft. For that reason, the radar on the nose of his Eagle was switched off.

Simple in concept, the overall system was murderously complex in execution. The fighters had to know their precise position in three dimensions, and so did the AEW bird supporting them. Beyond that, radar pulses from the E-767 were precisely timed. The result was mere mathematics. Knowing the position of the transmitter, and their own position, the Eagles could then receive the radar reflections and plot the blips as though the data were generated by their own onboard radar systems. A meld of Soviet-developed bi-static radars and American airborne-radar technology, this system took the idea one step further. The AEW radar was frequency-agile, able to switch instantly from a longwave search mode to a shortwave fire-control mode, and it could actually guide air-to-air missiles fired by the fighters. The radar was also of sufficient size and power that it could, everyone thought, defeat stealth technology.

In only a few minutes it was clear that the system worked. The four air-to-air missiles on his wings were dummies, with no rocket motors. The seekerheads were real, however, and onboard instruments showed that the missiles were tracking inbound and outbound airliners even more clearly than they would have done from the Eagle's own radar. It was a first, a genuinely new piece of military technology. Only a few years earlier, Japan would probably have offered it for sale, almost certainly to America, because this sort of thing had value beyond gold. But the world had changed, and the Americans would probably have not seen the point in spending the money for it. Besides, Japan wasn't about to sell this to anyone. *Not now,* Sato thought. *Especially not now.*

Their hotel was not necessarily an especially good one. Though it catered to foreign visitors, the management recognized that not all *gaijin* were wealthy. The rooms were small, the corridors narrow, the ceilings low, and a breakfast of a glass of juice, a cup of coffee, and one croissant cost only fifty dollars instead of the hundred or so charged elsewhere. As the saying in the U.S. government went, Clark and Chavez were "living off the economy," frugally, as Russians would have to do. It wasn't all that great a hardship. Crowded and intense as Japan was, it was still far more comfortable than Africa had been, and the food, while strange, was exotic and interesting enough that the novelty hadn't quite worn off yet. Ding might have grumped about the desire for a burger, but to say such a thing, even in Russian, would have broken cover. Returning after an eventful day, Clark inserted the key card in the slot on the door and twisted the knob. He didn't even stop when he felt and removed the small piece of tape on the inside surface of the knob. Inside, he merely held it up to show Ding, then headed to the bathroom to flush it away.

Chavez looked around the room, wondering if it was bugged, wondering if this spook stuff was all it was cracked up to be. It certainly seemed so mysterious. The tape on the doorknob. Somebody wanted a meet. Nomuri. It had to be him. The fieldcraft was clever, Chavez told himself. Whoever had left the marker had just walked down the corridor, and his hand had probably just tapped the knob, a gesture that even a careful observer might have missed. Well, that was the idea.

"I'm going to head out for a drink," "Klerk" announced in Russian. *I'll see what's up.*

"Vanya, you do too much of that." *Fine.* It was his regular routine in any case.

"Some Russian you are," Clark said for the microphones, if any, as he went out the door.

How the hell, Chavez wondered, *am I supposed to get any studying done?* He'd been forced to leave his books in Korea — they were all in English, of course. He couldn't take notes or go over things. *If I have to lose time on my master's,* Ding thought, *I'm going to ask the Agency to reimburse me for the blown courses.*

The bar, half a block away, was most agreeable. The room was dark. The booths were small and separated by solid partitions, and a mirror behind the ranks of liquor bottles made countersurveillance easy. Better yet, the barstools were almost all taken, which forced him to look elsewhere after a show of disappointment. Clark strolled all the way to the back. Nomuri was waiting.

"Taking chances, aren't we?" John said over the music. A waitress came up. He ordered a vodka, neat, specifying a local one to save money.

"Orders from home," Nomuri told him. He stood without another word, clearly offended that a gaijin had taken the seat without asking permission first and left without even a polite bow.

Before the drink arrived, Clark reached under the table, finding a package taped in place there. In a

350

moment it was in his lap, and would soon find its way inside his waistband behind his back. Clark always bought his working clothes in a full cut — the Russian disguise helped even more — and his shoulders provided ample overhang for hiding things, yet another reason, he thought, to stay in shape.

The drink arrived, and he took his time knocking it back, looking at the bar mirror and searching the reflections for faces that might have appeared in his memory before. It was a never-ending drill, and, tiring as it was, one he'd learned the hard way not to ignore. He checked his watch twice, both times unobtrusively, then a third time immediately before standing, leaving behind just enough cash to pay for the drink. Russians weren't known as big tippers.

The street was busy, even in the late evening. Clark had established the routine nightcap over the past week, and on every other night he would roam the local shops. This evening he selected a bookstore first, one with long, irregular rows. The Japanese were a literate people. The shop always had people in it. He browsed around, selecting a copy of *The Economist*, then wandered more, aimlessly toward the back, where he saw a few men eyeing the manga racks. Taller than they, he stood right behind a few, close but not too close, keeping his hands in front of him, shielded by his back. After five or so minutes he made his way to the front and paid for the magazine, which the clerk politely bagged for him. The next stop was an electronics store, where he looked at some CD players. This time he bumped into two people, each time politely asking their pardon, a phrase which he'd troubled himself to learn before anything else at Monterey. After that he headed back out onto the street and back to the hotel, wondering how much of the preceding fifteen minutes had been a total waste of time. *None of it*, Clark told himself. *Not a single second*.

In the room he tossed Ding the magazine. It drew

a look of its own before the younger man spoke. "Don't they have anything in Russian?"

"It's good coverage of the difficulties between this country and America. Read and learn. Improve your language skills."

Great, just fucking great, Chavez thought, reading the words for their real meaning. *We've been activated, for-real.* He'd never finish the master's now, Ding grumped. Maybe they just didn't want to jack his salary up, as CIA regulations specified for a graduate degree.

Clark had other things to do. The package Nomuri had transferred held a computer disk and a device that attached to a laptop. He switched it on, then inserted the disk into the slot. The file he opened contained only three sentences, and seconds after reading it, Clark had erased the disk. Next he started composing what to all intents and purposes was a news dispatch.

The computer was a Russian-language version of a popular Japanese model, with all the additional Cyrillic letters, and the hard part for Clark was that although he read and spoke Russian like a native, he was used to typing (badly enough) in English. The Russian-style keyboard drove him crazy, and he sometimes wondered if someone would ever pick up on this small chink in his cover armor. It took over an hour to type up the news article, and another thirty to do the more important part. He saved both items to the hard drive, then turned the machine off. Flipping it over, he removed the modem from its modular port and replaced it with the new one Nomuri had brought.

"What time is it in Moscow?" he asked tiredly.

"Same as always, six hours behind us, remember?"

"I'm going to send it to Washington, too."

"Fine," "Chekov" grunted. "I'm sure they'll love it, Ivan Sergeyevich."

Clark attached the phone line to the back of his computer and used the latter to dial up the fiberoptic line to Moscow. Transferring the report took less than a minute. He repeated the operation for the Interfax office in the American capital. It was pretty slick, John thought. The moment before the modem at one end linked up with the modem at the other sounded just like static — which it was. The mating signal was just a rough hiss unless you had a special chip, and he never called anyone but Russian press-agency offices. That the office in Washington might be tapped by the FBI was something else again. Finished, he kept one file and erased the other. Another day done, serving his country. Clark brushed his teeth before collapsing into his single bed.

"That was a fine speech, Goto-san." Yamata poured a generous amount of saké into an exquisite porcelain cup. "You made things so clear."

"Did you see how they responded to me!" The little man was bubbling now, his enthusiasm making his body swell before his host's eyes.

"And tomorrow you will have your cabinet, and the day after you will have a new office, Hiroshi."

"You're certain?"

A nod and a smile that conveyed true respect. "Of course I am. My colleagues and I have spoken with our friends, and they have come to agree with us that you are the only man suited to save our country."

"When will it begin?" Goto asked, suddenly sobered by the words, remembering exactly what his ascension would mean.

"When the people are with us."

"Are you sure we can — "

"Yes, I am sure." Yamata paused. "There is one problem, however."

"What is that?"

"Your lady friend, Hiroshi. If the knowledge be-

353

comes public that you have an American mistress, it compromises you. We cannot afford that," Yamata explained patiently. "I hope you will understand."

"Kimba is a most pleasant diversion for me," Goto objected politely.

"I have no doubt of it, but the Prime Minister can have his choice of diversions, and in any case we will be busy in the next month." The amusing part was that he could build up the man on one hand and reduce him on the other, just as easily as he manipulated a child. And yet there was something disturbing about it all. More than one thing. How much had he told the girl? And what to do with her now?

"Poor thing, to send her home now, she will never know happiness again."

"Undoubtedly true, but it must be done, my friend. Let me handle it for you? Better it should be done quietly, discreetly. You are on the television every day now. You cannot be seen to frequent that area as a private citizen would. There is too great a danger."

The man about to be Prime Minister looked down, sipping his drink, so transparently measuring his personal pleasure against his duties to his country, surprising Yamata yet again — but no, not really. Goto was Goto, and he'd been chosen for his elevation as much — more — for his weaknesses than his strengths.

"*Hai,*" he said after reflection. "Please see to it."

"I know what to do," Yamata assured him.

354

15

A Damned, Foolish Thing

Behind Ryan's desk was a gadget called a STU-6. The acronym probably meant "secure telephone unit," but he had never troubled himself to find out. It was about two feet square, and contained in a nicely made oak cabinet handcrafted by the inmates of a federal prison. Inside were a half dozen green circuit-boards, populated with various chips whose function was to scramble and unscramble telephone signals. Having one of these in the office was one of the better government status symbols.

"Yeah," Jack said, reaching back for the receiver.

"MP here. Something interesting came in. SANDALWOOD," Mrs. Foley said, her voice distinct on the digital line. "Flip on your fax?"

"Go ahead and send it." The STU-6 did that, too, fulfilling the function with a simple phone line that headed to Ryan's facsimile printer. "Did you get the word to them — "

"Yes, we did."

"Okay, wait a minute . . ." Jack took the first page and started reading it. "This is Clark?" he asked.

"Correct. That's why I'm fast-tracking it over to you. You know the guy as well as I do."

"I saw the TV coverage. CNN says their crew got

a little roughed up. . . ." Ryan worked his way down the first page.

"Somebody bounced a soda can off the producer's head. Nothing more serious than a headache, but it's the first time anything like that has happened over there — that Ed and I remember, anyway."

"Goddamn it!" Ryan said next.

"I thought you'd like that part."

"Thanks for the heads-up, Mary Pat."

"Glad to help." The line went dead.

Ryan took his time. His temper, he knew, was always his greatest enemy. He decided to give himself a moment to stand and head out of his office to the nearest water cooler, which was tucked in his secretary's office. Foggy Bottom, he'd heard, had once been a nice marsh before some fool had decided to drain it. What a pity the Sierra Club hadn't been around then to force an environmental-impact statement. They were so good at obstructing things, and didn't much care whether the things they halted were useful or not, and as a result they occasionally did some public good. But not this time, Ryan told himself, sitting back down. Then he lifted the STU-6 and punched the speed-dial button for State.

"Good morning, Mr. Secretary," the National Security Advisor said pleasantly. "What's the story about the demonstration outside the Tokyo Embassy yesterday?"

"You saw CNN the same as I did, I'm sure," Hanson replied, as though it were not the function of an American embassy mission to provide better information than any citizen could get with his oatmeal.

"Yes, I did, as a matter of fact, but I would really like to have the opinion of embassy personnel, like maybe the political officer, maybe even the DCM," Ryan said, allowing a little of his irritation to show. Ambassador Chuck Whiting was a recent political appointee, a former senator who had then become a

Washington lawyer, and had actually represented some Japanese business interests, but the Deputy Chief of Mission was an experienced man and a Japan specialist who knew the culture.

"Walt decided to keep his people in. He didn't want to provoke anything. I'm not going to fault him for that."

"That may be, but I have in my hand an eyewitness report from an experienced field officer who — "

"I have it, too, Ryan. It looks alarmist to me. Who is this guy?"

"As I said, an experienced field officer."

"Umm-hmm, I see he knows Iran." Ryan could hear the crackle of paper over the phone. "That makes him a spook. I guess that colored his thinking a little. How much experience in Japan?"

"Not much, but — "

"There you are. Alarmist, as I said. You want me to follow up on it, though?"

"Yes, Mr. Secretary."

"Okay, I'll call Walt. Anything else? I'm prepping for Moscow, too."

"Please, let's light a fire under them?"

"Fine, Ryan. I'll make sure that gets through. Remember, it's already nighttime over there, okay?"

"Fine." Ryan replaced the phone in its cradle and swore. *Mustn't wake up the Ambassador.* He had several options. Typically, he took the most direct. He lifted his desk phone and punched the button for the President's personal secretary.

"I need to talk to the boss for a few."

"Thirty minutes?"

"That'll be fine, thank you."

The delay was explained by a ceremony in the East Room that Ryan had had on his daily schedule sheet, too, but had forgotten about. It was just too big for the Oval Office, which suited the secretarial staff. Ten

TV cameras and a good hundred or so journalists watched as Roger Durling affixed his signature to the Trade Reform Act. The nature of the legislation demanded a number of pens, one for each letter of his name, which made the signing a lengthy and haphazard process. The first went, naturally enough, to Al Trent, who had authored the bill. The rest went to committee chairmen in the House and Senate, and also to selected minority members without whom the bill could not possibly have sailed through Congress as rapidly as it had. There was the usual applause, the usual handshakes, and a new entry was made in the United States Code, Annotated. The Trade Reform Act was now federal law.

One of the TV crews was from NHK. Their faces were glum. Next they would drive to the Commerce Department to interview the legal team that was analyzing Japanese laws and procedures for rapid duplication. It would be an unusually educational experience for the foreign journalists.

Like most senior government officials, Chris Cook had a TV in his office. He watched the signing on C-SPAN and, with it, saw the indefinite postponement of his entry into the "private" sector. It made him uneasy to accept outside payments while still a federal employee. They were going into a safe bank account, but it was illegal, wasn't it? He didn't really mean to break the law. Amity between America and Japan was important to him. It was now breaking down, and unless it could be rapidly restored, his career would stagnate and effectively end despite all the promise it had shown for so many years. And he needed the money. He had a dinner with Seiji scheduled for tonight. They had to discuss ways of making things right again, the Deputy Assistant Secretary of State told himself, returning to his work.

★ ★ ★

On Massachusetts Avenue, Seiji Nagumo was watching the same TV channel and was just as unhappy. Nothing would ever be the same again, he thought. Perhaps the new government . . . no, Goto was a demagogic fool. His posturing and blustering would only make things worse. The sort of action needed was . . . what?

For the first time in his career, Nagumo had no idea what that might be. Diplomacy had failed. Lobbying had failed. Even espionage, if one could call it that, had failed. Espionage? Was that the proper term? Well, technically, yes, he admitted. He was now paying money for information. Cook and others. At least they were well placed, at least he'd been able to warn his government, at least the Foreign Ministry knew that he'd done his best, as much as any man could do — more, really. And he'd keep trying, working through Cook to affect the way the Americans interpreted Japanese laws. But the Americans had a term for it: rearranging the deck chairs on the *Titanic*.

Reflection only made it worse, and soon the only word for what he felt was anguish. His countrymen would suffer, America, the world. All because of one traffic accident that had killed six inconsequential people. It was madness.

Madness or not, it was how the world worked. A messenger came into his office and handed over a sealed envelope for which Nagumo had to sign. He waited until his office door closed again before he opened it.

The cover sheet told him much. The dispatch was eyes-only. Even the Ambassador would never learn of what he was now reading. The instructions on the next two pages made his hand shake.

Nagumo remembered his history. Franz Ferdinand, June 28, 1914, in the cursed city of Sarajevo, a titled nonentity, a man of such little consequence that no

359

one of importance had troubled himself to attend the funeral, but his murder had been the "damned, foolish thing" to start the first war to span the globe. In this case the inconsequential people had been a police officer and some females.

And on such trivialities, *this* would happen? Nagumo went very pale, but he had no choice in the matter, because his life was driven by the same forces that turned the world on its axis.

Exercise DATELINE PARTNERS began at the scheduled time. Like most such war games, it was a combination of free play and strict rules. The size of the Pacific Ocean made for ample room, and the game would be played between Marcus Island, a Japanese possession, and Midway. The idea was to simulate a conflict between the U.S. Navy and a smaller but modern frigate force, played by the Japanese Navy. The odds were heavily loaded against the latter, but not completely so. Marcus Island — called Minami Tori-shima on their charts — was, for the purposes of the exercise, deemed to be a continental land mass. In fact the atoll consisted of a mere 740 acres, scarcely large enough for a meteorological station, a small fishing colony, and a single runway, from which would fly a trio of P-3C patrol aircraft. These could be administratively "shot down" by American fighters, but would return to life the next day. The commercial fishermen who also maintained a station on the island to harvest squid, kelp, and the occasional swordfish for their home markets welcomed the increased activity. The airmen had brought a cargo of beer which they would exchange for the fresh catch in what had become a friendly tradition.

Two of the three Orions lifted off before dawn, angling north and south, to search for the American carrier fleet. Their crewmen, aware of the trade problems between the two countries, concentrated on their mission. It was not an unknown mission to the Japanese Navy, after all. Their forefathers had done the same thing two generations before, in Kawasaki H8K2 flying boats — the same contractor that had built these Orions — to search for the marauding carriers commanded in turns by Halsey and Spruance. Many of the tactics they would employ today were based on lessons learned from that earlier conflict. The P-3Cs themselves were Japanese models of an American design that had begun life as turboprop airliners, then matured into rugged, powerful, if somewhat slow maritime patrol aircraft. As with most Japanese military aircraft, the American products had stopped at the basic profile. The power plants had since been developed and improved, giving the Orions a cruising speed boosted to 350 knots. The internal electronics were particularly good, especially the sensors designed to detect emissions from ships and aircraft. That was their mission for the moment, to fly out in large pie-shaped segments, listening for radar and radio signals that would announce the presence of American ships and aircraft. Reconnaissance: Find the enemy. That was the mission, and from press accounts and conversations with family members who worked in their country's economy, thinking of Americans as the enemy didn't even come all that hard.

Aboard *John Stennis*, Captain Sanchez watched the dawn patrol — a term beloved of all fighter pilots — shoot off the cats to establish an outer Combat Air Patrol. With the Tomcats off, next in line to go were the S-3 Vikings, anti-submarine birds with long legs to sweep the area the fleet would transit this day. Last went the Prowlers, the electronic bird-dogs, designed to detect and jam enemy radar signals. It was always exciting to watch from his perch at Pri-Fly. Almost as good as shooting off himself, but he was the CAG, and was supposed to command rather than merely lead his men now. His Alpha Strike force of Hornets was spotted on the deck, loaded with blue practice missiles for the discovery of the enemy battle force, the pilots sitting in their squadron ready rooms, mainly reading magazines or trading jokes because they were already briefed in on the mission.

Admiral Sato watched his flagship disengage from the oiler *Homana*, one of four supporting his fleet. The captain of the fleet-support ship lofted his cap and waved encouragement. Sato returned the gesture as the oiler put her rudder over to depart the battle force. He now had enough fuel to drive his ships hard. The contest was an interesting one, essentially guile against brute force, not an unusual situation for his country's navy, and for this task he would employ traditional Japanese tactics. His sixteen surface warships were split into three groups, one of eight and two of four, widely separated. Similar to Yamamoto's plan for the Battle of Midway, his operational concept was far more practical now, because with GPS navigation their position was always known, and with satellite communications links they could exchange messages in relative security. The Americans probably expected that he would keep his ships close to his "homeland," but he would not. He would take the issue to the enemy as best he could, since passive defense was not the way of his people, a fact that the Americans had learned and then forgotten, hadn't they? That was an amusing thought.

"Yes, Jack?" The President was in another good mood, flush from signing a new law which, he hoped, would solve a major problem for his country, and by the by make his reelection chances look rosy indeed. It would be a shame to ruin his day, Ryan thought, but his job wasn't political, at least not that kind of political.

"You might want to look at this." He handed the fax sheet over without sitting down.

"Our friend Clark again?" Durling asked, leaning back in his chair and reaching for his reading glasses. He had to use them for normal correspondence, though his speeches and TelePrompTers had large-enough type to protect his presidential vanity.

"I presume State has seen this. What do they say?" the President asked when he finished it.

"Hanson calls it alarmist," Jack reported. "But the ambassador kept his troops inside for the event because he didn't want to cause an 'incident.' This is the only eyewitness report we have aside from the TV people."

"I haven't read the text of his speech yet. I have it here somewhere." Durling gestured at his desk.

"Might be a good idea to do so. I just did."

The President nodded. "And what else? I know there's more."

"And I told Mary Pat to activate THISTLE." He explained briefly what that was.

"You really should get my permission first."

"That's what I'm here for, sir. You know a little about Clark. He doesn't scare easily. THISTLE includes a couple of people in their Foreign Ministry and MITI. I think we want to know what they're thinking."

"They're not enemies," Durling observed.

"Probably not," Jack conceded, for the first time allowing for the fact that the proper response wasn't *certainly not*, a fact the President noted with a raised eyebrow. "We still need to know, sir. That's my recommendation."

"Okay. Approved. What else?"

"I also told her to get Kimberly Norton out, soonest. It ought to happen in the next twenty-four hours."

"Sending Goto a message, are we?"

"That's part of it. Simpler version is, we know she's there, and she's an American citizen and — "

"And I have kids, too. Also approved. Save the piety for church, Jack," Durling ordered with a smile. "How will it go?"

"If she agrees to come out, they drive her to the airport and fly her to Seoul. They have clothes for her, and a fresh passport, and first-class tickets for her and an escort she'll meet at the terminal. She changes planes to a KAL flight to New York. We check her into a hotel, settle her down, and debrief. We fly her parents in from Seattle, and explain to them that it's to be kept quiet. The girl will probably need psychological counseling — I mean, really need it. That will help with the low profile. The FBI will assist on that one. Her father's a cop. He should play along." And that was neat and tidy enough for anyone, wasn't it?

The President gave Ryan a nod. "So then, what do we tell Goto about it?"

"That's your decision, Mr. President. I would recommend nothing at the moment. Let's debrief the girl first. Say a week or so, and then the Ambassador will check in for the usual courtesy visit to present your greetings to a new head of government — "

"And ask him politely how his countrymen will react if Mr. Nationalist turned out to be dipping his wick in a round-eye. Then we extend a small olive branch, right?" Durling caught on quickly enough, Jack thought.

"That's my recommendation, sir."

"A very small one," the President noted dryly.

"Just one olive on it for the moment," Ryan conceded.

"Approved," Durling said again, adding more sharply, "Next are you going to suggest what olive branch to offer?"

"No, sir. Have I pushed too much?" Jack asked,

realizing just how far he had gone.

Durling almost apologized for speaking crossly to his National Security Advisor. "You know, Bob was right about you."

"Excuse me?"

"Bob Fowler," Durling said, waving Ryan into a chair. "You ticked me off pretty bad when I brought you in the first time."

"Sir, I was a burn-out then, remember?" Jack did. The nightmares hadn't stopped yet. He saw himself, sitting there in the National Military Command Center, telling people what they had to do, but in the nightmare they couldn't see or hear him, as the Hot Line message kept coming in, taking his country closer and closer to the war he had in fact probably stopped. The full story on that had never been written in the open media. Just as well. Everyone who had been there knew.

"I didn't understand that then. Anyway" — Durling raised his arms to stretch — "when we dropped the ball last summer, Bob and I talked some things over up at Camp David. He recommended you for the job. Surprised?" the President asked with a twisty grin.

"Very," Jack admitted quietly. Arnie van Damm had never told him that story. Ryan wondered why.

"He said you're one levelheaded son of a bitch when the crap hits the fan. He also said you were an opinionated, pushy son of a bitch the rest of the time. Good judge of character, Bob Fowler." Durling gave him a moment to absorb that. "You're a good man in a storm, Jack. Do us both a favor and remember that this is as far as you can act without my approval. You've already had another pissing contest with Brett, haven't you?"

"Yes, sir." Jack bobbed his head like a schoolboy. "Just a little one."

"Don't push so hard. He's my Secretary of State."

"I understand, sir."

"All ready for Moscow?"

"Cathy is really looking forward to it," Ryan answered, pleased with the change of subject and noting that Durling had handled him very well indeed.

"It'll be good to see her again. Anne really likes her. Anything else?"

"Not right now."

"Jack, thanks for the heads-up," Durling said to conclude the meeting on a positive note.

Ryan left the office by the west door, walking past the (Teddy) Roosevelt Room and heading toward his office. Ed Kealty was in again, he saw, working in his office. He wondered when that one would break, realizing that the President, however pleased with the events of this day, still had that scandal hanging over him. *That sword again,* Jack thought. He had gone a little close to the edge this time, and it was his mission to make the President's job easier, not harder. There was more to it, after all, than foreign entanglements — and politics, something he had tried to keep at arm's length for years, was as real as anything else.

Fowler? Damn.

It would be a safe time to do it, they knew. Goto was giving a speech on TV tonight, his maiden broadcast as Prime Minister, and whatever he said, it guaranteed that he wouldn't be with his young mistress that evening. Perhaps the night's mission would be an interesting and useful counterpoint to what the politician had to say, a reply, of sorts, from America. They both liked that idea.

John Clark and Ding Chavez were walking along the block at the proper time, looking across the crowded street at the nondescript building. They always seemed that way, John thought. Maybe someone would tumble to the idea that a garish façade or an

366

office tower was actually better camouflage, or maybe not. More likely it was boredom talking again. A man came out and removed his sunglasses with his left hand. He smoothed his hair, stroking the back of his head twice with his left hand, then moved off. Nomuri had never ascertained the location of Kim Norton's room. Moving in that close was a risk, but the orders had come to take that risk, and now, having given the signal, he walked off toward where he'd left his car. Ten seconds later Nomuri was lost in the crowded sidewalk, Clark saw. He could do that. He had the right height and looks. So did Ding. With his size, glossy black hair, and complexion, Chavez at a distance could almost blend in here. The haircut he'd imposed on his partner helped even more. From behind he was just another person on the sidewalk. That was useful, Clark told himself, feeling ever more conspicuous, especially at a moment like this.

"Showtime," Ding breathed. Both men crossed the street as unobtrusively as possible.

Clark was dressed as a businessman, but rarely had he felt more naked. Neither he nor Ding had so much as a folding pocket knife. Though both men were well skilled in unarmed combat, both had enough experience to prefer arms — the better to keep one's enemies at a distance.

Luck smiled on them. There was no one in the tiny lobby of the building to note their presence. The two men took the stairs up. Second floor, all the way back, left side.

Nomuri had done his job well. The corridor was empty. Clark had the lead, and headed quickly down the dimly lit passage. The lock was a simple one. With Ding standing guard, he took out his burglar tools and defeated it, then opened the door quickly. They were already inside before they realized that the mission was a bust.

Kimberly Norton was dead. She lay on a futon,

wearing a medium-expensive silk kimono that was bunched just below the knees, exposing her lower legs. Postmortem lividity was beginning to color the underside of her body as gravity drew her blood downward. Soon the top of the body would be the color of ash, and the lower regions would be maroon. Death was so cruel, John thought. It wasn't enough that it stole life. It also stole whatever beauty the victim had once possessed. She'd been pretty — well, that was the point, wasn't it? John checked the body against the photograph, a passing resemblance to his younger daughter, Patsy. He handed the picture to Ding. He wondered if the lad would make the same connection.

"It's her."

"Concur, John," Chavez observed huskily. "It's her." Pause. "Shit," he concluded quietly, examining the face for a long moment that made his face twist with anger. *So,* Clark thought, *he sees it too.*

"Got a camera?"

"Yeah." Ding pulled a compact 35mm out of his pants pocket. "Play cop?"

"That's right."

Clark stooped down to examine the body. It was frustrating. He wasn't a pathologist, and though he had much knowledge of death, more knowledge still was needed to do this right. There . . . in the vein on the top of her foot, a single indentation. Not much more than that. So she'd been on drugs? If so, she'd been a careful user, John thought. She'd always cleaned the needle and . . . He looked around the room. There. A bottle of alcohol and a plastic bag of cotton swabs, and a bag of plastic syringes.

"I don't see any other needle marks."

"They don't always show, man," Chavez observed.

Clark sighed and untied the kimono, opening it. She'd been wearing nothing under it.

368

"Fuck!" Chavez rasped. There was fluid inside her thighs.

"That's a singularly unsuitable thing to say," Clark whispered back. It was as close as he'd come to losing his temper in many years. *"Take your pictures."*

Ding didn't answer. The camera flashed and whirred away. He recorded the scene as a forensic photographer might have done. Clark then started to rearrange the kimono, uselessly giving the girl back whatever dignity that death and men had failed to rob from her.

"Wait a minute . . . left hand."

Clark examined it. One nail was broken. All the others were medium-long, evenly coated with a neutral polish. He examined the others. There was something under them.

"Scratched somebody?" Clark asked.

"See anyplace she scratched herself, Mr. C?" Ding asked.

"No."

"Then she wasn't alone when it happened, man. Check her ankles again," Chavez said urgently.

On the left one, the foot with the puncture, the underside of the ankle revealed bruises almost concealed by the building lividity. Chavez shot his last frame.

"I thought so."

"Tell me why later. We're out of here," John said, standing.

Within less than a minute they were out the back door, down the meandering alley, and back on a main thoroughfare to wait for their car.

"That was close," Chavez observed as the police car pulled up to Number 18. There was a TV crew fifteen seconds behind.

"Don't you just love it? They're going to tie up everything real nice and neat . . . What is it, Ding?"

"Ain't right, Mr. C. Supposed to look like an OD, right?"

"Yeah, why?"

"You OD on smack, man, it just stops. Boom, bye-bye. I seen a guy go out like that back in the old days, never got the sticker out of his arm, okay? Heart stops, lungs stop, gone. You don't get up and set the needle down and then lay back down, okay? Bruises on the leg. Somebody stuck her. She was murdered, John. And probably she was raped, too."

"I saw the paraphernalia. All U.S.-made. Nice setup. They close the case, blame the girl and her family, give their own people an object lesson." Clark looked over as the car pulled around the corner. "Good eye, Ding."

"Thanks, boss." Chavez fell silent again, his anger building now that he had nothing to do but think it over. "You know, I'd really like to meet that guy."

"We won't."

Time for a little perverse fantasy: "I know, but I used to be a Ninja, remember? It might be real fun, especially barehanded."

"That just breaks bones, pretty often your own bones."

"I'd like to see his eyes when it happens."

"So put a good scope on the rifle," Clark advised.

"True," Chavez conceded. "What kind of person gets off on that, Mr. C?"

"One sick motherfucker, Domingo. I met a few, once."

Just before they got into the car, Ding's black eyes locked on Clark.

"Maybe I will meet this one personally, John. *El fado* can play tricks. Funny ones."

"Where is she?" Nomuri asked from behind the wheel.

"Drive," Clark told him.

"You should have heard the speech," Chet said,

moving up the street and wondering what had gone wrong.

"The girl's dead," Ryan told the President barely two hours later, 1:00 P.M., Washington time.

"Natural causes?" Durling asked.

"Drug overdose, probably not self-administered. They have photos. We ought to have them in thirty-six hours. Our guys just got clear in time. The Japanese police showed up pretty fast."

"Wait a minute. Back up. You're saying murder?"

"That's what our people think, yes, Mr. President."

"Do they know enough to make that evaluation?"

Ryan took his seat and decided that he had to explain a little bit. "Sir, our senior officer knows a few things about the subject, yes."

"That was nicely phrased," the President noted dryly. "I don't want to know any more about that subject, do I?"

"No reason for it right now, sir, no."

"Goto?"

"Possibly one of his people. Actually the best indicator will be how their police report it. If anything they tell us is at variance with what we've learned from our own people, then we'll know that somebody played with the data, and not all that many people have the ability to order changes in police reports." Jack paused for a moment. "Sir, I've had another independent evaluation of the man's character." He went on to repeat Kris Hunter's story.

"You're telling me that you believe he had this young girl killed, and will use his police to cover it up? And you already knew he likes that sort of thing?" Durling flushed. "You wanted me to extend this bastard an olive branch? What the hell's the matter with you?"

Jack took a deep breath. "Okay, yes, Mr. President,

I had that coming. The question is, now what do we do?"

Durling's face changed. "You didn't deserve that, sorry."

"Actually I do deserve it, Mr. President. I could have told Mary Pat to get her out some time ago — but I didn't," Ryan observed bleakly. "I didn't see this one coming."

"We never do, Jack. Now what?"

"We can't tell the legal attaché at the embassy because we don't 'know' about this yet, but I think we prep the FBI to check things out after we're officially notified. I can call Dan Murray about that."

"Shaw's designated hitter?"

Ryan nodded. "Dan and I go back a ways. For the political side, I'm not sure. The transcript of his TV speech just came in. Before you read it, well, you need to know what sort of fellow we're dealing with."

"Tell me, how many common *bastards* like that run countries?"

"You know that better than I do, sir." Jack thought about that for a moment. "It's not entirely a bad thing. People like that are weak, Mr. President. Cowards, when you get down to it. If you have to have enemies, better that they have weaknesses."

He might make a state visit, Durling thought. *We might have to put him up at Blair House, right across the street. Throw a state dinner: we'll walk out into the East Room and make pretty speeches, and toast each other, and shake hands as though we're bosom buddies. Be damned to that!* He lifted the folder with Goto's speech and skimmed through it.

"That son of a bitch! '*America will have to understand,*' my ass!"

"Anger, Mr. President, isn't an effective way of dealing with problems."

"You're right," Durling admitted. He was silent

for a moment, then he smiled in a crooked way. "You're the one with the hot temper, as I recall."

Ryan nodded. "I've been accused of that, yes, sir."

"Well, that's two big ones we have to deal with when we get back from Moscow."

"Three, Mr. President. We need to decide what to do about India and Sri Lanka." Jack could see from the look on Durling's face that the President had allowed himself to forget about that one.

Durling had allowed himself to semiforget another problem as well.

"How much *longer* will I have to wait?" Ms. Linders demanded.

Murray could see her pain even more clearly than he heard it. How did you explain this to people? Already the victim of a vile crime, she'd gotten it out in the open, baring her soul for all manner of strangers. The process hadn't been fun for anyone, but least of all for her. Murray was a skilled and experienced investigator. He knew how to console, encourage, chivvy information out of people. He'd been the first FBI agent to listen to her story, in the process becoming as much a part of her mental-health team as Dr. Golden. After that had come another pair of agents, a man and a woman who specialized more closely in cases of this type. After them had come two separate psychiatrists, whose questioning had necessarily been somewhat adversarial, both to establish finally that her story was true in all details and to give her a taste of the hostility she would encounter.

Along the way, Murray realized, Barbara Linders had become even more of a victim than she'd been before. She'd built her self up, first, to reveal herself to Clarice, then again to do the same with Murray, then again, and yet once more still. Now she looked forward to the worst ordeal of all, for some of the

373

members of the Judiciary Committee were allies of Ed Kealty, and some would take it upon themselves to hammer the witness hard either to curry favor with the cameras or to demonstrate their impartiality and professionalism as lawyers. Barbara knew that. Murray had himself walked her through the expected ordeal, even hitting her with the most awful of questions — always preceded with as gentle a preamble as possible, like, "One of the things you can expect to be asked is — "

It took its toll, and a heavy toll at that. Barbara — they were too close now for him to think of her as Ms. Linders — had shown all the courage one could expect of a crime victim and more besides. But courage was not something one picked out of the air. It was something like a bank account. You could withdraw only so much before it was necessary to stop, to take the time to make new deposits. Just the waiting, the not knowing when she would have to take her seat in the committee room and make her opening statement in front of bright TV lights, the certainty that she would have to bare her soul for the entire world . . . it was like a robber coming into the bank night after night to steal from her hard-won accumulation of inner resolve.

It was hard enough for Murray. He had built his case, had the prosecutor lined up, but he was the one close to her. It was *his* mission, Murray told himself, to show this lady that men were not like Ed Kealty, that a man was as repulsed by such acts as women were. He was her knight-errant. The disgrace and ultimate imprisonment of that criminal was now his mission in life even more than it was hers.

"Barb, you have to hang in there, kid. We're going to get this bastard, but we can't do it the right way unless . . ." He mouthed the words, putting conviction he didn't feel into them. Since when did politics enter into a criminal case? The law had been violated. They had their witnesses, their physical evidence, but now they were stuck in a holding pattern that was as damaging to this victim as any defense lawyer might be.

"It's taking too long!"

"Two more weeks, maybe three, and we go to bat, Barb."

"Look, I *know* something is happening, okay? You think I'm dumb? He's not out making speeches and opening bridges and stuff now, is he? Somebody told him and he's building up his case, isn't he?"

"I think what's happening is that the President is deliberately holding him in close so that when this does break, he won't be able to fall back on a high public profile as a defense. The President is on our side, Barb. I've briefed him in on this case myself, and he said, 'A criminal is a criminal,' and that's *exactly* what he should have said."

Her eyes came up to meet his. They were moist and desperate. "I'm coming apart, Dan."

"No, Barb, you're not," Murray lied. "You're one tough, smart, brave lady. You're going to come through this. He's the one who's going to come apart." Daniel E. Murray, Deputy Assistant Director of the Federal Bureau of Investigation, reached his hand across the table. Barbara Linders took it, squeezing it as a child might with her father, forcing herself to believe and to trust, and it shamed him that she was paying such a price because the President of the United States had to subordinate a criminal case to a question of politics. Perhaps it made sense in the great scheme of things, but for a cop the great scheme of things usually came down to one crime and one victim.

16

Payloads

The final step in arming the H-11/SS-19 missiles necessarily had to await official word from the nation's Prime Minister. In some ways the final payoff was something of a disappointment. They had originally hoped to affix a full complement of warheads, at least six each, to the nose of each bird, but to do that would have meant actually testing the trans-stage bus in flight, and *that* was just a little too dangerous. The covert nature of the project was far more important than the actual number of warheads, those in authority had decided. And they could always correct it at a later date. They'd deliberately left the top end of the Russian design intact for that very reason, and for the moment a total of 10 one-megaton warheads would have to do.

One by one, the individual silos were opened by the support crew, and one by one the oversized RVs were lifted off the flatcar, set in place, then covered with their aerodynamic shrouds. Again the Russian design served their purposes very well indeed. Each such operation took just over an hour, which allowed the entire procedure to be accomplished in a single night by the crew of twenty. The silos were resealed, and it was done; their country was now a nuclear power.

"Amazing," Goto observed.

"Actually very simple," Yamata replied. "The government funded the fabrication and testing of the 'boosters' as part of our space program. The plutonium came from the Monju reactor complex. Designing and building the warheads was child's play. If some Arabs can do a crude warhead in a cave in Lebanon, how hard can it be for our technicians?" In fact, everything but the warhead-fabrication process had been government funded in one way or another, and Yamata was sure that the informal consortium that had done the latter would be compensated as well. Had they not done it all for their country? "We will immediately commence training for the Self-Defense Force personnel to take over from our own people — once you assign them to us for that purpose, Goto-san."

"But the Americans and the Russians . . . ?"

Yamata snorted. "They are down to one missile each, and those will be officially blown up this week, as we will all see on television. As you know, their missile submarines have been deactivated. Their Trident missiles are already all gone, and the submarines are lined up awaiting dismantlement. A mere ten working ICBMs give us a marked strategic advantage."

"But what if they try to build more?"

"They can't — not very easily," Yamata corrected himself. "The production lines have been closed down, and in accordance with the treaty, the tooling has all been destroyed under international inspection. To start over would take months, and we would find out very quickly. Our next important step is to launch a major naval-construction program" — for which Yamata's yards were ready — "so that our supremacy in the Western Pacific will be unassailable. For the moment, with luck and the help of our friends, we will have enough to see us through. Before they will be able to challenge us, our strategic position will have improved to the point where they will have to accept our position and then treat with us as equals."

"So I must now give the order?"

"Yes, Prime Minister," Yamata replied, again explaining to the man his job function.

Goto rubbed his hands together for a moment and looked down at the ornate desk so newly his. Ever the weak man, he temporized. "It is true, my Kimba was a drug addict?"

Yamata nodded soberly, inwardly enraged at the remark. "Very sad, is it not? My own chief of security, Kaneda, found her dead and called the police. It seems that she was very careful about it, but not careful enough."

Goto sighed quietly. "Foolish child. Her father is a policeman, you know. A very stern man, she said. He didn't understand her. I did," Goto said. "She was a kind, gentle spirit. She would have made a fine geisha."

It was amazing how people transformed in death, Yamata thought coldly. That foolish, shameless girl had defied her parents and tried to make her own way in the world, only to find that the world was not tolerant of the unprepared. But because she'd had the ability to give Goto the illusion that he was a man, now she was a kind and gentle spirit.

"Goto-san, can we allow the fate of our nation to be decided by people like that?"

"No." The new Prime Minister lifted his phone. He had to consult a sheet on his desk for the proper number. "Climb Mount Niitaka," he said when the connection was made, repeating an order that had been given more than fifty years earlier.

In many ways the plane was singular, but in others quite ordinary. The VC-25B was in fact the Air

Force's version of the venerable Boeing 747 airliner. A craft with fully thirty years of history in its design, and still in serial production at the plant outside Seattle, it was painted in colors that had been chosen by a politically selected decorator to give the proper impression to foreign countries, whatever that was. Sitting alone on the concrete ramp, it was surrounded by uniformed security personnel "with authorization," in the dry Pentagonese, to use their M16 rifles far more readily than uniformed guards at most other federal installations. It was a more polite way of saying, "Shoot first and ask questions later."

There was no jetway. People had to climb stairs into the aircraft, just as in the 1950s, but there was still a metal detector, and you still had to check your baggage — this time to Air Force and Secret Service personnel who X-rayed everything and opened much of it for visual inspection.

"I hope you left your Victoria's Secret stuff at home," Jack observed with a chuckle as he hoisted the last bag on the counter.

"You'll find out when we get to Moscow," Professor Ryan replied with an impish wink. It was her first state trip, and everything at Andrews Air Force Base was new for her.

"Hello, Dr. Ryan! We finally meet." Helen D'Agustino came over and extended her hand.

"Cathy, this is the world's prettiest bodyguard," Jack said, introducing the Secret Service agent to his wife.

"I couldn't make the last state dinner," Cathy explained. "There was a seminar up at Harvard."

"Well, this trip ought to be pretty exciting," the Secret Service agent said, taking her leave smoothly to continue her duties.

Not as exciting as my last one, Jack thought, remembering another story that he couldn't relate to anyone.

"Where's she keep her gun?" Cathy asked.

"I've never searched her for it, honey," Jack said with a wink of his own.

"Do we go aboard now?"

"I can go aboard whenever I want," her husband replied. "Color me important." So much the better to board early and show her around, he decided, heading her toward the door. Designed to carry upwards of three hundred passengers in its civilian incarnation, the President's personal 747 (there was another backup aircraft, of course) was outfitted to hold a third of that number in stately comfort. Jack first showed his wife where they would be sitting, explaining that the pecking order was very clear. The closer you were to the front of the aircraft, the more important you were. The President's accommodations were in the nose, where two couches could convert into beds. The Ryans and the van Damms would be in the next area, twenty feet or so aft in a space that could seat eight, but only five in this case. Joining them would be the President's Director of Communications, a harried and usually frantic former TV executive named Tish Brown, recently divorced. Lesser staff members were sorted aft in diminishing importance until you got to the media, deemed less important still.

"This is the kitchen?" Cathy asked.

"Galley," Jack corrected. It was impressive, as were the meals prepared here, actually *cooked* from fresh ingredients and not reheated as was the way on airliners.

"It's bigger than ours!" she observed, to the amused pleasure of the chief cook, an Air Force master sergeant.

"Not quite, but the chef's better, aren't you, Sarge?"

"I'll turn my back now. You can slug him, ma'am. I won't tell."

Cathy merely laughed at the jibe. "Why isn't he upstairs in the lounge?"

"That's almost all communications gear. The President likes to wander up there to talk to the crew, but the guys who live there are mainly cryppies."

"Cryppies?"

"Communications guys," Jack explained, leading his wife back to their seats. The seats were beige leather, extra wide and extra soft, with recently added swing-up TV screens, personal phones, and other features which Cathy started to catalog, down to the presidential seal on the belt-buckles.

"Now I know what first-class really means."

"It's still an eleven-hour flight, babe," Jack observed, settling in while others boarded. With luck he'd be able to sleep most of the way.

The President's televised departure statement followed its own pattern. The microphone was always set up so that Air Force One loomed in the background, to remind everyone of who he was and to prove it by showing his personal plane. Roy Newton watched more for timing than anything else. Statements like this never amounted to much, and only C-SPAN carried them at all, though the network newsies were always there with cameras in case the airplane blew up on takeoff. Concluding his remarks, Durling took his wife, Anne, by the arm and walked to the stairs, where a sergeant saluted. At the door of the aircraft, the President and the First Lady turned to give a final wave as though already on the campaign trail — in a very real way this trip was part of that almost-continuous process — then went inside. C-SPAN switched back to the floor of the House, where various junior members were giving brief speeches under special orders. The President would be in the air for eleven hours, Newton knew, more time than he needed.

It was time to go to work.

The ancient adage was true enough, he thought, arranging his notes. If more than one person knew it, it wasn't a secret at all. Even less so if you both knew part of it and also knew who knew the rest, because then you could sit down over dinner and let on that you knew, and the other person would think that you knew it all, and would then tell you the parts you hadn't learned quite yet. The right smiles, nods, grunts, and a few carefully selected words would keep your source going until it was all there in plain sight. Newton supposed it was not terribly different for spies. Perhaps he would have been a good one, but it didn't pay any better than his stint in Congress — not even as well, in fact — and he'd long since decided to apply his talent to something that could make him a decent living.

The rest of the game was a lot easier. You had to select the right person to give the information to, and that choice was made merely by reading the local papers carefully. Every reporter had a hot-button item, something for which he or she had a genuinely passionate interest, and for that reason reporters were no different from anyone else. If you knew what buttons to push, you could manipulate anyone. What a pity it hadn't quite worked with the people in his district, Newton thought, lifting the phone and punching the buttons.

"Libby Holtzman."

"Hi, Libby, this is Roy. How are things?"

"A little slow," she allowed, wondering if her husband, Bob, would get anything good on the Moscow trip with the presidential party.

"How about dinner?" He knew that her husband was away.

"What about?" she asked. She knew it wasn't a tryst or something similarly foolish. Newton was a player, and usually had something interesting to tell.

"It'll be worth your time," he promised. "Jockey Club, seven-thirty?"

"I'll be there."

Newton smiled. It was all fair play, wasn't it? He'd lost his congressional seat on the strength of an accusation about influence-peddling. It hadn't been strong enough to have merited prosecution (someone else had influenced that), but it had been enough, barely, to persuade 50.7 percent of the voters in that off-year election that someone else should have the chance to represent them. In a presidential-election year, Newton thought, he would almost certainly have eked out a win, but congressional seats once lost are almost never regained.

It could have been much worse. This life wasn't so bad, was it? He'd kept the same house, kept his kids in the same school, then moved them on to good colleges, kept his membership in the same country club. He just had a different constituency now, no ethics laws to trouble his mind about — not that they ever had, really — and it sure as hell paid a lot better, didn't it?

DATELINE PARTNERS was being run out via computer-satellite relay — three of them, in fact. The Japanese Navy was linking all of its data to its fleet-operations center in Yokohama. The U.S. Navy did the same into Fleet-Ops at Pearl Harbor. Both headquarters offices used a third link to swap their own pictures. The umpires who scored the exercise in both locations thus had access to everything, but the individual fleet commanders did not. The purpose of the game was to give both sides realistic battle training, for which reason cheating was not encouraged — "cheating" was a concept by turns foreign and integral with the fighting of wars, of course.

Pacific Fleet's type commanders, the admirals in charge of the surface, air, submarine, and service forces, respectively, watched from their chairs as the game unfolded, each wondering how his underlings would perform.

"Sato's no dummy, is he?" Commander Chambers noted.

"The boy's got some beautiful moves," Dr. Jones opined. A senior contractor with his own "special-access" clearance, he'd been allowed into the center on Mancuso's parole. "But it isn't going to help him up north."

"Oh?" SubPac turned and smiled. "You know something I don't?"

"The sonar departments on *Charlotte* and *Asheville* are damned good, Skipper. My people worked with them to set up the new tracking software, remember?"

"The CO's aren't bad either," Mancuso pointed out.

Jones nodded agreement. "You bet, sir. They know how to listen, just like you did."

"God," Chambers breathed, looking down at the new four-ring shoulder boards and imagining he could feel the added weight. "Admiral, you ever wonder how we would have made it without Jonesy here?"

"We had Chief Laval with us, remember?" Mancuso said.

"Frenchy's son is the lead sonarman on *Asheville*, Mr. Chambers." For Jones, Mancuso would always be "skipper" and Chambers would always be a lieutenant. Neither officer objected. It was one of the rules of the naval service that bonded officers and (in this case, former) enlisted personnel.

"I didn't know that," SubPac admitted.

"Just joined up with her. He was on *Tennessee* before. Very sharp kid, made first-class three years out of his A-school."

"That's faster than you did it," Chambers observed. "Is he that good?"

384

"Sure as hell. I'm trying to recruit him for my business. He got married last year, has a kid on the way. It shouldn't be too hard to bribe him out into civilian life."

"Thanks a lot, Jonesy," Mancuso growled. "I oughta kick your ass outa here."

"Oh, come on, Skipper. When's the last time we got together for some real fun?" In addition to which, Jones's new whale-hunting software had been incorporated in what was left of the Pacific SOSUS system. "About time for an update."

The fact that both sides had observers in the other's headquarters was something of a complication, largely because there were assets and capabilities in both cases that were not strictly speaking shared. In this case, SOSUS-generated traces that might or might not be the Japanese submarine force northwest of Kure were actually better than what appeared on the main plotting board. The real traces were given to Mancuso and Chambers. Each side had two submarines. Neither American boat showed up on the traces, but the Japanese boats were conventionally powered, and had to go periodically to snorkeling depth in order to run their diesels and recharge their batteries. Though the Japanese submarines had their own version of the American Prairie-Masker systems, Jones's new software had gone a long way to defeat that countermeasure. Mancuso and the rest retired to the SubPac plotting room to examine the newest data.

"Okay, Jonesy, tell me what you see," Mancuso ordered, looking at the paper printouts from the underwater hydrophones that littered the bottom of the Pacific.

The data was displayed both electronically on TV-type displays and on fan-fold paper of the sort once used for computer printouts for more detailed analysis. For work like this, the latter was preferred, and there were two sets. One of them had already been marked up by the oceanographic technicians of the local SOSUS detachment. To make this a double-blind analysis, and to see if Jones still knew how, Mancuso kept separate the set already analyzed by his people.

Still short of forty, Jones had gray already in his thick dark hair, though he chewed gum now instead of smoking. The intensity was still there, Mancuso saw. Dr. Ron Jones flipped pages like an accountant on the trail of embezzlement, his finger tracing down the vertical lines on which frequencies were recorded.

"We assume that they'll snort every eight hours or so?" he asked.

"That's the smart thing, to keep their batteries fully charged," Chambers agreed with a nod.

"What time are they operating on?" Jones asked. Typically, American submarines at sea adjusted their clocks to Greenwich Mean Time — recently changed to "Universal Time" with the diminution of the Royal Navy, whose power had once allowed the prime meridian to be defined by the British.

"I presume Tokyo," Mancuso replied. "That's us minus five."

"So we start looking for patterns, midnight and even hours their time." There were five of the wide-folded sheets. Jones flipped one complete set at a time, noting the time references in the margins. It took him ten minutes.

"Here's one, and here's another. These two are possible. This one's also possible, but I don't think so. I'll put money down on this one . . . and this one for starters." His fingers tapped on seemingly random lines of dots.

"Wally?"

Chambers turned to the other table and flipped the marked-up sets to the proper time settings. "Jonesy, you fuckin' witch!" he breathed. It had taken a team of skilled technicians — experts all — over two hours to do what Jones had accomplished in a few minutes before their again-incredulous eyes.

The civilian contractor pulled a can of Coke from the nearby cooler and popped it open. "Gentlemen," he asked, "who's the all-time champ?"

That was only part of it, of course. The printouts merely gave bearing to a suspected noise source, but there were several of the bottom-sited SOSUS arrays, and triangulation had already been accomplished, nailing the datum points down to radii of ten to fifteen nautical miles. Even with Jones's improvements in the system, that still left a lot of ocean to search.

The phone rang. It was Commander-in-Chief Pacific Fleet. Mancuso took the call and made his recommendations for vectoring *Charlotte* and *Asheville* onto the suspected contacts. Jones observed the exchange and nodded approval.

"See what I mean, Skipper? You always did know how to listen."

Murray had been out discussing a few budgetary matters with the Assistant-Director-in-Charge of the Washington Field Office, therefore missing the phone call. The top-secret dispatch from the White House was tucked away in secure files, and then his secretary had been called out to bring a sick child home from school. As a result, the handwritten message from Ryan had been unconscionably late in coming to his attention.

"The Norton girl," he said, walking into Director Shaw's office.

"Bad?"

"Dead," Murray said, handing the paper over. Shaw scanned it quickly.

"Shit," the FBI Director whispered. "Did she have a prior history of drug use?"

"Not that I recall."

"Word from Tokyo?"

"I haven't checked in with the Leg-At yet. Bad

timing for that, Bill."

Shaw nodded, and the thought in his mind was transparent. Ask any FBI agent for the case he bragged about, and it is always kidnapping. It was really how the Bureau had made its name back in the 1930s. The Lindbergh Law had empowered the FBI to assist any local police force as soon as the possibility existed that the victim could have been taken across a state line. With the mere possibility — the victims were rarely actually transported so far — the whole weight and power of America's premier law-enforcement agency descended on the case like a pack of especially hungry wolves. The real mission was always the same: to get the victim back alive, and there the results were excellent. The secondary objective was to apprehend, charge, and try the subjects in question, and there the record, statistically speaking, was better still. They didn't know yet if Kimberly Norton had been a kidnap victim. They did know that she would be coming home dead. That single fact, for any FBI agent, was a professional failure.

"Her father's a cop."

"I remember, Dan."

"I want to go out there and talk it over with O'Keefe." Part of it was because Captain Norton deserved to hear it from other cops, not through the media. Part of it was because the cops on the case *had* to do it, to admit their failure to him. And part of it would be for Murray to take a look at the case file himself, to be sure for himself that all that might have been done, had been done.

"I can probably spare you for a day or two," Shaw replied. "The Linders case is going to wait until the President gets back anyway. Okay, get packed."

"This is better than the Concorde!" Cathy gushed at the Air Force corporal who served dinner. Her husband almost laughed. It wasn't often that Caroline Ryan's eyes went quite so wide, but then he was long accustomed to this sort of service, and the food was certainly better than she customarily ate in the Hopkins physicians' dining room. And there the plates didn't have gold trim, one of the reasons that Air Force One had so much pilferage.

"Wine for madam?" Ryan lifted the bottle of Russian River chardonnay and poured as his plate came down.

"We don't drink wine on the chicken farm, you see," she told the corporal with a small measure of embarrassment.

"Everybody's this way the first time, Dr. Ryan. If you need anything, please buzz me." She headed back to the galley.

"See, Cathy, I told you, stick with me."

"I wondered how you got used to flying," she noted, tasting the broccoli. "Fresh."

"The flight crew's pretty good, too." He gestured to the wineglasses. Not a ripple.

"The pay isn't all that great," Arnie van Damm said from the other side of the compartment, "but the perks ain't too bad."

"The blackened redfish isn't bad at all."

"Our chef stole the recipe from the Jockey Club. Best Cajun redfish in town," van Damm explained. "I think he had to trade his potato soup for it. Fair deal," Arnie judged.

"He gets the crust just right, doesn't he?"

One of Washington's few really excellent restaurants, the Jockey Club was located in the basement of the Ritz Carlton Hotel on Massachusetts Avenue. A quiet, dimly lit establishment, it had for many years been a place for "power" meals of one sort or another.

All the food here is good, Libby Holtzman thought,

especially when someone else paid for it. The previous hour had handled all manner of small talk, the usual exchange of information and gossip that was even more important in Washington than most American cities. That was over now. The wine was served, the salad plates gone, and the main course on the table. "So, Roy, what's the big item?"

"Ed Kealty." Newton looked up to watch her eyes.

"Don't tell me, his wife is finally going to leave the rat?"

"He's probably going to be the one leaving, as a matter of fact."

"Who's the unlucky bimbo?" Mrs. Holtzman asked with a wry smile.

"Not what you think, Libby. Ed's going away." You always wanted to make them wait for it.

"Roy, it's eight-thirty, okay?" Libby observed, making her position clear.

"The FBI has a case running on Kealty. Rape. More than one, in fact. One of the victims killed herself."

"Lisa Beringer?" The reason for her suicide had never been adequately explained.

"She left a letter behind. The FBI has it now. They also have several other women who are willing to testify."

"Wow," Libby Holtzman allowed herself to say. She set her fork down. "How solid is this?"

"The man running the case is Dan Murray, Shaw's personal attack dog."

"I know Dan. I also know he won't talk about this." You rarely got an FBI agent to discuss evidentiary matters in a criminal case, certainly not before it was presented. That sort of leak almost always came from an attorney or court clerk. "He doesn't just do things by the book — he *wrote* the book." It was literally true. Murray had helped draft many of the Bureau's official procedures.

"He might, this one time."

"Why, Roy?"

"Because Durling is holding things up. He thinks he needs Kealty for his clout on the Hill. You notice that Eddie-boy has been in the White House a lot lately? Durling spilled it all to him so that he can firm up his defense. At least," Newton said to cover himself, "that's what people are telling me. It does seem a little out of character, doesn't it?"

"Obstruction of justice?"

"That's the legal term, Libby. Technically speaking, well, I'm not quite sure it meets the legal test." Now the hook was well in the water, and the bait worm was wiggling very nicely.

"What if he was just holding it off to keep it from competing with the trade bill?" The fish was giving it a look, but wondering about the shiny, barbed thing behind the worm. . . .

"This one goes back further than that, Libby. They've been sitting on it for quite a while, that's what I hear. It does make a great excuse, though, doesn't it?" It was a very enticing worm, though.

"If you think politics takes precedence over a sexual-assault case. How solid is the case?"

"If it goes in front of a jury, Ed Kealty is going to spend time in a federal penitentiary."

"That solid?" My, what a juicy fat worm it was.

"Like you said, Murray's a good cop."

"Who's the U.S. Attorney on the case?"

"Anne Cooper. She's been full-time on this for weeks." One hell of a good worm, in fact. That barbed, shiny thing wasn't all that dangerous, was it?

Newton took an envelope from his pocket and set it on the tablecloth. "Names, numbers, details, but you didn't get them from me, okay?" The worm appeared to dance in the water, and it was no longer apparent that the hook was the thing really moving.

391

"What if I can't verify anything?"

"Then there's no story, and my sources are wrong, and I hope you enjoyed dinner." Of course, the worm might just go away.

"Why, Roy? Why you, why the story?" Circling, circling. But how did this worm ever get here?

"I've never liked the guy. You know that. We butted heads on two big irrigation bills, and he killed a defense project in my state. But you really want to know why? I have daughters, Libby. One's a senior at U-Penn. Another one's just starting University of Chicago Law School. They both want to follow in their dad's footsteps, and I don't want my little girls staffing on the Hill with *bastards* like Ed Kealty around." Who really cared how the worm got in the water, anyway?

With a knowing nod, Libby Holtzman took the envelope. It went into her purse without being opened. Amazing how they never noticed the hook until it was too late. Sometimes not even then. The waiter was disappointed when both diners passed on the dessert cart, settling for just a quick espresso before paying the bill.

"Hello?"

"Barbara Linders?" a female voice asked.

"Yes. Who's this?"

"Libby Holtzman from the *Post*. I live a few blocks away from you. I'd like to know if I might come over and talk about a few things."

"What things?"

"Ed Kealty, and why they've decided not to prosecute the case."

"They *what?*"

"That's what we're hearing," the voice told her.

"Wait a minute. They warned me about this," Linders said suspiciously, already giving part of the game away.

"They always warn you about something, usually the wrong thing. Remember, I was the one who did the story last year about Congressman Grant and that nasty little thing he had going on in his district office? And I was also the one who nailed that bastard undersecretary in Interior. I keep a close eye on cases like this, Barbara," the voice said, sister-to-sister. It was true. Libby Holtzman had nearly bagged a Pulitzer for her reporting on political sex-abuse cases.

"How do I know it's really you?"

"You've seen me on TV, right? Ask me over and you'll see. I can be there in five minutes."

"I'm going to call Mr. Murray."

"That's fine. Go ahead and call him, but promise me one thing?"

"What's that?"

"If he tells you the same thing about why they're not doing anything, then we can talk." The voice paused. "In fact, how about I come over right now anyway? If Dan tells you the right thing, we can just have a cup of coffee and do some background stuff for later. Fair enough?"

"Okay . . . I guess that's okay. I have to call Mr. Murray now." Barbara Linders hung up and dialed another number from memory.

"Hi, this is Dan — "

"Mr. Murray!" Barbara said urgently, her faith in the world so badly shaken already.

" — and this is Liz," another voice said, obviously now on tape. "We can't come to the phone right now . . ." both voices said together —

"Where are you when I need you?" Ms. Linders demanded of the recording machine, hanging up in a despairing fury before the humorous recording delivered her to the beep. Was it possible? Could it be true?

This is Washington, her experience told her. *Anything could be true.*

393

Barbara Linders looked around the room. She'd been in Washington for eleven years. What did she have to show for it? A one-bedroom apartment with prints on the wall. Nice furniture that she used alone. Memories that threatened her sanity. She was so alone, so damned alone with them, and she had to let them go, get them out, strike back at the man who had wrecked her life so thoroughly. And now that would be denied her, too? Was it possible? The most frightening thing of all was that Lisa had felt this way. She knew that from the letter she'd kept, a photocopy of which was still in the jewelry box on her bureau. She'd kept it both as a keepsake of her best friend and to remind herself not to go as dangerously far into despair as Lisa had. Reading that letter a few months ago had persuaded her to open up to her gynecologist, who had in turn referred her to Clarice Golden, starting the process that had led her — where? The door buzzed then, and Barbara went to answer it.

"Hi! Recognize me?" The question was delivered with a warm and sympathetic smile. Libby Holtzman was a tall woman with thick ebony hair that framed a pale face and warm brown eyes.

"Please come in," Barbara said, backing away from the door.

"Did you call Dan?"

"He wasn't home . . . or maybe he just left the machine on," Barbara thought. "You know him?"

"Oh, yes. Dan's an acquaintance," Libby said, heading toward the couch.

"Can I trust him? I mean, *really* trust him."

"Honestly?" Holtzman paused. "Yes. If he were running the case all by himself, yes, you could. Dan's a good man. I mean that."

"But he's not running the case by himself, is he?"

Libby shook her head. "It's too big, too political. The other thing about Murray is, well, he's a very loyal man. He does what he's told. Can I sit down, Barbara?"

"Please." Both sat on the couch.

"You know what the press does? It's our job to keep an eye on things. I like Dan. I admire him. He really is a good cop, an honest cop, and I'll bet you that everything he's done with you, well, he's acted like your big tough brother, hasn't he?"

"Every step of the way," Barbara confirmed. "He's been my best friend in all the world."

"That wasn't a lie. He's one of the good guys. I know his wife, Liz, too. The problem is, not everyone is like Dan, and that's where we come in," Libby told her.

"How do you mean?"

"When somebody tells a guy like Dan what he has to do, mostly they do it. They do it because they have to, because that's what the rules are — and you know something? He hates it, almost as much as you do. My job, Barbara, is to help people like Dan, because I can get the bastards off their backs, too."

"I can't . . . I mean, I just can't — "

Libby reached out and stopped her with a gentle touch on the hand.

"I'm not going to ask you to give me anything on the record, Barbara. That could mess up the criminal case, and you know I want this one to be handled through the system just as much as you do. But can you talk to me off the record?"

"Yes! . . . I think so."

"Do you mind if I record this?" The reporter pulled a small recorder from her purse.

"Who will hear it?"

"The only other person will be my AME — assistant managing editor. We do that to make sure that we have good sources. Except for that, it's like talking to your lawyer or doctor or minister. Those are the rules, and we never break them."

Intellectually speaking, Barbara knew that, but here and now in her apartment, the ethical rules of journalism seemed a thin reed. Libby Holtzman could see it in her eyes.

"If you want, I can just leave, or we can talk without the recorder, but" — a disarming smile — "I hate taking shorthand. You make mistakes that way. If you want to think about it a little while, that's okay, too. You've had enough pressure. I know that. I know what this can be like."

"That's what Dan says, but he *doesn't!* He doesn't *really.*"

Libby Holtzman looked straight into her eyes. She wondered if Murray had seen the same pain and felt it as deeply as she did now. Probably so, she thought, quite honestly, probably in a slightly different way, because he was a man, but he *was* a good cop, and he was probably just as mad about the way the case was going as she now felt.

"Barbara, if you just want to talk about . . . things, that's okay, too. Sometimes we just need a friend to talk to. I don't have to be a reporter all the time."

"Do you know about Lisa?"

"Her death was never really explained, was it?"

"We were best friends, we shared everything . . . and then when he — "

"Are you sure Kealty was involved with that?"

"I'm the one who found the letter, Libby."

"What can you tell me about that?" Holtzman asked, unable to restrain her journalistic focus now.

"I can do better than tell you." Linders rose and disappeared for a moment. She returned with the photocopies and handed them over.

It only took two minutes to read the letter once and then once again. Date, place, method. *A message from beyond the grave,* Libby thought. What was more dangerous than ink on paper?

"For what's on here, and what you know, he could

go to prison, Barbara."

"That's what Dan says. He smiles when he says it. He wants it to happen."

"Do you?" Holtzman asked.

"Yes!"

"Then let me help."

17

Strike One

It's called the miracle of modern communications only because nothing modern is supposed to be a curse. In fact, those on the receiving end of such information were often appalled by what they got.

It had been a smooth flight, even by the standards of Air Force One, on which many passengers — mainly the younger and more foolish White House staffers — often refused to buckle their seat belts as a show of . . . something, Ryan thought. The Air Force flight crew was as good as any, he knew, but it hadn't prevented one incident on final at Andrews, where a thunderbolt had blown the nosecone off the aircraft carrying the Secretary of Defense and his wife, rather to everyone's discomfiture. And so he always kept his belt on, albeit loosely, just as the flight crew did.

"Dr. Ryan?" The whisper was accompanied by a shake of his shoulders.

"What is it, Sarge?" There was no sense in grumbling at an innocent NCO.

"Mr. van Damm needs you upstairs, sir."

Jack nodded and moved his seat to the upright position. The sergeant handed him a coffee mug on the way. A clock told him it was nine in the morning, but it didn't say *where* it was nine in the morning, and Ryan could not at the moment remember what zone the clock was set on. It was all theoretical anyway. How many time zones could dance inside an airliner?

The upper deck of the VC-25B contrasted sharply with the lower deck. Instead of plush appointments, the compartment here was lined with military-style electronics gear whose individual boxes had chromed bars for easy removal and replacement. A sizable team of communications specialists was always at work, tapped into every source of information one might imagine: digital radio, TV, and fax, every single channel encrypted. Arnie van Damm stood in the middle of the area, and handed something over. It turned out to be a facsimile copy of the *Washington Post*'s late edition, about to hit the street, four thousand miles and six hours away.

VICE PRESIDENT IMPLICATED IN SUICIDE, the four-column headline announced. FIVE WOMEN CHARGE EDWARD KEALTY WITH SEXUAL ABUSE.

"You woke me up for this?" Ryan asked. It was nowhere near his area of responsibility, was it?

"You're named in the story," Arnie told him.

"What?" Jack scanned the piece. " 'National Security Advisor Ryan is one of those briefed in on the affair.' Okay, I guess that's true, isn't it?"

"Keep going."

" 'The White House told the FBI four weeks ago not to present the case to the Judiciary Committee.' That's not true."

"This one's a beautiful combination of what is and what isn't." The Chief of Staff was in an even fouler mood than Ryan.

"Who leaked?"

"I don't know, but Libby Holtzman ran this piece, and her husband is sleeping aft. He likes you. Get him and talk to him."

"Wait a minute, this is something that a little time

and truth will settle out, Arnie. The President hasn't done anything wrong that I know about."

"His political enemies can call the delay obstruction of justice."

"Come on." Jack shook his head in disbelief. "No way that would stand up to examination."

"It doesn't have to, damn it. We're talking politics, remember, not facts, and we have *elections* coming up. Talk to Bob Holtzman. Now," van Damm ordered. He didn't do it often with Ryan, but he did have the authority.

"Tell the Boss yet?" Jack asked, folding up his copy.

"We'll let him sleep for a while. Send Tish up on the way, will you?"

"Okay." Ryan headed back down and shook Tish Brown awake, pointed upstairs, then headed aft to a flight attendant — crew member, he corrected himself. "Get Bob Holtzman up here, will you?" Through an open port he could see that it was light outside. Maybe it was nine o'clock where they were going? Yeah, they were scheduled to arrive in Moscow at two in the afternoon, local time. The head cook was sitting in his galley, reading a copy of *Time*. Ryan went in and got his own coffee refill.

"Can't sleep, Dr. Ryan?"

"Not anymore. Duty calls."

"I have rolls baking, if you want."

"Great idea."

"What is it?" Bob Holtzman asked, sticking his head in. Like every man aboard at the moment, he needed a shave. Jack merely handed over the story.

"What gives?"

Holtzman was a fast reader. "Jesus, is this true?"

"How long has Libby been on this one?"

"It's news to me — oh, shit, sorry, Jack."

Ryan nodded with more smile than he felt. "Yeah, I just woke up, too."

"Is it true?"

"This is on background?"

"Agreed."

"The FBI's been running the case for some time now. The dates in Libby's piece are close, and I'd have to check my office logs for the exact ones. I got briefed in right around the time the trade thing blew up because of Kealty's security clearance — what I can tell him, what I can't, you know how that goes, right?"

"Yes, I understand. So what's the status of the case?"

"The chairman and ranking member of Judiciary have been briefed in. So have Al Trent and Sam Fellows on Intelligence. Nobody's putting a stopper on this one, Bob. To the best of my knowledge, the President's played a straight game the whole way. Kealty's going down, and after the impeachment proceedings, if it goes that far — "

"It *has* to go that far," Holtzman pointed out.

"I doubt it." Ryan shook his head. "If he gets a good lawyer, they'll cut some sort of deal. They have to, like it was with Agnew. If he goes through impeachment and then a Senate trial, God help him in front of a jury."

"Makes sense," Holtzman conceded. "You're telling me the meat of the story's wrong."

"Correct. If there's any obstruction going on, I don't know about it, and I *have* been briefed in on this."

"Have you spoken with Kealty?"

"No, nothing substantive. On 'business' stuff I brief his national-security guy and he briefs his boss. I wouldn't be good at that, would I? Two daughters."

"So you know about the facts of the case?"

"Not the specifics, no. I don't need to know. I do know Murray pretty well. If Dan says the case is solid, well, then I figure it is." Ryan finished off the rest of his coffee and reached for a fresh roll. "The President is *not* obstructing this one. It's been delayed so it wouldn't conflict with other things. That's all."

"You're not supposed to do that either, you know," Holtzman pointed out, getting one for himself.

"Goddamn it, Bob! Prosecutors schedule cases, too, don't they? All this is, is scheduling." Holtzman read Jack's face and nodded.

"I'll pass that one along."

It was already too late for proper damage-control. Most of the political players in Washington are early risers. They have their coffee, read their papers in great detail, check their fax machines for additional material, and often take early phone calls, or in a recent development, log onto computer services to check electronic mail, all in an effort to leave their homes with a good feel for the shape the new day will take. In the case of many members, facsimile copies of the late-edition story by Liz Holtzman had brief cover pages indicating that this might be a matter of great personal interest. Different code phrases were used, depending on which PR firm had originated the transmission, but all were the same. The Members in question had been compelled to mute their op-position to TRA. This opportunity, on the other hand, was seen as something of a payback for the earlier transgression. In few cases would the opportunity be missed.

The comments were mainly delivered off the rec-ord. "This looks like a very serious matter" was the phrase most often used. "It's unfortunate that the President saw fit to interfere in a criminal matter" was another favorite. Early calls to Director William Shaw of the FBI were met with "no comment" com-ments, usually with the additional clarification that the policy of the FBI was to decline comment on any possible criminal case, lest the subsequent legal proceedings be tainted and the rights of the accused compromised. The clarification was rarely if ever conveyed to the public; in that way "no comment" acquired its own very special spin.

The accused in this case awoke in his house on the grounds of the Naval Observatory on Massachusetts Avenue, North West, to find his senior aides downstairs and waiting for him.

"Oh, shit," Ed Kealty observed. It was all he had to say. There was little point in denying the story. His people knew him too well for that. He was a man of an amorous nature, they all rationalized, a trait not uncommon in public life, though he was fairly discreet about it.

"Lisa Beringer," the Vice President breathed, reading. "Can't they let the poor girl rest in peace?" He remembered the shock of her death, the way she'd died, slipping off her seat belt and driving into a bridge abutment at ninety miles per hour, how the medical examiner had related the inefficiency of the method. She'd taken several minutes to die, still alive and whimpering when the paramedics had arrived. Such a sweet, nice kid. She just hadn't understood how things were. She'd wanted too much back from him. Maybe she'd thought that it was different with her. Well, Kealty thought, everybody thought they were different.

"He's hanging you out to dry," Kealty's senior aide observed. The important part of this, after all, was the political vulnerability of their principal.

"Sure as hell." *That son of a bitch*, the Vice President thought. *After all the things I've done.* "Okay — ideas?"

"Well, of course we deny everything, indignantly at that," his chief of staff began, handing over a sheet of paper. "I have a press release for starters, then we will have a press conference before noon." He'd already called half a dozen former and current female staffers who would stand beside their boss. In every case it was a woman whose bed he had graced with his presence, and who remembered the time with a smile. Great men had flaws, too. In Edward Kealty's case, the flaws were more than balanced by his commitment to the things that mattered.

Kealty read quickly down the page. *The only defense against a completely false accusation is the truth . . . there is no basis in fact whatever to these accusations . . . my public record is well known, as is my support for women's and minority rights . . . I request* ("demand" was the wrong word to use, his personal counsel thought) *an immediate airing of the allegations and the opportunity to defend myself vigorously . . . clearly no coincidence with the upcoming election year . . . regret that such a groundless accusation will affect our great President, Roger Durling —*

"Get that son of a bitch on the phone right now!"

"Bad time for a confrontation, Mr. Vice President. You 'fully expect his support,' remember?"

"Oh, yes, I do, don't I?" That part of the release wouldn't so much be a warning shot across the bow as one aimed right at the bridge, Kealty thought. Either Durling would support him or else risk political meltdown in the primaries.

What else would happen this year? Though too late to catch the morning papers in most of America — too late even for *USA Today* — the Kealty story had been caught by the broadcast media as part of their own pre-show media surveys. For many in the investment community, that meant National Public Radio's "Morning Edition" show, a good program to listen to during the drives from New Jersey and Connecticut because of its repeating two-hour length. "A copyrighted story in this morning's *Washington Post* . . ." The coverage on it began at the top of both hourly segments, with a preamble like a warning

404

bell to get the listener's attention, and though political stories out of Washington were about as common as the local weather report, "rape" and "suicide" were words with unequivocal meaning.

"Shit," a thousand or so voices breathed simultaneously in the same number of expensive automobiles. *What else is going to happen?* The volatility of the market had not ended yet, and something like this was sure to exert the kind of downward pressure that never really made any economic sense but was so real that everyone knew it would happen, and because of that planned for it, and because of *that* made it even more real in what computer engineers called a feedback loop. The market would drop again today. It had trended down for eleven of the past fourteen days, and though the Dow was replete with bargains by any technical measure, the little guys would make their nervous sell orders, and the mutual funds, driven by calls from more little guys, would do the same, adding institutional momentum to a totally artificial situation. The entire system was called a true democracy, but if it was, then a herd of nervous cattle was a democracy, too.

"Okay, Arnie." President Durling didn't bother asking who had leaked it. He was a sufficiently sophisticated player in the game that he knew it didn't matter. "What do we do?"

"I talked to Bob Holtzman," Ryan told the Boss, prompted by a look from the chief of staff.

"And?"

"And, I think he believed me. Hell, I was telling the truth, wasn't I?" It was a question rather than a rhetorical expression.

"Yes, you were, Jack. Ed's going to have to handle this one himself." The relief on Ryan's face was so obvious as to offend the Chief Executive. "Did you think I was really going to do this?"

"Of course not," Ryan answered at once.

"Who knows?"

"On the airplane?" van Damm asked. "I'm sure Bob spread it around some."

"Well, let's clobber it right now. Tish," Durling said to his communications director, "let's get a release put together. The Judiciary Committee's been briefed in, and I have *not* put any pressure on them at all."

"What do we say about the delay?" Tish Brown asked.

"We decided jointly with the leadership that the matter deserved to have — what?" The President looked up at the ceiling. "It deserved to have a clear field . . ."

"Sufficiently serious — no, it is sufficiently *important* to deserve a Congress undistracted by other considerations?" Ryan offered. *Not bad,* he thought.

"I'll make a politician out of you yet," Durling said with a grudging smile.

"You're not going to say anything directly about the case," van Damm went on, giving the President advice in the form of an order.

"I know, I know. I can't say anything on the facts of the matter because I can't allow myself to interfere with the proceedings or Kealty's defense, except to say that any citizen is innocent until the facts demonstrate otherwise; America is founded on . . . and all that stuff. Tish, write it up. I'll deliver it on the airplane before we land, and then maybe we can do what we're supposed to be doing. Anything else?" Durling asked.

"Secretary Hanson reports that everything is set up. No surprises," Ryan said, finally getting to his own briefing. "Secretary Fiedler has the monetary-support agreement ready for initialing, too. On that end, sir, it's going to be a nice, smooth visit."

"How reassuring that is," the President observed

dryly. "Okay, let me get cleaned up." Air Force One or not, traveling in such close proximity to others was rarely comfortable. Presidential privacy was a tenuous commodity under the best of circumstances, but at least in the White House you had real walls between yourself and others. Not here. An Air Force sergeant strained at his leash to lay out Durling's clothing and shaving things. The man had already spent two hours turning the Presidential shoes from black leather into chrome, and it would have been ungracious to push the guy off. People were so damned eager to show their loyalty. Except for the ones you needed to, Durling thought as he entered the small washroom.

"We got more of 'em."

Sanchez emerged from the head adjacent to CIC to see people gathered around the central plotting table. There were now three groups of the diamond shapes that denoted enemy surface ships. *Charlotte*, moreover, had position on a "V" shape that meant an enemy submarine, and *Asheville* supposedly had a good sniff also. Best of all, the joint patrol line of S-3 Viking ASW aircraft two hundred miles in advance of the battle group had identified what appeared to be a patrol line of other submarines. Two had been caught snorting, one on SOSUS and one by sonobuoys, and, using a line defined by those two positions, two others had been found. Now they even had a predictable interval between boats for the aircraft to concentrate on.

"Sunset tomorrow?" the CAG asked.

"They like the rising sun, don't they? Let's catch 'em at dinner, then."

"Fine with me." Sanchez lifted the phone at his place to alert his wing operations officer.

"Takes long enough," Jones murmured.

"I seem to remember when you were able to stand watches for a real long time," Wally Chambers told the civilian.

"I was young and dumb then." *I smoked, too*, he remembered. Such good things for concentration and alertness. But most submarines didn't allow people to smoke at all. Amazing that some crews hadn't mutinied. What was the Navy coming to. "See what I told you about my software?"

"You telling us that even you can be replaced by a computer?"

The contractor's head turned. "You know, Mr. Chambers, as you get older you have to watch the coffee intake."

"You two going at it again?" Admiral Mancuso rejoined them after shaving in the nearby head.

"I think Jonesy was planning to hit Banzai Beach this afternoon." Captain Chambers chuckled, sipping at his decaf. "He's getting bored with the exercise."

"They do take a while," SubPac confirmed.

"Hey, guys, we're validating my product, aren't we?"

"If you want some insider information, yeah, I'm going to recommend you get the contract." Not the least reason for which was that Jones had underbid IBM by a good 20 percent.

"Next step, I just hired two guys from Woods Hole. That never occurred to the suits at Big Blue."

"What do you mean?"

"We're going to decode whale talk, now that we can hear it so much better. Greenpeace is going to love us. The submarine mission for the next decade: making the seas safe for our fellow mammals. We can also track those Jap bastards who hunt them."

"What do you mean?" Chambers asked.

"You want funding? I have an idea that'll keep it for you."

408

"What's that, Jonesy?" Mancuso asked.

"The Woods Hole guys think they have the alarm calls for three species identified: for humpback, fins, and seis. They got them by listening in with hydrophones while they were hanging out with whalers. I can program that for active — it's in the freq range we transmit on. So what we can do is have subs trail along with the whalers and broadcast the call, and guess what? The whalers won't find shit. No whale in his right mind will get within twenty miles of another whale screaming that he's being mugged. Not much solidarity in the cetacean community."

"You turning tree-hugger on us?" Chambers wondered. But he thought about it and nodded slowly.

"All those people have to tell their friends in Congress is that we're doing good scientific work. Okay? Not that they love us, not that they approve of our power plants, just that we're doing good work. What I'm giving you guys is a mission for the next ten years." Jones was also giving his company work for at least that long, but that was beside the point. Mancuso and the submarine community needed the work. "Besides, I used to enjoy listening to them when we were on *Dallas*."

"Signal from *Asheville*," a communications specialist reported from the door. "They have acquired their target."

"Well, they're pretty good," Jones said, looking down at the plot. "But we're still the big kid on the block."

Air Force One floated into the usual soft landing at Sheremetyevo Airport one minute early. There was a collective sigh as the thrust-reversers cut in, slowing the heavy aircraft rapidly. Soon everyone started hearing the click of seat belts coming off.

"What woke you up so early?" Cathy asked her husband.

"Political stuff at home. I guess I can tell you now." Ryan explained on, then remembered he had the fax still folded in his pocket. He handed it over, cautioning his wife that it wasn't all true.

"I always thought he was slimy." She handed it back.

"Oh, don't you remember when he was the Conscience of Congress?" Jack asked quietly.

"Maybe he was, but I never thought he had one of his own."

"Just remember — "

"If anybody asks, I'm a surgeon here to meet with my Russian colleagues and do a little sightseeing." Which was entirely true. The state trip would make considerable demands on Ryan's time in his capacity as a senior Presidential advisor. But it wasn't all that different from a normal family vacation either. Their tastes in sightseeing overlapped, but didn't entirely coincide, and Cathy knew that her husband loathed shopping in any form. It was something odd about men in general and her husband in particular.

The aircraft turned onto the taxiway, and things started to happen. President and Mrs. Durling emerged from their compartment, all ready to present themselves as the embodiment of their country. People remained seated to let them pass, aided by the intimidating presence of both Secret Service and Air Force security people.

"Hell of a job," Ryan breathed, watching the President put on his happy face, and knowing that it was at least partially a lie. He had to do so many things, and make each appear as though it were the only thing he had to do. He had to compartmentalize everything, when on one task to pretend that the others didn't exist. Maybe like Cathy and her patients. Wasn't that an interesting thought? They heard band

410

music when the door opened, the local version of "Ruffles and Flourishes."

"I guess we can get up now."

The protocol was already established. People hunched at the windows to watch the President reach the bottom of the steps, shake hands with the new Russian President and the U.S. Ambassador to the Russian Republic. The rest of the official party then went down the steps, while the press deplaned from the after door.

It was very different from Ryan's last trip to Moscow. The airport was the same, but the time of day, the weather, and the whole atmosphere could not have been more different. It only took one face to make that clear, that of Sergey Nikolayevich Golovko, chairman of the Russian Foreign Intelligence Service, who stood behind the front rank of dignitaries. In the old days he would not have shown his face at all, but now his blue eyes were aimed right at Ryan, and they twinkled with mirth as Jack led his wife down the stairs and to their place at the bottom.

The initial signs were a little scary, as was not unusual when political factors interfered with economic forces. Organized labor was flexing its muscles, and doing it cleverly for the first time in years. In cars and their associated components alone, it was possible that hundreds of thousands of jobs would be coming back to the fold. The arithmetic was straightforward: nearly ninety billion dollars of products had arrived from overseas in the last year and would now have to be produced domestically. Sitting down with their management counterparts, labor came to the collective decision that the only thing missing was the government's word that TRA would not be a paper tiger, soon to be cast away in the name of international amity. To get that assurance, however, they had to work Congress. So the lobbying was already under

411

way, backed by the realization that the election cycle was coming up. Congress could not do one thing with one hand and something else with the other. Promises were made, and action taken, and for once both crossed party lines. The media were already commenting on how well it was working.

It wasn't just a matter of hiring employees. There would have to be a huge increase in capacity. Old plants and those operating under their capacity would need to be upgraded and so preliminary orders were put in for tooling and materials. The instant surge came as something of a surprise despite all the warnings, because despite their expertise even the most astute observers had not seen the bill for the revolution it really was.

But the blip on the statistical reports was unmistakable. The Federal Reserve kept all manner of measuring criteria on the American economy, and one of them was orders for such things as steel and machine tools. The period during which TRA had traveled through Congress and to the White House had seen a jump so large as to be off the graph paper. Then the governors saw a vast leap in short-term borrowing, largely from auto-related industries that had to finance their purchases from various specialty suppliers. The rise in orders was inflationary, and inflation was already a long-standing concern. The rise in borrowing would deplete the supply of money that could be borrowed. That had to be stopped, and quickly. The governors decided that instead of the quarter-point rise in the discount rate that they had already approved, and word of which had already leaked, the jump would be a full half-point, to be announced at close of business the following day.

Commander Ugaki was in the control room of his submarine, as usual chain-smoking and drinking copious amounts of tea that occasioned hourly trips to

412

his cabin and its private head, not to mention hacking coughs that were exacerbated by the dehumidified air (kept unusually dry to protect onboard electronic systems). He knew they had to be out there, at least one, perhaps two American submarines — *Charlotte* and *Asheville*, his intelligence briefs had told him — but it wasn't the boats he feared. It was the crews. The American submarine force had been reduced drastically in size, but evidently not in quality. He'd expected to detect his adversary for DATELINE PARTNERS hours before. Perhaps, Ugaki told himself, they hadn't even had a sniff of him yet, but he wasn't sure of that, and over the past thirty-six hours he'd come fully to the realization that this was no longer a game, not since he'd received the code phrase "Climb Mount Niitaka." How confident he had been a week earlier, but now he was at sea and underwater. The transition from theory to reality was striking.

"Anything?" he asked his sonar officer, getting a headshake for an answer.

Ordinarily, an American sub on an exercise like this was "augmented," meaning that a sound source was switched on, which increased the amount of radiated noise she put in the water. Done to simulate the task of detecting a *Russian* submarine, it was in one way arrogant and in another way very clever of the Americans. They so rarely played against allies or even their own forces at the level of their true capabilities that they had learned to operate under a handicap — like a runner with weighted shoes. As a result, when they played a game without the handicap, they were formidable indeed.

Well, so am I! Ugaki told himself. Hadn't he grown up tracking Russian subs like the Americans? Hadn't he gotten in close of a Russian Akula? Patience. The true samurai is patient. This was not a task for a merchant, after all.

"It *is* like tracking whales, isn't it?" Commander Steve Kennedy observed.

"Pretty close," Sonarman 1/c Jacques Yves Laval, Jr., replied quietly, watching his display and rubbing his ears, sweaty from the headphones.

"You feel cheated?"

"My dad got to play the real game. All I ever heard growing up, sir, was what he could tell me about going up north and stalking the big boys on their own turf." Frenchy Laval was a name well known in the submarine community, a great sonarman who had trained other great sonarmen. Now retired as a master chief, his son carried on the tradition.

The hell of it was, tracking whales had turned out to be good training. They were stealthy creatures, not because they sought to avoid detection, but simply because they moved with great efficiency, and the submarines had found that moving in close enough to count and identify the members of individual pods or families was at least diverting if not exactly exciting. For the sonarmen anyway, Kennedy thought. Not much for weapons department. . . .

Laval's eyes focused on the waterfall display. He settled more squarely into his chair and reached for a grease pencil, tapping the third-class next to him.

"Two-seven-zero," he said quietly.

"Yeah."

"What you got, Junior?" the CO asked.

"Just a sniff, sir, on the sixty-hertz line." Thirty seconds later: "Firming up."

Kennedy stood behind the two watch-standers. There were now two dotted lines, one in the sixty-hertz frequency portion of the display, another on a higher-frequency band. The electric motors on the Japanese Harushio-class submarine used sixty-cycle A/C electrical current. An irregular series of dots, yellow on the dark screen, started cascading down in a column under the "60" frequency heading like droplets falling in slow motion from a leaky faucet, hence the appellation "waterfall display." Junior Laval let it grow for a few more seconds to see if it might be random and decided that it was probably not.

"Sir, I think we might want to start a track now. Designate this contact Sierra-One, possible submerged contact, bearing settling down on two-seven-four, strength is weak."

Kennedy relayed the information to the fire-control tracking party fifteen feet away. Another technician activated the ray-path analyzer, a high-end Hewlett-Packard minicomputer programmed to examine the possible paths through the water that the identified acoustical signal might have followed. Though widely known to exist, the high-speed software for this piece of kit was still one of the Navy's most closely held secrets, a product, Kennedy remembered, of Sono-systems, a Groton-based company run by one of Frenchy Laval's top protégés. The computer chewed on the input data for perhaps a thousand microseconds and displayed its reply.

"Sir, it's direct path. My initial range estimate is between eight and twelve thousand yards."

"Set it up," the approach officer told the petty officer on the fire-control director.

"This one ain't no humpback," Laval reported three minutes later. "I have three lines on the guy now, classify Sierra-One as a definite submarine contact, operating on his electric motors." Junior told himself that Laval *père* had made his rep stalking HEN-class Russian subs, which were about as hard to track as an earthquake. He adjusted his headphones. "Bearing steady at two-seven-four, getting hints of a blade rate on the guy."

"Solution light," the lead fire-controlman reported. "I have a valid solution for tube three on target Sierra-One."

415

"Left ten-degrees rudder, come to new course one-eight-zero," Kennedy ordered next to get a cross-bearing, from which would come a better range-gate on the target, and also data on the sub's course and speed. "Let's slow her down, turns for five knots."

The stalk was always the fun part.

"If you do that, you're cutting your own throat with a dull knife," Anne Quinlan said in her customarily direct way.

Kealty was sitting in his office. Ordinarily the number-two man in any organization would be in charge when number-one was away, but the miracle of modern communications meant that Roger could do everything he needed to do at midnight over Antarctica if he had to. Including putting out a press statement from his aircraft in Moscow that he was hanging his Vice President out to dry.

Kealty's first instinct was to proclaim to the entire world that he knew he had the confidence of his President. That would hint broadly that the news stories were true, and muddy the waters sufficiently to give him room to maneuver, the thing he needed most of all.

"What we need to know, Ed," his chief of staff pointed out, not for the first time, "is who the hell started this." That was the one thing the story had left out, clever people that reporters were. She couldn't ask him how many of the women in his office he'd visited with his charms. For one thing he probably didn't remember, and for another, the hard part would be identifying those he hadn't.

"Whoever it was, it was somebody close to Lisa," another staffer observed. That insight made light bulbs flash inside every head in the office.

"Barbara."

"Good guess," the "Chief" — which was how Quinlan liked to be identified — thought. "We need

416

to confirm that, and we need to settle her down some."

"Woman scorned," Kealty murmured.

"Ed, I don't want to hear any of that, okay?" the Chief warned. "When the hell are you going to learn that 'no' doesn't mean 'maybe later'? Okay, I'll go see Barbara myself, and maybe we can talk her out of this, but, goddammit, this is the last time, okay?"

18

Easter Egg

"Is this where the dresser was?" Ryan asked.

"I keep forgetting how well informed you are," Golovko observed, just to flatter his guest, since the story was actually widely known.

Jack grinned, still feeling more than a little of Alice-through-the-Looking-Glass. There was a completely ordinary door in the wall now, but until the time of Yuri Andropov, a large wooden clothes cabinet had covered it, for in the time of Beriya and the rest, the entrance to the office of Chairman of the KGB had to be hidden. There was no door off the main corridor, and none visible even in the anteroom. The melodrama of it had to have been absurd, Ryan thought, even to Lavrentiy Beriya, whose morbid fear of assassination — though hardly unreasonable — had dreamed up this obtuse security measure. It hadn't helped him avoid death at the hands of men who'd hated him even more than they'd feared him. Still and all, wasn't it bizarre enough just for the President's National Security Advisor to enter the office of the Chairman of the *Russian* Foreign Intelligence Service? Beriya's ashes must have been stirring up somewhere, Ryan thought, in whatever sewer they'd dropped the urn. He turned to look at his host, his mind imagining the oak bureau still, and halfway wishing they'd kept the old name of KGB, Committee for State Security, just for tradition's sake.

"Sergey Nikolay'ch, has the world really changed so much in the past — God, only ten years?"

"Not even that, my friend." Golovko waved Jack to a comfortable leather chair that dated back to the building's previous incarnation as home office of the Rossiya Insurance Company. "And yet we have so far to go."

Business, Jack thought. Well, Sergey had never been bashful about that. Ryan remembered looking into the wrong end of a pistol in this man's hand. But that had all taken place before the so-called end of history.

"I'm doing everything I can, Sergey. We got you the five billion for the missiles. That was a nice scam you ran on us, by the way." Ryan checked his watch. The ceremony was scheduled for the evening. One Minuteman-III and one SS-19 left — if you didn't count the SS-19s in Japan that had been reconfigured to launch satellites.

"We have many problems, Jack."

"Fewer than a year ago," Ryan observed, wondering what the next request would be. "I know you advise President Grushavoy on more than just intelligence matters. Come on, Sergey, things are getting better. You know that."

"Nobody ever told us that democracy would be so hard."

"It's hard for us, too, pal. We rediscover it every day."

"The frustration is that we know we have everything we need to make our country prosperous. The problem is in making everything work. Yes, I advise my president on many things — "

"Sergey, if you're not one of the best-informed people in your country, I would be very surprised."

"Hmm, yes. Well, we are surveying eastern Siberia,

419

so many things, so many resources. We have to hire Japanese to do it for us, but what they are finding . . ." His voice trailed off.

"You're building up to something, Sergey. What is it?"

"We think they do not tell us everything. We dug up some surveys done in the early thirties. They were in archives in the Ministry of the Interior. A deposit of gadolinium in an unlikely place. At the time there were few uses for that metal, and it was forgotten until some of my people did a detailed search of old data. Gadolinium now has many uses, and one of their survey teams camped within a few kilometers of the deposit. We know it's real. The thirties team brought back samples for assay. But it was not included in their last report."

"And?" Jack asked.

"And I find it curious that they lied to us on this," Golovko observed, taking his time. You didn't build up to a play like this all that quickly.

"How are you paying them for the work?"

"The agreement is that they will assist us in the exploitation of many of the things they find for us. The terms are generous."

"Why would they lie?" Ryan inquired.

Golovko shook his head. "I do not know. It might be important to find out. You are a student of history, are you not?"

It was one of the things that each respected about the other. Ryan might have written off Golovko's concerns as yet another example of Russian paranoia — sometimes he thought that the entire concept had been invented in this country — but that would have been unfair. Russia had fought Japan under the Czar in 1904–1905 and lost, along the way giving the Japanese Navy a landmark victory at the Battle of the Tsushima Strait. That war had gone a long way toward destroying the Romanovs and to elevating Japan to world-power status, which had led to their involvement in two world wars. It had also inflicted a bleeding sore on the Russian psyche that Stalin had remembered well enough to recover the lost territories. The Japanese had also been involved in post–World War I efforts to topple the Bolsheviks. They'd put a sizable army into Siberia, and hadn't been all that enthusiastic about withdrawing it. The same thing had happened again, in 1938 and 1939, with more serious consequences this time, first at the hands of Marshal Blyukher, and then a guy named Zhukov. Yes, there was much history between Russia and Japan.

"In this day and age, Sergey?" Ryan asked with a wry expression.

"You know, Jack, as bright a chap as you are, you are still an American, and your experience with invasions is far less serious than ours. Are we panicked about this? No, of course not. Is it something worthy of close attention? Yes, Ivan Emmetovich, it is."

He was clearly building up to something, and with all the time he'd taken, it had to be something big, Ryan thought. Time to find out what it was: "Well, Sergey Nikolay'ch, I suppose I can understand your concern, but there isn't very much I can — " Golovko cut him off with a single word.

"THISTLE."

"Lyalin's old network. What about it?"

"You have recently reactivated it." The Chairman of RVS saw that Ryan had the good grace to blink in surprise. A bright, serious man, Ryan, but still not really someone who would have made a good field officer. His emotions were just too open. Perhaps, Sergey thought, he should read a book on Ireland, the better to understand the player in the ancient leather chair. Ryan had strengths and weaknesses, neither of which he completely understood.

"What gives you that idea?" the American asked

as innocently as he could, knowing that he'd reacted, again, baited by this clever old pro. He saw Golovko smile at his discomfort and wondered if the liberalization of this country had allowed people to develop a better sense of humor. Before Golovko would just have stared impassively.

"Jack, we are professionals, are we not? I know this. How I know it is my concern."

"I don't know what cards you're holding, my friend, but before you go any further, we need to decide if this is a friendly game or not."

"As you know, the real Japanese counterintelligence agency is the Public Safety Investigation Division of their Justice Ministry." The expositional statement was as clear as it had to be, and was probably truthful. It also defined the terms of the discourse. This was a friendly game. Golovko had just revealed a secret of his own, though not a surprising one.

You had to admire the Russians. Their expertise in the espionage business was world-class. No, Ryan corrected himself. They *were* the class of the world. What better way to run agents in any foreign country than first to establish a network within the country's counterintelligence services? There was still the lingering suspicion that they had in fact controlled MI-5, Britain's Security Service, for some years, and their deep and thorough penetration of CIA's own internal-security arm was still an embarrassment to America.

"Make your play," Ryan said. *Check to the dealer . . .*

"You have two field officers in Japan covered as Russian journalists. They are reactivating the network. They are very good, and very careful, but one of their contacts is compromised by PSID. That can happen to anyone," Golovko observed fairly. He didn't even gloat, Jack saw. Well, he was too professional for that, and it was a fairly friendly game by most standards. The other side of the statement was as clear as it could be: with a simple gesture

Sergey was in a position to burn Clark and Chavez, creating yet another international incident between two countries that had enough problems to settle. That was why Golovko didn't gloat. He didn't have to.

Ryan nodded. "Okay, pal. I just folded. Tell me what you want."

"We would like to know why Japan is lying to us, and anything else that in Mrs. Foley's opinion might be of interest to us. In return we are in a position to protect the network for you." He didn't add, *for the time being.*

"How much do they know?" Jack asked, considering the spoken offer. Golovko was suggesting that Russia cover an American intelligence operation. It was something new, totally unprecedented. They put a very high value on the information that might be developed. High as hell, Jack thought. *Why?*

"Enough to expel them from the country, no more." Golovko opened a drawer and handed over a sheet of paper. "This is all Foleyeva needs to know."

Jack read and pocketed it. "My country has no desire to see any sort of conflict between Russia and Japan."

"Then we are agreed?"

"Yes, Sergey. I will recommend approval of your suggestion."

"As always, Ivan Emmetovich, a pleasure to do business with you."

"Why didn't you activate it yourself?" Ryan asked, wondering how badly rolled he'd been that day.

"Lyalin held out on the information. Clever of him. We didn't have enough time to — persuade? Yes, persuade him to give it over — before we gave him to your custody."

Such a nice turn of phrase, Jack thought. *Persuade.* Well, Golovko had come up under the old system. It was too much to expect that he would have been

423

entirely divorced from it. Jack managed a grin.

"You know, you were great enemies." And with Golovko's single suggestion, Jack thought behind clinically impassive eyes, perhaps now there would be the beginning of something else. Damn, how much crazier would this world get?

It was six hours later in Tokyo, and eight hours earlier in New York. The fourteen-hour differential and the International Dateline created many opportunities for confusion. It was Saturday the fourteenth in some places and Friday in others.

At three in the morning, Chuck Searls left his home for the last time. He'd rented a car the previous day — like many New Yorkers, he had never troubled himself to purchase one — for the drive to La Guardia. The Delta terminal was surprisingly full for the first flight of the day to Atlanta. He'd booked a ticket through one of the city's many travel agencies, and paid cash for the assumed name he would hereafter be using from time to time, which was not the same as the one on the passport he had also acquired a few months ago. Sitting in 2-A, a first-class seat whose wide expanse allowed him to turn slightly and lean his head back, he slept most of the way to Atlanta, where his baggage was transferred to a flight to Miami. There wasn't much, really. Two lightweight suits, some shirts, and other immediate necessities, plus his laptop computer. In Miami he'd board another flight under another name and head southeast to paradise.

George Winston, former head of the Columbus Group, was not a happy man despite the plush surroundings of his home in Aspen. A wrenched knee saw to that. Though he now had the time to indulge his newly discovered passion for skiing, he was a little too inexperienced and perhaps a little too old to use the expert slopes. It hurt like a sonuvabitch. He rose from his bed at three in the morning and limped into the bathroom for another dose of the painkiller the doctor had prescribed. Once there he found that the combination of wakefulness and lingering pain offered little hope of returning to sleep. It was just after five in New York, he thought, about the time he usually got up, always early to get a jump on the late-risers, checking his computer and the *Journal* and other sources of information so that he could be fully prepared for his opening moves on the market.

He missed it, Winston admitted to himself. It was a hell of a thing to say to the face in the mirror. Okay, so he'd worked too hard, alienated himself from his own family, driven himself into a state little different from drug addiction, but getting out was a . . . mistake?

Well, no, not exactly that, he thought, hobbling into his den as quietly as he could manage. It was just that you couldn't empty something and then attempt to fill it with nothing, could you? He couldn't sail his *Cristobol* all the time, not with kids in school. In fact there was only one thing in his life that he'd been able to do all the time, and that had damned near killed him, hadn't it?

Even so . . .

Damn, you couldn't even get the *Journal* out here at a decent hour. And this was civilization? Fortunately, they did have phone lines. Just for old times' sake, he switched on his computer. Winston was wired into nearly every news and financial service there was, and he selected his personal favorite. It was good to do it early in the morning. His wife would yell again if she saw him up to his old tricks, which meant that he was nowhere near as current on the Street as he liked to be, player or not. Well, okay, he had a few hours, and it wasn't as though he'd be riding a helicopter to the top of the mountain at dawn, was it? No skiing at all, the doc had told him firmly. Not for at least a week, and then he'd confine himself to the bunny slopes. It wouldn't look that bad, would it? He'd pretend to be teaching his kids . . . damn!

He'd gotten out too soon. No way he could have known, of course, but in the last few weeks the market had begged aloud for a person with his talents to swoop down and make his moves. He would have moved on steel three weeks ago, made his killing, and then moved on to . . . Silicon Alchemy. Yeah, that was one he would have snapped up in one big hurry. They had invented a new sort of screen for laptop computers, and now with Japan's products under a cloud, the issue had exploded. Who was it who'd quarterbacked the IPO? That Ryan guy, good instincts for the business, pissing away his time in government service now. *What a waste of talent,* Winston told himself, feeling the ache in his leg and trying not to add that he was pissing away his time in the middle of the night at a ski resort he couldn't use for the next week at best.

Everything on the Street seemed so unnecessarily shaky, he thought, checking trend lines on stocks he considered good if stealthy bellwethers. That was one of the tricks, spotting trends and indicators before the others did. One of the tricks? Hell, the *only* trick. How he did it was surprisingly hard to teach. He supposed that it was the same in any field. Some people just did it, and he was one of them. Others tried to do the same by cheating, seeking out information in underhanded ways, or by falsely creating trends that they could then exploit. But that was . . . cheating, wasn't it? And what was the point of making money that way? Beating the others fairly and at their own game, *that* was the real art of trading, and at the end of the day what he liked to hear was the way others would come up and say, "You son of a bitch!" The tone of the comment made all the difference.

There was no reason for the market to be so unsteady, he thought. People hadn't thought the things through, that was all.

The Hornets went off behind the first wave of Tomcats. Sanchez taxied his fighter to the starboard-side bow cat, feeling the towbar that formed part of his nosewheel gear slip into the proper slot on the shuttle. His heavily loaded fighter shuddered at full power as the deck crewmen gave the aircraft a last visual check. Satisfied, the catapult officer made the ready signal, and Sanchez fired off a salute and set his head back on the back of his ejection seat. A moment later, steam power flung him off the bow and into the air. The Hornet settled a bit, a feeling that was never entirely routine, and he climbed into the sky, retracting his landing gear and heading toward the rendezvous point, his wings heavy with fuel tanks and blue practice missiles.

They were trying to be clever, and almost succeeding, but "almost" didn't really count in this game. Satellite photos had revealed the presence of the three inbound surface groups. Sanchez would lead the Alpha Strike against the big one, eight ships, all tin cans. Two separated pairs of Tomcats would deal with the P-3s they had out; for the first time they'd hunt actively with their search radars instead of being under EMCOM. It would be a single rapier thrust — no, more the descending blow of a big and heavy club. Intermittent sweeps of an E-2C Hawkeye radar aircraft determined that the Japanese had not deployed fighters to Marcus, which would have been clever if difficult for them, and in any case they would not have been able to surge enough of them to matter, not against two full carrier air wings. Marcus just wasn't a big enough island, as Saipan or Guam was.

That was his last abstract thought for a while. On Bud's command via a low-power radio circuit, the formation began to disperse according to its carefully structured plan.

"Hai." Sato lifted the growler phone on *Mutsu*'s bridge.

"We just detected low-power radio voice traffic. Two signals, bearing one-five-seven, and one-nine-five, respectively."

"It's about time," Sato told his group-operations officer. *I thought they'd never get around to their attack.* In a real-war situation he would do one thing. In this particular case, he'd do another. There was little point in letting the Americans know the sensitivity of his ELINT gear. "Continue as before."

"Very well. We still have the two airborne radars. They appear to be flying racetrack patterns, no change."

"Thank you." Sato replaced the phone and reached for his tea. His best technicians were working the electronic-intelligence listening gear, and they had tapes collecting the information taken down by every sensor for later study. That was really the important part of this phase of the exercise, to learn all they could about how the U.S. Navy made its deliberate attacks.

"Action stations?" *Mutsu*'s captain asked quietly.

"No need," the Admiral replied, staring thought-fully at the horizon, as he supposed a fighting sailor did.

Aboard Snoopy One, an EA-6B Prowler, the flight crew monitored all radar and radio frequencies. They found and identified six commercial-type search radars, none of them close to the known location of the Japanese formation. They weren't making it much of a contest, everyone thought. Normally these games were a lot more fun.

The captain of the port at Tanapag harbor looked out from his office to see a large car-carrier working her way around the southern tip of Managaha Island. That was a surprise. He ruffled through the papers on his desk to see where the telex was to warn him of her arrival. Oh, yes, there. It must have come in during the night. MV *Orchid Ace* out of Yokohama. Cargo of Toyota Land Cruisers diverted for sale to the local Japanese landowners. Probably a ship that had been scheduled for transit to America. So now the cars would come here and clog the local roads some more. He grumped and lifted his binoculars to give her a look and saw to his surprise another lump on the horizon, large and boxy. Another car carrier? That was odd.

Snoopy One held position and altitude, just under the visual horizon from the "enemy" formation, about one hundred miles away. The electronic warriors in the two backseats had their hands ready on the power switches for the onboard jammers, but the Japanese didn't have any of their radars up, and there was nothing to jam. The pilot allowed herself a look to the southeast and saw a few flashes, yellow glints off the gold-impregnated canopies of the inbound Alpha Strike, which was now angling down to the deck to stay out of radar coverage as long as possible before popping up to loose their first "salvo" of administrative missiles.

"Tango, tango, tango," Commander Steve Kennedy said into the gertrude, giving the code word for a theoretical or "administrative" torpedo launch. He'd held contact with the Harushio-class for nine hours, taking the time to get acquainted with the contact, and to get his crew used to something more demanding than getting heartbeats on a pregnant hump-back. Finally bored with the game, it was time to light up the underwater telephone and, he was sure, scare the bejeebers out of Sierra-One after giving him ample time to counterdetect. He didn't want anyone to say later that he hadn't given the other guy a fair break. Not that this sort of thing was supposed to be fair, but Japan and America were friends, despite the news stuff they'd been getting on the radio for the past few weeks.

"Took his time," Commander Ugaki said. They'd tracked the American 688 for almost forty minutes. So they were good, but not that good. It had been so hard for them to detect *Kurushio* that they'd made their attack as soon as they had a track, and, Ugaki thought, he'd let them have their first shot. So. The CO looked at his own fire-control director and the four red solution lights.

He lifted his own gertrude phone to reply in a voice full of good-natured surprise: "Where did you come from?"

Those crewmen who were in earshot — every man aboard spoke good English — were surprised at the captain's announcement. Ugaki saw the looks. He would brief them in later.

"Didn't even 'tango' back. I guess he wasn't at GQ." Kennedy keyed the phone again. "As per exercise instructions, we will now pull off and turn on our augmenter." On his command, USS *Asheville* turned right and increased speed to twenty knots. She'd pull away to twenty thousand yards to restart the exercise, giving the "enemy" a better chance at useful training.

"Conn, sonar."

"Conn, aye."

"New contact, designate Sierra-Five, bearing two-

430

eight-zero, twin-screw diesel surface ship, type unknown. Blade rate indicates about eighteen knots," SM/1c Junior Laval announced.

"No classification?"

"Sounds a little, well, little, Cap'n, not the big boomin' sounds of a large merchantman."

"Very well, we'll run a track. Keep me posted."

"Sonar, aye."

It was just too easy, Sanchez thought. The *Enterprise* group was probably having a tougher time with their Kongo-class DDGs up north. He was not pressing it, but holding his extended flight of four at three hundred feet above the calm surface, at a speed of just four hundred knots. Each of the four fighter-attack aircraft of Slugger Flight carried four exercise Harpoon missiles, as did the four trailing in Mauler. He checked his heads-up display for location. Data loaded into his computer only an hour before gave him a probable location for the formation, and his GPS navigation system had brought him right to the programmed place. It was time to check to see how accurate their operational intelligence was.

"Mauler, this is lead, popping up — now!" Sanchez pulled back easily on the stick. "Going active — now!" With the second command he flipped on his search radar.

There they were, big as hell on the display. Sanchez selected the lead ship in the formation and spun up the seeker heads in the otherwise inert missiles hanging from his wings. He got four ready lights. "This is Slugger-Lead. Launch launch launch! Rippling four vampires."

"Two, launching four."

"Three, launch four."

"Four, launching three, one abort on the rail." About par for the course, Sanchez thought, framing a remark for his wing maintenance officer.

431

In a real attack the aircraft would have angled back down to the surface after firing their missiles so as not to expose themselves. For the purposes of the exercise they descended to two hundred feet and kept heading in to simulate their own missiles. Onboard recorders would take down the radar and tracking data from the Japanese ships in order to evaluate their performance, which so far was not impressive.

Faced with the irksome necessity of allowing women to fly in real combat squadrons off real carriers, the initial compromise had been to put them in electronic-warfare aircraft, hence the Navy's first female squadron commander was Commander Roberta Peach of VAQ-137, "The Rooks." The most senior female carrier aviator, she deemed it her greatest good fortune that *another* naval aviator, female, already had the call sign "Peaches," which allowed her to settle on "Robber," a name she insisted on in the air.

"Getting signals now, Robber," the lead EWO in the back of her Prowler reported. "Lots of sets lighting off."

"Shut 'em back down," she ordered curtly.

"Sure are a lot of 'em . . . targeting a Harm on an SPG-51. Tracking and ready."

"Launching now," Robber said. Shooting was her prerogative as aircraft commander. As long as the SPG-51 missile-illumination radar was up and radiating, the Harm antiradar missile was virtually guaranteed to hit.

Sanchez could see the ships now, gray shapes on the visual horizon. An unpleasant screech in his headphones told him that he was being illuminated with both search and fire-control radar, never a happy bit of news even in an exercise, all the more so that the "enemy" in this case had American-designed SM-2

432

Standard surface-to-air missiles with whose performance he was quite familiar. It looked like a Hatakaze-class. Two SPG-51C missile radars. Only one single-rail launcher. She could guide only two at a time. His aircraft represented two missiles. The Hornet was a larger target than the Harpoon was, and was not going as low or as fast as the missile did. On the other hand, he had a protective jammer aboard, which evened the equation somewhat. Bud eased his stick to the left. It was against safety rules to fly directly over a ship under circumstances like this, and a few seconds later he passed three hundred yards ahead of the destroyer's bow. At least one of his missiles would have hit, he judged, and that one was only a five-thousand-ton tin can. One Harpoon warhead would ruin her whole day, making his follow-up attack with cluster munitions even more deadly.

"Slugger, this is lead. Form up on me."

"Two — "

"Three — "

"Four," his flight acknowledged.

Another day in the life of a naval aviator, the CAG thought. Now he could look forward to landing, going into CIC, and spending the rest of the next twenty-four hours going over the scores. It just wasn't very exciting anymore. He'd splashed real airplanes, and anything else wasn't the same. But flying was still flying.

The roar of aircraft overhead was usually exhilarating. Sato watched the last of the gray American fighters climb away, and lifted his binoculars to see their direction. Then he rose and headed below to the CIC.

"Well?" he asked.

"Departure course is as we thought." Fleet-Ops tapped the satellite photo that showed both American battle groups, still heading west, into the prevailing winds, to conduct flight operations. The photo was only two hours old. The radar plot showed the American aircraft heading to the expected point.

"Excellent. My respects to the captain, make course one-five-five, maximum possible speed." In less than a minute, *Mutsu* shuddered with increased engine power and started riding harder through the gentle Pacific swells for her rendezvous with the American battle force. Timing was important.

On the floor of the New York Stock Exchange, a young trader's clerk made a posting error on Merck stock at exactly 11:43:02 Eastern Standard Time. It actually went onto the system and appeared on the board at 23⅛, well off the current value. Thirty seconds later he typed it in again, inputting the same amount. This time he got yelled at. He explained that the damned keyboard was sticky, and unplugged it, switching it for a new one. It happened often enough. People spilled coffee and other things in this untidy place. The correction was inputted at once, and the world returned to normal. In the same minute something similar happened with General Motors stock, and someone made the same excuse. It was safe. The people at her particular kiosk didn't interact all that much with the people who did Merck. Neither had any idea what they were doing, just that they were being paid $50,000 to make an error that would have no effect on the system at all. Had they not done it — they did not know — another pair of individuals had been paid the same amount of money to do the same thing ten minutes later.

In the Stratus mainframe computers at the Depository Trust Company — more properly in the software that resided in them — the entries were noted, and the Easter Egg started to hatch.

★ ★ ★

The cameras and lights were all set up in St. Vladimir Hall of the Great Kremlin Palace, the traditional room for finalizing treaties and a place that Jack had visited at another time and under very different circumstances. In two separate rooms, the President of the United States and the President of the Russian Republic were having their makeup put on, something that was probably more irksome to the Russian, Ryan was sure. Looking good for the cameras was not a traditional requirement for local political figures. Most of the guests were already seated, but the senior members of both official parties could be more relaxed. Final preparations were just about complete. The crystal glasses were on their trays, and the corks on the champagne bottles were unwrapped, awaiting only the word to be popped off.

"That reminds me. You never did send me any of that Georgian champagne," Jack told Sergey.

"Well, today it can be done, and I can get you a good price."

"You know, before, I would have had to turn it in because of ethics laws."

"Yes, I know that every American official is a potential crook," Golovko noted, checking around to see that everything was done properly.

"You should be a lawyer." Jack saw the lead Secret Service agent come through the door, and headed to his seat. "Some place, isn't it, honey?" he asked his wife.

"The czars knew how to live," she whispered back as the TV lights all came on. In America, all the networks interrupted their regular programming. The timing was a little awkward, with the eleven-hour differential between Moscow and the American West Coast. Then there was Russia, which had at least ten time zones of its own, a result of both sheer size and, in the case of Siberia, proximity to the Arctic Circle.

But this was something everyone would want to see.

The two presidents came out, to the applause of the three hundred people present. Roger Durling and Eduard Grushavoy met at the mahogany table and shook hands warmly as only two former enemies could. Durling, the former soldier and paratrooper with Vietnam experience; Grushavoy, also a former soldier, a combat engineer who had been among the first to enter Afghanistan. Trained to hate one another in their youth, now they would put a final end to it all. On this day, they would set aside all the domestic problems that both lived with on every day of the week. For today, the world would change by their hands.

Grushavoy, the host, gestured Durling to his chair, then moved to the microphone.

"Mister President," he said through an interpreter whom he didn't really need, "it is my pleasure to welcome you to Moscow for the first time . . ."

Ryan didn't listen to the speech. It was predictable in every phrase. His eyes fixed on a black plastic box that sat on the table exactly between the chairs of the two chiefs of state. It had two red buttons and a cable that led down to the floor. A pair of TV monitors sat against the near wall, and in the rear of the room, large projection TVs were available for everyone to watch. They showed similar sites.

"Hell of a way to run a railroad," an Army major noted, twenty miles from Minot, North Dakota. He'd just screwed in the last wire. "Okay, circuits are live. Wires are hot." Only one safety switch prevented the explosives from going, and he had his hand on it. He'd already done a personal check of everything, and there was a full company of military police patrolling the area because Friends of the Earth was threatening to protest the event by putting people where the explosives were, and as desirable as it might be just to blow the bastards up, the officer would have to disable the firing circuit if that happened. *Why the* hell, he wondered, *would anybody protest this?* He'd already wasted an hour trying to explain that to his Soviet counterpart.

"So like the steppes here," the man said, shivering in the wind. They both watched a small TV for their cue.

"It's a shame we don't have the politicians around here to give us some hot air." He took his hand off the safety switch. Why couldn't they just get on with it?

The Russian officer knew his American English well enough to laugh at the remark, feeling inside his oversized parka for a surprise he had in waiting for the American.

"Mr. President, the hospitality we have experienced in this great city is proof positive that there should be, can be, and *will* be a friendship between our two peoples — just as strong as our old feelings were, but far more productive. Today, we put an end to war," Durling concluded to warm applause, returning to shake Grushavoy's hand again. Both men sat down. Oddly, now they had to take their orders from an American TV director who held a headset to his face and talked very quickly.

"Now," men said in two languages, "if the audience will turn to the TVs . . ."

"When I was a lieutenant in the pioneers," the Russian President whispered, "I loved blowing things up."

Durling grinned, leaning his head in close. Some things were not for microphones. "You know the job I always wanted as a boy — do you have it over here?"

"What is that, Roger?"

"The guy who runs the crane with the big iron

437

ball for knocking buildings down. It *has to be* the best job in the whole world."

"Especially if you can put your parliamentary opposition in the building first!" It was a point of view that both shared.

"Time," Durling saw from the director.

Both men put their thumbs on their buttons.

"On three, Ed?" Durling asked.

"Yes, Roger!"

"One," Durling said.

"Two," Grushavoy continued.

"Three!" both said, pressing them down.

The two buttons closed a simple electrical circuit that led to a satellite transmitter outside. It took roughly a third of a second for the signal to go up to the satellite and come back down, then another third for the result to retrace the same path, and for a long moment a lot of people thought that something had gone wrong. But it hadn't.

"Whoa!" the Major observed when a hundred pounds of Composition-Four went off. The noise was impressive, even from half a mile, and there followed the tower of flame from the ignition of the solid-fuel rocket motor. That part of the ceremony had been tricky. They'd had to make sure that the thing would burn from the top only. Otherwise the missile might have tried to fly out of the silo, and *that* would just not have done at all. In fact the whole exercise was unnecessarily complicated and dangerous. The cold wind drove the toxic exhaust smoke to the east, and by the time it got to anything important, it would just be a bad smell, which was pretty much what you could say about the political conditions that had occasioned the existence of the burning rocket motor, wasn't it? There was a certain awe to it, though. The world's largest firework, burning backwards for about three minutes before there was nothing left but smoke. A sergeant activated the silo fire-suppression system, which actually worked, rather to the Major's surprise.

"You know, we had a drawing to see who'd get to do this. I won," the officer said, getting to his feet.

"I was just ordered to come. I am glad I did. Is it safe now?"

"I think so. Come on, Valentin. We have one more job to do, don't we?"

Both men got into an HMMWV, the current incarnation of the Army jeep, and the Major started it up, heading for the silo from upwind. Now it was just a hole in the ground, generating steam. A CNN crew followed, still giving a live feed as the vehicle bumped across the uneven prairie. Their vehicle stopped two hundred yards away, somewhat to their annoyance, while the two officers dismounted their vehicle, carrying gas masks against the possibility that there was still enough smoke to be a health concern. There wasn't. Just the nasty smell. The American officer waved the TV crew in and waited for them to get ready. That took two minutes.

"Ready!" the unit director said.

"Are we in agreement that the silo and missile are destroyed?"

"Yes, we are," the Russian replied with a salute. Then he reached behind his back and pulled two crystal glasses from his pockets. "Would you hold these please, Comrade Major?"

Next came a bottle of Georgian champagne. The Russian popped the cork with a wide grin and filled both glasses.

"I teach you Russian tradition now. First you drink," he said. The TV crew loved it.

"I think I know that part." The American downed the champagne. "And now?"

"The glasses may never be used for a lesser purpose.

439

Now you must do as I do." With that the Russian turned and poised himself to hurl his glass into the empty hole. The American laughed and did the same.

"Now!" With that, both glasses disappeared into the last American Minuteman silo. They disappeared in the steam, but both could hear them shatter against the scorched concrete walls.

"Fortunately, I have two more glasses," Valentin said, producing them.

"Son of a bitch," Ryan breathed. It turned out that the American at the Russian silo had had a similar idea, and was now explaining what "Miller time!" meant. Unfortunately, aluminum cans didn't break when thrown.

"Overly theatrical," his wife thought.

"It isn't exactly Shakespeare, but if t'were done when t'were done, then at least it's done, honey." Then they heard the corks popping off amid the sounds of applause.

"Is the five-billion-dollars part true?"

"Yep."

"So, Ivan Emmetovich, we can be truly friends now?" Golovko asked, bringing glasses. "We finally meet, Caroline," he said graciously to Cathy.

"Sergey and I go way back," Jack explained, taking the glass and toasting his host.

"To the time I had a gun to your head," the Russian observed. Ryan wondered if it were an historical reference . . . or a toast to the event?

"*What?*" Cathy asked, almost choking on her drink.

"You never told her?"

"Jesus, Sergey!"

"What are you two talking about?"

"Dr. Ryan, once upon a time your husband and I had a . . . professional disagreement that ended up with myself holding a pistol in his face. I never told you, Jack, that the gun wasn't loaded."

"Well, I wasn't going anywhere anyway, was I?"

"What *are* you two talking about? Is this some inside joke?" Cathy demanded.

"Yeah, honey, that's about right. How is Andrey Il'ich doing?"

"He is well. In fact, if you would like to see him, it can be arranged."

Jack nodded. "I'd like that."

"Excuse me, but who exactly are you?"

"Honey," Jack said. "This is Sergey Nikolayevich Golovko, Chairman of the Russian Foreign Intelligence Service."

"KGB? You know each other?"

"Not KGB, madam. We are much smaller now. Your husband and I have been . . . competitors for years now."

"Okay, and who won?" she asked.

Both men had the same thought, but Golovko said it first: "Both of us, of course. Now, if you will permit, let me introduce you to my wife, Yelena. She is a pediatrician." That was something CIA had never bothered to find out, Jack realized.

He turned to look at the two presidents, enjoying the moment despite being surrounded by newsies. It was the first time he'd actually been to an event like this, but he was sure they weren't always this chummy. Perhaps it was the final release of all that tension, the realization that, yes, Virginia, it really was over. He saw people bringing in yet more champagne. It was pretty good stuff, and he fully intended to have his share of it. CNN would soon tire of the party, but these people would not. All the uniforms, and politicians, and spies, and diplomats. Hell, maybe they would all really be friends.

19

Strike Two, 1-800-RUN

Though the overall timing was fortuitous, the plan for exploiting the chance was exquisite, the product of years of study and modeling and simulation. In fact the operation had already begun when six major commercial banks in Hong Kong started going short on U.S. Treasury bonds. These had been bought a few weeks earlier, part of a complex exchange for yen holdings done as a classic hedge against monetary fluctuations. The banks themselves were about to undergo a trauma — a change in ownership of the very ground upon which they stood — and the two factors made their massive purchases seem an entirely ordinary move to maximize their liquidity and flexibility at the same time. In liquidating the bonds, they were just cashing in, albeit in a large way, on the relative change in values of dollar and yen. They would realize a 17 percent profit from the move, in fact, then buy yen, which, currency experts all over the world were now saying, had reached a hard floor and would soon rebound. Still, two hundred ninety *billion* dollars of U.S. bonds were on the market briefly, and undervalued at that. They were soon snapped up by European banks. The Hong Kong bankers made the proper electronic entries, and the transaction was concluded. Next they wired the fact to Beijing, uneasily happy to show that they had followed orders and demonstrated obeisance to their soon-to-be political masters. So much the better, all thought, that they had taken a profit on the deal.

In Japan the transaction was noted. Fourteen hours off the local time of New York City, still the world's foremost trading center, it was not terribly unusual for Tokyo traders to work hours usually associated with night watchmen, and in any case the wire services that communicated financial information never ceased transmitting data. It would have surprised some people to learn that the people in the trading offices were very senior indeed, and that a special room had been established on the top floor of a major office building during the last week. Called the War Room by its current occupants, it had telephone lines leading to every city in the world with major trading activities and computer displays to show what was happening in all of them.

Other Asian banks went next, repeating the same procedure as in Hong Kong, and the people in the War Room watched their machines. Just after noon, New York time, Friday, which was 2:03 A.M. on Saturday in Tokyo, they saw another three hundred million dollars of U.S. bonds dumped into the market, these at a price even more attractive than that just offered in Hong Kong, and these, also, were rapidly bought by other European bankers for whom the working day and week were just coming to an end. As yet nothing grossly unusual had happened. Only then did the Japanese banks make their move, well covered by the activity of others. The Tokyo banks as well started selling off their U.S. Treasuries, clearly taking action to firm up the yen, it appeared. In the process, however, the entire world's ready surplus-dollar capacity had been used up in a period of minutes. It could be written off as a mere coincidence, but the currency traders — at least those not at lunch

443

in New York — were now alerted to the fact that any further trading on those notes would be unsettling, however unlikely that might be, what with the known strength of the dollar.

The state dinner was reflective of traditional Russian hospitality, made all the more intense by the fact that it celebrated the end of two generations of nuclear terror. The Metropolitan of the Russian Orthodox Church intoned a long and dignified invocation. Himself twice the victim of political imprisonment, his invitation to rejoice was heartfelt, moving a few to tears, which were soon banished by the start of the feast. There was soup, and caviar, and fowl, and fine beef; and huge quantities of alcohol which, for just this once, everyone felt free to imbibe. The real work of the trip was done. There really were no secrets left to hide. Tomorrow was Saturday, and everyone would have the chance to sleep late.

"You, too, Cathy?" Jack asked. His wife was not normally a heavy drinker, but tonight she was knocking it back.

"This champagne is wonderful." It was her first state dinner overseas. She'd had a good day of her own with local ophthalmic surgeons, and had invited two of the best, full professors both, to come to the Wilmer Institute and acquaint themselves with her specialty area. Cathy was in the running for a Lasker Award for her work with laser surgery, the product of eleven years of clinical research, and the reason she had not accepted a department chairmanship twice offered by University of Virginia. Her big paper announcing the breakthrough would soon be published in *NEJM*, and for her as well, this night and this trip were the culmination of many things.

"You're going to pay for it tomorrow," her husband warned. Jack was going easier on all the drinks, though he had already exceeded his normal nightly limit, which was one. It was the toasts that would do everyone in, he knew, having been through Russian banquets before. It was just a cultural thing. The Russians could drink most Irishmen under any table, something he'd once learned the hard way, but most of the American party either hadn't learned that lesson or simply didn't care this night. The National Security Advisor shook his head. They'd sure as hell learn it tomorrow morning. The main course arrived just then, and deep red wine filled the glasses.

"Oh, God, my dress is going to split wide open!"

"That should add to the official entertainment," her husband observed, earning a glare from across the table.

"You are far too skinny," Golovko observed, sitting next to her and giving voice to another Russian prejudice.

"So how old are your children?" Yelena Golovko asked. Also thin by Russian standards, she was a professor of pediatrics, and a very pleasant dinner companion.

"An American custom," Jack replied, pulling out his wallet and showing the pictures. "Olivia — I call her Sally. This is little Jack, and this is our newest."

"Your son favors you, but the girls are the image of their mother."

Jack grinned. "A good thing, too."

The great trading firms are just that, but it's a mystery to the average stockholder just how they trade. Wall Street was a vast collection of misnomers, beginning with the street itself, which is the approximate width of a back alley in most American residential areas, and even the sidewalks seem overly narrow for the degree of traffic they serve. When purchase orders came in to a major house, like the largest of them, Merrill Lynch, the traders did not go looking, physically or electronically, for someone willing to sell that particular issue. Rather, every day the company itself bought measured holdings of issues deemed likely to trade, and then awaited consumer interest in them. Buying in fairly large blocks made for some degree of volume discounting, and the sales, generally, were at a somewhat higher price. In this way the trading houses made money on what bookies called a "middle" position, typically about one eighth of a point. A point was a dollar, and thus an eighth of a point was twelve and a half cents. Seemingly a tiny margin of profit for a stock whose share value could be anything up to hundreds of dollars in the case of some blue chips, it was a margin repeated on many issues on a daily basis, compounded over time to a huge potential profit if things went well. But they didn't always go well, and it was also possible for the houses to lose vast sums in a market that fell more rapidly than their estimates. There were many aphorisms warning of this. On the Hong Kong market, a large and active one, it was said that the market "went up like an escalator and down like an elevator," but the most basic saying was hammered into the mind of every new "rocket scientist" on the huge computer-trading floor of Merrill Lynch headquarters on the Lower West Side: "Never assume that there is a buyer for what you want to sell." But everyone did assume that, of course, because there always was, at least as far back as the collective memory of the firm went, and that was pretty far.

Most of the trading was not to individual investors, however. Since the 1960s, mutual funds had gradually assumed control of the market. Called "institutions" and grouped under that title with banks, insurance companies, and pension-fund managers, there were actually far more such "institutions" than there were stock issues on the New York Stock Exchange, rather like having hunters outnumbering the game, and the institutions controlled pools of money so vast as to

446

defy comprehension. They were so powerful that to a large extent their policies could actually have a large effect on individual issues and even, briefly, the entire market, and in many cases the "institutions" were controlled by a small number of people — in many cases, just one.

The third and largest wave of Treasury-note sales came as a surprise to everyone, but most of all to the Federal Reserve Bank headquarters in Washington, whose staff had noted the Hong Kong and Tokyo transactions, the first with interest, the second with a small degree of alarm. The Eurodollar market had made things right, but that market was now mainly closed. These were more Asian banks, institutions that set their benchmarks not in America, but in Japan, and whose technicians had also noted the dumping and done some phoning around the region. Those calls had ended up in a single room atop an office tower, where very senior banking officials said that they'd been called in from a night's sleep to see a situation that looked quite serious to them, occasioning the second wave of sales, and that they recommended a careful, orderly, but rapid movement of position away from the dollar.

U.S. Treasury notes were the debt instruments of the United States government and also the principal retaining wall for the value of American currency. Regarded for fifty years as the safest investment on the planet, T-Bills gave both American citizens and everyone else the ability to put their capital in a commodity that represented the world's most powerful economy, protected in turn by the world's most powerful military establishment and regulated by a political system that enshrined rights and opportunities through a Constitution that all admired even though they didn't always quite understand it. Whatever the faults and failings of America — none of them mysteries to sophisticated international investors — since

447

1945 the United States had been the one place in all the world where money was relatively safe. There was an inherent vitality to America from which all strong things grew. Imperfect as they were, Americans were also the world's most optimistic people, still a young country by the standards of the rest of the world, with all the attributes of vigorous youth. And so, when people had wealth to protect, mixed with uncertainty on how to protect it, most often they bought U.S. Treasury notes. The return wasn't always inviting, but the security was.

But not today. Bankers worldwide saw that Hong Kong and Tokyo had bailed out hard and fast, and the excuse over the trading wires that they were moving their positions from the dollar to the yen just didn't explain it all, especially after a few phone calls were made to inquire why the move had been made. Then the word arrived that more Japanese banks were moving out their bond holdings in a careful, orderly, and rapid movement. With that, bankers throughout Asia started doing the same. The third wave of selling was close to six hundred billion dollars, almost all short-term notes with which the current U.S. administration had chosen to finance its spending deficit.

The dollar was already falling, and with the start of the third wave of selling, all in a period of less than ninety minutes, the drop grew steeper still. In Europe, traders on their way home heard their cellular phones start beeping to call them back. Something unexpected was afoot. Analysts wondered if it had anything to do with the developing sex scandal within the American government. Europeans always wondered at the American fixation with the sexual dalliances of politicians. It was foolish, puritanical, and irrational, but it was also real to the American political scene, and that made it a relevant factor in how they handled American securities. The value of three-month U.S. Treasury notes was already down 19/32 of a point — bond values were expressed in such fractions — and as a result of that the dollar had fallen four cents against the British pound, even more against the Deutschmark, and more still again against the yen.

"What the hell is going on?" one of the Fed's board members asked. The whole board, technically known as the Open Market Committee, was grouped around a single computer screen, watching the trend in a collective mood of disbelief. There was no reason for this chaos that any of them could identify. Okay, sure, there was the flap over Vice President Kealty, but he was the *Vice* President. The stock market had been wavering up and down for some time due to the lingering confusion over the effects of the Trade Reform Act. But what kind of evil synergy was this? The problem, they knew without discussing, was that they might never really know what was happening. Sometimes there was no real explanation. Sometimes things just happened, like a herd of cattle deciding to stampede for no reason that the drovers ever understood. When the dollar was down a full hundred basis points — meaning one percent of value — they all walked into the sanctity of their boardroom and sat down. The discussion was rapid and decisive. There was a run on the dollar. They had to stop it. Instead of the half-point rise in the Discount Rate they had planned to announce at the end of the working day, they would go to a full point. A strong minority actually proposed more than that, but agreed to the compromise. The announcement would be made immediately. The head of the Fed's public-relations department drafted a statement for the Chairman to read for whatever news cameras would answer the summons, and the statement would go out simultaneously on every wire service.

When brokers returned to their desks from lunch, what had been a fairly calm Friday was something else entirely. Every office had a news board that gave shorthand announcements of national and international events, because such things had effects on the market. The notification that the Fed had jacked up its benchmark rate by a full point shocked most trading rooms to a full fifteen or thirty seconds of silence, punctuated by not a few *Holy shit*s. Technical traders modeling on their computer terminals saw that the market was already reacting. A rise in the discount rate was a sure harbinger of a brief dip in the Dow, like dark clouds were of rain. This storm would not be a pleasant one.

The big houses, Merrill Lynch, Lehman Brothers, Prudential-Bache, and all the rest, were highly automated, and all were organized along similar lines. In almost every case there was a single large room with banks of computer terminals. The size of the room was invariably dictated by the configuration of the building, and the highly paid technicians were crowded in almost as densely as a Japanese corporate office, except that in the American business centers people weren't allowed to smoke. Few of the men wore their suit jackets, and most of the women wore sneakers.

They were all very bright, though their educational backgrounds might have surprised the casual visitor. Once peopled with products of the Harvard or Wharton business schools, the new crop of "rocket scientists" were just that — largely holders of science degrees, especially mathematics and physics. MIT was the current school of choice, along with a handful of others. The reason was that the trading houses all used computers, and the computers used highly complex mathematical models both to analyze and predict what the market was doing. The models were based on painstaking historical research that covered the NYSE all the way back to when it was a place under the shade of a buttonwood tree. Teams of historians and mathematicians had plotted every move in the market. These records had been analyzed, compared with all identifiable outside factors, and given their own mathematically drawn measure of reality, and the result was a series of very precise and inhumanly intricate models for how the market had worked, did work, and would work. All of this data, however, was dedicated to the idea that dice *did* have a memory, a concept beloved of casino owners, but false.

You needed to be a mathematical genius, everyone said (especially the mathematical geniuses), to understand how this thing operated. The older hands kept out of the way for the most part. People who had learned business in business schools, or even people who had started as clerks and made their way up the ladder through sheer effort and savvy, had made way for the new generation — not really regretting it. The half-life of a computer jockey was eight years or so. The pace on the floor was killing, and you had to be young and stupid, in addition to being young and brilliant, to survive out there. The older hands who had worked their way up the hard way let the youngsters do the computer-driving, since they themselves had only a passing familiarization with the equipment, and took on the role of supervising, marking trends, setting corporate policy, and generally being the kindly uncle to the youngsters, who regarded the supervisory personnel as old farts to whom you ran in time of trouble.

The result was that nobody was really in charge of anything — except, perhaps, the computer models, and everyone used the same model. They came in slightly different flavors, since the consultants who had generated them had been directed by each trading house to come up with something special, and the result was prosperity for the consultants, who did essentially the same work for each customer but billed

451

each for what they claimed was a unique product.

The result, in military terms, was an operational doctrine both identical and inflexible across the industry. Moreover, it was an operational philosophy that everyone knew and understood only in part.

The Columbus Group, one of the largest mutual-fund fleets, had its own computer models. Controlling billions of dollars, its three main funds, Niña, Pinta, and Santa Maria, were able to purchase large blocks of equities at rock-bottom prices, and by those very transactions to affect the price of individual issues. That vast market power was in turn commanded by no more than three individuals, and that trio reported to a fourth man who made all of the really important decisions. The rest of the firm's rocket scientists were paid, graded, and promoted on their ability to make recommendations to the seniors. They had no real power per se. The word of the boss was law, and everybody accepted that as a matter of course. The boss was invariably a man with his own fortune in the group. Each of his dollars had the same value as the dollar of the smallest investor, of whom there were thousands. It ran the same risks, reaped the same benefits, and occasionally took the same losses as everyone else's dollar. That, really, was the only security built into the entire trading system. The ultimate sin in the brokerage business was to place your own interests before those of your investors. Merely by putting your interests alongside theirs, there came the guarantee that everyone was in it together, and the little guys who had not the barest understanding of how the market worked rested secure in the idea that the big boys who did know were looking after things. It was not unlike the American West in the late nineteenth century, where small cattle ranchers entrusted their diminutive herds to those of the large ranchers for the drive to the railheads.

It was 1:50 P.M. when Columbus made its first

move. Calling his top people together, Raizo Yamata's principal lieutenant briefly discussed the sudden run on the dollar. Heads nodded. It was serious. Pinta, the medium-risk fund of the fleet, had a goodly supply of Treasury notes, always a good parking place in which to put cash in anticipation of a better opportunity for later on. The value of these notes was falling. He announced that he was ordering their immediate transfer for Deutschmarks, again the most stable currency in Europe. The Pinta manager nodded, lifted his phone, and gave the order, and another huge transaction was made, the first by an American trader.

"I don't like the way this afternoon is going," the vice-chairman said next. "I want everybody close." Heads nodded again. The storm clouds were coming closer, and the herd was getting restless with the first shafts of lightning. "What bank stocks are vulnerable to a weak dollar?" he asked. He already knew the answer, but it was good form to ask.

"Citibank," the Niña manager replied. He was responsible for the blue-chip fund's management. "We have a ton of their stock."

"Start bailing out," the vice-chairman ordered, using the American idiom. "I don't like the way the banks are exposed."

"All of it?" The manager was surprised. Citibank had just turned in a pretty good quarterly statement.

A serious nod. "All of it."

"But — "

"All of it," the vice-chairman said quietly. "Immediately."

At the Depository Trust Company the accelerated trading activity was noted by the staffers whose job it was to note every transaction. Their purpose was to collate everything at the end of the trading day, to note which buyer had purchased which stock from which seller, and to post the money transfers from and to the appropriate accounts, in effect acting as the automated bookkeeper for the entire equities market. Their screens showed an accelerating pace of activity, but the computers were all running Chuck Searls' Electra-Clerk 2.4.0 software, and the Stratus mainframes were keeping up. There were three outputs off each machine. One line went to the monitor screens. Another went to tape backups. A third went to a paper printout, the ultimate but most inconvenient record-keeping modality. The nature of the interfaces demanded that each output come from a different internal board inside the computers, but they were all the same output, and as a result nobody bothered with the permanent records. After all, there were a total of six machines divided between two separate locations. This system was as secure as people could make it.

Things could have been done differently. Each sale/purchase order could have been sent out immediately, but that was untidy — the sheer administrative volume would have taxed the abilities of the entire industry. Instead, the purpose of DTC was to bring order out of chaos. At the end of each day, the transactions were organized by trading house, by stock issue, and by client, in a hierarchical way, so that each house would write a limited number of checks — funds transfers were mostly done electronically, but the principle held. This way the houses would both save on administrative expense and generate numerous means by which every player in the game could track and measure its own activity for the purposes of internal audit and further mathematical modeling of the market as a whole. Though seemingly an operation of incomprehensible complexity, the use of computers made it as routine and far more efficient than written entries in a passbook savings account.

"Wow, somebody's dumping on Citibank," the sys-con said.

The floor of the New York Stock Exchange was divided into three parts, the largest of which had once been a garage. Construction was under way on a fourth trading room, and local doomsayers were already noting that every time the Exchange had increased its space, something bad had happened. Some of the most rational and hard-nosed business types in all the world, this community of professionals had its own institutional superstitions. The floor was actually a collection of individual firms, each of which had a specialty area and responsibility for a discrete number of issues grouped by type. One firm might have eight to fifteen pharmaceutical issues, for example. Another managed a similar number of bank stocks. The real function of the NYSE was to provide both liquidity and a benchmark. People could buy and sell stocks anywhere from a lawyer's office to a country-club dining room. Most of the trading in major stocks happened in New York because . . . it happened in New York, and that was that. The New York Stock Exchange was the oldest. There were also the American Stock Exchange, Amex, and the newer National Association of Securities Dealers Automatic Quotation, whose awkward name was compensated for by a snappy acronym, NASDAQ. The NYSE was the most traditional in organization, and some would say that it had been dragged kicking and screaming into the world of automation. Somewhat haughty and stodgy — they regarded the other markets as the minor leagues and themselves as the majors — it was staffed by professionals who stood for most of the day at their kiosks, watching various displays, buying and selling and, like the trading houses, living off the "middle" or "spread" positions which they anticipated. If the stock market and its investors were the herd, they were the cowboys, and their job was to keep track of things, to set the benchmark prices to which everyone referred, to keep the herd organized and contained, in return for which the best of them made a very good living that compensated for a physical working environment which at best was chaotic and unpleasant, and at its worst really was remarkably close to standing in the way of a stampede.

The first rumblings of that stampede had already started. The sell-off of Treasury notes was duly reported on the floor, and the people there traded nervous looks and headshakes at the unreasonable development. Then they learned that the Fed had responded sharply. The strong statement from the chairman didn't — couldn't — disguise his unease, and would not have mattered in any case. Few people listened to the statement beyond the announcement of a change in the Discount Rate. That was the news. The rest of it was spin control, and investors discounted all of that, preferring to rely on their own analysis.

The sell orders started coming. The floor trader who specialized in bank stocks was stunned by the phone call from Columbus, but that didn't matter. He announced that he had "five hundred Citi at three," meaning five hundred thousand shares of the stock of First National City Bank of New York at eighty-three dollars, two full points under the posted price, clearly a move to get out in a hurry. It was a good, attractive price, but the market hesitated briefly before snapping them up, and then at "two and a half."

Computers also kept track of trading because the traders didn't entirely trust themselves to stay on top of everything. A person could be on the phone and miss something, after all, and therefore, to a remarkable degree, major institutions were actually managed by computers, or more properly the software that

456

resided on them, which was in turn written by people who established discrete sets of monitoring criteria. The computers didn't understand the market any more than those who programmed them, of course, but they did have instructions: If "A" happens, then do "B." The new generation of programs, generically called "expert systems" (a more attractive term than "artificial intelligence") for their high degree of sophistication, were updated on a daily basis with the status of benchmark issues from which they electronically extrapolated the health of whole segments of the market. Quarterly reports, industry trends, changes in management, were all given numerical values and incorporated in the dynamic databases that the expert systems examined and acted upon, entirely without the judgmental input of human operators.

In this case the large and instant drop in the value of Citibank stock announced to the computers that they should initiate sell orders on other bank stocks. Chemical Bank, which had had a rough time of late, the computers remembered, had also dropped a few points in the last week, and at the three institutions that used the same program, sell orders were issued electronically, dropping that issue an instant point and a half. That move on Chemical Bank stock, linked with the fall of Citibank, attracted the immediate attention of other expert systems with the same operational protocols but different benchmark banks, a fact that guaranteed a rippling effect across the entire industry spectrum. Manufacturers Hanover was the next major bank stock to head down, and now the programs were starting to search their internal protocols for what a fall in bank-stock values indicated as the *next* defensive move in other key industries.

With the money realized by the Treasury sales, Columbus started buying gold, both in the form of stocks and in gold futures, starting a trend from currency and into precious metals. The sudden jump there went out on the wires as well, and was noted by traders, both human and electronic. In all cases the analysis was pretty much the same: a sell-off of government bonds, plus a sudden jump in the Discount Rate, plus a run on the dollar, plus a building crash in bank stocks, plus a jump in precious metals, all combined to announce a dangerous inflationary predictor. Inflation was always bad for the equities market. You didn't need to have artificial intelligence to grasp that. Neither computer programs nor human traders were panicking yet, but everyone was leaning forward and watching the wires for developing trends, and everyone wanted to be ahead of the trend, the better to protect their own and their clients' investments.

By this time the bond market was seriously rattled. Half a billion dollars, dumped at the right time, had shaken loose another ten. The Eurodollar managers who had been called back to their offices were not really in a fit state to make rational decisions. The days and weeks had been long of late with the international trade situation, and arriving singly back at their offices, each asked the others what the devil was going on, only to learn that a lot of U.S. Treasuries had been sold very short, and that the trend was continuing, now augmented by a large and very astute American institution. But *why?* they all wanted to know. That set them to looking at additional data on the wires, trying to catch up with the information streaming from America. Eyes squinted, heads shook, and these traders, lacking the time to review everything, turned to their own expert systems to make the analyses, because the reasons for the swift movements were simply not obvious enough to be real.

But it didn't really matter why, did it? It had to be real. The Fed had just gone up a full point on the discount rate, and that hadn't happened by accident. For the moment, they decided, in the absence of guidance from their governments and central banks, they would defer buying U.S. Treasuries. They also began immediate examinations of their equity holdings, because stocks looked as though they were going to drop, and drop rapidly.

". . . between the people of Russia and the people of America," President Grushavoy concluded his toast, the host answering President Durling, the guest, as the protocol for such things went. Glasses were raised and tipped. Ryan allowed a drop or two of the vodka to pass his lips. Even with these thimble glasses, you could get pretty wasted — waiters stood everywhere to replenish them — and the toasting had just begun. He'd never been to a state affair this . . . loose. The entire diplomatic community was here — or at least the ambassadors from all the important countries were present. The Japanese Ambassador in particular seemed jovial, darting from table to table for snippets of conversation.

Secretary of State Brett Hanson stood next, raising his glass and stumbling through a prepared ode to the far-seeing Russian Foreign Ministry, celebrating their cooperation not merely with the United States, but all of Europe. Jack checked his watch: 10:03 local time. He already had three and a half drinks down, and deemed himself to be the most sober person in the room. Cathy was getting a little giggly on him. *That* hadn't happened in a very long time, and he knew that he'd be razzing her about it for years to come.

"Jack, you have no taste for our vodka?" Golovko asked. He also was hitting it pretty hard, but Sergey appeared to be used to it.

"I don't want to make too much of a fool out of myself," Ryan replied.

"It would be difficult for you to do that, my friend," the Russian observed.

"That's because you're not married to him," Cathy

noted with a twinkle in her eye.

"Now wait a minute," a bond specialist said to his computer in New York. His firm managed several large pension funds, which were responsible for the retirement security of over a million union workers. Just back from a normal lunch at his favorite deli, he was offering Treasuries at bargain prices on orders from upstairs, and for the moment they were just sitting out there awaiting a buyer. Why? A cautious order appeared from a French bank, apparently a hedge against inflationary pressure on the franc. That was a mere billion, bid at $1^7/_{32}$ off the opening value, the international equivalent of armed robbery. But Columbus, he saw, had bitten the bullet and taken the francs, converting them almost instantly into D-marks in a hedge move of its own. Still digesting his corned-beef sandwich, the man felt his lunch turn into a ball of chilled lead.

"Somebody making a run on the dollar?" he asked the trader next to him.

"Sure looks that way," she answered. In an hour, future options on the dollar had dropped the maximum-allowed limit for a day after having climbed all morning.

"Who?"

"Whoever it is, Citibank just took one in the back. Chemical's sliding, too."

"Some kind of correction?" he wondered.

"Correction *from* what? *To* what?"

"So what do I do? Buy? Sell? Hide?" He had decisions to make. He had the life savings of real people to protect, but the market wasn't acting in a way he understood. Things were going in the shitter, and he didn't know why. In order to do his job properly, he had to know.

"Still heading west to meet us, *Shoho*," Fleet Operations told Admiral Sato. "We should have them on radar soon."

"*Hai.* Thank you, *Issa*," Sato replied, an edge on his good humor now. He wanted it that way, wanted his people to see him like that. The Americans had won the exercise, which was hardly a surprise. Nor was it surprising that the crewmen he saw were somewhat depressed as a result. After all the workups and drills, they'd been administratively annihilated, and the resentment they felt, while not terribly professional, was entirely human. *Again,* they thought, the Americans have done it to us *again.* That suited the fleet commander. Their morale was one of the most important considerations in the operation, which, the crewmen didn't know, was not over, but actually about to begin.

The event that had started with T-Bills was now affecting all publicly traded bank issues, enough so that the chairman of Citibank called a press conference to protest against the collapse of his institution's stock, pointing to the most recent earnings statement and demonstrable financial health of one of the country's largest banks. Nobody listened. He would have been better advised to make a few telephone calls to a handful of chosen individuals, but that might not have worked either.

The one banker who could have stopped things that day was giving a speech at a downtown club when his beeper went off. He was Walter Hildebrand, president of the New York branch of the Federal Reserve Bank, and second in importance only to the man who ran the headquarters in Washington. Himself a man of great inherited wealth who had nonetheless started at the bottom of the financial industry (albeit living in a comfortable twelve-room condo as he did so) and earned his way to the top, Hildebrand had also earned his current job, which he viewed as his best opportunity for real public service. A canny financial analyst, he had published a book examining the crash of October 19, 1987, and the role played by his predecessor at the New York Fed, Gerry Lornigan, in saving the market. Having just delivered a speech on the ramifications of the Trade Reform Act, he looked down at his beeper, which unsurprisingly told him to call the office. But the office was only a few blocks away, and he decided to walk back instead of calling, which would have told him to go to the NYSE. It would not have mattered.

Hildebrand walked out of the building by himself. It was a clear, crisp day, a good one to walk off some of his lunch. He hadn't troubled himself to use a bodyguard, as some of his antecedents had, though he did have a pistol-carry permit and sometimes used it.

The streets of lower Manhattan are narrow and busy, populated mostly by delivery trucks and yellow-painted taxicabs that darted from corner to corner like drag racers. The sidewalks were just as narrow and crowded. Just walking around meant taking a crooked path, with many sidesteps. The clearest path was most often that closest to the curb, and that is what Hildebrand took, moving as rapidly as the circumstances permitted, the faster to get to his office. He didn't note the presence of another man, just behind him, only three feet, in fact, a well-dressed man with dark hair and an ordinary face. It was just a matter of waiting for the right moment, and the nature of the traffic here made it inevitable that the moment would come. That was a relief to the dark-haired man, who didn't want to use his pistol for the contract. He didn't like noise. Noise attracted looks. Looks could be remembered, and though he planned to be on a plane to Europe in just over two hours, there was no such thing as being too careful. So, his head swiveled, watching the traffic ahead and behind, he chose the moment with care.

They were approaching the corner of Rector and Trinity. The traffic light ahead turned green, allowing a two-hundred-foot volume of automobiles to surge forward another two hundred feet. Then the light behind changed as well, releasing the pent-up energy of a corresponding number of vehicles. Some of them were cabs, which raced especially fast because cabs loved to change lanes. One yellow cab jumped off the light and darted to its right. A perfect situation. The dark-haired man increased his pace until he was right behind Hildebrand, and all he had to do was push. The president of the New York Fed tripped on the curb and fell into the street. The cabdriver saw it, and turned the wheel even before he had a chance to swear, but not far enough. For all that, the man in the camel-hair overcoat was lucky. The cab stopped as fast as its newly refurbished brakes allowed, and the impact speed was under twenty miles per hour, enough to catapult Walter Hildebrand about thirty feet into a steel lightpole and break his back. A police officer on the other side of the street responded at once, calling for an ambulance on his portable radio.

The dark-haired man blended back into the crowd and headed for the nearest subway station. He didn't know if the man was dead or not. It wasn't really necessary to kill him, he'd been told, which had seemed odd at the time. Hildebrand was the first banker he'd been told not to kill.

The cop hovering over the fallen businessman noted the beeper's repeated chirping. He'd call the displayed number as soon as the ambulance arrived. His main concern right now was in listening to the cabdriver protest that it wasn't his fault.

The expert systems "knew" that when bank stocks dropped rapidly, confidence in the banks themselves was invariably badly shaken, and that people would think about moving their money out of the banks that appeared to be threatened. That would force the banks in turn to pressure their lenders to pay back loans, or, more importantly to the expert systems and their ability to read the market a few minutes faster than everyone else, because banks were turning into investment institutions themselves, to liquidate their own financial holdings to meet the demands of depositors who wanted their deposits back. Banks were typically cautious investors on the equity market, sticking mainly to blue chips and other bank stocks, and so the next dip, the computers thought, would be in the major issues, especially the thirty benchmark stocks that made up the Dow Jones Industrial Average. As always, the imperative was to see the trend first and to move first, thus safeguarding the funds that the big institutions had to protect. Of course, since all the institutions used essentially the same expert systems, they all moved at virtually the same time. With the sight of a single thunderbolt just a little too close to the herd, all of the herd members started moving away from it, in the same direction, slowly at first, but moving.

The men on the floor of the exchange knew it was coming. Mostly people who received programmed-trade orders, they had learned from experience to predict what the computers would do. *Here it comes* was the murmur heard in all three trading rooms, and the very predictability of it should have been an indicator of what was really happening, but it was hard for the cowboys just to stay outside the herd, try to find a way to direct it, turn it, pacify it — and not be engulfed by it. If *that* happened, they stood to lose because a serious downward turn could obliterate the thin margins on which their firms depended.

The head of the NYSE was now on the balcony, looking down, wondering where the hell Walt Hildebrand was. That's all they needed, really. Everybody

464

listened to Walt. He lifted his cellular phone and called his office again, only to hear from Walt's secretary that he hadn't returned to the office from his speech yet. Yes, she *had* beeped him. She really had.

He could see it start. People moved more rapidly on the floor. Everyone was there now, and the sheer volume of noise emanating from the floor was reaching deafening levels. Always a bad sign when people started shouting. The electronic ticker told its own tale. The blue chips, all three-letter acronyms as well known to him as the names of his children, were accounting for more than a third of the notations, and the numbers were trending sharply down. It took a mere twenty minutes for the Dow to drop fifty points, and as awful and precipitous as that was, it came as a relief. Automatically, the computers at the New York Stock Exchange stopped accepting computer-generated sell orders from their electronic brethren. The fifty-point mark was called a "speed bump." Set in place after the 1987 crash, its purpose was to slow things down to a human pace. The simple fact that everyone overlooked was that people could take the instructions — they didn't even bother calling them recommendations anymore — from their computers and forward the sell orders themselves by phone or telex or electronic mail, and all the speed bump accomplished was to add another thirty seconds to the transaction process. Thus, after a hiatus of no more than a minute, the trading pace picked up yet again and the direction was down.

By this time, the panic within the entire financial community was quite real, reflected in a tenseness and a low buzz of conversation in every trading room of every one of the large institutions. Now CNN issued a live special report from its own perch over the floor of the former NYSE garage. The stock ticker on their "Headline News" service told the tale to investors who also liked to keep track of more human

465

events. For others, there was now a real human being to say that the Dow Jones Industrial Average had dropped fifty points in the blink of an eye, and was now down twenty more points, and the downward spiral was not reversing itself. There followed questions from the anchorperson in Atlanta, and resulting speculation on the cause of the event, and the reporter who hadn't had time to check her sources for information, winged it on her own, and said that there was a worldwide run on the dollar that the Fed had failed to stop. She couldn't have picked a worse thing to say. Now everyone knew what was happening, after a fashion, and the public got involved in the stampede.

Although investment professionals looked upon the public's lack of understanding for the investment process with contempt, they failed to recognize the crucial element of similarity they shared with them. The public merely accepted the fact that the Dow going up was good and its going down was bad. It was exactly the same for the traders, who thought they really understood the system. The investment professionals knew far more about the mechanics of the market but had lost track of the foundation of its value. For them, as for the public, reality had become trends, and they often expressed their bets by use of derivatives, which were moving numerical indicators that over the years had become increasingly disconnected from what the individual stock designations truly represented. Stock certificates were not, after all, theoretical expressions, but individual segments of ownership in corporations that had a physical reality. Over time the "rocket scientists" on the floor of this room had forgotten that, and even schooled as they were in mathematical models and trend analysis, the underlying value of that which they traded was foreign to them — the facts had become more theoretical than the theory that was now breaking down before their eyes. Denied a foundation in what they were doing, lacking an anchor on which to hold fast in the storm sweeping across the room and the whole financial system, they simply did not know what to do, and the few supervisory personnel who did lacked the numbers and the time with which to settle their young traders down.

None of this really made sense at all. The dollar should have been strong and should grow stronger after a few minor rumbles. Citibank had just turned in a good if not spectacular earnings statement, and Chemical Bank was fundamentally healthy as well after some management restructuring, but the stocks on both issues had dropped hard and fast. The computer programs said that the combination of factors meant something very bad, and the *expert systems* were *never* wrong, were they? Their foundation was historically precise, and they saw into the future better than people could. The technical traders believed the models despite the fact that they did not see the reasoning that had led the models to make the recommendations displayed on their computer terminals; in exactly the same way, ordinary citizens now saw the news and knew that something bad was happening without understanding why it was bad, and wondered what the hell to do about it.

The "professionals" were as badly off as the ordinary citizens catching news flashes on TV or radio, or so it seemed. In fact, it was far worse for them. Understanding the mathematical models as well as they did became not an asset, but a liability. To the average citizen what he saw was incomprehensible at first, and as a result, few took any action at all. They watched and waited, or in many cases just shrugged since they had no stocks of their own. In fact they did, but didn't know it. The banks, insurance companies, and pension funds that managed the citizens' money had huge positions in all manner of public issues. Those institutions were all managed by "professionals" — whose education and experience told them that they *had to* panic. And panic they did, beginning a process that the man in the street soon recognized for what it was. That was when the telephone calls from individuals began, and the downslope became steeper for everyone.

What was already frightening became worse. The first calls came from the elderly, people who watched TV during the day and chatted back and forth on the phone, sharing their fears and their shock at what they saw. Many of them had invested their savings in mutual funds because they gave higher yields than bank accounts — which was why banks had gotten into the business as well, to protect their own profits. The mutual funds were taking huge hits now, and though the hits were limited mainly to the blue chips at the moment, when the calls came in from individual clients to cash in their money and get out, the institutions had to sell off as yet untroubled issues to make up for the losses in others that should have been safe but were not. Essentially, they were throwing away equities that had held their value to this point, for which procedure the timeless aphorism was "to throw good money after bad." It was almost an exact description for what they had to do.

The necessary result was a general run, the drop of every stock issue on every exchange. By three that afternoon, the Dow was down a hundred seventy points. The Standard and Poor's Five Hundred was actually showing worse results, but the NASDAQ Composite Index was the worst of all, as individual investors across America dialed their 1-800 numbers to their mutual funds.

The heads of all the exchanges staged a conference call with the assembled commissioners of the Securities and Exchange Commission in Washington, and for the first confused ten minutes all the voices demanded answers to the same questions that the others were simultaneously asking. Nothing at all was accomplished. The government officials requested information and updates, essentially asking how close the herd was to the edge of the canyon, and how fast it was approaching the abyss, but not contributing a dot to the effort to turn the cattle to safety. The head of the NYSE resisted his instinct to shut down or somehow slow down the trading. In the time they talked — a bare twenty minutes — the Dow dropped another ninety points, having blown through two hundred points of free-fall and now approaching three. After the SEC commissioners broke off to hold their own in-house conference, the exchange heads violated federal guidelines and talked together about taking remedial action, but for all their collective expertise, there was nothing to be done now.

Now individual investors were blinking on "hold" buttons across America. Those whose funds were managed through banks learned something especially disquieting. Yes, their funds were in banks. Yes, those banks were federally insured. But, *no,* the mutual funds the banks managed in order to serve the needs of their depositors were *not* protected by the FDIC. It wasn't merely the interest income that was at risk, but the *principal* as well. The response to that was generally ten or so seconds of silence, and, in not a few cases, people got into their cars and drove to banks to get cash for what other deposits they did have.

The NYSE ticker was now running fourteen minutes late despite the high-speed computers that recorded the changing values of issues. A handful of stocks actually managed to increase, but those were mainly precious metals. Everything else fell. Now all the major networks were running live feeds from the Street. Now everyone knew. Cummings, Cantor, and Carter, a firm that had been in business for one hundred twenty years, ran out of cash reserves, forcing its chairman to make a frantic call to Merrill Lynch. That placed the chairman of the largest house in a delicate position. The oldest and smartest pro around, he had nearly broken his hand half an hour earlier by pounding on his desk and demanding answers that no one had. Thousands of people bought stock not just through, but also *in,* his corporation because of its savvy and integrity. The chairman could make a strategic move to protect a fellow bulwark of the entire system against a panic with no foundation to it, or he could refuse, guarding the money of his stockholders. There was no right answer to this one. Failure to help CC&C would — could — take the panic to the next stage and so damage the market that the money he saved by not helping the rival firm would just as soon be lost anyway. Extending help to CC&C might turn into nothing more than a gesture, without stopping anything, and again losing money that belonged to others.

"Holy shit," the chairman breathed, turning to look out the windows. One of the nicknames for the house was "the Thundering Herd." Well, the herd was sure as hell thundering now . . . He measured his responsibility to his stockholders against his responsibility to the whole system upon which they and everyone else depended. The former had to come first. Had to. There was no choice. Thus one of the system's most important players flung the entire financial network over a cliff and into the waiting abyss.

Trading on the floor of the exchange stopped at 3:23 P.M., when the Dow achieved its maximum allowable fall of five hundred points. That figure merely reflected the value of thirty stock issues, and the fall in others well exceeded the benchmark loss of the biggest of the blue chips. The ticker took another thirty minutes to catch up, offering the illusion of further activity while the people on the floor looked at one another, mostly in silence, standing on a wood floor so covered with paper slips as to give the appearance of snow. It was a Friday, they all told themselves. Tomorrow was Saturday. Everyone would be at home. Everyone would have a chance to take a few deep breaths and think. That's all that had to happen, really, just a little thought. None of it made sense. A whole lot of people had been badly hurt, but the market would bounce back, and over time those with the wit and the courage to stand fast would get it all back. *If,* they told themselves, *if everyone used the time intelligently, and if nothing else crazy happened.*

They were almost right.

At the Depository Trust Company, people sat about with ties loose in their collars, and made frequent trips to the restrooms because of all the coffee and soda they'd drunk on this most frantic of afternoons, but there was some blessing to be had. The market had closed early, and so they could start their work early. With the inputs from the major trading centers concluded, the computers switched from one mode of operation to another. The taped recordings of the day's transactions were run through the machines for collation and transmission. It was close to six in the evening when a bell sounded on one of the workstations.

"Rick, I've got a problem here!"

Rick Bernard, the senior system controller, came over and looked at the screen to see the reason for the alert bell.

The last trade they could identify, at exactly noon of that day, was for Atlas Milacron, a machine-tool company flying high with orders from the auto companies, six thousand shares at 48½. Since Atlas was listed on the New York Stock Exchange, its stock

471

was identified by a three-letter acronym, AMN in this case. NASDAQ issues used four-letter groups.

The next notation, immediately after AMN 6000 48½, was AAA 4000 67⅛, and the one under that AAA 9000 51¼. In fact, by scrolling down, all entries made after 12:00:01 showed the same three-letter, meaningless identifier.

"Switch over to Beta," Bernard said. The storage tape on the first backup computer system was opened. "Scroll down."

"Shit!"

In five minutes all six systems had been checked. In every case, every single trade had been recorded as gibberish. There was no readily accessible record for any of the trades made after twelve noon. No trading house, institution, or private investor could know what it had bought or sold, to or from whom, or for how much, and none could therefore know how much money was available for other trades, or for that matter, to purchase groceries over the weekend.

20

Strike Three

The party broke up after midnight. The official entertainment was a sort of ballet-in-the-round. The Bolshoy hadn't lost its magic, and the configuration of the room allowed the guests to see the dancers at much closer hand than had ever been possible, but finally the last hand had been clapped red and hurt from the encores, and it was time for security personnel to help their charges to the door. Nearly everyone had a roll to his or her walk, and sure enough, Ryan saw, he *was* the most sober person in the room, including his wife.

"What do you think, Daga?" Ryan asked Special Agent Helen D'Agustino. His own bodyguard was getting coats.

"I think, just once, I'd like to be able to party with the principals." Then she shook her head like a parent disappointed with her children.

"Oh, Jack, tomorrow I'm going to feel awful," Cathy reported. The vodka here was just too smooth.

"I told you, honey. Besides," her husband added nastily, "it's *already* tomorrow."

"Excuse me, I have to help with JUMPER." Which was the Secret Service code name for the President, a tribute to his paratrooper days.

Ryan was surprised to see an American in ordinary

473

business attire — the formal dinner had been black-tie, another recent change in the Russian social scene — waiting outside the doors. He led his wife over that way.

"What is it?"

"Dr. Ryan, I need to see the President right away."

"Cathy, could you stay here for a second." To the embassy official: "Follow me."

"Oh, Jack . . ." his wife griped.

"You have it on paper?" Ryan asked, holding his hand out.

"Here, sir." Ryan took the fax sheets and read them while walking across the room.

"Holy shit. Come on." President Durling was still chatting with President Grushavoy when Ryan appeared with the junior man in his wake.

"Some party, Jack," Roger Durling observed pleasantly. Then his face changed. "Trouble?"

Ryan nodded, adopting his Advisor's face. "We need Brett and Buzz, Mr. President, right now."

"There they are." The SPY-1D radar on *Mutsu* painted the forward edge of the American formation on the raster screen. Rear Admiral — *Shoho* — Sato looked at his operations officer with an impassive expression that meant nothing to the rest of the bridge crew but quite a bit to the Captain — *Issa* — who knew what Exercise DATELINE PARTNERS was really all about. Now it was time to discuss the matter with the destroyer's commanding officer. The two formations were 140 nautical miles apart and would rendezvous in the late afternoon, the two officers thought, wondering how *Mutsu*'s CO would react to the news. Not that he had much choice in the matter.

Ten minutes later, a *Socho,* or chief petty officer, went out on deck to check out the Mark 68 torpedo launcher on the port side. First opening the inspection hatch on the base of the mount, he ran an electronic

474

diagnostic test on all three "fish" in the three-tube launcher. Satisfied, he secured the hatch, and one by one opened the aft hatches on each individual tube, removing the propeller locks from each Mark 50 torpedo. The *Socho* was a twenty-year veteran of the sea, and completed the task in under ten minutes. Then he lifted his tools and walked over to the starboard side to repeat it for the identical launcher on the other side of his destroyer. He had no idea why he had been ordered to perform the tasks, and hadn't asked.

Another ten minutes and *Mutsu* went to flight quarters. Modified from her original plans, the destroyer now sported a telescoping hangar that allowed her to embark a single SH-60J antisubmarine helicopter that was also useful for surveillance work. The crew had to be roused from sleep and their aircraft pre-flighted, which required almost forty minutes, but then it lifted off, first sweeping around the formation, then moving forward, its surface-scanning radar examining the American formation that was still heading west at eighteen knots. The radar picture was downlinked to flagship *Mutsu*.

"These will be the two carriers, three thousand meters apart," the CO said, tapping the display screen.

"You have your orders, Captain," Sato said.

"*Hai*," *Mutsu*'s commander replied, keeping his feelings to himself.

"What the hell happened?" Durling asked. They had assembled in a corner, with Russian and American security personnel to keep others away.

"It looks like there was a major conniption on the Street," Ryan replied, having had the most time to consider the event. It wasn't exactly a penetrating analysis.

"Cause?" Fiedler asked.

"No reason for it that I know about," Jack said,

looking around for the coffee he'd ordered. He needed some, and the other three men needed it even more.

"Jack, you have the most recent trading experience," Secretary of the Treasury Fiedler observed.

"Start-ups, IPOs, not really working the Street, Buzz." The National Security Advisor paused, gesturing to the fax sheets. "It's not as though we have a lot to go on. Somebody got nervous on T-Bills, most likely guess right now is that somebody was cashing in on relative changes between the dollar and the yen, and things got a little out of hand."

"A little?" Brett Hanson interjected, just to let people know he was here.

"Look, the Dow took a big fall, down to a hard floor, and there are two days for people to regroup. It's happened before. We're flying back tomorrow night, right?"

"We need to do something now," Fiedler said. "Some sort of statement."

"Something neutral and reassuring," Ryan suggested. "The market's like an airplane. It'll pretty much fly itself if you leave it alone. This has happened before, remember?"

Secretary Bosley Fiedler — "Buzz" went back to Little League baseball — was an academic. He'd written books on the American financial system without ever having actually played in it. The good news was that he knew how to take a broad, historical view on economics. His professional reputation was that of an expert on monetary policy. The bad news, Ryan saw now, was that Fiedler had never been a trader, or even thought that much about it, and consequently lacked the confidence that a real player would have had with this situation, which explained why he had immediately asked Ryan for an opinion. Well, that was a good sign, wasn't it? He knew what he didn't know. No wonder everybody said he was smart.

"We put in speed bumps and other safeguards as a result of the last time. This event blew right through them. In less than three hours," SecTreas added uneasily, wondering, as an academic would, why good theoretical measures had failed to work as expected.

"True. It'll be interesting to see why. Remember, Buzz, it *has* happened before."

"Statement," the President said, giving a one-word order.

Fiedler nodded, thinking for a moment before speaking. "Okay, we say that the system is fundamentally sound. We have all manner of automated safeguards. There is no underlying problem with the market or with the American economy. Hell, we're growing, aren't we? And TRA is going to generate at least half a million manufacturing jobs in the coming year. That's a hard number, Mr. President. That's what I'll say for now."

"Defer anything else until we get back?" Durling asked.

"That's my advice," Fiedler confirmed. Ryan nodded agreement.

"Okay, get hold of Tish and put it out right away."

There was an unusual number of charter flights, but Saipan International Airport wasn't all that busy an airport despite its long runways, and increased business made for increased fees. Besides, it was a weekend. Probably some sort of association, the tower chief thought as the first of the 747s out of Tokyo began its final approach. Of late Saipan had become a much more popular place for Japanese businessmen. A recent court decision had struck down the constitutional provision prohibiting foreign ownership of land and now allowed them to buy up parcels. In fact, the island was more than half foreign-owned now, a source of annoyance to many of the native Chamorros people, but not so great an annoyance as

477

to prevent many of them from taking the money and moving off the land. It was bad enough already. On any given weekend, the number of Japanese on Saipan outnumbered the citizens, and typically treated the owners of the island like . . . natives.

"Must be a bunch going to Guam, too," the radar operator noted, examining the line of traffic heading farther south.

"Weekend. Golf and fishing," the senior tower controller observed, looking forward to the end of his shift. The Japs — he didn't like them very much — were not going to Thailand as much for their sex trips. Too many had come home with nasty gifts from that country. Well, they did spend money here — a lot of it — and for the privilege of doing it for this weekend they'd boarded their jumbo-jets at about two in the morning . . .

The first JAL 747 charter touched down at 0430 local time, slowing and turning at the end of the runway in time for the next one to complete its final approach. Captain Torajiro Sato turned right onto the taxiway and looked around for anything unusual. He didn't expect it, but on a mission like this — *Mission?* he asked himself. That was a word he hadn't used since his F-86 days in the Air Self-Defense Force. If he'd stayed, he would have been a *Sho* by now, perhaps even commanding his country's entire Air Force. Wouldn't that have been grand? Instead — instead he'd left that service and started with Japan Air Lines, at the time a place of far greater respect. He'd hated that fact then, and now hoped that it would change for all time. It would be an Air *Force* now, even if someone lesser than he was actually in command.

He was still a fighter pilot at heart. You didn't have much chance to do anything exciting in a 747. He'd been through one serious inflight emergency eight years before, a partial hydraulic failure, and handled it so skillfully that he hadn't bothered telling the passengers. No one outside the flight deck had even noticed. His feat was now a routine part of the simulator training for 747 captains. Beyond that frantic but satisfying moment, he strove for precision. He was something of a legend in an airline known worldwide for its excellence. He could read weather charts like a fortune-teller, pick the precise tar-strip on a runway where his main gear would touch, and had never once been more than three minutes off an arrival time.

Even taxiing on the ground, he drove the monstrous aircraft as though it were a sports car. So it was today, as he approached the jetway, adjusted his power settings, nosewheel steering, and finally the brakes, to come to a precise stop.

"Good luck, *Nisa*," he told Lieutenant Colonel Seigo Sasaki, who'd ridden the jump seat in the cockpit for the approach, scanning the ground for the unusual and seeing nothing.

The commander of the special-operations group hustled aft. His men were from the First Airborne Brigade, ordinarily based at Narashino. There were two companies aboard the 747, three hundred eighty men. Their first mission was to assume control of the airport. It would not be difficult, he hoped.

The JAL personnel at the gate had not been briefed for the events of the day, and were surprised to see that all the people leaving the charter flight were men, all about the same age, all carrying identical barrel-bags, and that the first fifty or so had the tops unzipped and their hands inside. A few held clipboards on which were diagrams of the terminal, as it had not been possible to perform a proper rehearsal for the mission. While baggage handlers struggled with the cargo containers out of the bottom of the aircraft, other soldiers headed for the baggage area, and simply walked through EMPLOYEES ONLY signs to start unpacking the heavy weapons. At another jetway, a second airliner arrived.

Colonel Sasaki stood in the middle of the terminal now, looking left and right, watching his teams of ten or fifteen men fan out and, he saw, doing their job quietly and well.

"Excuse me," a sergeant said pleasantly to a bored and sleepy security guard. The man looked up to see a smile, and down to see that the barrel bag over the man's shoulder was open, and that the hand in it held a pistol. The guard's mouth gaped comically and the private disarmed him without a struggle. In less than two minutes, the other six guards on terminal duty were similarly taken into custody. A lieutenant led a squad to the security office, where three more men were disarmed and handcuffed. All the while continuous if terse radio messages were flowing in to their colonel.

The tower chief turned when the door opened — a guard had handed over the pass card and punched in the entry code on the keypad without the need for much encouragement — to see three men with automatic rifles.

"What the hell — "

"You will continue your duties as before," a captain, or *ichii,* told him. "My English is quite good. Please do not do anything foolish." Then he lifted his radio microphone and spoke in Japanese. The first phase of Operation KABUL was completed thirty seconds early, and entirely without violence.

The second load of soldiers took over airport security. These men were in uniform to make sure that everyone knew what was going on, and they took their places at all entrances and control points, commandeering official vehicles to set additional security points on the access roads into the airport. This wasn't overly hard, as the airport was on the extreme southern part of the island, and all approaches were from the north. The commander of the second detachment relieved Colonel Sasaki. The former would control the arrival of the remaining First Airborne Brigade elements tasked to Operation KABUL. The latter had other tasks to perform.

Three airport buses pulled up to the terminal, and Colonel Sasaki boarded the last after moving around to make sure that all his men were present and properly organized. They drove immediately north, past the Dan Dan Golf Club, which adjoined the airport, then left on Cross Island Road, which took them in sight of Invasion Beach. Saipan is by no means a large island, and it was dark — there were very few streetlights — but that didn't lessen the cold feeling in Sasaki's stomach. He had to run this mission on time and on profile or risk catastrophe. The Colonel checked his watch. The first aircraft would now be landing on Guam, where the possibility of organized resistance was very real. Well, that was the job of First Division. He had his own, and it had to be done before dawn broke.

The word got out very quickly. Rick Bernard placed his first call to the chairman of the New York Stock Exchange to report his problem and to ask for guidance. On the assurance that this was no accident, he made the obvious recommendation and Bernard called the FBI, located close to Wall Street in the Javits Federal Office Building. The senior official here was a deputy director, and he dispatched a team of three agents to the primary DTC office located in midtown.

"What seems to be the problem?" the senior agent asked. The answer required ten minutes of detailed explanation, and was immediately followed by a call direct to the Deputy-Director-in-Charge.

MV *Orchid Ace* had been alongside long enough

to off-load a hundred cars. All of them were Toyota Land Cruisers. Taking down the security shack and its single drowsy guard proved to be another bloodless exercise, which allowed the buses to enter the fenced storage lot. Colonel Sasaki had enough men in the three buses to give each a crew of three, and they all knew what to do. The police substations at Koblerville and on Capitol Hill would be the first places approached, now that his men had the proper transport. His own part of the mission was at the latter site, at the home of the Governor.

It was really a coincidence that Nomuri had spent the night in town. He'd actually given himself an evening off, which happened rarely enough, and he found that recovery from a night on the town was facilitated by a trip to the bathhouse, something his ancestors had gotten right about a thousand years earlier. After washing, he got his towel and headed to the hot tub, where the foggy atmosphere would clear his head better than aspirin could. He would emerge from this civilized institution refreshed, he thought.

"Kazuo," the CIA officer observed. "Why are you here?"

"Overtime," the man replied with a tired smile.

"Yamata-san must be a demanding boss," Nomuri observed, sliding himself slowly into the hot water, not really meaning anything by the remark. The reply made his head turn.

"I have never seen history happen before," Taoka said, rubbing his eyes and moving around a little, feeling the tension bleed from his muscles, but altogether too keyed up to be sleepy after ten hours in the War Room.

"Well, my history for last night was a very nice hostess," Nomuri said with a raised eyebrow. A nice lady of twenty-one years, too, he didn't add. A very bright young lady, who had many other people contesting for her attention, but Nomuri was far closer to her age, and she enjoyed talking to someone like him. It wasn't all about money, Chet thought, his eyes closed over a smiling face.

"Mine was somewhat more exciting than that."

"Really? I thought you said you were working." Nomuri's eyes opened reluctantly. Kazuo had found something more interesting than sexual fantasy?

"I was."

It was just something about the way he said it. "You know, Kazuo, when you start telling a story, you must finish it."

A laugh and a shake of the head. "I shouldn't, but it will be in the papers in a few hours."

"What's that?"

"The American financial system crashed last night."

"Really? What happened?"

The man's head turned and he spoke the reply very quietly indeed. "I helped do it to them."

It seemed very odd to Nomuri, sitting in a wooden tub filled with 107-degree water, that he felt a chill.

"*Wakarémasen.*" I don't understand.

"It will be clear in a few days. For now, I must go back." The salaryman rose and walked out, very pleased with himself for sharing his role with one friend. What good was a secret, after all, if at least one person didn't know that you had it? A secret could be a grand thing, and one so closely held in a society like this was all the more precious.

What the hell? Nomuri wondered.

"There they are." The lookout pointed, and Admiral Sato raised his binoculars to look. Sure enough, the clear Pacific sky backlit the mast tops of the lead screen ships, FFG-7 frigates by the look at the cross-trees. The radar picture was clear now, a classic circular formation, frigates on the outer ring, destroyers inward of that, then two or three Aegis cruisers not very different from his own flagship. He checked the time. The Americans had just set the morning watch. Though warships always had people on duty, the real work details were synchronized with daylight, and people would now be rousing from their bunks, showering, and heading off for breakfast.

The visual horizon was about twelve nautical miles away. His squadron of four ships was heading east at thirty-two knots, their best possible continuous speed. The Americans were westbound at eighteen.

"Send by blinker light to the formation: Dress ships."

Saipan's main satellite uplink facility was off Beach Road, close to the Sun Inn Motel, and operated by MTC Micro Telecom. It was an entirely ordinary civilian facility whose main construction concern had been protection against autumnal typhoons that regularly battered the island. Ten soldiers, commanded by a major, walked up to the main door and were able to walk right in, then approach the security guard, who simply had no idea what was happening, and, again, didn't even attempt to reach for his sidearm. The junior officer with the detail was a captain trained in signals and communications. All he had to do was point at the various instruments in the central control room. Phone uplinks to the Pacific satellites that transferred telephone and other links from Saipan to America were shut down, leaving the Japan links up — they went to a different satellite, and were backed up with cable — without interfering with downlinked signals. At this hour it was not overly surprising that no single telephone circuit to America was active at the moment. It would stay that way for quite some time.

"Who are you?" the Governor's wife asked.

"I need to see your husband," Colonel Sasaki replied. "It's an emergency."

The fact of that statement was made immediately clear by the first shot of the evening, caused when the security guard at the legislature building managed to get his pistol out. He didn't get a round off — an eager paratrooper sergeant saw to that — but it was enough to make Sasaki frown angrily and push past the woman. He saw Governor Comacho, walking to the door in his bathrobe.

"What is this?"

"You are my prisoner," Sasaki announced, with three other men in the room now to make it clear that he wasn't a robber. The Colonel found himself embarrassed. He'd never done anything like this before, and though he was a professional soldier, his culture as much as any other frowned upon the invasion of another man's house regardless of the reason. He found himself hoping that the shots he'd just heard hadn't been fatal. His men had such orders.

"What?" Comacho demanded. Sasaki just pointed to the couch.

"You and your wife, please sit down. We have no intention of harming you."

"What is this?" the man asked, relieved that he and his wife weren't in any immediate danger, probably.

"This island now belongs to my country," Colonel Sasaki explained. It couldn't be so bad, could it? The Governor was over sixty, and could remember when that had been true before.

"A goddamned long way for her to come," Commander Kennedy observed after taking the message. It turned out that the surface contact was the *Muroto*, a cutter from the Japanese Coast Guard that occasionally supported fleet operations, usually as a

485

practice target. A fairly handsome ship, but with the low freeboard typical of Japanese naval vessels, she had a crane installed aft for the recovery of practice torpedoes. It seemed that *Kurushio* had expected the opportunity to get off some practice shots in DATE-LINE PARTNERS. Hadn't *Asheville* been told about that?

"News to me, Cap'n," the navigator said, flipping through the lengthy op-order for the exercise.

"Wouldn't be the first time the clerks screwed up." Kennedy allowed himself a smile. "Okay, we've killed them enough." He keyed his microphone again. "Very well, Captain, we'll replay the last scenario. Start time twenty minutes from now."

"Thank you, Captain," the reply came on the VHF circuit. "Out."

Kennedy replaced the microphone. "Left ten-degrees rudder, all ahead one third. Make your depth three hundred feet."

The crew in the attack center acknowledged and executed the orders, taking *Asheville* east for five miles. Fifty miles to the west, USS *Charlotte* was doing much the same thing, at exactly the same time.

The hardest part of Operation KABUL was on Guam. Approaching its hundredth year as an American-flag possession, this was the largest island in the Marianas chain, and possessed a harbor and real U.S. military installations. Only ten years earlier, it would have been impossible. Not so long ago, the now-defunct Strategic Air Command had based nuclear bombers here. The U.S. Navy had maintained a base for missile submarines, and the security obtaining to both would have made anything like this mission a folly. But the nuclear weapons were all gone — the missiles were, anyway. Now Andersen Air Force base, two miles north of Yigo, was really little more than a commercial airport. It supported trans-Pacific flights by the

American Air Force. No aircraft were actually based there any longer except for a single executive jet used by the base commander, itself a leftover from when 13th Air Force had been headquartered on the island. Tanker aircraft that had once been permanently based on Guam were now transient reserve formations that came and went as required. The base commander was a colonel who would soon retire, and he had under him only five hundred men and women, mostly technicians. There were only fifty armed USAF Security Police. It was much the same story at the Navy base whose airfield was now co-located with the Air Force. The Marines who had once maintained security there because of the nuclear weapons stockpile had been replaced by civilian guards, and the harbor was empty of gray hulls. Still, this was the most sensitive part of the overall mission. The airstrips at Andersen would be crucial to the entire operation.

"Pretty ships," Sanchez thought aloud, looking through his binoculars from his chair in Pri-Fly. "Nice tight interval on the formation, too." The four Kongos were on a precise reciprocal heading, about eight miles out, the CAG noted.

"They have the rails lined?" the Air Boss asked. There seemed to be a white line down the sides of all four of the inbound destroyers.

"Rendering honors, yeah, that's nice of them." Sanchez lifted the phone and punched the button for the navigation bridge. "Skipper? CAG here. It seems that our friends are going formal on us."

"Thanks, Bud." The Commanding Officer of *Johnnie Reb* made a call to the battle-group commander on *Enterprise*.

"What?" Ryan said, answering the phone.

"Takeoff in two and a half hours," the President's

secretary told him. "Be ready to leave in ninety minutes."

"Wall Street?"

"That's right, Dr. Ryan. He thinks we need to be home a little early. We've informed the Russians. President Grushavoy understands."

"Okay, thanks," Ryan said, not really meaning it. He'd hoped to scoot out to see Narmonov for an hour or so. Then the real fun part came. He reached over and shook his wife awake.

A groan: "Don't even say it."

"You can sleep the rest of it off on the airplane. We have to be packed and ready in an hour and a half."

"What? Why?"

"Leaving early," Jack told her. "Trouble at home. Wall Street had another meltdown."

"Bad?" Cathy opened her eyes, rubbing her forehead and thankful it was still dark outside until she looked at the clock.

"Probably a bad case of indigestion."

"What time is it?"

"Time to get ready to leave."

"We need maneuvering room," Commander Harrison said.

"No dummy is he?" Admiral Dubro asked rhetorically. The opposition, Admiral Chandraskatta, had turned west the night before, probably catching on, finally, that the *Eisenhower/Lincoln* battle force was not where he'd suspected after all. That clearly left a single alternative, and therefore he'd headed west, forcing the Americans against the island chain that India mostly owned. Half of the U.S. Navy's Seventh Fleet was a powerful collection of ships, but their power would be halved again if their location became known. The whole point of Dubro's operations to this point had been to keep the other guy guessing.

488

Well, he'd made his guess. Not a bad one, either.

"What's our fuel state?" Dubro asked, meaning that of his escort ships. The carriers could steam until the food ran out. Their nuclear fuel would not do so for years.

"Everybody's up to ninety percent. Weather's good for the next two days. We can do a speed run if we have to."

"You thinking the same thing I am?"

"He's not letting his aircraft get too close to the Sri Lankan coast. They might show on air-traffic-control radars and people might ask questions. If we head northeast, then east, we can race past Dondra Head at night and curl back around south. Even money nobody sees us."

The Admiral didn't like even-money odds. That meant it was just as likely somebody *would* see the formation, and the Indian Fleet could then turn northeast, forcing either a further move by the Americans away from the coast they might or might not be protecting — or a confrontation. You could play this sort of game only so long, Dubro thought, before somebody asked to see the cards.

"Get us through today without being spotted?"

That one was obvious, too. The formation would send aircraft at the Indians directly from the south, hopefully pulling them south. Harrison presented the scheme for the coming day's air operations.

"Make it so."

Eight bells rang over the ship's 1-MC intercom system. 1600 hours. The afternoon watch was relieved and replaced with the evening watch. Officers and men, and, now, women, moved about to and from their duty stations. *Johnnie Reb*'s air wing was standing down, mainly resting and going over results of the now-concluded exercise. The Air Wing's aircraft were about half parked on the flight deck, with the other half struck down in the hangar bay. A few were being worked on, but the maintenance troops were mostly standing down, too, enjoying a pastime the Navy called Steel Beach. It sure was different now, Sanchez thought, looking down at the non-skid-covered steel plates. Now there were women sunning themselves, too, which occasioned the increased use of binoculars by the bridge crew, and had generated yet another administrative problem for his Navy. What varieties of bathing suits were proper for U.S. Navy sailors? Much to the chagrin of some, but the relief of many, the verdict was one-piece suits. But even those could be worth looking at, if properly filled, the CAG thought, returning his glasses to the approaching Japanese formation.

The four destroyers came in fast and sharp, knocking down a good thirty knots, the better to make a proper show for their hosts and erstwhile enemies. The proper signal flags were snapping in the breeze, and white-clad crewmen lined the rails.

"Now hear this," the 1-MC system blared for all to hear. "Attention to port. Man the rails. Stand by to render honors." Those crewmen in presentable uniforms headed to the portside galleries off the flight deck, organized by sections. It was an awkward evolution for a carrier, and required quite a bit of time to set up, especially on a Steel Beach day. Having it done at change of watch made it a little easier. There was a goodly supply of properly uniformed sailors to perform the duty before going to their berthing spaces to change into their tanning outfits.

Sato's last important act of the operation was to send out a satellite transmission with a time check. Downlinked to fleet headquarters, it was immediately rebroadcast on a different circuit. The last chance to stop the operation had passed by. The die was now cast, if not yet thrown. The Admiral left *Mutsu*'s CIC

490

and headed back to the bridge, leaving his operations officer in charge while he conned the squadron.

The destroyer came abeam of United States Ships *Enterprise* and *John Stennis*, exactly between the two carriers, less than two thousand meters to each. She was doing thirty knots, with all stations manned except for the vacancies caused by the people standing at the ships' rails. At the moment that his bridge crossed the invisible line between those of the two American carriers, the sailors on the rails saluted port and starboard in a very precise rendition of courtesy at sea.

A single whistle from the bosun's pipe over the speakers: "Hand salute . . . Two!" the orders came over the speakers, and the sailors on the galleries of *Johnnie Reb* brought their hands down. Immediately thereafter they were dismissed with three notes from the bosun's mate of the watch.

"Gee, can we go home now?" The Air Boss chuckled. Exercise DATELINE PARTNERS was now fully concluded, and the battle force could return to Pearl Harbor for one more week of upkeep and shore leave before deploying to the IO. Sanchez decided to stay in the comfortable leather chair and read over some documents while enjoying the breeze. The combined speed of the two intermingled formations made for a rapid passage.

"Whoa!" a lookout said.

The maneuver was German in origin, formally called a *Gefechtskehrtwendung*, "battle turn." On signal-flag hoist, all four destroyers turned sharply to the right, the aftermost ship first. As soon as her bow showed movement, the next ship put her rudder over, and the next, and then the flagship last. It was a move calculated to attract the admiration of the Americans, and something of a surprise in the close space between the two carriers. In a matter of sec-

491

onds, the Japanese destroyers had smartly reversed course, now heading *west* at thirty knots, and overtaking the carriers they had only a moment before approached from the other direction. A few people on the bridge crew whistled approval at the ship-handling skills. Already the rails on all four of the Aegis destroyers were cleared.

"Well, that was pretty sharp," Sanchez commented, looking down at his documents again.

USS *John Stennis* was steaming normally, all four of her propellers turning at 70rpm, with Condition-Three set. That meant that all spaces were manned with the exception of the embarked air wing, which had stood down after several days on higher activity. There were lookouts arrayed around the island structure, for the most part looking in their assigned areas of responsibility, though all had sneaked at least one long look at the Japanese ships, because they were, after all, different from the U.S. ships. Some used hand-held 7 × 50 marine binoculars, many of Japanese manufacture. Others leaned on far more massive 20 × 120 "Big Eyes," spotting binoculars, which were mounted on pedestals all around the bridge.

Admiral Sato was not sitting down in his command chair, though he was holding his binoculars up. It was a pity, really. They were such proud, beautiful ships. Then he remembered that the one to port was *Enterprise*, an ancient name in the United States Navy, and that a ship that had borne the name before this one had tormented his country, escorting Jimmy Doolittle to the Japanese coast, fighting at Midway, Eastern Solomons, Santa Cruz, and every other major fleet engagement, many times hit, but never severely. The name of an honored enemy, but an enemy. That was the one he'd watch. He had no idea who *John Stennis* had been.

Mutsu had passed well beyond the carriers, almost

reaching the trailing plane-guard destroyers before turning, and the overtake now seemed dreadfully slow. The Admiral wore his white gloves, and held his binoculars just below the rail, watching the angle to the carrier change.

"Bearing to Target One is three-five-zero. Target Two bearing now zero-one-zero. Solution light," the petty officer reported. The *Isso* wondered what was going on and why, most of all wondered how he might live to tell this tale someday, and thought that probably he would not.

"I'll take it now," the ops officer said, sliding into the seat. He'd taken the time to acquaint himself with the torpedo director. The order had already been given, and all he'd needed was the light. The officer turned the key in the enable-switch lock, flipped the cover off the button for the portside array, and pressed. Then he did the same for the starboard side.

The three-tube mounts on both sides of the ship snapped violently outboard to an angle of about forty degrees off the centerline. The hemispherical weather covers on all six tubes popped off. Then the "fish" were launched by compressed air, diving into the water, left and right, about ten seconds apart. The propellers were already turning when they were ejected into the sea, and each trailed control wires that connected them to *Mutsu*'s Combat Information Center. The tubes, now empty, rotated back to their standby position.

"Fuck me!" a lookout said on *Johnnie Reb*.

"What was that, Cindy?"

"They just launched a fuckin' fish!" she said. She was a petite seaman (*that* term hadn't changed yet) apprentice, only eighteen years old, on her first ship, and was learning profanity to fit in with the saltier members of the crew. Her arm shot out straight. "I saw him launch — there!"

"You sure?" the other nearby lookout asked, swinging his Big Eyes around. Cindy had only hand-helds.

The young woman hesitated. She'd never done anything like this before, and wondered what her chief might do if she were wrong. "Bridge, Lookout Six, the last ship in the Jap line just launched a torpedo!" The way things were set up on the carrier, her announcement was carried over the bridge speakers.

One level down, Bud Sanchez looked up. "What was that?"

"Say again, Look-Six!" the OOD ordered.

"I said I *saw* that Jap destroyer launch a torpedo off her starboard side!"

"This is Look-Five. I didn't see it, sir," a male voice said.

"I fucking saw it!" shouted a very excited young female voice, loudly enough that Sanchez heard this exclamation over the air, rather than on the bridge speakers. He dropped his papers, jumped to his feet, and sprinted out the door to the lookout gallery. The Captain tripped on the steel ladder, ripping his pants and bloodying one knee, and was swearing when he got to the lookouts.

"Talk to me, honey!"

"I saw it, sir, I *really did!*" She didn't even know who Sanchez was, and the silver eagles on his collar made him important enough to frighten her even worse than the idea of inbound weapons, but she had seen it and she was standing her ground.

"I didn't see it, sir," the senior seaman announced.

Sanchez trained his binoculars on the destroyer, now only about two thousand yards away. What . . . ? He next shoved the older seaman off the Big Eyes and trained them in on the quarterdeck of the Japanese flagship. There was the triple-tube launcher, trained in as it should be . . .

. . . but the fronts of the tubes were black, not gray. The weather covers were off . . . Without looking, Captain Rafael Sanchez ripped the phones off the senior lookout.

"Bridge, this is CAG. Torpedoes in the water! Torpedoes inbound from port quarter!" He trained the glasses aft, looking for trails on the surface but seeing none. Not that it mattered. He swore violently and stood back up to look at Seaman-Apprentice Cynthia Smithers. "Right or wrong, sailor, you did just fine," he told her as alarms started sounding all over the ship. Only a second later, a blinker light started flashing at *Johnnie Reb* from the Japanese flagship.

"Warning, warning, we just had a malfunction, we have launched several torpedoes," *Mutsu*'s CO said into the TBS microphone, shamed by the lie as he listened to the open talk-between-ships FM circuit.

"*Enterprise*, this is *Fife*, there are torpedoes in the water," another loud voice proclaimed even more loudly.

"Torpedoes — where?"

"They're ours. We have a flash fire in CIC," *Mutsu* announced next. "They may be armed." *Stennis*, he saw, was turning already, the water boiling at her stern with increased power. It wouldn't matter, though with luck nobody would be killed.

"What do we do now, sir?" Smithers asked.

"A couple of Hail Marys, maybe," Sanchez replied darkly. They were ASW torpedoes, weren't they? Little warheads. They couldn't really hurt something as big as *Johnnie Reb*, could they? Looking down at the deck, people were up and running now, mainly carrying their sunbathing towels as they raced to their duty stations.

"Sir, I'm supposed to report to Damage Control Party Nine on the hangar deck."

"No, stay right here," Sanchez ordered. "You can leave," he told the other one.

John Stennis was heeling hard to port now. The radical turn to starboard was taking hold and the deck rumbled with the sudden increase of power to her engines. One nice thing about the nuclear-powered carriers. They had horses to burn, but the ship weighed over ninety thousand tons and took her time accelerating. *Enterprise*, less than two miles away, was slower on the trigger, just starting to show turn now. *Oh, shit* . . .

"Now hear this, now hear this, stream the Nixie!" the OOD's voice called over the speakers.

The three Mark 50 antisubmarine torpedoes heading toward *Stennis* were small, smart instruments of destruction designed to punch small, fatal holes into submarine hulls. Their ability to harm a ship of ninety thousand tons was small indeed, but it was possible to choose which sort of damage they would inflict. They were spaced about a hundred meters apart, racing forward at sixty knots, each guided by a thin insulated wire. Their speed advantage over the target and the short range almost guaranteed a hit, and the turn-away maneuver undertaken by the American carrier merely offered the ideal overtake angle because they were all targeted on the screws. After traveling a thousand yards, the seeker head on the first "fish" went active. The sonar picture it generated was reported back to *Mutsu*'s CIC as a violently bright target of yellow on black, and the officer on the director steered it straight in, with the other two following automatically. The target area grew closer. Eight hundred meters, seven, six . . .

"I have you both," the officer said. A moment later the sonar picture showed the confused jamming from the American Nixie decoy, which mimicked the ultrasonic frequencies of the torpedo seeker-heads. Another feature built into the new ones had a powerful pulsing magnetic field to trick the under-the-keel influence-exploders the Russians had developed. But the Mark 50 was a contact weapon, and by controlling them with the wire, he could force them to ignore the acoustical interference. It wasn't fair, wasn't sporting at all, but then, who ever said war was supposed to be that way? he asked the director, who did not answer.

It was a strange disconnect of sight, sound, and feel. The ship hardly shuddered at all when the first column of water leaped skyward. The noise was unmistakably real, and, coming without warning, it made Sanchez jump on the port-after corner of the island. His initial impression was that it hadn't been all that bad a deal, that maybe the fish had exploded in *Johnnie Reb*'s wake. He was wrong.

The Japanese version of the Mark 50 had a small warhead, only sixty kilograms, but it was a shaped charge, and the first of them exploded on the boss of number-two propeller, the inboard postside shaft. The shock immediately ripped three of the screw's five blades off, unbalancing a propeller now turning at a hundred-thirty RPM. The physical forces involved were immense, and tore open the shaft fittings and the skegs that held the entire propulsion system in place. In a moment the aftermost portion of the shaft alley was flooded, and water started entering the ship through her most vulnerable point. What happened forward was even worse.

Like most large warships, *John Stennis* was steam-powered. In her case two nuclear reactors generated power by boiling water directly. That steam went into a heat exchanger where other water was boiled (but not made radioactive as a result) and piped aft to a high-pressure turbine. The steam hit the turbine blades, causing them to turn much like the vanes of a windmill, which is all the turbine really was; the steam was then piped aft to a low-pressure turbine to make use of the residual energy. The turbines had efficient turning rates, far faster than the propeller could attain, however, and to lower the shaft speed to something the ship could really use, there was a set of reduction gears, essentially a shipboard version of an automobile transmission, located between them. The finely machined barrel-shaped wheels in that bit of marine hardware were the most delicate element of the ship's drivetrain, and the blast energy from the warhead had traveled straight up the shaft, jamming the wheels in a manner that they were not designed to absorb. The added asymmetrical writhing of the unbalanced shaft rapidly completed the destruction of the entire Number Two drivetrain. Sailors were leaping from their feet with the noise even before the second warhead struck, on Number Three.

That explosion was on the outer edge of the starboard-inboard propeller, and the collateral damage took half a blade off Number Four. Damage to Number Three was identical with Number Two. Number Four was luckier. This engine-room crew threw the steam controls to reverse with the first hint of vibration. Poppet valves opened at once, hitting the astern-drive blades and stopping the shaft before the damage got as far as the reduction gears, just in time for the third torpedo to complete the destruction of the starboard-outboard prop.

The All-Stop bell sounded next, and the crewmen in all four turbine rooms initiated the same procedure undertaken moments earlier by the crew on the starboard side. Other alarms were sounding. Damage-control parties raced aft and below to check the flooding, as their carrier glided to a lengthy and crooked halt. One of her rudders was damaged as well.

"What the hell was that all about?" one engineman asked another.

"My God," Sanchez breathed topside. Somehow

the damage to *Enterprise*, now two miles away, seemed even worse than that to his ship. Various alarms were still sounding, and below on the navigation bridge, voices were screaming for information so loudly that the need for telephone circuits seemed superfluous. Every ship in the formation was maneuvering radically now. *Fife*, one of the plane-guard 'cans, had reversed course and was getting the hell out of Dodge, her skipper clearly worried about other possible fish in the water. Somehow Sanchez knew there weren't. He'd seen three explosions aft on *Johnnie Reb* and three under *Enterprise*'s stern.

"Smithers, come with me."

"Sir, my battle-station — "

"They can handle it without you, and there's nothing much to look out for now. We're not going much of anywhere for a while. You're going to talk to the Captain."

"Jesus, sir!" The exclamation was not so much profanity as a prayer to be spared that ordeal.

The CAG turned. "Take a deep breath and listen to me: you might be the only person on this whole goddamned ship who did their job right over the last ten minutes. Follow me, Smithers."

"Shafts two and three are blown away, Skipper," they heard a minute later on the bridge. The ship's CO was standing in the middle of the compartment, looking like a man who'd been involved in a traffic accident. "Shaft four is damaged also . . . shaft one appears okay at the moment."

"Very well," the skipper muttered, then added for himself, "What the hell . . ."

"We took three ASW torps, sir," Sanchez reported. "Seaman Smithers here saw the launch."

"Is that a fact?" The CO looked down at the young seaperson. "Miss, you want to sit over in my chair. When I'm finished keeping my ship afloat I want to talk to you." Then came the hard part. The Captain of USS *John Stennis* turned to his communications officer and started drafting a signal to CincPacFlt. It would bear the prefix NAVY BLUE.

"Conn, Sonar, torpedo in the water, bearing two-eight-zero, sounds like one of their Type 89s," "Junior" Laval reported, not in an overly excited way. Submarines were regularly shot at by friends.

"All ahead flank!" Commander Kennedy ordered. Exercise or not, it was a torpedo, and it wasn't something to feel comfortable about. "Make your depth six hundred feet."

"Six hundred feet, aye," the chief of the boat replied from his station as diving officer. "Ten degrees down-angle on the planes." The helmsman pushed forward on the yoke, angling USS *Asheville* toward the bottom, taking her below the layer.

"Estimated range to the fish?" the Captain asked the tracking party.

"Three thousand yards."

"Conn, Sonar, lost him when we went under the layer. Still pinging in search mode, estimate the torpedo is doing forty or forty-five knots."

"Turn the augmenter off, sir?" the XO asked.

Kennedy was tempted to say yes, the better to get a feel for how good the Japanese torpedo really was. To the best of his knowledge no American sub had yet played against one. It was supposedly the Japanese version of the American Mark 48.

"There it is," Sonar called. "It just came under the layer. Torpedo bearing steady at two-eight-zero, signal strength is approaching acquisition values."

"Right twenty degrees rudder," Kennedy ordered. "Stand by the five-inch room."

"Speed going through thirty knots," a crewman reported as *Asheville* accelerated.

"Right twenty-degrees rudder, aye, no new course given."

"Very well," Kennedy acknowledged. "Five-inch room, launch decoy now-now-now! Cob, take her up to two hundred!"

"Aye," the chief of the boat replied. "Up ten on the planes!"

"Making it hard?" the executive officer asked.

"No freebies."

A canister was ejected from the decoy-launcher compartment, called the five-inch room for the diameter of the launcher. It immediately started giving off bubbles like an Alka-Seltzer tablet, creating a new, if immobile, sonar target for the torpedo's tracking sonar. The submarine's fast turn created a "knuckle" in the water, the better to confuse the Type 89 fish.

"Through the layer," the technician on the bathythermograph reported.

"Mark your head!" Kennedy said next.

"Coming right through one-nine-zero, my rudder is twenty-right."

"Rudder amidships, steady up on two-zero-zero."

"Rudder amidships, aye, steady up on two-zero-zero."

"All ahead one-third."

"All ahead one-third, aye." The enunciator changed positions, and the submarine slowed down, now back at two hundred feet, over the layer, having left a lovely if false target behind.

"Okay." Kennedy smiled. "Now let's see how smart that fish is."

"Conn, Sonar, the torpedo just went right through the knuckle." The tone of the report was just a little off, Kennedy thought.

"Oh?" the CO went forward a few steps, entering sonar. "Problem?"

"Sir, that fish just went right through the knuckle like it didn't see it."

"Supposed to be a pretty smart unit. You suppose it just ignores decoys like the ADCAP does?"

501

"Up-Doppler," another sonarman said. "Ping-rate just changed . . . frequency change, it might have us, sir."

"Through the layer? That is clever." It was going a little fast, Kennedy thought, like real combat, even. Was the new Japanese torpedo really that good, had it really just ignored the decoy and the knuckle? "We recording all this?"

"You bet, sir," Sonarman 1/c Laval said, reaching up to tap the tape machine. A new cassette was taking all this in, and another video system was recording the display on the waterfall screens. "There go the motors, just increased speed. Aspect change . . . it's got us, zero aspect on the fish, screw noises just faded." Meaning that the engine noise of the torpedo was now somewhat blocked by the body of the weapon. It was headed straight in.

Kennedy turned his head to the tracking party. "Range to fish?"

"Under two thousand, sir, closing fast now, estimate torpedo speed sixty knots."

"Two minutes to overtake at this speed."

"Look at this, sir." Laval tapped the waterfall display. It showed the track of the torpedo, and also showed the lingering noise of the decoy, still generating bubbles. The Type 89 had drilled right through the center of it.

"What was that?" Laval asked the screen. A large low-frequency noise had just registered on the screen, bearing three-zero-five. "Sounded like an explosion, way off, that was a CZ signal, not direct path." A convergence-zone signal meant that it was a long way away, more than thirty miles.

Kennedy's blood turned a little cold at that piece of news. He stuck his head back into the attack center. "Where are *Charlotte* and the other Japanese sub?"

"Northwest, sir, sixty or seventy miles."

"All ahead flank!" That order just happened automatically. Not even Kennedy knew why he'd given it.

"All ahead flank, aye," the helmsman acknowledged, turning the enunciator dial. These exercises sure were exciting stuff. Before the engine order was acknowledged, the skipper was on his command phone again:

"Five-inch room, launch two, now-now-now!"

The ultrasonic targeting sonar on a homing torpedo is too high in frequency to be heard by the human ear. Kennedy knew that the energy was hitting his submarine, reflecting off the emptiness within, because the sonar waves stopped at the steel-air boundary, bouncing backward to the emitter that generated them.

It couldn't be happening. If it were, others would have noted it, wouldn't they? He looked around. The crew was at battle stations. All watertight doors were closed and dogged down as they would be in combat. *Kurushio* had launched an exercise torpedo, identical to a warshot in everything but the warhead, for which an instrument package was substituted. They were also designed *not* to hit their targets, but to turn away from them, because a metal-to-metal strike could break things, and fixing those things could be expensive.

"It's still got us, sir."

But the fish had run *straight through* the knuckle . . .

"Take her down fast!" Kennedy ordered, knowing it was too late for that.

USS *Asheville* dropped her nose, taking a twenty-degree down-angle, back over thirty knots with the renewed acceleration. The decoy room launched yet another bubble canister. The increased speed degraded sonar performance, but it was clear from the display that the Type 89 had again run straight through the false image of a target and just kept coming.

"Range under five hundred," the tracking part said. One of its members noticed that the Captain was pale and wondered why. Well, nobody likes losing, even in an exercise.

Kennedy thought about maneuvering more as *Asheville* ducked under the layer yet again. It was too close to outrun. It could outturn him, and every attempt to confuse it had failed. He was just out of ideas. He'd had no time to think it all through.

"Jesus!" Laval took his headphones off. The Type 89 was now alongside the submarine's towed-array sonar, and the noise was well off the scale. "Should turn away any second now . . ."

The Captain just stood there, looking around. Was he crazy? Was he the only one who thought —

At the last second, Sonarman 1/c Laval looked aft to his commanding officer. *"Sir, it didn't turn!"*

21

Navy Blue

Air Force One lifted off a few minutes sooner than expected, speeded on her way by the early hour. Reporters were already up and moving before the VC-25B reached her cruising altitude, coming forward to ask the President for a statement explaining the premature departure. Cutting short a state trip was something of a panic reaction, wasn't it? Tish Brown handled the journalists, explaining that the unfortunate developments on Wall Street commanded a quick return so that the President could reassure the American people . . . and so forth. For the moment, she went on, it might be a good idea for everyone to catch up on sleep. It was, after all, a fourteen-hour flight back to Washington, with the headwinds that blew across the Atlantic at this time of year, and Roger Durling needed his sleep, too. The ploy worked for several reasons, not the least of which was that the reporters were suffering from too much alcohol and not enough sleep, like everyone else aboard — except the flight crew, all hoped. Besides, there were Secret Service agents and armed Air Force personnel between them and the President's accommodations. Common sense broke out, and everyone returned back to the seating area. Soon things were quieted down, and nearly every passenger aboard was either asleep or feigning it. Those who weren't asleep wished they were.

Johnnie Reb's commanding officer was, by federal law, an aviator. The statute went back to the 1930s, and had been drafted to prevent battleship sailors from taking over the new and bumptious branch of the Old Navy. As such, he had more experience flying airplanes than in driving ships, and since he'd never had a command afloat, his knowledge of shipboard systems consisted mainly of things he'd picked up along the way rather than from a matter of systematic study and experience. Fortunately, his chief engineer was a black-shoe destroyer sailor with a command under his belt. The skipper did know, however, that water was supposed to be outside the hull, not inside.

"How bad, ChEng?"

"Bad, sir." The Commander gestured to the deck plates, still covered with an inch of water that the pump was gradually sending over the side. At least the holes were sealed now. That had taken three hours. "Shafts two and three are well and truly trashed. Bearings shot, tail shafts twisted and split, reduction gears ground up to junk — no way anybody can fix them. The turbines are okay. The reduction gears took all the shock. Number One shaft's okay. Some shock damage to the aft bearings. That I can fix myself. Number four screw is damaged, not sure how bad, but we can't turn it without risking the shaft bearings. Starboard rudder is jammed over, but I can deal with that, another hour, maybe, and it'll be 'midships. May have to replace it, depending on how bad it looks. We're down to one shaft. We can make ten, eleven knots, and we can steer, badly."

"Time to fix?"

"Months — four or five is my best guess right now, sir." All of which, the Commander knew, would require him to be here, overseeing the yard crews, essentially rebuilding half the ship's power plant — maybe three quarters. He hadn't fully evaluated the damage to Number Four yet. That was when the Captain really lost his temper. It was about time, the ChEng thought.

"If I could launch an air strike, I'd sink those sunzabitches!" But launching anything on the speed generated by a single shaft was an iffy proposition. Besides, it had been an accident, and the skipper really didn't mean it.

"You have my vote on that one, sir," ChEng assured him, not really meaning it either, because he added: "Maybe they'll be nice enough to pay for the repairs." His reward was a nod.

"We can start moving again?"

"Number One shaft is a little out from shock damage, but I can live with it, yes, sir."

"Okay, get ready to answer bells. I'm taking this overpriced barge back to Pearl."

"Aye aye, sir."

Admiral Mancuso was back in his office, reviewing preliminary data on the exercise when his yeoman came in with a signal sheet.

"Sir, looks like two carriers are in trouble."

"What did they do, collide?" Jones asked, sitting in the corner and reviewing other data.

"Worse," the yeoman told the civilian.

ComSubPac read the dispatch. "Oh, that's just great." Then his phone rang; it was the secure line that came directly from PacFltOps. "This is Admiral Mancuso."

"Sir, this is Lieutenant Copps at Fleet Communications. I have a submarine emergency beacon, located approximately 31-North, 175-East. We're refining that position now. Code number is for *Asheville*, sir. There is no voice transmission, just the beacon. I am initiating a SUBMISS/SUBSUNK. The nearest naval aircraft are on the two carriers — "

"Dear God." Not since *Scorpion* had the U.S. Navy lost a sub, and he'd been in high school then. Mancuso shook his head clear. There was work to be done. "Those two carriers are probably out of business, mister."

"Oh?" Oddly enough, Lieutenant Copps hadn't heard that yet.

"Call the P-3s. I have work to do."

"Aye aye, sir."

Mancuso didn't have to look at anything. The water in that part of the Pacific Ocean was three miles deep, and no fleet submarine ever made could survive at a third of that depth. If there were an emergency, and if there were any survivors, any rescue would have to happen within hours, else the cold surface water would kill them.

"Ron, we just got a signal. *Asheville* might be down."

"*Down?*" That word was not one any submariner wanted to hear, even if it was a gentler expression than *sunk*. "Frenchy's kid . . ."

"And a hundred twenty others."

"What can I do, Skipper?"

"Head over to SOSUS and look at the data."

"Aye aye, sir." Jones hustled out the door while SubPac lifted his phone and started punching buttons. He already knew that it was an exercise in futility. All PacFlt submarines now carried the AN/BST-3 emergency transmitters aboard, set to detach from their ships if they passed through crush depth or if the quartermaster of the watch neglected to wind the unit's clockwork mechanism. The latter possibility, however, was unlikely. Before the explosive bolts went, the BST made the most godawful noise to chide the neglectful enlisted man . . . *Asheville* was almost certainly dead, and yet he had to follow through in the hope of a miracle. Maybe a

508

few crewmen had gotten off.

Despite Mancuso's advice, the carrier group did get the call. A frigate, USS *Gary*, went at once to maximum sustainable speed and sprinted north toward the area of the beacon, responding as required by the laws of man and the sea. In ninety minutes she'd be able to launch her own helicopter for a surface search and further serve as a base for other helos to continue the rescue operation if necessary. *John Stennis* turned slowly into the wind and managed to launch a single S-3 Viking ASW aircraft, whose onboard instruments were likely to be useful for a surface search. The Viking was overhead in less than an hour. There was nothing to be seen on radar except for a Japanese coast-guard cutter, heading in for the beacon, about ten miles out. Contact was established, and the white cutter verified its notice of the emergency radio and intentions to search for survivors. The Viking circled the transmitter. There was a slick of diesel oil to mark the ship's grave, and a few bits of floating debris, but repeated low passes and four sets of eyes failed to spot anything to be rescued.

The "Navy Blue" prefix on a signal denoted information that would be of interest to the entire fleet, perhaps sensitive in nature, less often highly classified; in this case it was something too big to be kept a secret. Two of Pacific Fleet's four aircraft carriers were out of business for a long time. The other two, *Eisenhower* and *Lincoln*, were in the IO, and were likely to remain there. Ships know few secrets, and even before Admiral Dubro got his copy of the dispatch, word was already filtering through his flagship. No chief swore more vilely than the battle-force commander, who already had enough to worry about. The same response greeted the signals personnel who

509

informed the senior naval officers on Pentagon duty.

Like most intelligence officers in a foreign land in time of danger, Clark and Chavez didn't have a clue. If they had, they would probably have caught the first plane anywhere. Spies have never been popular with anyone, and the Geneva Protocols merely affirmed a rule for time of war, mandating their death as soon after apprehension as was convenient, usually by firing squad.

Peacetime rules were a little more civilized, but generally with the same end result. It wasn't something CIA emphasized in its recruiting interviews. The international rules of espionage allowed for this unhappy fact by giving as many field intelligence officers as possible diplomatic covers, along with which came immunity from harm. Those were called "legal" agents, protected by international treaty as though they really were the diplomats their passports said they were. Clark and Chavez were "illegals," and not so protected — in fact, John Clark had never once been given a "legal" cover. The importance of this became clear when they left their cheap hotel for a meeting with Isamu Kimura.

It was a pleasant afternoon made less so by the looks they got as *gaijin;* no longer a mixture of curiosity and distaste, now there was genuine hostility. The atmosphere had changed materially since their arrival here, though remarkably things immediately became more cordial when they identified themselves as Russians, which prompted Ding to speculate on how they might make their cover identity more obvious to passersby. Unfortunately civilian clothing did not offer that option, and so they had to live with the looks, generally feeling the way a wealthy American might in a high-crime neighborhood.

Kimura was waiting at the agreed-upon place, an inexpensive drinking establishment. He already had a few drinks in him.

"Good afternoon," Clark said pleasantly in English. A beat. "Something wrong?"

"I don't know," Kimura said when the drinks came. There were many ways of speaking that phrase. This way indicated that he knew something. "There is a meeting of the ministers today. Goto called it. It's been going on for hours. A friend of mine in the Defense Agency hasn't left his office since Thursday night."

"*Da* — so?"

"You haven't seen it, have you? The way Goto has been speaking about America." The MITI official finished off the last of his drink and raised his hand to order another. Service, typically, was fast.

They could have said that they'd seen the first speech, but instead "Klerk" asked for Kimura's read on the situation.

"I don't know," the man replied, saying the same thing again while his eyes and tone told a somewhat different story. "I've never seen anything like this. The — what is the word? — rhetoric. At my ministry we have been waiting for instructions all week. We need to restart the trade talks with America, to reach an understanding, but we have no instructions. Our people in Washington are doing nothing. Goto has spent most of his time with Defense, constant meetings, and with his zaibatsu friends. It's not the way things are here at all."

"My friend," Clark said with a smile, his drink now untouched after a single sip, "you speak as though there is something serious in the air."

"You don't understand. There is nothing in the air. Whatever is going on, MITI is not a part of it."

"And?"

"MITI is part of *everything* here. My Minister is there now, finally, but he hasn't told us anything." Kimura paused. Didn't these two know anything?

511

"Who do you think makes our foreign policy here? Those dolts in the Foreign Ministry? They report to *us*. And the Defense Agency, who cares what they think about anything? We are the ones who shape our country's policies. We work with the zaibatsu, we coordinate, we . . . represent business in our relations with other countries and their markets, we make the position papers for the Prime Minister to give out. That's why I entered the ministry in the first place."

"But not now?" Clark asked.

"Now? Goto is meeting with them himself, and spends the rest of his time with people who don't matter, and only now is my Minister called in — well, yesterday," Kimura corrected himself. "And he's still there."

The man seemed awfully rattled, Chavez told himself, over what seemed to be little more than some bureaucratic turf-fighting. The Ministry of International Trade and Industry was being outmaneuvered by someone else. So?

"You are upset that the industry leaders meet directly with your Prime Minister," he asked.

"So much, and so long, yes. They're supposed to work through us, but Goto has always been Yamata's lapdog." Kimura shrugged. "Perhaps they want to make policy directly now, but how can they do that without us?"

Without me, the man means, Chavez thought with a smile. Dumb-ass bureaucrat. CIA was full of them, too.

It wasn't all the way thought through, but such things never were. Most of the tourists who came to Saipan were Japanese, but not quite all of them. The Pacific island was a good place for a lot of things. One of them was deep-sea fishing, and the waters here were not as crowded as those around Florida

512

and the Gulf of California. Pete Burroughs was sunburned, exhausted, and thoroughly satisfied with an eleven-hour day at sea. It was just the perfect thing, the computer engineer told himself, sitting in the fighting chair and sipping a beer, to get a person over a divorce. He'd spent the first two hours getting offshore, then three hours trolling, then four hours fighting against the biggest goddamned albacore tuna he'd ever seen. The real problem would be convincing his fellow workers that it wasn't a lie. The monster was too big to mount over his mantel, and besides, his ex- had the house and the fireplace. He'd have to settle for a photo, and everyone knew the stories about that, damn it. Blue-screen technology had reached fishermen. For twenty bucks you could have your choice of monster fish hanging from its electronic tail behind you. Now, if he'd caught a shark, he could have taken home the jaw and teeth, but an albacore, magnificent as it was, was just tuna fish. Well, what the hell, his wife hadn't believed his stories about the late nights at work either. The bitch. Good news, bad news. She didn't like fishing either, but now he could fish all he wanted. Maybe even fish for a new girl. He popped open another beer.

The marina didn't look very busy for a weekend. The main port area was, though, three big commercial ships, ugly ones, he thought, though he didn't know exactly what they were on first sight. His company was in California, though not close to the water, and most of his fishing was of the freshwater sort. This trip had been a life's ambition. Tomorrow, maybe, he'd get something else. For the moment, he looked left at the albacore. Had to be at least seven hundred pounds. Nowhere close to the record, but one hell of a lot bigger than the monster salmon he'd gotten the year before with his trusty Ted Williams spinning rig. The air shook again, spoiling his moment with his fish. The overhead shadow announced another goddamned 747 coming out of the airport. It wouldn't be long before this place was spoiled, too. Hell, it already was. About the only good news was that the Japanese who came here to kick loose and screw Filipina bar girls didn't like to fish much.

The boat's skipper brought them in smartly. His name was Oreza, a retired Master Chief Quartermaster, U.S. Coast Guard. Burroughs left the fighting chair, headed topside, and sat down next to him.

"Get tired of talking to your fish?"

"Don't like drinking alone, either."

Oreza shook his head. "Not when I'm driving."

"Bad habit from the old days?"

The skipper nodded. "Yeah, I guess. I'll buy you one at the club, though. Nice job on the fish. First time, you said?"

"First time in blue water," Burroughs said proudly.

"Coulda fooled me, Mr. Burroughs."

"Pete," the engineer corrected.

"Pete," Oreza confirmed. "Call me Portagee."

"You're not from around here."

"New Bedford, Massachusetts, originally. Winters are too cold. I served here once, long time back. There used to be a Coast Guard station down at Punta Arenas, closed now. The wife and I liked the climate, liked the people, and, hell, the competition statewide for this sort of business is too stiff," Oreza explained. "What the hell, the kids are all grown. So anyway, we ended up coming out here."

"You know how to handle a boat pretty well."

Portagee nodded. "I ought to. I've been doing it thirty-five years, more if you count going out with my pop." He eased to port, coming around Mañagaha Island. "The fishing out of New Bedford's gone to hell, too."

"What are those guys?" Burroughs asked, pointing to the commercial port.

"Car carriers. When I came in this morning they

were moving jeeps out of that one." The skipper shrugged. "More goddamned cars. You know, when I came here it was kinda like Cape Cod in the winter. Now it's more like the Cape in the summer. Wall-to-goddamned-wall." Portagee shrugged. More tourists made for more crowding, spoiling the island, but also bringing him more business.

"Expensive place to live?"

"Getting that way," Oreza confirmed. Another 747 flew off the island. "That's funny . . ."

"What?"

"That one didn't come out of the airport."

"What do you mean?"

"That one came out of Kobler. It's an old SAC runway, BUFF field."

"BUFF?"

"Big Ugly Fat Fucker," Portagee explained. "B-52s. There's five or six runways in the islands that can take big birds, dispersal fields from the bad old days," he went on. "Kobler's right next to my old LORAN station. I'm surprised they still keep it up. Hell, I didn't know they did, even."

"I don't understand."

"There used to be a Strategic Air Command base on Guam. You know, nukes, all that big shit? In case the crap hit the fan, they were supposed to disperse off Andersen Air Force Base so one missile couldn't get them all. There's two big-bird runways on Saipan, the airport and Kobler, two more on Tinian, leftovers from World War Two, and two more on Guam."

"They're still good to use?"

"No reason why not." Oreza's head turned. "We don't get many hard-freezes here to rip things up." The next 747 came off Saipan International, and in the clear evening sky they could see yet another coming in from the eastern side of the island.

"This place always this busy?"

515

"No, most I've ever seen. Goddamned hotels must be packed solid." Another shrug. "Well, that means the hotels'll be interested in buying that fish off ya."

"How much?"

"Enough to cover the charter, Pete. That's one big fish you brought in. But tomorrow you have to get lucky again."

"Hey, you find me another big boy like our friend down there, and I don't care what you charge."

"I love it when people say that." Oreza eased back on the throttles as he approached the marina. He aimed for the main dock. They needed the hoist to get the fish off. The albacore was the third-largest he'd ever brought in, and this Burroughs guy wasn't all that bad a charter.

"You make a living at this?"

Portagee nodded. "With my retirement pay, yeah, it's not a bad life. Thirty-some years I drove Uncle's boats, and now I get to drive me own — and she's paid for."

Burroughs was looking at the commercial ships now. He lifted the skipper's binoculars. "You mind?"

"Strap around your neck if you don't mind." Amazing that people thought the strap was some sort of decoration.

"Sure." Burroughs did that, adjusting the focus for his eyes and examining *Orchid Ace*. "Ugly damned things . . ."

"Not made to be pretty. Made to carry cars." Oreza started the final turn in.

"That's no car. Looks like some kind of construction thing, bulldozer, like . . ."

"Oh?" Portagee called for his mate, a local kid, to come topside and work the lines. Good kid, fifteen, might try for the Coast Guard and spend a few years learning the trade properly. Oreza was working on that.

"The Army have a base here?"

"Nope. The Air Force and Navy still have some folks down on Guam, but not even much there anymore." There. He killed his throttles, and the *Springer* drifted to a halt, just perfect. Again, Oreza thought, as always taking pleasure from doing a seaman's job just so. A man on the dock turned the crank to swing the hoist over his fantail, giving a thumbs-up when he saw the size of the fish. Watching to see that the boat was tied up properly, Oreza sat back, killed his engines, and thought about the evening's first beer.

"Here, take a look." Burroughs handed the glasses over.

Portagee turned in his chair and readjusted the binoculars to his eyes before training them in on the car carrier down the coast. He knew how the ships were arranged. He'd done safety inspection on them while on shore duty with the Coast Guard. He'd inspected this very ship, in fact, one of the first built-for-the-purpose automobile ferries, designed to carry trucks and other cargo as well as private cars. Some of the decks had a lot of overhead . . .

"What?"

"You know what it is?"

"No." It was a tracked vehicle. It was in shadows because the sun was low in the sky, but the paintwork was definitely dark, and it had a large box of some sort on the back. Then something clicked. It was some kind of missile launcher. He remembered seeing them on TV during the Persian Gulf War, just before his retirement. Oreza stood to get a slightly better angle. There were two others in the parking lot. . . .

"Oh, okay, I got it, some sort of exercise," Burroughs said, heading down the ladder to the main deck. "See, that's a fighter plane over there. My cousin used to fly it before he went with American. It's an F-15 Eagle, Air Force bird."

Oreza turned the glasses and caught the fighter circling. Sure enough, there were two of them flying in a nice tight military formation, F-15 Eagle fighters, circling the center of the island in a classic display of protection for one's native soil . . . except for one thing. The national emblem on the wings was a solid red circle.

Again, Jones preferred the paper printouts to an electronic display. The latter was better for live-action, but on high-speed playback got the eyes tired too fast, and this was a job that demanded care. Lives might depend on it, he told himself, already thinking that was a lie. Two senior chief oceanographic technicians went through the pages with him. They started with midnight, and had to check carefully. The submarine-exercise area off Kure atoll had been chosen for its proximity to a series of hydrophones, part of the Pacific SOSUS system. The near array was one of the last ever implanted, and was the size of a garage or small house. Actually part of a mega-array, it was electronically linked to another installation fifty nautical miles away, but that one was older, smaller, and less capable. A cable that linked them both, leading first to Kure, then to Midway, where there was a satellite uplink to back up the cable that led all the way to Pearl Harbor. The ocean was in fact crisscrossed with such cables. For quite some time during the Cold War, the U.S. Navy had laid almost as much as Bell Telephone, occasionally chartering the latter's ships for the task.

"Okay, there's *Kurushio* snorting," Jones said, circling the black marks in red.

"How the hell did you ever beat Masker?" one of the chiefs asked in surprise.

"Well, it is a good system, but you ever really listen to it?"

"I haven't been at sea in ten years," the senior chief replied.

"When I was on *Dallas*, we played games with

Moosbrugger for a week, down at AUTEC in the Bahamas."

"The Moose has a big rep."

"And it's a no-shit rep, too. We couldn't hold her, she couldn't hold us, it was a real mother," Jones went on, speaking now not like a civilian contractor with a doctorate, but like the proud sonarman he'd been, and, he realized, still was. "They had a helicopter pilot who was giving us fits, too. Anyway" — he flipped another page — "then I figured it out. Masker sounds like rain hitting the surface, like a spring shower. Not real noisy, but the freqs are unique, you can get a good cut on 'em. Then I realized all we had to do was see what the topside weather was like. If it's blue sky, and you hear rain bearing zero-two-zero, that's the guy. It was clear yesterday northwest of Kure. I checked with Fleet Weather before I came over."

The senior chief nodded and smiled. "I'll remember that one, sir."

"Okay, we have the Jap here at midnight. Now let's see what else we can find. He flipped forward to the next fan-fold page. Had circumstances been different he might have seen it as a paper Slinky, one of his new son's favorite toys. "That's gotta be *Asheville*, probably sprinting off to restart a scenario. She's wearing a speed screw, isn't she?"

"I don't know."

"I do. I don't think we would have gotten this many hits on her with a patrol screw. Let's plot this out."

"Running a plot, already have some of it," another chief reported. The process was largely computer-aided now. Once it had been a real black art.

"Posit?" Jones looked up.

"Position's right about here, same as the beacon, almost. Sir," the chief said patiently, making a black mark on the plastic-covered wall chart, "we know where she is, I mean, the rescue — "

"Ain't gonna be no rescue." Jones looked up and stole a cigarette from a passing seaman. *There, I finally said it out loud.*

"You can't smoke in here," one of the chiefs said. "We have to go outside — "

"Give me a light and follow me on this," Jones ordered. He flipped another page, checking the 60Hz line. "Nothing . . . nothing. Those diesel boats are pretty good . . . but if they're quiet, they ain't snorting, and if they ain't snorting they ain't going very far . . . *Asheville* sprinted out this way, and probably then she came back in . . ." Another page.

"No rescue, sir?" It had taken fully thirty seconds for the question to be asked.

"How deep's the water?"

"I know that, but the escape trunks . . . I mean, I've seen it, there's three of them."

Jones didn't even look up, taking a puff off his first smoke in years. "Yeah, the mom's hatch, that's what we called it on *Dallas.* 'See, mom, if anything goes wrong, we can get out right there.' Chief, you don't get off one of these things, okay? You don't. That ship is dead, and so's her crew. I want to see why."

"But we already have the crush sounds."

"I know. I also know that two of our carriers had a little accident today." Those sounds were on the SOSUS printouts, too.

"What are you saying?"

"I'm not saying anything." Another page. At the bottom of it was a large black blotch, the loud sound that marked the death of USS *Asheville* and all —

"What the fuck is this?"

"We think it's a double-plot, sir. The bearing's almost the same as the *Asheville* sound, and we think the computer — "

"The time's off, goddamn it, a whole four minutes." He flipped back three pages. "See, that's somebody else."

"*Charlotte?*"

It was then that Jones felt even colder. His head swam a little from the cigarette, and he remembered why he'd quit. The same signature on the paper, a diesel boat snorting, and, later, a 688-class sprinting. The sounds were so close, nearly identical, and the coincidence of the bearing from the new seafloor array could have made almost anyone think . . .

"Call Admiral Mancuso and find out if *Charlotte* has checked in."

"But — "

"Right now, Senior Chief!"

Dr. Ron Jones stood up and looked around. It was the same as before, almost. The people were the same, doing the same work, displaying the same competence, but something was missing. The thing that wasn't the same was . . . what? The large room had a huge chart of the Pacific Ocean on its back wall. Once that chart had been marked with red silhouettes, the class shapes of Soviet submarines, boomers, and fast-attacks, often with black silhouettes in attendance, to show that Pacific SOSUS was tracking "enemy" subs, quarterbacking American fast-attacks onto them, vectoring P-3C Orion ASW birds in to follow them, and occasionally to pounce on and harry them, to let them know who owned the oceans of the world. Now the marks on the wall chart were of whales, some of them with names, just as with the Russian subs, but these names were things like "Moby and Mabel," to denote a particular pod with a well-known alpha-pair to track by name. There wasn't an enemy now, and the urgency had gone. They weren't thinking the way he'd once thought, heading "up north" on *Dallas*, tracking people they might one day have to kill. Jones had never really expected *that*, not really-really, but the possibility

521

was something he'd never allowed himself to forget. These men and women, however, had. He could see it, and now he could hear it from the way the chief was talking to SubPac on the phone.

Jones walked across the room and just took the receiver away. "Bart, this is Ron. Has *Charlotte* checked in?"

"We're trying to raise her now."

"I don't think you're going to, Skipper," the civilian said darkly.

"What do you mean?" The reply caught the meaning. The two men had always communicated on a nonverbal level.

"Bart, you better come over here. I'm not kidding, Cap'n."

"Ten minutes," Mancuso promised.

Jones stubbed his smoke out in a metal waste can and returned to the printouts. It was not an easy thing for him now, but he flipped to the pages where he'd stopped. The printouts were made with pencils that were located on metal shuttle-bars, marking received noises in discrete frequency ranges, and the marks were arranged with the low frequencies on the left, and the higher ones on the right. Location within the range columns denoted bearing. The tracks meandered, looking to all the world like aerial photographs of sand dunes in some trackless desert, but if you knew what to look for, every spidery trace and twist had meaning. Jones slowed his analysis, taking in every minute's record of reception and sweeping from left to right, making marks and notes as he went. The chiefs who'd been assisting him stood back now, knowing that a master was at work, that he saw things they should have seen, but had not, and knowing why a man younger than they called an admiral by his first name.

"Attention on deck," some voice called presently, "Submarine Force, Pacific, arriving." Mancuso came in, accompanied by Captain Chambers, his operations officer, and an aide who kept out of the way. The Admiral just looked at Jones's face.

"You raise *Charlotte* yet, Bart?"

"No."

"Come here."

"What are you telling me, Jonesy?"

Jones took the red pen to the bottom of the page. "There's the crush, that's the hull letting go."

Mancuso nodded, letting out a breath. "I know, Ron."

"Look here. That's high-speed maneuvering — "

"Something goes wrong, you go max power and try to drive her up to the roof," Captain Chambers observed, not seeing it yet, or more probably not wanting to, Jones thought. Well, Mr. Chambers had always been a pretty nice officer to work for.

"But she wasn't heading straight for the roof, Mr. Chambers. Aspect changes, here and here," Jones said, moving the pen upward on the printout page, backwards in time, marking where the width of the traces varied, and the bearings changed subtly. "She was turning, too, at max power on a speed screw. This is probably a decoy signature. And this" — his hand went all the way to the right — "is a fish. Quiet one, but look at the bearing rates. It was turning, too, chasing *Asheville*, and that gives these traces here, all the way back to this time-point here." Ron circled both traces, and though separated on the paper by fourteen inches, the shallow twists and turns were almost identical. The pen moved again, upwards on the sheet, then shot across to another frequency column. "To a launch transient. Right there."

"Fuck," Chambers breathed.

Mancuso leaned over the paper sheet, next to Jones, and he saw it all now. "And this one?"

"That's probably *Charlotte*, also maneuvering

briefly. See, here and here, look like aspect changes on these traces to me. No transients because it was probably too far away, same reason we don't have a track on the fish." Jones moved the pen back to the track of USS *Asheville*. "Here. That Japanese diesel boat launched on her. Here. *Asheville* tried to evade and failed. Here's the first explosion from the torpedo warhead. Engine sounds stop here — she took the hit from aft. Here's the internal bulkheads letting go. Sir, *Asheville* was sunk by a torpedo, probably a Type 89, right about the same time that our two carriers had their little accident."

"It's not possible," Chambers thought.

When Jones turned his head, his eyes looked like the buttons on a doll's face. "Okay, sir, then you tell me what these signals denote." Somebody had to goad him into reality.

"Christ, Ron!"

"Settle down, Wally," ComSubPac said quietly, looking at the data and searching for another plausible interpretation. He had to look, even in the knowledge that there was no other possible conclusion.

"Wasting your time, Skipper." Jones tapped the track of USS *Gary*. "Somebody better tell that frigate that it ain't a rescue she's on. She's sailing in harm's way. There's two SSKs out there with warshots, and they already used them twice." Jones walked to the wall chart. He had to search around for a red marker, lifted it, and drew two circles, both about thirty miles in diameter. "Somewhere here. We'll get a better cut on them when they snort next. Who's the surface track, by the way?"

"Reportedly a coast-guard cutter, one of theirs, heading in for the rescue," SubPac answered.

"We might want to think about killing it," Jones suggested, marking that contact in red also, then setting the pen down. He'd just taken the final step. The surface ship whose position he'd marked was not "she," but rather *it*. An enemy. A target.

"We have to see CINCPAC," Mancuso said.

Jones nodded. "Yes, sir, I think we do."

22

The Global Dimension

The bomb was impressive. It exploded outside the Trincomalee Tradewinds, a new luxury hotel mainly built with Indian money. A few people, none closer than half a block away, would remember the vehicle, a small white delivery truck that had been big enough to contain half a ton of AMFO, an explosive mixture composed of nitrogen-based fertilizer and diesel fuel. It was a concoction easily made up in a bathtub or laundry basin, and in this case sufficient to rip the façade off the ten-story hotel, killing twenty-seven people and injuring another hundred or so in the process. Scarcely had the noise died when a telephone call came in to the local Reuters office.

"The final phase of liberation has begun," the voice said, probably reading the words off a prepared statement, as terrorists often did. "The Tamil Tigers will have their homeland and their autonomy or there will be no peace in Sri Lanka. This is only the beginning of the end of our struggle. We will explode one bomb per day until we achieve our goal." Click.

For more than a hundred years, Reuters had been one of the world's most efficient news services, and the Colombo office was no exception, even on a weekend. In ten minutes the report went out on the wire — a satellite link today — to the agency's London

526

headquarters, where it was instantly relayed across the global news network as a "flash" story.

Many U.S. agencies routinely monitor the news-wire services, including the intelligence services, the FBI, Secret Service, and the Pentagon. This was also true of the White House Signals Office, and so it was that twenty-five minutes after the bomb went off, an Air Force sergeant put his hand on Jack Ryan's shoulder. The National Security Advisor's eyes opened to see a finger pointed topside.

"Flash traffic, sir," the voice whispered.

Ryan nodded sleepily, slipped off his seat belt, and thanked God that he hadn't drunk too much in Moscow. In the dim lights of the cabin everyone else was conked out. To keep from waking his wife it was necessary to step over the table. He almost tripped, but the sergeant grabbed his arm.

"Thank you, ma'am."

"No problem, sir." Ryan followed her to the spiral stairs and headed up to the communications area on the upper deck.

"What gives?" He resisted the temptation to ask the time. It would have begged another question: the time in Washington, the time where the plane was now, or the time where the flash traffic had originated. Just another sign of progress, Ryan thought, heading to the thermal printer, you had to ask when "now" was. The communications watch officer was an Air Force first lieutenant, black, slim, and pretty.

"Good morning, Dr. Ryan. The National Security Office said to flag this one for you." She handed over the slippery paper Jack hated. The thermal printers were quiet, though, and this communications room, like all the others, was noisy enough already. Jack read the Reuters dispatch, too new as yet to have any analysis from CIA or elsewhere.

"That's the indicator we were looking for. Okay, let's get a secure phone."

"Some other stuff that's just come in," an airman said, handing over more papers. "The Navy had a bad day."

"Oh?" Ryan sat down in a padded chair and flipped on a reading light. "Oh, shit," he said next. Then he looked up. "Coffee, please, Lieutenant?" The officer sent an enlisted man for a cup.

"First call?"

"NMCC, the senior watch officer." The National Security Advisor checked his watch, did the arithmetic, and decided that he'd gotten about five hours of sleep total. It was not likely that he'd get much more between here, wherever that was, and Washington.

"Line three, Dr. Ryan. Admiral Jackson on the other end."

"This is SWORDSMAN," Ryan said, using his official Secret Service code name. They'd tried to hang GUNFIGHTER on him, a token of backhanded respect for his earlier life.

"This is SWITCHBOARD. Enjoying the flight, Jack?" It was a constant amazement to Ryan that the secure digital comm links had such high transmission quality. He could recognize his friend's voice, and even his humorous tone. He could also tell that it was somewhat forced.

"These Air Force drivers are pretty good. Maybe you should think about learning from them. Okay, what gives? What are you doing in the shop?"

"Pac Fleet had a little incident a few hours ago."

"So I see. Sri Lanka first," SWORDSMAN ordered.

"Nothing much more than the wire dispatch. We have some still photos, too, and we expect video in a half-hour or so. The consulate in Trincomalee is reporting in now. They confirm the incident. One American citizen injured, they think, just one, and not real serious, but he's asking to be evac'd soonest. Mike is being painted into a corner. He's going to try an' maneuver out of it when the sun goes down. Our estimate is that our friends are starting to get real frisky. Their amphibs are still alongside, but we've lost track of that brigade. The area they've been using to play games in appears empty. We have overheads three hours old, and the field is empty."

Ryan nodded. He slid the plastic blind off the window by his chair. It was dark outside. There were no lights to be seen below. Either they were over the ocean already or there were clouds down there. All he could see was the blinking strobe on the aircraft's wingtip.

"Any immediate dangers there?"

"Negative," Admiral Jackson thought. "We estimate a week to take positive action, minimum, but we also estimate that positive action is now likely. The folks up the river concur. Jack," Robby added, "Admiral Dubro needs instructions on what he can do about things, and he needs them soon."

"Understood." Ryan was making notes on an Air Force One scratchpad that the journalists hadn't managed to steal yet. "Stand by." He looked up at the Lieutenant. "ETA to Andrews?"

"Seven and a half hours, sir. Winds are pretty stiff. We're approaching the Icelandic coast now."

Jack nodded. "Thank you. Robby, we're seven and a half out. I'll be talking to the Boss before we get in. Start thinking about setting a briefing up two hours after we get in."

"Roger that."

"Okay. Now, what the hell happened to those carriers?"

"Supposedly one of the Jap 'cans had a little malfunction and rippled off her Mark 50s. They caught both CVNs in the ass. *Enterprise* has damage to all four shafts. *Stennis* has three down. They report no fatalities, some minor injuries."

"Robby, how the hell — "

"Hey, SWORDSMAN, I just work here, remember."

"How long?"

"Four to six months to effect repairs, that's what we have now. Wait, stand by, Jack." The voice stopped, but Ryan could hear murmurs and papers shuffling. "Wait a minute — something else just came in."

"Standing by." Ryan sipped his coffee and returned to the task of figuring out what time it was.

"Jack, something bad. We have a SUBMISS/SUB-SUNK in Pac Fleet."

"What's that?"

"USS *Asheville*, that's a new 688, her BST-3 just started howling. *Stennis* has launched a bird to check it out, and a 'can's heading up there, too. This ain't good."

"What's the crew? Like a hundred?"

"More, one-twenty, one-thirty. Oh, damn. Last time this happened, I was a mid."

"We had an exercise going with them, didn't we?"

"DATELINE PARTNERS, yes, just ended yesterday. Until a couple hours ago, looked like a good exercise. Things went in the shitter in a hurry . . ." Jackson's voice trailed off. "Another signal. First report, *Stennis* launched a Hoover — "

"What?"

"S-3 Viking, ASW bird. Four-man crew. They report no survivors from the sub. Shit," Jackson added, even though it wasn't exactly a surprise. "Jack, I need to do some work here, okay?"

"Understood. Keep me posted."

"Will do. Out." The line went dead.

Ryan finished off his coffee and dropped the plastic cup into a basket bolted to the floor of the aircraft. There was no point in waking the President just yet. Durling would need his sleep. He was coming home to a financial crisis, a political mess, maybe a brewing war, in the Indian Ocean, and now the situation with

530

Japan would only get worse after this damned-fool accident in the Pacific. Durling was entitled to a little good luck, wasn't he?

By coincidence Oreza's personal car was a white Toyota Land Cruiser, a popular vehicle on the island. He and his charter were walking toward it when two more just like it pulled into the marina's parking lot. Six people got out and walked straight toward them. The former Command Master Chief stopped dead in his tracks. He'd left Saipan just before dawn, having picked Burroughs up at the hotel himself, the better to catch the tuna chasing their own food in the early morning. Though traffic on the way in to the dock had been . . . well, a little busier than usual, the world had held its normal shape.

But not now. Now there were Japanese fighters circling over the island, and now six men in fatigues and pistol belts were walking toward him and his charter. It was like something from a movie, he thought, one of those crazy TV mini-things from when the Russians were real.

"Hello, how was the fishing?" the man asked. He had O-3 rank, Oreza saw, and a parachutist's badge on the left breast pocket. Smiling, just as pleasant and friendly as he could be.

"I bagged one hell of an albacore tuna," Pete Burroughs said, his pride amplified by the four beers he'd drunk on the way in.

A wider smile. "Ah! Can I see it?"

"Sure!" Burroughs reversed his path and led them back to the dock, where the fish was still hanging head-down from the hoist.

"This is your boat, Captain Oreza?" the soldier asked. Only one other man had followed their captain down. The others stayed behind, watching closely, as though under orders not to be too . . . something, Portagee thought. He also took note of the fact that this officer had troubled himself to learn his name.

"That's right, sir. Interested in a little fishing?" he asked with an innocent smile.

"My grandfather was a fisherman," the *ishii* told them.

Portagee nodded and smiled. "So was mine. Family tradition."

"Long tradition?"

Oreza nodded as they got to *Springer*. "More than a hundred years."

"Ah, a fine boat you have. May I look at it?"

"Sure, jump aboard." Portagee went first and waved him over. The sergeant who'd walked down with his captain, he saw, stayed on the dock with Mr. Burroughs, keeping about six feet away from him. There was a pistol in the man's holster, a SIG P220, the standard sidearm of the Japanese military. By this time all kinds of alarm were lighting off in Oreza's brain.

"What does 'Springer' denote?"

"It's a kind of hunting dog."

"Ah, yes, very good." The officer looked around. "What sort of radios do you need for a boat like this. Expensive?"

"I'll show you." Oreza led him into the salon. "Your people make it, sir, NEC, a standard marine VHF and a backup. Here's my GPS nav system, depth finder, fish-finder, radar." He tapped each instrument. They were in fact all Japanese-made, high quality, reasonably priced, and reliable as hell.

"You have guns aboard?"

Click. "Guns? What for?"

"Don't many islanders own guns?"

"Not that I know of." Oreza shook his head. "Anyway, I've never been attacked by a fish. No, I don't have any, even at home."

Clearly the officer was pleased by that news.

"Oreza, what sort of name is that?" It sounded native to the Ishii.

"Originally, you mean? Way back, my people come from Portugal."

"Your family here a long time?"

Oreza nodded. "You bet." Five years was a long time, wasn't it? A husband and wife constituted a family, didn't they?

"The radios, VHF you say, short-range?" The man looked around for other instruments, but clearly there were none.

"Mainly line-of-sight, yes, sir."

The captain nodded. "Very good. Thank you. Beautiful boat. You take great pride in it, yes?"

"Yes, sir, I do."

"Thank you for showing me around. You can go now," the man said finally, not quite knowing how discordant the final sentence was. Oreza escorted him to the dock and watched him leave, rejoining his men without another word.

"What was — "

"Pete, you want to button it for a minute?" The command was delivered in his Master Chief's voice, and had the desired effect. They walked off to Oreza's car, letting the others pull away, marching as soldiers did to a precise one hundred twenty paces per minute, the sergeant a step to his captain's left and half a pace behind, walking exactly in step. By the time the fisherman got to his car it was clear that yet another Toyota Land Cruiser was at the entrance to the marina parking lot, not really doing anything but sitting there, with three men inside, all in uniform.

"Some kind of exercise? War games? What gives?" Burroughs asked once they were in Oreza's car.

"Beats the shit out of me, Pete." He started up and headed out of the lot, turning right to go south on Beach Road. In a few minutes they passed by the commercial docks. Portagee took his time, obeying

533

all rules and limits, and blessing his luck that he had the same model car and color the soldiers used.

Or almost. The vehicles off-loading from *Orchid Ace* now were mainly olive-green. A steady cab-rank of airport buses off-loaded people in uniforms of the same color. They appeared to be going to a central point, then dispersing either to the parked military vehicles or to the ship, perhaps to off-load their assigned units.

"What are those big boxy things?"

"It's called MLRS, Multiple-Launch Rocket System." There were six of them now, Oreza saw.

"What's it for?" Burroughs asked.

"Killing people," Portagee replied tersely. As they drove by the access road to the docks, a soldier waved them on vigorously. More trucks, deuce-and-a-halfs. More soldiers, maybe five or six hundred. Oreza continued south. Every major intersection had a Land Cruiser in place, and no less than three soldiers, some with pistol belts, occasionally one with a slung rifle. It took a few minutes to realize that there wasn't a single police car in evidence. He turned left onto Wallace Highway.

"My hotel?"

"How about dinner at my place tonight?" Oreza headed up the hill, past the hospital, finally turning left into his development. Though a man of the sea, he preferred a house in high ground. It also afforded a fine view of the southern part of the island. His was a home of modest size with lots of windows. His wife, Isabel, was an administrator at the hospital, and the home was close enough that she could walk to work if the mood suited her. The mood this evening was not a happy one. As soon as he pulled into the driveway, his wife was out the door.

"Manni, what's going on?" Her ancestry was like his. Short, round, and dark-complected, now her swarthy skin was pale.

"Let's go inside, okay? Honey, this is Pete Burroughs. We went fishing today." His voice was calm, but his eyes swept around. The landing lights of four aircraft were visible to the east, lined up a few miles apart, approaching the island's two large runways. When the three of them were inside, and the doors shut, the talking could start.

"The phones are out. I tried to call Rachel and I got a recording. The overseas lines are down. When I went to the mall — "

"Soldiers?" Portagee asked his wife.

"*Lots* of 'em, and they're all — "

"Japs." Master Chief Quartermaster Manuel Oreza, United States Coast Guard, retired, completed the thought.

"Hey, that's not the polite way to — "

"Neither's an invasion, Mr. Burroughs."

"What?"

Oreza lifted the kitchen phone and hit the speed-dial button for his daughter's house in Massachusetts.

"We're sorry, but a cable problem has temporarily interrupted Trans-Pacific service. Our people are working on the problem. Thank you for your patience — "

"My ass!" Oreza told the recording. "Cable, hell, what about the satellite dishes?"

"Can't call out?" Burroughs was slow to catch on, but at least this was something he knew about.

"No, doesn't seem that way."

"Try this." The computer engineer reached into his pocket and pulled out his cellular phone.

"I have one," Isabel said. "It doesn't work either. I mean it's fine for local calls, but — "

"What number?"

"Area code 617," Portagee said, giving the rest of the number.

"Wait, I need the USA prefix."

"It's not going to work," Mrs. Oreza insisted.

535

"You don't have satellite phones here yet, eh?" Burroughs smiled. "My company just got us all these things. I can download on my laptop, send faxes with it, all that stuff. Here." He handed the phone over. "It's ringing."

The entire system was new, and the first such phone had not yet been sold in the islands yet, a fact that the Japanese military had troubled itself to learn in the past week, but the service was global, even if the local marketing people hadn't started selling the things here. The signal from the small device went to one of thirty-five satellites in a low-orbit constellation to the nearest ground station. Manila was the closest, beating Tokyo by a mere thirty miles, though even one mile would have been enough for the executive programming that ran the system. The Luzon ground station had been in operation for only eight weeks, and immediately relayed the call to another satellite, this one a Hughes bird in geosynchronous orbit over the Pacific, back down to a ground station in California, and from there via fiberoptic to Cambridge, Massachusetts.

"Hello?" the voice said, somewhat crossly, since it was 5:00 A.M. in America's Eastern Time Zone.

"Rachel?"

"Daddy?"

"Yeah, honey."

"You okay out there?" his daughter asked urgently.

"What do you mean?"

"I tried to call Mom, but the recording said you had a big storm and the lines were down."

"There wasn't any storm, Rach," Oreza said without much thought on the matter.

"What's the matter, then?"

Jesus, where do I start? Portagee asked himself. What if nobody . . . was that possible?

"Uh, Portagee," Burroughs said.

536

"What is it?" Oreza asked.

"What's what, Daddy?" his daughter asked also, of course.

"Wait a minute, honey. What is it, Pete?" He put his hand over the receiver.

"You mean like, invasion, like war, taking over, all that stuff?"

Portagee nodded. "Yes, sir, that's what it looks like."

"Turn the phone off, now!" The urgency in his voice was unmistakable. Nobody had thought any of this through yet, and both were coming to terms with it from different directions and at different speeds.

"Honey, I'll be back, okay? We're fine. 'Bye." Oreza thumbed the CLEAR button. "What's the problem, Pete?"

"This isn't some joke, right? You're not doing a number to mess with my head, tourist games and all that stuff, are you?"

"Jesus, I need a beer." Oreza opened the refrigerator and took one out. That it was a Japanese brand did not for the moment matter. He tossed one to his guest. "Pete, this ain't no play-acting, okay? In case you didn't notice, we seen at least a battalion of troops, mechanized vehicles, fighters. And that asshole on the dock was real interested in the radio on my boat."

"Okay." Burroughs opened his beer and took a long pull. "Let's say this is a no-shitter. You can DF one of those things."

"Dee-eff? What do you mean?" A pause while he dusted off some long-unused memories. "Oh . . . yeah."

It was busy at the headquarters of Commander-in-Chief Pacific. CINCPAC was a Navy command, a tradition that dated back to Admiral Chester Nimitz. At the moment people were scurrying about. They were almost all in uniform. The civilian employees were rarely in on weekends, and with a few exceptions it was too late for them anyway. Mancuso saw the collective mood as he came through security, people looking down with harried frowns, moving quickly the better to avoid the heavy atmosphere of an office in considerable turmoil. Nobody wanted to be caught in the storm.

"Where's Admiral Seaton?" ComSubPac asked the nearest yeoman. The petty officer just pointed to the office suite. Mancuso led the other two in that direction.

"Where the hell have you been?" CINCPAC demanded as they came into his inner office.

"SOSUS, sir. Admiral, you know Captain Chambers, my operations officer. This is Dr. Ron Jones — "

"The sonarman you used to brag on?" Admiral David Seaton allowed himself a pleasant moment. It was brief enough.

"That's right, sir. We were just over at SOSUS checking the data on — "

"No survivors, Bart. Sorry, but the S-3 crew says — "

"Sir, they were killed," Jones interrupted, tired of the preliminaries. His statement stopped everything cold.

"What do you mean, Dr. Jones?" CINCPAC asked after perhaps as much as a second.

"I mean *Asheville* and *Charlotte* were torpedoed and sunk by Japanese submarines, sir."

"Now wait a minute, son. You mean *Charlotte*, too?" Seaton's head turned. "Bart, what is this?" SubPac didn't get a chance to answer.

"I can prove it, sir." Jones held up the sheaf of papers under his arm. "I need a table with a light over it."

Mancuso's face was pretty grim. "Sir, Jonesy appears to be right. These were not accidents."

538

"Gentlemen, I have fifteen Japanese officers in the operations room right now trying to explain how the fire control on their 'cans works and — "

"You have Marines, don't you?" Jones asked coldly. "They carry guns, don't they?"

"Show me what you have." Dave Seaton gestured at his desk.

Jones walked CINCPAC through the printouts, and if Seaton wasn't exactly a perfect audience, he surely was a quiet one. On further examination, the SOSUS traces even showed the surface ships and the Mark 50 antisub torpedoes that had crippled half of PacFlt's carriers. The new array off Kure was really something, Jones thought.

"Look at the time, sir. All of this happened over a period of what? Twenty minutes or so. You have two hundred fifty dead sailors out there, and it wasn't any accident."

Seaton shook his head like a horse shedding troublesome insects. "Wait a minute, I haven't had any word — I mean, the threat board is blank. There aren't any indications at all that — "

"There are now, sir." Jones wasn't letting up at all.

"But — "

"Goddamn it, Admiral!" Jones swore. "Here it is, black and white, okay? There are other copies of this back at the SOSUS building, there's a tape record, and I can show it to you on a fucking TV screen. You want your own experts to go over there, well, shit, they're right here, ain't they?" The contractor pointed to Mancuso and Chambers. "We have been *attacked*, sir."

"What are the chances that this is some sort of mistake?" Seaton asked. His face was as ghostly pale as the cloth of his undress-white uniform shirt.

"Just about zero. I suppose you could wait for them to take an ad out in *The New York Times* if you want

539

additional confirmation." Diplomacy had never been Jones's strongest suit, and he was too angry to consider it anyway.

"Listen, mister — " Seaton began, but then he bit off his words, and instead looked up at his type commander. "Bart?"

"I can't argue with the data, sir. If there were a way to dispute it, Wally or I would have found it. The people at SOSUS concur. It's hard for me to believe, too," Mancuso conceded. "*Charlotte* has failed to check in and — "

"Why didn't her beacon go off?" CINCPAC asked.

"The gadget is located on the sail, aft corner. Some of my skippers weld them down. The fast-attack guys resisted putting them aboard last year, remember? Anyway, the fish could have destroyed the BST or for some reason it didn't deploy properly. We have that noise indicator at *Charlotte*'s approximate location, and she has failed to respond to an emergency order to communicate with us. There is no reason, sir, to assume that she's still alive." And now that Mancuso had said it, it was official. There was one more thing that needed to be said.

"You're telling me we're at war." The statement was delivered in an eerily quiet voice. ComSubPac nodded.

"Yes, sir, I am."

"I didn't have any warning at all," Seaton objected.

"Yeah, you have to admire their sense of tradition, don't you?" Jones observed, forgetting that the last time there had been ample warning, all of it unheeded.

Pete Burroughs didn't finish his fifth beer of the day. The night had not brought peace. Though the sky was clear and full of stars, brighter lights continued to approach Saipan from the east, taking advantage of the trade winds to ease their approach into the island's two American-built runways. Each jumbo jet had to be carrying at least two hundred soldiers, probably closer to three. They could see the two airfields. Oreza's binoculars were more than adequate to pick out the aircraft and the fuel trucks that scurried about to fill up the arriving jets so that they could rapidly go home to make another shuttle run. It didn't occur to anyone to keep a count until it was a few hours too late.

"Car coming in," Burroughs warned, alerted by the glow of turning lights. Oreza and he retreated to the side of the house, hoping to be invisible in the shadows. The car was another Toyota Land Cruiser, which drove down the lane, reversed direction at the end of the cul-de-sac, and headed back out after having done not very much of anything but look around and perhaps count the cars in the various driveways — more likely to see if people were gathered in an inopportune way. "You have any idea what to do?" he asked Oreza when it was gone.

"Hey, I was Coast Guard, remember? This is Navy shit. No, more like Marine shit."

"It sure is deep shit, man. You suppose anybody knows?"

"They gotta. Somebody's gotta," Portagee said, lowering the glasses and heading back into the house. "We can watch from inside our bedroom. We always leave the windows open anyway." The cool evenings here, always fresh and comfortable from the ocean breezes, were yet another reason for his decision to move to Saipan. "What exactly do you do, Pete?"

"Computer industry, several things really. I have a masters in EE. My real specialty area is communications, how computers talk to each other. I've done a little government work. My company does plenty, but mostly on another side of the house." Burroughs looked around the kitchen. Mrs. Oreza had prepared

541

a light dinner, a good one, it appeared, though it was growing cold.

"You were worried about having people track in on your phone."

"Maybe just being paranoid, but my company makes the chips for scanners that the Army uses for just that purpose."

Oreza sat down and started shoveling some of the stir-fry onto his plate. "I don't think anything's paranoid anymore, man."

"I hear ya, Skipper." Burroughs decided to do the same, and looked at the food with approval. "Y'all trying to lose weight?"

Oreza grunted. "We both need to, Izzy and me. She's been taking classes in low-fat stuff."

Burroughs looked around. Though the home had a dining room, like most retired couples (that's how he thought of them, even though they clearly were not), they ate at a small table in their kitchen. The sink and counter were neatly laid out, and the engineer saw the steel mixing and serving bowls. The stainless steel gleamed. Isabel Oreza, too, ran a tight ship, and it was plain enough who was the skipper at home.

"Do I go to work tomorrow?" she asked, her mind drifting, trying to come to terms with the change in local affairs.

"I don't know, honey," her husband replied, his own thoughts stopped cold by the question. What would he do? Go fishing again as though nothing at all had happened?

"Wait a minute," Pete said, still looking at the mixing bowls. He stood, took the two steps needed to reach the kitchen counter, and lifted the largest bowl. It was sixteen inches in diameter and a good five or six inches deep. The bottom was flat, perhaps a three-inch circle, but the rest of it was spherical, almost parabolic in shape. He pulled his sat-phone out of his shirt pocket. He'd never measured the antenna, but now, extending it, he saw it was less than four inches in length. Burroughs looked over at Oreza. "You have a drill?"

"Yeah, why?"

"DF, hell. I got it!"

"You lost me, Pete."

"We drill a hole in the bottom, put the antenna through it. The bowl's made out of steel. It reflects radio waves just like a microwave antenna. Everything goes up. Hell, it might even make the transmitter more efficient."

"You mean like, E.T. phone home?"

"Close enough, Cap'n. What if nobody's phoned home on this one?" Burroughs was still trying to think it through, coming to terms slowly with a very frightening situation. "Invasion" meant "war." War, in this case, was between America and Japan, and however bizarre that possibility was, it was also the only explanation for the things he'd seen that day. If it was a war, then he was an enemy alien. So were his hosts. But he'd seen Oreza do some very fancy footwork at the marina.

"Let me get my drill. How big a hole you need?" Burroughs handed over the sat-phone. He'd been tempted to toss it through the air, but stopped himself on the realization that it was perhaps his most valuable possession. Oreza checked the diameter of the little button at the end of the slim metal whip and went for his tool kit.

"Hello?"

"Rachel? It's Dad."

"You sure you're okay? Can I call you guys now?"

"Honey, we're fine, but there's a problem here." How the hell to explain this? he wondered. Rachel Oreza Chandler was a prosecuting attorney in Boston, actually looking forward to leaving government ser-

543

vice and becoming a criminal lawyer in private practice, where the job satisfaction was rarer, but the pay and hours were far better. Approaching thirty, she was now at the stage where she worried about her parents in much the same way they'd once worried about her. There was no sense in worrying Rachel now, he decided. "Could you get a phone number for me?"

"Sure, what number?"

"Coast Guard Headquarters. It's in D.C., at Buzzard's Point. I want the watch center. I'll wait," he told her.

The attorney put one line on hold and dialed D.C. information. In a minute she relayed the number, hearing her father repeat it word for word back to her. "That's right. You sure things are okay? You sound a little tense."

"Mom and I are just fine, honest, baby." She hated it when he called her that, but it was probably too late to change him. Poppa would just never be PC.

"Okay, you say so. I hear that storm was really bad. You have electricity back yet?" she asked, forgetting that there hadn't been a storm at all.

"Not yet, honey, but soon, probably," he lied. "Later, baby."

"Coast Guard Watch Center, Chief Petty Officer Obrecki, this is a nonsecure line," the man said, just as rapidly as possible to prevent the person on the other end from understanding a single word.

"Are you telling me that that fuzzy-cheeked infant who sailed on *Panache* with me made *chief?*" It was good enough to startle the man at the other end, and the reply was comprehensible.

"This is Chief Obrecki. Who's this?"

"*Master* Chief Oreza," was the answer.

"Well, how the hell are you, Portagee? I heard you retired." The chief of the watch leaned back

544

in his chair. Now that he was a chief himself, he could refer to the man at the other end by his nickname.

"I'm on Saipan. Okay, kid, listen up: put your watch officer on right now."

"What's the matter, Master Chief?"

"No time, okay? Let's do it."

"Fair enough." Obrecki put the call on hold. "Commander, could you pick up on one, ma'am?"

"NMCC, this is Rear Admiral Jackson," Robby said, tired and in a very foul mood. Only reluctantly did he lift the phone, on the recommendation of a youngish Air Force major.

"Admiral, this is Lieutenant Commander Powers, Coast Guard, over at Buzzard's Point. I have a call on the line from Saipan. The caller is a retired Command Master Chief. One of ours."

Damn it, I have a broke carrier division out there, his mind raged. "That's nice, Commander. You want to clue me in fast? It's busy here."

"Sir, he reports a whole lot of Japanese troops on the island of Saipan."

Jackson's eyes came up off the dispatches on his desk. "What?"

"I can patch him over now, sir."

"Okay," Robby said guardedly.

"Who's this?" another voice asked, old and gruff. He sounded like a chief, Robby thought.

"I'm Rear Admiral Jackson, in the National Military Command Center." He didn't have to order a tape on the line. They were all taped.

"Sir, this is Master Chief Quartermaster Manuel Oreza, U.S. Coast Guard, retired, serial number three-two-eight-six-one-four-zero-three-zero. I retired five years ago and moved to Saipan. I operate a fishing boat here. Sir, there are a lot — and I mean a whole goddamned pisspot full — of Japanese troops, uniformed and carrying arms, on this-here rock, right now, sir."

Jackson adjusted his hand on the phone, gesturing for another officer to pick up. "Master Chief, I hope you understand that I find that a little bit hard to believe, okay?"

"Shit, sir, you oughta see it from my side. I am looking out my window right now. I can see down on the airport and Kobler Field. I count a total of six jumbo-jet aircraft, four at the airport and two at Kobler. I observed a pair of F-15 Eagle fighters with meatball markings circling over the island a few hours ago. Question, sir, is there any sort of joint exercise under way at this time?" the voice asked. It was stone sober, Jackson thought. It sure as hell sounded like a command master chief.

The Air Force major listening fifteen feet away was scribbling notes, though an invitation to Jurassic Park would have seemed somewhat more realistic.

"We just concluded a joint exercise, but Saipan didn't have anything to do with it."

"Sir, then this ain't no fuckin' exercise. There are three car-carrier-type merchant ships tied alongside the dock up the coast from me. One of 'em's named *Orchid Ace*. I have personally observed military-type vehicles, I think MLRS — Mike Lima Romeo Sierra — six of those sitting in the parking lot at the commercial dock area. Admiral, you check with the Coast Guard and pull my package. I did thirty years in CG blue. I ain't dickin' around, sir. Check for yourself, the phone lines to the rock are out. The story is supposedly that we had a big windstorm, took lines down and stuff. Ain't been no windstorm, Admiral. I was out fishing all day, okay? Check with your weather pukes to confirm that one, too. There are Japanese troops on this island, wearing fatigue uniforms and under arms."

"You got a count, Master Chief?"

546

The best confirmation of this insane tale, Robby thought, was the embarrassed tone of the answer to that question. "No, sir, sorry, I didn't think to count the airplanes. I'd guess three to six arrivals per hour, over the last six hours at least, probably more, but that's just a guess, sir. Wait . . . Kobler, one of the birds is moving, like to take off. It's a 747, but I can't make out the markings."

"Wait. If the phones are out, how are you talking to me?" Oreza explained, giving Jackson a conventional number to call back on. "Okay, Master Chief. I'm going to do some checking here. I'll be back to you in less than an hour. Fair enough?"

"Yes, sir, I figure we done our part." The line went dead.

"Major!" Jackson shouted without looking up. When he did that, he saw the man was there.

"Sir, I know he sounded normal and all, but — "

"But call Andersen Air Force Base right now."

"Roger." The young pilot went back to his desk and flipped open his Autovon directory. Thirty seconds later he looked up and shook his head, a curious look on his face.

"Is someone telling me," Jackson asked the ceiling, "that a U.S. Air Force base dropped off the net today and nobody *noticed?*"

"Admiral, CINCPAC on your STU, sir, it's coded as CRITIC traffic." CRITIC was a classification of priority even higher than FLASH, and not a prefix often used, even by a Theater Commander in Chief. *What the hell,* Jackson thought. *Why not ask?*

"Admiral Seaton, this is Robby Jackson. Are we at war, sir?"

His part in the exercise seemed easy enough, Zhang Han San thought. Just one flight to one place, to talk first with one person, then another, and it had gone even more easily than he'd expected.

547

Well, he shouldn't have been surprised, he thought, returning to the airport in the back of the embassy car. Korea would be cut off, certainly for a period of months, and perhaps indefinitely. To do anything else would have carried with it great dangers for a country whose military had been downsized and whose next-door neighbor was the nation with the world's largest standing army, and an historical enemy at that. Han hadn't even been forced to bring up that unseemly thought. He'd simply delivered an observation. There seemed to be difficulties between America and Japan. Those difficulties did not pertain directly to the Republic of Korea. Nor would it appear that the Republic had any immediate ability to ameliorate those differences, except perhaps as an honest broker of influence when diplomatic negotiations were undertaken, at which time the good offices of the Republic of Korea would be most welcome indeed by all sides in the dispute, certainly by Japan.

He'd taken no particular pleasure at the discomfort his mild words had given to his hosts. There was much to admire in the Koreans, a fact lost on Japan in their blind racism, Zhang thought. With luck, he might firm up the trading relationship between the PRC and the ROK, and they, too, would profit from the ultimate objective — and why not? The ROKs had no reason to love the Russians, and even less to love the Japanese. They simply had to get over their regrettable friendship with America and become part of a new reality. It was sufficient to the moment that they had indeed seen things his way, and that America's one remaining ally in this part of the world was off the playing field, their president and foreign minister having seen the light of reason. And with luck, the war, such as it was, might already be over for all intents and purposes.

"Ladies and gentlemen." The voice came from the

548

living room, where Mrs. Oreza had left the TV on. "In ten minutes there will be a special announcement. Please stay tuned."

"Manni?"

"I heard it, honey."

"You have a blank tape for your VCR?" Burroughs asked.

23

Catching Up

Robby Jackson's day had started off badly enough. He'd had bad ones before, including a day as a lieutenant commander at Naval Air Test Center, Patuxent River, Maryland, in which a jet trainer had decided without any prompting at all to send him and his ejection seat flying through the canopy, breaking his leg in the process and taking him off flight status for months. He'd seen friends die in crashes of one sort or another, and even more often had participated in searches for men whom he'd rarely found alive, more often locating a slick of jet fuel and perhaps a little debris. As a squadron commander and later as a CAG, he'd been the one who'd written the letters to parents and wives, telling them that their man, and most recently, their little girl, had died in the service of their country, each time asking himself what he might have done differently to prevent the necessity of the exercise. The life of a naval aviator was filled with such days.

But this was worse, and the only consolation was that he was deputy J-3, responsible to develop operations and plans for his country's military. Had he been part of J-2, the intelligence boys, his sense of failure would have been complete indeed.

"That's it, sir, Yakota, Misawa, and Kadena are

550

all off the net. Nobody's picking up."

"How many people?" Jackson asked.

"Total, about two thousand, mainly mechanics, radar controllers, loggies, that sort of thing. Maybe an airplane or two in transit, but not many of those. I have people checking now," the Major replied. "How about the Navy?"

"We have people at Andersen on Guam, co-located with your base. The port, too, maybe a thousand people total. It's a lot smaller than it used to be." Jackson lifted his secure phone and punched in the numbers for CINCPAC. "Admiral Seaton? This is Jackson again. Anything else?"

"We can't raise anybody west of Midway, Rob. It's starting to look real."

"How does this thing work?" Oreza asked.

"I hate to say this, but I'm not sure. I didn't bother reading the manual," Burroughs admitted. The sat-phone was sitting on the coffee table, its antenna extended through the drill hole in the bottom of the mixing bowl, which was in turn sitting atop two piles of books. "I'm not sure if it broadcasts its position to the satellites periodically or not." For which reason they felt it necessary to maintain the comical arrangement.

"You turn mine off by putting the antenna back down," Isabel Oreza observed, causing two male heads to turn. "Or you can just take the batteries out, right?"

"Damn." Burroughs managed to say it first, but not by much. He lifted the bowl off, put the little antenna back in its hole, then flipped off the battery cover and withdrew the two AAs. The phone was now completely off. "Ma'am, if you want to get into the master's program at Sanford, use me as a reference, okay?"

"Ladies and gentlemen." Heads turned in the living

551

room to see a smiling man in green fatigues. His English was letter-perfect. "I am General Tokikichi Arima of the Japanese Ground Self-Defense Forces. Please allow me to explain what has happened today.

"First of all, let me assure you that there is no cause for alarm. There was an unfortunate shooting at the police substation adjacent to your parliament building, but the two police officers who were hurt in the exchange are both doing well in your local hospital. If you have heard rumors of violence or death, those rumors are not true," the General assured the twenty-nine thousand citizens of Saipan.

"You probably want to know what has happened," he went on. "Early today, forces under my command began arriving on Saipan and Guam. As you know from your history, and indeed as some of the older citizens on this island well remember, until 1944 the Mariana Islands were possessions of Japan. It may surprise some of you to know that since the court decision several years ago allowing Japanese citizens to purchase real estate in the islands, the majority of the land on Saipan and Guam is owned by my countrymen. You also know of our love and affection for these islands and the people who live here. We have invested billions of dollars here and created a renaissance in the local economy after years of shameful neglect by the American government. Therefore, we're not really strangers at all, are we?

"You probably also know that there have been great difficulties between Japan and America. Those difficulties have forced my country to rethink our defense priorities. We have, therefore, decided to reestablish our ownership of the Mariana Islands as a purely defensive measure to safeguard our own shores against possible American action. In other words, it is necessary for us to maintain defense forces here and therefore to bring the Marianas back into our country.

"Now." General Arima smiled. "What does this mean to you, the citizens of Saipan?

"Really, it means nothing at all. All businesses will remain open. We, too, believe in free enterprise. You will continue to manage your own affairs through your own elected officials, with the additional benefit that you will have status as Japan's forty-eighth prefecture, with full parliamentary representation in the Diet. That is something you have not had as an American commonwealth — which is just another word for colony, isn't it? You will have dual citizenship rights. We will respect your culture and your language. Your freedom to travel will not be impeded. Your freedoms of speech, press, religion, and assembly will be the same as those enjoyed by all Japanese citizens, and totally identical with the civil rights you now enjoy. In short, nothing is going to change in your daily life at all." Another charming smile.

"The truth of the matter is that you will greatly benefit from this change in government. As part of Japan, you will be part of the world's most vibrant and dynamic economy. Even more money will come to your island. You will see prosperity such as you have never dreamed of," Arima assured his audience. "The only changes you will experience will be positive ones. On that you have my word and the word of my government.

"Perhaps you say that such words are easy to speak, and you are correct. Tomorrow you will see people on the streets and roads of Saipan, surveying, taking measurements, and interviewing local citizens. Our first important task will be to improve the roads and highways of your island, something neglected by the Americans. We want your advice on the best way to do this. In fact, we will welcome your help and participation in everything we do.

"Now," Arima said, leaning forward somewhat, "I know that some among you will find these developments unwelcome, and I wish to apologize sincerely for that. We have no desire to harm anyone here, but you must understand that any attack upon one of my men or any Japanese citizen will be treated as a violation of the law. I am also responsible to take certain security measures to protect my troops and to bring this island into compliance with Japanese law.

"All firearms owned by private citizens on Saipan must be surrendered in the next few days. You may bring them into your local police stations. If you have a sales record for the guns, or if you can demonstrate their commercial value, we will pay you the fair cash value for them. Similarly, we must ask that any own-ers of 'ham' radios turn them over to us for a short period of time, and, please, not to use them until you do. Again, we will pay in cash the full value of your property, and in the case of the radios, when we return them to you, you may keep the money as a token of our thanks for your cooperation. Aside from that" — another smile — "you will hardly notice that we are here. My troops are under orders to treat everyone on this island as fellow citizens. If you ex-perience or even see a single incident in which a Jap-anese soldier is impolite to a local citizen, I want you to come to my headquarters and report it. You see, our law applies to us, too.

"For the moment, please go about your normal lives." A number came up on the screen. "If you have any specific questions, please call this number or feel free to come to my headquarters at your par-liament building. We will be glad to help you in any way we can. Thank you for listening. Good night."

"This message will be repeated every fifteen min-utes on Channel Six, the public-access channel," an-other voice said.

"Son of a bitch," Oreza breathed.

"I wonder who their ad agency is," Burroughs

554

noted, going to punch the rewind button on the VCR.

"Can we believe it?" Isabel asked.

"Who knows? You have any guns?"

Portagee shook his head. "Nope. I don't even know if this rock has a registration law. Have to be crazy to take on soldiers anyway, right?"

"It makes it a lot easier for them if they don't have to watch their backs." Burroughs started putting the batteries back in his sat-phone. "You have the number for that admiral?"

"Jackson."

"Master Chief Oreza, sir. You got a tape machine running?"

"Yes, I do. What you got?"

"Well, sir, it's official," Oreza reported dryly. "They just made the announcement on TV. We taped it. I'm turning the tape on now. I'll hold the phone right next to the speaker."

General Tokikichi Arima, Jackson wrote down on a pad. He handed it to an Army sergeant. "Have the intel boys identify this name."

"Yessir." The sergeant vanished in an instant.

"Major!" Robby called next.

"Yes, Admiral?"

"The sound quality is pretty good. Have a copy of the tape run over to the spooks for voice-stress analysis. Next, I want a typed transcript ASAP ready to fax out to half a million places."

"Right."

For the rest of the time, Jackson just listened, an island of calm in a sea of madness, or so it seemed.

"That's it," Oreza told him when it ended. "You want the call-in number, Admiral?"

"Not right now, no. Good job, Master Chief. Anything else to report?"

"The airplanes are still shuttling in. I counted fourteen since we talked last."

"Okay." Robby made the proper notes. "You feel like you're in any particular danger?"

"I don't see people running around with guns, Admiral. You notice they didn't say anything about American nationals on the island?"

"No, I didn't. Good point." *Ouch.*

"I ain't real comfortable about this, sir." Oreza gave him a quick reprise of the incident on his boat.

"I can't say that I blame you, Master Chief. Your country is working on the problem, okay?"

"You say so, Admiral. I'm shutting down for a while."

"Fair enough. Hang in there," Jackson ordered. It was a hollow directive, and both men knew it.

"Roger that. Out."

Robby sat the phone back in the cradle. "Opinions?"

"You mean aside from, 'It's all fuckin' crazy'?" a staff officer inquired.

"It may be crazy to us, but it's sure as hell logical to somebody." There was no sense in clobbering the officer for the statement, Jackson knew. It would take a bit more time before they really came to terms with the situation. "Does anybody *not* believe the information we have now?" He looked around. Seven officers were present, and people weren't selected for duty in the NMCC for their stupidity.

"It may be crazy, sir, but everything keeps coming down the same way. Every post we've tried to link with is off the air. They're all supposed to have duty officers, but nobody's answering the phone. Satellite links are down. We have four Air Force bases and an Army post off the air. It's real, sir." The staffer redeemed herself with the follow-up.

"Anything from State? Any of the spook shops?"

"Nothing," a colonel from J-2 replied. "I can give you a satellite pass over the Marianas in about an hour. I've already told NRO and I-TAC about the tasking and the priority."

"KH-11?"

"Yes, sir, and all the cameras are up. Weather is clear. We'll get good overheads," the intelligence officer assured him.

"No storm in the area yesterday?"

"Negative," another officer said. "Ain't no reason for phone service to be out. They have Trans-Pac cable and satellite uplinks. I called the contractor that operates the dishes. They had no warning at all. They've been sending their own signals to their people, requesting information, no reply."

Jackson nodded. He'd waited this long only to get the confirmation he needed to take the next step.

"Okay, let's get a warning signal drafted, distribution to all the CINCs. Alert SecDef and the Chiefs. I'm calling the President now."

"Dr. Ryan, NMCC on the STU with CRITIC traffic. Admiral Robert Jackson again." The use of "CRITIC" caused heads to turn as Ryan lifted the secure phone.

"Robby, this is Jack. What's happening?" Everyone in the communications room saw the National Security Advisor turn pale. "Robby, are you serious?" He looked at the communications watch officer. "Where are we now?"

"Approaching Goose Bay, Labrador, sir. About three hours out."

"Get Special Agent d'Agustino up here, would you, please?" Ryan took his hand off the phone. "Robby, I need hard copy . . . okay . . . he's still asleep, I think. Give me thirty minutes to get organized here. Call me if you need me."

Jack got out of his chair and made his way to the lav just aft of the flight deck. He managed to avoid looking in the mirror when he washed his hands. The

Secret Service agent was waiting for him when he emerged.

"Not much sleep for you, eh?"

"Is the Boss up yet?"

"Sir, he left orders not to do that until we were an hour out. I just checked with the pilot and — "

"Kick him loose, Daga, right now. Then get Secretaries Hanson and Fiedler up. Arnie, too."

"What's the matter, sir?"

"You'll be in there to hear it." Ryan took the roll of fax paper off the secure machine and started reading. He looked up. "I'm not kidding, Daga. Right now."

"Any danger to the President?"

"Let's assume that there is," Jack replied. He thought for a second. "Where's the nearest fighter base, Lieutenant?"

The *what?* on her face was quite obvious. "Sir, there are F-15s at Otis on Cape Cod, and F-16s at Burlington, Vermont. Both are Air National Guard groups tasked to continental air defense."

"You call them and tell them that the President would like to have some friends around ASAP." The nice thing about talking to lieutenants was that they weren't used to asking why an order was given, even when there was no obvious reason for it. The same thing didn't apply to the Secret Service.

"Doc, if you need to do that, then I need to know, too, right now."

"Yeah, Daga, I guess so." Ryan tore off the top section of the thermal fax paper when he got to the second page of the transmission.

"Holy shit," the agent thought aloud, handing it back. "I'll wake the President up. You need to tell the pilot. They do things a little differently at times like this."

"Fair enough. Fifteen minutes, Daga, okay?"

"Yes, sir." She headed down the circular stairs

while Jack went forward to the flight deck.

"One-six-zero minutes to go, Dr. Ryan. Has been a long one, hasn't it?" the Colonel at the controls asked pleasantly. The smile faded instantly from his face.

It was mere chance that took them past the American Embassy. Maybe he'd just wanted to see the flag, Clark thought. It was always a pleasant sight in a foreign land, even if it did fly over a building designed by some bureaucrat with the artistic sense of —

"Somebody's worried about security," Chavez said.

"Yevgeniy Pavlovich, I know your English is good. You need not practice it on me."

"Excuse me. The Japanese are concerned with a riot, Vanya? Except for that one incident, there hasn't been much hooliganism . . ." His voice trailed off. There were two squads of fully armed infantrymen arrayed around the building. That seemed very odd indeed. Over here, Ding thought, one or two police officers seemed enough to —

"Yob'tvoyu mat."

Clark was proud of the lad just then. Foul as the imprecation was, it was also just what a Russian would have said. The reason for it was also clear. The guards around the embassy perimeter were looking in as much as they were looking out, and the Marines were nowhere to be seen.

"Ivan Sergeyevich, something seems very odd."

"Indeed it does, Yevgeniy Pavlovich," John Clark said evenly. He didn't let the car slow down, and hoped the troops on the sidewalk wouldn't notice the two gaijin driving by and take down their license number. It might be a good time to change rental cars.

"The name is Arima, first name Tokikichi, sir, Lieutenant General, age fifty-three." The Army sergeant was an intelligence specialist. "Graduated their National Defense Academy, worked his way up the line as an infantryman, good marks all the way. He's airborne qualified. Took the senior course at Carlisle Barracks eight years ago, did just fine. 'Politically astute,' the form sheet says. Well connected. He's Commanding General of their Eastern Army, a rough equivalent of a corps organization in the U.S. Army, but not as heavy in corps-level assets, especially artillery. That's two infantry divisions, First and Twelfth, their First Airborne Brigade, First Engineer Brigade, Second Anti-Air Group, and other administrative attachments."

The sergeant handed over the folder, complete with a pair of photos. *The enemy has a face now,* Jackson thought. *At least one face.* Jackson examined it for a few seconds and closed the folder back. It was about to go to Condition FRANTIC in the Pentagon. The first of the Joint Chiefs was in the parking lot, and he was the lucky son of a bitch to give them the news, such as it was. Jackson assembled his documents and headed off to the Tank, a pleasant room, actually, located on the outside of the building's E-Ring.

Chet Nomuri had spent the day meeting at irregular hours with three of his contacts, learning not very much except that something very strange was afoot, though nobody knew what. His best course of action, he decided, was to head back to the bathhouse and hope Kazuo Taoka would turn up. He finally did, by which time Nomuri had spent so much time soaking in the blisteringly hot water that his body felt like pasta that had been in the pot for about a month.

"You must have had a day like I did," he managed to say with a crooked smile.

"How was yours?" Kazuo asked, his smile tired but enthusiastic.

"There is a pretty girl at a certain bar. Three

560

months I've worked on her. We had a vigorous afternoon." Nomuri reached below the surface of the water, feigning agony in an obvious way. "It may never work again."

"I wish that American girl was still around," Taoka said, settling in the tub with a prolonged *Ahhhhh.* "I am ready for someone like her now."

"She's gone?" Nomuri asked innocently.

"Dead," the salaryman said, easily controlling his sense of loss.

"What happened?"

"They were going to send her home. Yamata sent Kaneda, his security man, to tidy things up. But it seems she used narcotics, and she was found dead of an overdose. A great pity," Taoka observed, as if he were describing the demise of a neighbor's cat. "But there are more where she came from."

Nomuri just nodded with weary impassivity, remarking to himself that this was a side of the man he hadn't seen before. Kazuo was a fairly typical Japanese salaryman. He'd joined his company right out of college, starting off in a position little removed from clerkship. After serving five years, he'd been sent off to a business school, which in this country was the intellectual equivalent of Parris Island, with a touch of Buchenwald. There was just something outrageous about how this country operated. He expected that things would be different. It was a foreign land, after all, and every country was different, which was fundamentally a good thing. America was the proof of that. America essentially lived off the diversity that arrived at her shores, each ethnic community adding something to the national pot, creating an often boiling but always creative and lively national mix. But now he truly understood why people came to the U.S., especially people from this country.

Japan demanded much of its citizens — or more properly, its culture did. The boss was always right.

561

A good employee was one who did as he was told. To advance you had to kiss a lot of ass, sing the company song, exercise like somebody in goddamned boot camp every morning, showing up an hour early to show how sincere you were. The amazing part was that anything creative happened here at all. Probably the best of them fought their way to the top despite all this, or perhaps were smart enough to disguise their inner feelings until they got to a position of real authority, but by the time they got there they must have accumulated enough inner rage to make Hitler look like a pansy. Along the way they bled those feelings off with drinking binges and sexual orgies of the sort he'd heard about in this very hot tub. The stories about jaunts to Thailand and Taiwan and most recently the Marianas were especially interesting, stuff that would have made his college chums at UCLA blush. Those things were all symptoms of a society that cultivated psychological repression, whose warm and gentle façade of good manners was like a dam holding back all manner of repressed rage and frustration. That dam occasionally leaked, mostly in an orderly, controlled way, but the strain on the dam was unchanging, and one result of that strain was a way of looking at others, especially *gaijin*, in a manner that insulted Nomuri's American-cultivated egalitarian outlook. It would not be long, he realized, before he started hating this place. That would be unhealthy and unprofessional, the CIA officer thought, remembering the repeated lessons from the Farm: a good field spook identified closely with the culture he attacked. But he was sliding in the other direction, and the irony was that the deepest reason for his growing antipathy was that his roots sprang from this very country.

"You really want more like her?" Nomuri asked, eyes closed.

"Oh, yes. Fucking Americans will soon be our national sport." Taoka chuckled. "We had a fine time of it the past two days. And I was there to see it all happen," his voice concluded in awe. It had all paid off. Twenty years of toeing the line had brought its reward, to have been there in the War Room, listening to it all, following it all, seeing history written before his eyes. The salaryman had made his mark, and most importantly of all, he'd been noticed. By Yamata-san himself.

"So what great deeds have happened while I was performing my own, eh?" Nomuri asked, opening his eyes and giving off a leering smile.

"We just went to war with America, and we've won!" Taoka proclaimed.

"War? *Nan ja?* We accomplished a takeover of General Motors, did we?"

"A real war, my friend. We crippled their Pacific Fleet and the Marianas Islands are Japanese again."

"My friend, you cannot tolerate too much alcohol," Nomuri thought, really believing what he'd just said to the blowhard.

"I have not had a drink in four days!" Taoka protested. "What I told you is true!"

"Kazuo," Chet said patiently as though to a bright child, "you tell stories with a skill and style better than any man I have ever met. Your descriptions of women make my loins swell as though I were there myself." Nomuri smiled. "But you exaggerate."

"Not this time, my friend, truly," Taoka said, really wanting his friend to believe him, and so he started giving details.

Nomuri had no real military training. Most of his knowledge of such affairs came from reading books and watching movies. His instructions for operating in Japan had nothing to do with gathering information on the Japanese Self-Defense Forces, but rather with trade and foreign-affairs matters. But Kazuo Taoka *was* a fine storyteller, with a keen eye for detail, and it took only three minutes before Nomuri had to close his eyes again, a smile fixed on his lips. Both actions were the result of his training in Yorktown, Virginia, as was that of his memory, which struggled now to record every single word while another part of his consciousness wondered how the hell he was going to get the information out. His other reaction was one that Taoka could neither see nor hear, a quintessential Americanism, spoken within the confines of the CIA officer's mind: *You motherfuckers!*

"Okay, JUMPER is up and pretty much put together," Helen d'Agustino said. "JASMINE" — the code name for Anne Durling — "will be in another cabin. SecState and SecTreas are up and having their coffee. Arnie van Damm is probably in better shape than anybody aboard. Showtime. How about the fighters?"

"They'll join up in about twenty minutes. We went with the F-15s out of Otis. Better range, they'll follow us all the way down. I'm really being paranoid on that, ain't I?"

Daga's eyes gave off a coldly professional smile. "You know what I've always liked about you, Dr. Ryan?"

"What's that?"

"I don't have to explain security to you like I do with everybody else. You think just like I do." It was a lot for a Secret Service agent to say. "The President is waiting, sir." She led him down the stairs.

Ryan bumped into his wife on the way forward. Pretty as ever, she was not suffering from the previous night despite her husband's warning, and on seeing Jack she almost made a joke that it was he who'd had the prob—

"What's the matter?"

"Business, Cathy."

"Bad?"

564

Her husband just nodded and went forward, past a Secret Service agent and an armed Air Force security policeman. The two convertible couches had been made up. President Durling was sitting down in suit pants and white shirt. His tie and jacket were not in evidence at this time. A silver pot of coffee was on the low table. Ryan could see out the windows on both sides of the nose cabin. They were flying a thousand feet or so above fleecy cumulus clouds.

"I hear you've been up all night, Jack," Durling said.

"Since before Iceland, whenever that was, Mr. President," Ryan told him. He hadn't washed, hadn't shaved, and his hair probably looked like Cathy's after a long procedure under a surgical cap. Worse still was the look in his eyes as he prepared to deliver grimmer news than he'd ever spoken.

"You look like hell. What's the problem?"

"Mr. President, based on information received over the last few hours, I believe that the United States of America is at war with Japan."

"What you need is a good chief to run this for you," Jones observed.

"Ron, one more of those, and I'll toss you in the brig, okay? You've thrown enough weight around for one day," Mancuso replied in a weary voice. "Those people were under my command, remember?"

"Have I been that much of a jerk?"

"Yeah, Jonesy, you have." Chambers handled that answer. "Maybe Seaton needed to be brought up short once, but you overdid it big-time. And now we need solutions, not smartass bullshit."

Jones nodded but kept his own counsel. "Very well, sir. What assets do we have?"

"Best estimate, they have eighteen boats deployable. Two are in overhaul status and are probably unavailable for months at least," Chambers replied, doing the enemy first. "With *Charlotte* and *Asheville* out of the game, we have a total of seventeen. Four of those are in yard-overhaul and unavailable. Four more are in bobtail-refits alongside the pier here or in 'Dago. Another four are in the IO. Maybe we can shake those loose, maybe we can't. That leaves five. Three of those are with the carriers for the 'exercise,' one's right down below at the pier. The last one's at sea up in the Gulf of Alaska doing workups. That has a new CO — what, just three weeks since he relieved?"

"Correct." Mancuso nodded. "He's just learning the job."

"Jesus, the cupboard's *that* bare?" Jones was now regretting his comment on having a good chief around. The mighty United States Pacific Fleet, as recently as five years ago the most powerful naval force in the history of civilization, was now a frigate navy.

"Five of us, eighteen of them, and they're all spun-up to speed. They've been running ops for the last couple of months." Chambers looked at the wall chart and frowned. "That's one big fuckin' ocean, Jonesy." It was the way he added the last statement that worried the contractor.

"The four in refits?"

"That order's out. 'Expedite readiness for sea.' And that brings the number to nine, in a couple of weeks, if we're lucky."

"Mr. Chambers, sir?"

Chambers turned back. "Yeah, Petty Officer Jones?"

"Remember when we used to head up north, all alone, tracking four or five of the bad guys at once?"

The operations officer nodded soberly, almost nostalgically. His reply was quiet. "Long time ago, Jonesy. We're dealing with SSKs now, on their home turf and — "

566

"Did you trade your balls in to get that fourth stripe on your shoulder?" Chambers turned around in an instant rage.

"You listen to me, *boy*, I — " But Ron Jones just snarled back.

" 'I,' hell, *you*, used to be a kickass *officer!* I trusted you to know what to do with the data I gave you, just like I trusted him — " Jones pointed to Admiral Mancuso. "When I sailed with you guys, we were the class of the whole fuckin' world. And if you did your job right as a CO, and if *you*'ve been doing your job right as a type-commander, Bart, then those kids out there still are. Goddamn it! When I tossed my bag down the hatch on *Dallas* the first time, I trusted you guys to know your damned job. Was I wrong, gentlemen? Remember the motto on *Dallas*? 'First in Harm's Way'! What the hell's the matter here?" The question hung in the air for several seconds. Chambers was too angry to take it in. SubPac was not.

"We look that bad?" Mancuso asked.

"Sure as hell, sir. Okay, we took it in the ass from these bastards. Time to start thinking about catchup. We're the varsity, aren't we? Who's better suited to it than we are?"

"Jones, you always did have a big mouth," Chambers said. Then he looked back at the chart. "But I guess maybe it is time to go to work."

A chief petty officer stuck his head in the door. "Sir, *Pasadena* just checked in from down the hill. Ready in all respects to get under way, the CO requests orders."

"How's he loaded?" Mancuso replied, knowing that if he'd really done his job right over the past few days the question would have been unnecessary.

"Twenty-two ADCAPs, six Harpoons, and twelve T-LAM-Cs. They're all warshots," the chief replied. "He's ready to rock, sir."

ComSubPac nodded. "Tell him to stand by for mission orders."

"Aye aye, sir."

"Good skipper?" Jones asked.

"He got the Battle-E last year," Chambers said. "Tim Parry. He was my XO on *Key West*. He'll do."

"So now all he needs is a job."

Mancuso lifted the secure phone for CINCPAC. "Yeah."

"Signal from State Department," the Air Force communications officer said, entering the room. "The Japanese Ambassador requests an urgent meeting with the President."

"Brett?"

"We see what he has to say," SecState said. Ryan nodded agreement.

"Any chance at all that this is some kind of mistake?" Durling asked.

"We expect some hard intelligence anytime now from a satellite pass over the Marianas. It's dark there, but that won't matter much." Ryan had finished his briefing, and on completion the data he'd managed to deliver seemed very thin. The baseline truth here was that what had evidently taken place was so wildly beyond the limits of reason that he himself would not be fully satisfied until he saw the overheads himself.

"If it's real, then what?"

"That will take a little time," Ryan admitted. "We want to hear what their ambassador has to say."

"What are they really up to?" Treasury Secretary Fiedler asked.

"Unknown, sir. Just pissing us off, it isn't worth the trouble. We have nukes. They don't. It's all crazy . . ." Ryan said quietly. "It doesn't make any sense at all." Then he remembered that in 1939, Germany's biggest trading partner had been . . . France. History's most often repeated lesson was that logic was not a constant in the behavior of nations. The study of history was not always bilateral. And the lessons learned from history depended on the quality of the student. Worth remembering, Jack thought, because the other guy might forget.

"It's got to be some kind of mistake," Hanson announced. "A couple of accidents. Maybe our two subs collided under the water and maybe we have some excitable people on Saipan. I mean it doesn't make any sense at all."

"I agree, the data does not form any clear picture, but the individual pieces — damn it, I *know* Robby Jackson. I *know* Bart Mancuso."

"Who's that?"

"ComSubPac. He owns all our subs out there. I sailed with him once. Jackson is deputy J-3, and we've been friends since we were both teaching at Annapolis." Lo, these many years ago.

"Okay," Durling said. "You've told us everything you know?"

"Yes, Mr. President. Every word, without any analysis."

"Meaning you don't really have any?" The question stung some, but this was not a time for embroidering. Ryan nodded.

"Correct, Mr. President."

"So for now, we wait. How long to Andrews?"

Fiedler looked out a window. "That's the Chesapeake Bay below us now. We can't be too far out."

"Press at the airport?" he asked Arnie van Damm.

"Just the ones in the back of the plane, sir."

"Ryan?"

"We firm up our information as fast as we can. The services are all on alert."

"What are those fighters doing out there?" Fiedler asked. They were now flying abeam Air Force One, in a tight two-ship element about a mile away, their pilots wondering what this was all about. Ryan wondered if the press would take note of it. Well, how long could this affair remain a secret?

"My idea, Buzz," Ryan said. Might as well take responsibility for it.

"A little dramatic, don't you think?" SecState inquired.

"We didn't expect to have our fleet attacked either, sir."

"Ladies and gentlemen, this is Colonel Evans. We're now approaching Andrews Air Force Base. We all hope you've enjoyed the flight. Please bring your seats back to the upright position and . . ." In the back, the junior White House aides ostentatiously refused to fasten their seat belts. The cabin crew did what they were supposed to do, of course.

Ryan felt the main gear thump down on runway Zero-One Right. For the majority of the people aboard, the press, it was the end. For him it was just the beginning. The first sign was the larger than normal complement of security police waiting at the terminal building, and some especially nervous Secret Service agents. In a way it was a relief to the National Security Advisor. Not everyone thought it was some sort of mistake, but it would be so much better, Ryan thought, if he were wrong, just this once. Otherwise they faced the most complex crisis in his country's history.

24

Running in Place

If there was a worse feeling than this one, Clark didn't know what it might be. Their mission in Japan was supposed to have been easy: evacuate an American citizen who had gotten herself into a tight spot and ascertain the possibility of reactivating an old and somewhat dusty intelligence network.

Well, that was the idea, the officer told himself, heading to his room. Chavez was parking the car. They'd decided to rent a new one, and again the clerk at the counter had changed his expression on learning that their credit card was printed in both Roman and Cyrillic characters. It was an experience so new as to have no precedent at all. Even at the height (or depths) of the Cold War, Russians had treated American citizens with greater deference than their own countrymen, and whether that had resulted from curiosity or not, the privilege of being American had been an important touchstone for a lonely stranger in a foreign and hostile land. Never had Clark felt so frightened, and it was little consolation that Ding Chavez didn't have the experience to realize just how unusual and dangerous their position was.

It was therefore something of a relief to feel the piece of tape on the underside doorknob. Maybe Nomuri could give him some useful information.

Clark went in the room only long enough to use the bathroom before heading right back out. He saw Chavez in the lobby and made the appropriate gesture: *Stay put.* Clark noticed with a smile that his junior partner had stopped at a bookstore and purchased a copy of a Russian-language newspaper, which he carried ostentatiously as a kind of defensive measure. Two minutes later, Clark was looking in the window of the camera shop again. There wasn't much street traffic, but enough that he wasn't the only one around. As he stood looking at the latest automated wonder from Nikon, he felt someone bump into him.

"Watch where you're going," a gruff voice said in English and moved on. Clark took a few seconds before heading in the other direction, turning the corner and heading down an alley. A minute later he found a shadowy place and waited. Nomuri was there quickly.

"This is dangerous, kid."

"Why do you think I hit you with that signal?" Nomuri's voice was low and shaky.

It was fieldcraft from a TV series, about as realistic and professional as two kids sneaking a smoke in the boys' room of their junior high. The odd part was that, important as it was, Nomuri's message occupied about one minute. The rest of the time was concerned with procedural matters.

"Okay, number one, no contact at all with your normal rat-line. Even if they're allowed out on the street, you don't know them. You don't go near them. Your contact points are gone, kid, you understand?" Clark's mind was going at light-speed toward nowhere at the moment, but the most immediate priority was survival. You had to be alive in order to accomplish something, and Nomuri, like Chavez and himself, were "illegals," unlikely to receive any sort of clemency after arrest and totally separated from any support from their parent agency.

Chet Nomuri nodded. "That leaves you, sir."

"That's right, and if you lose us, you return to your cover and you don't do anything. Got that? Nothing at all. You're a loyal Japanese citizen, and you stay in your hole."

"But — "

"But nothing, kid. You are under my orders now, and if you violate them, you answer to me!" Clark softened his voice. "Your first priority is always survival. We don't issue suicide pills and we don't expect movie-type bullshit. A dead officer is a dumb officer." *Damn,* Clark thought, had the mission been different from the very beginning, they would have had a routine established — dead-drops, a whole collection of signals, a selection of cutouts — but there wasn't time to do that now, and every second they talked here in the shadows there was the chance that some Tokyo-ite would let his cat out, see a Japanese national talking to a gaijin, and make note of it. The paranoia curve had risen fast, and would only get steeper.

"Okay, you say so, man."

"And don't forget it. Stick to your regular routine. Don't change anything except maybe to back off some. Fit in. Act like everybody else does. A nail that sticks up gets hammered down. Hammers hurt, boy. Now, here's what I want you to do." Clark went on for a minute. "Got it?"

"Yes, sir."

"Get lost." Clark headed down the alley, and entered his hotel through the delivery entrance, thankfully unwatched at this time of night. Thank God, he thought, that Tokyo had so little crime. The American equivalent would be locked, or have an alarm, or be patrolled by an armed guard. Even at war, Tokyo was a safer place than Washington, D.C.

"Why don't you just buy a bottle instead of going out to drink?" "Chekov" asked, not for the first time, when he came back into the room.

"Maybe I should." Which reply made the younger officer's eyes jerk up from his paper and his Russian practice. Clark pointed to the TV, turned it on, and found CNN Headline News, in English.

Now for my next trick. How the hell do I get the word in? he wondered. He didn't dare use the fax machine to America. Even the Washington Interfax office was far too grave a risk, the one in Moscow didn't have the encryption gear needed, and he couldn't go through the Embassy's CIA connection either. There was one set of rules for operating in a friendly country, and another for a hostile one, and nobody had expected the rules that made the rules to change without warning. That he and other CIA officers should have provided forewarning of the event was just one more thing to anger the experienced spy; the congressional hearings on that one were sure to be entertaining if he lived long enough to enjoy them. The only good news was that he had the name of a probable suspect in the murder of Kimberly Norton. That, at least, gave him something to fantasize about, and his mind had little other useful activity to undertake at the moment. At the half-hour it was clear that even CNN didn't know what was going on, and if CNN didn't know, then nobody did. Wasn't that just great, Clark thought. It was like the legend of Cassandra, the daughter of King Priam of Troy who always knew what was happening, and who was always ignored. But Clark didn't even have a way of getting the word out . . . did he?

I wonder if . . . ? No. He shook his head. That was too crazy.

"All ahead full," the Commanding Officer of *Eisenhower* said.

"All ahead full, aye," the quartermaster on the enunciator pushed the handles forward. A moment later the inner arrow rotated to the same position. "Sir, engine room answers all ahead full."

"Very well." The CO looked over at Admiral Dubro. "Care to lay any bets, sir?"

The best information, oddly enough, came from sonar. Two of the battle group's escorts had their towed-array sonars, called "tails," streamed, and their data, combined with that of two nuclear submarines to the formation's starboard, indicated that the Indian formation was a good way off to the south. It was one of those odd instances, more common than one might expect, where sonar far outperformed radar, whose electronic waves were limited by the curve of the earth, while sound waves found their own deep channels. The Indian fleet was over a hundred fifty miles away, and though that was spitting distance for jet attack aircraft, the Indians were looking to their south, not the north, and it further appeared that Admiral Chandraskatta didn't relish night-flight operations and the risks they entailed for his limited collection of Harriers. Well, both men thought, night landings on a carrier weren't exactly fun.

"Better than even," Admiral Dubro replied after a moment's analysis.

"I think you're right."

The formation was blacked out, not an unusual circumstance for warships, all its radars turned off, and the only radios in use were line-of-sight units with burst-transmission capability, which broadcast for hundredths of seconds only. Even satellite sets generated side-lobes that could betray their position, and their covert passage south of Sri Lanka was essential.

"World War Two was like this," the CO went on, giving voice to his nerves. They were depending on the most human of fundamentals. Extra lookouts had been posted, who used both regular binoculars and "night-eye" electronic devices to sweep the horizon for silhouettes and mast-tops, while others on lower decks looked closer in for the telltale "feather" of a submarine periscope. The Indians had two submarines out on which Dubro did not have even an approximate location. They were probably probing south, too, but if Chandraskatta was really as smart as he feared, he would have left one close in, just as insurance. Maybe. Dubro's deception operation had been a skillful one.

"Admiral?" Dubro's head turned. It was a signalman. "FLASH Traffic from CINCPAC." The petty officer handed over the clipboard and held a red-covered flashlight over the dispatch so that the battle-group commander could read it.

"Did you acknowledge receipt?" the Admiral asked before he started reading.

"No, sir, you left orders to chimp everything down."

"Very good, sailor." Dubro started reading. In a second he was holding both the clipboard and the flashlight. "Son of a bitch!"

Special Agent Robberton would drive Cathy home, and with that notification, Ryan again became a government functionary rather than a human being with a wife and family. It was a short walk to Marine One, its rotor already turning. President and Mrs. Durling, JUMPER and JASMINE, had done the requisite smiles for the cameras and had used the opportunity of the long flight to beg off answering any questions. Ryan trailed behind like some sort of equerry.

"Take an hour to get caught up," Durling said as the helicopter landed on the south lawn of the White House. "When is the Ambassador scheduled in?"

"Eleven-thirty," Brett Hanson replied.

"I want you, Arnie, and Jack there for the meeting."

"Yes, Mr. President," the Secretary of State acknowledged.

The usual photographers were there, but most of

576

the White House reporters whose shouted questions so annoyed everyone were still back at Andrews collecting their bags. Inside the ground-floor entrance was a larger contingent of Secret Service agents than normal. Ryan headed west and was in his office two minutes later, shedding his coat and sitting down at a desk already decorated with call slips. Those he ignored for the moment, as he lifted the phone and dialed CIA.

"DDO, welcome back, Jack," Mary Pat Foley said. Ryan didn't bother asking how she knew it was him. Not that many had her direct line.

"How bad?"

"Our embassy personnel are safe. The embassy has not as yet been entered, and we're destroying everything." Station Tokyo, as all CIA stations had become in the last ten years, was completely electronic now. Destroying files was a question of seconds and left no telltale smoke. "Ought to be done by now." The procedure was straightforward. The various computer disks were erased, reformatted, erased again, then subjected to powerful hand-held magnets. The bad news was that some of the data was irreplaceable, though not so much so as the people who had generated it. There was now a total of three "illegals" in Tokyo, the net human-intelligence assets of the United States in what was — probably — an enemy country.

"What else?"

"They're letting people travel back and forth to their homes, with escort. Actually they're playing it pretty cool," Mrs. Foley said, her surprise not showing. "It's not like Teheran in '79, anyway. For communications they're letting us use satellite links so far, but those are being electronically monitored. The embassy has one STU-6 operating. The rest have been deactivated. We still have TAPDANCE capability, too," she finished, mentioning the random-pad cipher

577

that all embassies now used through the National Security Agency's communications net.

"Other assets?" Ryan asked, hoping that his own secure line was not compromised, but using cover procedure even so.

"Without the legals they're pretty much cut off." The worry in her voice was clear with that answer, along with quite a bit of self-reproach. The Agency still had operations in quite a few countries that did not absolutely require embassy personnel as part of the loop. But Japan wasn't one of them, and even Mary Pat couldn't make hindsight retroactive.

"Do they even know what's going on?" It was an astute question, the Deputy Director (Operations) thought, and another needle in her flesh.

"Unknown," Mrs. Foley admitted. "They didn't get any word to us. They either do not know or have been compromised." Which was a nicer way of saying arrested.

"Other stations?"

"Jack, we got caught with our knickers down, and that's a fact." For all the grief that it had to cause her, Ryan heard, she was reporting facts like a surgeon on the OR. What a shame that Congress would grill her unmercifully for the intelligence lapse. "I have people in Seoul and Beijing shaking the bushes, but I don't expect anything back from them for hours."

Ryan was rummaging through his pink call sheets. "I have one here, an hour old, from Golovko . . ."

"Hell, call the bastard," Mary Pat said at once. "Let me know what he says."

"Will do." Jack shook his head, remembering what the two men had talked about. "Get down here fast. Bring Ed. I need a gut call on something but not over the phone."

"Be there in thirty," Mrs. Foley said.

Jack spread out several faxes on his desk, and scanned them quickly. The Pentagon's operations people had been faster than the other agencies, but now DIA was checking in, quickly followed by State. The government was awake — nothing like gunfire to accomplish that, Jack thought wryly — but the data was mainly repetitive, different agencies learning the same thing at different times and reporting in as though it were new. He flipped through the call sheets again, and clearly the majority of them would say the same thing. His eyes came back to the one from the chairman of the Russian Foreign Intelligence Service. Jack lifted the phone and made the call, wondering which of the phones on Golovko's desk would ring. He took out a scratch pad, noting the time. The Signals Office would take note of the call, of course, and tape it, but he wanted to keep his own notes.

"Hello, Jack."

"Your private line, Sergey Nikolay'ch?"

"For an old friend, why not?" The Russian paused, ending the joviality for the day. "I presume you know."

"Oh, yeah." Ryan thought for a moment before going on. "We were caught by surprise," he admitted. Jack heard a very Russian grunt of sympathy.

"So were we. Completely. Do you have any idea what the madmen are up to?" the RVS Chairman asked, his voice a mixture of anger and concern.

"No, I see nothing at the moment that makes any sense at all." And perhaps that was the most worrying part of all.

"What plans do you have?"

"Right now? None," Ryan said. "Their ambassador is due here in less than an hour."

"Splendid timing on his part," the Russian commented. "They've done this to you before, if memory serves."

"And to you," Ryan said, remembering how the Russo-Japanese War had begun. *They do like their surprises.*

579

"Yes, Ryan, and to us." And *that*, Jack knew, was why Sergey had made the call, and why his voice showed genuine concern. Fear of the unknown wasn't limited to children, after all, was it? "Can you tell me what sort of assets you have in place to deal with the crisis?"

"I'm not sure at the moment, Sergey," Ryan lied. "If your Washington *rezidentura* is up to speed, you know I just got in. I need time to get caught up. Mary Pat is on her way down to my office now."

"Ah," Jack heard over the line. Well, it was an obvious lie he'd told, and Sergey was a wise old pro, wise enough to know. "You were very foolish not to have activated THISTLE sooner, my friend."

"This is an open line, Sergey Nikolay'ch." Which was partially true. The phone call was routed through the American Embassy in Moscow on a secure circuit, but from there on it was a standard commercial line, probably, and therefore subject to possible bugging.

"You need not be overly concerned, Ivan Emmetovich. Do you recall our conversation in my office?"

Oh, yeah. Maybe the Russians really did have the Japanese counterintelligence chief under their control. If so, he was in a position to know if the phone call was secure or not. And if so, there were some other cards in his hand. Nice ones. Was he offering Ryan a peek?

Think fast, Jack, Ryan commanded himself. *Okay, the Russians have another network up and running . . .*

"Sergey, this is important: you did not have any warning?"

"Jack, on my honor as a spy" — Ryan could almost hear the twisted smile that must be framing the answer — "I just had to tell my President that I was caught with my fly unbuttoned, and the embarrassment to me is even greater than what — "

Jack didn't bother listening to the embroidery.

Okay. The Russians *did* have another spy network operating in Japan, but they had probably not received any warning either, had they? No, the danger from that sort of double-dealing was just too great. Next fact: their second network was inside the Japanese government itself; had to be if they had PSID penetrated. But THISTLE was mainly a *commercial* spy net — always had been — and Sergey had just told him that the U.S. had been foolish not to have activated it sooner. The novelty of what he knew distracted Jack from a more subtle implication surrounding the admission of fault from Moscow.

"Sergey Nikolay'ch, I'm short of time here. You are building to something. What is it?"

"I propose cooperation between us. I have the approval of President Grushavoy to make the offer." He didn't say *full* cooperation, Jack noted, but the offer was startling even so.

Never, not ever, not once except in bad movies had KGB and CIA really cooperated on anything important. Sure, the world had changed plenty, but KGB, even in its new incarnation, still worked to penetrate American institutions and remained good at it. That was why you didn't let them in. But he'd just made the offer anyway. Why?

The Russians are scared. Of what?

"I will present that to my President after consulting with Mary Pat." Ryan wasn't yet sure how he would present it. Golovko, however, knew the value of what he'd just laid on the American's desk. It would not require much insight to speculate on the probable reply.

Again, Ryan could hear the smile. "If Foleyeva does not agree, I will be most surprised. I will be in my office for a few more hours."

"So will I. Thanks, Sergey."

"Good day, Dr. Ryan."

"Well, that sounded interesting," Robby Jackson

said in the doorway. "Looks like you had a long night, too."

"In an airplane, yet. Coffee?" Jack asked.

The Admiral shook his head. "One more cup and I might shake apart." He came in and sat down.

"Bad?"

"And getting worse. We're still trying to tally how many uniformed people we have in Japan — there are some transients. An hour ago a C-141 landed at Yakota and promptly went off the air. The god-damned thing just headed right in," Robby said. "Maybe a radio problem, more likely they didn't have the gas to go anywhere else. Flight crew of four, maybe five — I forget. State is trying to run a tally for how many businessmen are there. It ought to generate an approximate number, but there are tourists to consider also."

"Hostages." Ryan frowned.

The Admiral nodded. "Figure the ten thousand as a floor figure."

"The two subs?"

Jackson shook his head. "Dead, no survivors. *Stennis* has recovered her airplane and is heading for Pearl at about twelve knots. *Enterprise* is trying to make turns on one shaft, and is under tow, she's making maybe six. Maybe none if the engine damage is as bad as the CO told us. They've sent a big salvage tug to help with that. We've sent some P-3s to Midway to do antisubmarine patrols. If I were the other side, I'd try to finish them off. *Johnnie Reb* ought to be okay, but *Big-E* is a hell of a ripe target. CINCPAC is worried about that. We're out of the power-projection business, Jack."

"Guam?"

"All the Marianas are off the air, except for one thing." Jackson explained about Oreza. "All he tells us is how bad things are."

"Recommendations?"

"I have people looking at some ideas, but for starters we need to know if the President wants us to try. Will he?" Robby asked.

"Their ambassador will be here soon."

"Good of him. You didn't answer my question, Dr. Ryan."

"I don't know the answer yet."

"There's a confidence-builder."

For Captain Bud Sanchez the experience was unique. It was not quite a miracle that he'd recovered the S-3 Viking without incident. The "Hoover" was a docile aircraft floating in, and there had been a whole twenty knots of wind over the deck. Now his entire air wing was back aboard, and his aircraft carrier was running away.

Running away. Not heading into harm's way, the creed of the United States Navy, but limping back to Pearl. The five squadrons of fighters and attack aircraft on the deck of *John Stennis* just sat there, lined up in neat rows on the flight deck, all ready for combat operations but except in a really dire emergency unable to take off. It was a question of wind and weight. Carriers turned into the wind to launch and recover aircraft, and needed the most powerful engines placed aboard ships to give the greatest possible airflow over the bow. The moving air added to the takeoff impulse generated by the steam catapults to give lift to the aircraft flung into the air. Their ability to take off was directly governed by that airflow, and more significantly from a tactical point of view, the magnitude of the airflow governed the weight they could carry aloft — which meant fuel and weapons. As it was, he could get airplanes off, but without the gas needed to stay aloft long or to hunt across the ocean for targets, and without the weapons needed to engage those targets. He judged that he had the ability to use fighters to defend the fleet against an air threat out to a radius of perhaps a hundred miles. But there was no air threat, and though they knew the position of the retiring Japanese formations, he did not have the ability to reach them with his attack birds. But then, he didn't have orders to allow him to do it anyway.

Night at sea is supposed to be a beautiful thing, but it was not so this time. The stars and gibbous moon reflected off the calm surface of the ocean, making everyone nervous. There was easily enough light to spot the ships, blackout or not. The only really active aircraft of his wing were the antisubmarine helicopters whose blinking anticollision lights sparkled mainly forward of the carriers, aided also by those of some of *Johnnie Reb*'s escorts. The only good news was that the slow fleet speed made for excellent performance by the sonar systems on the destroyers and frigates, whose large-aperture arrays were streamed out in their wakes. Not too many. The majority of the escorts had lingered behind with *Enterprise*, circling her in two layers like bodyguards for a chief of state, while one of their number, an Aegis cruiser, tried to help her along with a towing wire, increasing her speed of advance to a whole six and a half knots at the moment. Without a good storm over the bow, *Big-E* could not conduct flight operations at all.

Submarines, historically the greatest threat to carriers, might be out there. Pearl Harbor said that they had no contacts at all in the vicinity of the now-divided battle force, but that was an easy thing to say from a shore base. The sonar operators, urged by nervous officers to miss nothing, were instead finding things that weren't there: eddies in the water, echoes of conversing fish, whatever. The nervous state of the formation was manifested by the way a frigate five miles out increased speed and turned sharply left, her sonar undoubtedly pinging away now, probably at nothing more than the excited imag-

584

ination of a sonarman third-class who might or might not have heard a whale fart. Maybe two farts, Captain Sanchez thought. One of his own Seahawks was hovering low over the surface, dipping her sonar dome to do her own sniffing. *One thousand three hundred miles back to Pearl Harbor,* Sanchez thought. Twelve knots. That came to four and a half days. Every mile of it under the threat of submarine attack.

The other question was: what genius had thought that pulling back from the Western Pacific had been a good idea? Was the United States a global power or not? Projecting power around the world was important, wasn't it? Certainly it *had* been, Sanchez thought, remembering his classes at the War College. Newport had been his last "tour" prior to undertaking the position of Commander, Air Wing. The U.S. Navy had been the balance of power over the entire world for two generations, able to intimidate merely by existing, merely by letting people see the pictures in their updated copies of *Jane's Fighting Ships.* You could never know where those ships were. You could only count the empty berths in the great naval bases and wonder. Well, there wouldn't be much wondering now. The two biggest graving docks at Pearl Harbor would be full for some time to come, and if the news of the Marianas was correct, America lacked the mobile firepower to take them back, even if Mike Dubro decided to act like Seventh Cavalry and race back home.

"Hello, Chris, thank you for coming."

The Ambassador would arrive at the White House in only a few minutes. The timing was impossible, but whoever in Tokyo was making decisions had not troubled himself with Nagumo's convenience, the embassy official knew. It was awkward for another reason as well. Ordinarily a city that took little note of foreigners, Washington would soon change, and now for the first time, Nagumo was gaijin.

"Seiji, what the hell happened out there?" Cook asked.

Both men belonged to the University Club, a plush establishment located next door to the Russian Embassy and, boasting one of the best gyms in town, a favored place for a good workout and a quick meal. A Japanese commercial business kept a suite of rooms there, and though they would not be able to use this rendezvous again, for the moment it did guarantee anonymity.

"What have they told you, Chris?"

"That one of your navy ships had a little accident. Jesus, Seiji, aren't things bad enough without that sort of mistake? Weren't the goddamned gas tanks bad enough?" Nagumo took a second before responding. In a way it was good news. The overall events were being kept somewhat secret, as he had predicted and the Ambassador had hoped. He was nervous now, though his demeanor didn't show it.

"Chris, it was not an accident."

"What do you mean?"

"I mean there was a battle of sorts. I mean that my country feels itself to be very threatened, and that we have taken certain defensive measures to protect ourselves."

Cook just didn't get it. Though he was part of the State Department's Japan specialists, he'd not yet been called in for a full briefing and knew only what he'd caught on his car radio, which was thin enough. It was beyond Chris's imagination, Nagumo saw, to consider that his country could be attacked. After all, the Soviets were gone, weren't they? It was gratifying to Seiji Nagumo. Though appalled at the risks that his country was running and ignorant of the reasons for them, he was a patriot. He loved his country as much as any man. He was also part of its culture. He had orders and instructions. Within the confines

586

of his own mind he could rage at them, but he'd decided, simply, that he was a soldier of his country, and that was that. And Cook was the real gaijin, not himself. He kept repeating it to himself.

"Chris, our countries are at war, after a fashion. You pushed us too far. Forgive me, I am not pleased by this, you must understand that."

"Wait a minute." Chris Cook shook his head as his face twisted into a very quizzical expression. "You mean war? Real war?"

Nagumo nodded slowly, and spoke in a reasonable, regretful tone. "We have occupied the Mariana Islands. Fortunately this was accomplished without loss of life. The brief encounter between our two navies may have been more serious, but not greatly so. Both sides are now withdrawing away from one another, which is a good thing."

"You've killed our people?"

"Yes, I regret to say, some people may have lost their lives on both sides." Nagumo paused and looked down as though unable to meet his friend's eyes. He'd already seen there the emotions he'd expected. "Please, don't blame me for this, Chris," he went on quietly in a voice clearly under very tight control. "But these things have happened. I had no part in it. Nobody asked me for an opinion. You know what I would have said. You know what I would have counseled." Every word was true and Cook knew it.

"Christ, Seiji, what can we do?" The question was a manifestation of his friendship and support, and as such, very predictable. Also predictably, it gave Nagumo the opening he'd expected and needed.

"We have to find a way to keep things under control. I do not want my country destroyed again. We have to stop this and stop it quickly." Which was his country's objective and therefore his own. "There is no room in the world for this . . . this abomination. There are cooler heads in my country. Goto is a fool.

There" — Nagumo threw up his hands — "I have said it. He *is* a fool. Do we allow our countries to do permanent damage to one another because of fools? What of your Congress, what of that Trent maniac with his Trade *Reform* Act. Look what his *reforms* have brought us to!" He was really into it now. Able to veil his inner feelings, like most diplomats, he was now discovering acting talents made all the more effective by the fact that he really believed in what he was saying. He looked up with tears in his eyes. "Chris, if people like us don't get this thing under control — my God, then what? The work of generations, gone. Your country and mine, both badly hurt, people dead, progress thrown away, and for what? Because fools in my country and yours could not work out difficulties on *trade?* Christopher, you must help me stop this. You must!" Mercenary and traitor or not, Christopher Cook was a diplomat, and his professional creed was to eliminate war. He had to respond, and he did.

"But what can you really do?"

"Chris, you know that my position is really more senior than my post would indicate," Nagumo pointed out. "How else could I have done the things for you to make our friendship what it is?"

Cook nodded. He'd suspected as much.

"I have friends and influence in Tokyo. I need time. I need negotiating space. With those things I can soften our position, give Goto's political opponents something to work with. We have to put that man in the asylum he belongs in — or shoot him yourself. That maniac might destroy my country, Chris! For God's sake, you must help me stop him." The last statement was an entreaty from the heart.

"What the hell can I do, Seiji? I'm just a DASS, remember? A little Indian, and there's a bunch of chiefs."

"You are one of the few people in your State Department who really understand us. They will seek your counsel." A little flattery. Cook nodded.

"Probably. If they're smart," he added. "Scott Adler knows me. We talk."

"If you can tell me what your State Department wants, I can get that information to Tokyo. With luck I can have my people inside the Foreign Ministry propose it first. If we can accomplish that much, then your ideas will appear to be our ideas, and we can more easily accommodate your wishes." It was called *judo*, "the gentle art," and consisted mainly of using an enemy's strength and movements against himself. Nagumo thought he was making a very skillful use of it now. It had to appeal to Cook's vanity that he might be able to manage foreign policy himself through cleverness. It appealed to Nagumo's that he'd thought up this gambit.

Cook's face twisted into disbelief again. "But if we're at war, how the hell will — "

"Goto is not completely mad. We will keep the embassies open as a line of communication. We will offer you a return of the Marianas. I doubt the offer will be completely genuine, but it will be placed on the table as a sign of good faith. There," Seiji said, "I have now betrayed my country." As planned.

"What will be acceptable to your government as an end-game scenario?"

"In my opinion? Full independence for the Northern Marianas; an end to their commonwealth status. For reasons of geography and economics they will fall into our sphere of influence in any case. I think it is a fair compromise. We do own most of the land there," Nagumo reminded his guest. "That is a guess on my part, but a good one."

"What about Guam?"

"As long as it is demilitarized, it remains U.S. territory. Again a guess, but a good one. Time will be necessary for a full resolution of the various issues,

589

but I think we can stop this war before it goes further."

"What if we do not agree?"

"Then many people will die. We are diplomats, Chris. It is our mission in life to prevent that." One more time: "If you can help me, just to let us know what you want us to do so that I can get our side moving in that direction, you and I can end a war, Chris. Please, can you help me?"

"I won't take money for this, Seiji," Cook said by way of a reply.

Amazing. The man had principles after all. So much the better that they were not accompanied by insight.

The Japanese Ambassador arrived, as instructed, at the East Wing entrance. A White House usher opened the door on the stretch Lexus, and the Marine at the door saluted, not having been told not to. He walked in alone, unaccompanied by a bodyguard, and he passed through the metal detectors without incident, then turned west, past a long corridor including, among other things, the entrance to the President's own movie theater. There were portraits of other presidents, sculptures by Frederic Remington, and other reminders of America's frontier history. The walk itself was intended to give the man a sense of the size of the country to which he represented his own. A trio of Secret Service agents escorted him up to the State Floor of the building, an area he knew well, then farther west to the wing from which the United States was administered. The looks, he saw, were not unfriendly, merely correct, but that was quite different from the cordiality he ordinarily received in this building. As a final touch, the meeting was held in the Roosevelt Room. It held the Nobel Prize won by Theodore for negotiating the end of the Russo-Japanese War.

If the mode of arrival was supposed to overawe him, the Ambassador thought, then the final act was counterproductive. The Americans, and others, were known for such foolish theatrics. The Indian Treaty Room in the adjacent Old Executive Office Building had been designed to overawe savages. This one reminded him of his country's first major conflict, which had raised Japan to the ranks of the great nations by the defeat of another member of that club, czarist Russia, a country far less great than she had appeared, internally corrupt, strewn with dissension, given to posturing and bluster. Much like America, in fact, the Ambassador thought. He needed such ideas right now to keep his knees from trembling. President Durling was standing, and took his hand.

"Mr. Ambassador, you know everyone here. Please be seated."

"Thank you, Mr. President, and thank you for receiving me on such short and urgent notice." He looked around the conference table as Durling went to his seat at the opposite end, nodding to each of them. Brett Hanson, Secretary of State; Arnold van Damm, the Chief of Staff; John Ryan, National Security Advisor. The Secretary of Defense was also in the building, he knew, but not here. How interesting. The Ambassador had served many years in Washington, and knew much of Americans. There was anger in the faces of the men seated; though the President controlled his emotions admirably, just like the security people who stood at the doors, his look was that of a soldier. Hanson's anger was outrage. He could not believe that anyone would be so foolish as to threaten his country in any way — he was like a spoiled child resenting a failing grade on an exam from a fair and scrupulous teacher. Van Damm was a politician, and regarded him as a *gaijin* — a curious little man. Ryan showed the least anger of all, though it was there, indicated more in the way he held his pen than in the fixed stare of his blue cat's eyes. The Ambassador had never dealt with Ryan beyond a few chance encounters at state functions. The same was true of most of the embassy staff, and though his background was well known to all Washington insiders, Ryan was known to be a European specialist and therefore ignorant of Japan. That was good, the Ambassador thought. Were he more knowledgeable, he might be a dangerous enemy.

"Mr. Ambassador, you requested this meeting," Hanson said. "We will let you begin."

Ryan endured the opening statement. It was lengthy and prepared and predictable, what any country would say under these circumstances, added to which was a little national spice. It wasn't their fault; they'd been pushed, treated as lowly vassals despite years of faithful and productive friendship. They, too, regretted this situation. And so forth. It was just diplomatic embroidery, and Jack let his eyes do the work while his ears filtered out the noise.

More interesting was the demeanor of the speaker. Diplomats in friendly circumstances tended to the florid, and in hostile, they droned, as though embarrassed to speak their words. Not this time. The Japanese Ambassador showed overt strength that spoke of pride in his country and her actions. Not quite defiant, but not embarrassed either. Even the German ambassador who'd given word of Hitler's invasion to Molotov had shown grief, Jack remembered.

For his part, the President listened impassively, letting Arnie show the anger and Hanson show the shock, Jack saw. Good for him.

"Mr. Ambassador, war with the United States of America is not a trivial thing," the Secretary of State said when the opening statement was concluded.

The Ambassador didn't flinch. "It is only a war if you wish it to be. We do not have the desire to destroy your country, but we do have our own se-

592

curity interests." He went on to state his country's position on the Marianas. They'd been Japanese territory before, and now they were again. His country had a right to its own defensive perimeter. And that, he said, was that.

"You do know," Hanson said, "that we have the ability to destroy your country?"

A nod. "Yes, I do. We well remember your use of nuclear weapons on our country."

Jack's eyes opened a little wider at that answer. On his pad he wrote, *nukes?*

"You have something else to say," Durling observed, entering the conversation.

"Mr. President — my country also has nuclear arms."

"Delivered how?" Arnie asked with a snort. Ryan blessed him silently for the question. There were times when an ass had his place.

"My country has a number of nuclear-tipped intercontinental missiles. Your own people have seen the assembly plant. You can check with NASA if you wish." The Ambassador read off the name and the dates in a very matter-of-fact way, noting that Ryan took them down like a good functionary. The room became so quiet that he could hear the scratching of the man's pen. More interesting still were the looks on the other faces.

"Do you threaten us?" Durling asked quietly.

The Ambassador looked straight into the man's eyes, twenty feet away. "No, Mr. President, I do not. I merely state a fact. I say again, this is a war only if you wish it so. Yes, we know you can destroy us if you wish, and we cannot destroy you, though we can cause you great harm. Over what, Mr. President? A few small islands that are historically our possessions anyway? They have been Japanese in all but name for years now."

"And the people you killed?" van Damm asked.

"I regret that sincerely. We will of course offer compensation to the families. It is our hope that we can conclude matters. We will not disturb your embassy or its personnel, and we hope that you will grant us the same courtesy, to maintain communications between our governments. Is it so hard," he asked, "to think of us as equals? Why did you feel the need to hurt us? There was a time when a single airplane crash, due to a mistake made by your people at Boeing, killed more of my citizens than the number of American lives lost in the Pacific. Did we scream at you? Did we threaten your economic security, your very national survival? No. We did not. The time has come for my country to take her place in the world. You've withdrawn from the Western Pacific. We must now look to our own defenses. To do that we need what we need. How can we be sure that, having crippled our nation in economic terms, you will not at some later time seek to destroy us physically?"

"We would never do that!" Hanson objected.

"Easily said, Mr. Secretary. You did it once before, and as you yourself just pointed out, you retain that ability."

"We didn't start that war," van Damm pointed out.

"You did not?" the Ambassador asked. "By cutting off our oil and trade, you faced us with ruin, and a war resulted. Just last month you threw our economy into chaos, and you expected us to do nothing — because we had not the ability to defend ourselves. Well, we do have that ability," the Ambassador said. "Perhaps now we can treat as equals.

"So far as my government is concerned, the conflict is over. We will take no further action against Americans. Your citizens are welcome in my country. We will amend our trade practices to accommodate your laws. This entire incident could be presented to your public as an unfortunate accident, and we can reach an agreement between ourselves on the Marianas. We stand ready to negotiate a settlement that will serve the needs of your country and of mine. That is the position of my government." With that, the Ambassador opened his portfolio and extracted the "note" which the rules of international behavior required. He rose and handed it to the Secretary of State.

"If you require my presence, I stand at your service. Good day." He walked back to the door, past the National Security Advisor, who didn't follow the Ambassador with his eyes as the others did. Ryan had said nothing at all. That might have been disturbing in a Japanese, but not in an American, really. He'd simply had nothing to say. Well, he was a European specialist, wasn't he?

The door closed and Ryan waited another few seconds before speaking.

"Well, that was interesting," Ryan observed, checking his page of notes. "He only told us one thing of real importance."

"What do you mean?" Hanson demanded.

"Nuclear weapons and the delivery systems. The rest was embroidery, really meant for a different audience. We still don't know what they're really doing."

25

All the King's Horses

It hadn't made the media yet, but that was about to change. The FBI was already looking for Chuck Searls. They already knew that it wouldn't be easy, and the truth of the matter is that all they could do, on the basis of what they had, was to question him. The six programmers who'd worked to some greater or lesser extent on the Electra-Clerk 2.4.0 program had all been interviewed, and all of them denied knowledge of what they all referred to as the "Easter Egg," in every case with a mixture of outrage at what had been done and admiration at how. Only three widely separated lines of code, and it had taken all six of them working together twenty-seven hours to find it. Then had come the really bad news: all six of them, plus Searls, had had access to the raw program. They were, after all, the six senior programmers at the firm, and like people with identical security clearances, each could access it whenever he or she wished, up to the very moment that it left the office on the toaster-disk. In addition, while there were records of access, each of them also had the ability to fiddle the coding on the master computer and either erase the access-time reference or mix it with the others. For that matter, the Easter Egg could have been in there for the months it had taken to perfect the program, so finely crafted it was. Finally, one of them admitted quite freely, any of them could have done it. There were no fingerprints on computer programs. Of greater importance for the moment, there was no way of undoing what Electra-Clerk 2.4.0 had done.

What it had done was sufficiently ghastly that the FBI agents on the case were joking grimly that the advent of sealed thermopane windows in Wall Street office buildings was probably saving thousands of lives. The last identifiable trade had been put up at 12:00:00, and beginning at 12:00:01, all the records were gobbledygook. Literally billions — in fact, hundreds of billions of dollars in transactions had disappeared, lost in the computer-tape records of the Depository Trust Company.

The word had not yet gotten out. The event was still a secret, a tactic first suggested by the senior executives of DTC, and so far approved by both the governors of the Securities and Exchange Commission and the New York Stock Exchange. They'd had to explain the reasons for it to the FBI. In addition to all the money lost in a crash such as had taken place on Friday, there would also have been quite a bit of money made through "puts," the name for derivative trades used by many brokers as hedges, and a means that allowed profit on a *falling* market. In addition, every house kept its own records of trades, and therefore, theoretically, it *was* possible over time to reconstruct everything that had been erased by the Easter Egg. But if word of the DTC disaster got out, it was possible that unscrupulous or merely desperate traders would fiddle their own records. It was unlikely in the case of the larger houses, but virtually inevitable in the case of smaller ones, and such manipulation would be nearly impossible to prove — a classic case of one person's word against another's, the worst sort of criminal evidence. Even the biggest and most honorable trading houses had their miscreants, either real or potential. There was just too much money involved, further complicated by the ethical duty of traders to safeguard the money of their clients.

For that reason, over two hundred agents had visited the offices and homes of the chief executive officers of every trading establishment within a hundred-mile radius of New York. It was a feat easier than most had feared, since many of the executives were using their weekend as a frantic work period, and in most cases they cooperated, turning over their own computerized records. It was estimated that 80 percent of the trades that had taken place after noon Friday were now in the possession of federal authorities. That was the easy part. The hard part, the agents had just learned, would be to analyze them, to connect the trade made by every house with the corresponding trade of every other. As irony would have it, a programmer from Searls' company had, without prompting, sketched out the minimum requirements for the task: a high-end workstation for every company-set of records, integrated through yet another powerful mainframe no smaller than a Cray Y-MP (there was one at CIA, and three more at NSA, he told them), along with a very slick custom program. There were thousands of traders and institutions, some of whom had executed millions of transactions. The permutations, he'd said to the two agents who were able to keep up with his fast-forward discourse, were probably on the order of ten to the sixteenth power . . . maybe eighteenth. The latter number, he'd had to explain, was a million cubed, a million times a million *times* a million. A very large number. Oh, one other thing: they'd better be damned sure that they had the records of every house and every trade or the whole thing could fall apart. Time required to resolve all the trades? He'd been unwilling to speculate on that, which didn't please the agents who had to return to their office in the Javits Federal Office Building and explain all this to their boss, who refused even to use his office computer to type letters. The term *Mission: IMPOSSIBLE* came to their minds on the short drive back to their offices.

And yet it had to be done. It wasn't just a matter of stock trades, after all. Each transaction had also held a monetary value, real money that had changed electronic hands, moving from one account to another, and though electronic, the complex flow of money had to be accounted for. Until all of the transactions were resolved, the amount of money in the account of every trading house, every institution, every bank, and ultimately every private citizen in America — even those who did not play the market — could not be known. In addition to paralyzing Wall Street, the entire American banking system was now frozen in place, a conclusion that had been reached about the time that Air Force One had touched down at Andrews Air Force Base.

"Oh, shit," commented the Deputy Director in Charge of the New York Field Division of the Federal Bureau of Investigation. In this he was more articulate than investigators from other federal agencies who were using his northwest-corner office as a conference room. The others mainly just looked at the cheap carpet on the floor and gulped.

The situation had to get worse, and it did. One of the DTC employees told the tale to a neighbor, an attorney, who told someone else, a reporter, who made a few phone calls and drafted a story for *The New York Times*. That flagship paper called the Secretary of the Treasury who, just back from Moscow and not yet briefed on the magnitude of the situation, declined to comment but forgot to ask the *Times* to demur. Before he could correct that mistake, the story was set up to run.

Secretary of the Treasury Bosley Fiedler practically ran through the tunnel connecting the Treasury Building with the White House. Not a man accustomed to strenuous exercise, he was puffing hard when he made it into the Roosevelt Room, just missing the departure of the Japanese Ambassador.

"What is it, Buzz?" President Durling asked.

Fiedler caught his breath and gave a five-minute summary of what he'd just learned via teleconference with New York. "We can't let the markets open," he concluded. "I mean, they *can't* open. Nobody can trade. Nobody knows how much money they have. Nobody knows who owns what. And the banks . . . Mr. President, we have a major problem here. Nothing even remotely like this has ever happened before."

"Buzz, it's just money, right?" Arnie van Damm asked, wondering why it all had to happen in one day after what had been a rather pleasant few months.

"No, it's not just money." Heads turned because Ryan was the one who answered the question. "It's confidence. Buzz here wrote a book about that back when I was working for Merrill Lynch." Perhaps a friendly reference would steady the man down some, he thought.

"Thank you, Jack." Fiedler sat down and sipped a glass of water. "Use the 1929 crash as an example. What was really lost? The answer in monetary terms is, nothing. A lot of investors lost their shirts, and margin calls made it all worse, but what people don't often grasp is that the money they lost was money already given to others."

"I don't understand," Arnie said.

"Nobody really does. It's one of those things that's too simple. In the market people expect complexity, and they forget the forest is made up of individual trees. Every investor who lost money first *gave* his money to another trader, in return for which he received a stock certificate. He traded money for something of value, but that something of value fell, and that's what the crash was. *But* the first guy, the guy who gave the certificate and got the money *before the crash* — notionally he did the smart thing, he didn't lose anything, did he? Therefore the amount of money out in the economy in 1929 *did not change at all.*"

"Money doesn't just evaporate, Arnie," Ryan explained. "It goes from one place to another place. It doesn't just go away. The Federal Reserve Bank controls that." It was clear, however, that van Damm didn't understand.

"But then, why the *hell* did the Great Depression happen?"

"Confidence," Fiedler replied. "A huge number of people really got slammed in '29 because of margin calls. They bought stock while putting up an amount less than the value of the transaction. Today we call that sort of thing leveraging. Then they were unable to cover their exposure when they had to sell off. The banks and other institutions took a huge beating because they had to cover the margins. You ended up with a lot of little people who were left with nothing but debts they couldn't begin to pay back, and banks who were cash-short. Under those circumstances people stop doing things. They're *afraid* to risk what they have left. The people who got out in time and still have money — the ones who have not actually been hurt — they see what the rest of the economy is like and do nothing also, they just sit tight because it simply looks scary out there. *That*'s the problem, Arnie.

"You see, what makes an economy isn't wealth, but the *use* of wealth, all the transactions that occur every day, from the kid who cuts your grass for a buck to a major corporate acquisition. If that stops, everything stops." Ryan nodded approval to Fiedler.

601

It was a superb little lecture.

"I'm still not sure I get it," the chief of staff said. The President was still listening.

My turn. Ryan shook his head. "Not many people get it. Like Buzz said, it's too simple. You look for activity, not inactivity, as an indication of a trend, but inactivity is the real danger here. If I decide to sit still and do nothing, then my money doesn't circulate. I don't buy things, and the people who make the things I would have bought are out of work. That's a frightening thing to them, and to their neighbors. The neighbors get so scared that they hold on to their money — why spend it when they might need it to eat when they lose *their* jobs, right? And on, and on, and on. We have a real problem here, guys," Jack concluded. "Monday morning the bankers are going to find out that they don't know what they have, either. The banking crisis didn't really start until 1932, well after the stock market came unglued. Not this time."

"How bad?" The President asked this question.

"I don't know," Fiedler replied. "It's never happened before."

" 'I don't know' doesn't cut it, Buzz," Durling said.

"Would you prefer a lie?" the Secretary of the Treasury asked. "We need the chairman of the Fed in here. We're facing a lot of problems. The first big one is a liquidity crisis of unprecedented proportions."

"Not to mention a shooting war," Ryan pointed out for those who might have forgotten.

"Which is the more serious?" President Durling asked.

Ryan thought about it for a second. "In terms of real net harm to our country? We have two submarines sunk, figure about two hundred fifty sailors dead. Two carriers crippled. They can be fixed. The Marianas are under new ownership. Those are all bad things," Jack said in a measured voice, thinking as he spoke. "But they do not genuinely affect our national security because they do not pertain to the real strength of our country. America is a shared idea. We're people who think in a certain way, who believe that they can do the things they want to do. Everything else follows from that. It's confidence, optimism, the one thing that other countries find so strange about us. If you take that away, hell, we're no different from anybody else. The short answer to your question, Mr. President, is that the economic problem is far more dangerous to us than what the Japs just did."

"You surprise me, Jack," Durling said.

"Sir, like Buzz said, would you prefer a lie?"

"What the hell is the problem?" Ron Jones asked. The sun was already up, and USS *Pasadena* was visible, still tied to her pier, the national ensign hanging forlornly in the still air. A fighting ship of the United States Navy was doing nothing at all, and the son of his mentor was dead at the hands of an enemy. Why wasn't anyone doing something about it?

"She doesn't have orders," Mancuso said, "because I don't have orders, because CINCPAC doesn't have orders, because National Command Authority hasn't issued any orders."

"They awake there?"

"SecDef's supposed to be in the White House now. The President's been briefed in by now, probably," ComSubPac thought.

"But he can't get his thumb out," Jones observed.

"He's the President, Ron. We do what he says."

"Yeah, like Johnson sent my dad to Vietnam." Jones turned to look at the wall chart. By the end of the day the Japanese surface ships would be out of range for the carriers, which couldn't launch strikes anyway. USS *Gary* had concluded her search for sur-

vivors, mainly out of fear of lingering Japanese submarines out there, but for all the world looking as
though she'd been chased off the site by a Coast Guard
cutter. The intelligence they did have was based on
satellite information because it hadn't been thought
prudent even to send a P-3C out to shadow the surface
force, much less prosecute the submarine contacts.
"First out of harm's way, eh?"

Mancuso decided not to get angry this time. He
was a flag officer and paid to think like one. "One
thing at a time. Our most important assets at risk
are those two carriers. We have to get 'em in, and
we have to get 'em fixed. Wally is planning operations
right now. We have to gather intelligence, think it
over, and then decide what we can do."

"And then see if he'll let us?"

Mancuso nodded. "That's how the system works."

"Great."

The dawn was pleasing indeed. Sitting on the upper
deck of the 747, Yamata had taken a window seat
on the portside, looking out the window and ignoring
the buzz of conversation around him. He had scarcely
slept in three days and still the rush of power and
elation filled him like a flood. This was the last pre-
scheduled flight in. Mainly administrative personnel,
along with some engineers and civilians who would
start to put the new government in place. The bureaucrats with that task had been fairly clever in their
way. Of course, everyone on Saipan would have a
vote, and the elections would be subject to international scrutiny, a political necessity. There were about
twenty-nine thousand local citizens, but that didn't
count Japanese, many of whom now owned land,
homes, and business enterprises. Nor did it count soldiers, and others staying in hotels. The hotels — the
largest were Japanese-owned, of course — would be
considered condominiums, and all those in the condo

units, residents. As Japanese citizens they each had a vote. The soldiers were citizens as well, and also had the franchise, and since their garrison status was indeterminate, they were also considered residents. Between the soldiers and the civilians, there were thirty-one thousand Japanese on the island, and when elections were held, well, his countrymen were assiduous in making use of their civil rights, weren't they? *International scrutiny*, he thought, staring out to the east, *be damned.*

It was especially pleasing to watch from thirty-seven thousand feet the first muted glow on the horizon, which seemed much like a garnish for a bouquet of still-visible stars. The glow brightened and expanded, from purple to deep red, to pink, to orange, and then the first sliver of the face of the sun, not yet visible on the black sea below, and it was as though the sunrise were for him alone, Yamata thought, long before the lower people got to enjoy and savor it. The aircraft turned slightly to the right, beginning its descent. The downward path through the early-morning air was perfectly timed, seeming to hold the sun in place all the way down, just the yellow-white sliver, preserving the magical moment for several minutes. The sheer glory moved Yamata nearly to tears. He still remembered the faces of his parents, their modest home on Saipan. His father had been a minor and not terribly prosperous merchant, mainly selling trinkets and notions to the soldiers who garrisoned the island. His father had always been very polite to them, Raizo remembered, smiling, bowing, accepting their rough jokes about his polio-shriveled leg. The boy who had watched thought it normal to be deferential to men carrying arms, wearing his nation's uniform. He'd learned different since, of course. They were merely servants. Whether they carried on the samurai tradition or not — the very word *samurai* was a derivation of the verb "to serve," he reminded himself, clearly implying a master, no? — it was they who looked after and protected their betters, and it was their betters who hired them and paid them and told them what to do. It was necessary to treat them with greater respect than they really deserved, but the odd thing was that the higher they went in rank, the better they understood what their place really was.

"We will touch down in five minutes," a colonel told him.

"*Dozo.*" A nod rather than a bow, because he was sitting down, but even so the nod was a measured one, precisely of the sort to acknowledge the service of an underling, showing him both politeness and superiority in the same pleasant gesture. In time, if this colonel was a good one and gained general's rank, then the nod would change, and if he proceeded further, then someday, if he were lucky, Yamata-san might call his given name in friendship, single him out for a smile and a joke, invite him for a drink, and in his advancement to high command, learn who the master really was. The Colonel probably looked forward to achieving that goal. Yamata buckled his seat belt and smoothed his hair.

Captain Sato was exhausted. He'd just spent far too much time in the air, not merely breaking but shredding the crew-rest rules of his airline, but he, too, could not turn away from his duty. He looked off to the left and saw in the morning sky the blinking strokes of two fighters, probably F-15s, one of them, perhaps, flown by his son, circling to protect the soil of what was once again their country. *Gently,* he told himself. There were soldiers of his country under his care, and they deserved the best. One hand on the throttles, the other on the wheel, he guided the Boeing airliner down an invisible line in the air toward a point his eyes had already selected. On his command to the copilot, the huge flaps went down all the way.

Sato eased back on the yoke, bringing up the nose and flaring the aircraft, letting it settle, floating it in until only the screech of rubber told them that they were on the ground.

"You are a poet," the copilot said, once more impressed by the man's skill.

Sato allowed himself a smile as he engaged reverse-thrust. "You taxi in." Then he keyed the cabin intercom.

"Welcome to Japan," he told the passengers.

Yamata didn't shout only because the remark surprised him so. He didn't wait for the aircraft to stop before he unbuckled. The door to the flight deck was right there, and he had to say something.

"Captain?"

"Yes, Yamata-san?"

"You understand, don't you?"

His nod was that of a proud professional, and in that moment one very much akin to the zaibatsu. *"Hai."* His reward was a bow of the finest sincerity, and it warmed the pilot's heart to see Yamata-san's respect.

The businessman was not in a hurry, not now. The bureaucrats and administrative soldiers worked their way off the aircraft into waiting buses that would take them to the Hotel Nikko Saipan, a large modern establishment located in the center of the island's west coast, which would be the temporary administrative headquarters for the occupa— for the new government, Yamata corrected himself. It took five minutes for all of them to deplane, after which he made his own way off to another Toyota Land Cruiser whose driver, this time, was one of his employees who knew what to do without being told, and knew that this was a moment for Yamata to savor in silence.

He scarcely noticed the activity. Though he'd caused it to happen, it was less important than its anticipation had been. Oh, perhaps a brief smile at the sight of the military vehicles, but the fatigue was real now, and his eyes drooped despite an iron will that commanded them to be bright and wide. The driver had planned the route with care, and managed to avoid the major tieups. Soon they passed the Marianas Country Club again, and though the sun was up, there were no golfers in evidence. There was no military presence either except for two satellite uplink trucks on the edge of the parking lot, newly painted green after having been appropriated from NHK. No, we mustn't harm the golf course, now without a doubt the most expensive single piece of real estate on the island.

It was right about here, Yamata thought, remembering the shape of the hills. His father's rude little store had been close to the north airfield, and he could remember the A6M Type-Zero fighters, the strutting aviators, and the often overbearing soldiers. Over there had been the sugarcane processing plant of Nanyo Kohatsu Kaisha, and he could remember stealing small bits of the cane and chewing on them. And how fair the breezy mornings had been. Soon they were on his land. Yamata shook off the cobwebs by force of will and stepped out of the car, walking north now.

It was the way his father and mother and brother and sister must have come, and he imagined he could see his father, hobbling on his crippled leg, struggling for the dignity that his childhood disease had always denied him. Had he served the soldiers in those last days, bringing them what useful things he had? Had the soldiers in those last days set aside their crude insults at his physical condition and thanked him with the sincerity of men for whom death was now something seen and felt in its approach? Yamata chose to believe both. And they would have come down this draw, their retreat toward death protected by the last rear-guard action of soldiers in their last moment of perfection.

It was called Banzai Cliff by the locals, Suicide Cliff by the less racist. Yamata would have to have his public-relations people work on changing the name to something more respectful. July 9, 1944, the day organized resistance ended. The day the Americans had declared the island of Saipan "secure."

There were actually two cliffs, curved and facing inward as though a theater; the taller of them was two hundred forty meters above the surface of the beckoning sea. There were marble columns to mark the spot, built years earlier by Japanese students, shaped to represent children kneeling in prayer. It would have been here that they'd approached the edge, holding hands. He could remember his father's strong hands. Would his brother and sister have been afraid? Probably more disoriented than fearful, he thought, after twenty-one days of noise and horror and incomprehension. Mother would have looked at father. A warm, short, round woman whose jolly musical laugh rang again in her son's ears. The soldiers had occasionally been gruff with his father, but never with her. And never with the children. And the last service the soldiers had rendered had been to keep the Americans away from them at that final moment, when they'd stepped off the cliff. Holding hands, Yamata chose to believe, each holding a child in a final loving embrace, proudly refusing to accept captivity at the hands of barbarians, and orphaning their other son. Yamata could close his eyes and see it all, and for the first time the memory and the imagined sight made his body shudder with emotion. He'd never allowed himself anything more than rage before, all the times he'd come here over the years, but now he could truly let the emotions out and weep with pride, for he had repaid his debt of honor to those who had given him birth, and his debt of honor to those who had done them to death. In full.

The driver watched, not knowing but understanding, for he knew the history of this place, and he too was moved to tears as a shaking man of sixty-odd years clapped his hands to call the attention of sleeping relatives. From a hundred meters away, he saw the man's shoulders rack with sobs, and after a time, Yamata lay down on his side, in his business suit, and went to sleep. Perhaps he would dream of them. Perhaps the spirits of whoever it was, the driver thought, would visit him in his sleep and say what things he needed to hear. But the real surprise, the driver thought, was that the old bastard had a soul at all. Perhaps he'd misjudged his boss.

"Damn if they ain't organized," Oreza said to himself, looking through his binoculars, the cheap ones he kept in the house.

The living-room window afforded a view of the airports, and the kitchen gave one of the harbor. *Orchid Ace* was long gone, and another car ferry had taken her berth, *Century Highway No. 5*, her name was, and this one was unloading jeep-type vehicles and trucks. Portagee was fairly strung-out, having forced himself to stay up all night. He'd now done twenty-seven hours without sleep, some of them spent working hard on the ocean west of the island. He was too old for that sort of thing, the master chief knew. Burroughs, younger and smarter, had curled up on the living-room rug and was snoring away.

Oreza wished for a cigarette for the first time in years. They were good for staying alert. You just needed them at a time like this. They were what a warrior used — at least that's what the World War II movies proclaimed. But this wasn't World War II, and he wasn't a warrior. For all he'd done in his over thirty years in the United States Coast Guard, he'd never fired a shot in anger, even on his one Vietnam tour. Someone else had always been on the gun. He didn't know *how* to fight.

"Up all night?" Isabel asked, dressed for her job. It was Monday on this side of the International Dateline, and a workday. She looked down and saw that the pad of note paper usually kept next to the phone was covered with scribbles and numbers. "Does it matter?"

"I don't know, Izz."

"Want some breakfast?"

"It can't hurt," Pete Burroughs said, stretching as he came into the kitchen. "I think I conked out around three." A moment's consideration. "I feel like . . . hell," he said, in deference to the lady in the room.

"Well, I have to be at my desk in an hour or so," Mrs. Oreza observed, pulling open the refrigerator. Breakfast in this house consisted of a selection of cold cereals and skim milk, Burroughs saw, along with toast made of the bread baked from straw. Toss in a little fruit, he thought, and he could have been back in San Jose. The coffee he could already smell. He found a cup and poured some.

"Somebody really knows how to do this right."

"It's Manni," Isabel said.

Oreza smiled for the first time in hours. "I learned it from my first chief. The right blend, the right proportions, and a pinch of salt."

Probably in the dark of the moon and after sacrificing a goat, Burroughs thought. If so, however, the goat had died for a noble cause. He took a long sip and came over to check Oreza's tally sheet.

"That many?"

"Could be conservative. It's two flying hours from here to Japan. That's four on the round-trip. Let's be generous and say ninety minutes on the ground at each end. Seven-hour cycle. Three and a half trips per airplane per day. Each flight about three hundred, maybe three-fifty soldiers per hop. That means every plane brings in a thousand men. Fifteen airplanes operating over one day, that means a whole division of troops. You suppose the Japs have more than fifteen 747s?" Portagee asked. "Like I said, conservative. Now it's just a matter of bringing their mobile equipment in."

"How many ships for that?"

Another frown. "Not sure. During the Persian Gulf War — I was over there then doing port-security work . . . damn. Depends on what ships you use and how you pack them. I'll be conservative again. Twenty large merchant hulls just to ferry in the gear. Trucks, jeeps, all kinds of stuff you'd never think of. It's like moving a cityful of people. They need to resupply fuel. This rock doesn't grow enough food; that has to come in by ship, too, and the population of this place just doubled. The water supply might be stretched." Oreza looked down and made a notation on that. "Anyway, they came to stay. That's for damned sure," he said, heading for the table and his Special K, wishing for three eggs up, bacon, white-bread toast with butter, hash-browns, and all the cholesterol that went with it. Damn turning fifty!

"What about me?" the engineer asked. "I seen you pass for a local. I sure as hell can't."

"Pete, you're my charter, and I'm the captain, okay? I am responsible for your safety. That's the law of the sea, sir."

"We're not at sea anymore," Burroughs pointed out.

Oreza was annoyed by the truth of the observation. "My daughter's the lawyer. I try to keep things simple. Eat your breakfast. I need some sleep, and you have to take over the forenoon watch."

"What about me?" Mrs. Oreza asked.

"If you don't show up for work — "

" — somebody will wonder why."

"It'll be nice to know if they told the truth about

612

the cops who got shot," her husband went on. "I've been up all night, Izz. I haven't heard a single shot. Every crossroads seems to be manned, but they're not doing anything to anybody." He paused. "I don't like it either, honey. One way or another we have to deal with it."

"Did you do it, Ed?" Durling asked bluntly, his eyes boring in on his Vice President. He cursed the man for forcing him to deal with one more problem among the multiple crises hanging over his presidency now. But the *Post* piece gave him no choice.

"Why are you hanging me out to dry? Why didn't you at least *warn* me of this?"

The President waved around the Oval Office. "There are a lot of things you can do in here and there are things you can't do. One of them is to interfere with a criminal investigation."

"Don't give me that! A lot of people have — "

"Yeah, and they all paid a price for it, too." *It's not my ass that needs to be covered*, Roger Durling didn't say. *I'm not risking mine for yours.* "You didn't answer my question."

"Look, Roger!" Ed Kealty snarled back. The President stopped him with a raised hand and a quiet voice.

"Ed, I have an economy in meltdown. I have dead sailors in the Pacific Ocean. I can't spare the energy for this. I can't spare the political capital. I can't spare the time. Answer my question," Durling commanded.

The Vice President flushed, his head snapping to the right before he spoke. "All right, I like women. I've never hidden that from anyone. My wife and I have an understanding." His head came back. "But I have *never*, *NEVER* molested, assaulted, raped, or forced myself on anybody in my whole fucking life. Never. I don't *have* to."

613

"Lisa Beringer?" Durling said, consulting his notes for the name.

"She was a sweet thing, very bright, very sincere, and she begged me to — well, you can guess. I explained to her that I couldn't. I was up for reelection that year, and besides she was too young. She deserved somebody her age to marry and give her kids and a good life. She took it hard, started drinking — maybe something else, but I don't think so. Anyway, one night she headed off on the Beltway and lost it, Roger. I was there for the funeral. I still talk with her parents. Well," Kealty said, "not lately, I guess."

"She left a note, a letter behind."

"More than one." Kealty reached into his coat pocket and handed two envelopes over. "I'm surprised nobody noticed the date on the one the FBI has. Ten days before her death. This one is a week later, and this one is the day she was killed. My staff found them. I suppose Barbara Linders found the other one. None were ever mailed. I think you'll find some differences between them, all three, as a matter of fact."

"The Linders girl says that you — "

"Drugged her?" Kealty shook his head. "You know about my drinking problem, you knew it when you asked me in. Yeah, I'm an alcoholic, but I had my last drink two years ago." A crooked smile. "My sex life is even better now. Back to Barbara. She was sick that day, the flu. She went to the pharmacy on the Hill and got a prescription, and — "

"How do you know that?"

"Maybe I keep a diary. Maybe I just have a good memory. Either way, I know the date this happened. Maybe one of my staffers checked the records of the pharmacy, and maybe the medication she took had a label on the bottle, one that says don't drink while using these capsules. I didn't know that, Roger. When

I have a cold — well, back then, anyway, I used brandy. Hell," Kealty admitted, "I used booze for a lot of things. So I gave some to her, and she became very cooperative. A little too cooperative, I suppose, but I was half in the bag myself, and I figured it was just my well-known charm."

"So what are you telling me? You're not guilty?"

"You want to say I'm an alley cat, can't keep it zipped? Yeah, I guess so. I've been to priests, to doctors, to a clinic once — covering that up was some task. Finally I went to the head of neuroscience at Harvard Medical School. They think there's a part of the brain that regulates our drives, just a theory, but a good one. It goes along with hyperactivity. I was a hyperactive child. I still don't ever sleep more than six hours a night. Roger, I am all those things, but I am not a rapist."

So there it was, Durling thought. Not a lawyer himself, he had appointed, consulted, and heard enough of them to know what he'd been told. Kealty could defend himself on two grounds: that the evidence against him was more equivocal than the investigators imagined, and that it wasn't really his fault. The President wondered which of the defenses might be true. Neither? One? Both?

"So what are you going to do?" he asked the Vice President, using much the same voice he'd summoned a few hours earlier for the Ambassador from Japan. He was increasingly sympathetic with the man sitting across from him, in spite of himself. What if the guy really was telling the truth? How could he know — and that was what the jury would say, after all, if it got that far; and if a jury would think that, then what would the Judiciary hearings be like? Kealty still had a lot of markers out on the Hill.

"Somehow I just don't think anyone's going to print up DURLING/KEALTY bumper stickers this summer, right?" The question came with a smile of sorts.

"Not if I have anything to say about it," the President confirmed, cold again. This wasn't a time for humor.

"I don't want to hurt you, Roger. I did two days ago. If you'd warned me, I could have told you these things sooner, saved everybody a lot of time and trouble. Including Barbara. I lost track of her. She's very good on civil-rights stuff, a good head on her, and a good heart. It was only that one time, you know. And she stayed in my office afterwards," Kealty pointed out.

"We've covered that, Ed. Tell me what you want."

"I'll go. I'll resign. I don't get prosecuted."

"Not good enough," Durling said in a neutral voice.

"Oh, I'll admit my weaknesses. I'll apologize to you, honorable public servant that you are, for any harm I might have done to your presidency. My lawyers will meet with their lawyers, and we'll negotiate compensation. I leave public life."

"And if that's not good enough?"

"It will be," Kealty said confidently. "I can't be tried in a court until the constitutional issues are resolved. Months, Roger. All the way to summer, probably, maybe all the way to the convention. You can't afford that. I figure the worst-case scenario for you is, the Judiciary Committee sends the bill of impeachment to the floor of the House, but the House doesn't pass it, or maybe does, narrowly, and then the Senate trial ends up with a hung jury, so to speak. Do you have any idea how many favors I've done there, and in the Senate?" Kealty shook his head. "It's not worth the political risk to you, and it distracts you and Congress from the business of government. You need all the time you have. Hell, you need more than that." Kealty stood and headed toward the door to the President's right, the one that was so perfectly blended into the curved, eggshell-white walls and gold trim. He spoke his final words without turning. "Anyway, it's up to you now."

It angered President Roger Durling that, in the end, the easy way out might be the just way out, as well — but nobody would ever know. They would only know that his final action was politically expedient in a moment of history that demanded political expediency. An economy potentially in ruins, a war just started — he didn't have the time to fool with this. A young woman had died. Others claimed to have been molested. But what if the dead young girl had died for other reasons, and what if the others — *Goddamn it,* he swore in his mind. That was something for a jury to decide. But it had to pass through three separate legal procedures before a jury could decide, and then any defense lawyer with half a brain could say that a fair trial was impossible anyway after C-SPAN had done its level best to tell the whole world every bit of evidence, tainting everything, and denying Kealty his constitutional right to a fair and impartial trial before disinterested jurors. That ruling was likely enough in a Federal district court trial, and even more so on appeal — and would gain the victims nothing. And what if the bastard actually was, technically speaking, innocent of a crime? An open zipper, distasteful though it was, did not constitute a crime.

And neither he nor the country needed the distraction. Roger Durling buzzed his secretary.

"Yes, Mr. President?"

"Get me the Attorney General."

He'd been wrong, Durling thought. Sure, he could interfere with a criminal investigation. He had to. And it was easy. Damn.

617

26

Catch-up

"He really said that?" Ed Foley leaned forward. It was easier for Mary Pat to grasp it than for her husband.

"Sure enough, and it's all on his honor as a spy," Jack confirmed, quoting the Russian's words.

"I always did like his sense of humor," the DDO said, getting her first laugh of the day, and probably the last. "He's studied us so hard that he's more American than Russian."

Oh, Jack thought, *that's it.* That explained Ed. The opposite was true of him. A Soviet specialist for nearly all of his career, he was more Russian than American. The realization occasioned his own smile.

"Thoughts?" the National Security Advisor asked.

"Jack, it gives them the ID of the only three humint assets we have on the ground over there. Bad joss, man," Edward Foley said.

"That's a consideration," Mary Patricia Foley agreed. "But there's another consideration. Those three assets are cut off. Unless we can communicate with them, they might as well not be there. Jack, how serious is this situation?"

"We are for all practical purposes at war, MP." Jack had already relayed the gist of the meeting with the Ambassador, including his parting comment.

She nodded. "Okay, they're giving a war. Are we going to come?"

"I don't know," Ryan admitted. "We have dead people out there. We have U.S. territory with another flag flying over it right now. But our ability to respond effectively is severely compromised — and we have this little problem at home. Tomorrow the markets and the banking system are going to have to come to terms with some very unpleasant realities."

"Interesting coincidence," Ed noted. He was too old a hand in the intelligence business to believe in coincidences. "What's going to happen with that stuff, Jack? You know a lot about it."

"I don't have a clue, guys. It's going to be bad, but how bad, and how it's going to be bad . . . nobody's been here before. I suppose the good news is that things can't fall further. The bad news is the mentality that goes with the situation will be like a person trapped in a burning building. You may be safe where you are, but you can't get out, either."

"What agencies are looking into things?" Ed Foley asked.

"Just about all of them. The Bureau's the lead agency. It has the most available investigators. The SEC is better suited to it, but they don't have the troops for something this big."

"Jack, in a period of less than twenty-four hours, somebody leaked the news on the Vice President" — he was in the Oval Office right now, they all knew — "the market went in the crapper, and we had the attack on Pacific Fleet, and you just told us the most harmful thing to us is this economic thing. If I were you, sir — "

"I see your point," Ryan said, cutting Ed off a moment too soon for a complete picture. He made a few notes, wondering how the hell he'd be able to prove anything, as complex as the market situation was. "Is anybody that smart?"

"Lots of smart people in the world, Jack. Not all of them like us." It was very much like talking with Sergey Nikolay'ch, Ryan thought, and like Golovko, Ed Foley was an experienced pro for whom paranoia was always a way of life and often a tangible reality. "But we have something immediate to consider here."

"These are three good officers," Mary Pat said, taking the ball from her husband. "Nomuri's been doing a fine job sliding himself into their society, taking his time, developing a good network of contacts. Clark and Chavez are as good a team of operators as we have. They have good cover identities and they ought to be pretty safe."

"Except for one thing," Jack added.

"What's that?" Ed Foley asked, cutting his wife off.

"The PSID knows they're working."

"Golovko?" Mary Pat asked. Jack nodded soberly. "That son of a bitch," she went on. "You know, they still are the best in the world." Which was not an altogether pleasant admission from the Deputy Director (Operations) of the Central Intelligence Agency.

"Don't tell me they have the head of Japanese counterintel under their control?" her husband inquired delicately.

"Why not, honey? They do it to everybody else." Which was true. "You know, sometimes I think we ought to hire some of their people just to give lessons." She paused for a second. "We don't have a choice."

"Sergey didn't actually come out and say that, but I don't know how else he could have known. No," Jack agreed with the DDO, "we don't really have any choice at all."

Even Ed saw that now, which was not the same as liking it. "What's the *quid* on this one?"

"They want everything we get out of THISTLE.

They're a little concerned about this situation. They were caught by surprise, too, Sergey tells me."

"But they have another network operating there. He told you that, too," MP observed. "And it has to be a good one, too."

"Giving them the 'take' from THISTLE in return for not being hassled is one thing — and a pretty big thing. This goes too far. Did you think this one all the way through, Jack? It means that they'll actually be running our people for us." Ed didn't like that one at all, but on a moment's additional consideration, it was plain that he didn't see an alternative either.

"Interesting circumstances, but Sergey says he was caught with his drawers down. Go figure." Ryan shrugged, wondering yet again how it was possible for three of the best-informed intelligence professionals in his country *not* to be able to understand what was going on.

"A lie on his part?" Ed wondered. "On the face of it, that doesn't make a whole lot of sense."

"Neither does lying," Mary Pat said. "Oh, I love these *matryoshka* puzzles. Okay, at least we know there are things we don't know yet. That means we have a lot of things to find out, the quicker the better. If we let RVS run our people . . . it's risky, Jack, but — damn, I don't see that we have a choice."

"I tell him yes?" Jack asked. He had to get the President's approval, too, but that would be easier than getting theirs.

The Foleys traded a look and nodded.

An oceangoing commercial tug was located by a helicopter fifty miles from the *Enterprise* formation, and in a remarkable set of circumstances, the frigate *Gary* took custody of the barge and dispatched the tug to the carrier, where she could relieve the Aegis cruiser, and, by the way, increase *Big-E*'s speed of advance to nine knots. The tug's skipper contemplated the magnitude of the fee he'd garner under the Lloyd's Open Form salvage contract, which the carrier's CO had signed and ferried back by helicopter. The typical court award was 10 to 15 percent of the value of the property salved. A carrier, an air wing, and six thousand people, the tugboat crew thought. What was 10 percent of three billion dollars? Maybe they'd be generous and settle for five.

It was a mixture of the simple and the complex, as always. There were now P-3C Orion patrol aircraft operating out of Midway to support the retreating battle force. It had taken a full day to reactivate the facilities at the midocean atoll, possible only because there was a team of ornithologists there studying the goonies. The Orions were in turn supported by C-130s of the Hawaiian Air National Guard. However it had happened, the admiral who still flew his flag on the crippled aircraft carrier could look at a radar picture with four antisubmarine aircraft arrayed around his fleet and start to feel a little safer. His outer ring of escorts were hammering the ocean with their active sonars, and, after an initial period of near panic, finding nothing much to worry about. He'd make Pearl Harbor by Friday evening, and maybe with a little wind could get his aircraft off, further safeguarding them.

The crew was smiling now, Admiral Sato could see, as he headed down the passageway. Only two days before, they'd been embarrassed and shamed by the "mistake" their ship had made. But not now. He'd gone by ship's helicopter to all four of the Kongos personally to deliver the briefings. Two days away from the Marianas, they now knew what they had accomplished. Or at least part of it. The submarine incidents were still guarded information, and for the moment they knew that they had avenged a great wrong to their country, done so in a very clever way, allowing Japan to reclaim land that was historically hers — and without, they thought, taking lives in the process. The initial reaction had been shock. Going to war with America? The Admiral had explained that, no, it was not really a war unless the Americans chose to make an issue of it, which he thought unlikely, but also something, he warned them, for which they had to be prepared. The formation was spread out now, three thousand meters between ships, racing west at maximum sustainable speed. That was using up fuel at a dangerous rate, but there would be a tanker at Guam to refuel them, and Sato wanted to be under his own ASW umbrella as soon as possible. Once at Guam he could consider future operations. The first one had been successful. With luck there would not have to be a second, but if there were, he had many things to consider.

"Contacts?" the Admiral asked, entering the Combat Information Center.

"Everything in the air is squawking commercial," the air-warfare officer replied.

"Military aircraft all carry transponders," Sato reminded him. "And they all work the same way."

"Nothing is approaching us." The formation was on a course deliberately offset from normal commercial air corridors, and on looking at the billboard display, the Admiral could see that traffic was in all those corridors. True, a military-surveillance aircraft could see them from some of the commercial tracks, but the Americans had satellites that were just as good. His intelligence estimates had so far proved accurate. The only threat that really concerned him was from submarines, and that one was manageable. Submarine-launched Harpoon or Tomahawk missiles were a danger with which he was prepared to deal. Each of the destroyers had her SPY-1D radar up and operating, scanning the surface. Every fire-control director was manned. Any inbound cruise missile would be detected and engaged, first by his American-made (and Japanese-improved) SM-2MR missiles, and behind those weapons were CIWS gatling-gun point-defense systems. They would stop most of the inbound "vampires," the generic term for cruise missiles. A submarine *could* close and engage with torpedoes, and one of the larger warheads could kill any ship in his formation. But they would hear the torpedo coming in, and his ASW helicopters would do their very best to pounce on the attacking sub, deny her the chance to continue the engagement, and just maybe kill her. The Americans didn't have all that many submarines, and their commanders would be correspondingly cautious, especially if he managed to add a third kill to the two already accomplished.

What would the Americans do? Well, what *could* they do now? he asked himself. It was a question he'd asked himself again and again, and he always had the same answer. They'd drawn down too much. They depended on their ability to deter, forgetting that deterrence hinged on the perceived ability to take action if deterrence failed: the same old equation of *don't-want-to* but *can*. Unfortunately for them, the Americans had leaned too much on the former and neglected the latter, and by all the rules Sato knew, by the time they *could* again, their adversary would be able to stop them. The overall strategic plan he'd helped to execute was not new at all — just better-executed than it had been the first time, he thought, standing close to the triple billboard display and watching the radar symbols of commercial aircraft march along their defined pathways, their very action proclaiming that the world was resuming its normal shape without so much as a blip.

The hard part always seemed to come after the decisions were made, Ryan knew. It wasn't making them that wore on the soul so much as having to live with them. Had he done the right things? There was no measure except hindsight, and that always came too late. Worse, hindsight was always negative because you rarely looked back to reconsider things that had gone right. At a certain level, things stopped being clear-cut. You weighed options, and you weighed the factors, but very often you knew that no matter which way you jumped, somebody would be hurt. In those cases the idea was to hurt the least number of people or things, but even then real people were hurt who would otherwise not be hurt at all, and you were choosing, really, whose lives would be injured — or lost — like a disinterested god-figure from mythology. It was worse still if you knew some of the players, because they had faces your mind could see and voices it could hear. The ability to make such decisions was called moral courage by those who didn't have to do it, and stress by those who did.

And yet he had to do it. He'd undertaken this job in the knowledge that such moments would come. He'd placed Clark and Chavez at risk before in the East African desert, and he vaguely remembered worrying about that, but the mission had come off and after *that* it had seemed like trick-or-treat on Halloween, a wonderfully clever little game played by nation against nation. The fact that a real human being in the person of Mohammed Abdul Corp had lost his life as a result — well, it was easy to say, now, that he'd deserved his fate. Ryan had allowed himself to file that entire memory away in some locked drawer, to be dredged out years later should he ever succumb to the urge to write memoirs. But now the memory was back, removed from the files by the necessity to put the lives of real men at risk again. Jack locked his confidential papers away before heading toward the Oval Office.

"Off to see the boss," he told a Secret Service agent

in the north-south corridor.

"SWORDSMAN heading to JUMPER," the agent said into his microphone, for to those who protected everyone in what to them was known as the House, they were as much symbols as men, designations, really, for what their functions were.

But I'm not a symbol, Jack wanted to tell him. *I'm a man,* with doubts. He passed four more agents on the way, and saw how they looked at him, the trust and respect, how they *expected* him to know what to do, what to tell the Boss, as though he were somehow greater than they, and only Ryan knew that he wasn't. He'd been foolish enough to accept a job with greater responsibilities than theirs, that's all, greater than he'd ever wanted.

"Not fun, is it?" Durling said when he entered the office.

"Not much." Jack took his seat.

The President read his advisor's face and mind at the same time, and smiled. "Let's see. I'm supposed to tell you to relax, and you're supposed to tell me the same thing, right?"

"Hard to make a correct decision if you're over-stressed," Ryan agreed.

"Yeah, except for one thing. If you're not stressed, then it isn't much of a decision, and it's handled at a lower level. The hard ones come here. A lot of people have commented on that," the President said. It was a remarkably generous observation, Jack realized, for it voluntarily took some of the burden off his shoulders by reminding him that he did, after all, merely *advise* the President. There was greatness in the man at the ancient oak desk. Jack wondered how difficult a burden it was to bear, and if its discovery had come as a surprise — or merely, perhaps, as just one more necessity with which one had to deal.

"Okay, what is it?"

"I need your permission for something." Ryan ex-

626

plained the Golovko offers — the first made in Moscow, and the second only a few hours earlier — and their implications.

"Does this give us a larger picture?" Durling asked.

"Possibly, but we don't have enough to go with."

"And?"

"A decision of this type always goes up to your level," Ryan told him.

"Why do I have to — "

"Sir, it reveals both the identity of intelligence officers and methods of operation. I suppose technically it doesn't have to be your decision, but it is something you should know about."

"You recommend approval." Durling didn't have to ask.

"Yes, sir."

"We can trust the Russians?"

"I didn't say *trust*, Mr. President. What we have here is a confluence of needs and abilities, with a little potential blackmail on the side."

"Run with it," the President said without much in the way of consideration. Perhaps it was a measure of his trust in Ryan, thus returning the burden of responsibility back to his visitor. Durling paused for a few seconds before posing his next question. "What are they up to, Jack?"

"The Japanese? On the face of it, this makes no objective sense at all. What I keep coming back to is, why kill the submarines? Why kill *people?* It just doesn't seem necessary to have crossed that threshold."

"Why do this to their most important trading partner?" Durling added, making the most obvious observation. "We haven't had a chance to think it through, have we?"

Ryan shook his head. "Things have certainly piled up on us. We don't even know the things we don't know yet."

The President cocked his head to the side. "What?"

Jack smiled a little. "That's something my wife likes to say about medicine. You have to know the things you don't know. You have to figure out what the questions are before you can start looking for answers."

"How do we do that?"

"Mary Pat has people out asking questions. We go over all the data we have. We try to infer things from what we know, look for connections. You can tell a lot from what the other guy is trying to do and how he's going about it. My biggest one now, why did they kill the two subs?" Ryan looked past the President, out the window to the Washington Monument, that fixed, firm obelisk of white marble. "They did it in a way that they think will allow us a way out. We can claim it was a collision or something — "

"Do they really expect that we'll just accept the deaths and — "

"They offered us the chance. Maybe they don't expect it, but it's a possibility." Ryan was quiet for perhaps thirty seconds. "No. No, they couldn't misread us that badly."

"Keep thinking out loud," Durling commanded.

"We've cut our fleet too far back — "

"I don't need to hear that now," was the answer, an edge on it.

Ryan nodded and held a hand up. "Too late to worry why or how, I know that. But the important thing is, they know it, too. Everybody knows what we have and don't have, and with the right kind of knowledge and training, you can infer what we can do. Then you structure your operations on a combination of what you can do, and what *he* can do about it."

"Makes sense. Okay, go on."

"With the demise of the Russian threat, the submarine force is essentially out of business. That's because a submarine is only good for two things, really. Tactically, submarines are good for killing other subs. But strategically, submarines are limited. They cannot control the sea in the same way as surface ships do. They can't project power. They can't ferry troops or goods from one place to another, and that's what sea control really means." Jack snapped his fingers. "But they *can* deny the sea to others, and Japan is an island-nation. So they're afraid of sea-denial." Or, Jack added in his own mind, maybe they just did what they could do. They crippled the carriers because they could not easily do more. Or could they? Damn, it was still too complicated.

"So we could strangle them with submarines?" Durling asked.

"Maybe. We did it once before. We're down to just a few, though, and that makes their countersub task a lot easier. But their ultimate trump against such a move on our part is their nuclear capacity. They counter a strategic threat to them with a strategic threat to us, a dimension they didn't have in 1941. There's something missing, sir." Ryan shook his head, still looking at the monument through the thick, bullet-resistant windows. "There's something big we don't know."

"The why?"

"The why may be it. First I want to know the *what*. What do they want? *What* is their end-game objective?"

"Not why they're doing it?"

Ryan turned his head back to meet the President's eyes. "Sir, the decision to start a war is almost never rational. World War One, kicked off by some fool killing some other fool, events were skillfully manipulated by Leopold something-or-other, 'Poldi,' they called him, the Austrian Foreign Minister. Skilled manipulator, but he didn't factor in the simple fact that his country lacked the power to achieve what he wanted. Germany and Austria-Hungary started the war. They both lost. World War Two, Japan and Germany took on the whole world, never occurred to them that the rest of the world might be stronger. Particularly true of Japan." Ryan went on. "They never really had a plan to defeat us. Hold on that for a moment. The Civil War, started by the South. The South lost. The Franco-Prussian War, started by France. France lost. Almost every war since the Industrial Revolution was initiated by the side which ultimately *lost*. Q.E.D., going to war is not a rational act. Therefore, the thinking behind it, the *why* isn't necessarily important, because it is probably erroneous to begin with."

"I never thought of that, Jack."

Ryan shrugged. "Some things are too obvious, like Buzz Fiedler said earlier today."

"But if the *why* is not important, then the *what* isn't either, is it?"

"Yes, it is, because if you can discern the objective, if you can figure out what they want, then you can deny it to them. That's how you start to defeat an enemy. And, you know, the other guy gets so interested in what he wants, so fixed on how important it is, that he starts forgetting that somebody else might try to keep him from getting it."

"Like a criminal thinking about hitting a liquor store?" Durling asked, both amused and impressed by Ryan's discourse.

"War is the ultimate criminal act, an armed robbery writ large. And it's always about greed. It's always a nation that wants something another nation has. And you defeat that nation by recognizing what it wants and denying it to them. The seeds of their defeat are usually found in the seeds of their desire."

"Japan, World War Two?"

"They wanted a real empire. Essentially they

630

wanted exactly what the Brits had. They just started a century or two too late. They never planned to defeat us, merely to — " He stopped suddenly, an idea forming. "Merely to achieve their goals and force us to acquiesce. Jesus," Ryan breathed. "That's it! It's the same thing all over again. The same methodology. The same objective?" he wondered aloud.

It's there, the National Security Advisor told himself. *It's all right there.*

If you can find it. If you can find it all.

"But we have a first objective of our own," the President pointed out.

"I know."

George Winston supposed that, like an old fire horse, he had to respond to the bells. His wife and children still in Colorado, he was over Ohio now, sitting in the back of his Gulfstream, looking down at the crab-shape of city lights. Probably Cincinnati, though he hadn't asked the drivers about their route into Newark.

His motivation was partially personal. His own fortune had suffered badly in the events of the previous Friday, drawn down by hundreds of millions. The nature of the event, and the way his money was spread around various institutions, had guaranteed a huge loss, since he'd been vulnerable to every variety of programmed trading system. But it wasn't about money. Okay, he told himself, so I lost two hundred mill'. I have lots more where that came from. It was the damage to the entire system, and above all the damage done to the Columbus Group. His baby had taken a huge hit, and like a father returning to the side of his married daughter in time of crisis, he knew that it would always be his. *I should have been there,* Winston told himself. *I could have seen it and stopped it. At least I could have protected my investors.* The full effects weren't in yet, but it was so bad as to be almost beyond comprehension. Winston had to do something, had to offer his expertise and counsel. Those investors were still his people.

It was an easy ride into Newark. The Gulfstream touched down smoothly and taxied off to the general-aviation terminal, where a car was waiting, and one of his senior former employees. He wasn't wearing a tie, which was unusual for the Wharton School graduate.

Mark Gant hadn't slept in fifty hours, and he leaned against the car for stability because the very earth seemed to move under him, to the accompaniment of a headache best measured on the Richter Scale. For all that, he was glad to be here. If anyone could figure this mess out, it was his former boss. As soon as the private jet stopped, he walked over to stand at the foot of the stairs.

"How bad?" was the first thing George Winston said. There was warmth between the two men, but business came first.

"We don't know yet," Gant replied, leading him to the car.

"Don't know?" The explanation had to wait until they got inside. Gant handed over the first section of the *Times* without comment.

"Is this for real?" A speed-reader, Winston scanned across the opening two columns, turning back to page 21 to finish a story framed by lingerie ads.

Gant's next revelation was that the manager Raizo Yamata had left behind was gone. "He flew back to Japan Friday night. He said to urge Yamata-san to come to New York to help stabilize the situation. Or maybe he wanted to gut himself open in front of his boss. Who the fuck knows?"

"So who the hell's in charge, Mark?"

"Nobody," Gant answered. "Just like everything else here."

632

"Goddamn it, Mark, *somebody* has to be giving the orders!"

"We don't have any instructions," the executive replied. "I've called the guy. He's not at the office — hey, I left messages, tried his house, Yamata's house, everybody's friggin' house, everybody's friggin' office. Zip-o, George. Everybody's running for cover. Hell, for all I know the dumb fuck took a header off the biggest building in town."

"Okay, I need an office and all the data you have," Winston said.

"*What* data?" Gant demanded. "We don't have shit. The whole system went down, remember?"

"You have the records of our trades, don't you?"

"Well, yeah, I have our tapes — a copy, anyway," Gant corrected himself. "The FBI took the originals."

A brilliant technician, Gant's first love had always been mathematics. Give Mark Gant the right instructions and he could work the market like a skilled cardsharp with a new deck of Bicycles. But like most of the people on the Street, he needed someone else to tell him what the job was. Well, every man had some limitations, and on the plus side of the ledger, Gant was smart, honest, and he knew what his limitations were. He knew when to ask for help. That last quality put him in the top 3 or 4 percent.

So he must have gone to Yamata and his man for guidance . . .

"When all this was going down, what instructions did you have?"

"Instructions?" Gant rubbed his unshaven face and shook his head. "Hell, we busted our ass to stay ahead of it. If DTC gets its shit together, we'll come out with most of our ass intact. I laid a mega-put on GM and made a real killing on gold stocks, and — "

"That's not what I mean."

"He said to run with it. He got us out of the bank

633

stocks in one big hurry, thank God. Damn if he didn't see that one coming first. We were pretty well placed before it all went down. If it hadn't been for all the panic calls — I mean, Jesus, George, it finally happened, y'know? One-eight-hundred-R-U-N. Jesus, if people had just kept their heads." A sigh. "But they didn't, and now, with the DTC fuckup . . . George, I don't know what's going to be opening up tomorrow, man. If this is true, if they can rebuild the house by tomorrow morning, hey, man, I don't know. I just don't," Gant said as they entered the Lincoln Tunnel.

The whole story of Wall Street in one exhausted paragraph, Winston told himself, looking at the glossy tile that made up the interior of the tunnel. Just like the tunnel, in fact. You could see forward and you could see behind, but you couldn't see crap to the sides. You couldn't see outside the limited perspective.

And you had to.

"Mark, I'm still a director of the firm."

"Yes, so?"

"And so are you," Winston pointed out.

"I know that, but — "

"The two of us can call a board meeting. Start making calls," George Winston ordered. "As soon as we're out of this damned hole in the ground."

"For when?" Gant asked.

"For *now*, goddamn it!" Winston swore. "Those who're out of town, I'll send my jet for."

"Most of the guys are in the office." Which was the only good news he'd heard since Friday afternoon, George thought, nodding for his former employee to go on. "I suppose most everyone else is closed."

They cleared the tunnel about then. Winston pulled the cellular phone from its holder and handed it over.

"Start calling." Winston wondered if Gant knew

what he was going to request at the meeting. Probably not. A good man in a tunnel, he had never outgrown his limitations.

Why the hell did I ever leave? Winston demanded of himself. It just wasn't safe to leave the American economy in the hands of people who didn't know how it worked.

"Well, that worked," Admiral Dubro said. Fleet speed slowed to twenty knots. They were now two hundred miles due east of Dondra Head. They needed more sea room, but getting this far was success enough. The two carriers angled apart, their respective formations dividing and forming protective rings around the centerpieces, *Abraham Lincoln* and *Dwight D. Eisenhower*. In another hour the formations would be outside of visual contact, and that was good, but the speed run had depleted bunkers, and that was very bad. The nuclear-powered carriers perversely were also tankers of a sort. They carried tons of bunker fuel for their conventionally powered escorts, and were able to refuel them when the need arose. It soon would. The fleet oilers *Yukon* and *Rappahannock* were en route from Diego Garcia with eighty thousand tons of distillate fuel between them, but this game was getting old in a hurry. The possibility of a confrontation compelled Dubro to keep all his ships' bunkers topped off. Confrontation meant potential battle, and battle always necessitated speed, to go into harm's way, and to get the hell out of it, too.

"Anything from Washington yet?" he asked next.

Commander Harrison shook his head. "No, sir."

"Okay," the battle-force commander said with a dangerous calm. Then he headed off to communications. He'd solved a major operational problem, for the moment, and now it was time to scream at someone.

27

Piling On

Everything was running behind, at maximum speed, largely in circles, getting nowhere at amazing speed. A city both accustomed to and dedicated to the prevention of leaks, Washington and its collection of officials were too busy with four simultaneous crises to respond effectively to any of them. None of that was unusual, a fact that would have been depressing to those who ought to be dealing with it, a digression for which, of course, they didn't have time. The only good news, Ryan thought, is that the biggest story hadn't quite leaked. Yet.

"Scott, who're your best people for Japan?"

Adler was still a smoker or had bought a pack on his way over from Foggy Bottom. It required all of Ryan's diminishing self-control not to ask for one, but neither could he tell his guest not to light up. They all had to deal with stress in their own ways. The fact that Adler's had once been Ryan's was just one more inconvenience in a weekend that had gone to hell faster than he'd thought possible.

"I can put a working group together. Who runs it?"

"You do," Jack answered.

"What will Brett say?"

"He'll say, 'Yes, sir,' when the President tells him,"

636

Ryan replied, too tired to be polite.

"They have us by the balls, Jack."

"How many potential hostages?" Ryan asked. It wasn't just the residual military people. There had to be thousands of tourists, businessmen, reporters, students . . .

"We have no way of finding out, Jack. None," Adler admitted. "The good news is that we have no indications of adverse treatment. It's not 1941, at least I don't think so."

"If that starts . . ." Most Americans had forgotten the manner of treatment accorded foreign prisoners. Ryan was not one of them. "Then we start going crazy. They have to know that."

"They know us a lot better than they did back then. So much interaction. Besides, we have tons of their people over here, too."

"Don't forget, Scott, that their culture is fundamentally different from ours. Their religion is different. Their view of man's place in nature is different. The value they place on human life is different," the National Security Advisor said darkly.

"This isn't a place for racism, Jack," Adler observed narrowly.

"Those are all facts. I didn't say they're inferior to us. I said that we're not going to make the mistake of thinking they're motivated in the same way we are — okay?"

"That's fair, I suppose," the Deputy Secretary of State conceded.

"So I want people who really understand their culture in here to advise me. I want people who think like they do." The trick would be finding space for them, but there were offices downstairs whose occupants could move out, albeit kicking and screaming about how important protocol and political polling were.

"I can find a few," Adler promised.

"What are we hearing from the embassies?"

"Nobody knows much of anything. One interesting development in Korea, though."

"What's that?"

"The defense attaché in Seoul went to see some friends about getting some bases moved up in alert level. They said no. That's the first time the ROKs ever said no to us. I guess their government is still trying to figure all this out."

"It's too early to start that, anyway."

"Are we going to do anything?"

Ryan shook his head. "I don't know yet." Then his phone buzzed.

"NMCC on the STU, Dr. Ryan."

"Ryan," Jack said, lifting the phone. "Yes, put him through. Shit," he breathed so quietly that Adler hardly caught it. "Admiral, I'll be back to you later today."

"Now what?"

"The Indians," Ryan told him.

"I call the meeting to order," Mark Gant said, tapping the table with his pen. Only two more than half of the seats were filled, but that was a quorum. "George, you have the floor."

The looks on all the faces troubled George Winston. At one level the men and women who determined policy for the Columbus Group were physically exhausted. At another they were panicked. It was the third that caused him the most pain: the degree of hope they showed at his presence, as though he were Jesus come to clean out the temple. It wasn't supposed to be this way. No one man was supposed to have that sort of power. The American economy was too vast. Too many people depended on it. Most of all, it was too complex for one man or even twenty to comprehend it all. That was the problem with the models that everyone depended on. Sooner or later it came down to trying to gauge and measure and regulate something that simply was. It existed. It worked. It functioned. People needed it, but nobody really knew how it worked. The Marxists' illusion that they did know had been their fundamental flaw. The Soviets had spent three generations trying to command an economy to work instead of just letting it go on its own, and had ended up beggars in the world's richest nation. And it was not so different here. Instead of controlling it, they tried to live off it, but in both cases you had to have the illusion that you understood it. And nobody did, except in the broadest sense.

At the most basic level it all came down to needs and time. People had needs. Food and shelter were the first two of those. So other people grew the food and built the houses. Both required time to do, and since time was the most precious commodity known to man, you had to compensate people for it. Take a car — people needed transportation, too. When you bought a car, you paid people for the time of assembly, for the time required to fabricate all the components; ultimately you were paying miners for the time required to dig the iron ore and bauxite from the ground. That part was simple enough. The complexity began with all of the potential options. You could drive more than one kind of car. Each supplier of goods and services involved in the car had the option to get what he needed from a variety of sources, and since time was precious, the person who used his time most efficiently got a further reward. That was called competition, and competition was a never-ending race of everyone against everyone else. Fundamentally, every business, and in a sense every single person in the American economy, was in competition with every other. Everyone was a worker. Everyone was also a consumer. Everyone provided something for others to use. Everyone selected products and services

639

from the vast menu that the economy offered. That was the basic idea.

The true complexity came from all the possible interactions. Who bought what from whom. Who became more efficient, the better to make use of their time, benefiting both the consumers and themselves at once. With everyone in the game, it was like a huge mob, with everyone talking to everyone else. You simply could not keep track of all the conversations.

And yet Wall Street held the illusion that it could, that its computer models could predict in broad terms what would happen on a daily basis. It was not possible. You could analyze individual companies, get a feel for what they were doing right and wrong. To a limited degree, from one or a few such analyses you could see trends and profit by them. But the use of computers and modeling techniques had gone too far, extrapolating farther and farther away from baseline reality, and while it had worked, after a fashion, for years, that had only magnified the illusion. With the collapse three days earlier, the illusion was shattered, and now they had nothing to cling to. *Nothing but me,* George Winston thought, reading their faces.

The former president of the Columbus Group knew his limitations. He knew the degree to which he understood the system, and knew roughly where that understanding ended. He knew that nobody could quite make the whole thing work, and that train of thought took him almost as far as he needed to go on this dark night in New York.

"This looks like a place without a leader. Tomorrow, what happens?" he asked, and all the "rocket scientists" averted their eyes from his, looking down at the table, or in some cases sharing a glance with the person who happened to be across it. Only three days before, someone would have spoken, offered an opinion with some greater or lesser degree of confidence. But not now, because nobody knew. Nobody had the first idea. And nobody spoke up.

"You have a president. Is he telling you anything?" Winston asked next. Heads shook.

It was Mark Gant, of course, who posed the question, as Winston had known he would.

"Ladies and gentlemen, it is the board of directors which selects our president and managing director, isn't it? We need a leader now."

"George," another man asked. "Are you back?"

"Either that or I'm doing the goddamnedest out-of-body trip you people have ever seen." It wasn't much of a joke, but it did generate smiles, the beginning of a little enthusiasm for something.

"In that case, I submit the motion that we declare the position of president and managing director to be vacant."

"Second."

"There is a motion on the floor," Mark Gant said, rather more strongly. "Those in favor?"

There was a chorus of "ayes."

"Oppose?"

Nothing.

"The motion carries. The presidency of the Columbus Group is now vacant. Is there a further motion from the floor?"

"I nominate George Winston to be our managing director and president," another voice said.

"Second."

"Those in favor?" Gant asked. This vote was identical except in its growing enthusiasm.

"George, welcome back." There was a faint smattering of applause.

"Okay." Winston stood. It was his again. His next comment was desultory: "Somebody needs to tell Yamata." He started pacing the room.

"Now, first thing: I want to see everything we have

on Friday's transactions. Before we can start thinking about how to fix the son of a bitch, we need to know how it got broke. It's going to be a long week, folks, but we have people out there that we have to protect."

The first task would be hard enough, he knew. Winston didn't know if anyone could fix it, but they had to start with examining what had gone so badly wrong. He knew he was close to something. He had the itchy feeling that went with the almost-enough information to move on a particular issue. Part of it was instinct, something he both depended on and distrusted until he could make the itch go away with hard facts. There was something else, however, and he didn't know what it was. He did know that he needed to find it.

Even good news could be ominous. General Arima was spending a good deal of time on TV, and he was doing well at it. The latest news was that any citizen who wanted to leave Saipan would be granted free air fare to Tokyo for later transit back to the States. Mainly what he said was that nothing important had changed.

"My ass," Pete Burroughs growled at the smiling face on the tube.

"You know, I just don't believe this," Oreza said, back up after five hours of sleep.

"I do. Check out that knoll southeast of here."

Portagee rubbed his heavy beard and looked. Half a mile away, on a hilltop recently cleared for another tourist hotel (the island had run out of beach space), about eighty men were setting up a Patriot missile battery. The billboard radars were already erected, and as he watched, the first of four boxy containers was rolled into place.

"So what are we going to do about this?" the engineer asked.

"Hey, I drive boats, remember?"

"You used to wear a uniform, didn't you?"

"Coast Guard," Oreza said. "Ain't never killed nobody. And that stuff" — he pointed to the missile site — "hell, you probably know more about it than I do."

"They make 'em in Massachusetts. Raytheon, I think. My company makes some chips for it." Which was the extent of Burroughs's knowledge. "They're planning to stay, aren't they?"

"Yeah." Oreza got his binoculars and started looking out windows again. He could see six road junctions. All were manned by what looked like ten men or so — a squad; he knew that term — with a mixture of the Toyota Land Cruisers and some jeeps. Though many had holsters on their pistol belts, no long guns were in evidence now, as though they didn't want to make it look like some South American junta from the old days. Every vehicle that passed — they didn't stop any that he saw — received a friendly wave. *PR*, Oreza thought. *Good PR*.

"Some kind of fuckin' love-in," the master chief said. And that would not have been possible unless they were confident as hell. Even the missile crew on the next hill over, he thought. They weren't rushing. They were doing their jobs in an orderly, professional way, and that was fine, but if you expected to use the things, you moved more snappily. There was a difference between peacetime and wartime activity, however much you said that training was supposed to eliminate the difference between the two. He turned his attention back to the nearest crossroads. The soldiers there were not the least bit tense. They looked and acted like soldiers, but their heads weren't scanning the way they ought to on unfriendly ground.

It might have been good news. No mass arrests and detainments, the usual handmaiden of invasions. No overt display of force beyond mere presence. You

643

would hardly know that they were here, except that they were sure as hell here, Portagee told himself. And they planned to stay. And they didn't think anybody was going to dispute that. And he sure as hell was in no position to change their view on anything.

"Okay, here are the first overheads," Jackson said. "We haven't had much time to go over them, but — "

"But we will," Ryan completed the sentence. "I'm a carded National Intelligence Officer, remember? I can handle the raw."

"Am I cleared for this?" Adler asked.

"You are now." Ryan switched on his desk light, and Robby dialed the combination on his attaché case. "When's the next pass over Japan?"

"Right about now, but there's cloud cover over most of the islands."

"Nuke hunt?" Adler asked. Admiral Jackson handled the answer.

"You bet your ass, sir." He laid out the first photo of Saipan. There were two car-carriers at the quay. The adjacent parking lot was spotted with orderly rows of military vehicles, most of them trucks.

"Best guess?" Ryan asked.

"An augmented division." His pen touched a cluster of vehicles. "This is a Patriot battery. Towed artillery. This looks like a big air-defense radar that's broken down for transport. There's a twelve-hundred-foot hill on this rock. It'll see a good long way, and the visual horizon from up there is a good fifty miles." Another photo. "The airports. Those are five F-15 fighters, and if you look here, we caught two of their F-3s in the air coming in on final."

"F-3?" Adler asked.

"The production version of the FS-X," Jackson explained. "Fairly capable, but really a reworked F-16. The Eagles are for air defense. This little puppy is

644

a good attack bird."

"We need more passes," Ryan said in a voice suddenly grave. Somehow it was real now. Really real, as he liked to say, metaphysically real. It was no longer the results of analysis or verbal reports. Now he had photographic proof. His country was sure as hell at war.

Jackson nodded. "Mainly we need pros to go over these overheads, but, yeah, we'll be getting four passes a day, weather permitting, and we need to examine every square inch of this rock, and Tinian, and Rota, and Guam, and all the little rocks."

"Jesus, Robby, can we do it?" Jack asked. The question, though posed in the simplest terms, had implications that even he could not yet appreciate. Admiral Jackson was slow to lift his eyes from the overhead photos, and his voice suddenly lost its rage as the naval officer's professional judgment clicked in.

"I don't know yet." He paused, then posed a question of his own. "Will we try?"

"I don't know that, either," the National Security Advisor told him. "Robby?"

"Yeah, Jack?"

"Before we decide to try, we have to know if we can."

Admiral Jackson nodded. "Aye aye."

He'd been awake most of the night listening to his partner's snoring. What was it about this guy? Chavez asked himself groggily. How the hell could he sleep? Outside, the sun was up, and the overwhelming sounds of Tokyo in the morning beat their way through windows and walls, and still John was sleeping. Well, Ding thought, he was an old guy and maybe he needed his rest. Then the most startling event of their entire stay in the country happened. The phone rang. That caused John's eyes to snap

645

open, but Ding got the phone first.

"*Tovarorischiy,*" a voice said. "All this time in-country and you haven't called me?"

"Who is this?" Chavez asked. As carefully as he'd studied his Russian, hearing it on the phone here and now made the language sound like Martian. It wasn't hard for him to make his voice seem sleepy. It was hard, a moment later, to keep his eyeballs in their sockets.

A jolly laugh that had to be heartfelt echoed down the phone line. "Yevgeniy Pavlovich, who else would it be? Scrape the stubble from your face and join me for breakfast. I'm downstairs."

Domingo Chavez felt his heart stop. Not just miss a beat — he would have sworn it stopped until he willed it to start working again, and when it did, it went off at warp-factor-three. "Give us a few minutes."

"Ivan Sergeyevich had too much to drink again, *da?*" the voice asked with another laugh. "Tell him he grows too old for that foolishness. Very well, I will have some tea and wait."

All the while Clark's eyes were fixed on his, or for the first few seconds, anyway. Then they started sweeping the room for dangers that had to be around, so pale his partner's face had become. Domingo was not one to get frightened easily, John knew, but whatever he'd heard on the phone had almost panicked the kid.

Well. John rose and switched on the TV. If there were danger outside the door, it was too late. The window offered no escape. The corridor outside could well be jammed full of armed police, and his first order of business was to head for the bathroom. Clark looked in the mirror as the water ran from the flushing toilet. Chavez was there before the handle came back up.

"Whoever was on the phone called me 'Yevgeniy.'

He's waiting downstairs, he says."

"What did he sound like?" Clark asked.

"Russian, right accent, right syntax." The toilet stopped running, and they couldn't speak anymore for a while.

Shit, Clark thought, looking in the mirror for an answer, but finding only two very confused faces. Well. The intelligence officer started washing up and thinking over possibilities. *Think.* If it had been the Japanese police, would they have bothered to . . . ? No. Not likely. Everyone regarded spies as dangerous in addition to being loathsome, a curious legacy of James Bond movies. Intelligence officers were about as likely to start a firefight as they were to sprout wings and fly. Their most important physical skills were running and hiding, but nobody ever seemed to grasp that, and if the local cops were on to them, then . . . then he would have awakened to a pistol in his face. And he hadn't, had he? *Okay.* No immediate danger. Probably.

Chavez watched in no small amazement as Clark took his time washing his hands and face, shaving carefully, and brushing his teeth before he relinquished the bathroom. He even smiled when he was done, because that expression was necessary to the tone of his voice.

"Yevgeniy Pavlovich, we must appear *kulturny* for our friend, no? It's been so many months." Five minutes later they were out the door.

Acting skills are no less important to intelligence officers than to those who work the legitimate theater, for like the stage, in the spy business there are rarely opportunities for retakes. Major Boris Il'ych Scherenko was the deputy *rezident* of RVS Station Tokyo, awakened four hours earlier by a seemingly innocuous call from the embassy. Covered as Cultural Attaché, he'd most recently been busy arranging the final details for a tour of Japan by the St. Petersburg Ballet. For fifteen years an officer of the First Chief (Foreign) Directorate of the KGB, he now fulfilled the same function for his newer and smaller agency. His job was even more important now, Scherenko thought. Since his nation was far less able to deal with external threats, it needed good intelligence more than ever. Perhaps that was the reason for this lunacy. Or maybe the people in Moscow had gone completely mad. There was no telling. At least the tea was good.

Awaiting him in the embassy had been an enciphered message from Moscow Center — that hadn't changed — with names and detailed descriptions. It made identification easy. Easier than understanding the orders he had.

"Vanya!" Scherenko nearly ran over, seizing the older man's hand for a hearty handshake, but forgoing the kiss that Russians are known for. That was partly to avoid offending Japanese sensibilities and partly because the American might slug him, passionless people that they were. Madness or not, it was a moment to savor. These were two senior CIA officers, and tweaking their noses in public was not without its humor. "It's been so long!"

The younger one, Scherenko saw, was doing his best to conceal his feelings, but not quite well enough. KGB/RVS didn't know anything about him. But his agency did know the name John Clark. It was only a name and a cursory description that could have fit a Caucasian male of any nationality. One hundred eighty-five to one hundred ninety centimeters. Ninety kilos. Dark hair. Fit. To that Scherenko added, blue eyes, a firm grip. Steady nerve. Very steady nerve, the Major thought.

"Indeed it has. How is your family, my friend?"

Add excellent Russian to that, Scherenko thought, catching the accent of St. Petersburg. As he cataloged the physical characteristics of the American, he saw two sets of eyes, one blue, one black, doing the same to him.

"Natalia misses you. Come! I am hungry! Breakfast!" He led the other two back to his corner booth.

"CLARK, JOHN (none?)", the thin file in Moscow was headed. A name so nondescript that other cover names were unknown and perhaps never assigned. Field officer, paramilitary type, believed to perform special covert functions. More than two (2) Intelligence Stars for courage and/or proficiency in field operations. Brief stint as a Security and Protective Officer, during which time no one had troubled himself to get a photo, Scherenko thought. Typical. Staring at him across the table now, he saw a man relaxed and at ease with the old friend he'd met for the first time perhaps as much as two minutes earlier. Well, he'd always known that CIA had good people working for them.

"We can talk here," Scherenko said more quietly, sticking to Russian.

"Is that so . . . ?"

"Scherenko, Boris Il'ych, Major, deputy *rezident*," he said, finally introducing himself. Next he nodded to each of his guests. "You are John Clark — and Domingo Chavez."

"And this is the fucking Twilight Zone," Ding muttered.

" 'Plum blossoms bloom, and pleasure women buy new scarves in a brothel room.' Not exactly Pushkin, is it? Not even Pasternak. Arrogant little barbarians." He'd been in Japan for three years. He'd arrived expecting to find a pleasant, interesting place to do business. He'd come to dislike many aspects of Japanese culture, mainly the assumed local superiority to everything else in the world, particularly offensive to a Russian who felt exactly the same way.

"Would you like to tell us what this is all about, Comrade Major?" Clark asked.

Scherenko spoke calmly now. The humor of the event was now behind them all, not that the Americans had ever appreciated it. "Your Maria Patricia Foleyeva placed a call to our Sergey Nikolayevich Golovko, asking for our assistance. I know that you are running another officer here in Tokyo, but not his name. I am further instructed to tell you, Comrade *Klerk,* that your wife and daughters are fine. Your younger daughter made the dean's list at her university again, and is now a good candidate for admission to medical school. If you require further proof of my bonafides, I'm afraid I cannot help you." The Major noted a thin expression of pleasure on the younger man's face and wondered what that was all about.

Well, that settles that, John thought. *Almost.* "Well, Boris, you sure as hell know how to get a man's attention. Now, maybe you can tell us what the hell is going on."

"We didn't see it either," Scherenko began, going over all the high points. It turned out that his data was somewhat better than what Clark had gotten from Chet Nomuri, but did not include quite everything. Intelligence was like that. You never had the full picture, and the parts left out were always important.

"How do you know we can operate safely?"

"You know that I cannot — "

"Boris Il'ych, my life is in your hands. You know I have a wife and two daughters. My life is important to me, and to them," John said reasonably, making himself appear all the more formidable to the pro across the table. It wasn't about fear. John knew that he was a capable field spook, and Scherenko gave the same impression. "Trust" was a concept both central to and alien from intelligence operations. You had to trust your people, and yet you could never trust them all the way in a business where du-

650

alisms were a way of life.

"Your cover works better for you than you think. The Japanese think that you are Russians. Because of that, they will not trouble you. We can see to that," the deputy *rezident* told them confidently.

"For how long?" Clark asked rather astutely, Scherenko thought.

"Yes, there is always that question, isn't there?"

"How do we communicate?" John asked.

"I understand that you require a high-quality telephone circuit." He handed a card under the table. "All of Tokyo is now fiberoptic. We have several similar lines to Moscow. Your special communications gear is being flown there as we speak. I understand it is excellent. I would like to see it," Boris said with a raised eyebrow.

"It's just a ROM chip, man," Chavez told him. "I couldn't even tell you which one it is."

"Clever," Scherenko thought.

"How serious are they?" the younger man asked him.

"They appear to have moved a total of three divisions to the Marianas. Their navy has attacked yours." Scherenko gave what details he knew. "I should tell you that our estimate is that you will face great difficulties in taking your islands back."

"How great?" Clark asked.

The Russian shrugged, not without sympathy. "Moscow believes it unlikely. Your capabilities are almost as puny as ours have become."

And that's *why this is happening,* Clark decided on the spot. That was why he had a new friend in a foreign land. He'd told Chavez, practically on their first meeting, a quote from Henry Kissinger: "Even paranoids have enemies." He sometimes wondered why the Russians didn't print that on their money, rather like America's *E pluribus unum.* The hell of it was, they had a lot of history to back that one up. And so, for that matter, did America.

"Keep talking."

"We have their government intelligence organs thoroughly penetrated, also their military, but THISTLE is a commercial network, and I gather you have developed better data than I have. I'm not sure what that means." Which wasn't strictly true, but Scherenko was distinguishing between what he knew and what he thought; and, like a good spook, giving voice only to the former for now.

"So we both have a lot of work to do."

Scherenko nodded. "Feel free to come to the chancery."

"Let me know when the communications gear gets to Moscow." Clark could have gone on, but held back. He wouldn't be completely sure until he got the proper electronic acknowledgment. So strange, he thought, that he needed it, but if Scherenko was telling the truth about his degree of penetration in the Japanese government, then he could have been "flipped" himself. And old habits died especially hard in this business. The one comforting thing was that his interlocutor knew that he was holding back, and didn't appear to mind for the moment.

"I will."

It didn't take many people to crowd the Oval Office. The premier power room in what Ryan still hoped was the world's most powerful nation was smaller than the office he'd occupied during his return to the investment business — and in fact smaller than his corner office in the West Wing, Jack realized for the first time.

They were all tired. Brett Hanson was especially haggard. Only Arnie van Damm looked approximately normal, but, then, Arnie always looked as though he were coming off a bender. Buzz Fiedler looked to be in something close to despair. The Secretary of Defense was the worst of all, however. It was he who had supervised the downsizing of the American military, who had told Congress almost on a weekly basis that our capabilities were far in excess of our needs. Ryan remembered the testimony on TV, the internal memos that dated back several years, the almost desperate objections by the uniformed chiefs of staff which they had faithfully not leaked to the media. It wasn't hard to guess what SecDef was thinking now. This brilliant bureaucrat, so confident in his vision and his judgment, had just run hard into the flat, unforgiving wall called reality.

"The economic problem," President Durling said, much to SecDef's relief.

"The hard part is the banks. They're going to be running scared until we rectify the DTC situation. So many banks now make trades that they don't know what their own reserves are. People are going to try to cash in their mutual-fund holdings controlled by those banks. The Fed Chairman has already started jawboning them."

"Saying what?" Jack asked.

"Saying they had an unlimited line of credit. Saying that the money supply will be enough for their needs. Saying that they can loan all the money they want."

"Inflationary," van Damm observed. "That's very dangerous."

"Not really," Ryan said. "In the short term inflation is like a bad cold, you take aspirin and chicken soup for it. What happened Friday is like a heart attack. You treat *that* first. If the banks don't open for business as usual . . . Confidence is the big issue. Buzz is right."

Not for the first time, Roger Durling blessed the fact that Ryan's first departure from government had taken him back into the financial sector.

"And the markets?" the President asked SecTreas.

"Closed. I've talked to all of the exchanges. Until

653

the DTC records are re-created, there will be no organized trading."

"What does that mean?" Hanson asked. Ryan noticed that the Defense Secretary wasn't saying anything. Ordinarily such a confident guy, too, Jack thought, quick to render an opinion. In other circumstances he would have found the man's newly found reticence very welcome indeed.

"You don't *have* to trade stocks on the floor of the NYSE," Fiedler explained. "You can do it in the country-club men's room if you want."

"And people will," Ryan added. "Not many, but some."

"Will it matter? What about foreign exchanges?" Durling asked. "They trade our stocks all over the world."

"Not enough liquidity overseas," Fiedler answered. "Oh, there's some, but the New York exchanges make the benchmarks that everybody uses, and without those nobody knows what the values are."

"They have records of the tickers, don't they?" van Damm asked.

"Yes, but the records are compromised, and you don't gamble millions on faulty information. Okay, it's not really a bad thing that the information on DTC leaked. It gives us a cover story that we can use for a day or two," Ryan thought. "People can relate to the fact that a system fault had knocked stuff down. It'll hold them off from a total panic for a while. How long to fix the records?"

"They still don't know," Fiedler admitted. "They're still trying to assemble the records."

"We probably have until Wednesday, then." Ryan rubbed his eyes. He wanted to get up and pace, just get his blood circulating, but only the President did that in the Oval Office.

"I had a conference call with all the exchange heads. They're calling everyone in to work, like for a normal day. They have orders to shuffle around and look busy for the TV cameras."

"Nice idea, Buzz," the President managed to say first. Ryan gave SecTreas a thumbs-up.

"We have to come up with some sort of solution fast," Fiedler went on. "Jack's probably right. By late Wednesday it's a real panic, and I can't tell you what'll happen," he ended soberly. But the news wasn't all that bad for this evening. There was a little breathing space, and there were other breaths to be taken.

"Next," van Damm said, handling this one for the Boss, "Ed Kealty is going to go quietly. He's working out a deal with Justice. So that political monkey is off our backs. Of course" — the Chief of Staff looked at the President — "then we have to fill that post soon."

"It'll wait," Durling said. "Brett . . . India."

"Ambassador Williams has been hearing some ominous things. The Navy's analysis is probably right. It appears that the Indians may be seriously contemplating a move on Sri Lanka."

"Great timing," Ryan heard, looking down, then he spoke.

"The Navy wants operational instructions. We have a two-carrier battle force maneuvering around. If it's time to bump heads, they need to know what they are free to do." He had to say that because of his promise to Robby Jackson, but he knew what the answer would be. That pot wasn't boiling quite yet.

"We've got a lot on the plate. We'll defer that one for now," the President said. "Brett, have Dave Williams meet with their Prime Minister and make it clear to her that the United States does not look kindly upon aggressive acts anywhere in the world. No bluster. Just a clear statement, and have him wait for a reply."

"We haven't talked to them that way in a long

time," Hanson warned.

"It's time to do so now, Brett," Durling pointed out quietly.

"Yes, Mr. President."

And now, Ryan thought, *the one we've all been waiting for*. Eyes turned to the Secretary of Defense. He spoke mechanically, hardly looking up from his notes.

"The two carriers will be back at Pearl Harbor by Friday. There are two graving docks for repairs, but to get the ships fully mission-capable will require months. The two submarines are dead, you know that. The Japanese fleet is retiring back to the Marianas. There has been no additional hostile contact of any kind between fleet units.

"We estimate about three divisions have been air-ferried to the Marianas. One on Saipan, most of two others on Guam. They have air facilities that we built and maintained . . ." His voice droned on, giving details that Ryan already knew, towards a conclusion that the National Security Advisor already feared.

Everything was too small in size. America's navy was half what it had been only ten years before. There remained the ability to sea-lift only one full division of troops capable of forced-entry assault. Only one, and that required moving all the Atlantic Fleet ships through Panama and recalling others from the oceans of the world as well. To land such troops required support, but the average U.S. Navy frigate had one 3-inch gun. Destroyers and cruisers had but two 5-inch guns each, a far cry from the assembled battleships and cruisers that had been necessary to take the Marianas back in 1944. Carriers, none immediately available, the closest two in the Indian Ocean, and those together did not match the Japanese air strength on Guam and Saipan today, Ryan thought, for the first time feeling anger over the affair. It had taken him long enough to get over the disbelief, Jack told himself.

"I don't think we can do it," SecDef concluded, and it was a judgment that no one in the room was prepared to dispute. They were too weary for recriminations. President Durling thanked everyone for the advice and headed upstairs for his bedroom, hoping to get a little sleep before facing the media in the morning.

He took the stairs instead of the elevator, thinking along the way as Secret Service agents at the top and bottom of the stairs watched. A shame for his presidency to end this way. Though he'd never really desired it, he'd done his best, and his best, only a few days earlier, hadn't been all that bad.

28

Transmissions

The United 747-400 touched down at Moscow's Scheremetyevo Airport thirty minutes early. The Atlantic jetstream was still blowing hard. A diplomatic courier was first off, helped that way by a flight attendant. He flashed his diplomatic passport at the end of the jetway, where a customs officer pointed him toward an American embassy official who shook his hand and led him down the concourse.

"Come with me. We even have an escort into town." The man smiled at the lunacy of the event.

"I don't know you," the courier said suspiciously, slowing down. Ordinarily his personality and his diplomatic bag were inviolable, but everything about this trip had been unusual, and his curiosity was thoroughly aroused.

"There's a laptop computer in your bag. There's yellow tape around it. It's the only thing you're carrying," said the chief of CIA Station Moscow, which was why the courier didn't know him. "The code word for your trip is STEAMROLLER."

"Fair enough." The courier nodded on their way down the terminal corridor. An embassy car was waiting — it was a stretched Lincoln, and looked to be the Ambassador's personal wheels. Next came a lead car which, once off the airport grounds, lit off a rotating light, the quicker to proceed downtown. On the whole it struck the courier as a mistake. Better to have used a Russian car for this. Which raised a couple of bigger questions. Why the hell had he been rousted at zero notice from his home to ferry a goddamned portable computer to Moscow? If everything was so goddamned secret, why were the Russians in on it? And if it were this goddamned important, why wait for a commercial flight? A State Department employee of long standing, he knew that it was foolish to question the logic of government operations. It was just that he was something of an idealist.

The rest of the trip went normally enough, right to the embassy, set in west-central Moscow, by the river. Inside the building, the two men went to the communications room, where the courier opened his bag, handed over its contents, and headed off for a shower and a bed, his questions never to be answered, he was sure.

The rest of the work had been done by Russians at remarkable speed. The phone line to Interfax led in turn to RVS, thence by military fiberoptic line all the way to Vladivostok, where another similar line, laid by Nippon Telephone & Telegraph, led to the Japanese home island of Honshu. The laptop had an internal modem, which was hooked to the newly installed line and switched on. Then it was time to wait, typically, though everything else had been done at the best possible speed.

It was one-thirty when Ryan got home to Peregrine Cliff. He'd dispensed with his GSA driver, instead letting Special Agent Robberton drive him, and he pointed the Secret Service agent toward a guest room before heading to his own bed. Not surprisingly, Cathy was still awake.

"Jack, what's going on?"

"Don't you have to work tomorrow?" he asked as

his first dodge. Coming home had been something of a mistake, if a necessary one. He needed fresh clothing more than anything else. A crisis was bad enough. For senior Administration officials to look frazzled and haggard was worse, and the press would surely pick up on it. Worst of all, it was visually obvious. The average Joe seeing the tape on network TV would know, and worried officers made for worried troopers, a lesson Ryan remembered from the Basic Officers' Course at Quantico. And so it was necessary to spend two hours in a car that would better have been spent on the sofa in his office.

Cathy rubbed her eyes in the darkness. "Nothing in the morning. I have to deliver a lecture tomorrow afternoon on how the new laser system works to some foreign visitors."

"From where?"

"Japan and Taiwan. We're licensing the calibration system we developed and — what's wrong?" she asked when her husband's head snapped around.

It's just paranoia, Ryan told himself. *Just a dumb coincidence, nothing more than that. Can't be anything else.* But he left the room without a word. Robberton was undressing when he got to the guest room, his holstered pistol hanging on the bedpost. The explanation took only a few seconds, and Robberton lifted a phone and dialed the Secret Service operations center two blocks from the White House. Ryan hadn't even known that his wife had a code name.

"SURGEON" — well, that was obvious, Ryan thought — "needs a friend tomorrow . . . at Johns Hopkins . . . oh, yeah, she'll be fine. See ya." Robberton hung up. "Good agent, Andrea Price. Single, willowy, brown hair, just joined the detail, eight years on the street. I worked with her dad when I was a new agent. Thanks for telling me that."

"See you around six-thirty, Paul."

"Yeah." Robberton lay right down, giving every

indication of someone who could go to sleep at will. A useful talent, Ryan thought.

"What was *that* all about?" Caroline Ryan demanded when her husband returned to the bedroom. Jack sat down on the bed to explain.

"Cathy, uh, tomorrow at Hopkins, there's going to be somebody with you. Her name is Andrea Price. She's with the Secret Service. And she'll be following you around."

"Why?"

"Cathy, we have several problems now. The Japanese have attacked the U.S. Navy, and have occupied a couple of islands. Now, you can't — "

"They did *what?*"

"You can't tell that to anyone," her husband went on. "Do you understand? You can't tell that to anybody, but since you are going to be with some Japanese people tomorrow, and because of who I am, the Secret Service wants to have somebody around you, just to make totally certain that things are okay." There would be more to it than that. The Secret Service was limited in manpower, and was not the least bit reticent about asking for assistance from local police forces. The Baltimore City Police, which maintained a high-profile presence at Johns Hopkins at all times — the hospital complex was not located in the best of areas — would probably assign a detective to back up Ms. Price.

"Jack, are we in any danger?" Cathy asked, remembering distant times and distant terrors, when she'd been pregnant with little Jack, when the Ulster Liberation Army had invaded their home. She remembered how pleased she'd been, and the shame she'd felt for it, when the last of them had been executed for multiple murder — ending, she'd thought, the worst and most fearful episode of her life.

For his part, Jack realized that it was just one more thing that they hadn't thought through. If America

661

were at war, he was the National Security Advisor to the President, and, yes, that made him a high-value target. And his wife. And his three children. Irrational? What about war was not?

"I don't think so," he replied after a moment's consideration, "but, well, we might want to — we might have some additional houseguests. I don't know. I'll have to ask."

"You said they attacked our navy?"

"Yes, honey, but you can't — "

"That means war, doesn't it?"

"I don't know, honey." He was so exhausted that he was asleep thirty seconds after hitting the pillow, and his last conscious thought was a recognition that he knew very little of what he needed to know in order to answer his wife's questions, or, for that matter, his own.

Nobody was sleeping in lower Manhattan, at least nobody whom others might think important. It occurred to more than one tired trading executive to observe that they were really earning their money now, but the truth of the matter was that they were accomplishing very little. Proud executives all, they looked around trading rooms filled with computers whose collective value was something only the accounting department knew, and whose current utility was approximately zero. The European markets would soon open. And do what? everyone wondered. There was ordinarily a nightwatch here whose job it was to trade European equities, to keep track of the Eurodollar market, the commodities and metals market, and all the economic activity that occurred on the eastern side of the Atlantic as well as the western. On most days it was like the prologue to a book, a precursor to the real action, interesting but not overly vital except, perhaps, for flavor, because the real substance was decided here in New York City.

But none of that was true today. There was no guessing what would happen this day. Today Europe was the only game in town, and all of the rules had been swept away. The people who manned the computers for this part of the watch cycle were often considered second-string by those who showed up at eight in the morning, which was both untrue and unfair, but in any community there had to be internal competition. This time, as they showed up at their accustomed and ungodly hour, the people who did this regularly noted the presence of front-row executives, and felt a combination of unease and exhilaration. Here was their chance to show their stuff. And here was their chance to screw up, live and in color.

It started exactly at four in the morning, Eastern Standard Time.

"Treasuries." The word was spoken simultaneously in twenty houses as European banks that still had enormous quantities of U.S. T-Bills as a hedge against the struggling European economies and their currencies suddenly felt quite uneasy about holding them. It seemed odd to some that the word had been slow to get out to their European cousins on Friday, but it was always that way, really, and the opening moves, everyone in New York thought, were actually rather cautious. It was soon clear why. There were plenty of "asks," but not many "bids." People were trying to sell Treasury Notes, but the interest in buying them was less enthusiastic. The result was prices that dropped just as fast as European confidence in the dollar.

"This is a steal, down three thirty-seconds already. What can we do?" That question, too, was asked in more than one place, and in each the answer was identical:

"Nothing," a word in every case spoken with disgust. There followed something else, usually a variant

663

of *Fucking Europeans,* depending on the linguistic peculiarities of the senior executives in question. So it had started again, a run on the dollar. And America's biggest weapon for fighting back was out of business because of a computer program everyone had trusted. The No Smoking signs in several of the trading rooms were ignored. They didn't have to worry about ashes in the equipment, did they? They really couldn't use the fucking computers for anything today. It was, one executive snorted to a colleague, a good day for some maintenance on the systems. Fortunately, not everybody felt that way.

"Okay, here's where it started, then?" George Winston asked. Mark Gant ran his finger down the screen display.

"Bank of China, Bank of Hong Kong, Imperial Cathay Bank. They bought these up about four months ago, hedging against the yen, and very successfully, it appears. So, Friday, they dumped them to cash in and bought up a truckload of Japanese treasuries. With the movement that happened here, it looks like they turned twenty-two percent on the overall transaction."

They were the first, Winston saw, and being first in the trend, they cashed in big. That sort of hit was of a magnitude to cause more than a few expensive dinners in Hong Kong, a city well suited to the indulgence.

"Look innocent to you?" he asked Gant with a stifled yawn.

The executive shrugged. He was tired, but having the boss back in the saddle gave everyone new energy. "Innocent, hell! It's a brilliant move. They saw something coming, I suppose, or they were just lucky."

Luck, Winston thought, *there was always that.* Luck was real, something any senior trader would admit over drinks, usually after two or three, the number required to get past the usual "brilliance" bullshit.

Sometimes it just felt right, and you did it because of that, and that's all there was to it. If you were lucky, it worked, and if not, you hedged.

"Keep going," he ordered.

"Well, then other banks started doing the same thing." The Columbus Group had some of the most sophisticated computer systems on the Street, able to track any individual issue and category of issues over time, and Gant was a quintessential computer jockey. They next watched the sell-off of other T-Bills by other Asian banks. Interestingly, the Japanese banks were slower off the mark than he would have expected. It was no disgrace to be a little behind Hong Kong. The Chinese were good at this thing, especially those trained by the Brits, who had largely invented modern central banking and were still pretty slick at it. But the Japs were faster than the Thais, Winston thought, or at least they should have been . . .

It was instinct again, just the gut-call of a guy who knew how to work the Street: "Check Japanese treasuries, Mark."

Gant typed in a command, and the rapid advance in the value of the yen was obvious — so much so, in fact, that they hardly needed to track it via computer. "Is this what you want?"

Winston leaned down, looking at the screen. "Show me what Bank of China did when they cashed in."

"Well, they sold off to the Eurodollar market and bought yen. I mean, it's the obvious play — "

"But look who they bought the yen from," Winston suggested.

"And what they paid for it . . ." Gant turned his head and looked at his boss.

"You know why I was always honest here, Mark? You know why I never screwed around, not ever, not even once, not even when I had an in-the-bank sure thing?" George asked. There was more than one reason, of course, but why confuse the issue? He pressed his fingertip to the screen, actually leaving a fingerprint on the glass. He almost laughed at the symbolism. "That's why."

"That doesn't really mean anything. The Japanese knew they could jack it up some and — " Gant didn't quite get it yet, Winston saw. He needed to hear it in his own terms.

"Find the trend, Mark. Find the trend there." *Well, son of a bitch,* he told himself, heading to the men's room. *The trend is my friend.* Then he thought of something else:

Fuck with my financial market, will you?

It wasn't much consolation. He had given his business over to a predator, Winston realized, and the damage was well and truly done. His investors had trusted him and he had betrayed that trust. Washing his hands, he looked up into the mirror over the sink, seeing the eyes of a man who'd left his post, deserted his people.

But you're back now, by God, and there's a ton of work to be done.

Pasadena had finally sailed, more from embarrassment than anything else, Jones thought. He'd listened to Bart Mancuso's phone conversation with CINC-PAC, explaining that the submarine was loaded with weapons and so filled up with food that her passageways were completely covered with cartons of canned goods, enough for sixty days or more at sea. That was a sign of the not-so-good old days, Jones thought, remembering what the long deployments had been like, and so USS *Pasadena*, warship of the U.S. Navy, was now at sea, heading west at about twenty knots, using a quiet screw, not a speed screw, he thought. Otherwise he might have gotten a hit on her. The submarine had just passed within fifteen nautical miles of a SOSUS emplacement, one of the new ones that could hear the fetal heartbeat of an unborn whale calf. *Pasadena* didn't have orders yet, but she'd be in the right place if and when they came, with her crew running constant drills, leaning down, getting that at-sea feeling that came to you when you needed it. That was something.

Part of him dearly wished to be there, but that was part of his past now.

"I don't see nothin', sir." Jones blinked and looked back at the fan-fold page he'd selected.

"Well, you have to look for other things," Jones said. Only a Marine with a loaded pistol would get him out of SOSUS now. He'd made that clear to Admiral Mancuso, who had in turn made it clear to others. There had been a brief discussion of getting Jones a special commission, perhaps to Commander's rank, but Ron had quashed that idea himself. He'd left the Navy a Sonarman 1/c, and that was as good a rank as he'd ever wanted. Besides, it would not have looked good to the chiefs who really ran this place and had already accepted him as one of their own.

Oceanographic Technician 2/c Mike Boomer had been assigned to Jones as personal assistant. The kid had the makings of a good student, Dr. Jones thought, even if he'd left service in P-3s because of chronic airsickness.

"All these guys are using Prairie-Masker systems when they snort. It sounds like rain on the surface, remember? Rain on the surface is on the thousand-hertz line. So, we look for rain" — Jones slid a weather photo on the table — "where there ain't no rain. Then we look for sixty-hertz hits, little ones, short ones, brief ones, things you might otherwise ignore, that happen to be where the rain is. They use sixty-hertz generators and motors, right? Then we look for transients, just little dots that look like background noise, that are also where the rain is. Like this." He marked the sheet with a red pen, then looked to the station's command master chief, who was leaning over the other side of the table like a curious god.

"I heard stories about you when I was working the Ref-Tra at Dam Neck. I thought they were sea stories."

"Got a smoke?" the only civilian in the room asked. The master chief handed one over. The antismoking signs were gone and the ashtrays were out. SOSUS was at war, and perhaps the rest of PacFlt would soon catch up. *Jesus, I'm home*, Jones told himself. "Well, you know the difference between a sea story and a fairy tale."

"What's that, sir?" Boomer asked.

"A fairy tale starts, 'Once upon a time,' " Jones said with a smile, marking another 60hz hit on the sheet.

"And a sea story starts, 'No shit,' " the master chief concluded the joke. Except this little fucker really was that good. "I think you have enough to run a plot, Dr. Jones."

"I think we have a track on an SSK, Master Chief."

"Shame we can't prosecute."

Ron nodded slowly. "Yeah, me, too, but now we know we can get hits on the guys. It's still going to be a mother for P-3s to localize them. They're good boats, and that's a fact." They couldn't get too carried away. All SOSUS did was to generate lines of bearing. If more than one hydrophone set got a hit on the same sound source, you could rapidly triangulate bearings into locations, but those locations were circles, not points, and the circles were as much as twenty miles across. It was just physics, neither friend nor enemy. The sounds that most easily traveled long distances were of the lower frequencies, and for any sort of wave, only the higher frequencies gave the best resolution.

"We know where to look the next time he snorts, too. Anyway, you can call Fleet Operations and tell them there's nobody close to the carriers. Here, here,

here, surface groups." He made marks on the paper. "Also heading west at good speed, and not being real covert about it. All target-track bearings are opening. It's a complete disengagement. They're not looking for any more trouble."

"Maybe that's good."

Jones crushed out the cigarette. "Yeah, Master Chief, maybe it is, if the flags get their shit together."

The funny part was that things had actually calmed down. Morning TV coverage of the Wall Street crash was clinically precise, and the analysis exquisite, probably better than Americans were getting at home, Clark thought, what with all the economics professors doing the play-by-play, along with a senior banker for color commentary. Perhaps, a newspaper editorialized, America will rethink her stance vis-à-vis Japan. Was it not clear that the two countries genuinely needed each other, especially now, and that a strong Japan served American interests as well as local ones? Prime Minister Goto was quoted in a conciliatory way, though not in front of a camera, in language that was for him decidedly unusual and widely covered for that reason.

"Fucking Twilight Zone," Chavez observed in a quiet moment, breaking language cover because he just had to. What the hell, he thought, they were under Russian operational control now. What rules did matter now?

"*Russkiy*," his senior replied tolerantly.

"*Da, tovarisch,*" was the grumbled reply. "Do you have any idea what's going on. Is it a war or not?"

"The rules sure are funny," Clark said, in English, he realized. *It's getting to me, too.*

There were other *gaijin* back on the street, most of them apparently Americans, and the looks they were getting were back to the ordinary suspicion and curiosity, the current hostility level down somewhat from the previous week.

"So what do we do?"

"We try the Interfax number our friend gave us." Clark had his report all typed up. It was the only thing he knew to do, except for keeping his contacts active and fishing for information. Surely Washington knew what he had to tell them, he thought, going back into the hotel. The clerk smiled and bowed, a little more politely this time, as they headed to the elevator. Two minutes later they were in the room. Clark took the laptop from its carry-case, inserted the phone plug in the back, and switched it on. Another minute, and the internal modem dialed the number he'd gotten over breakfast, linking to a line across the Sea of Japan to the Siberian mainland, thence to Moscow, he supposed. He heard the electronic trilling of a ringing phone and waited for linkup.

The station chief had gotten over the cringing associated with having a Russian intelligence officer in the embassy communications room, but he hadn't quite gotten to the whimsy stage yet. The noise from the computer startled him.

"Very clever technique," the visitor said.

"We try."

Anyone who had ever used a modem would recognize the sound, the rasp of running water, or perhaps a floor-polishing brush, just a digital hiss, really, of two electronic units attempting to synchronize themselves so that data could be exchanged. Sometimes it took but a few seconds, sometimes as many as five or even ten. In fact, it only took one second or so with these units, and the remaining hiss was actually the random-appearing digital code of 19,200 characters of information crossing the fiberoptic line per second — first in one direction, then the other. When the real transmission was concluded, formal lockup was achieved, and the guy at the other end sent his twenty column-inches for the day. Just to be on the safe side, the Russians would make sure that the report would be carried in two papers the next day, on page 3 in both cases. No sense in being too obvious.

Then came the hard part for the CIA station chief. On command, he printed two copies of the same report, one of which went to the RVS officer. Was Mary Pat going through change-of-life or something?

"His Russian is very literary, even classical. Who taught him my language?"

"I honestly don't know," the station chief lied, successfully as it turned out. The hell of it was, the Russian was right. That occasioned a frown.

"Want me to help with the translation?"

Shit. He smiled. "Sure, why not?"

"Ryan." A whole five hours of sleep, Jack grumped, lifting the secure carphone. Well, at least he wasn't doing the driving.

"Mary Pat here. We have something. It'll be on your desk when you get there."

"How good?"

"It's a start," the DDO said. She was very economical in her use of words. Nobody really trusted radiophones, secure or not.

"Hello, Dr. Ryan. I'm Andrea Price." The agent was already dressed in a lab coat, complete with picture-pass clipped to the lapel, which she held up. "My uncle is a doctor, GP in Wisconsin. I think he'd like this." She smiled.

"Do I have anything to worry about?"

"I really don't think so," Agent Price said, still smiling. Protectees didn't like to see worried security personnel, she knew.

"What about my children?"

671

"There are two agents outside their school, and one more is in the house across from the day-care center for your little one," the agent explained. "Please don't worry. They pay us to be paranoid, and we're almost always wrong, but it's like in your business. You always want to be wrong on the safe side, right?"

"And my visitors?" Cathy asked.

"Can I make a suggestion?"

"Yes."

"Get them all Hopkins lab coats, souvenirs, like. I'll eyeball them all when they change." That was pretty clever, Cathy Ryan thought.

"You're carrying a gun?"

"Always," Andrea Price confirmed. "But I've never had to use it, never even took it out for an arrest. Just think of me as a fly on the wall," she said.

More like a falcon, Professor Ryan thought, but at least a tame one.

"How are we supposed to do that, John?" Chavez asked in English. The shower was running. Ding was sitting on the floor, and John on the toilet.

"Well, we seen 'em already, haven't we?" the senior officer pointed out.

"Yeah, in the fuckin' factory!"

"Well, we just have to find out where they went." On the face of it, the statement was reasonable enough. They just had to determine how many and where, and oh, by the way, whether or not there were really nukes riding on the nose. No big deal. All they knew was that they were SS-19–type launchers, the new improved version thereof, and that they'd left the factory by rail. Of course, the country had over twenty-eight thousand kilometers of rail lines. It would have to wait. Intelligence officers often worked banker's hours, and this was one of those cases. Clark decided to get into the shower to clean off before heading for bed. He didn't know what to do, yet, or how to go about it, but worrying himself to death would not improve his chances, and he'd long since learned that he worked better with a full eight hours under his belt, and occasionally had a creative thought while showering. Sooner or later Ding might learn those tricks as well, he thought, seeing the expression on the kid's face.

"Hi, Betsy," Jack said to the lady waiting in his office's anteroom. "You're up early. And who are you?"

"Chris Scott. Betsy and I work together."

Jack waved them into his office, first checking his fax machine to see if Mary Pat had transmitted the information from Clark and Chavez, and, seeing it there, decided it could wait. He knew Betsy Fleming from his CIA days as a self-taught expert on strategic weapons. He supposed Chris Scott was one of the kids recruited from some university with a degree in what Betsy had learned the hard way. At least the younger one was polite about it, saying that he worked *with* Betsy. So had Ryan, once, years ago, while concerned with arms-control negotiations. "Okay, what do we have?"

"Here's what they call the H-11 space booster." Scott opened his case and pulled out some photos. Good ones, Ryan saw at once, made with real film at close range, not the electronic sort shot through a hole in someone's pocket. It wasn't hard to tell the difference, and Ryan immediately recognized an old friend he'd thought dead and decently buried less than a week before.

"Sure as hell, the SS-19. A lot prettier this way, too." Another photo showed a string of them on the assembly building's floor. Jack counted them and grimaced. "What else do I need to know?"

"Here," Betsy said. "Check out the business end."

"Looks normal," Ryan observed.

"That's the point. The nose assembly *is* normal," Scott pointed out. "Normal for supporting a warhead bus, not for a commo-sat payload. We wrote that up a while back, but nobody paid any attention to it," the technical analyst added. "The rest of the bird's been fully re-engineered. We have estimates for the performance enhancements."

"Short version?"

"Six or seven MIRVs each and a range of just over ten thousand kilometers," Mrs. Fleming replied. "Worst-case, but realistic."

"That's a lot. Has the missile been certified, tested? Have they tested a bus that we know of?" the National Security Advisor asked.

"No data. We have partial stuff on flight tests of the launcher from surveillance in the Pacific, stuff AMBER BALL caught, but it's equivocal on several issues," Scott told him.

"Total birds turned out?"

"Twenty-five we know about. Of those, three have been used up in flight tests, and two are at their launch facility being mated up with orbital payloads. That leaves twenty."

"What payloads?" Ryan asked almost on a whim.

"The NASA guys think they are survey satellites. Real-time-capable photo-sats. So probably they are," Betsy said darkly.

"And so probably they've decided to enter the overhead-intelligence business. Well, that makes sense, doesn't it?" Ryan made a couple of notes. "Okay, the downside, worst-case threat is twenty launchers with seven MIRVs each, for a total of one hundred forty?"

"Correct, Dr. Ryan." Both were professional enough that they didn't editorialize on how bad that threat was. Japan had the theoretical capacity to cut the hearts out of one hundred forty American cities.

674

America could quickly reconstitute the ability to turn their Home Islands into smoke and fire as well, but that wasn't a hell of a lot of consolation, was it? Forty-plus years of MAD, thought to be ended less than seven days before, and now it was back again, Ryan thought. Wasn't that just wonderful?

"Do you know anything about the assets that produced these photos?"

"Jack," Betsy said in her normal June Cleaver voice, "you know I never ask. But whoever it was, was overt. You can tell that from the photos. These weren't done with a Minox. Somebody covered as a reporter, I bet. Don't worry. I won't tell." Her usual impish smile. She had been around long enough that she knew all the tricks.

"They're obviously high-quality photos," Chris Scott went on, wondering how the hell Betsy had the clout to call this man by his first name. "Slow, small-grain film, like what a reporter uses. They let NASA guys into the factory, too. They wanted us to know."

"Sure as hell." Mrs. Fleming nodded agreement.

And the Russians, Ryan reminded himself. *Why them?* "Anything else?"

"Yeah, this." Scott handed over two more photos. It showed a pair of modified railroad flatcars. One had a crane on it. The other showed the hardpoints for installing another. "They evidently transport by rail instead of truck. I had a guy look at the railcar. It's apparently standard gauge."

"What do you mean?" Ryan asked.

"The width between the rails. Standard gauge is what we use and most of the rest of the world. Most of the railways in Japan are narrow gauge. Funny they didn't copy the road transporters the Russians made for the beast," Scott said. "Maybe their roads are too narrow or maybe they just prefer to do it this way. There's a standard-gauge line from here to Yoshinobu. I was a little surprised by the rigging gear. The cradles in the railcar seem to roughly match the dimensions of the transport cocoon that the Russians designed for the beast. So they copied everything but the transporter. That's all we have, sir."

"Where are you off to next?"

"We're huddling across the river with the guys at NRO," Chris Scott answered.

"Good," Ryan said. He pointed at both of them. "You tell them this one's hotter 'n' hell. I want these things found and found yesterday."

"You know they'll try, Jack. And they may have done us a favor by rolling these things out on rails," Betsy Fleming said as she stood.

Jack organized the photos and asked for another complete set before he dismissed his visitors. Then he checked his watch and called Moscow. Ryan supposed that Sergey was working long hours, too.

"Why the hell," he began, "did you sell them the SS-19 design?"

The reply was harsh. Perhaps Golovko was sleep-deprived as well. "For money, of course. The same reason you sold them Aegis, the F-15, and all — "

Ryan grimaced, mainly at the justice in the retort. "Thanks, pal. I guess I deserved that. We estimate they have twenty available."

"That would be about right, but we haven't had people visit their factory yet."

"We have," Ryan told him. "Want some pictures?"

"Of course, Ivan Emmetovich."

"They'll be on your desk tomorrow," Jack promised. "I have our estimate. I'd like to hear what your people think." He paused and then went on. "We are worst-casing at seven RVs per missile, for a total of one-forty."

"Enough for both of us," Golovko observed. "Remember when we first met, negotiating to remove those fucking things?" He heard Ryan's snort over the phone. He didn't hear what his colleague was thinking.

The first time I was close to those things, aboard your missile submarine, Red October, *yeah, I remember that. I remember feeling my skin crawl like I was in the presence of Lucifer himself.* He'd never had the least bit of affection for ballistic weapons. Oh, sure, maybe they'd kept the peace for forty years, maybe the thought of them had deterred their owners from the intemperate thoughts that had plagued chiefs of state for all of human history. Or just as likely, mankind had just been lucky, for once.

"Jack, this is getting rather serious," Golovko said. "By the way, our officer met with your officers. He reports favorably on them — and thank you, by the way, for the copy of their report. It included data we did not have. Not vitally important, but interesting even so. So tell me, do they know to seek out these rockets?"

"The order went out," Ryan assured him.

"To my people as well, Ivan Emmetovich. We will find them, never fear," Golovko felt the need to add. He had to be thinking the same thing: the only reason the missiles had not been used was that both sides had possessed them, because it was like threatening a mirror. That was no longer true, was it? And so came Ryan's question:

"And then what?" he asked darkly. "What do we do then?"

"Do you not say in your language, 'One thing at a time'?"

Isn't this just great? Now I have a friggin' Russian *trying to cheer me up!*

"Thank you, Sergey Nikolay'ch. Perhaps I deserved that as well."

"So why did we sell Citibank?" George Winston asked.

677

"Well, he said to look out for banks that were vulnerable to currency fluctuations," Gant replied. "He was right. We got out just in time. Look, see for yourself." The trader typed another instruction into his terminal and was rewarded with a graphic depiction of what First National City Bank stock had done on Friday, and sure enough it had dropped off the table in one big hurry, largely because Columbus, which had purchased the issue in large quantities over the preceding five weeks, had held quite a bit, and in selling it had shaken faith in the stock badly. "Anyway, that set off an alarm in our program — "

"Mark, Citibank is one of the benchmark stocks in the model, isn't it?" Winston asked calmly. There was nothing to be gained by leaning on Mark too hard.

"Oh." His eyes opened a little wider. "Well, yes, it is, isn't it?"

That was when a very bright light blinked on in Winston's mind. It was not widely known how the "expert systems" kept track of the market. They worked in several interactive ways, monitoring both the market as a whole and also modeling benchmark stocks more closely, as general indicators of developing market trends. Those were stocks which over time had tracked closely with what everything else was doing, with a bias toward general stability, those that both dropped and rose more slowly than more speculative issues, steady performers. There were two reasons for it, and one glaring mistake. The reasons were that while the market fluctuated every day, even in the most favorable of circumstances, the idea was to not only bag an occasional killing on a high-flyer, but also to hedge your money on safe stocks — not that any stock was truly safe, as Friday had proven — when everything else became unsettled. For those reasons, the benchmark stocks were those that over time had provided safe havens. The mistake was a common one: dice have no memory. Those benchmark stocks were such because the companies they represented had historically good management. Management could change over time. So it was not the stocks that were stable. It was the management, and that was only something from the past, whose currency had to be examined periodically — despite which, those stocks were used to grade trends. And a trend was a trend only *because people thought it was,* and in thinking so, they made it so. Winston had regarded benchmark stocks only as predictors of what the *people* in the market would do, and for him trends were always psychological, predictors of how people would follow an artificial model, not the performance of the model itself. Gant, he realized, didn't quite see it that way, like so many of the technical traders.

And in selling off Citibank, Columbus had activated a little alarm in its own computer-trading system. And even someone as bright as Mark had forgotten that Citibank was part of the goddamned model!

"Show me other bank stocks," Winston ordered.

"Well, Chemical went next," Gant told, him, pulling up that track as well. "Then Manny-Hanny, and then others, too. Anyway, we saw it coming, and we jumped into metals and the gold stocks. You know, when the dust settles, it's going to turn out that we did okay. Not great, but pretty okay," Gant said, calling up his executive program for overall transactions, wanting to show something he'd done right. "I took the money from a quick flip on Silicon Alchemy and laid this put on GM and — "

Winston patted him on the shoulder. "Save that for later, Mark. I can see it was a good play."

"Anyway, we were ahead of the trends all the way. Yeah, we got a little hurt when the calls came in and we had to dump a lot of solid things, but that happened to everybody — "

"You don't see it, do you?"

679

"See what, George?"

"We *were* the trend."

Mark Gant blinked his eyes, and Winston could tell.

He didn't see it.

29

Written Records

The presentation went very well, and at the end of it Cathy Ryan was handed an exquisitely wrapped box by the Professor of Ophthalmic Surgery from Chiba University, who led the Japanese delegation. Unwrapping it, she found a scarf of watered blue silk, embroidered with gold thread. It looked to be more than a hundred years old.

"The blue goes so well with your eyes, Professor Ryan," her colleague said with a smile of genuine admiration. "I fear it is not a sufficiently valuable gift for what I have learned from you today. I have hundreds of diabetic patients at my hospital. With this technique we can hope to restore sight for most of them. A magnificent breakthrough, Professor." He bowed, formally and with clear respect.

"Well, the lasers come from your country," Cathy replied. She wasn't sure what emotion she was supposed to have. The gift was stunning. The man was as sincere as he could be, and his country might be at war with hers. But why wasn't it on the news? If there were a war, why was this foreigner not under arrest? Was she supposed to be gracious to him as a learned colleague or hostile to him as an enemy? What the hell was going on? She looked over at Andrea Price, who just leaned against the back wall and

681

smiled, her arms crossed across her chest.

"And you have taught us how to use them more efficiently. A stunning piece of applied research." The Japanese professor turned to the others and raised his hands. The assembled multitude applauded, and a blushing Caroline Ryan started thinking that she just might get the Lasker statuette for her mantelpiece after all. Everyone shook her hand before leaving for the bus that waited to take them back to the Stouffer's on Pratt Street.

"Can I see it?" Special Agent Price asked after all were gone and the door safely closed. Cathy handed the scarf over. "Lovely. You'll have to buy a new dress to go with it."

"So there never was anything to worry about," Dr. Ryan observed. Interestingly, once she'd gotten fifteen seconds into her lecture, she'd forgotten about it anyway. Wasn't that interesting?

"No, like I told you, I didn't expect anything." Price handed the scarf back, not without some reluctance. The little professor was right, she thought. It did go nicely with her eyes. "Jack Ryan's wife" was all she'd heard, and then some. "How long have you been doing this?"

"Retinal surgery?" Cathy closed her notebook. "I started off working the front end of the eye, right up to the time little Jack was born. Then I had an idea about how the retina is attached naturally and how we might reattach bad ones. Then we started looking at how to fix blood vessels. Bernie let me run with it, and I got a research grant from NIH to play with, and one thing led to another . . ."

"And now you're the best in the world at this," Price concluded the story.

"Until somebody with better hands comes along and learns how to do it, yes." Cathy smiled. "I suppose I am, for a few more months, anyway."

"So how's the champ?" Bernie Katz asked, entering

the room and seeing Price for the first time. The pass on her coat puzzled him. "Do I know you?"

"Andrea Price." The agent gave Katz a quick and thorough visual check before shaking hands. He actually found it flattering until she added, "Secret Service."

"Where were the cops like you when I was a kid?" the surgeon asked gallantly.

"Bernie was one of my first mentors here. He's department chairman now," Cathy explained.

"About to be overtaken in prestige by my colleague. I come bearing good news. I have a spy on the Lasker Committee. You're in the finals, Cathy."

"What's a Lasker?" Price asked.

"There's one step up from a Lasker Prize," Bernie told her. "You have to go to Stockholm to collect it."

"Bernie, I'll never have one of those. A Lasker is hard enough."

"So keep researching, girl!" Katz hugged her and left.

I want it, I want it, I want it! Cathy told herself silently. She didn't have to give voice to the words. It was plain for Special Agent Price to see. Damn, didn't this beat guarding politicians?

"Can I watch one of your procedures?"

"If you want. Anyway, come on." Cathy led her back to her office, not minding her at all now. On the way they walked through the clinic, then one of the labs. In the middle of a corridor, Dr. Ryan stopped dead in her tracks, reached into her pocket, and pulled out a small notebook.

"Did I miss something?" Price asked. She knew she was talking too much, but it took time to learn the habits of your protectees. She also read Cathy Ryan as the type who didn't like being protected, and so needed to be made comfortable about it.

"You'll have to get used to me," Professor Ryan

683

said, smiling as she scribbled a few notes. "Whenever I have an idea, I write it down right away."

"Don't trust your memory?"

"Never. You can't trust your memory with things that affect live patients. One of the first things they teach you in medical school." Cathy shook her head as she finished up. "Not in this business. Too many opportunities to screw up. If you don't write it down, then it never happened."

That sounded like a good lesson to remember, Andrea Price told herself, following her principal down the corridor. The code name, SURGEON, was perfect for her. Precise, smart, thorough. She might even have made a good agent except for her evident discomfort around guns.

It was already a regular routine, and in many ways that was not new. For a generation, the Japanese Air Self-Defense Force had responded to Russian fighter activity out of the forward base at Dolinsk Sokol — at first in cooperation with the USAF — and one of the regular tracks taken by the Soviet Air Force had earned the name "Tokyo Express," probably an unknowing reference to a term invented in 1942 by the United States Marines on Guadalcanal.

For security reasons the E-767s were based with the 6th Air Wing at Komatsu, near Tokyo, but the two F-15Js that operated under the control of the E-767 now aloft over the town of Nemuro at the northeast tip of the island of Hokkaido were actually based on the Home Island at Chitose. These were a hundred miles offshore, and each carried eight missiles, four each of heat-seekers and radar-homers. All were warshots now, requiring only a target.

It was after midnight, local time. The pilots were well rested and alert, comfortably strapped into their ejection seats, their sharp eyes scanning the darkness while fingers made delicate course-corrections on the sticks. Their own targeting radars were switched off, and though their aircraft still flashed with anticollision strobe lights, those were easily switched off should the necessity arise, making them visually nonexistent.

"Eagle One-Five," the digital radio told the element leader, "check out commercial traffic fifty kilometers zero-three-five your position, course two-one-five, angels three-six."

"Roger, Kami," the pilot replied on keying his radio. Kami, the call sign for the orbiting surveillance aircraft, was a word with many meanings, most of them supernatural like "soul" or "spirit." And so they had rapidly become the modern manifestation of the spirits guarding their country, with the F-15Js as the strong arms that gave power to the will of those spirits. On command, the two fighters came right, climbing on a shallow, fuel-efficient slope for five minutes until they were at thirty-seven thousand feet, cruising outbound from their country at five hundred knots, their radars still off, but now they received a digital feed from the Kami that appeared on their own sets, one more of the new innovations and something the Americans didn't have. The element leader alternated his eyes up and down. A pity, he thought, that the hand-off display didn't integrate with his head-up display. Maybe the next modification would do that.

"There," he said over his low-power radio.

"I have it," his wingman acknowledged.

Both fighters turned to the left now, descending slowly behind what appeared to be an Air Canada 767-ER. Yes, the floodlit tail showed the maple-leaf logo of that airline. Probably the regular transpolar flight out of Toronto International into Narita. The timing was about right. They approached from almost directly astern — not quite exactly, lest an overly quick overtake result in a ramming — and the buffet told them that they were in the wake turbulence of a "heavy," a wide-bodied commercial transport. The flight leader closed until he could see the line of cabin lights, and the huge engine under each wing, and the stubby nose of the Boeing product. He keyed his radio again.

"Kami, Eagle One-Five."

"Eagle."

"Positive identification, Air Canada Seven-Six-Seven Echo Romeo, inbound at indicated course and speed." Interestingly, the drill for the BARCAP — Barrier Combat Air Patrol — was to use English. That was the international language of aviation. All their pilots spoke it, and it worked better for important communications.

"Roger." And on further command, the fighters broke off to their programmed patrol area. The Canadian pilot of the airliner would never know that two armed fighters had closed to within three hundred meters of his aircraft — but then he had no reason to expect that any would, because the world was at peace, at least this part of it.

For their part, the fighter-drivers accepted their new duties phlegmatically along with the modification in their daily patterns of existence. For the indefinite future no less than two fighters would hold this patrol station, with two more back at Chitose at plus-five alert, and another four at plus-thirty. Their wing commander was pressing for permission to increase his alert-status further still, for despite what Tokyo said, their nation *was* at war, and that was what he'd told his people. The Americans were formidable adversaries, he'd said in his first lecture to his pilots and senior ground-staff. Clever ones, devious, and dangerously aggressive. Worst of all, at their best they were utterly unpredictable, the reverse of the Japanese who, he'd gone on, tended to be highly predictable. Perhaps that was why he'd been posted to this command, the pilots thought. If things went further, the first contact with hostile American forces would be here. He wanted to be ready for it, despite the huge price of money, fuel, and fatigue that attended it. The pilots thoroughly approved. War was a serious business, and though new to it, they didn't shrink from its responsibilities.

The time factor would soon become his greatest frustration, Ryan thought. Tokyo was fourteen hours ahead of Washington. It was dark there now, and the next day, and whatever clever idea he might come up with would have to wait hours until implementation. The same was true in the IO, but at least he had direct comms to Admiral Dubro's battle force. Getting word to Clark and Chavez meant going via Moscow, and then farther either by contact via RVS officer in Tokyo — not something to be done too frequently — or by reverse-modem message whenever Clark lit up his computer for a dispatch to the Interfax News Agency. There would necessarily be a time lag in anything he did, and that could get people killed.

It was about information. It always was, always would be. The real trick was in finding out what was going on. What was the other side doing? What were they thinking?

What is it that they want to accomplish? he asked himself.

War was always about economics, one of the few things that Marx had gotten right. It was just greed, really, as he'd told the President, an armed robbery writ large. At the nation-state level, the terms were couched in terms such as Manifest Destiny or *Lebensraum* or other political slogans to grab the attention and ardor of the masses, but that's what it came down to: *They have it. We want it. Let's get it.*

And yet the Mariana Islands weren't worth it. They were simply not worth the political or economic cost. This affair would ipso facto cost Japan her most lucrative trading partner. There could be no recovery from this, not for years. The market positions so carefully established and exploited since the 1960s would be obliterated by something politely termed public resentment but far more deeply felt than that. For what possible reason could a country so married to the idea of business turn its back on practical considerations?

But war is never rational, Jack. You told the President that yourself.

"So tell me, what the hell are they thinking?" he commanded, instantly regretting the profanity.

They were in a basement conference room. For the first meeting of the working group, Scott Adler was absent, off with Secretary Hanson. There were two National Intelligence Officers, and four people from State, and they looked as puzzled and bemused as he did, Ryan thought. Wasn't that just great. For several seconds nothing happened. Hardly unexpected, Jack thought. It was always a matter of clinical interest for him when he asked for real opinions from a group of bureaucrats: who would say what?

"They're mad and they're scared." It was Chris Cook, one of the commercial guys from State. He'd done two tours at the embassy in Tokyo, spoke the language passably well, and had run point on several rounds of the trade negotiations, always taking back seat to senior men and women, but usually the guy who did the real work. That was how things were, and Jack remembered resenting that others sometimes got the credit for his ideas. He nodded at the comment, seeing that the others around the table did the same, grateful that someone else had taken the initiative.

"I know why they're mad. Tell me why they're scared."

"Well, hell, they still have the Russians close by, and the Chinese, both still major powers, but we've withdrawn from the Western Pacific, right? In their mind, it leaves them high and dry — and now it looks to them like we've turned on them. That makes us potential enemies, too, doesn't it? Where does that leave them? What real friends do they have?"

"Why take the Marianas?" Jack asked, reminding himself that Japan had not *been* attacked by those countries in historically recent times, but had done so herself to all of them. Cook had made a perhaps unintended point. How did Japan respond to outside threats? By attacking first.

"It gives them defensive depth, bases outside their home islands."

Okay, that makes sense, Jack thought. Satellite photos less than an hour old hung on the wall. There were fighters now on the airstrips at Saipan and Guam, along with E-2C Hawkeye airborne-early-warning birds of the same type that operated off American carriers. That created a defensive barrier that extended twelve hundred miles almost due south from Tokyo. It could be seen as a formidable wall against American attacks, and was in essence a reduced version of Japanese grand strategy in the Second World War. Again Cook had made a sound observation.

"But are we really a threat to them?" he asked.

"We certainly are now," Cook replied.

"Because they forced us to be," one of the NIOs snarled, entering the discussion. Cook leaned across the table at him.

"Why do people start wars? Because they're afraid of something! For Christ's sake, they've gone through more governments in the last five years than the Italians. The country is politically unstable. They have real economic problems. Until recently their currency's been in trouble. Their stock market's gone down the tubes because of our trade legislation, and we've faced them with financial ruin, and you ask *why* they got a little paranoid? If something like this happened to us, what the hell would we do?" the Deputy Assistant Secretary of State demanded, rather cowing the National Intelligence Officer, Ryan saw.

Good, he thought. A lively discussion was usually helpful, as the hottest fire made the strongest steel.

"My sympathy for the other side is mitigated by the fact that they have invaded U.S. territory and violated the human rights of American citizens." The reply to Cook's tirade struck Ryan as somewhat arch. The response was that of a lead hound on the scent of a crippled fox, able to play with the quarry instead of the other way around for a change. Always a good feeling.

"And we've already put a couple hundred thousand of their citizens out of work. What about their rights?"

"Fuck their rights! Whose side are you on, Cook?"

The DASS just leaned back into his chair and smiled as he slid the knife in. "I thought I was supposed to tell everyone what they're thinking. Isn't that what we're here for? What they're thinking is that we've jerked them around, bashed them, belittled them, and generally let them know that we tolerate them through sufferance and not respect since before I was born. We've never dealt with them as equals, and they think that they deserve better from us, and they don't like it. And you know," Cook went on, "I don't blame them for feeling that way. Okay, so now they've lashed out. That's wrong, and I deplore it, but we need to recognize that they tried to do it in as nonlethal a way as possible, consistent with their strategic goals. That's something we need to consider here, isn't it?"

"The Ambassador says his country is willing to let it stop here," Ryan told them, noting the look in Cook's eyes. Clearly he'd been thinking about the situation, and that was good. "Are they serious?"

He'd asked another tough question again, something that the people around the table didn't much like. Tough questions required definitive answers, and such answers could often be wrong. It was toughest for the NIOs. The National Intelligence Officers were senior people from CIA, DIA, or NSA, usually. One of them was always with the President to give him an opinion in the event of a rapidly evolving crisis. They were supposed to be experts in their fields, and they were, as, for that matter, was Ryan, who'd been an NIO himself. But there was a problem with such people. An NIO was generally a serious, tough-minded man or woman. They didn't fear death, but they *did* fear being wrong on a hard call. For that reason, even putting a gun to one's head didn't guarantee an unequivocal answer to a tough question. He looked from face to face, seeing that Cook did the same, with contempt on his face.

"Yes, sir, I think it likely that they are. It's also likely that they will offer us something back. They know that they have to let us save face here, too. We can count on it, and that will work in our favor if we choose to negotiate with them."

"Would you recommend that?"

A smile and a nod. "It never hurts you to talk with somebody, no matter what the situation is, does it? I'm a State Department puke, remember? I have to recommend that. I don't know the military side. I don't know if we can contest this thing or not. I presume we can, and that they know we can, and that they know they're gambling, and that they're even more scared than we are. We can use that in our favor."

"What can we press for?" Ryan asked, chewing on his pen.

"Status quo ante," Cook replied at once. "Complete withdrawal from the Marianas, restoration of the islands and their citizens to U.S. rule, reparations to the families of the people killed, punishment of those responsible for their deaths." Even the NIOs nodded at that, Ryan saw. He was already starting to like Cook. He spoke his mind, and what he said had a logic to it.

"What will we get?" Again the answer was plain and simple.

"Less." *Where the hell has Scott Adler been hiding this guy?* Ryan thought. *He speaks my language.* "They have to give us something, but they won't give it all back."

"And if we press?" the National Security Advisor asked.

"If we want it all back, then we may have to fight for it," Cook said. "If you want my opinion, that's dangerous." Ryan excused the facile conclusion. He was, after all, a State Department puke, and part of that culture.

"Will the Ambassador have the clout to negotiate?"

"I think so, yes," Cook said after a moment. "He has a good staff, he's a very senior professional diplomat. He knows Washington and he knows how to play in the bigs. That's why they sent him here."

Jaw, jaw is better than war, war. Jack remembered the words of Winston Churchill. And that was true, especially if the former did not entirely preclude the threat of the latter.

"Okay," Ryan said. "I have some other things that need doing. You guys stay here. I want a position paper. I want options. I want multiple opening positions for both sides. I want end-game scenarios. I want likely responses on their part to *theoretical* military moves on our part. Most of all," he said directly to the NIOs, "I want a feel for their nuclear capacity, and the conditions under which they might feel the need to make use of it."

"What warning will we have?" The question, surprisingly, came from Cook. The answer, surprisingly, came from the other NIO, who felt the need, now, to show something of what he knew.

"The Cobra Dane radar on Shemya still works. So do the DSPS satellites. We'll get launch warning and impact prediction if it comes to that. Dr. Ryan, have we done anything — "

"The Air Force has air-launched cruise missiles in the stockpile. They would be carried in by B-1 bombers. We also have the option of rearming Tomahawk cruise missiles with W-80 warheads as well for launch by submarines or surface ships. The Russians know that we may exercise that option, and they will not object so long as we keep it quiet."

"That's an escalation," Cook warned. "We want to be careful about that."

"What about their SS-19s?" the second NIO inquired delicately.

"They think they need them. It will not be easy to talk them out of 'em." Cook looked around the table. "We have nuked their country, remember. It's a very sensitive subject, and we're dealing with people motivated by paranoia. I recommend caution on that issue."

"Noted," Ryan said as he stood. "You know what I want, people. Get to work." It felt a little good to be able to give an order like that, but less so to have to do it, and less still in anticipation of the answers he would receive for his questions. But you had to start somewhere.

"Another hard day?" Nomuri asked.

"I thought with Yamata gone it would get easier," Kazuo said. He shook his head, leaning back against the fine wood rim of the tub. "I was wrong."

The others nodded curt agreement at their friend's observation, and they all missed Taoka's sexual stories now. They needed the distraction, but only Nomuri knew why they had ended.

"So what is going on? Now Goto says that we need

693

America. Last week they were our enemies, and now we are friendly again? This is very confusing for a simple person like me," Chet said, rubbing his closed eyes, and wondering what the bait would draw. Developing his rapport with these men had not been easy because they and he were so different, and it was to be expected that he would envy them, and they him. He was an entrepreneur, they thought, who ran his own business, and they the senior salarymen of major corporations. They had security. He had independence. They were expected to be overworked. He marched to his own drum. They had more money. He had less stress. And now they had knowledge, and he did not.

"We have confronted America," one of their number said.

"So I gather. Isn't that highly dangerous?"

"In the short term, yes," Taoka said, letting the blisteringly hot water soothe his stress-knotted muscles. "Though I think we have already won."

"But won *what*, my friend? I feel I have started watching a mystery in the middle of the show, and all I know is that there's a pretty, mysterious girl on the train to Osaka." He referred to a dramatic convention in Japan, mysteries based on how efficiently the nation's trains ran.

"Well, as my boss tells it," another senior aide decided to explain, "it means true independence for our country."

"Aren't we independent already?" Nomuri asked in open puzzlement. "There are hardly any American soldiers here to annoy us anymore."

"And those under guard now," Taoka observed. "You don't understand. Independence means more than politics. It means economic independence, too. It means not going to others for what we need to survive."

"It means the Northern Resource Area, Kazuo,"

694

another of their number said, going too far, and knowing it from the way two pairs of eyes opened in warning.

"I wish it would mean shorter days and getting home on time for a change instead of sleeping in a damned coffin-tube two or three nights a week," one of the more alert ones said to alter the course of the conversation.

Taoka grunted. "Yes, how can one get a girl in there?" The guffaws that followed that one were forced, Nomuri thought.

"You salarymen and your secrets! Ha!" the CIA officer snapped. "I hope you do better with your women." He paused. "Will all this affect my business?" A good idea, he thought, to ask a question like that.

"For the better, I should think," Kazuo said. There was general agreement on that point.

"We must all be patient. There will be hard times before the good ones truly come."

"But they *will* come," another suggested confidently. "The really hard part is behind us."

Not if I can help it, Nomuri didn't tell them. But what the hell did "Northern Resource Area" mean? It was so like the intelligence business that he knew he'd heard something important, quite without knowing what the hell it was all about. Then he had to cover himself with a lengthy discourse on his new relationship with the hostess, to be sure, again, that they would remember this, and not his questions.

It was a shame to have to arrive in the darkness, but that was mere fortune. Half of the fleet had diverted for Guam, which had a far better natural harbor, because all the people in these islands had to see the Japanese Navy — Admiral Sato was weary of the "Self-Defense Force" title. His was a *navy* now, composed of fighting ships and fighting men that had tasted battle, after a fashion, and if historians would later comment that their battle had not been a real one or a fair one, well, what military textbook did *not* cite the value of surprise in offensive operations? None that he knew of, the Admiral told himself, seeing the loom of Mount Takpochao through his binoculars. There was already a powerful radar there, up and operating, his electronics technicians had told him an hour earlier. Yet another important factor in defending what was again his country's native soil.

He was alone on the starboard bridge wing in the pre-dawn gloom. Such an odd term, he thought. Gloom? Not at all. There was a wonderful peace to this, especially when you were alone to keep it to yourself, and your mind started editing the distractions out. Above his head was the faint buzz of electronic gear, like a hive of slumbering bees, and that noise was soon blanked out. There was also the distant hum of the ship's systems, mostly the engines, and air-conditioning blowers, he knew, shrugging it off. There were no human noises to trouble him. The captain of *Mutsu* enforced good bridge discipline. The sailors didn't speak unless they had reason to, concentrating on their duties as they were supposed to do. One by one, Admiral Sato eliminated the extraneous noises. That left only the sound of the sea, the wonderful swish of steel hull parting the waves. He looked down to see it, the fan-shaped foam whose white was both brilliant and faint at the same time, and aft the wide swath was a pleasant fluorescent green from the disturbance of phytoplankton, tiny creatures that came to the surface at night for reasons Sato had never troubled himself to understand. Perhaps to enjoy the moon and stars, he told himself with a smile in the darkness. Ahead was the island of Saipan, just a space on the horizon blacker than the darkness itself; it seemed so because it occulted the stars on the western horizon, and a seaman's mind

696

knew that where there were no stars on a clear night, then there had to be land. The lookouts at their stations atop the forward superstructure had seen it long before him, but that didn't lessen the pleasure of his own discovery, and as with sailors of every generation there was something special to a landfall, because every voyage ended with discovery of some sort. And so had this one.

More sounds. First the jerky whirs of electrical motors turning radar systems, then something else. He knew he was late noticing it, off to starboard, a deep rumble, like something tearing, growing rapidly in intensity until he knew it could only be the roar of an approaching aircraft. He lowered his binoculars and looked off to the right, seeing nothing until his eyes caught movement close aboard, and two dart shapes streaked overhead. *Mutsu* trembled in their wake, giving Admiral Sato a chill followed by a flush of anger. He pulled open the door to the wheelhouse.

"What the hell was that?"

"Two F-3s conducting an attack drill," the officer of the deck replied. "They've been tracking them in CIC for several minutes. We had them illuminated with our missile trackers."

"Will someone tell those 'wild eagles' that flying directly over a ship in the dark risks damage to us, and foolish death to them!"

"But, Admiral — " the OOD tried to say.

"*But* we are a valuable fleet unit and I do not wish one of my ships to have to spend a month in the yard having her mast replaced because some damned fool of an aviator couldn't see us in the dark!"

"*Hai.* I will make the call at once."

Spoiling my morning that way, Sato fumed, going back out to sit in the leather chair and doze off.

Was he the first guy to figure it out? Winston asked himself. Then he asked himself why he should find that surprising. The FBI and the rest were evidently trying to put things back together, and their main effort was probably to defend against fraud. Worse, they were also going over all the records, not just those of the Columbus Group. It had to be a virtual ocean of data, and they would have been unfamiliar with the stuff, and this was a singularly bad time for on-the-job training.

The TV told the story. The Chairman of the Federal Reserve Bank had been on all the morning talk shows, which had to have kept his driver busy in D.C. this day, followed by a strong public statement in the White House Press Room, followed by a lengthy interview on CNN. It was working, after a fashion, and TV showed that as well. A lot of people had shown up at banks before lunch, surprised there to find piles of cash trucked out the previous night to make what in military terms was probably called a show of force. Though the Chairman had evidently jawboned every major banker in the country, the reverse was true of the tellers meeting depositors at their windows: *Oh, you want cash? Well, of course we have all you need.* In not a few cases, by the time people got home they started to feel a new variety of paranoia — *keep all this cash at home?* — and by afternoon some had even begun coming back to redeposit.

That would be Buzz Fiedler's work, too, and a good man he was, Winston thought, for an academic. The Treasury Secretary was only buying time, and doing so with money, but it was a good tactic, good enough to confuse the public into believing things were not as bad as they appeared.

Serious investors knew better. Things were bad, and the play in the banks was a stopgap measure at best. The Fed was dumping cash into the system. Though a good idea for a day or so, the net effect by the end of the week had to be to weaken the dollar further still, and already American T-Bills were about as popular in the global financial community as plague rats. Worst of all, though Fiedler had prevented a banking panic for the time being, you could hold back a panic only so long, and unless you could restore confidence in a real way, the longer you played stop-gap games, the worse would be the renewed panic if those measures failed, for then there would be no stopping it. That was what Winston really expected.

Because the Gordian knot around the throat of the investment system would not soon be untied.

Winston thought he had decoded the likely cause of the event, but along the way he'd learned that there might not be a solution. The sabotage at DTC had been the master stroke. Fundamentally, no single person knew what he owned, what he'd paid for it, when he'd gotten it, or what cash he had left; and the absence of knowledge was metastatic. Individual investors didn't know. Institutions didn't know. The trading houses didn't know. Nobody knew.

How would the real panic start? In short order, pension funds would have to write their monthly checks — but would the banks honor them? The Fed would encourage them to do so, but somewhere along the line there would be one bank that would not, due to troubles of its own — just one, such things always began in a single place, after all — and that would start yet another cascade, and the Fed would have to step in again by boosting the money supply, and *that* could start a hyperinflationary cycle. That was the ultimate nightmare. Winston well remembered the way that inflation had affected the market and the country in the late 1970s, the "malaise" that had indeed been real, the loss of national confidence that had manifested itself with nutcases building cabins in the Northwestern mountains and bad movies about life after the apocalypse. And even then inflation had topped out at what? Thirteen percent or so.

Twenty-percent interest rates. A country strangling from nothing more than the loss of confidence that had resulted from gasoline lines and a vacillating president. Those times might well seem nostalgic indeed.

This would be far worse, something not like America at all, something from the Weimar Republic, something from Argentina in the bad old days, or Brazil under military rule. And it wouldn't stop just with America, would it? Just as in 1929, the ripple effects would spread far, crippling economies across the world, well beyond even Winston's capacity for prediction. He would not be badly hurt personally, George knew. Even the 90-percent diminution of his personal wealth would leave a vast and comfortable sum — he always hedged some of his bets on issues that owned physically real things, like oil or gold; and he had his own gold holdings, real metal bars in vaults, like a miser of old — and since major depressions were ultimately *deflationary,* the relative value of his diverse holdings would actually increase after a time. He knew that he and his family would survive and thrive, but the cost to those less fortunate than himself was economic and social chaos. And he wasn't in the business just for himself, was he? Over time he'd come to think long at night about the little guys who'd seen his TV ads and entrusted him with their savings. It was a magic word, trust. It meant that you had an obligation to the people who gave it to you. It meant that they believed what you said about yourself, and that you had to prove that it was real, not merely to them, but to yourself as well. Because if you failed, then houses were not bought, kids not educated, and the dreams of real people not unlike yourself would die aborning. Bad enough just in America, Winston thought, but this event would — could — affect the entire world.

And he had to know what he'd done. It was not an accident. It had been a well-considered plan, executed with style. *Yamata. That clever son of a bitch,* Winston thought. Perhaps the first Japanese investor he'd ever respected. The first one who'd really understood the game both tactically and strategically. Well, that was sure as hell the case. The look on his face, those dark eyes over the champagne glass. *Why didn't you see it then?* So that was the game after all, wasn't it?

But no. It couldn't be the entire game. A part of it, perhaps, a tactic aimed at something else. What? What could be so important that Raizo Yamata was willing to kiss off his personal fortune, and along the way destroy the very global markets upon which his own corporations and his own national economy depended? That was not something to enter the mind of a businessman, certainly not something to warm the soul of a maven on the Street.

It was strange to have it all figured out and yet not understand the sense of it. Winston looked out the window as the sun set on New York Harbor. He had to tell somebody, and that somebody had to understand what this was all about. Fiedler? Maybe. Better somebody who knew the Street . . . and knew other things, too. But who?

"Are they ours?" All four lay alee in Laolao Bay. One of their number was tucked alongside an oiler, doubtless taking on fuel.

Oreza shook his head. "Paint's wrong. The Navy paints its ships darker, bluer, like."

"They look like serious ships, man." Burroughs handed the binoculars back.

"Billboard radars, vertical-launch cells for missiles, antisub helicopters. They're Aegis 'cans, like our Burke class. They're serious, all right. Airplanes are afraid of 'em." As Portagee watched, a helicopter lifted off one and headed for the beach.

"Report in?"

"Yeah, good idea."

Burroughs went into the living room and put the batteries back in his phone. The idea of completely depowering it was probably unnecessary, but it was safe, and neither man was interested in finding out how the Japanese treated spies, for that was what they were. It was also awkward, putting the antenna through the hole in the bottom of the serving bowl and then holding it next to your head, but it did give a certain element of humor to the exercise, and they needed a reason to smile at something.

"NMCC, Admiral Jackson."

"You have the duty again, sir?"

"Well, Master Chief, I guess we both do. What do you have to report?"

"Four Aegis destroyers offshore, east side of the island. One's taking fuel on now from a small fleet oiler. They showed up just after dawn. Two more car carriers at the quay, another on the horizon outbound. We counted twenty fighter aircraft a while ago. About half of them are F-15s with twin tails. The other half are single tails, but I don't know the type. Otherwise nothing new to tell you about."

Jackson was looking at a satellite photo only an hour old showing four ships in line-ahead formation, and fighters dispersed at both the airfields. He made a note and nodded.

"What's it like there?" Robby asked. "I mean, they hassling anybody, arrests, that sort of thing?" He heard the voice at the other end snort.

"Negative, sir. Everybody's just nice as can be. Hell, they're on TV all the time, the public-access cable channel, telling us how much money they plan to spend here and all the things they're gonna do for us." Jackson heard the disgust in the man's voice.

"Fair enough. I might not always be here. I do have to get a little sleep, but this line is set aside

702

for your exclusive use now, okay?"

"Roger that, Admiral."

"Play it real cool, Master Chief. No heroic shit, okay?"

"That's kid stuff, sir. I know better," Oreza assured him.

"Then close down, Oreza. Good work." Jackson heard the line go dead before he set his phone down. "Better you than me, man," he added to himself. Then he looked over at the next desk.

"Got it on tape," an Air Force intelligence officer told him. "He confirms the satellite data. I'm inclined to believe that he's still safe."

"Let's keep him that way. I don't want anybody calling out to them without my say-so," Jackson ordered.

"Roge-o, sir." *I don't think we can anyway,* he didn't add.

"Tough day?" Paul Robberton asked.

"I've had worse," Ryan answered. But this crisis was too new for so confident an evaluation. "Does your wife mind . . . ?"

"She's used to having me away, and we'll get a routine figured out in a day or so." The Secret Service agent paused. "How's the Boss doing?"

"As usual he gets the hard parts. We all dump on him, right?" Jack admitted, looking out the window as they turned off Route 50. "He's a good man, Paul."

"So are you, doc. We were all pretty glad to get you back." He paused. "How tough is it?" The Secret Service had the happy circumstance of needing to know almost everything, which was just as well, since they overheard almost everything anyway.

"Didn't they tell you? The Japanese have built nukes. And they have ballistic launchers to deliver them."

Paul's hands tightened on the wheel. "Lovely. But

703

they can't be that crazy."

"On the evening of December 7, 1941, USS *Enterprise* pulled into Pearl Harbor to refuel and rearm. Admiral Bill Halsey was riding the bridge, as usual, and looked at the mess from the morning's strike and said, 'When this war is over, the Japanese language will be spoken only in hell.' " Ryan wondered why he'd just said that.

"That's in your book. It must have been a good line for the guys around him."

"I suppose. If they use their nukes, that's what'll happen to them. Yeah, they have to know that," Ryan said, his fatigue catching up with him.

"You need about eight hours, Dr. Ryan, maybe nine," Robberton said judiciously. "It's like with us. Fatigue really messes up your higher-brain functions. The Boss needs you sharp, doc, okay?"

"No argument there. I might even have a drink tonight," Ryan thought aloud.

There was an extra car in the driveway, Jack saw, and a new face that looked out the window as the official car pulled into the parking pad.

"That's Andrea. I already talked with her. Your wife had a good lecture today, by the way. Everything went just fine."

"Good thing we have two guest rooms." Jack chuckled as he walked into the house. The mood was happy enough, and it seemed that Cathy and Agent Price were getting along. The two agents conferred while Ryan ate a light dinner.

"Honey, what's going on?" Cathy asked.

"We're involved in a major crisis with Japan, plus the Wall Street thing."

"But how come — "

"Everything that's happened so far has been at sea. It hasn't broken the news yet, but it will."

"War?"

Jack looked up and nodded. "Maybe."

"But the people at Wilmer today, they were just as nice — you mean they don't know either?"

Ryan nodded. "That's right."

"That doesn't make any sense!"

"No, honey, it sure doesn't." The phone rang just then, the regular house phone. Jack was the closest and picked it up. "Hello?"

"Is this Dr. John Ryan?" a voice asked.

"Yeah. Who's this?"

"George Winston. I don't know if you remember, but we met last year at the Harvard Club. I gave a little speech about derivatives. You were at the next table over. By the way, nice job on the Silicon Alchemy IPO."

"Seems like a while ago," Ryan said. "Look, it's kinda busy down here, and — "

"I want to meet with you. It's important," Winston said.

"What about?"

"I'll need fifteen or twenty minutes to explain it. I have my G at Newark. I can be down whenever you say." The voice paused. "Dr. Ryan, I wouldn't be asking unless I thought it was important."

Jack thought about it for a second. George Winston was a serious player. His rep on the Street was enviable: tough, shrewd, honest. And, Ryan remembered, he'd sold control of his fleet to somebody from Japan. Somebody named Yamata — a name that had turned up before.

"Okay, I'll squeeze you in. Call my office tomorrow about eight for a time."

"See you tomorrow then. Thanks for listening." The line went dead. When he looked over at his wife, she was back at work, transcribing notes from her carry-notebook to her laptop computer, an Apple Powerbook 800.

"I thought you had a secretary for that," he observed with a tolerant smile.

705

"She can't think about these things when she writes up my notes. I can." Cathy was afraid to relate Bernie's news on the Lasker. She'd picked up several bad habits from her husband. One of them was his Irish-peasant belief in luck, and how you could spoil luck by talking about it. "I had an interesting idea today, just after the lecture."

"And you wrote it right down," her husband observed. Cathy looked up with her usual impish smile.

"Jack, if you don't write it down — "

"Then it never happened."

30

Why Not?

The dawn came up like thunder in this part of the world, or so the poem went. Sure as hell the sun was hot, Admiral Dubro told himself. It was almost as hot as his temper. His demeanor was normally pleasant, but he had simmered in both tropical heat and bureaucratic indifference for long enough. He supposed that the policy weenies and the planning weenies and the political weenies had the same take on things: he and his battle force could dance around here indefinitely without detection, doing their Ghostbusters number and intimidating the Indians without actual contact. A fine game, to be sure, but not an endless one. The idea was to get your battle force in close without detection and then *strike* at the enemy without warning. A nuclear-powered carrier was good at that. You could do it once, twice, even three times if the force commander had it together, but you couldn't do it forever, because the other side had brains, too, and sooner or later a break would go the wrong way.

In this case it wasn't the players who'd goofed. It was the water boy, and it hadn't even been much of an error. As his operations people had reconstructed events, a single Indian Sea Harrier at the very end of its patrol arc had had his look-down radar on and gotten a hit on one of Dubro's oilers, which were now racing northeast to refill his escort ships whose bunkers were nearly two thirds empty after the speed run south of Sri Lanka. An hour later another Harrier, probably stripped of weapons and carrying nothing but fuel tanks, had gotten close enough for a visual. The replenishment-group commander had altered course, but the damage was done. The placement of the two oilers and their two-frigate escort could only have meant that Dubro was now east-by-south of Dondra Head. The Indian fleet had turned at once, satellite photos showed, split into two groups, and headed northeast as well. Dubro had little choice but to allow the oilers to continue on their base course. Covertness or not, his oil-fueled escorts were dangerously close to empty bunkers, and that was a hazard he could not afford. Dubro drank his wake-up coffee while his eyes burned holes in the bulkhead. Commander Harrison sat across from the Admiral's desk, sensibly not saying much of anything until his boss was ready to speak.

"What's the good word, Ed?"

"We still have them outgunned, sir," the Force Operations Officer replied. "Maybe we need to demonstrate that."

Outgunned? Dubro wondered. Well, yes, that was true, but only two thirds of his aircraft were fully mission-capable now. They'd been away too long from base. They were running out of the stores needed to keep the aircraft operating. In the hangar bay, aircraft sat with inspection hatches open, awaiting parts that the ship no longer had. He was depending on the replenishment ships for those, for the parts flown into Diego Garcia from stateside. Three days after delivery, he'd be back to battery, after a fashion, but his people were tired. Two men had been hurt on the flight deck the day before. Not because they were stupid. Not because they were inexperienced. Because they'd been doing it too damned long, and fatigue was even more dangerous to the mind than to the body, especially in the frenetic environment of a carrier's flight deck. The same was true of everyone in the battle force, from the lowliest striker to . . . himself. The strain of continuous decision-making was starting to tell. And all he could do about that was to switch to decaf.

"How are the pilots?" Mike Dubro asked.

"Sir, they'll do what you tell them to do."

"Okay, we do light patrolling today. I want a pair of Toms up all the time, at least four more on plus-five, fully armed for air-to-air. Fleet course is one-eight-zero, speed of advance twenty-five knots. We link up with the replenishment group and get everyone topped off. Otherwise, we do a stand-down. I want people rested insofar as that is possible. Our friend is going to start hunting tomorrow, and the game is going to get interesting."

"We start going head-to-head?" the ops officer asked.

"Yeah." Dubro nodded. He checked his watch. Nighttime in Washington. The people with brains would be heading for bed now. He'd soon make another demand for instructions, and he wanted the smart ones to pass it along, preferably with a feel for the urgency of his situation. Pay-or-play time was grossly overdue, and all he could be sure of now was that it would come unexpectedly — and after that, Japan? Harrison and his people were already spending half of their time on that.

The tradecraft, again, was of the bad-TV variety, and the only consolation was that maybe the Russians were right. Maybe Scherenko had told them the truth. Maybe they were not in any real danger from the PSID. That seemed a very thin reed to Clark, none of whose education had encouraged him to trust Russians to do anything pleasant to Americans.

"The wheel may be crooked," he whispered to himself — in English, damn it! In any event, what they'd done was laughably simple. Nomuri had parked his car in the same lease-garage that the hotel maintained for its guests, and now Nomuri had a key to Clark's rental car, and over the left-side visor was a computer disk. This Clark retrieved and handed to Chavez, who slid it into their laptop. An electronic chime announced the activation of the machine as Clark headed out into the traffic. Ding copied the file over to the hard-disk and erased the floppy, which would soon be disposed of. The report was verbose. Chavez read it silently before turning the car radio on, then relayed the high points in whispers over the noise.

"Northern Resource Area?" John asked.

"*Da.* A curious phrase," Ding agreed, thinking. It occurred to him that his diction was better in Russian than English, perhaps because he'd learned English on the street, and Russian in a proper school from a team of people with a genuine love for it. The young intelligence officer dismissed the thought angrily.

Northern Resource Area, he thought. Why did that sound familiar? But they had other things to do, and that was tense enough. Ding found that while he liked the paramilitary end of being a field officer, this spy stuff was not exactly his cup of tea. Too scary, too paranoid.

Isamu Kimura was at the expected meeting site. Fortunately his job allowed him to be in and out a lot, and to sit down with foreigners as a matter of routine. One benefit was that he had an eye for safe places. This one was on the docks, thankfully not overly busy at the moment, but at the same time a location where such a meeting would not be overly out of character. It was also a hard one to bug. There were still harbor sounds to mask quiet conversation.

Clark was even more uneasy, if that were possible.

With any covert recruitment there was a period during which open contact was safe, but the safety diminished linearly over time at a rapid but unknown rate, and there were other considerations. Kimura was motivated by — what? Clark didn't know why Oleg Lyalin had been able to recruit him. It wasn't money. The Russians had never paid him anything. It wasn't ideology. Kimura wasn't a Communist in his political creed. Was it ego? Did he think he was worthy of a better post that someone else had taken? Or, most dangerously of all, was he a patriot, the eccentric personal sort who judged what was good for his country in his own mind? Or, as Ding might have observed, was he just fucked up? Not a very elegant turn of phrase, but in Clark's experience not an unknown state of affairs, either. The simple version was that Clark didn't know; worse, any motivation for treason simply justified betraying your country to another, and there was something in him that refused to feel comfortable with such people. Perhaps cops didn't like dealing with their informants either, John told himself. Small comfort, that.

"What's so important?" Kimura asked, halfway down a vacant quay. The idle ships in Tokyo Bay were clearly visible, and he wondered if the meeting place had been selected for just that reason.

"Your country has nuclear weapons," Clark told him simply.

"What?" First the head turned, then the feet stopped, then a very pale look came over his face.

"That's what your ambassador in Washington told the American president on Saturday. The Americans are in a panic. At least that's what Moscow Center has told us." Clark smiled in a very Russian way. "I must say that you've won my professional admiration to have done it so openly, especially buying our own rockets to be the delivery vehicles. I must also tell you that the government of my country is decidedly displeased by this development."

"The rockets could easily be aimed at us." Chavez added dryly, "They make people nervous."

"I had no idea. Are you sure?" Kimura started walking again, just to get his blood flowing.

"We have a highly placed source in the U.S. government. It is not a mistake." Clark's voice, Ding noted, was coldly businesslike: *Ah, your car has a scratch on the bumper. I know a good man to fix it.*

"So that's why they thought they could get away with it." Kimura didn't have to say any more, and it was plain that a piece of the puzzle had just dropped into place in his mind. He took a few breaths before speaking again: "This is madness."

And those were three of the most welcome words John had heard since calling home from Berlin to hear that his wife had safely delivered their second child. Now it was time for real hardball. He spoke without smiling, fully into his role as a senior Russian intelligence officer, trained by the KGB to be one of the best in the world:

"Yes, my friend. Any time you frighten a major power, that is truly madness. Whoever is playing this game, I hope they know how dangerous it is. Please heed my words, *Gospodin* Kimura. My country is gravely concerned. Do you understand? *Gravely* concerned. You've made fools of us before America and the entire world. You have weapons that can threaten my country as easily as they can threaten America. You have initiated action against the United States, and we do not see a good reason for it. That makes you unpredictable in our eyes, and a country with nuclear-tipped rockets and political instability is not a pleasant prospect. This crisis is going to expand unless sensible people take proper action. We are not concerned about your commercial disagreements with America, but when the possibility of real war exists, then we are concerned."

Kimura was still pale at the prospect.

"What is your rank, Klerk-san?"

"I am a full colonel of the Seventh Department, Line PR, the First Chief Directorate of the Committee for State Security."

"I thought — "

"Yes, the new name, the new designation, what rubbish," Clark observed with a snort. "Kimura-san, I am an intelligence officer. My job is to protect my country. I'd expected this posting to be a simple, pleasant one, but now I find myself — did I tell you about our Project RYAN?"

"You mentioned it once, but — "

"Upon the election of the American President Reagan — I was a captain then, like Chekov here — our political masters looked at the ideological beliefs of the man and feared that he might actually consider a nuclear strike against our country. We immediately launched a frantic effort to discern what those chances were. We eventually decided that it was a mistake, that Reagan, while he hated the Soviet Union, was not a fool.

"But now," Colonel Klerk went on, "what does my country see? A nation with covertly developed nuclear weapons. A nation that has for no good reason chosen to attack a country that is more business partner than enemy. A nation which more than once has attacked Russia. And so the orders I received sound very much like Project RYAN. Do you understand me now?"

"What do you want?" Kimura asked, already knowing the answer.

"I want to know the location of those rockets. They left the factory by rail. I want to know where they are now."

"How can I possibly — " Clark cut him off with a look.

"How is your concern, my friend. I tell you what

713

I must have." He paused for effect. "Consider this, Isamu: events like this acquire a life of their own. They suddenly come to dominate the men who started them. With nuclear weapons in the equation, the possible consequences — in a way you know about them, and in a way you do not. I do know," Colonel Klerk went on. "I've seen the briefings of what the Americans were once able to do to us, and what we were able to do to them. It was part of Project RYAN, yes? To frighten a major power is a grave and foolish act."

"But if you find out, then what?"

"That I do not know. I do know that my country will feel much safer with the knowledge than without. Those are my orders. Can I force you to help us? No, I cannot. But if you do not help us, then you help to place your country at risk. Consider that," he said with the coldness of a coroner. Clark shook his hand in an overtly friendly way and walked off.

"Five-point-seven, five-point-six, five-point-eight from the East German judge . . ." Ding breathed when they were far enough away. "Jesus, John, you *are* a Russian."

"You bet your ass, kid." He managed a smile.

Kimura stayed on the dock for a few minutes, looking out across the bay at the dormant ships. Some were car carriers, more were conventional container ships, with seamanlike lines to slice through the waves as they plied their commerce on the seas. This seemingly ordinary aspect of civilization was almost a personal religion for Kimura. Trade drew nations together in need, and in needing one another they ultimately came to find a good reason to keep the peace, however acrimonious their relations might be otherwise. Kimura knew enough history to realize that it didn't always work that way, however.

You are breaking the law, he told himself. *You are disgracing your name and your family. You are dishon-*

714

oring your friends and co-workers. You are betraying your country.

But, damn it! *whose* country was he betraying? The *people* selected the members of the Diet, and their elected representatives selected the Prime Minister — but the people really had had no say whatever in this. They, like his ministry, like the members of the Diet, were mere spectators. They were being lied to. His country was at war, and the people didn't really know! His country had troubled itself to build nuclear arms, and the people didn't know. Who had given that order? The government? The government had just changed over — again — and surely the time involved meant . . . what?

Kimura didn't know. He knew the Russian was right, to some extent anyway. The dangers involved were not easily predicted. His country was in such danger as had not existed in his lifetime. His nation was descending into madness, and there were no doctors to diagnose the problem, and the only thing Kimura could be sure of was the fact that it was so far over his head that he didn't know where or how to begin.

But someone must do something. At what point, Kimura asked himself, did a traitor become a patriot, and a patriot a traitor?

He should have been resentful, Cook thought, finally getting to bed. But he wasn't. The day had gone exceptionally well, all things considered. The others were praying for him to step on his weenie. That was plain enough, especially the two NIOs. They were so damned smart — they thought, Cook told himself with a broad smile at the ceiling. But they didn't know diddly. Did they know they didn't know? Probably not. They always acted superior, but when crunch time came and you hit them with a question — well, then, it was always *on one hand,* sir, followed by *on the other hand,* sir. How the hell could you make policy on that basis?

Cook, on the *other* hand, did know, and the fact that Ryan was aware of it, had instantly elevated him to de facto leadership of the working group, which had been met with both resentment and relief by the others around the table. *Okay,* they were now thinking, *we'll let* him *take the risks.* All in all, he thought he'd managed things rather well. The others would both back him up and distance themselves from him, making their notations on the positions he generated to cover their asses should things go badly, as they secretly hoped, but also staying within the group's overall position to bask in the light of success if things went well. They'd hope for that, too, but not as much, bureaucrats being what they were.

So the preliminaries were done. The opening positions were set. Adler would head the negotiating team. Cook would be his second. The Japanese Ambassador would lead the other side, with Seiji Nagumo as *his* second. The negotiations would follow a pattern as structured and stylized as Kabuki theater. Both sides of the table would posture and the real action would take place during coffee or tea breaks, as the members of the respective teams talked quietly with their counterparts. That would allow Chris and Seiji to trade information, to control the negotiations, and just maybe to keep this damned-fool thing from getting worse than it already was.

They're going to be giving you money for providing information, the voice persisted. Well, yes, but Seiji was going to be giving him information, too, and the whole point was to defuse the situation and to *save lives!* he answered back. The real ultimate purpose of diplomacy was to keep the peace, and that meant saving lives in the global context, like doctors but with greater efficiency, and doctors got paid well, didn't they? Nobody dumped on them for the money they made. That noble profession, in their white coats, as opposed to the cookie-pushers at Foggy Bottom. What made them so special?

It's about restoring the peace, *damn it!* The money didn't matter. That was a *side issue.* And since it *was* a side issue, he deserved it, didn't he? Of course he did, Cook decided, closing his eyes at last.

The engineers were working hard, Sanchez saw, back at his chair in Pri-Fly. They'd repacked and realigned two bearings on the tailshaft, held their collective breath, and cracked their throttles a little wider on Number One. Eleven knots, edging toward twelve, enough to launch some aircraft for Pearl Harbor, enough to get the COD aboard with a full collection of engineers to head below and help the ChEng make his evaluation of the situation. As one of the senior officers aboard, Sanchez would learn of their evaluation over lunch. He could have flown off to the beach with the first group of fighters, but his place was aboard. *Enterprise* was far behind now, fully covered by P-3s operating out of Midway, and Fleet Intelligence was more and more confident that there were no hostiles about, enough that Sanchez was starting to believe them. Besides, the antisubmarine aircraft had dropped enough sonobuoys to constitute a hazard to navigation.

The crew was up now, and still a little puzzled and angry. They were up because they knew they'd make Pearl early, and were no doubt relieved that whatever danger they feared was diminishing. They were puzzled because they didn't understand what was going on. They were angry because their ship had been injured, and by now they had to know that two submarines had been lost, and though the powers-that-were had worked to conceal the nature of the losses, ships do not keep secrets well. Radiomen took them down, and yeomen delivered them, and stewards overheard what officers said. *Johnnie Reb* had nearly six thousand people aboard, and the facts, as reported, sometimes got lost amid the rumors, but sooner or later the truth got out. The result would be predictable: rage. It was part of the profession of arms. However much the carrier sailors might disparage the bubbleheads on the beach, however great the rivalry, they were brothers (and, now, sisters), comrades to whom loyalty was owed.

But owed how? What would their orders be? Repeated inquiries to CINCPAC had gone unanswered. Mike Dubro's Carrier Group Three had *not* been ordered to make a speed-run back to WestPac, and that made no sense at all. Was this a war or not? Sanchez asked the sunset.

"So how did you learn this?" Mogataru Koga asked. Unusually, the former prime minister was dressed in a traditional kimono, now that he was a man of leisure for the first time in thirty years. But he'd taken the call and extended the invitation quickly enough, and listened with intense silence for ten minutes.

Kimura looked down. "I have many contacts, Koga-san. In my post I must."

"As do I. Why have I not been told?"

"Even within the government, the knowledge has been closely held."

"You are not telling me everything." Kimura wondered how Koga could know that, without realizing that a look in the mirror would suffice. All afternoon at his desk, pretending to work, he'd just looked down at the papers in front of him, and now he could not remember a single document. Just the questions. What to do? Whom to tell? Where to go for guidance?

"I have sources of information that I may not reveal, Koga-san." For the moment his host accepted that with a nod.

"So you tell me that we have attacked America,

718

and that we have constructed nuclear weapons?"

A nod. *"Hai."*

"I knew Goto was a fool, but I didn't think him a madman." Koga considered his own words for a moment. "No, he lacks the imagination to be a madman. He's always been Yamata's dog, hasn't he?"

"Raizo Yamata has always been his . . . his — "

"Patron?" Koga asked caustically. "That's the polite term for it." Then he snorted and looked away, and his anger now had a new target. *Exactly what you tried to stop. But you failed to do it, didn't you?*

"Koga often seeks his counsel, yes."

"So. Now what?" he asked a man clearly out of his depth. The answer was entirely predictable.

"I do not know. This matter is beyond me. I am a bureaucrat. I do not make policy. I am afraid for us now, and I don't know what to do."

Koga managed an ironic smile and poured some more tea for his guest. "You could well say the same of me, Kimura-san. But you still have not answered a question for me. I, too, have contacts remaining. I knew of the actions taken against the American Navy last week, after they happened. But I have not heard about the nuclear weapons." Just speaking those two words gave the room a chill for both men, and Kimura marveled that the politician could continue to speak evenly.

"Our ambassador in Washington told the Americans, and a friend at the Foreign Ministry — "

"I too have friends at the Foreign Ministry," Koga said, sipping his tea.

"I cannot say more."

The question was surprisingly gentle. "Have you been speaking with Americans?"

Kimura shook his head. "No."

The day usually started at six, but that didn't make it easy, Jack thought. Paul Robberton had gotten the

719

papers and started the coffee, Andrea Price turned to also, helping Cathy with the kids. Ryan wondered about that until he saw an additional car parked in the driveway. So the Secret Service thought it was a war. His next step was to call the office, and a minute later his STU-6 started printing the morning faxes. The first item was unclassified but important. The Europeans were trying to dump U.S. T-Bills, and nobody was buying them, still. One such day could be seen as an aberration. Not a second one. Buzz Fiedler and the Fed Chairman would be busy again, and the trader in Ryan worried. It was like the Dutch kid with his thumb in the dike. What happened when he spotted another leak? And even if he could reach it, what about the third?

News from the Pacific was unchanged, but getting more texture. *John Stennis* would make Pearl Harbor early, but *Enterprise* was going to take longer than expected. No evidence of Japanese pursuit. Good. The nuke hunt was under way, but without results, which wasn't surprising. Ryan had never been to Japan, a failing he regretted. His only current knowledge was from overhead photographs. In winter months when the skies over the country were unusually clear, the National Reconnaissance Office had actually used the country (and others) to calibrate its orbiting cameras, and he remembered the elegance of the formal gardens. His other knowledge of the country was from the historical record. But how valid was that knowledge now? History and economics made strange bedfellows, didn't they?

The usual kisses sent Cathy and the kids on their way, and soon enough Jack was in his official car for Washington. The sole consolation was that it was shorter than the former trip to Langley.

"You should be rested, at least," Robberton observed. He would never have talked so much to a political appointee, but somehow he felt far more at ease with this guy. There was no pomposity in Ryan.

"I suppose. The problems are still there."

"Wall Street still number one?"

"Yeah." Ryan looked at the passing countryside after locking the classified documents away. "I'm just starting to realize, this could take the whole world down. The Europeans are trying to sell off their treasuries. Nobody's buying. The market panic might be starting there today. Our liquidity is locked up, and a lot of theirs is in our T-Bills."

"Liquidity means cash, right?" Robberton changed lanes and speeded up. His license plate told the state cops to leave him alone.

"Correct. Nice thing, cash. Good thing to have when you get nervous — and not being able to get it, that *makes* people nervous."

"You like talking 1929, Dr. Ryan? I mean, that bad?"

Jack looked over at his bodyguard. "Possibly. Unless they can untangle the records in New York — it's like having your hands tied in a fight, like being at a card table with no money, if you can't play, you just stand there. Damn." Ryan shook his head. "It's just never happened before, and traders don't much like that either."

"How can people so smart get so panicked?"

"What do you mean?"

"What did anybody take away? Nobody blew up the mint" — he snorted — "it would have been our case!"

Ryan managed a smile. "You want the whole lecture?"

Paul's hands gestured on the wheel. "My degree's in psychology, not economics." The response surprised him.

"Perfect. That makes it easy."

The same worry occupied Europe. Just short of

noon, a conference call for the central bankers of Germany, Britain, and France resulted in little more than multilingual confusion over what to do. The past years of rebuilding the countries of Eastern Europe had placed an enormous strain on the economies of the countries of Western Europe, who were in essence paying the bill for two generations of economic chaos. To hedge against the resulting weakness of their own currencies, they'd bought dollars and American T-Bills. The stunning events in America had occasioned a day of minor activity, all of it down but nothing terribly drastic. That had all changed, however, after the last buyer had purchased the last discounted lot of American Treasuries — for some the numbers were just too good — with money taken from the liquidation of equities. That buyer already thought it had been a mistake and cursed himself for again riding the back of a trend instead of the front. At 10:30 A.M. local time, the Paris market started a precipitous slide, and inside of an hour, European economic commentators were talking about a domino effect, as the same thing happened in every market in every financial center. It was also noted that the central banks were trying the same thing that the American Fed had attempted the previous day. It wasn't that it had been a bad idea. It was just that such ideas only worked once, and European investors weren't buying. They were bailing out. It came as a relief when people started buying up stocks at absurdly low prices, and they were even grateful that the purchases were being made in yen, whose strength had reasserted itself, the only bright light on the international financial scene.

"You mean," Robberton said, opening the basement door to the West Wing. "You mean to tell me that it's *that* screwed up?"

"Paul, you think you're smart?" Jack asked. The

question took the Secret Service man aback a little.

"Yeah, I do. So?"

"So why do you suppose that anybody else is smarter than you are? They're not, Paul," Ryan went on. "They have a different job, but it isn't about brains. It's about education and experience. Those people don't know crap about running a criminal investigation. Neither do I. Every tough job requires brains, Paul. But you can't know them all. Anyway, bottom line, okay? No, they're not any smarter than you, and maybe not *as* smart as you. It's just that it's *their* job to run the financial markets, and your job to do something else."

"Jesus," Robberton breathed, dropping Ryan off at his office door. His secretary handed off a fistful of phone notes on his way in. One was marked *Urgent!* and Ryan called the number.

"That you, Ryan?"

"Correct, Mr. Winston. You want to see me. When?" Jack asked, opening his briefcase and pulling the classified things out.

"Anytime, starting ninety minutes from now. I have a car waiting downstairs, a Gulfstream with warm motors, a car waiting at D.C. National." His voice said the rest. It was urgent, and no-shit serious. On top of that came Winston's reputation.

"I presume it's about last Friday."

"Correct."

"Why me and not Secretary Fiedler?" Ryan wondered.

"You've worked there. He hasn't. If you want him to sit in on it, fine. He'll get it. I think you'll get it faster. Have you been following the financial news this morning?"

"It sounds like Europe's getting squirrelly on us."

"And it's just going to get worse," Winston said. And he was probably right, Jack knew.

"You know how to fix it?" Ryan could almost hear

the head at the other end shake in anger and disgust.

"I wish. But maybe I can tell you what really happened."

"I'll settle for that. Come down as quick as you want," Jack told him. "Tell the driver West Executive Drive. The uniformed guards will be expecting you at the gate."

"Thanks for listening, Dr. Ryan." The line clicked off, and Jack wondered how long it had been since the last time George Winston had said *that* to anyone. Then he got down to his work for the day.

The one good thing was that the railcars used to transport the "H-11" boosters from the assembly plant to wherever were standard gauge. That accounted for only about 8 percent of Japanese trackage and was, moreover, something discernible from satellite photographs. The Central Intelligence Agency was in the business of accumulating information, most of which would never have any practical use, and most of which, despite all manner of books and movies to the contrary, came from open-source material. It was just a matter of finding a railway map of Japan to see where all the standard-gauge trackage was and starting from there, but there were now over two thousand miles of such trackage, and the weather over Japan was not always clear, and the satellites were not always directly overhead, the better to see into valleys that littered a country composed largely of volcanic mountains.

But it was also a task with which the Agency was familiar. The Russians, with their genius and mania for concealing everything, had taught CIA's analysts the hard way to look for the unlikely spots first of all. An open plain, for example, was a likely spot, easy to approach, easy to build, easy to service, and easy to protect. That was how America had done it in the 1960s, banking incorrectly on the hope that missiles would never become accurate enough to hit such small, rugged point targets. Japan would have learned from that lesson. Therefore, the analysts had to look for the difficult places. Woods, valleys, hills, and the very selectivity of the task ensured that it would require time. Two updated KH-11 photosatellites were in orbit, and one KH-12 radar-imaging satellite. The former could resolve objects down to the size of a cigarette pack. The latter produced a monochrome image of far less resolution, but could see through clouds, and, under favorable circumstances, could actually penetrate the ground, down to as much as ten meters; in fact it had been developed for the purpose of locating otherwise invisible Soviet missile silos and similarly camouflaged installations.

That was the good news. The bad news was that each individual frame of imagery had to be examined by a team of experts, one at a time; that every irregularity or curiosity had to be reexamined and graded; that the time involved despite — indeed, because of — the urgency of the task was immense. Analysts from the CIA, the National Reconnaissance Office, and the Intelligence and Threat Analysis Center (I-TAC) were grouped together for the task, looking for twenty holes in the ground, knowing nothing other than the fact that the individual holes could be no less than five meters across. There could be one large group of twenty, or twenty individual and widely separated holes. The first task, all agreed, was to get new imagery of the whole length of standard-gauge rails. Weather and camera angles impeded some of that task, and now on the third day of the hunt, 20 percent of the needed mapping still remained undone. Already thirty potential sites had been identified for further scrutiny from new passes at slightly different light levels and camera angles which would allow stereo-optic viewing and additional computer enhancement. People on the analysis team were talking again about the 1991 Scud-hunts. It was not a pleasant memory for them. Though many lessons had been learned, the main one was this: it wasn't really all that hard to hide one or ten or twenty or even a hundred relatively small objects within the borders of a nation-state, even a very open, very flat one. And Japan was neither. Under the circumstances, finding all of them was a nearly impossible task. But they had to try anyway.

It was eleven at night, and his duties to his ancestors were done for the moment. They would never be fully carried out, but the promises to their spirits he'd made so many years before were now accomplished. What had been Japanese soil at the time of his birth was now again Japanese soil. What had been his family's land was now again his family's land. The nation that had humbled his nation and murdered his family had finally been humbled, and would remain so for a long, long time. Long enough to assure his country's position, finally, among the great nations of the world.

In fact, even greater than he'd planned, he noted. All he had to do was look at the financial reports coming into his hotel suite via facsimile printer. The financial panic he'd planned and executed was now moving across the Atlantic. Amazing, he thought, that he hadn't anticipated it. The complex financial maneuvers had left Japanese banks and businesses suddenly cash-rich, and his fellow zaibatsu were seizing the opportunity to buy up European equities for themselves and their companies. They'd increase the national wealth, improve their position in the various European national economies, *and* publicly appear to be springing to the assistance of others. Yamata judged that Japan would bend some efforts to help Europe out of her predicament. His country needed markets after all, and with the sudden increase in

Japanese ownership of their private companies, perhaps now European politicians would listen more attentively to their suggestions. Not certain, he thought, but possible. What they would definitely listen to was power. Japan was facing down America. America would never be able to confront his country, not with her economy in turmoil, her military defanged, and her President politically crippled. And it was an election year as well. The finest strategy, Yamata thought, was to sow discord in the house of your enemy. That he had done, taking the one action that had simply not occurred to the bonehead military people who'd led his country down the path of ruin in 1941.

"So," he said to his host. "How may I be of service?"

"Yamata-san, as you know, we will be holding elections for a local governor." The bureaucrat poured a stiff shot of a fine Scotch whiskey. "You are a landowner, and have been so for some months. You have business interests here. I suggest that you might be a perfect man for the job."

For the first time in years, Raizo Yamata was startled.

In another room in the same hotel an admiral, a major, and a captain of Japan Air Lines held a family reunion.

"So, Yusuo, what will happen next?" Torajiro asked.

"What I think will happen next is that you will return to your normal flight schedule back and forth to America," the Admiral said, finishing his third drink. "If they are as intelligent as I believe them to be, then they will see that the war is already over."

"How long have you been in on this, Uncle?" Shiro inquired with deep respect. Having now learned of what his uncle had done, he was awed by the man's audacity.

"From when I was a *nisa,* supervising construction of my first command in Yamata-san's yards. What is it? Ten years now. He came down to see me, and we had dinner and he asked some theoretical questions. Yamata learns quickly for a civilian," the Admiral opined. "I tell you, I think there is much more to this than meets the eye."

"How so?" Torajiro asked.

Yusuo poured himself another shot. His fleet was safe, and he was entitled to unwind, he thought, especially with his brother and nephew, now that all the stress was behind him. "We've spoken more and more in the past few years, but most of all right before he bought that American financial house. And so, now? My little operation happens the same day that their stock market crashes . . . ? An interesting coincidence, is it not?" His eyes twinkled. "One of my first lessons to him, all those years ago. In 1941 we attacked America's periphery. We attacked the arms but not the head or the heart. A nation can grow new arms, but a heart, or a head, that's far harder. I suppose he listened."

"I've flown over the head part many times," Captain Torajiro Sato noted. One of his two normal runs was to Dulles International Airport. "A squalid city."

"And you shall do so again. If Yamata did what I think, they will need us again, and soon enough," Admiral Sato said confidently.

"Go ahead, let him through," Ryan said over the phone.

"But — "

"But if it makes you feel better, pop it open and look, but if he says not to X-ray it, don't, okay?"

"But we were told just to expect one, and there's two."

"It's okay," Jack told the head uniformed guard at the west entrance. The problem with increased se-

728

curity alerts was that they mainly kept you from getting the work done that was necessary to resolve the crisis. "Send them both up." It took another four minutes by Jack's watch. They probably did pop the back off the guy's portable computer to make sure there wasn't a bomb there. Jack rose from his desk and met them at the anteroom door.

"Sorry about that. Remember the old Broadway song, 'The Secret Service Makes Me Nervous'?" Ryan waved them into his office. He assumed the older one was George Winston. He vaguely remembered the speech at the Harvard Club, but not the face that had delivered it.

"This is Mark Gant. He's my best technical guy, and he wanted to bring his laptop."

"It's easier this way," Gant explained.

"I understand. I use them, too. Please sit down." Jack waved them to chairs. His secretary brought in a coffee tray. When cups were poured, he went on. "I had one of my people track the European markets. Not good."

"That's putting it mildly, Dr. Ryan. We may be watching the beginning of a global panic," Winston began. "I'm not sure where the bottom is."

"So far Buzz is doing okay," Jack replied cautiously. Winston looked up from his cup.

"Ryan, if you're a bullshitter, I've come to the wrong place. I thought you knew the Street. The IPO you did with Silicon Alchemy was nicely crafted — now, was that you or did you take the credit for somebody else's work?"

"There's only two people who talk to me like that. One I'm married to. The other has an office about a hundred feet that way." Jack pointed. Then he grinned. "Your reputation precedes you, Mr. Winston. Silicon Alchemy was *all* my work. I have ten percent of the stock in my personal portfolio. That's how much I thought of the outfit. If you ask around about my rep, you'll find I'm not a bullshitter."

"Then you know it's today," Winston said, still taking the measure of his host.

Jack bit his lip for a moment and nodded. "Yeah. I told Buzz the same thing Sunday. I don't know how close the investigators are to reconstructing the records. I've been working on something else."

"Okay." Winston wondered what else Ryan might be working on but dismissed the irrelevancy. "I can't tell you how to fix it, but I think I can show you how it got broke."

Ryan turned for a second to look at his TV. CNN Headline News had just started its thirty-minute cycle with a live shot from the floor of the NYSE. The sound was all the way down, but the commentator was speaking rapidly and her face was not smiling. When he turned back, Gant had his laptop flipped open and was calling up some files.

"How much time do we have for this?" Winston asked.

"Let me worry about that," Jack replied.

31

The How and the What

Treasury Secretary Bosley Fiedler had not allowed
himself three consecutive hours of sleep since the return from Moscow, and his stride through the tunnel
connecting the Treasury Building with the White
House meandered sufficiently to make his bodyguards
wonder if he might need a wheelchair soon. The
Chairman of the Federal Reserve was hardly in better
shape. The two had been conferring, again, in the
Secretary's office when the call arrived — *Drop everything and come here* — peremptory even for somebody like Ryan, who frequently short-circuited the
workings of the government. Fiedler started talking
even before he walked through the open door.

"Jack, in twenty minutes we have a conference call
with the central banks of five Euro— who's this?"
SecTreas asked, stopping three paces into the room.

"Mr. Secretary, I'm George Winston. I'm president
and managing director of — "

"Not anymore. You sold out," Fiedler objected.

"I'm back as of the last rump-board meeting. This
is Mark Gant, another of my directors."

"I think we need to listen to what they have to
say," Ryan told his two new arrivals. "Mr. Gant,
please restart your rain dance."

"Damn it, Jack, I have twenty minutes. Less now,"

the Secretary of the Treasury said, looking at his watch.

Winston almost snarled, but instead spoke as he would have to another senior trader: "Fiedler, the short version is this: the markets were deliberately taken down by a systematic and highly skillful attack, and I think I can prove that to your satisfaction. Interested?"

The SecTreas blinked very hard. "Why, yes."

"But how . . . ?" the Fed Chairman asked.

"Sit down and we'll show you," Gant said. Ryan made way and the two senior officials took their places on either side of him and his computer. "It started in Hong Kong . . ."

Ryan walked to his desk, dialed the Secretary's office, and told his secretary to route the conference call to his room in the West Wing. A typical executive secretary, she handled the irregularity better than her boss could ever have done. Gant, Jack saw, was a superb technician, and his second stint at explaining matters was even more efficient than his first. The Secretary and the Chairman were also good listeners who knew the jargon. Questions were not necessary.

"I didn't think something like this was possible," the Chairman said eight minutes into the exposition. Winston handled the response.

"All the safeguards built into the system are designed to prevent accidents and catch crooks. It never occurred to anybody that somebody would pull something like this. Who would deliberately lose so much money?"

"Somebody with bigger fish to fry," Ryan told him.

"What's bigger than — "

Jack cut him off. "Lots of things, Mr. Winston. We'll get to that later." Ryan turned his head. "Buzz?"

"I'll want to confirm this with my own data, but

732

it looks pretty solid." SecTreas looked over at the Chairman.

"You know, I'm not even sure it's a criminal violation."

"Forget that," Winston announced. "The real problem is still here. Crunch time is today. If Europe keeps going down, then we have a global panic. The dollar's in free-fall, the American markets can't operate, most of the world's liquidity is paralyzed, and all the little guys out there are going to catch on as soon as the media figure out what the hell is going down. The only thing that's prevented that to this point is that financial reporters don't know crap about what they cover."

"Otherwise they'd be working for us," Gant said, rejoining the conversation. "Thank God their sources are keeping it zipped for the time being, but I'm surprised it hasn't broken out all the way yet." Just maybe, he thought, the media didn't want to start a panic either.

Ryan's phone rang and he went to answer it. "Buzz, it's your conference call." The Secretary's physical state was apparent when he rose. The man wavered and grabbed the back of a chair to steady himself. The Chairman was only a touch more agile, and if anything both men were yet more shaken by what they had just learned. Fixing something that had broken was a sufficiently difficult task. Fixing something deliberately and maliciously destroyed could hardly be easier. And it had to be fixed, and soon, lest every nation in Europe and North America join the plunge into a deep, dark canyon. The climb out of it would require both years and pain, and that was under the best of political circumstances — the long-term political ramifications of such a vast economic dislocation could not possibly be grasped at this stage, though Ryan was already recoiling from that particular horror.

Winston looked at the National Security Advisor's face, and it wasn't hard to read his thoughts. His own elation at the discovery was gone now that he'd given the information over to others. There ought to have been something else for him to say: how to fix matters. But all of his intellectual energy had been expended in building his case for the prosecution, as it were. He hadn't had the chance yet to take his analysis any further.

Ryan saw that and nodded with a grim smile of respect. "Good job."

"It's my fault," Winston said, quietly so as not to disturb the conference call proceeding a few feet away. "I should have stayed in."

"I've bailed out once myself, remember?" Ryan got back into a chair. "Hey, we all need a change from time to time. You didn't see this coming. It happens all the time. Especially here."

Winston gestured angrily. "I suppose. Now we can identify the rapist, but how the hell do you get un-raped? Once it's happened, it's happened. But those were my investors he fucked. Those people came to *me*. Those people *trusted* me." Ryan admired the summation. That was how people in the business were supposed to think.

"In other words, now what?"

Gant and Winston traded a look. "We haven't figured that one out."

"Well, so far you've outperformed the FBI and SEC. You know, I haven't even bothered checking how my portfolio did."

"Your ten percent of Silicon Alchemy won't hurt you. Long term," Winston said, "new communications gadgets always make out, and they have a couple of honeys."

"Okay, that's settled for now." Fiedler rejoined the group. "All the European markets are shut down, just like we are, until we can get things sorted out."

Winston looked up. "All that means is, there's a hell of a flood, and you're building the levee higher and higher. And if you run out of sandbags before the river runs out of water, then the damage will only be worse when you lose control."

"We're all open to suggestions, Mr. Winston," Fiedler said gently. George's reply matched it in kind.

"Sir, for what it's worth, I think you've done everything right to this point. I just don't see a way out."

"Neither do we," the Chairman of the Federal Reserve Board observed.

Ryan stood. "For the moment, gentlemen, I think we need to brief the President."

"What an interesting idea," Yamata said. He knew he'd had too much to drink. He knew that he was basking in the sheer satisfaction of carrying out what had to be the most ambitious financial gambit in history. He knew that his ego was expanding to its fullest size since — when? Even reaching the chairmanship of his conglomerate hadn't been this satisfactory. He'd crushed a whole nation and had altered the course of his own, and yet he had never even considered public office of any kind. And why not? he asked himself. Because that had always been a place for lesser men.

"For the moment, Yamata-san, Saipan will have a local governor. We will hold internationally supervised elections. We need a candidate," the Foreign Ministry official went on. "It must be someone of stature. It would be helpful if it were a man known and friendly to Goto-san, and a man with local interests. I merely ask that you consider it."

"I will do that." Yamata stood and headed for the door.

Well. He wondered what his father would have thought of that. It would mean stepping down from

735

chairmanship of his corporation . . . but — but what? What corporate worlds had he failed to conquer? Was it not time to move on? To retire honorably, to enter the formal service of his nation. After the local government situation was cleared up . . . then? Then to enter the Diet with great prestige, because the insiders would know, wouldn't they? *Hai,* they would know who had truly served the interests of the nation, who more than the Emperor Meiji himself had brought Japan to the first rank of nations. When had Japan ever had a political leader worthy of her place and her people? Why should he *not* take the honor due him? It would all require a few years, but he had those years. More than that, he had vision and the courage to make it real. Only his peers in business knew of his greatness now, but that could change, and his family name would be remembered for more than building ships and televisions and all the other things. Not a trademark. A name. A heritage. Would that not make his father proud?

"Yamata?" Roger Durling asked. "Tycoon, right, runs a huge company? I may have bumped into him at some reception or other when I was Vice President."

"Well, that's the guy," Winston said.

"So what are you saying he did?" the President asked.

Mark Gant set up his computer on the President's desk, this time with a Secret Service agent immediately behind him and watching every move, and this time he took it slow because Roger Durling, unlike Ryan, Fiedler, and the Fed Chairman, didn't really understand all the ins and outs. He did prove to be an attentive audience, however, stopping the presentation to ask questions, making a few notes, and three times asking for a repeat of a segment of the presentation. Finally he looked over to the Secretary of the Treasury.

"Buzz?"

"I want our people to verify the information independently — "

"That won't be hard," Winston told them. "Any one of the big houses will have records almost identical to this. My people can help organize it for you."

"If it's true, Buzz?"

"Then, Mr. President, this situation comes more under Dr. Ryan's purview than mine," SecTreas replied evenly. His relief was tempered with anger at the magnitude of what had been done. The two outsiders in the Oval Office didn't yet understand that.

Ryan's mind was racing. He'd ignored Gant's repeated explanation of the "how" of the event. Though the presentation to the President was clearer and more detailed than the first two times — the man would have made a fine instructor at a business school — the important parts were already fixed in the National Security Advisor's mind. Now he had the how, and the how told him a lot. This plan had been exquisitely planned and executed. The timing of the Wall Street takedown and the carrier/submarine attack had not been an accident. It was therefore a fully integrated plan. Yet it was also a plan which the Russian spy network had not uncovered, and that was the fact that kept repeating itself to him.

Their existing net is inside the Japanese government. It is probably concentrated on their security apparatus. But that net failed to give them strategic warning for the military side of the operation, and Sergey Nikolay'ch hasn't connected Wall Street with the naval action yet.

Break the model, Jack, he told himself. *Break the paradigm.* That's when it became clearer.

"That's why they didn't get it," Ryan said almost to himself. It was like driving through patches of fog; you got into a clear spot followed by another clouded one. "It wasn't really their government at all. It really was Yamata and the others. That's why they want THISTLE back." Nobody else in the room knew what he was talking about.

"What's that?" the President asked. Jack turned his eyes to Winston and Gant, then shook his head. Durling nodded and went on. "So the whole event was one big plan?"

"Yes, sir, but we still don't know it all."

"What do you mean?" Winston asked. "They cripple us, start a worldwide panic, and you say there's *more?*"

"George, how often have you been over there?" Ryan asked, mainly to get information to the others.

"In the last five years? I guess it comes out to an average of about once a month. My grandchildren will be using up the last of my frequent-flyer miles."

"How often have you met with government people over there?"

Winston shrugged. "They're around a lot. But they don't matter very much."

"Why?" the President asked.

"Sir, it's like this: there're maybe twenty or thirty people over there who really run things, okay? Yamata is the biggest fish in that lake. The Ministry of International Trade and Industry is the interface between the big boys in the corporate arena and the government, plus the way they grease the skids themselves with elected officials, and they do a *lot* of that stuff. It's one of the things Yamata liked to show off when we negotiated his takeover of my Group. At one party there were two ministers and a bunch of parliamentary guys, and their noses got real brown, y'know?" Winston reflected that at the time he'd thought it a good demeanor for elected officials. Now he wasn't quite so sure.

"How freely can I speak?" Ryan asked. "We may need their insights."

Durling handled that: "Mr. Winston, how good are

you at keeping secrets?"

The investor had himself a good chuckle. "Just so long as you don't call it insider stuff, okay? I've never been hassled by the SEC, and I don't want to start."

"This one'll come under the Espionage Act. We're at war with Japan. They've sunk two of our submarines and crippled two aircraft carriers," Ryan said, and the room changed a lot.

"Are you serious?" Winston asked.

"Two-hundred-and-fifty-dead-sailors serious, the crews of USS *Asheville* and USS *Charlotte*. They've also seized the Mariana Islands. We don't know yet if we can take those islands back. We have upwards of ten thousand American citizens in Japan as potential hostages, plus the population of the islands, plus military personnel in Japanese custody."

"But the media — "

"Haven't caught on yet, remarkably enough," Ryan explained. "Maybe it's just too crazy."

"Oh." Winston got it after another second. "They wreck our economy, and we don't have the political will to . . . has anybody ever tried anything like this before?"

The National Security Advisor shook his head. "Not that I know of."

"But the real danger to us — is this problem here. That son of a bitch," George Winston observed.

"How do we fix it, Mr. Winston?" President Durling asked.

"I don't know. The DTC move was brilliant. The takedown was pretty cute, but Secretary Fiedler here might have smarted his way out of that with our help," Winston added. "But with no records, everything's paralyzed. I have a brother who's a doctor, and once he told me . . ."

Ryan's eyeballs clicked at that remark, clicked hard enough that he didn't listen to the rest. Why was that important?

"The time estimate came in last night," the Fed Chairman was saying now. "They need a week. But we don't really have a week. This afternoon we're meeting with all the heads of the big houses. We're going to try and . . ."

The problem is that there are no records, Jack thought. *Everything's frozen in place because there are* no records *to tell people what they own, how much money they . . .*

"Europe is paralyzed, too . . ." Fiedler was talking now, while Ryan stared down at the carpet. Then he looked up:

"If you don't write it down, it never happened." Conversation in the room stopped, and Jack saw that he might as well have said, *The crayon is purple.*

"What?" the Fed Chairman asked.

"My wife — that's what she says. 'If you don't write it down, then it never happened.' " He looked around. They still didn't understand. Which wasn't overly surprising, as he was still developing the thought himself. "She's a doc, too, George, at Hopkins, and she always has this damned little notebook with her, and she's always stopping dead in her tracks to take it out and make a note because she doesn't trust her memory."

"My brother's the same way. He uses one of those electronic things," Winston said. Then his eyeballs went out of focus. "Keep going."

"There are no records, no really official records of any of the transactions, are there?" Jack went on. Fiedler handled the answer.

"No. Depository Trust Company crashed for fair. And as I just said, it'll take — "

"Forget that. We don't have the time, do we?"

That depressed SecTreas again. "No, we can't stop it."

"Sure we can." Ryan looked at Winston. "Can't we?"

President Durling had been covering the snippets

740

of conversation like a spectator at a tennis match, and the stress of the situation had placed a short fuse on his temper. "What the hell are you people talking about?"

Ryan almost had it now. He turned to his President. "Sir, it's simple. We say it never happened. We say that after noon on Friday, the exchanges simply stopped functioning. Now, can we get away with that?" Jack asked. He didn't give anyone a chance to answer, however. "Why not? Why *can't* we get away with it? There are no records to prove that we're wrong. *Nobody* can prove a single transaction from twelve noon on, can they?"

"With all the money that everyone lost," Winston said, his mind catching up rapidly, "it won't look all that unattractive. You're saying we restart . . . Friday, maybe, Friday at noon . . . just wipe out the intervening week, right?"

"But nobody will buy it," the Fed Chairman observed.

"Wrong." Winston shook his head. "Ryan's got something here. First of all, they *have* to buy it. You can't do a transaction — you can't execute one, I mean, without written records. So nobody can prove that they did anything without waiting for reconstruction of the DTC records. Second, most people went to the cleaners, institutions, banks, everybody, and they'll all want a second chance. Oh, yeah, they'll buy into it, pal. Mark?"

"Step in a time machine and do Friday all over again?" Gant's laugh was grim at first. Then it changed. "Where do we sign up?"

"We can't do that to everything, not all the trades," the Fed Chairman objected.

"No, we can't," Winston agreed. "The international T-Bill transactions were outside our control. But what we can do, sir, is conference with the European banks, show them what's happened, and then

741

together with them — "

Now it was Fiedler: "Yes! They dump yen and buy dollars. Our currency regains its position and theirs falls. The other Asian banks will then think about reversing their positions. The European central banks will play ball, I think."

"You'll have to keep the Discount Rate up," Winston said. "That'll sting us some, but it's one hell of a lot better than the alternative. You keep the rate up so that people stop dumping T-Bills. We want to generate a move away from the yen, just like they did to us. The Europeans will like that because it will limit the Japs' ability to scoop up their equities like they started doing yesterday." Winston got off his chair and started pacing a little as he was wont to do. He didn't know that he was violating a White House protocol, and even the President didn't want to interrupt him, though the two Secret Service agents in the room kept a close eye on the trader. Clearly his mind was racing through the scenario, looking for holes, looking for flaws. It took perhaps two minutes, and everyone waited for his evaluation. Then his head came up. "Dr. Ryan, if you ever decide to become a private citizen again, we need to talk. Gentlemen: this *will* work. It's just so damned outrageous, but maybe that works in our favor."

"What happens Friday, then?" Jack asked.

Gant spoke up: "The market will drop like a rock."

"What's so damned great about that?" the President demanded.

"Because then, sir," Gant went on, "it'll bounce after about two hundred points, and close . . . ? It'll close down, oh, maybe a hundred, maybe not even that much. The following Monday everybody catches his breath. Some people look for bargains. Most, probably, are still nervous. It drops again, probably ends up pretty stagnant, down another fifty at most. The rest of the week, things settle out. Figure by

742

the following Friday, the market has restabilized down one, maybe one-fifty, from the Friday-noon position. The drop will have to happen because of what the Fed has to do with the Discount Rate, but we're used to that on the Street." Only Winston fully appreciated the irony in the fact that Gant had it almost exactly right. He himself could hardly have done it better. "Bottom line, it's a major hiccup, but no more than that."

"Europe?" Ryan asked.

"It'll be rougher over there because they're not as well organized, but their central banks have somewhat more power," Gant said. "Their governments can also interfere more in the marketplace. That's both a help and a hurt. But the end result is going to be the same. It has to be, unless everyone signs on to the same suicide pact. People in our business don't do that."

Fiedler's turn: "How do we sell it?"

"We get the heads of the major institutions together just as fast as we can," Winston replied. "I can help if you want. They listen to me, too."

"Jack?" the President asked with a turn of the head.

"Yes, sir. And we do it right away."

Roger Durling gave it a few more seconds of thought before turning to the Secret Service agent next to his desk. "Tell the Marines to get my chopper over here. Tell the Air Force to get something warmed up for New York."

Winston demurred. "Mr. President, I have my own."

Ryan took that one. "George, the Air Force guys are better. Trust me."

Durling rose and shook hands all around before the Secret Service agents conducted the others downstairs and out onto the South Lawn to await the helicopter flight to Andrews. Ryan stayed put.

"Will it really work? Can we really fix it that easily?" The politician in Roger Durling distrusted magic fixes to anything. Ryan saw the doubts and framed his answer appropriately.

"It ought to. They need something up there, and they will surely want it to work. The crucial element is that they have to know that the takedown was a deliberate act. That makes it artificial, and if they believe that it was artificial, then it's easier for everyone to accept an irregular fix to it."

"I guess we'll see." Durling paused. "Now what does that tell us about Japan?"

"It tells us that their government isn't the prime moving force behind this. That's good news and bad news. The good news is that the effort will be poorly organized at some levels, that the Japanese people are disconnected from the effort, and that there may be elements in their government very uncomfortable with the undertaking."

"The bad news?" the President asked.

"We still don't know what their overall objective is. The government is evidently doing what it's told. It has a solid strategic position in WestPac, and we still don't know what to do about it. Most important of all — "

"The nukes." Durling nodded. "That's their trump. We've never been at war against someone with nuclear arms, have we?"

"No, sir. That's a new one, too."

The next transmission from Clark and Chavez went out just after midnight Tokyo time. This time Ding had drafted the article. John had run out of interesting things to say about Japan. Chavez, being younger, did an article that was lighter, about young people and their attitudes. It was just the cover, but you have to work hard on those, and Ding, it turned out, had learned how to write coherently at George Mason University.

"Northern Resource Area?" John asked, typing the question on the computer screen. Then he turned the machine on the coffee table.

I should have seen it sooner. It's in one of the books back at Seoul, mano. Indonesia, belonged to the Dutch back then, was the Southern *Resource Area when they kicked off Big Mistake No. 2. Care to guess what the Northern one was?*

Clark just took one look and pushed the computer back. "Yevgeniy Pavlovich, go ahead and send it." Ding erased the dialog on the screen and hooked up the modem to the phone. The dispatch went out seconds later. Then the two officers traded a look. It had been a productive day after all.

The timing for once could scarcely have been better: 00:08 in Tokyo was 18:08 in Moscow and 10:08 both at Langley and in the White House, and Jack was just reentering his office after his time at the opposite corner of the West Wing when his STU-6 started warbling.

"Yeah."

"Ed here. We just got something important from our people in-country. The fax is coming over now. A copy's on the way to Sergey, too."

"Okay, standing by." Ryan flipped the proper switch and heard the facsimile printer start to turn out its copy.

Winston wasn't all that easy a man to impress. The VC-20 version of the Gulfstream-III business jet, he saw, was as nicely appointed as his personal aircraft — the seats and carpet were not as plush, but the communications gear was fabulous . . . even enough to make a real techno-weenie like Mark happy, he thought. The two older men took the chance to catch up on sleep while he observed the Air Force crewmen run through their preflight checklist. It really wasn't at all different from what his crewmen did, but Ryan had been right. It somehow made a difference to see military-type insignia on their shoulders. Three minutes later the executive jet was airborne and heading north for New York's La Guardia, with the added benefit that they already had a priority approach set up, which would save fifteen minutes at the top end of the trip. As he listened, the sergeant working the communications bay was arranging an FBI car to meet them at the general-aviation terminal, and evidently the Bureau was now calling everyone who mattered in the markets for a meeting at their own New York headquarters. How remarkable, he thought, to see the government acting in an efficient manner. What a pity they couldn't do that all the time.

Mark Gant was not paying attention to any of that. He was working on his computer, preparing what he called the case for the prosecution. He'd need about twenty minutes to get the exhibits printed up on acetate sheets for an overhead projector, something the FBI ought to be prepared for, they both hoped. From that point on . . . who would deliver the information? *Probably me,* Winston thought. He'd let Fiedler and the Fed Chairman propose the solution, and that was fair. After all, a government guy had come up with it.

Brilliant, George Winston told himself with an admiring chuckle. *Why didn't I think of that? What else . . . ?*

"Mark, make a note. We'll want to fly the European central-bank boys over here to see this. I don't think doing it over a teleconference line will really cut it."

Gant checked his watch. "We'll have to call right after we get in, George, but if we do the timing ought to work out okay. The evening flights into New York — yeah, they'll get in in the morning, and probably

746

we can coordinate everything for a Friday restart."

Winston looked aft. "We'll tell them when we get in. I think they need to catch some Z's for right now."

Gant nodded agreement. "It's going to work, George. That Ryan guy is pretty smart, isn't he?"

Now was a time to take it slow, Jack told himself. He was almost surprised that his phone hadn't rung yet, but on reflection he realized that Golovko was reading the same report, was looking at the same map on his wall, and was also telling himself to think it through as slowly and carefully as circumstances allowed.

It was starting to make sense. Well, almost. "Northern Resource Area" had to mean Eastern Siberia. The term "Southern Resource Area," as Chavez had stated in his report, had once been the term used by the Japanese government in 1941 to identify the Dutch East Indies, back when their prime strategic objective had been oil, then the principal resource needed for a navy and now the most important resource for any industrialized nation needing power to run its economy. Japan was the world's largest importer of oil despite an earnest effort to switch over to nuclear power for electricity. And Japan had to import so much else; only coal was in natural abundance. Supertankers were largely a Japanese invention, the more efficiently to move oil from the Persian Gulf fields to Japanese terminals. But they needed other things, too, and since she was an island nation, those commodities all had to come by sea, and Japan's navy was small, far too small to secure the sea-lanes.

On the other hand, Eastern Siberia was the world's last unsurveyed territory, and Japan was now conducting the survey, and the sea-lanes from the Eurasian mainland to Japan — *Hell, why not just build a railroad tunnel and do it the easy way?* Ryan asked himself.

747

Except for one thing. Japan was stretching her abilities to accomplish what she had already done, even with a gravely diminished American military *and* a five-thousand-mile buffer of Pacific waters between the American mainland and her own home islands. Russia's military capacity was even more drastically reduced than America's, but an invasion was more than a political act. It was an act against a people, and the Russians had not lost their pride. The Russians would fight, and they were still far larger than Japan. The Japanese had nuclear weapons on ballistic launchers, and the Russians, like the Americans, did not — but the Russians did have bombers, and fighter-bombers, and cruise missiles, all with nuclear capability, and bases close to Japan, and the political will to make use of them. There would have to be one more element. Jack leaned back, staring at his map. Then he lifted his phone and speed-dialed a direct line.

"Admiral Jackson."

"Robby? Jack. I have a question."

"Shoot."

"You said that one of our attachés in Seoul had a little talk with — "

"Yeah. They told him to sit tight and wait," Jackson reported.

"What *exactly* did the Koreans say?"

"They said . . . wait a minute. It's only half a page, but I have it here. Stand by." Jack heard a drawer open, probably a locked one. "Okay, paraphrasing, that sort of decision is political not military, many considerations to be looked at, concern that the Japanese could close their harbors to trade, concern about invasion, cut off from us, they're hedging. We haven't gone back to them yet," Robby concluded.

"OrBat for their military?" Jack asked. He meant "order of battle," essentially a roster of a nation's military assets.

"I have one around here."

"Short version," Ryan ordered.

"A little larger than Japan's. They've downsized since reunification, but what they retained is high-quality. Mainly U.S. weapons and doctrine. Their air force is pretty good. I've played with them and — "

"If you were an ROK general, how afraid would you be of Japan?"

"I'd be wary," Admiral Jackson replied. "Not afraid, but wary. They don't like Japan very much, remember."

"I know. Send me copies of that attaché report and the ROK OrBat."

"Aye aye." The line clicked off. Ryan called CIA next. Mary Pat still wasn't available, and her husband picked up. Ryan didn't bother with preliminaries.

"Ed, have you had any feedback from Station Seoul?"

"The ROKs seem very nervous. Not much cooperation. We've got a lot of friends in the KCIA, but they're clamming up on us, no political direction as yet."

"Anything different going on over there?"

"Well, yes," Ed Foley answered. "Their air force is getting a little more active. You know they have established a big training area up in the northern part of the country, and sure enough they're running some unscheduled combined-arms exercises. We have some overheads of it."

"Next, Beijing," Ryan said.

"A whole lot of nothing. China is staying out of this one. They say that they want no part of this, they have no interest in this. It doesn't concern them."

"Think about that, Ed," Jack ordered.

"Well, sure, it does concern them . . . oh . . ."

It wasn't quite fair and Ryan knew it. He now had fuller information than anyone else, and a huge head start on the analysis.

"We just developed some information. I'll have it sent over as soon as it's typed up. I want you down here at two-thirty for a skull session."

"We'll be there," the almost-DDO promised.

And there it was, right on the map. You just needed the right information, and a little time.

Korea was not a country to be intimidated by Japan. The latter country had ruled the former for almost fifty years earlier in the century, and the memories for Koreans were not happy ones. Treated as serfs by their conquerors, to this day there were few quicker ways to get dead than to refer to a Korean citizen as a Jap. The antipathy was real, and with the growing Korean economy and the competition to Japan that it made, the resentment was bilateral. Most fundamental of all was the racial element. Though Korea and Japan were in fact countries of the same genetic identity, the Japanese still regarded Koreans as Hitler had once regarded Poles. The Koreans, moreover, had their own warrior tradition. They'd sent two divisions of troops to Vietnam, had built a formidable military of their own to defend against the now-dead madmen to their north. Once a beaten-down colony of Japan, they were now tough, and very, very proud. So what, then, could have cowed them out of honoring treaty commitments to America?

Not Japan. Korea had little to fear from direct attack, and Japan could hardly use her nuclear weapons on Korea. Wind patterns would transport whatever fallout resulted right back to the country that had sent the weapons.

But immediately to Korea's north was the world's most populous country, with the world's largest standing army, and *that* was enough to frighten the ROKs, as it would frighten anyone.

Japan needed and doubtless wanted direct access to natural resources. It had a superb and fully developed economic base, a highly skilled manpower pool, all manner of high-tech assets. But Japan had a relatively small population in proportion to her economic strength.

China had a vast pool of people, but not as yet highly trained, a rapidly developing economy still somewhat lacking in high technology. And like Japan, China needed better access to resources.

And to the immediate north of both China and Japan was the world's last unexploited treasure house.

Taking the Marianas would prevent or at least hinder the approach of America's principal strategic arm, the U.S. Navy, from approaching the area of interest. The only other way to protect Siberia was from the west, through all of Russia. Meaning that the area was in fact cut off from outside assistance. China had her own nuclear capacity to deter Russia, and a larger land army to defend the conquest. It was a considerable gamble, to be sure, but with the American and European economies in a shambles, unable to help Russia, yes, it did all make good strategic sense. Global war on the installment plan.

The operational art, moreover, was not new in the least. First cripple the strong enemy, then gobble up the weak one. Exactly the same thing had been attempted in 1941–1942. The Japanese strategic concept had never been to conquer America, but to cripple the larger country so severely that acquiescence to her southern conquests would become a political necessity. Pretty simple stuff, really, Ryan told himself. You just had to break the code. That's when the phone rang. It was his number-four line.

"Hello, Sergey," Ryan said.

"How did you know?" Golovko demanded.

Jack might have answered that the line was set aside for the Russian's direct access, but didn't. "Because you just read the same thing I did."

"Tell me what you think?"

"I think you are their objective, Sergey Nikolay'ch. Probably for next year." Ryan's voice was light, still in the flush of discovery, which was always pleasant despite the nature of the new knowledge.

"Earlier. Autumn, I should imagine. The weather will work more in their favor that way." Then came a lengthy pause. "Can you help us, Ivan Emmetovich? No, wrong question. *Will* you help us?"

"Alliances, like friendships, are always bilateral," Jack pointed out. "You have a president to brief. So do I."

32

Special Report

As an officer who had once hoped to command a ship like this one, Captain Sanchez was glad he'd chosen to remain aboard instead of flying his fighter off to the Naval Air Station at Barbers Point. Six gray tugboats had nudged USS *John Stennis* into the graving dock.

There were over a hundred professional engineers aboard, including fifty new arrivals from Newport News Shipbuilding, all of them below and looking at the power plant. Trucks were lined up on the perimeter of the graving dock, and with them hundreds of sailors and civilian yard employees, like doctors or EMTs, Bud imagined, ready to switch out body parts.

As Captain Sanchez watched, a crane lifted the first brow from its cradle, and another started turning, to lift what looked like a construction trailer, probably to rest on the flight deck. The gate on the dock wasn't even closed yet. Somebody, he saw, was in a hurry.

"Captain Sanchez?"

Bud turned to see a Marine corporal. He handed over a message form after saluting. "You're wanted at CINCPACFLT Operations, sir."

"That's totally crazy," the president of the New

753

York Stock Exchange said, managing to get the first word in.

The big conference room at the FBI's New York office looked remarkably like a courtroom, with seats for a hundred people or more. It was about half empty, and the majority of people present were government employees of one sort or another, mainly FBI and SEC officials who'd been working the takedown case since Friday evening. But the front row was filled entirely with senior traders and institution chairmen.

George had just taken them through his version of the events of the previous week, using an overhead projector to display trends and trades and going slowly because of the fatigue level that had to affect the judgment of everyone trying to understand what he was saying. The Fed Chairman just then entered the room, having made his calls to Europe. He gave Winston and Fiedler a thumbs-up and took a seat in the back for the moment.

"It may be crazy, but that's what happened."

The NYSE head thought about that. "That's all well and good," he said after a few seconds, meaning that it wasn't well and good at all, and everybody knew it. "But we're still stuck in the middle of a swamp, and the alligators are gathering around us. I don't think we can hold them off much longer." There was general agreement on that point. Everyone in the front row was surprised to see their former colleague smile.

Winston turned to the Secretary of the Treasury. "Buzz, why don't you deliver the good news?"

"Ladies and gentlemen, there is a way out," Fiedler said confidently. His next sixty seconds generated incredulous silence. The traders didn't even have the wit to turn and look at one another. But if they didn't exactly nod with approval, neither did anyone object, even after a seemingly endless period of consideration.

The first to speak, predictably, was the managing director of Cummings, Carter, and Cantor. CCC had died around 3:15 on the previous Friday, caught moving the wrong way, its cash reserves wiped out, and then denied help from Merrill Lynch in a move which, in fairness, the managing director could not really fault.

"Is it legal?" he asked.

"Neither the United States Department of Justice nor the Securities and Exchange Commission will consider your cooperation to be any sort of violation. I will say," Fiedler added, "that any attempt to exploit the situation will be dealt with very severely indeed — but if we all work together, antitrust and other considerations will be set aside in the interests of national security. That is irregular, but it is now on record, and you all heard me say it. Ladies and gentlemen, that is the intention and the word of the United States government."

Well, damn, the assembled multitude thought. Especially the law-enforcement people.

"Well, you all know what happened to us at Triple-C," the director said, looking around, and his natural skepticism was tempered with the beginnings of genuine relief. "I don't have a choice here. I have to buy into this."

"I have something to add." Now the Fed Chairman walked to the front of the room. "I just finished calling the central-bank heads of Britain, France, Germany, Switzerland, Belgium, and the Netherlands. They're all flying here tonight. We'll get together right here tomorrow morning to set up a system by which they also can cooperate in this effort. We *are* going to stabilize the dollar. We *are* going to fix the T-Bill market. The American banking system will *not* go down on us. I am going to propose to the Open Market Committee that anyone who holds on to U.S. Treasuries — that is, extends the three-month and six-month notes for one renewal cycle — gets an *extra* fifty basis points as a reward from the U.S. government for helping us through this situation. We will also give the same bonus to anyone who buys T-Bills in the next ten days after the markets reopen."

Smart move, Winston thought. *Very smart move.* That would draw foreign money into America, away from Japan, and really firm up the dollar — while attacking the yen. The Asian banks that dumped on the dollar would get it in the back of the neck for the move. *So two could play the game, eh?*

"You need legislation for that," a treasuries expert objected.

"We'll get it, we'll have ink on paper by Friday-a-week. For the moment, that is the policy of the Federal Reserve, approved and supported by the President of the United States," the Chairman added.

"They're giving us our life back, people," Winston said, pacing up and down again in front of the wooden rail. "We have been *attacked* by people who wanted to take us down. They wanted to cut our heart out. Well, looks like we have some pretty good doctors here. We're going to be sick for a while, but by the end of next week it's going to be okay."

"Friday noon, eh?" the NYSE asked.

"Correct," Fiedler told him, staring hard now and waiting for a response. The executive gave it another few seconds of thought, then stood.

"You will have the full cooperation of the New York Stock Exchange." And the prestige of the NYSE was enough to overcome any doubts. Full cooperation was inevitable, but speed in the decision cycle was vital, and in ten more seconds the market officials were standing, smiling, and thinking about getting their shops back together.

"There will be no program trading until further notice," Fiedler said. "Those 'expert systems' nearly killed us. Friday is going to be exciting under the

756

best of circumstances. We want people to use their brains, not their Nintendo systems."

"Agreed," NASDAQ said for the rest.

"We need to rethink those things anyway," Merrill Lynch announced thoughtfully.

"We will coordinate through this office. Think things through," the Fed Chairman told them. "If you have ideas on how to make the transition go more smoothly, we want to know about it. We will reconvene at six. Ladies and gentlemen, we are in this together. For the next week or so we are not competitors. We are team members."

"I have about a million individual investors depending on my house," Winston reminded them. "Some of you have more. Let's not forget that." There was nothing like an appeal to honor. It was a virtue that all craved, even those who lacked it. Fundamentally, honor was itself a debt, a code of behavior, a promise, something inside yourself that you owed to the others who saw it in you. Everyone in this room wanted all the others to look and see a person worthy of respect and trust, and honor. An altogether useful concept, Winston thought, most particularly in time of trouble.

And then there was one, Ryan thought. The way it always seemed to work at this level, you took care of the simple jobs first and saved the really tough ones for last.

The mission now was more to prevent war than to execute it, but the latter would be part of the former.

The control of Eastern Siberia by Japan and China would have the effect of creating a new — what? Axis? Probably not that. Certainly a new world economic powerhouse, a rival to America in all categories of power. It would give Japan and China a huge competitive advantage in economic terms.

757

That in and of itself was not an evil ambition. But the methods were. The world had once operated by rules as simple as those of any jungle. If you got it first, it was yours — but only if you had the strength to hold it. Not terribly elegant, nor especially fair by contemporary standards, but the rules had been accepted because the stronger nations generally gave citizens political stability in return for loyalty, and that was usually the first step in the growth of a nation. After a while, however, the human need for peace and security had grown into something else — a desire for a stake in the governance of their country. From 1789, the year that America had ratified its Constitution, to 1989, the year that Eastern Europe had fallen, a mere two centuries, something new had come into the collective mind of mankind. It was called by many names — democracy, human rights, self-determination — but it was fundamentally a recognition that the human will had its own force, and mainly for good.

The Japanese plan sought to deny that force. But the time for the old rules was past, Jack told himself. The men in this room would have to see to it.

"So," his briefing concluded, "that's the overall situation in the Pacific."

The Cabinet Room was full, except for the seat of the Secretary of the Treasury, whose senior deputy was sitting in. Around the roughly diamond-shaped table were the heads of the various departments of the Executive Branch. Senior members of Congress and the military had seats against the four walls.

The Secretary of Defense was supposed to speak next. Instead of rising to the lectern as Ryan went back to his place, however, he flipped open his leather folder of notes and scarcely looked up from them.

"I don't know that we can do this," SecDef began, and with those words the men and women of the President's Cabinet shifted uneasily in their chairs.

758

"The problem is as much technical as anything. We cannot project sufficient power to — "

"Wait a minute," Ryan interrupted. "I want to make a few items clear for everyone, okay?" There were no objections. Even the Defense Secretary seemed relieved that he didn't have to speak.

"Guam is U.S. Territory, has been for almost a century. The people there are our citizens. Japan took the island away from us in 1941, and in 1944 we took it back. People died to do that."

"We think we can get Guam back through negotiations," Secretary Hanson said.

"Glad to hear that," Ryan replied. "What about the rest of the Marianas?"

"My people think it's unlikely that we will get them back through diplomatic means. We'll work on it, of course, but — "

"But *what?*" Jack demanded. There was no immediate answer. "All right, let's make another thing clear. The Northern Marianas were *never* a legal possession of Japan, despite what their ambassador told us. They were a Trust Territory under the League of Nations, and so they were *not* war booty to us when we took them in 1944 along with Guam. In 1947 the United Nations declared them a Trust Territory under the protection of the United States. In 1952 Japan officially renounced all claims to sovereignty to the islands. In 1978, the *people* of the Northern Marianas opted to become a Commonwealth, politically unified with the United States, and they elected their first governor — we took long enough to let them do that, but they did. In 1986 the U.N. decided that we had faithfully fulfilled our responsibilities to those people, and in the same year the people of those islands all got U.S. citizenship. In 1990 the U.N. Security Council closed out the trusteeship for good.

"Do we all have that? The citizens of those islands

are *American* citizens, with U.S. passports — not because we made them do it, but because they freely chose to be. That's called self-determination. We brought the idea to those rocks, and the people there must have thought that we were serious about it."

"You can't do what you can't do," Hanson said. "We can negotiate — "

"Negotiate, hell!" Jack snarled back. "Who says we can't?"

SecDef looked up from his notes. "Jack, it could take years to rebuild . . . the things we've deactivated. If you want to blame someone, well, blame me."

"If we can't do it — what's it going to cost?" the Secretary of Health and Human Services asked. "We have things we have to do *here!*"

"So we let a foreign country strip the citizenship rights of Americans because it's *too hard* to defend them?" Ryan asked more quietly. "Then what? What about the next time it happens? Tell me, when did we stop being the United States of America? It's a matter of political will, that's all," the National Security Advisor went on. "Do we have any?"

"Dr. Ryan, we live in a real world," the Secretary of the Interior pointed out. "All those people on those islands, can we put their lives at risk?"

"We used to say that freedom had a greater value than life. We used to say the same thing about our political principles," Ryan replied. "And the result is the world which those principles built. The things we call rights — nobody just *gave* them to us. No, sir. Those ideas are things we fought for. Those are things people died for. The people on those islands are American citizens. Do we owe them anything?"

Secretary Hanson was uncomfortable with this line of thought. So were others, but they deferred to him, grateful to be able to do so. "We can negotiate from a position of strength — but we have to go carefully."

"How carefully?" Ryan asked quietly.

"Damn it, Ryan, we can't risk nuclear attack over a few thousand — "

"Mr. Secretary, what's the magic number, then? A million? Our place in the world is based on a few very simple ideas — and a lot of people lost their lives for those ideas."

"You're talking philosophy," Hanson shot back. "Look, I have my negotiating team together. We'll get Guam back."

"No, sir, we're going to get them *all* back. And I'll tell you why." Ryan leaned forward, looking up and down the table. "If we don't, then we cannot prevent a war between Russia on one side and Japan and China on the other. I think I know the Russians. They will fight for Siberia. They have to. The resources there are their best chance for bootstrapping their country into the next century. That war could go nuclear. Japan and China probably don't think it'll go that far, people, but I'm telling you it will. You know why?

"If we cannot deal with this situation effectively, then who can? The Russians will think they're alone. Our influence with them will be zero, they'll have their backs against a wall, and they'll lash out the only way they can, and the butcher's bill will be like nothing the world has ever seen, and I'm not ready for another dark age.

"So we don't have a choice. You can name any reason you want, but it all comes down to the same thing: we have a debt of honor to the people on those islands who decided that they wanted to be Americans. If we don't defend that principle, we don't defend anything. And nobody will trust us, and nobody will respect us, not even ourselves. If we turn our back on them, then we are not the people we say we are, and everything we've ever done is a lie."

Through it all, President Durling sat quietly in his place, scanning faces, most especially his Secretary

761

of Defense, and behind him, against the wall, the Chairman of the Joint Chiefs, the man SecDef had picked to assist him in the dismantlement of the American military. Both men were looking down, and it was clear that both men were unworthy of the moment. It was also clear that their country could not afford to be.

"How can we do it, Jack?" Roger Durling asked.

"Mr. President, I don't know yet. Before we try, we have to decide if we are going to or not, and that, sir, is your call."

Durling weighed Ryan's words, and weighed the desirability of polling his cabinet for their opinions, but the faces told him something he didn't like. He remembered his time in Vietnam when he'd told his troopers that, yes, it all mattered, even though he knew that it was a lie. He'd never forgotten the looks on their faces, and though it was not widely known, every month or so now, in the dark of night, he'd walk down to the Vietnam Memorial, where he knew the exact location of every name of every man who had died under his command, and he visited those names one by one, to tell them that, yes, it really had mattered somehow, that in the great scheme of events their deaths had contributed to something, and that the world had changed for the better, too late for them, but not too late for their fellow citizens. President Durling thought of one other thing: nobody had ever taken land away from America. Perhaps it all came down to that.

"Brett, you will commence negotiations immediately. Make it clear that the current situation in the Western Pacific is in no way acceptable to the United States government. We will settle for nothing less than a complete restoration of the Mariana Islands to their antebellum condition. Nothing less," Durling repeated.

"Yes, Mr. President."

"I want plans and options for the removal of Japanese forces from those islands should negotiations fail," JUMPER told the Secretary of Defense. The latter nodded but his face told the tale. SecDef didn't think it could be done.

Admiral Chandraskatta thought it had taken long enough, but he was patient, and he knew that he could afford to be. *What will happen now?* he wondered.

It could have gone more quickly. He'd been a little slow in his methods and plans, trying to learn the thought patterns of his adversary, Rear Admiral Michael Dubro. He was a clever foe, skilled at maneuvering, and because he was clever, he'd been quick to think that his own foe was stupid. It had been obvious for a week that the American formation lay to the southwest, and by moving south, he'd cajoled Dubro into moving north, then east. Had his assessment been wrong, then the American fleet would still have had to go to the same spot, east of Dondra Head, forcing the fleet oilers to cut the corner. Sooner or later they would pass under the eyes of his air patrols, and, finally, they had. Now all he had to do was follow them, and Dubro couldn't divert them except to the east. And that meant diverting his entire fleet to the east, away from Sri Lanka, opening the way for his navy's amphibious formation to load its cargo of soldiers and armored vehicles. The only alternative was for the Americans to confront his fleet and offer battle.

But they wouldn't do that — would they? No. The only sensible thing for America to do was to recall Dubro and his two carriers to Pearl Harbor, there to await the political decision on whether or not to confront Japan. They had divided their fleet, violating the dictum of Alfred Thayer Mahan, which Chandraskatta had learned at the Naval War College at Newport, Rhode Island, along with his classmate,

Yusuo Sato, not so many years before, and he remembered the theoretical discussions they'd had on walks along the seawall, watching the yachts and wondering how small navies could defeat big ones.

Arriving at Pearl Harbor, Dubro would confer with the intelligence and operations staffs of his Pacific Fleet command and they would do their sums, and then they would see that it probably could not be done. How angry and frustrated they would be, the Indian Admiral thought.

But first he would teach them a lesson. Now he was hunting them. For all their speed and cleverness, they were tied to a fixed point, and sooner or later you just ran out of maneuvering room. Now he could force them away, and allow his country to take her first imperial step. A small one, almost inconsequential in the great game, but a worthy opening move nonetheless because the Americans would withdraw, allowing his country to move, as Japan had moved. By the time America had built its strength back up, it would be too late to change things. It was all about space and time, really. Both worked against a country crippled by internal difficulties and therefore robbed of her purpose. How clever of the Japanese to see to that.

"It went better than I expected," Durling said. He'd walked over to Ryan's office for the chat, a first for both of them.

"You really think so?" Jack asked in surprise.

"Remember, I inherited most of the cabinet from Bob." The President sat down. "Their focus is domestic. That's been my problem all along."

"You need a new SecDef and a new Chairman," the National Security Advisor observed coldly.

"I know that, but the timing is bad for it." Durling smiled. "It gives you a slightly wider purview, Jack. But I have a question to ask you first."

"I don't know if we can bring it off." Ryan was doodling on his pad.

"We have to take the missiles out of play first."

"Yes, sir, I know that. We'll find them. At least I expect that we will one way or another. The other wild cards are hostages, and our ability to hit the islands. This war, if that's what it is, has different rules. I'm not sure what those rules are yet." Ryan was still working on the public part of the problem. How would the American people react? How would the Japanese?

"You want some input from your commander in chief?" Durling asked.

That was good enough to generate another smile. "You bet."

"I fought in a war where the other side made the rules," Durling observed. "It didn't work out very well."

"Which leads me to a question," Jack said.

"Ask it."

"How far can we go?"

The President considered. "That's too open-ended."

"The enemy command authority is usually a legitimate target of war, but heretofore those people have been in uniform."

"You mean going after the zaibatsu?"

"Yes, sir. Our best information is that they're the ones giving the orders. But they're civilians, and going directly after them could seem like assassination."

"We'll cross that bridge when we get to it, Jack." The President stood to leave, having said what he'd come in to say.

"Fair enough." *A slightly wider purview,* Ryan thought. That could mean many things. Mainly it meant that he had the opportunity to run with the ball, but all alone, unprotected. *Well,* Jack thought, *you've done that before.*

"What have we done?" Koga asked. "What have we allowed them to do?"

"It's so easy for them," responded a political aide of long standing. He didn't have to say who *them* was. "We cannot ourselves assert our power, and divided, it's just so easy for them to push us in any direction they want . . . and over time — " The man shrugged.

"And over time the policy of our country has been decided by twenty or thirty men elected by no one but their own corporate boardrooms. But this far?" Koga asked. "But *this* far?"

"We are where we are. Would you prefer that we deny it?" the man asked.

"And who protects the people now?" the former — that word was bitter indeed — Prime Minister asked, leading with his chin and knowing it.

"Goto, of course."

"We cannot permit that. You know what he follows." Koga's counselor nodded, and would have smiled but for the gravity of the moment. "Tell me," Mogataru Koga asked. "What is honor? What does it dictate now?"

"Our duty, Prime Minister, is to the people," replied a man whose friendship with the politician went back to Tokyo University. Then he remembered a quote from a Westerner — Cicero, he thought. "The good of the people is the highest law."

And that said it all, Koga thought. He wondered if treason always began that way. It was something he'd sleep on, except that he knew that he wouldn't sleep at all that night. *This morning,* Koga thought with a grunt, checking his watch.

"We're sure that it has to be standard-gauge track?"

"You can resection the photos we have yourself," Betsy Fleming told him. They were back in the Pen-

766

tagon headquarters of the National Reconnaissance Office. "The transporter-car our people saw is standard gauge."

"Disinformation, maybe?" the NRO analyst asked.

"The diameter of the SS-19 is two-point-eight-two meters," Chris Scott replied, handing over a fax from Russia. "Throw in another two hundred seventy centimeters for the transport container. I ran the numbers myself. The narrow-gauge track over there would be marginal for an object of that width. Possible, but marginal."

"You have to figure," Betsy went on, "that they're not going to take too many chances. Besides, the Russians also considered a rail-transport mode for the Mod-4 version, and designed the bird for that, and the Russian rail gauge — "

"Yeah, I forgot that. It is larger than our standard, isn't it?" The analyst nodded. "Okay, that does make the job easier." He turned back to his computer and executed a tasking order that he'd drafted a few hours earlier. For every pass over Japan, the narrow-focus high-resolution cameras would track down along precise coordinates. Interestingly, AMTRAK had the best current information on Japanese railroads, and even now one of their executives was being briefed in on the security rules pertaining to overhead imagery. It was a pretty simple briefing, really. Tell anyone what you see, and figure on a lengthy vacation at Marion, Illinois.

The computer-generated order went to Sunnyvale, California, from there to a military communications satellite, and thence to the two orbiting KH-11 satellites, one of which would overfly Japan in fifty minutes, the other ten minutes after that. All three people wondered how good the Japanese were at camouflaging. The hell of it was, they might never find out. All they could do, really, was wait. They would look at the imagery in real-time as it came in, but unless there were overt signs pointing to what they sought, the real work would be done over hours and days. If they were lucky.

Kurushio was on the surface, never something to make a submarine commander happy. They wouldn't be here long. Fuel was coming aboard through two large-diameter hoses, and other stores, mainly food, were lowered by crane to crewmen waiting on the deck. His navy didn't have a proper submarine tender, Commander Ugaki knew. Mainly they used tank-landing ships for the purpose, but those were fulfilling other purposes now, and he was stuck with a mer-chantman whose crew was enthusiastic but unfamiliar with the tasks they were now attempting.

His was the last boat into Agana Harbor because he'd been the one farthest away from the Marianas when the occupation had begun. He'd fired only one torpedo, and was gratified to see how well the Type 89 had worked. That was good. The mer-chantmen didn't have the equipment to reload him properly, but, the captain told himself, he had fifteen more, and four Harpoon missiles, and if the Ameri-cans offered him that many targets, so much the bet-ter.

Those crewmen not on duty loading stores on the afterdeck were crowded forward, getting some sun as submariners often did — as indeed their captain was doing, bare-chested atop the sail, drinking tea and smiling for everyone to see. His next mission was to patrol the area west of the Bonins, to intercept any American ship — more likely a submarine — that attempted to close the Home Islands. It promised to be typical submarine duty, Ugaki thought: dull but demanding. He'd have to talk to his crew about how important it was.

"So where's the patrol line?" Jones asked, pushing the envelope again.

"Along 165-East for the moment," Admiral Mancuso said, pointing at the chart. "We're thin, Jonesy. Before I commit them to battle, I want them to get used to the idea. I want the COs to drill their people up. You're never ready enough, Ron. Never."

"True," the civilian conceded. He'd come over with SOSUS printouts to demonstrate that all known submarine contacts were off the screen. Two hydrophone arrays that were operated from the island of Guam were no longer available. Though connected by undersea cable to the rest of the network, they'd evidently been turned off by the monitoring facility on Guam, and nobody at Pearl had yet been able to trick them back on. The good news was that a backup array off Samar in the Philippines was still operating, but it could not detect the Japanese SSKs shown by satellite to be replenishing off Agana. They'd even gotten a good count. Probably, Mancuso thought. The Japanese still painted the hull numbers on the sails, and the satellite cameras could read them. Unless the Japanese, like the Russians and then the Americans, had learned to spoof reconnaissance efforts by playing with the numbers — or simply erased them entirely.

"It would be nice to have a few more fast-attacks, wouldn't it?" Jones observed after a minute's contemplation of the chart.

"Sure would. Maybe if we can get some direction from Washington . . ." His voice trailed off, and Mancuso thought a little more. The location of every sub under his command was marked with a black silhouette, even the ones in overhaul status. Those were marked in white, showing availability dates, which was not much help at the moment. But there were five such silhouettes at Bremerton, weren't there?

The *Special Report* card appeared on all the major

TV networks. In every case the hushed voice of an anchorperson told people that their network shows would be interrupted by a speech from the President about the economic crisis with which his administration had been dealing since the weekend. Then came the Presidential Seal. Those who had been following the events were surprised to see the President smiling.

"Good evening.

"My fellow Americans, last week we saw a major event take place in the American financial system.

"I want to begin my report to you by saying that the American economy is strong. Now" — he smiled — "that may seem a strange pronouncement given all that you've heard in the media and elsewhere. But let me tell you why that is so. I'll start off with a question:

"What has changed? American workers are still making cars in Detroit and elsewhere. American workers are still making steel. Kansas farmers have their winter wheat in and are preparing for a new planting season. They're still making computers in the Silicon Valley. They're still making tires in Akron. Boeing is still making airplanes. They're still pumping oil out of the ground in Texas and Alaska. They're still mining coal in West Virginia. All the things you were doing a week ago, you are still doing. So what has changed?

"What changed was this: some electrons traveled along some copper wires, telephone lines like this one" — the President held up a phone cord and tossed it aside on his desk — "and that's all," he went on in the voice of a good, smart neighbor come to the house to offer some kindly advice. "Not one person has lost his life. Not a single business has lost a building. The wealth of our nation is unchanged. Nothing has gone away.

"And yet, my fellow Americans, we have begun

to panic — over what?

"In the past four days we have determined that a deliberate attempt was made to tamper with the U.S. financial markets. The United States Department of Justice, with the assistance of some good Americans within those markets, is now building a criminal case against the people responsible for that. I cannot go further at the moment because even your President does not have the right to tamper with the right of any person to a fair and impartial trial. But we do know what happened and we do know that what happened is entirely artificial.

"Now, what are we going to do about it?" Roger Durling asked.

"The financial markets have been closed all week. They will reopen at noon on Friday and . . ."

33

Reversal Points

"It can't possibly work," Kozo Matsuda said over the translation. "Raizo's plan was perfect — better than perfect," he went on, talking as much to himself as the telephone receiver. Before the crash he'd worked in conjunction with a banker associate to use the opportunity to cash in on the T-Bill transactions, which had gone a long way to recapitalizing his troubled conglomerate. It had also made his cash account yen-heavy in the face of international obligations. But that was not a problem, was it? Not with the renewed strength of the yen and corresponding weakness of the American dollar. It might even make sense, he thought, to purchase American interests through intermediaries — a good strategic move once the American equities market resumed its free fall.

"When do the European markets open?" Somehow in the excitement of the moment he couldn't remember.

"London is nine hours behind us. Germany and Holland are eight. Four this afternoon," the man on the other end of the phone said. "Our people have their instructions." And those were clear: to use the renewed power of their national currency to buy as many European equities as possible so that when the financial panic ended, two or three years from now, Japan would be so enmeshed in that multinational economy as to be a totally integral part of it; so vital to their survival that separation would run the renewed danger of financial collapse. And they wouldn't risk that, not after recovery from the worst economic crisis in three generations, and certainly not after Japan had played so important and selfless a part in restoring prosperity to three hundred million Europeans. It was troubling that the Americans suspected a hand in what had taken place, but Yamata-san had assured them all that no records could possibly exist — wasn't that the masterstroke of the entire event, the elimination of records and their replacement with chaos? Businesses could not operate without precise financial records of their transactions, and denied those, they simply stopped. Rebuilding them would require weeks or months, Matsuda was sure, during which time the paralysis would allow Japan — more precisely, his fellow zaibatsu — to cash in, in addition to the brilliant strategic moves Yamata had executed through their government agencies. The integrated nature of the plan was the reason why all his fellows had signed on to it.

"It really doesn't matter, Kozo. We took Europe down, too, and the only liquidity left in the world is ours."

"Good one, Boss," Ryan said, leaning on the door-frame.

"A long way to go," Durling said, leaving his chair and heading out of the Oval Office before saying anything more. The President and National Security Advisor headed into the White House proper, past the technicians who alone had been allowed in. It wasn't time to face reporters yet.

"It's amazing how philosophical it is," Jack said as they took the elevator to the residential floor.

"Metaphysics, eh? You did go to a Jesuit school, didn't you?"

"Three, actually. What is reality?" Jack asked rhetorically. "Reality to them is electrons and computer screens, and if there's one thing I learned on the Street, it's that they don't know investments worth a damn. Except Yamata, I suppose."

"Well, he did all right, didn't he?" Durling asked.

"He should have left the records alone. If he'd left us in free-fall . . ." Ryan shrugged. "It might just have kept going. It just never occurred to him that we might not play by his rules." And that, Jack told himself, would be the key to everything. The President's speech had been a fine mix of things said and unsaid, and the targeting of the speech had been precise. It had been, in fact, the first PsyOp of a war.

"The press can't stay dumb forever."

"I know." Ryan even knew where the leak would start, and the only reason it hadn't happened already was the FBI. "But we need to keep them dumb just a little longer."

It started cautiously, not really as part of any operational plan at all, but more as a precursor to one. Four B-1B Lancer bombers lifted off from Elmendorf Air Force Base in Alaska, followed by two KC-10 tankers. The combination of latitude and time of year guaranteed darkness. Their bomb bays were fitted with fuel tanks instead of weapons. Each aircraft had a crew of four, pilot and copilot, plus two systems operators.

The Lancer was a sleek aircraft, a bomber equipped with a fighter's stick instead of a more conventional control yoke, and pilots who had flown both said that the B-1B felt and flew like a slightly heavy F-4 Phantom, its greater weight and larger size giving the bomber greater stability and, for now, a smoother ride. For the moment the staggered formation of six flew international route R-220, maintaining the lateral spacing expected of commercial air traffic.

A thousand miles and two hours out, passing Shemya and leaving ground-control radar coverage, the six aircraft turned north briefly. The tankers held steady while the bombers one by one eased underneath to take on fuel, a procedure that lasted about twelve minutes in each case. Finished, the bombers continued southwest while the tankers turned to land at Shemya, where they would refill their own tanks.

The four bombers descended to twenty-five thousand feet, which took them below the regular stream of commercial air traffic and allowed more freedom of maneuver. They continued close to R-220, the westernmost of the commercial flight tracks, skimming down past the Kamchatka Peninsula.

Systems were flipped on in the back. Though designed as a penetrating bomber, the B-1B fulfilled many roles, one of which was electronic intelligence. The body of any military aircraft is studded with small structures that look for all the world like the fins on fish. These objects are invariably antennas of one sort or another, and the graceful fairing has no more sinister purpose than to reduce drag. The Lancer had many of them, designed to gather in radar and other electronic signals and pass them along to internal equipment, which analyzed the data. Some of the work was done in real-time by the flight crew. The idea was for the bomber to monitor hostile radar, the better to allow its crew to avoid detection and deliver its bombs.

At the NOGAL reporting point, about three hundred miles outside the Japanese Air Defense Identification Zone, the bombers split into a patrol line, with roughly fifty miles separating the aircraft, and descended to ten thousand feet. Crewmen rubbed their hands together, pulled their seat belts a little tighter, and started concentrating. Cockpit chatter lessened to that required by the mission, and tape recorders were flipped on. Satellite monitoring told them that the Japanese Air Force had airborne-early-warning aircraft, E-767s, operating almost continuously, and those were the defensive assets that the bomber crews feared most. Flying high, the E-767s could see far. Mobile, they could move to deal with threats with a high degree of efficiency. Worst of all, they invariably operated in conjunction with fighters, and fighters had eyes in them, and behind the eyes were brains, and weapons with brains in them were the most frightening of all.

"Okay, there's the first one," one of the systems operators said. It wasn't really the first. For practice of sorts, they'd calibrated their equipment on Russian air-defense radars, but for the first time in the collective memory of all sixteen airmen, it wasn't Russian radars and fighters which concerned them. "Low-frequency, fixed, known location."

They were receiving what operators often called "fuzz." The radar in question was under the horizon and too far away to detect their semistealthy aircraft. As you can see a person holding a flashlight long before the light reveals your presence to the holder, so it was with radar. The powerful transmitter was as much a warning beacon to unwanted guests as a lookout for its owners. The location, frequency, pulse-repetition rate, and estimated power of the radar was noted and logged. A display on the electronic-warfare officer's board showed the coverage for that radar. The display was repeated on the pilot's console, with the danger area marked in red. He'd stay well clear of it.

"Next," the EWO said. "Wow, talk about power — this one's airborne. Must be one of their new ones. It's definitely moving south-to-north, now bearing two-zero-two."

"Copy," the pilot acknowledged quietly, his eyes

scanning all around the dark sky. The Lancer was really proceeding on autopilot, but his right hand was only inches from the stick, ready to jerk the bomber to the left, dive to the deck, and go to burner. There were fighters somewhere off to his right, probably two F-15s, but they would stay close to E-767s.

"Another one, one-nine-five, just appeared . . . different freq and — stand by," the electronics officer said. "Okay, major frequency change. He's probably in an over-the-horizon mode now."

"Could he have us?" the pilot asked, checking his avoidance screen again. Outside the red keep-out zone was a yellow section that the pilot thought of as the "maybe" zone. They were at most a few minutes away from entering that zone, and "maybe" seemed very worrisome indeed at the moment, nearly three thousand miles from Elmendorf Air Force Base.

"Not sure. It's possible. Recommend we come left," the EWO said judiciously. On that advice, he felt the aircraft bank five degrees. The mission wasn't about taking risks. It was about gathering information, as a gambler would observe a table before taking his seat and putting his chips in play.

"I think there's somebody out there," one of the E-767 operators said. "Zero-one-five, southerly course. Hard to hold it."

The rotodome atop the E-767 was like few others in the world, and all of them were Japanese. Three of them were operating on the eastern approaches to their country. Transmitting up to three million watts of electrical energy, it had four times the power of anything the Americans had aloft, but the true sophistication of the system lay not in its power but in its mode of delivery. Essentially a smaller version of the SPY radar carried on the Kongo-class destroyers, the array was composed of thousands of solid-state diodes that could scan both electronically and mechanically, and jump in frequency to suit the needs of the moment. For long-range detection, a relatively low frequency was best. However, though the waves curved around the visible horizon somewhat, it was at the cost of poor resolution. The operator was getting a hit on only every third sweep or so. The system software had not yet learned to distinguish clutter from the purposeful activities of a human mind, at least not in all cases, and not, unfortunately, at this frequency setting. . . .

"Are you sure?" the senior controller asked over the intercom line. He'd just called up the display himself and didn't see anything yet.

"Here." The first man moved his cursor and marked the contact when it reappeared. He wished they could improve that software. "Wait! Look here!" He selected another blip and marked it, too. It disappeared almost at once but came back in fifteen seconds. "See, southerly course — speed five hundred knots."

"Excellent." The senior controller activated his radio microphone and reported to his ground station that Japanese air defenses were being probed for the first time. The only surprise, really, was that it had taken them so long. *This is where things get interesting,* he thought, wondering what would happen next, now that the games had begun.

"No more of those Es?" the pilot asked.

"No, just the two. I thought I had a little fuzz a minute ago," the EWO said, "but it faded out." He didn't need to explain that with the sensitivity of his instruments, he was probably getting readings on garage-door openers as well. A moment later another ground radar was plotted. The patrol line angled back west one by one as they passed the coverage of the two E-767s, still on a southwesterly base course, now halfway down the largest home island, Honshu, which was well over three hundred miles to their right. The copilots of each of the four aircraft looked exclusively west now, while the aircraft commanders scanned for possible air traffic to their front. It was tense but routine, not unlike driving through a neighborhood in which one didn't want to live. So long as the lights were all green, you didn't get too worried — but you didn't like the looks your car got.

The crew of the third E-767 was unhappy, and their fighter escorts even more so. Enemy aircraft were looking at their coastline, and even if they were six hundred kilometers out, they still didn't belong in the neighborhood. But they switched their radar systems to standby. Probably EC-135s, they thought, surveillance aircraft, assembling an electronic order of battle for their country. And if the American mission were to gather information, then the smart thing to do was to deny them the information they wanted. And it was easy to do, or so the radar-controller officers told themselves.

We'll go closer in the next time, the aircraft commander told himself. First electronics experts would have to examine the data and try to determine what was and what wasn't safe, betting the lives of fellow Air Force officers with their conclusions. That was a happy thought. The crew relaxed, yawned, and started talking, mainly about the mission and what they had learned. Four and a half hours back to Elmendorf, and a shower, and some mandated crew rest.

The Japanese controllers were still not completely sure that they'd had contacts at all, but that would be determined by examining their onboard tapes. Their patrol patterns returned to their normal monitoring of commercial air traffic, and a few comments

779

were exchanged on why the devil that traffic still continued. The answers were mainly shrugs and raised eyebrows and even more uncertainty than had existed when they'd thought they were tracking contacts. There was just something about looking at a radar screen for more than a few hours. Sooner or later your imagination took over, and the more you thought about it, the worse it got. But that, they knew, was the same for the other side in the game, too.

The central-bank heads were accustomed to VIP treatment. Their flights all arrived at John F. Kennedy International within the same hour. Each was met by a senior diplomat from their respective countries' U.N. delegations, whisked past customs control, and sent to the city in a car with diplomatic tags. The common destination surprised them all, but the Federal Reserve Chairman explained that for convenience the New York FBI office was a better place for coordination than the local Federal Reserve bank, especially since it was large enough to accommodate the directors of the major trading houses — and since antitrust regulations were being suspended in the interest of American national security. That notification bemused the European visitors. Finally, they thought, America understood the national-security implications of financial matters. It had certainly taken them long enough.

George Winston and Mark Gant began their final briefing on the events of the previous week after an introduction from the Chairman and Secretary Fiedler, and by this time they had the presentation down pat.

"Bloody clever," the head of the Bank of England observed to his German counterpart.

"*Jawohl*," was the whispered reply.

"How do we prevent something like this from happening again?" one of them wondered aloud.

"Better record-keeping systems for starters," Fiedler replied alertly after something approaching a decent night's sleep. "Aside from that . . . ? It's something we need to study for a while. Of greater interest are the remedial measures which we must now consider."

"The yen must suffer for this," the French banker observed at once. "And we must help you to protect the dollar in order to protect our own currencies."

"Yes." The Fed Chairman nodded at once. "Jean-Jacques, I'm glad you see it the same way we do."

"And to save your equities markets, what will you do?" the head of the Bundesbank asked.

"This is going to sound somewhat crazy, but we think it will work," Secretary Fiedler began, outlining the procedures that President Durling had *not* revealed in his speech and whose execution depended to a large degree on European cooperation. The visitors shared a common look, first of incredulity, then of approval.

Fiedler smiled. "Might I suggest that we coordinate our activities for Friday?"

Nine in the morning was considered an ungodly hour for the commencement of diplomatic negotiations, which helped the situation. The American delegation arrived at the Japanese Embassy on Massachusetts Avenue, N.W., in private cars, the better to conceal the situation.

The formalities were observed in all particulars. The conference room was large, with a correspondingly large table. The Americans took their places on one side and the Japanese on the other. Handshakes were exchanged because these were diplomats and such things were to be expected. Tea and coffee were available, but most just poured glasses of ice water into crystal glasses. To the annoyance of the Americans, some of the Japanese smoked. Scott Adler wondered if they did it just to unsettle him, and so to break the ice he requested and got a smoke from the Ambassador's chief aide.

"Thank you for receiving us," he began in a measured voice.

"Welcome, again, to our embassy," the Japanese Ambassador replied with a friendly if wary nod.

"Shall we begin?" Adler asked.

"Please." The Ambassador leaned back in his chair and adopted a relaxed posture to show that he was at ease and that he would listen politely to the impending discourse.

"The United States is gravely concerned with developments in the Western Pacific," Adler began. *Gravely concerned* was the right turn of phrase. When nations are gravely concerned, it usually means that they are contemplating violent action. "As you know, the inhabitants of the Mariana Islands hold American citizenship, and do so because of their own wishes, freely expressed in an election almost twenty years ago. For that reason the United States of America will not under any circumstances accept Japanese occupation of those islands, and we req— no," Adler corrected himself, "we *demand* the return of those islands to U.S. sovereignty forthwith, and the immediate and total removal of Japanese armed forces from the territories in question. We similarly require the immediate release of any and all U.S. citizens held by your government. Failure to comply with these requirements will entail the most serious possible consequences."

Everyone in the room thought the opening position statement was unequivocal. If anything it was a little too strong, the Japanese diplomats thought, even those who deemed their country's actions to be madness.

"I personally regret the tone of your statement," the Ambassador replied, giving Adler a diplomatic slap across the face. "On the substantive issues, we will listen to your position and consider its merit against our own security interests." This was a diplomat's way of saying that Adler would now have to repeat what he had just said — with amplifications. It was an implicit demand for another statement, one that conceded something, in return for which was the implied promise that there might be a concession on the part of his government.

"Perhaps I did not make myself sufficiently clear," Adler said after a sip of water. "Your country has committed an act of war against the United States of America. The consequences of such acts are very grave. We offer your country the opportunity to withdraw from those acts without further bloodshed."

The other Americans sitting at the table communicated without words and without a look: *Hardball.* There had scarcely been time for the American team to develop its thoughts and approaches, and Adler had gone further than they'd expected.

"Again," the Ambassador said after his own moment of contemplation, "I find your tone personally regrettable. As you know, my country has legitimate security interests, and has been the victim of unfortunate legal actions which can have no effect other than severe damage to our economic and physical security. Article 51 of the United Nations Charter specifically recognizes the right of any sovereign nation to self-defense measures. We have done no more than that." It was a skillful parry, even the Americans thought, and the renewed request for civility suggested a real opening for maneuver.

The initial discussions went on for another ninety minutes, with neither side budging, each merely repeating words, with hardly a change of phrase. Then it was time for a break. Security personnel opened the French doors to the embassy's elegant garden, and everyone went out, ostensibly for fresh air but really for more work. The garden was too large to bug, especially with a brisk wind blowing through the trees.

"So, Chris, we've begun," Seiji Nagumo said, sipping his coffee — he'd chosen it to show how sympathetic he was with the American position; for the same reason, Christopher Cook was drinking tea.

"What did you expect us to say?" the Deputy Assistant Secretary of State asked.

"The opening position is not surprising," Nagumo conceded.

Cook looked away, staring at the wall that enclosed the garden. He spoke quietly. "What will you give up?"

"Guam, definitely, but it must be demilitarized," Nagumo replied in the same voice. "And you?"

"So far, nothing."

"You must give me something to work with, Chris," Nagumo observed.

"There's nothing *to* offer, except maybe a cessation of hostilities — before they actually start."

"When will that happen?"

"Not anytime soon, thank God. We do have time to work with. Let's make good use of it," Cook urged.

"I'll pass that along. Thank you." Nagumo wandered off to join a member of his delegation. Cook did the same, ending up three minutes later with Scott Adler.

"Guam, demilitarized. That's definite. Maybe more. That's not definite."

"Interesting," Adler thought. "So you were right on their allowing us to save face. Nice call, Chris."

"What will we offer them back?"

"*Gornisch,*" the Deputy Secretary of State said coldly. He was thinking about his father, and the tattoo on his forearm, and how he'd learned that a 9 was an upside-down 6, and how his father's freedom had been taken away by a country once allied with the owner of this embassy and its lovely if cold garden. It was somewhat unprofessional and Adler knew it. Japan had offered a safe haven during those years to a few lucky European Jews, one of whom had become a cabinet secretary under Jimmy Carter. Perhaps if his father had been one of those fortunate few, his attitude might have been different, but his father hadn't, and his wasn't. "For starters we lean on them hard and see what happens."

"I think that's a mistake," Cook said after a moment.

"Maybe," Adler conceded. "But they made the mistake first."

The military people didn't like it at all. It annoyed the civilians, who had established the site approximately five times as fast as these uniformed boneheads would have managed, not to mention doing it in total secrecy and less expensively.

"It never occurred to you to hide the site?" the Japanese general demanded.

"How could anyone find this?" the senior engineer shot back.

"They have cameras in orbit that can pick up a packet of cigarettes lying on the ground."

"And a whole country to survey." The engineer shrugged. "And we are in the bottom of a valley whose sides are so steep that an inbound ballistic warhead can't possibly hit it without striking those peaks first." The man pointed. "And now they do not even have the missiles they need to do it," he added.

The General had instructions to be patient, and he was, after his initial outburst. It was his site to command now. "The first principle is to deny information to the other side."

"So we hide it, then?" the engineer asked politely.
"Yes."

"Camouflage netting on the catenary towers?" They'd done it during the construction phase.

"If you have them, it's a good beginning. Later we can consider other more permanent measures."

"By train, eh?" The AMTRAK official noted after the completion of his briefing. "Back when I started in the business, I was with the Great Northern, and the Air Force came to us half a dozen times about how to move missiles around by rail. We ended up moving a lot of concrete in for them."

"So you've actually thought this one over a few times?" Betsy Fleming asked.

"Oh, yeah." The official paused. "Can I see the pictures now?" The goddamned security briefing had taken hours of unnecessary threats, after which he'd been sent back to his hotel to contemplate the forms — and to allow the FBI to run a brief security check, he imagined.

Chris Scott flipped the slide projector on. He and Fleming had already made their own analysis, but the purpose of having an outside consultant was to get a free and fresh opinion. The first shot was of the missile, just to give him a feel for the size of the thing. Then they went to the shot of the train car.

"Okay, it sure looks like a flatcar, longer than most, probably specially made for the load. Steel construction. The Japanese are good at this sort of thing. Good engineers. There's a crane to lift something. How much does one of these monsters weigh?"

"Figure a hundred tons for the missile itself," Betsy answered. "Maybe twenty for the transporter-container."

"That's pretty heavy for a single object, but not all that big a deal. Well within limits for the car and the roadbed." He paused for a moment. "I don't see any obvious electronics connections, just the usual brake lines and stuff. You expect them to launch off the cars?"

"Probably not. You tell us," Chris Scott said.

"Same thing I told the Air Force twenty-some years ago for the MX. Yeah, you can move them around, but it doesn't make finding them all that hard unless you assume that you're going to make a whole lot of railcars that look exactly alike — and even then, like for the mainline on the Northern, you have a fairly simple target. Just a long, thin line, and guess what, our mainline from Minneapolis to Seattle was longer than all the standard-gauge track in their country."

"So?" Fleming asked.

"So this isn't a launch car. It's just a transport car. You didn't need me to tell you that."

No, but it is nice to hear it from somebody else, Betsy thought.

"Anything else?"

"The Air Force kept telling me how delicate the damned things are. They don't like being bumped. At normal operating speeds you're talking three lateral gees and about a gee and a half of vertical acceleration. That's not good for the missile. Next problem is dimensional. That car is about ninety feet long, and the standard flatcar for their railroads is sixty or less. Their railroads are mainly narrow-gauge. Know why?"

"I just assumed that they picked — "

"It's all engineering, okay?" the AMTRAK executive said. "Narrow-gauge track gives you the ability to shoehorn into tighter spots, to take sharper turns, generally to do things smaller. But they went to standard gauge for the *Shin-Kansen* because for greater speed and stability you just need it wider. The length of the cargo and the corresponding length of the car to carry it means that if you turn too tightly, the car overlaps the next track and you run the risk of collision unless you shut down traffic coming the other way every time you move these things. That's why the missile is somewhere off the *Shin-Kansen* line. It has to be. Then next, there's the problem of the cargo. It really messes things up for everybody."

"Keep going," Betsy Fleming said.

"Because the missiles are so delicate, we would have been limited to low speed — it would have wrecked our scheduling and dispatching. We never wanted the job. The money to us would have been okay, but it would probably have hurt us in the long run. The same thing would be true of them, wouldn't it? Even worse. The *Shin-Kansen* line is a high-speed passenger routing. They meet timetables like you wouldn't believe, and they wouldn't much like things that mess them up." He paused. "Best guess? They used those cars to move the things from the factory to someplace else and that's all. I'd bet a lot of money that they did everything at night, too. If I were you I'd hunt around for these cars, and expect to find them in a yard somewhere doing nothing. Then I'd start looking for trackage off the mainline that doesn't go anywhere."

Scott changed slides again. "How well do you know their railroads?"

"I've been over there often enough. That's why they let you draft me."

"Well, tell me what you think of this one." Scott pointed at the screen.

"That's some bitchin' radar," a technician observed. The trailer had been flown up to Elmendorf to support the B-1 mission. The bomber crews were sleeping now, and radar experts, officer- and enlisted-rank, were going over the taped records of the snooper flight.

"Airborne phased array?" a major asked.

"Sure looks that way. Sure as hell isn't the APY-1

we sold them ten years back. We're talking over two million watts, and the way the signal strength jumps. Know what they've got here? It's a rotating dome, probably a single planar array," the master sergeant said. "So it's rotating, okay. But they can steer it electronically, too."

"Track and scan?"

"Why not? It's frequency-agile. Damn, I wish we had one of these, sir." The sergeant picked up a photo of the aircraft. "This thing is going to be a problem for us. All that power — makes you wonder if they might get a hit. Makes me wonder if they were tracking the 1s, sir."

"From that far out?" The B-1B was not strictly speaking a stealthy aircraft. From nose-on it did have a reduced radar signature. From abeam the radar cross section was considerably larger, though still smaller than any conventional airplane of similar physical dimensions.

"Yes, sir. I need to play with the tapes some."

"What will you look for?"

"The rotodome probably turns at about six rpm. The pulses we're recording ought to be at about that interval. Anything else, and they were steering the beam at us."

"Good one, Sarge. Run it down."

34

All Aboard

Yamata was annoyed to be back in Tokyo. His pattern of operation in thirty years of business had been to provide command guidance, then let a team of subordinates work out the details while he moved on to other strategic issues, and he'd fully expected it to go easier in this case rather than harder. After all, the twenty most senior zaibatsu were his staff now. Not that they thought of themselves that way. Yamata-san smiled to himself. It was a heady thought. Getting the government to dance to his tune had been child's play. Getting these men onboard had taken years of cajolery. But they *were* dancing to his tune, and they just needed the bandmaster around from time to time. And so he'd flown back on a nearly empty airliner to steady down their nerves.

"It's not possible," he told them.

"But he said — "

"Kozo, President Durling can say anything he wishes. I'm telling you that it is not possible for them to rebuild their records in anything less than several weeks. If they attempt to reopen their markets today all that will result is chaos. And chaos," he reminded them, "works in our favor."

"And the Europeans?" Tanzan Itagake asked.

"They will wake up at the end of next week and

discover that we have bought their continent," Yamata told them all. "In five years America will be our grocer and Europe will be our boutique. By that time the yen will be the world's most powerful currency. By that time we will have a fully integrated national economy and a powerful continental ally. Both of us will be self-sufficient in all our resource needs. We will no longer have a population that needs to abort its babies to keep from overpopulating our Home Islands. And," he added, "we will have political leadership worthy of our national status. That is our next step, my friends."

Indeed, Binichi Murakami thought behind an impassive face. He remembered that he'd signed on partly as a result of being accosted on the streets of Washington by a drunken beggar. How was it possible that someone as clever as himself could be influenced by petty anger? But it had happened, and now he was stuck with the rest. The industrialist sipped his saké and kept his peace while Yamata-san waxed rhapsodic about their country's future. He was really talking about his own future, of course, and Murakami wondered how many of the men around the table saw that. Fools. But that was hardly fair, was it? After all, he was one of them.

Major Boris Scherenko had no less than eleven highly placed agents within the Japanese government, one of whom was the deputy head of the PSID, a man he'd compromised some years before while on a sex and gambling trip to Taiwan. He was the best possible person to have under control — it was likely that he would one day graduate to chief of the agency and enable the Tokyo *rezidentura* both to monitor and influence counterintelligence activity throughout the country. What confused the Russian intelligence officer was that none of his agents had been of much help so far.

791

Then there was the issue of working with the Americans. Given his professional training and experience, it was as if he were heading the welcoming committee for diplomats arriving from Mars. The dispatch from Moscow made it easier to accept. Or somewhat easier. It appeared that the Japanese were planning to rob his country of her most precious potential asset, in conjunction with China, and to use that power base to establish themselves as the world's most powerful nation. And the strangest thing of all was that Scherenko did not think the plan crazy on its face. Then came his tasking orders.

Twenty missiles, he thought. It was one area he'd never targeted for investigation. After all, *Moscow* had sold the things to them. They must have considered the possibility that the missiles could be used for — but, no, of course they hadn't. Scherenko promised himself that he'd sit down with this Clark fellow, an experienced man, and after breaking the ice with a few drinks, inquire delicately if the American's political direction was as obtuse as that which he received, regardless of the government in question. Perhaps the American would have something useful to say. After all, their governments changed every four or eight years. Perhaps they were used to it.

Twenty missiles, he thought. *Six warheads each.* Once it had been normal to think of missiles as things that flew in thousands, and both sides had actually been mad enough to accept it as a strategic fact of life. But now, the possibility of a mere ten or twenty — at whom would they really be aimed? Would the Americans really stand up for their new . . . what? Friends? Allies? Associates? Or were they merely former enemies whose new status had not yet been decided in Washington? Would they help his country against the new/old danger? What kept coming back to him was, *twenty missiles times six warheads.* They would be evenly targeted, and surely enough to wreck his country. And if that were true, they would surely be enough to deter America from helping.

Well, then Moscow is right, Scherenko judged. Full cooperation now was the best way to avoid that situation. America wanted a location on the missiles, probably with the intention of destroying them. *And if they don't, we will.*

The Major personally handled three of the agents. His subordinates handled the others, and under his direction messages were prepared for distribution to dead-drops around the city. *What do you know about . . .* How many would answer his call for information? The danger was not so much that the people under his control would not have the information he needed, but that one or more of them would take this opportunity to report in to the government. In asking for something of this magnitude, he ran the risk of giving one of his agents the chance to redeem himself by turning patriot, to reveal the new orders and absolve himself of any guilt. But some risks you had to run. After midnight he took a walk, picking high-traffic areas to place his drops and making the appropriate wake-up signals to alert his people. He hoped that the half of PSID he controlled was the one covering this area. He thought so, but you could never be sure, could you?

Kimura knew he was running risks, but he'd gone beyond that kind of worry now. All he could really hope for was that he was acting as a patriot, and that somehow people would understand and honor that fact after his execution for treason. The other consolation was that he would not die alone.

"I can arrange a meeting with former Prime Minister Koga," he said simply.

Oh, shit, Clark thought at once. *I'm a goddamned spy,* he wanted to reply. *I'm not with the goddamned State Department.* The only good news at the moment was that Chavez didn't react at all. His heart had probably stopped, John told himself. *Like yours just did.*

"To what end?" he asked.

"The situation is grave, is it not? Koga-san has no part in this. He is still a man of political influence. His views should be of interest to your government."

Yeah, you might say that. But Koga was also a politician on the outside, and perhaps willing to trade the lives of some foreigners for an open door back into the government; or just a man who placed country ahead of personal gain — which possibility might cut in just about any direction Clark could imagine.

"Before I can commit to that, I need instructions from my government," John said. It was rarely that he temporized on anything, but this one was well beyond his experience.

"Then I would suggest that you get it. And soon," Kimura added as he stood and left.

"I always wondered if my master's in international relations would come in handy," Chavez observed, staring into his half-consumed drink. "Of course I have to live long enough to get the parchment." *Might be nice to get married, settle down, have kids, maybe even have a real life someday,* he didn't add.

"Good to see you still have a sense of humor, Yevgeniy Pavlovich."

"They're going to tell us to do it. You know that."

"*Da.*" Clark nodded, keeping his cover and now trying to think as a Russian would. Did the KGB manual have a chapter for this? he wondered. The CIA's sure as hell didn't.

As usual the tapes were clearer than the instant analysis of the operators. There had been three, perhaps four — more likely four, given American operational patterns, the intelligence officers opined — aircraft probing Japanese air defenses. Definitely not EC-135s, however. Those aircraft were based on a design almost fifty years old and studded with enough antennas to watch every TV signal in the hemisphere, and would have generated far larger radar returns. Besides, the Americans probably didn't have four such aircraft left. Therefore something else, probably their B-1B bomber, the intelligence people estimated. And the B-1B was a *bomber,* whose purpose was far more sinister than the collection of electronic signals. So the Americans were thinking of Japan as an enemy whose defenses would have to be penetrated for the purpose of delivering death, an idea new to neither side in this war — if war it was, the cooler heads added. But what else could it be? the majority of the analysts asked, setting the tone of the night's missions.

Three E-767s were again up and operating, again with two of them active and one waiting in the ambush role. This time the radars were turned up in power, and the parameters for the signal-processing software were electronically altered to allow for easier tracking of stealthy targets at long range. It was physics they depended on. The size of the antenna combined with the power of the signal and the frequency of the electronic waves made it possible to get hits on almost anything. That was both the good news and the bad news, the operators thought, as they received all manner of signals now. There was one change, however. When they thought they had a weak return from a moving object at long range, they started directing their fighters in that direction. The Eagles never got within a hundred miles. The return signals always seemed to fade out when the E-767 switched frequency from longwave acquisition to shortwave tracking, and that didn't bode well for the Ku-band needed for actual targeting. It did show them that the Americans were still probing, and that perhaps they knew they were being tracked. And, everyone

795

thought, if nothing else it was good training for the fighters. If this were truly a war, all the participants told themselves, then it was becoming more and more real.

"I don't buy it," the Colonel said.

"Sir, it looks to me like they were tracking you. They were sweeping you at double the rate that I can explain by the rotation of their dome. Their radar is completely electronic. They can steer their beams, and they *were* steering their beams." The sergeant's voice was reasonable and respectful, even though the officer who'd led the first probe was showing a little too much pride and not quite enough willingness to listen. He'd heard a little of what he was just told, but now he just shrugged it off.

"Okay, maybe they did get a few hits. We were broadside-aspect to them. Next time we'll deploy the patrol line farther out and do a direct penetration. That cuts our RCS by quite a bit. We have to tickle their line to see how they react."

Better you than me, pal, the sergeant thought. He looked out the window. Elmendorf Air Force Base was in Alaska and subject to dreadful winter weather — the worst enemy of any man-made machine. As a result the B-1s were all in hangars, which hid them from the satellite that Japan might or might not have operating. Still, nobody was sure about that.

"Colonel, I'm just a sergeant who diddles with O-scopes, but I'd be careful about that. I don't know enough about this radar to tell you for sure how good it is. My gut tells me it's pretty damned good."

"We'll be careful," the Colonel promised. "Tomorrow night we'll have a better set of tapes for you."

"Roger that, sir." *Better you than me, pal,* he thought again.

USS *Pasadena* had joined the north end of the patrol

line west of Midway. It was possible for the submarines to report in with their satellite radios without revealing their positions except to PacFlt SubOps.

"Not much of a line," Jones observed, looking at the chart. He'd just come over to confer on what SOSUS had on Japanese naval movements, which was at the moment not much. The best news available was that SOSUS, even with Jones's improved tracking software, wasn't getting anything on the line of *Olympia*, *Helena*, *Honolulu*, *Chicago*, and now *Pasadena*. "We used to have more boats than that just to cover the Gap."

"That's all the SSNs we have available, Ron," Chambers replied. "And, yeah, it ain't much. But if they forward-deploy their diesel boats, they'd better be real careful." Washington had given them that much by way of orders. An eastward move of Japanese warships would not be tolerated, and the elimination of one of their submarines would be approved, probably. It was just that the boat holding the contact had to call it in first for political approval. Mancuso and Chambers hadn't told Jones that. There was little sense in dealing with his temper again.

"We have a bunch of SSNs in storage — "

"Seventeen on the West Coast, to be exact," Chambers said. "Minimum six months to reactivate them, not countin' getting the crews spun up."

Mancuso looked up. "Wait a minute. What about my 726s?"

Jones turned. "I thought they were deactivated."

SubPac shook his head. "The environmental people wouldn't let me. They all have caretaker crews aboard."

"All five of them," Chambers said quietly. "*Nevada*, *Tennessee*, *West Virginia*, *Pennsylvania*, and *Maryland*. That's worth calling Washington about, sir."

"Oh, yeah," Jones agreed. The 726-class, more

797

commonly known by the name of the lead ship, *Ohio*, which was now high-quality razor blades, was far slower than the smaller 688-class of fast-attack boats, a lot less maneuverable and ten knots slower, but they were also quiet. More than that, they defined what quiet was.

"Wally, think we can scratch up crews for them?"

"I don't see why not, Admiral. We could have them moving in a week . . . ten days max, *if* we can get the right people."

"Well, that's something I can do." Mancuso lifted the phone for Washington.

The business day started in Central Europe at ten o'clock local time, which was nine o'clock in London, and a dark four o'clock in New York. That made it six in the evening in Tokyo after what had been at first an exciting week, then a dull one, which had allowed people to contemplate their brilliance at the killing they had made.

Currency traders in the Japanese capital were surprised when things started quite normally. Markets came up on-line much as a business might open its doors for customers waiting outside for a long-awaited sale. It had been announced that it would happen that way. It was just that nobody here had really believed it. As one man they phoned their supervisors for instructions, surprising them with the news from Berlin and the other European centers.

At the New York FBI office, machines wired into the international trading network showed exactly the same display as those on every other continent. The Fed Chairman and Secretary Fiedler watched. Both men had phones to their ears, linked into an encrypted conference line with their European counterparts.

The Bundesbank made the first move, trading five hundred billion yen for the current equivalent in dollars to the Bank of Hong Kong, a very cautious transaction to test the waters. Hong Kong handled it as a matter of course, seeing a marginal advantage in the German mistake. The Bundesbank was foolish enough to expect that the reopening of the New York equities markets would bolster the dollar. The transaction was executed, Fiedler saw. He turned to the Fed Chairman and winked. The next move was by the Swiss, and this one was a *trillion* yen for Hong Kong's remaining holding in U.S. Treasuries. That transaction, too, went through the wires in less than a minute. The next one was more direct. The Bern Commercial Bank took Swiss francs back from a Japanese bank, trading yen holdings for them, another dubious move occasioned by a phone call from the Swiss government.

The opening of European stock markets saw other moves. Banks and other institutions that had made a strategic move to buy up Japanese equities as a counterbalance to Japanese acquisitions in European markets now started selling them off, immediately converting the yen holdings to other currencies. That was when the first alarm light went on in Tokyo. The Europeans' actions might have appeared to be mere profit-taking, but the currency conversions bespoke a belief that the yen was going to fall and fall hard, and it was a Friday night in Tokyo, and their trading floors were closed except for the currency traders and others working the European markets.

"They should be getting nervous now," Fiedler observed.

"I would," Jean-Jacques said in Paris. What nobody quite wanted to say was that the First World Economic War had just begun in earnest. There was an excitement to it, even though it ran contrary to all their instincts and experience.

"You know, I don't have a model to predict this," Gant said, twenty feet away from the two government officials. The European action, helpful as it was, confounded all computer models and preconceptions.

"Well, pilgrim, that's why we've got brains and guts," George Winston responded deadpan.

"But what are our markets going to do?"

Winston grinned. "Sure as hell we're going to find out in, oh, about seven and a half hours. And you don't even have to shell out for the E-Ticket. Where's your sense of adventure?"

"I'm glad somebody's happy about this."

There were worldwide rules for currency trading. Trading stopped once a currency had fallen a certain amount, but not this time. The floor under the yen was yanked out by every European government, trading didn't stop, and the yen resumed its fall.

"They can't do that!" someone said in Tokyo. But they were doing it, and he reached for a phone, knowing even then what his instructions would be. The yen was being attacked. They had to defend it, and the only way was to trade the foreign-currency holdings they already owned in order to bring the yen holdings back home and out of the playing field of international speculation. Worst of all, there was no reason for this action. The yen was strong, especially against the American dollar. Soon it would replace it as the world's benchmark currency, especially if the American financial markets were foolish enough to reopen later in the day. The Europeans were making a sucker bet of such magnitude as to defy qualification, and since it didn't make sense, all the Japanese traders could do was to apply their own experience to the situation and act accordingly. The irony of the moment would have been delicious, had they been able to appreciate it. Their actions were virtually automatic. Francs, French and Swiss, British pounds, German D-marks, Dutch guilders, and Danish kroner were disbursed in vast quantities to purchase yen, whose relative value, everyone in Tokyo was sure, could only appreciate, especially if the Europeans pegged their currencies to the dollar.

There was an element of nervousness to it, but they did it, acting on the orders of their superiors, who were even now leaving their homes and catching cars or trains to the various commercial office buildings in which world trading was conducted. Equities were traded off in Europe as well, with the local currencies converted to yen. The expectation again was that when the American collapse resumed, the European currencies would fall, and with them the values of stock issues. Then Japan could reacquire even larger quantities of European stocks. The European moves were a sad case of misplaced loyalty, or confidence, or something, the people in Tokyo thought, but sad or not, it worked in their favor. And that was just fine. By noon London time a massive movement had taken place. Individual investors and smaller institutions, seeing what everyone else had done, had moved in — foolishly, the Japanese knew. Noon London time was seven in the morning on America's East Coast.

"My fellow Americans," President Durling said at exactly 7:05 A.M. on every TV network. "On Wednesday night I told you that today American financial markets are going to reopen . . ."

"Here it goes," Kozo Matsuda said, just back in his office and watching CNN. "He's going to say that they can't, and Europe is going to panic. Splendid," he told his aides, turning back to the TV. The American president was smiling and confident. Well, a politician had to know how to act, the better to lie to his citizens.

"The problems which the market experienced last week came from a deliberate assault on the American

801

economy. Nothing like this has ever happened before, and I am going to walk you through what happened, how it was done, and why it was done. We've spent an entire week accumulating this information, and even now Treasury Secretary Fiedler and the Chairman of the Federal Reserve Board are in New York, working with the heads of the great American financial institutions to set things aright.

"I am also pleased to report that we have had the time to consult with our friends in Europe, and that our historic allies have chosen to stand with us as faithfully in this time of difficulty as they have in other times.

"So what really happened last Friday?" Roger Durling asked.

Matsuda sat his drink down on his desk when he saw the first chart appear on the screen.

Jack watched him go through it. The trick as always was to make a complex story simple, and that task had involved two professors of economics, half of Fiedler's personal staff, and a governor of the Securities and Exchange Commission, all working in coordination with the President's best speechwriter. Even so, it took twenty-five minutes, six flip charts, and would require a number of government spokesmen talking who were even now on background to reporters whose briefings had started at 6:30.

"I told you Wednesday night that nothing — *nothing* of consequence had happened to us. Not one piece of property has been affected. Not one farm has lost anything. Each of you is the same person you were a week ago, with the same abilities, the same home, the same job, the same family and friends. What happened last Friday was an attack not on our country itself, but on our national confidence.

"Our confidence is a harder and tougher target than people realize, and that is something we're going to prove today."

Most of the people in the trading business were en route to their offices and missed the speech, but their employers had all taped it, and there were also printed copies on every desk and at every computer terminal. The trading day would not start until noon, moreover, and there were strategy sessions to be held everywhere, though nobody really had much idea of what to do. The most obvious response to the situation was indeed so obvious that no one knew whether or not to try it.

"They're doing it to us," Matsuda said, watching his screens. "What can we do to stop it?"

"It depends on what their stock market does," his senior technical trader replied, not knowing what else to say and not knowing what to expect, either.

"Do you think it'll work, Jack?" Durling asked. He had two speeches sitting in folders on his desk, and didn't know which he would be giving in the evening.

The National Security Advisor shrugged. "Don't know. It gives them a way out. Whether or not they make use of it is up to them."

"So now we just get to sit and wait?"

"That's about it, Mr. President."

The second session was held in the State Department. Secretary Hanson huddled with Scott Adler, who then met with his negotiating team and waited. The Japanese delegation arrived at 9:45.

"Good morning," Adler said pleasantly.

"A pleasure to see you again," the Ambassador replied, taking his hand, but not as confidently as on the day before. Not surprisingly, he had not had time to receive detailed instructions from Tokyo. Adler had halfway expected a request for a postponement of the session, but, no, that would have been too obvious a sign of weakness, and so the Ambassador, a skilled and experienced diplomat, was in the most precarious of diplomatic positions — he was forced to represent his government with nothing more to fall back on than his wits and his knowledge. Adler walked him to his seat, then returned to his side of the table. Since America was the host today, Japan got to speak first. Adler had placed a side bet with the Secretary as to the Ambassador's opening statement.

"First of all it needs to be said that my government objects in the strongest terms to the attack on our currency engineered by the United States . . ."

That's ten bucks you owe me, Mr. Secretary, Adler thought behind an impassive face.

"Mr. Ambassador," he replied, "that is something we could say just as easily. In fact, here is the data which we have developed on the events of last week." Binders appeared on the table and were slid across to the Japanese diplomats. "I need to tell you that we are now conducting an investigation that could well lead to the indictment of Raizo Yamata for wire- and securities fraud."

It was a bold play for a number of reasons. It showed everything that the Americans knew about the attack on Wall Street and pointed to the things yet to be learned. As such, it could have no effect other than to ruin the criminal case against Yamata and his allies, should it come to that. But that was a side issue. Adler had a war to stop, and stop quickly. He'd let the boys and girls at Justice worry about the other stuff.

"It might be better of course for your country to deal with this man and his acts," Adler offered next, giving generous maneuvering room to the Ambassador and his government. "The net effect of his actions, as may be seen today, will be to cause greater hardship to your country than to ours.

"Now, if we may, I should like us to return to the issue of the Mariana Islands."

The one-two punch predictably staggered the Japanese delegation. As was often the case, nearly everything was left unsaid: *We know what you did. We know how you did it. We are prepared to deal with all of it.* The brutally direct method was designed to conceal the real American problem — the inability to make an immediate military counter — but it also provided Japan with the ability to separate her government from the acts of certain of her citizens. And that, Ryan and Adler had decided the previous night, was the best means of achieving a quick and clean end to the situation. To that end, a large carrot was required.

"The United States seeks little more than a return to normal relations. The immediate evacuation of the Marianas will allow us to consider a more lenient interpretation of the Trade Reform Act. This, also, is something we are willing to place on the table for consideration." It was probably a mistake to hit him with this much, Adler thought, but the alternative was further bloodshed. By the end of the first session of formal negotiations, something remarkable had happened. Neither side had repeated a position. Rather, it had been, in diplomatic terms, a free-form exchange of views, few of them well considered.

"Chris," Adler whispered when he stood. "Find out what they're really thinking."

"Got it," Cook replied. He got himself some coffee and headed out to the terrace, where Nagumo stood on the edge, looking out toward the Lincoln Memorial.

"It's an elegant way out, Seiji," Cook offered.

"You push us too hard," Nagumo said without turning.

"If you want a chance to end this without getting

people killed, this is the best one."

"The best for you, perhaps. What of our interests?"

"We'll cut a deal on trade." Cook didn't understand it all. Unschooled in financial matters, he was as yet unaware of what was happening on that front. To him the recovery of the dollar and the protection of the American economy was an isolated act. Nagumo knew different. The attack his country had begun could be balanced only by a counterattack. The effect would not be restoration of the status quo ante, but, rather, serious damage to his own country's economy on top of preexisting damage from the Trade Reform Act. In this, Nagumo knew something that Cook did not: unless America acceded to Japanese demands for some territorial gain, then the war was quite real.

"We need time, Christopher."

"Seiji, there *isn't* time. Look, the media haven't picked up on this yet. That can change at any moment. If the public finds out, there's going to be hell to pay." Because Cook was right, he'd given Nagumo an opening.

"Yes, there may well be, Chris. But I am protected by my diplomatic status and you are not." He didn't need to say more than that.

"Now, wait a minute, Seiji . . ."

"My country needs more than what you offer," Nagumo replied coldly.

"We're giving you a way out."

"We must have more." There was no turning back now, was there? Nagumo wondered if the ambassador knew that yet. Probably not, he judged, from the way the senior diplomat was looking in his direction. It was suddenly clear to him. Yamata and his allies had committed his country to action from which there was no backing away, and he couldn't decide if they'd known it or not when they'd begun. But that didn't matter now. "We must have something," he went on, "to show for our actions."

At about that time, Cook realized how slow he'd been on the uptake. Looking in Nagumo's eyes, he saw it all. Not so much cruelty as resolve. The Deputy Assistant Secretary of State thought about the money sitting in a numbered account, and the questions that would be asked, and what possible explanation he might have for it.

It sounded like an old-fashioned school bell when the digital clock turned from 11:59:59 to 12:00:00.

"Thank you, H. G. Wells," a trader breathed, standing on the wooden floor of the New York Stock Exchange. The time machine was in operation. For the first time in his memory, at this hour of the day the floor was clean. Not a single paper slip lay there. The various traders at their kiosks looked around and saw some signs of normality. The ticker had been running for half an hour, showing the same data it had displayed the previous week, really as a way of synchronizing their minds with the new day, and everyone used it as a touchstone, a personal contact with reality that both was and was not.

It was a hell of a speech the President had given five hours earlier. Everyone on the floor had seen it at least once, most of them right here, followed by a pep talk from the head of the NYSE that would have done Knute Rockne proud. They had a mission that day, a mission that was more important than their individual well-being, and one that, if accomplished, would see to their long-term security as well as that of the entire country. They had spent the day reconstructing their activities of the previous Friday, to the point where every trader knew what quantities of which stock he or she held, what every position was. Some even remembered the moves they'd been planning to make, but most of those had been "up" moves rather than "down" ones, and their collective

807

memory would not allow them to follow through on them.

On the other hand, they remembered well the panic of the afternoon seven days before, and, knowing that it had been both artificial and malicious, no one wished to start it afresh. And besides, Europe had signaled its confidence in the dollar in the strongest terms. The bond market was as solidly fixed as though set in granite, and the first moves of the day had been to buy U.S. Treasuries to take advantage of the stunning deal offered by the Fed Chairman. That move was the best confidence-builder they'd ever seen.

For over ninety seconds by one trader's watch, exactly *nothing* happened on the floor of the exchange. The ticker simply displayed nothing. The phenomenon evoked snorts of disbelief from men whose minds raced to understand it. The little-guy investors, without a clue, were making few calls, and those who did were told by their brokers to sit tight. And for the most part that was what they did. Those who did make sell orders had them handled in-house by their brokerage houses from the reservoir of issues that they had on hand, left over from the previous week. But the big traders weren't doing anything, either. Each of them was waiting for somebody else to do something. The inactivity of merely a minute and a half seemed an eternity to people accustomed to frantic action, and when the first major play happened, it came as a relief.

That first big move of the day, predictably, came from the Columbus Group. It was a massive purchase of Citibank common. Seconds later, Merrill Lynch pushed the button for a similar acquisition of Chemical Bank.

"Yeah," a few voices said on the floor. It made sense, didn't it? Citibank was vulnerable to a fall in the dollar, but the Europeans had seen to it that the dollar was rising in value, and that made First National City Bank a good issue to pick up on. As a result, the first tick of the Dow Jones Industrial Average was *up*, defying every prediction of every computer.

"Yeah, we can do this," another floor trader observed. "I want a hundred Manny-Hanny at six," he announced. That would be the next bank to benefit from the increasing strength of the dollar, and he wanted a supply that he could move out at six and a quarter. The stocks that had led the slide the previous week would now lead a rise, and for the same reasons as before. Mad as it sounded, it made perfect sense, they all realized. And as soon as the rest of the market figured it out, they could all cash in on it.

The news ticker on the wall was up and running, again giving shorthand selections off the wire services. GM, it said, was rehiring twenty thousand workers for its plants around Detroit in anticipation of increased auto sales. The callback would take nine months, the announcement didn't say, and was the result of a call from the Secretaries of Commerce and Labor, but it was enough to excite interest in auto stocks, and that excited interest in machine tools. By 12:05:30, the Dow was up five points. Hardly a hiccup after the five-hundred-point plummet seven days before, but it looked like Everest on a clear day from the floor of the NYSE.

"I don't believe this," Mark Gant observed, several blocks away in the Javits Federal Office Building.

"Where the hell is it written down that computers are always right?" George Winston inquired with another forced grin. He had his own worries. Buying up Citibank was not without dangers, but his move, he saw, had the proper effect on the issue. When it had moved up three points, he initiated a slow sell-off to cash in, as other fund managers moved in to follow the trend. Well, that was predictable, wasn't it? The herd just needed a leader. Show them a trend and wait for them to follow, and if it was contrarian, so much the better.

"First impression — it's working," the Fed Chairman told his European colleagues. All the theories said it should, but theories seemed thin at moments like this. Both he and Secretary Fiedler were watching Winston, now leaning back in his chair, chewing on a pen and talking calmly into a phone. They could hear what he was saying. At least his voice was calm, though his body was that of a man in a fight, every muscle tense. But after another five minutes they saw him stretch tense muscles and smile and turn and say something to Gant, who merely shook his head in wonderment as he watched his computer screen do things that it didn't believe possible.

"Well, how about that," Ryan said.

"Is it good?" President Durling asked.

"Let's put it this way: if I were you I'd give your speechwriter a dozen long-stemmed red roses and tell her to plan on working here another four years or so."

"It's way too early for that, Jack," the President replied somewhat crossly.

Ryan nodded. "Yes, sir, I know. What I mean to tell you is, you did it. The markets may — hell, *will* fluctuate the rest of the day, but they're not going to free-fall like we initially expected. It's about confidence, Boss. You restored it, and that's a fact."

"And the rest of it?"

"They've got a chance to back down. We'll know by the end of the day."

"And if they don't?"

The National Security Advisor thought about that. "Then we have to figure a way to fight them without

810

hurting them too badly. We have to find their nukes and we have to settle this thing down before it really gets out of control."

"Is that possible?"

Ryan pointed to the screen. "We didn't think this was possible, did we?"

35

Consequences

It happened in Idaho, in a community outside Mountain Home Air Force Base. A staff sergeant based there had flown out to Andersen Air Force Base on Guam to work on the approach-control radars. His wife had delivered a baby a week after his departure, and she attempted to call him that evening to tell him about his new daughter, only to learn that the phones were out due to a storm. Only twenty years old and not well educated, she'd accepted the news with disappointment. The military comm links were busy, an officer had told her, convincingly enough that she'd gone home with tears in her eyes. A day later she'd talked to her mother and surprised her with the news that her husband didn't know about his daughter yet. Even in time of war, her mother thought, such news always got through — and what storm could possibly be worse than fighting a war?

So she called the local TV station and asked for the weatherman, a sagacious man of fifty who was excellent at predicting the tornadoes that churned through the region every spring, and, it was widely thought, saved five or ten lives each year with his instant analysis of which way the funnel clouds moved.

The weatherman in turn was the kind who enjoyed

being stopped in the local supermarkets with friendly comments, and took the inquiry as yet another compliment for his professional expertise, and besides, he'd never checked out the Pacific Ocean before. But it was easy enough. He linked into the NOAA satellite system and used a computer to go backwards in time to see what sort of storm had hammered those islands. The time of year was wrong for a typhoon, he knew, but it was the middle of an ocean, and storms happened there all the time.

But not this year and not this time. The satellite photos showed a few wispy clouds, but otherwise fair weather. For a few minutes he wondered if the Pacific Ocean, like Arkansas, was subject to fair-weather gales, but, no, that wasn't likely, since those adiabatic storms resulted mainly from variations in temperature and land elevation, whereas an ocean was both flat and moderate. He checked with a colleague who had been a Navy meteorologist to confirm it, and found himself left only with a mystery. Thinking that perhaps the information he had was wrong, he consulted his telephone book and dialed 011-671-555-1212, since a directory-assistance call was toll-free. He got a recording that told him that there had been a storm. Except there had *not* been a storm. Was he the first guy to figure that out?

His next move was to walk across the office to the news department. Within minutes an inquiry went out on one of the wire services.

"Ryan."

"Bob Holtzman, Jack. I have a question for you."

"I hope it's not about Wall Street," Jack replied in as unguarded a voice as he could muster.

"No, it's about Guam. Why are the phone lines out?"

"Bob, did you ask the phone company that?" Ryan tried.

"Yeah. They say there was a storm that took a lot of lines down. Except for a couple of things. One, there wasn't any storm. Two, there's an undersea cable *and* a satellite link. Three, a week is a long time. What's going on?" the reporter asked.

"How many people are asking?"

"Right now, just me and a TV station in Little Rock that put a request up on the AP wire. Another thirty minutes and it's going to be a lot more. What gives? Some sort of — "

"Bob, why don't you come on down here," Ryan suggested. *Well, it's not as though you expected this to last forever,* Jack told himself. Then he called Scott Adler's office. *But why couldn't it have waited one more day?*

Yukon was fueling her second set of ships. The urgency of the moment meant that the fleet oiler was taking on two escorts at a time, one on either beam, while her helicopter transferred various parts and other supplies around the formation, about half of them aircraft components to restore *Ike*'s aircraft to full-mission status. The sun would set in another thirty minutes, and the underway-replenishment operations would continue under cover of darkness. Dubro's battle force had darted east, the better to distance itself from the Indian formation, and again had gone to EMCON, with all radars off, and a deceptive placement of their surveillance aircraft. But they'd lost track of the two Indian carriers, and while the Hawkeyes probed cautiously, Dubro sweated.

"Lookouts report unknown aircraft inbound at two-one-five," a talker called.

The Admiral swore quietly, lifted his binoculars, and turned to the southwest. There. Two Sea Harriers. Playing it smart, too, he saw. They were at five thousand feet or so, tucked into the neat two-plane element used for tactical combat and air shows, flying straight and level, careful not to overfly any ship directly. Before they had passed over the first ring of escorts, a pair of Tomcats were above and behind them, ready to take them out in a matter of seconds if they showed hostile intent. But hostile intent meant loosing a weapon first, and in this day and age a loosed weapon most probably meant a hit, whatever happened to the launch aircraft. The Harriers flew overhead one time only. They seemed to be carrying extra fuel tanks and maybe a reconnaissance pod, but no weapons, this time. Admiral Chandraskatta was no fool, but then Dubro had never made that assumption. His adversary had played a patient game, sticking to his own mission and biding his time, and learning from every trick the Americans had shown him. None of this was of much comfort to the battle-force commander.

"Follow them back?" Commander Harrison asked dispassionately.

Mike Dubro shook his head. "Pull one of the Hummers in close and track by radar."

When the hell would Washington realize he had an imminent confrontation brewing?

"Mr. Ambassador," Scott Adler said, folding up the note an aide had just delivered. "It is likely that in the next twenty-four hours your occupation of the Marianas will become public knowledge. At that point the situation will go beyond our control. You have plenipotentiary powers to resolve this affair . . ."

But he didn't, as Adler had begun to suspect, despite assurances to the contrary. He could also see that he'd pushed the man too hard and too fast. Not that he'd had a choice in the matter. The entire affair had been going on for barely a week. In normal diplomatic practice it took that long just to select the kind of chairs the negotiators sat in. In that respect everything had been doomed from the beginning, but

815

Adler was a professional diplomat for whom hope was never dead. Even now as he concluded his latest statement, he looked into the man's eyes for something he'd be able to report to the White House.

"Throughout our talks we have heard about America's demands, but we have not heard a single word concerning my country's legitimate security interests. Today you have conducted a systematic attack on our financial and economic foundations and — "

Adler leaned forward. "Mr. Ambassador! A week ago your country did the same thing to us, as the information in front of you demonstrates. A week ago your country conducted an attack on the United States Navy. A week ago your country seized U.S. territory. In equity, sir, you have no place to criticize us for efforts necessary to the restoration of our own economic stability." He paused for a moment, reproving himself for the decidedly undiplomatic language of his outburst, but events had gone beyond such niceties — or they soon would. "We have offered you the opportunity to negotiate in good faith for a mutually acceptable interpretation of the Trade Reform Act. We will accept an apology and reparations for the losses to our Navy. We *require* the immediate evacuation of Japanese military forces from the Mariana Islands."

But things had already gone too far for that, and everyone at the table knew it. There just wasn't time. Adler felt the dreadful weight of inevitability. All his skills were useless now. Other events and other people had taken matters out of his hands, and the Ambassador's hands as well. He saw the same look on the man's face that must have been on his own.

His voice was mechanical. "Before I can respond to that, I must consult with my government. I propose that we adjourn so that consultations may be carried out."

Adler nodded more with sadness than anger. "As you wish, Mr. Ambassador. If you should need us, we will be available."

"My God, you kept all that quiet? *How?*" Holtzman demanded.

"Because you guys were all looking the other way," Jack answered bluntly. "You've always depended too much on us for information anyway." He instantly regretted those words. It had come out as too much of a challenge. *Stress, Jack.*

"But you lied to us about the carriers and you never told us about the submarines at all!"

"We're trying to stop this thing before it gets worse," President Durling said. "We're talking to them over at State right now."

"You've had a busy week," the journalist acknowledged. "Kealty's out?"

The President nodded. "He's talking with the Justice Department and with the victims."

"The big thing was getting the markets put back in place," Ryan said. "That was the real — "

"What do you mean? They've *killed* people!" Holtzman objected.

"Bob, why have you guys been hammering the Wall Street story so hard all week? Damn it, what was really scary about their attack on us was the way they wrecked the financial markets and did their run on the dollar. We had to fix that first."

Bob Holtzman conceded the point. "How the hell did you pull that one off?"

"God, who would have thunk it?" Mark Gant asked. The bell had just rung to close the abbreviated trading day. The Dow was down four and a quarter points, with four hundred million shares traded. The S&P 500 was actually up a fraction, as was NASDAQ, because the blue-chip companies had suffered more from general nerves than the smaller fry. But the bond market was the best of all, and the dollar was solid. The Japanese yen, on the other hand, had taken a fearful beating against every Western currency.

"The changes in bonds will drop the stock market next week," Winston said, rubbing his face and thanking Providence for his luck. Residual nerves in the market would encourage people to seek out safer places for their money, though the strength of the dollar would swiftly ameliorate that.

"By the end of the week?" Gant wondered. "Maybe. I'm not so sure. A lot of manufacturing stocks are still undervalued."

"Your move on Citibank was brilliant," the Fed Chairman said, taking a place next to the traders.

"They didn't deserve the hit they took last week, and everyone knew it. I was just the first to make the purchase," Winston replied matter-of-factly. "Besides, we came out ahead on the deal." He tried not to be too smug about it. It had just been another exercise in psychology; he'd done something both logical and unexpected to initiate a brief trend, then cashed in on it. Business as usual.

"Any idea how Columbus made out today?" Secretary Fiedler asked.

"Up about ten," Gant replied at once, meaning ten million dollars, a fair day's work under the circumstances. "We'll do better next week."

An FBI agent came over. "Call in from DTC. They're posting everything normally. That part of the system seems to be back to normal."

"What about Chuck Searls?" Winston asked.

"Well, we've taken his apartment completely apart. He had two brochures about New Caledonia, of all places. That's part of France, and we have the French looking for him."

"Want some good advice?"

"Mr. Winston, we always look for advice," the

818

agent replied with a grin. The mood in the room was contagious.

"Look in other directions, too."

"We're checking everything."

"Yeah, Buzz," the President said, lifting the phone. Ryan, Holtzman, and two Secret Service agents saw JUMPER close his eyes and let out a long breath. He'd been getting reports from Wall Street all afternoon, but it wasn't official for him until he heard it from Secretary Fiedler. "Thanks, my friend. Please let everybody know that I — good, thanks. See you tonight." Durling replaced the phone. "Jack, you are a good man in a storm."

"One storm left."

"So does that end it?" Holtzman asked, not really understanding what Durling had said. Ryan took the answer.

"We don't know yet."

"But — "

"But the incident with the carriers can be written off as an accident, and we won't know for sure what happened to the submarines until we look at the hulls. They're in fifteen thousand feet of water," Jack told him, cringing inwardly for saying such things. But this was war, and war was something you tried to avoid. *If possible*, he reminded himself. "There's the chance that we can both back away from this, write it off to a misunderstanding, a few people acting without authority, and if they get hammered for it, nobody else dies."

"And you're telling me all this?"

"It traps you, doesn't it?" Jack asked. "If the talks over at State work out, then you have a choice, Bob. You can either help us keep things quiet, or you can have a shooting war on your conscience. Welcome to the club, Mr. Holtzman."

"Look, Ryan, I can't — "

"Sure you can. You've done it before." Jack noted that the President sat there and listened, saying nothing. That was partly to distance himself from Ryan's maneuvering, but another part, perhaps, liked what he saw. And Holtzman was playing along.

"So what does all this mean?" Goto asked.

"It means that they will bluster," Yamata told him. *It means that our country needs leadership*, he couldn't say. "They cannot take the islands back. They lack the resources to attack us. They may have patched up their financial markets for now, but Europe and America cannot survive without us indefinitely, and by the time they realize that, we will not need them as we do now. Don't you see? This has always been about *independence* for us! When we achieve that, everything will change."

"And for now?"

"Nothing changes. The new American trade laws would have the same effect as hostilities. At least this way we get something for it, and we will have the chance of ruling our own house."

That's what it really came down to, the one thing that nobody but he ever quite saw. His country could make products and sell them, but so long as his country needed markets more than the markets needed his country, trade laws could cripple Japan, and his country would have no recourse at all. Always the Americans. It was always them, forcing an early end to the Russo-Japanese War, denying their imperial ambitions, allowing them to build up their economy, then cutting the legs out from under them, three times now, the same people who'd killed his family. Didn't they see? Now Japan had struck back, and timidity still prevented people from seeing reality. It was all Yamata could manage to rein in his anger at this small and foolish man. But he needed Goto, even though the Prime Minister was too stupid to realize that there was no going back.

"You're sure that they cannot . . . respond to our actions?" Goto asked after a minute or so of contemplation.

"Hiroshi, it is as I have been telling you for months. We cannot fail to win — unless we fail to try."

"Damn, I wish we could use these things to do our surveys." The real magic of overhead imagery lay not in individual photographs, but rather in pairs of photographs, generally taken a few seconds apart from the same camera, then transmitted down to the ground stations at Sunnyvale and Fort Belvoir. Real-time viewing was all well and good to excite the imagination of congressmen privy to such things or to count items in a hurry. For real work, you used prints, set in pairs and viewed through a stereoscope, which worked better than the human eyes for giving precise three-dimensionality to the photos. It was almost as good as flying over in a helicopter. *Maybe even better,* the AMTRAK official thought, *because you could go backwards as well as forwards.*

"The satellites cost a lot of money," Betsy Fleming observed.

"Yeah, like our whole budget for a year. This one's interesting." A team of professional photo-interpretation experts was analyzing every frame, of course, but the plain truth of the matter was that CIA and NRO had stopped being interested in the technical aspects of railroad-building decades ago. Tracking individual trains loaded with tanks or missiles was one thing. This was something else.

"How so?"

"The *Shin-Kansen* line is a revenue maker. This spur isn't going to make much money for them. Maybe they can cut a tunnel up here," he went on, manipulating the photos. "Maybe they can make it into that city — but me, I'd come the other way

821

and save the money on engineering. Of course it could just be a shunt to use for servicing the main-line."

"Huh?"

He didn't even lift his eyes from the stereo-viewer. "A place to stash work cars, snowblowers, that sort of thing. It is well sited for that purpose. Except that there's no such cars there."

The resolution on the photos was just fantastic. They'd been taken close to noon local time, and you could see the sun's glint on the rails of the mainline, and the spur as well. He figured that the width of the rails was about the resolution limit of the cameras, an interesting fact that he couldn't relay to anyone else. The ties were concrete, like the rest of the Bullet Train line, and the quality of the engineering was, well, something he'd envied for a long time. The official looked up reluctantly.

"No way it's a revenue line. The turns are all wrong. You couldn't do thirty miles per hour through there, and the train sets on that line cruise over a hundred. Funny, though, it just disappears."

"Oh?" Betsy asked.

"See for yourself." The executive stood to stretch, giving Mrs. Fleming a place at the viewer. He picked up a large-scale map of the valley and looked to see where things went. "You know, when Hill and Stevens built the Great Northern . . ."

Betsy wasn't interested. "Chris, take a look at this."

Their visitor looked up from the map. "Oh. The truck? I don't know what color they paint their — "

"Not green."

Time usually worked in favor of diplomacy, but not in this case, Adler thought as he entered the White House. He knew the way, and had a Secret Service agent to conduct him in case he got lost. The Deputy Secretary of State was surprised to see a reporter in

822

the Oval Office, even more so when he was allowed to stay.

"You can talk," Ryan told him. Scott Adler took a deep breath and started his report.

"They're not backing down on anything. The Ambassador isn't very comfortable with the situation, and it shows. I don't think he's getting much by way of instructions out of Tokyo, and that worries me. Chris Cook thinks they're willing to let us have Guam back in a demilitarized condition, but they want to keep the rest of the islands. I dangled the TRA at them, but no substantive response." He paused before going on. "It's not going to work. We can keep at it for a week or a month, but it's just not going to happen. Fundamentally they don't know what they're into. They see a continuum of engagement between the military and economic sides. They don't see the firebreak between the two. They don't see that they've crossed over a line, and they don't see the need to cross back."

"You're saying there's a war happening," Holtzman observed, to make things clear. It made him feel foolish to ask the question. He didn't notice the same aura of unreality surrounding everyone else in the room.

Adler nodded. "I'm afraid so."

"So what are we going to do about it?"

"What do you suppose?" President Durling asked.

Commander Dutch Claggett had never expected to be in this situation. A fast-track officer since his graduation from the U.S. Naval Academy twenty-three years earlier, his career had come to a screeching halt aboard USS *Maine*, when as executive officer he'd been present for the only loss of an American fleet-ballistic-missile submarine. The irony was that his life's ambition had been command of a nuclear submarine, but command of *Tennessee* meant nothing at

823

all now. It was just an entry on his first résumé when he entered the civilian job market. Her designed mission was to carry Trident-II sea-launched ballistic missiles, but the missiles were gone and the only reason that she still existed at all was because the local environmental movement had protested her dismantlement to Federal District Court, and the judge, a lifelong member of the Sierra Club, had agreed to the arguments, which were again on their way back to the United States Court of Appeals. Claggett had been in command of *Tennessee* for nine months now, but the only time he'd been under way had been to move from one side of the pier to another. Not exactly what he'd had in mind for his career. *It could be worse,* he told himself in the privacy of his cabin. He could have been dead, along with so many of the others from USS *Maine.*

But *Tennessee* was still all his — he didn't even share her with a second CO — and he was still a naval officer in command of a man-o'-war, technically speaking, and his reduced crew of eighty-five drilled every day because that was the life of the sea, even tied alongside a pier. His reactor plant, known to its operators as Tennessee Power and Light Company, was lit up at least once per week. The sonarmen played acquisition-and-tracking games against audio-tapes, and the rest of those aboard operated every shipboard system, down to tinkering with the single Mark 48 torpedo aboard. It had to be this way. The rest of the crew wasn't being SERB'd, after all, and it was his duty to them to maintain their professional standing should they get the transfers they all wanted to a submarine that actually went to sea.

"Message from SubPac, sir," a yeoman said, handing over a clipboard. Claggett took the board and signed first for receipt.

Report earliest date ready to put to sea.

"What the hell?" Commander Claggett asked the

bulkhead. Then he realized that the message ought to have come through Group at least, not straight from Pearl. He lifted his phone and dialed SubPac from memory. "Admiral Mancuso, please. *Tennessee* calling."

"Dutch? What's your matériel condition?" Bart Mancuso asked without preamble.

"Everything works, sir. We even had our ORSE two weeks ago, and we maxed it." Claggett referred to the Operational Reactor Safeguards Examination, still the Holy Grail of the Nuclear Navy, even for razor-blade fodder.

"I know. How soon?" Mancuso asked. The bluntness of the question was like something from the past.

"I need to load food and torps, and I need thirty people."

"Where are you weak?"

Claggett thought for a moment. His officers were on the young side, but he didn't mind that, and he had a good collection of senior chiefs. "Nowhere, really. I'm working these people hard."

"Okay, good. Dutch, I'm cutting orders to get you ready to sail ASAP. Group is getting into gear now. I want you moving just as fast as you can. Mission orders are on the way. Be prepared to stay at sea for ninety days."

"Aye aye, sir." Claggett heard the line go dead. A moment later he lifted his phone and called for his department heads and chiefs to meet in the wardroom. The meeting had not yet started when the phone rang again. It was a call from Group asking for Claggett's precise manpower needs.

"Your house has a fine view. Is it for sale?"

Oreza shook his head. "No, it's not," he told the man at the door.

"Perhaps you would think about it. You are a fisherman, yes?"

825

"Yes, sir, I am. I have a charter boat — "

"Yes, I know." The man looked around, clearly admiring the size and location of what was really a fairly ordinary tract house by American standards. Manuel and Isabel Oreza had bought it five years earlier, just barely beating the real-estate boom on Saipan. "I would pay much for this," the man said.

"But then where would I live?" Portagee asked.

"Over a million American dollars," the man persisted.

Strangely enough, Oreza felt a flash of anger at the offer. He still had a mortgage, after all, and paid the bill every month — actually his wife did, but that was beside the point. The typical American monthly ritual of pulling the ticket out of the book, filling out the check, tucking both in the preprinted envelope, and dropping it in the mail on the first day of the month — the entire procedure was proof to them that they did indeed own their first house after thirty-plus years of being government-service tumbleweeds. The house was *theirs.*

"Sir, this house is mine, okay? I live here. I like it here."

The man was as friendly and polite as he could be, in addition to being a pushy son of a bitch. He handed over a card. "I know. Please excuse my intrusion. I would like to hear from you after you have had a chance to consider my offer." And with that he walked to the next house in the development.

"What the hell?" Oreza whispered, closing the door.

"What was that all about?" Pete Burroughs asked.

"He wants to pay me a million bucks for the house."

"Nice view," Burroughs observed. "On the California coast this would go for a nice price. But not that much. You wouldn't believe what Japanese real-estate prices are."

826

"A million bucks?" *And that was just his opening offer,* Oreza reminded himself. The man had his Toyota Land Cruiser parked in the cul-de-sac, and was clearly walking from one house to another, seeing what he could buy.

"Oh, he'd turn it over for a lot more, or maybe if he was smart, just rent it."

"But then where would we live?"

"You wouldn't," Burroughs replied. "How much you want to bet they give you a first-class ticket stateside at the settlement. Think about it," the engineer suggested.

"Well, that's interesting," Robby Jackson thought. "Anything else happening?"

"The 'cans we saw before are gone now. Things are settling back down to — hell, they *are* normal now except for all the soldiers around."

"Any trouble?"

"No, sir, nothing. Same food ships coming in, same tankers, same everything. Air traffic has slowed down a lot. The soldiers are sort of dug in, but they're being careful how they do it. Not much visible anymore. There's still a lot of bush country on the island. I guess they're all hid in there. I ain't been goin' lookin', y'know?" Jackson heard him say.

"That's fine. Just stay cool, Master Chief. Good report. Let me get back to work."

"Okay, Admiral."

Jackson made his notes. He really should have turned this stuff over to somebody else, but Chief Oreza would want a familiar voice on the other end of the circuit, and everything was taped for the intelligence guys anyway.

But he had other things to do, too. The Air Force would be running another probe of Japanese air defenses tonight. The SSN patrol line would move west another hundred miles, and people would gather a lot of intelligence information, mainly from satellites. *Enterprise* would make Pearl Harbor today. There were two complete carrier air wings at Barbers Point Naval Air Station, but no carriers to put them on. The Army's 25th Infantry Division (Light) was still based at Schofield Barracks a few miles away, but there were no ships to put them on, either. The same was true of the First Marine Division at Camp Pendleton, California. The last time America had struck at the Mariana Islands, Operation FORAGER, 15 June 1944, he'd troubled himself to find out, there had been 535 ships, 127,571 troops. The combined ships of the entire U.S. Navy and every merchant ship flying the Stars and Stripes did not begin to approach the first number; the Army and Marines combined would have been hard pressed to find enough light-infantry troops to meet the second. Admiral Ray Spruance's Fifth Fleet — which no longer existed — had consisted of no less than *fifteen* fast carriers. PacFlt now had none. Five divisions had been tasked to the mission of retaking the islands, supported by over a thousand tactical aircraft, battleships, cruisers, destroyers. . . .

And you're the lucky son of a bitch who has to come up with a plan *to take the Marianas back. With what?*

We can't deal with them force-on-force, Jackson told himself. They did hold the islands, and their weapons, mainly American-designed, were formidable. The worst complication was the quantity of civilians. The "natives" — all of them American citizens — numbered almost fifty thousand, most of whom lived on Saipan, and any plan that took many of those lives in the name of liberation would be a weight his conscience was unready to bear. It was a whole new kind of war, with a whole new set of rules, few of which he had figured out yet. But the central issues were the same. The enemy has taken something of ours, and we have to take it back or America was no longer a great power. Jackson hadn't spent his entire adult life in uniform so that he could be around when that bit of history got written. Besides, what would he say to Master Chief Manuel Oreza?

We can't do it force-on-force. America no longer had the ability to move a large army except from one base to another. There was really no large army to move, and no large navy to move it. There were no useful advance bases to support an invasion. Or were there? America still owned most of the islands in the Western Pacific, and every one had an airstrip of one kind or other. Airplanes flew farther now, and could refuel in midair. Ships could stay at sea almost indefinitely, a skill invented by the U.S. Navy eighty years earlier and made more convenient still by the advent of nuclear power. Most importantly, weapons technology had improved. You didn't need a bludgeon anymore. There were rapiers now. And overhead imagery. *Saipan.* That's where the issue would be decided. Saipan was the key to the island chain. Jackson lifted his phone.

"Ryan."

"Robby. Jack, how free a hand do we have?"

"We can't kill many people. It's not 1945 anymore," the National Security Advisor told him. "And they have nuclear missiles."

"Yeah, well, we're looking for those, so they tell me, and I know that's our first target if we can find them. What if we can't?"

"We have to," Ryan replied. *Have to?* he wondered. His best intelligence estimate was that the command-and-control over those missiles was in the hands of Hiroshi Goto, a man of limited intelligence and genuine antipathy to America. A more fundamental issue was that he had no confidence at all in America's ability to predict the man's actions. What might seem irrational to Ryan could seem reasonable to Goto —

and to whoever else he depended upon for advice, probably Raizo Yamata, who had begun the entire business and whose personal motivations were simply unknown. "Robby, we have to take them out of play, and to do that, yeah, you have a free hand. I'll clear that with NCA," he added, meaning National Command Authority, the dry Pentagon term for the President.

"Nukes?" Jackson asked. It was his profession to think in such terms, Ryan knew, however horrid the word and its implications were.

"Rob, we don't want to do that unless there's no choice at all, but you are authorized to consider and plan for the possibility."

"I just had a call from our friend on Saipan. It seems somebody wants to pay top dollar for his house."

"We think they may try to stage elections — a referendum on sovereignty. If they can move people off the island, then, well, it makes them some points, doesn't it?"

"We don't want that to happen, do we?"

"No, we don't. I need a plan, Rob."

"We'll get one for you," the Deputy J-3 promised.

Durling appeared on TV again at nine in the evening, Eastern Time. There were already rumbles out. The TV anchors had followed their stories about developments on Wall Street with confused references to the carrier accident the previous week and to urgent negotiations between Japan and the United States over the Mariana Islands, where, they noted, communications were out following a storm that might never have happened. It was very discomforting for them to say what they didn't know. By this time Washington correspondents were trading information and sources, amazed at having missed something of this magnitude. That amazement translated itself into rage at their own government for concealing something of this dimension. Background briefings that had begun at eight helped to assuage them somewhat. Yes, Wall Street was the big news. Yes, it was more vital to the overall American well-being than some islands that not a few of their number had to be shown on a map. But, no, damn it, the government didn't have the right not to tell the media what was going on. Some of them, though, realized that the First Amendment guaranteed their freedom to find things out, not to demand information from others. Others realized that the Administration was trying to end the affair without bloodshed, which went part of the way to calming them down. But not all of the way.

"My fellow Americans," Durling began for the second time in the day, and it was immediately apparent that, as pleasing as the events of the afternoon had been, the news this evening would be bad. And so it was.

There is something about inevitability that offends human nature. Man is a creature of hope and invention, both of which belie the idea that things cannot be changed. But man is also a creature prone to error, and sometimes that makes inevitable the things that he so often seeks to avoid.

The four B-1B Lancer bombers were five hundred miles offshore now, again spread on a line centered due east of Tokyo. This time they turned directly in, took an exact westerly heading of two-seven-zero degrees, and dropped down to a low-penetration altitude. The electronic-warfare officers aboard each of the aircraft now knew more than they had two nights earlier. Now at least they could ask the right questions. Additional satellite information had fixed the location of every air-defense radar site in the country, and they knew they could beat those. The important part of this night's mission was to get a feel for the capabilities of the E-767s, and that demanded more circumspection.

The B-1B had been reworked many times since the 1970s. It had actually become slower rather than faster, but it had also become stealthy. Especially from nose-on, the Lancer had the radar cross section — the RCS — of a large bird, as opposed to the B-2A, which had the RCS of a sparrow attempting to hide from a hawk. It also had blazing speed at low-level, always the best way to avoid engagement if attacked, which the crews hoped to avoid. The mission for tonight was to "tickle" the orbiting early-warning aircraft, wait for them to react electronically, and then turn and run back to Elmendorf with better data than what they had already developed, from which a real attack plan could be formulated. The flight crews had forgotten only one thing. The air temperature was 31 degrees Fahrenheit on part of their aircraft and 35 on another.

Kami-Two was flying one hundred miles east of Choshi, following a precise north-south line at four hundred knots. Every fifteen minutes the aircraft reversed course. It had been up on patrol for seven hours, and was due to be relieved at dawn. The crew was tired but alert, not yet quite settled into the numbing routine of their mission.

The real problem was technical, which affected the operators badly. Their radar, sophisticated as it was, did them fewer favors than one might imagine. Designed to make the detection of stealthy aircraft possible, it had achieved its goal, perhaps — they didn't really know yet — through a number of incremental improvements in performance. The radar itself was immensely powerful, and being of solid-state construction, both highly reliable and precise in its operation. Internal improvements included reception gear cooled with liquid nitrogen to boost sensitivity by a factor of four, and signal-processing software that missed little. That was really the problem. The radar displays were TV tubes that showed a computer-generated picture called a raster-scan, rather than the rotating-analog readout known since the invention of radar in the 1930s. The software was tuned to find anything that generated a return, and at the power and sensitivity settings being used now, it was showing things that weren't really there. Migratory birds, for example. The software engineers had programmed in a speed gate to ignore anything slower than one hundred thirty kilometers per hour, else they would have been tracking cars on the highways to their west, but the software took every return signal before deciding whether to show it to the operator, and if anything lay on or beyond that ring a few seconds later, it was plotted as a possible moving aircraft contact. In that way, two albatrosses a few thousand meters apart became a moving aircraft in the mind of the onboard computer. It was driving the operators mad, and along with them the pilots of the two Eagle fighters that flew thirty kilometers outboard of the surveillance aircraft. The result of the software problem was irritation that had already transformed itself into poor judgment. In addition, with the current sensitivity of the overall system, the still-active streams of commercial aircraft looked for all the world like fleets of bombers, and the only good news was that Kami-One to their north was dealing with them, classifying and handing them off.

"Contact, one-zero-one, four hundred kilometers," a captain on one of the boards said into the intercom. "Altitude three thousand meters . . . descending. Speed five hundred knots."

"Another bird?" the colonel commanding the mission asked crossly.

"Not this one . . . contact is firming up."

★ ★ ★

Another aviator with the rank of colonel eased his stick down to take his bomber lower. The autopilot was off now. *In and out,* he told himself, scanning the sky ahead of him.

"There's our friend," one of the EWOs said. "Bearing two-eight-one."

Automatically, both pilot and copilot looked to their right. Unsurprisingly, they saw nothing. The copilot looked back in. At night you wanted to keep an eye on instruments. The lack of good external references meant you ran the risk of vertigo, the loss of spatial orientation, which all aviators feared. They seemed to be approaching some layered clouds. His eyes checked the external temperature gauges. Thirty-five, and that was good. Two or three degrees lower and you ran the risk of icing, and the B-1, like most military aircraft, didn't have deicing equipment. Well, the mission was electronic, not visual, and clouds didn't mean much to radar transmission or reception.

But clouds did mean moisture, and the copilot allowed himself to forget that the temperature gauge was in the nose, and the tail was quite a bit higher. The temperature there was thirty-one, and ice started forming on the bomber's tailfin. It wasn't even enough to cause any degradation in the controls. But it was enough to make a subtle change in the shape of the aircraft, whose radar cross section depended on millimeter tolerances.

"That's a hard contact," the Captain said on Kami-Two. He worked his controls to lock on it, transmitting the contact to the Colonel's own display. "Maybe another one now."

"I have it." The contact, he saw, was leveling out and heading straight for Tokyo. It could not possibly be an airliner. No transponder. The base course was wrong. The altitude was wrong. The penetration speed was wrong. It had to be an enemy. With that knowledge, he told his two fighters to head for it.

"I think I can start interrogating it more — "

"No," the Colonel replied over the IC phones.

The two F-15J fighters had just topped off their tanks and were well sited for the interception. The alpha-numeric symbols on the Kami's screens showed them close, and aboard the fighters the pilots could see the same display and didn't have to light off their own targeting radars. With their outbound speed of five hundred knots, and a corresponding speed on the inbound track, it wouldn't be long.

At the same time a report was downlinked to the regional air-defense headquarters, and soon many people were watching the electronic drama. There were now three inbound aircraft plotted, spaced out as though to deliver an attack. If they were B-1 bombers, everyone knew, they could be carrying real bombs or cruise missiles, and they were well within the launch radius for the latter. That created a problem for the air-defense commander, and the time of day did not make it better. His precise instructions were not yet precise enough, and there was no command guidance he could depend on in Tokyo. But the inbounds were within the Air Defense Identification Zone, and they were probably bombers, and — what? the General asked himself. For now he ordered the fighters to split up, each closing on a separate target. It was going too fast. He should have known better, but you couldn't plan for everything, and they were bombers, and they were too close, and they were heading in fast.

"Are we getting extra hits?" the aircraft commander asked. He planned to get no closer than one hundred miles to the airborne radar, and he already had his escape procedures in mind.

"Sir, that's negative. I'm getting a sweep every six

835

seconds, but no electronic steering on us yet."

"I don't think they can see us this way," the pilot thought aloud.

"If they do, we can get out of Dodge in a hurry." The copilot flexed his fingers nervously and hoped his confidence was not misplaced.

There could be no tally-ho call. The fighters were above the cloud layer. Descending through clouds under these circumstances ran risks. The orders came as something of an anticlimax after all the drills and preparation, and a long, boring night of patrolling. Kami-Two changed frequencies and began electronic beam-steering on all three of her inbound contacts.

"They're hitting us," the EWO reported at once. "Freq change, pulsing us hard on the Ku-band."

"Probably just saw us." That made sense, didn't it? As soon as they plotted an inbound track, they'd try to firm it up. It gave him a little more time to work with. He'd keep going in for another few minutes, the Colonel thought, just to see what happened.

"He's not turning," the Captain said. He should have turned away immediately, shouldn't he? everyone aboard wondered. There could only be one good reason why he hadn't, and the resulting order was obvious. Kami-Two changed frequencies again to fire-control mode, and an Eagle fighter loosed two radar-homing missiles. To the north, another Eagle was still just out of range of its newly assigned target. Its pilot punched burner to change that.

"Lock-up — somebody's locked-up on us!"

"Evading left." The Colonel moved the stick and increased power for a screaming dive down to the wavetops. A series of flares combined with chaff clouds emerged from the bomber's tail. They stopped almost at once in the cold air and hovered nearly motionless. The sophisticated radar aboard the E-767 identified the chaff clouds and automatically ignored them, steering its pencil-thin radar beam on the bomber, which was still moving. All the missile had to do was follow it in. All the years of design work were paying off now, and the onboard controllers commented silently to themselves on the unexpected situation. The system had been designed to protect against Russians, not Americans. How remarkable.

"I can't break lock." The EWO tried active jamming next, but the pencil beam that was hammering the aluminum skin of their Lancer was two million watts of power, and his jammers couldn't begin to deal with it. The aircraft lurched into violent corkscrew maneuvers. They didn't know where the missiles were, and they could only do what the manual said, but the manual, they realized a little late, hadn't anticipated this sort of adversary. When the first missile exploded on contact with the right wing, they were too close to the water for their ejection seats to be of any help.

The second B-1 was luckier. It took a hit that disabled two engines, but even with half power it was able to depart the Japanese coast too rapidly for the Eagle to catch up, and the flight crew wondered if they would make Shemya before something else important fell off of their hundred-million-dollar aircraft. The rest of the flight retreated as well, hoping that someone could tell them what had gone wrong.

Of greater moment, yet another hostile act had been committed, and four more people were dead, and turning back would now be harder still for both sides in a war without any discernible rules.

36

Consideration

It wasn't that much of a surprise, Ryan told himself, but it would be of little consolation to the families of the four Air Force officers. It ought to have been a simple, safe mission, and the one bleak positive was that sure enough it had learned something. Japan had the world's best air-defense aircraft. They would have to be defeated if they were ever to take out their intercontinental missiles — but taken out the missiles had to be. A considerable pile of documents lay on his desk. NASA reports of the Japanese SS-19. Tracking on the observed test-firings of the birds. Evaluation of the capabilities of the missiles. Guesses about the payloads. They were all guesses, really. He needed more than that, but that was the nature of intelligence information. You never had enough to make an informed decision, and so you had to make an uninformed decision and hope that your hunches were right. It was a relief when the STU-6 rang, distracting him from the task of figuring what he could tell the President about what he didn't know.

"Hi, MP. Anything new?"

"Koga wants to meet with our people," Mrs. Foley replied at once. "Preliminary word is that he's not very pleased with developments. But it's a risk," she added.

It would be so much easier if I didn't know those two, Ryan thought. "Approved," was what he said. "We need all the information we can get. We need to know who's really making the decisions over there."

"It's not the government. Not really. That's what all the data indicates. That's the only plausible reason why the RVS didn't see this coming. So the obvious question is — "

"And the answer to that question is yes, Mary Pat."

"Somebody will have to sign off on that, Jack," the Deputy Director (Operations) said evenly.

"Somebody will," the National Security Advisor promised.

He was the Deputy Assistant Commercial Attaché, a young diplomat, only twenty-five, who rarely got invited to anything important, and when he was, merely hovered about like a court page from a bygone era, attending his senior, fetching drinks, and generally looking unimportant. He was an intelligence officer, of course, and junior at that job as well. His was the task of making pickups from dead-drops while on his way into the embassy every morning that the proper signals were spotted, as they were this morning, a Sunday in Tokyo. The task was a challenge to his creativity because he had to make the planned seem random, had to do it in a different way every time, but not so different as to seem unusual. It was only his second year as a field intelligence officer, but he was already wondering how the devil people maintained their careers in this business without going mad.

There it was. A soda can — a red Coca-Cola in this case — lying in the gutter between the left-rear wheel of a Nissan sedan and the curb, twenty meters ahead, where it was supposed to be. It could not have been there very long. Someone would have picked it up and deposited it in a nearby receptacle. He admired the neatness of Tokyo and the civic pride it represented. In fact he admired almost everything about these industrious and polite people, but that only made him worry about how intelligent and thorough their counterintelligence service was. Well, he did have a diplomatic cover, and had nothing more to fear than a blemish on a career that he could always change — his cover duties had taught him a lot about business, should he decide to leave the service of his government, he kept telling himself. He walked down the crowded morning sidewalk, bent down, and picked up the soda can. The bottom of the can was hollow, indented for easy stacking, and his hand deftly removed the item taped there, and then he simply dropped the can in the trash container at the end of the block before turning left to head for the embassy. Another important mission done, even if all it had appeared to be was the removal of street litter from this most fastidious of cities. Two years of professional training, he thought, to be a trash collector. Perhaps in a few years he would start recruiting his own agents. At least your hands stayed clean that way.

On entering the embassy he found his way to Major Scherenko's office and handed over what he'd retrieved before heading off to his own desk for a brief morning's work.

Boris Scherenko was as busy as he'd ever expected to be. His assignment was supposed to be a nice, quiet, commercial-spying post, learning industrial techniques that his country might easily duplicate, more a business function than one of pure espionage. The loss of Oleg Lyalin's THISTLE network had been a professional catastrophe that he had labored for some time to correct without great success. The traitor Lyalin had been a master at insinuating himself into business operations while he himself had worked to effect a more conventional penetration of the Japanese government organs, and his efforts to duplicate the former's achievements had barely begun to bear fruit when his tasking had changed back to something else entirely, a mission as surprising to him as the current situation doubtless was to the Americans who had been so badly stung by their erstwhile allies. Just one more truism that the Americans had allowed themselves to forget. You couldn't trust anyone.

The package just delivered on his desk was at least easy to work with: two frames of thirty-five-millimeter film, black and white, already developed as a photographic negative. It was just a matter of peeling off the gray tape and unfolding it, a task that took some minutes. As sophisticated as his agency was, the actual work of espionage was often as tedious as assembling a child's birthday toys. In this case, he used a pocket knife and a bright light to remove the film, and nearly cut himself in the process. He placed the two frames in cardboard holders, which went one at a time into a slide-viewer. The next task was to transcribe the data onto a paper pad, which was just one more exercise in tedium. It was worth it, he saw at once. The data would have to be confirmed through other sources, but the news was good.

"There's your two cars," the AMTRAK executive said. It had been so obvious a place to look that a day had been required to realize it. The two oversized flatcars were at the Yoshinobu launch facility, and beside them were three transporter-containers for the SS-19/H-11 booster, just sitting there in the yard. "This might be another one, sticking out of the building."

"They have to have more than two, don't they?" Chris Scott asked.

"I would," Betsy Fleming replied. "But it could just mean a place to stash the cars. And it's the logical place."

841

"Here or at the assembly plant," Scott agreed with a nod.

Mainly they were waiting now for nonvisual data. The only KH-12 satellite in orbit was approaching Japan and already programmed to look at one small patch of a valley. The visual information had given them a very useful cue. Another fifty meters of the rail spur had disappeared from view between one KH-11 pass and another. The photos showed the catenary towers ordinarily used for stringing the overhead power lines needed for electrically powered trains, but the towers did not have wires on them. They had possibly been erected to make the spur look normal to commuters who traveled the route in the Bullet Trains, just one more exercise in hiding something in plain sight.

"You know, if they'd just left it alone . . ." the AMTRAK guy said, looking at the overheads again.

"Yeah," Betsy responded, checking the clock. But they hadn't. Somebody was hanging camouflage netting on the towers, just around the first turn in the valley. The train passengers wouldn't notice, and, given slightly better timing, the three of them wouldn't have either. "If you were doing this, what would you do next?"

"To hide it from you guys? That's easy," the executive said. "I'd park track-repair cars there. That way it would look ordinary as hell, and they have the room for it. They should have done it before. Do people make mistakes like this all the time?"

"It isn't the first," Scott said.

"And now you're waiting for what?" the man asked.

"You'll see."

Launched into orbit eight years earlier by the Space Shuttle Atlantis, the TRW-built KH-12 satellite had actually survived far beyond its programmed life, but

842

as was true of many products made by that company — the Air Force called it "TR-Wonderful" — it just kept on ticking. The radar-reconnaissance satellite was completely out of maneuvering fuel, however, which meant you had to wait for it to get to a particular place and hope that the operating altitude was suitable to what you wanted.

It was a large cylindrical craft, over thirty feet in length, with immense "wings" of solar receptors to power the onboard Ku-band radar. The solar cells had degraded over the years in the intense radiation environment, allowing only a few minutes of operation per revolution. The ground controllers had waited what seemed a long time for this opportunity. The orbital track was northwest-to-southeast, within six degrees of being directly overhead, close enough to see straight down into the valley. They already knew a lot. The geological history of the place was clear. A river now blocked with a hydroelectric dam had cut the gorge deep. It was more canyon than valley at this point, and the steep sides had been the deciding factor in putting the missiles here. The missiles could launch vertically, but incoming warheads would be blocked from hitting them by the mountains to east and west. It didn't make any difference whose warheads they were. The shape and course of the valley would have had the same effect on Russian RVs as Americans'. The final bit of genius was that the valley was hard rock. Each silo had natural armor. For all those reasons, Scott and Fleming had bet much of their professional reputations on the tasking orders for the KH-12.

"Right about now, Betsy," Scott said, checking the wall clock.

"What exactly will you see?"

"If they're there, we'll know it. You follow space technology?" Fleming asked.

"You're talking to an original Trekkie."

"Back in the 1980s, NASA orbited a mission, and the first thing they downloaded was a shot of the Nile delta, underground aquifers that feed into the Mediterranean Sea. We mapped them."

"The same one did the irrigation canals down in Mexico, right, the Mayans, I think. What are you telling me?" the AMTRAK official asked.

"It was our mission, not NASA's. We were telling the Russians that they couldn't hide their silos from us. They got the message, too," Mrs. Fleming explained. Right about then the secure fax machine started chirping. The signal from the KH-12 had been crosslinked to a satellite in geostationary orbit over the Indian Ocean, and from there to the U.S. mainland. Their first read on the signals would be unenhanced, but, they hoped, good enough for a fast check. Scott took the first image off the machine and set it on the table under a bright light, next to a visual print of the same place.

"Tell me what you see."

"Okay, here's the mainline . . . oh — this thing picks up the ties. The rails are too small, eh?"

"Correct." Betsy found the spur line. The concrete rail ties were fifteen centimeters in width, and made for a good, sharp radar return that looked like a line of offset dashes.

"It goes quite a way up the valley, doesn't it?" The AMTRAK guy's face was down almost on the paper, tracing with his pen. "Turn, turn. What are these?" he asked, touching the tip to a series of white circles.

Scott placed a small ruler on the sheet. "Betsy?"

"Dense-packed it, too. My, aren't we clever. It must have cost a fortune to do this."

"Beautiful work," Scott breathed. The rail spur curved left and right, and every two hundred meters was a silo, not three meters away from the marching ranks of rail ties. "Somebody really thought this one through."

"You lost me."

"Dense-pack," Mrs. Fleming said. "It means that if you attempt to hit the missile field, the first warhead throws so much debris into the air that the next warhead gets trashed on the way in."

"It means that you can't use nuclear weapons to take these boys out — not easily anyway," Scott went on. "Summarize what you know for me," he ordered.

"This is a rail line that doesn't make any commercial sense. It doesn't go anywhere, so it can't make money. It's not a service siding, too long for that. It's standard gauge, probably because of the cargo-dimension requirements."

"And they're stringing camouflage netting over it," Betsy finished the evaluation, and was already framing the National Intelligence Estimate they had to draft tonight. "Chris, this is the place."

"But I only count ten. There's ten more we have to find."

It was hard to think of it as an advantage, but the downsizing of the Navy had generated a lot of surplus staff, so finding another thirty-seven people wasn't all that hard. That brought *Tennessee*'s complement to one hundred twenty, thirty-seven short of an Ohio's normal crew size, a figure Dutch Claggett could accept. He didn't need the missile technicians, after all.

His crew would be heavy on senior petty officers, another burden he would bear easily, the CO told himself, standing atop the sail and watching his men load provisions under the glaring lights. The reactor plant was up and running. Even now his engineering officer was conducting drills. Just forward of the sail, a green Mark 48 ADCAP torpedo was sliding backwards down the weapons-loading hatch under the watchful eyes of a chief torpedoman. There were only sixteen of those torpedoes to be had, but he didn't expect to need that many for the mission he anticipated. *Asheville* and *Charlotte*. He'd known men on both, and if Washington got its thumb out, maybe he'd do something about that.

A car pulled up to the brow, and a petty officer got out, carrying a metal briefcase. He made his way aboard, dodging around the crewmen tossing cartons, then down a hatch.

"That's the software upgrade for the sonar systems," Claggett's XO said. "The one they've been tracking whales with."

"How long to upload it?"

"Supposedly just a few minutes."

"I want to be out of here before dawn, X."

"We'll make it. First stop Pearl?"

Claggett nodded, pointing to the other Ohios, also loading men and chow. "And I don't want any of those turkeys beating us there, either."

It wasn't a comfortable feeling, but the sight was worth it. *Johnnie Reb* rested on rows of wooden blocks, and towered above the floor of the dry dock like some sort of immense building. Captain Sanchez had decided to give things a look, and stood alongside the ship's commanding officer. As they watched, a traveling crane removed the remains of the number-three screw. Workers and engineers in their multicolored hard hats made way, then converged back on the skeg, evaluating the damage. Another crane moved in to begin the removal of number-four tailshaft. It had to be pulled straight out, its inboard extremity already disconnected from the rest of the assembly.

"Bastards," the skipper breathed.

"We can fix her," Sanchez noted quietly.

"Four months. If we're lucky," the Captain added. They just didn't have the parts to do it any faster. The key, unsurprisingly, was the reduction gears. Six complete gear sets would have to be manufactured, and that took time. *Enterprise*'s entire drivetrain was gone, and the efforts to get the ship to safety as quickly as possible had wrecked the one gear set that might have been repairable. Six months for her, *if* the contractor could get spun up in a hurry, and work three-shift weeks to get the job done. The rest of the repairs were straightforward.

"How quick to get number-one shaft back to battery?" Sanchez asked.

The Captain shrugged. "Two-three days, for what that's worth."

Sanchez hesitated before asking the next question. He should have known the answer, and he was afraid it would sound really stupid — oh, what the hell? He had to go off to Barbers Point anyway. And the only dumb questions, he'd told people for years, were the ones you didn't ask.

"Sir, I hate to sound stupid, but how fast will she go on two shafts?"

Ryan found himself wishing that the Flat Earth Society was right. In that case the world could have been a single time zone. As it was, the Marianas were fifteen hours ahead, Japan fourteen, Moscow eight. Western Europe's principal financial markets were five and six ahead, depending on the country. Hawaii was five hours behind. He had contacts in all of those places, and everyone was working on local time, and it was so different in every case that just keeping track of who was probably awake and who was probably asleep occupied much of his thoughts. He grunted to himself in bed, remembering with nostalgia the confusion that always came to him on long flights. Even now people were working in some of those places, none under his control; and he knew he had to sleep if he were going to be able to deal with any of them when the sun returned to where he lived and worked. But sleep wasn't coming, and all he saw was the pine decking that made up his bedroom ceiling.

"Any ideas?" Cathy asked.

Jack grunted. "I wish I'd stuck with merchant banking."

"And then who'd be running things?"

A long breath. "Somebody else."

"Not as well, Jack," his wife suggested.

"True," he admitted to the ceiling.

"How do you think people will react to this?"

"I don't know. I'm not even sure how I'm reacting to it," Jack admitted. "It's not supposed to be like this at all. We're in a war that doesn't make any sense. We just got rid of the last nuclear missiles ten days ago, and now they're back, and pointed at us, and we don't have any to point back at them, and if we don't stop this thing fast — I don't know, Cathy."

"Not sleeping doesn't help."

"Thank God, married to a doctor." He managed a smile. "Well, honey, you got us out of one problem anyway."

"How did I do that?"

"By being smart." By using your head all the time, his mind went on. His wife didn't do anything without thinking it through first. She worked pretty slowly by the standards of her profession. Perhaps that was normal for someone pushing the frontiers back, always considering and planning and evaluating — like a good intelligence officer, in fact — and then when everything was ready and you had it all figured out, zap with her laser. Yeah, that wasn't a bad way to operate, was it?

"Well, I think they've learned one lesson," Yamata

848

said. A rescue aircraft had recovered two bodies and some floating debris from the American bomber. The bodies would be treated with dignity, it had been decided. The names had already been telexed to Washington via the Japanese Embassy, and in due course the remains would be returned. Showing mercy was the proper thing to do, for many reasons. Someday America and Japan would be friends again, and he didn't want to poison that possibility. It was also bad for business.

"The Ambassador reports that they do not offer us anything," Goto replied after a moment.

"They have not as yet evaluated their position, and ours."

"Will they repair their financial systems?"

Yamata frowned. "Perhaps. But they still have great difficulties. They still need to buy from us, they still need to sell to us — and they cannot strike us effectively, as four of their airmen, possibly eight, just learned to their sorrow." Things had not gone entirely in accord with his plans, but, then, when had things ever really done that? "What we must do next is to show them that the people who live on Saipan prefer our rule to theirs. Then world opinion will work in our favor, and that will defuse the situation greatly."

And until then, Yamata thought, things were going well. The Americans would not soon again probe his country's mainland. They didn't have the ability to retake the islands, and by the time they did, well, Japan would have a new ally, and perhaps even new political leadership, wouldn't it?

"No, I am not being watched," Koga assured them.

"As a reporter — no, you know better than that, don't you?" Clark asked.

"I know you are an intelligence officer. I know Kimura here has been in contact with you." They were in a comfortable teahouse close to the Ara River.

Nearby was the boat-racing course built for the 1964 Olympics. It was also conveniently close to a police station, John reminded himself. Why, he wondered, had he always feared the attention of police officers? Under the circumstances, it seemed the proper thing to nod his understanding of the situation.

"In that case, Koga-san, we are at your mercy."

"I presume your government now knows what is going on. All of it," Koga went on distastefully. "I've spoken with my own contacts as well."

"Siberia," Clark said simply.

"Yes," Koga responded. "That is part of it. Yamata-san's hatred for America is another part, but most of all, it's pure madness."

"The Americans' reaction is not really a matter of my immediate concern, but I can assure you that my country will not meekly submit to an invasion of our soil," John said calmly.

"Even if China is involved?" Kimura asked.

"Especially if China is involved," Chavez said just to let everyone know he was there. "I presume that you study history, as we do."

"I fear for my country. The time for such adventures is long past, but the people who — do you really understand how policy decisions are made here? The will of the people is an irrelevance. I tried to change that. I tried to bring an end to the corruption."

Clark's mind was racing, trying to decide if the man was sincere or not. "We face similar problems, as you have probably heard. The question is, what do we do now?"

The torment on the man's face was clear. "I do not know. I asked for this meeting in the hope that your government will understand that not everyone here is mad."

"You must not think of yourself as a traitor, Koga-san," Clark said after a moment's consideration. "Truly you are not. What does a man do when he feels that his government is taking incorrect action? And you are correct in your judgment that the possible consequences of this current course of action could well be serious. My country has neither the time nor the energy to waste on conflict, but if it is forced on us, well, then we must react. Now I must ask you a question."

"Yes, I know." Koga looked down at the table. He thought about reaching for his drink, but was too afraid that his hand would shake.

"Will you work with us to prevent this from happening?" *This is something for somebody a hell of a lot more senior than I am,* John told himself, but he was here, and the senior pukes were not.

"Doing what?"

"I lack the seniority to tell you exactly what that might be, but I can convey requests from my government. At the very least we will ask you for information, and perhaps for influence. You are still respected within government circles. You still have friends and allies in the Diet. We will not ask you to compromise those things. They are too valuable to be thrown away."

"I can speak out against this madness. I can — "

"You can do many things, Koga-san, but please, for the sake of your country and mine, please do nothing without first considering the effects you will achieve by taking action." *My next career change,* Clark thought. *Political counselor.* "We are agreed, are we not, that the objective here is to avoid a major war?"

"*Hai.*"

"Any fool can start a war," Chavez announced, thanking Providence for his master's courses. "It takes a better man to prevent one, and it takes careful thought."

"I will listen to your counsel. I do not promise you that I will follow it. But I will listen."

851

Clark nodded. "That is all we can ask." The rest of the meeting was procedural. Another such rendezvous would be too dangerous. Kimura would handle messages from this point on. Clark and Chavez left first, heading back to their hotel by foot. It was a very different affair from dealing with Mohammed Abdul Corp. Koga was honorable, bright, and wanted to do the right thing, even if it entailed treason. But John realized that his words to the man hadn't just been part of the seduction dance. At a certain point, state policy became a matter of conscience, and he was grateful that this man seemed to have one.

"Straight board shut," the chief of the boat announced from his post on the port-forward corner of the attack center. As was normal, the submarine's most senior enlisted man was the diving officer. Every opening in the ship's hull was closed tight, the red circles on the diving board replaced now with red horizontal dashes. "Pressure in the boat."

"All systems aligned and checked for dive. The compensation is entered. We are rigged for dive," the OOD announced.

"Okay, let's take her down. Dive the ship. Make your depth one hundred feet." Claggett looked around the compartment, first checking the status boards, then checking the men. *Tennessee* hadn't been underwater for more than a year. Neither had her crew, and he looked around for any first-dive nerves as the officer of the deck gave the proper commands for the evolution. It was normal that a few of the younger men shook their heads, reminding themselves that they were submariners, after all, and supposedly used to this. The sounds of escaping air made that clear enough. *Tennessee* took a gentle five-degree down angle at the bow. For the next few minutes the submarine would be checked for trim to see that the ship was properly balanced and that all onboard systems really did work, as all tests and inspections had already made certain. That process required half an hour. Claggett could well have gone faster, and the next time he certainly would, but for the moment it was time to get everyone comfortable again.

"Mr. Shaw, come left to new course two-one-zero."

"Aye, helm, left ten degrees rudder, come to new course two-one-zero." The helmsman responded properly, bringing the submarine to her base course.

"All ahead full," Claggett ordered.

"All ahead full, aye." The full-speed bell would take *Tennessee* to twenty-six knots. There were actually four more knots of speed available with a flank bell. It was a little-known fact that someone had made a mistake with the Ohio-class of boomers. Designed for a maximum speed of just over twenty-six knots, the first full-power trials on the lead boat in the class had topped out at just over twenty-nine, and later models had been marginally faster still. Well, Claggett thought with a smile, the U.S. Navy had never been especially interested in slow ships; they were less likely to dodge out of harm's way.

"So far, so good," Claggett observed to his OOD.

Lieutenant Shaw nodded. Another officer on his way out of the Navy, he'd been tapped as the boat's navigator, and having served with Dutch Claggett before, he'd not objected to coming back one more time. "Speed's coming up nicely, Cap'n."

"We've been saving a lot of neutrons lately."

"What's the mission?"

"Not sure yet, but damned if we aren't the biggest fast-attack submarine ever made," Claggett observed.

"Time to stream."

"Then do it, Mr. Shaw."

A minute later the submarine's lengthy towed-sonar was allowed to deploy aft, guided into the ship's wake via the starboard-side after diving plane. Even at high speed, the thin-line array immediately began providing data to the sonarmen forward of the attack center. *Tennessee* was at full speed now, diving deeper to eight hundred feet. The increased water pressure eliminated the chance of cavitation coming off her sophisticated screw system. Her natural-circulation reactor plant gave off no pump noise. Her smooth lines created no flow noise at all. Inside, crewmen wore rubber-soled shoes. Turbines were mounted on decks connected to the hull via springs to isolate and decouple propulsion sounds. Designed to radiate no noise at all, and universally referred to even by the fast-attack community as "black holes," the class really was the quietest thing man had ever put to sea. Big, with nowhere near the speed and maneuverability of the smaller attack boats, *Tennessee* and her sisters were still ahead in the most important category of performance. Even whales had a hard time hearing one.

Force-on-force, Robby Jackson thought again. If that's impossible, then what? "Well, if we can't play this like a prizefight, then we play it like a card game," he said to himself, alone in his office. He looked up in surprise, then realized that he'd heard his own words spoken aloud.

It wasn't very professional to be angry, but Rear Admiral Jackson was indulging himself with anger for the moment. The enemy — that was the term he was using now — assumed that he and his colleagues in J-3 could not construct an effective response to their moves. To them it was a matter of space and time and force. Space was measured in thousands of miles. Time was being measured in months and years. Force was being measured in divisions and fleets.

What if they were wrong? Jackson asked himself.

Shemya to Tokyo was two thousand miles.

854

Elmendorf to Tokyo was another thousand. But space *was* time. Time to them was the number of months or years required to rebuild a navy capable of doing what had been done in 1944, but that wasn't in the cards, and therefore was irrelevant. And force wasn't everything you had. Force was what you managed to deliver to the places that needed to be hit. Everything else was wasted energy, wasn't it?

More important still was perception. His adversaries *perceived* that their own limiting factors applied to others as well. They defined the contest in their terms, and if that's how America played the game, then America would lose. So his most important task was to make up his own set of rules. And so he would, Jackson told himself. That's where he began, on a clear sheet of unlined white paper, with frequent looks at the world map on his wall.

Whoever had run the night watch at CIA was intelligent enough, Ryan thought. Intelligent enough to know that information received at three in the morning could wait until six, which bespoke a degree of judgment rare in the intelligence community, and one for which he was grateful. The Russians had transmitted the dispatch to the Washington *rezidentura,* and from there it had been hand-carried to CIA. Jack wondered what the uniformed guards at CIA had thought when they had let the Russian spooks through the gate. From there the report had been driven to the White House, and the courier had been waiting for Ryan in his anteroom when he came in.

"Sources report a total of nine (9) 'H-11' rockets at Yoshinobu. Another missile is at the assembly plant, being used as an engineering test-bed for a proposed structural upgrade. That leaves ten (10) or eleven (11) rockets unaccounted for, more probably the former, location as yet unknown. Good news, Ivan

Emmetovich. I presume your satellite people are quite busy. Ours are as well. Golovko."

"Yes, they are, Sergey Nikolay'ch," Ryan whispered, flipping open the second folder the courier had brought down. "Yes, they are."

Here goes nothing, thought Sanchez.

AirPac was a vice admiral, and in as foul a mood as every other officer at the Pearl Harbor Naval Base. Responsible for every naval aircraft and flight deck from Nevada west, his ought to have been the point command for the war that had begun only a few days earlier, but not only could he not tell his two active carriers in the Indian Ocean what he wanted, he could see his other two carriers, sitting side by side in dry docks. And likely to remain there for months, as a CNN camera crew was now making clear to viewers across the entire world.

"So what is it?" he asked his visitors.

"Do we have plans for visiting WestPac?" Sanchez asked.

"Not anytime soon."

"I can be ready to move in less than ten days," *Johnnie Reb*'s CO announced.

"Is that a fact?" AirPac inquired acidly.

"Number-one shaft's okay. If we fix number four, I can do twenty-nine, maybe thirty knots. Probably more. The trials on two shafts had the wheels attached. Eliminate the drag from those, maybe thirty-two."

"Keep going," the Admiral said.

"Okay, the first mission has to be to eliminate their airplanes, right?" Sanchez said. "For that I don't need Hoovers and 'Truders. *Johnnie Reb* can handle four squadrons of Toms and four more of Plastic Bugs, Robber's det of Queers to do the jamming, plus an extra det of Hummers. And guess what?"

AirPac nodded. "That almost equals their fighter strength on the islands." It was dicey. One carrier deck against two major island bases wasn't exactly . . . but the islands were pretty far apart, weren't they? Japan had other ships out there, and submarines, which is what he feared in particular. "It's a start, maybe."

"We need some other elements," Sanchez agreed. "Anybody going to say no when we ask?"

"Not at this end," the Admiral said after a moment's thought.

The CNN reporter had made her first live feed from atop the edge of the dry dock, and it showed the two nuclear-powered carriers sitting on their blocks, not unlike twin babies in side-by-side cradles. Somebody in CINCPAC's office must have paid a price for letting her in, Ryan thought, because the second feed was from much farther away, the flattops across the harbor but still clearly visible behind her back, as she said much the same things, adding that she had learned from informed sources that it could be as much as six months before *Stennis* and *Enterprise* could again put to sea.

Isn't that just great, Jack grumbled to himself. Her estimate was as good as the one sitting on his desk with *Top Secret* written on the folder in red lettering. Maybe it was even better, since her source was probably a yard worker with real experience in that largest of body and fender shops. She was followed by a learned commentator — this one a retired admiral working at a Washington think-tank — who said that taking the Marianas back would be extremely difficult at best.

The problem with a free press was that it gave out information to everyone, and over the past two decades it had become so good a source of information that his country's own intelligence services used it for all manner of time-critical data. For its part, the public had grown more sophisticated in its demands for news, and the networks had responded by improving both its collection and analysis. Of course, the press had its weaknesses. For real insider information it depended too much on leaks and not enough on shoeleather, especially in Washington, and for analysis it often selected people motivated less by facts than by an agenda. But for things that one could *see*, the press often worked better than trained intelligence officers on the government payroll.

The other side depended on it too, Jack thought. Just as he was watching his office TV, so were others, all over the world. . . .

"You look busy," Admiral Jackson said from the door.

"I'm waiting just as fast as I can." Ryan waved him to a seat. "CNN just reported on the carriers."

"Good," Robby replied.

"Good?"

"We can have *Stennis* back to sea in seven to ten days. Old pal of mine, Bud Sanchez, is the CAG aboard her, and he has some ideas I like. So does AirPac."

"A week? Wait a minute." Yet another effect of TV news was that people often believed it over official data, even though in this case the classified report was identical with —

Three were still in Connecticut, and the other three were undergoing tests in Nevada. Everything about them was untraditional. The fabrication plant, for example, was more like a tailor shop than an aircraft factory. The basic material for the airframes arrived in rolls, which were laid out on a long, thin table where computer-driven laser cutters sliced out the proper shapes. Those were then laminated and baked in an oven until the carbon-fiber fabric formed a sandwich stronger than steel, but far lighter — and, unlike steel, transparent to electromagnetic energy. Nearly twenty years of design work had gone into this, and the first pedestrian set of requirements had grown into a book as thick as a multivolume encyclopedia. A typical Pentagon program, it had taken too long and cost too much, but the final product, if not exactly worth the wait, was certainly worth having, even at twenty million dollars per copy, or, as the crews put it, ten million dollars per seat.

The three in Connecticut were sitting in an open-sided shed when the Sikorsky employees arrived. The onboard systems were fully functional, and they had each been flown only just enough by the company test pilots to make sure that they could fly. All the systems had been checked out properly through the onboard diagnostic computer which, of course, had also diagnosed itself. After fueling, the three were wheeled out onto the ramp and flown off just after dark, north to Westover Air Force Base, in western Massachusetts, where they would be loaded in a Galaxy transport of the 327th Military Airlift Squadron for a flight to a place northeast of Las Vegas that wasn't on any official maps, though its existence wasn't much of a secret. Back in Connecticut, three wooden mockups were wheeled into the shed, its open side visible from the residential area and highway three hundred yards uphill. People would even be seen to work on them all week.

Even if you didn't really know the mission yet, the requirements were pretty much the same. *Tennessee* reduced speed to twenty knots, five hundred miles off the coast.

"Engine room answers all ahead two-thirds, sir."

"Very well," Commander Claggett acknowledged. "Left twenty-degrees rudder, come to new course zero-three-zero." The helmsman repeated that order back, and Claggett's next command was, "Rig ship for ultraquiet."

He already knew the physics of what he was doing, but moved aft to the plotting table anyway, to recheck the ship's turning circle. The Captain, too, had to check everything he did. The sharp course reversal was designed to effect a self-noise check. All over the submarine, unnecessary equipment was switched off, and crewmen not on duty got into their individual bunks as their ship turned. The crew, Claggett noted, was already getting into the swing.

Trailing behind *Tennessee* at the end of a thousand-yard cable was her towed sonar array, itself a thousand feet long. In another minute the submarine was like a dog chasing her own lengthy tail, a bare thousand yards abeam of it, and still doing twenty knots while sonarmen listened on their own systems for noise from their own ship. Claggett's next stop was the sonar room, so that he could watch the displays himself. It was electronic incest of sorts, the best sonar systems ever made trying to locate the quietest ship ever made.

"There we are, sir." The lead sonarman marked his screen with a grease pencil. The Captain tried not to be too disappointed. *Tennessee* was doing twenty knots, and the array was only a thousand yards off for the few seconds required for the pass to be made.

"Nobody's that invisible, sir," Lieutenant Shaw observed.

"Bring her back to base course. We'll try it again at fifteen knots." To the sonar chief: "Put a good man on the tapes. So let's find that rattle aft, shall we?" Ten minutes later *Tennessee* commenced another self-noise check.

"It's all going to be done in the saddle, Jack. As I read this, time works for them, not for us." It wasn't that Admiral Jackson liked it. There didn't appear to be another way, and this war would be come-as-you-are and make up your own rules as you went along.

"You may be right on the political side. They want to stage the elections soon, and they seem awfully confident — "

"Haven't you heard? They're flying civilians in hand over fist," Jackson told him. "Why do that? I think they're all going to become instant residents, and they're all going to vote *Ja* on the *Anschluss*. Our friends with the phone can see the airport. The inbound flights have slacked off some, but look at the numbers. Probably fifteen thousand troops on the island. They can all vote. Toss in the Japanese tourists already there, and those who've flown in, and that's all she wrote, boy."

The National Security Advisor winced. "That is simple, isn't it?"

"I remember when the Voting Rights Act got passed. It made a big difference in Mississippi when I was a kid. Don't you just love how people can use law to their benefit?"

"It sure is a civilized war, isn't it?" *Nobody ever said they were stupid,* Jack told himself. The results of the election would be bogus, but all they really had to do was muddle things. The use of force required a clear cause. So negotiations were part of the strategy of delay. The other side was still determining the rules of the game. America did not yet have a strategy of action.

"That's what we need to change."

"How?"

Jackson handed over a folder. "Here's the information I need."

Mutsu had satellite communications, which included video that could be uplinked from fleet headquarters at Yokohama. It was a pretty sight, really,

Admiral Sato thought, and so good of CNN to give it to him. *Enterprise* with three propellers wrecked, and the fourth visibly damaged. *John Stennis* with two already removed, a third clearly beyond repair; the fourth, unfortunately, seemed to be intact. What was not visible was internal damage. As he watched, one of the huge manganese-bronze propellers was removed from the latter ship, and another crane maneuvered in, probably, the destroyer's engineering officer observed, to withdraw part of the starboard outboard shaft.

"Five months," he said aloud, then heard the reporter's estimate of six, pleasantly the opinion of some unnamed yard worker.

"That's what headquarters thinks."

"They can't defeat us with destroyers and cruisers," *Mutsu*'s captain observed. "But will they pull their two carriers out of the Indian Ocean?"

"Not if our friends continue to press them. Besides," Sato went on quietly, "two carriers are not enough, not against a hundred fighters on Guam and Saipan — more if I request it, as I probably will. It's really a political exercise now."

"And their submarines?" the destroyer's CO wondered, very nervous.

"So why can't we?" Jones asked.

"Unrestricted warfare is out," SubPac said.

"It worked before."

"They didn't have nuclear weapons before," Captain Chambers said.

"Oh." There was that, Jones admitted to himself. "Do we have a plan yet?"

"For the moment, keeping them away from us," Mancuso said. It wasn't exactly a mission to thrill Chester Nimitz, but you had to start somewhere. "What do you have for me?"

"I've gotten a couple of hits on snorting subs east

of the islands. Nothing good enough to initiate a hunt, but I don't suppose we're sending P-3s in there anyway. The SOSUS troops are up to speed, though. Nothing's going to slip past us." He paused. "One other thing. I got one touch" — a touch was less firm than a hit — "on somebody off the Oregon coast."

"*Tennessee*," Chambers said. "That's Dutch Claggett. He's due in here zero-two-hundred Friday."

Jones was impressed with himself. "Damn, a hit on an Ohio. How many others?"

"Four more, the last one leaves the pier in about an hour." Mancuso pointed at his wall chart. "I told each one to run over that SOSUS array for a noise check. I knew you'd be around to sniff after them. Don't get too cocky about it. They're doing a speed run into Pearl."

Jones nodded and turned. "Good one, Skipper."

"We haven't completely lost it yet, Dr. Jones."

"Goddamn it, Chief!" Commander Claggett swore.

"My fault, sir. Sure as hell." He took it like a man. It was a toolbox. It had been found stuck between a seawater pipe and the hull, where minor vibrations off the spring-suspended deck had made the wrenches inside rattle, enough that the submarine-towed sonar had detected the noise. "It isn't one of ours, probably a yard worker left it aboard."

Three other chief petty officers were there to share the experience. It could have happened to anyone. They knew what was coming next, too. Their captain took a deep breath before going on. A good show of anger was required, even for his chiefs.

"Every inch of the hull from the collision bulkhead to the tailshaft. Every loose nut, every bolt, every screwdriver. If it's layin' on the deck, pick it up. If it's loose, tighten it. No stoppin' till it's done. I want this ship so quiet I can hear the dirty jokes you're thinking about me."

"It'll get done, sir," the Chief of the Boat promised. *Might as well get used to no sleep,* he didn't say, and sure enough —

"You got it, COB, no sleep until this boat makes a tomb look noisy." On reflection, Claggett thought he could have picked a better metaphor.

The CO made his way back forward, reminding himself to thank his sonar chief for isolating the source of the noise. It was better to have found it the first day out, and he had to raise hell about it. Those were the rules. He had to command himself not to smile. The Captain, after all, was *supposed* to be a stern son of a bitch — when he found something wrong, that is, and in a few minutes the chiefs would relay all his wrath on to others and feel the same way about it.

Things had already changed, he saw, as he passed through the reactor spaces. Like doctors in an operating room, the reactor watch sat or stood as their assignments dictated, mainly watching, making a few notes at the proper times. At sea for less than a day, and already Xerox copies of *Think Quiet* were taped to both sides of every watertight door. Those few crewmen he encountered in the passageways made way for him, often with a curt, proud nod. *Yeah, we're pros, too, sir.* Two men were jogging in the missile room, a long and now useless compartment, and Claggett, as service etiquette dictated, made way for them, almost smiling again as he did so.

"Toolbox, right?" the executive officer asked when the CO reentered the Attack Center. "I had that happen to me on *Hampton* after our first refit."

"Yep." Claggett nodded. "Turn of the next watch, we do a fore-and-aft walkdown."

"Could be worse, sir. Once coming out of a yard overhaul, a guy I know had to reenter the dry dock. They found a friggin' extension ladder in the forward

864

ballast tank." Stories like that made submariners shiver.

"Toolbox, sir?" the sonar chief asked.

Now he could smile. Claggett leaned against the doorframe and nodded as he pulled out a five-dollar bill. "Good call, Chief."

"Wasn't all that much." But the chief petty officer pocketed the five anyway. On *Tennessee,* as on a lot of submarines, every wrench aboard had its handle dipped in liquid vinyl, which both gave a slightly better grip, especially to a sweaty hand, and also cut way back on the chance of rattling. "Some yard puke, I bet," he added with a wink.

"I only pay once," Claggett observed. "Any new contacts?"

"Single-screw low-speed diesel surface ship bearing three-four-one, way out. It's a CZ contact, designated Sierra-Thirty. They're working a plot now, sir." He paused for a moment, and his mood changed. "Cap'n?"

"What is it, Chief?"

"*Asheville* and *Charlotte — is it true?*"

Commander Claggett nodded again. "That's what they told me."

"We'll even the score, sir."

Roger Durling lifted the sheet of paper. It was handwritten, which was something the President rarely saw. "This is rather thin, Admiral."

"Mr. President, you're not going to authorize a systematic attack on their country, are you?" Jackson asked.

Durling shook his head. "No, that's more than I want. The mission is to get the Marianas back and to prevent them from carrying through on the second part of their plan."

Robby took a deep breath. This was what he'd been preparing for.

"There's a third part, too," Jackson announced. The two men with him froze.

"What's that, Rob?" Ryan asked after a moment.

"We just figured it out, Jack. The Indian task-force commander, Chandraskatta? He went to Newport a while back. Guess who was in the same class." He paused. "A certain Japanese admiral named Sato."

Ryan closed his eyes. Why hadn't somebody turned this up before? "So, three countries with imperial ambitions . . ."

"It looks that way to me, Jack. Remember the Greater East Asia Co-Prosperity Sphere? Good ideas keep coming back. We need to stop it all," Jackson said forcefully. "I spent twenty-some years training for a war that nobody wanted to fight — with the Russians. I'd rather train to keep the peace. That means stopping these guys right now."

"Will this work?" the President asked.

"No guarantees, sir. Jack tells me there's a diplomatic and political clock on the operation. This isn't Iraq. Whatever international consensus we have is just with the Europeans, and that'll evaporate sooner or later."

"Jack?" Durling asked.

"If we're going to do it, this is probably the way."

"Risky."

"Mr. President, yes, sir, it's risky," Robby Jackson agreed. "If you think diplomacy will work to get the Marianas back, fine. I don't especially want to kill anybody. But if I were in their shoes, I would not give those islands back. They need them for Phase Two, and if that happens, even if the Russians don't go nuke . . ."

A giant step backwards, Ryan thought. A new alliance of sorts, one that could stretch from the Arctic Circle to Australia. Three countries with nuclear capacity, a huge resource base, massive economies, and the political will to use violence to achieve their ends.

The Nineteenth Century all over again, played on a far larger field. Economic competition backed by force, the classic formula for unending war.

"Jack?" the President asked again.

Ryan nodded slowly. "I think we have to. You can pick any reason you want. They all come out the same way."

"Approved."

37

Going Deep

"Normalcy" was the word the various commentators consistently used, usually with adjectives like "eerie" and/or "reassuring" to describe the week's routine. People on the political left were gratified that the government was using diplomatic means to address the crisis, while those on the political right were enraged that the White House was low-keying everything. Indeed, it was the absence of leadership, and the absence of real policy statements that showed everyone that Roger Durling was a domestic-policy president who didn't have much of a clue on how to handle international crises. Further criticism found its way to the National Security Advisor, John P. Ryan, who, though he had supposedly good credentials in intelligence, had never really established himself as a player in national-security matters per se, and certainly was not taking a very forceful position now. Others found his circumspection admirable. The downsizing of the American military, pundits observed, made effective counteraction extremely difficult at best, and though lights remained on at the Pentagon throughout the nights, there obviously was no way to deal with the situation in the Marianas. As a result, other observers said in front of any TV camera with a red light, the Administration would do its best to appear to remain calm and steady while doing the best it could. Hence the illusion of normalcy to conceal the inherent weakness of the American position.

"You ask us to do nothing?" Golovko asked in exasperation.

"It's our battle to fight. If you move too soon, it alerts China, and it alerts Japan." Besides, Ryan could not add, what *can* you do? The Russian military was in far worse shape than America's. They could move additional aircraft to Eastern Siberia. Moving ground troops to firm up the light-strength formations of border guards could well trigger a Chinese response. "Your satellites are telling you the same thing ours are, Sergey. China isn't mobilizing."

"Yet." The single word had a sting to it.

"Correct. Not yet. And if we play our cards right, that won't happen." Ryan paused. "Any further information on the missiles?"

"We have several sites under surveillance," Golovko reported. "We have confirmed that the rockets at Yoshinobu are being used for civilian purposes. That is probably a cover for military testing, but nothing more than that. My technical people are quite confident."

"Don't you just love how confident they can be," Ryan observed.

"What are you going to do, Jack?" the Chairman of the RVS asked directly.

"Even as we speak, Sergey Nikolay'ch, we are telling them that their occupation of the islands is not acceptable." Jack paused for a breath and reminded himself that like it or not, he had to trust the man. "And if they don't leave on their own, we'll find a way to force them off."

"But *how?*" the man demanded, looking down at the estimates prepared by military experts in the nearby Defense Ministry.

"Ten, fifteen years ago, did you tell your political masters that we were worthy of your fear?"

"As you did of us," Golovko confirmed.

"We are more fortunate now. They don't fear us. They think they've already won. I cannot say more at the moment. Perhaps by tomorrow," Jack thought. "For now, instructions are on the way for you to relay to our people."

"It will be done," Sergey promised.

"My government will honor the wishes of the people on all of the islands," the Ambassador repeated, then added a new provision. "We also may be willing to discuss the difference in status between Guam and the rest of the Mariana Archipelago. American interest in that island does go back nearly a hundred years," he allowed for the first time.

Adler accepted the statement impassively, as the rules of the proceedings required. "Mr. Ambassador, the people of all those islands are American citizens. They are so by their own choice."

"And they will again have the opportunity to express that choice. Is it the position of your government that self-determination is only *allowed* one time?" he asked in reply. "That seems quite odd for a country with a tradition of easy immigration *and* emigration. As I have stated earlier, we will gladly permit dual citizenship for those natives who prefer to keep their American passports. We will compensate them for their property should they decide to leave, and . . ." The rest of his statement was the same.

As often as he had observed or engaged in it, diplomatic exchange, Adler thought, combined the worst aspects of explaining things to a toddler and talking with a mother-in-law. It was dull. It was tedious. It was exasperating. And it was necessary. A moment earlier, Japan had conceded something. It hadn't been unexpected. Cook had wheedled the information out of Nagumo the previous week, but now it was on the table. That was the good news. The bad news was that he was now expected to offer something in return. The rules of diplomatic exchange were based on compromise. You never got all of what you wanted, and you never gave the other guy all of what he wanted. The problem was that diplomacy assumed that neither side would ever be forced to give away anything of vital interest — and that both sides recognized what those vital interests were. But so often they didn't, and then diplomacy was fated to fail, much to the chagrin of those who falsely believed that wars were always the product of inept diplomats. Much more often they were the result of national interests so incompatible that compromise simply was not possible. And so now the Ambassador expected Adler to give just a little ground.

"Speaking for myself, I am gratified that you acknowledge the unconditional rights of the Guamian people to remain American citizens. I am further pleased to note that your country allow the people of the Northern Marianas to determine their own destiny. Do you assure me that your country will abide by the results of the election?"

"I believe we have made that clear," the Ambassador replied, wondering if he'd just won something or not.

"And the elections will be open to — "

"All residents of the islands, of course. My country believes in universal suffrage, as does yours. In fact," he added, "we will make an additional concession. In Japan the vote comes at age twenty, but for the purposes of this election, we will lower the voting age to eighteen. We want no one to protest that the plebiscite is unfair in any way."

You clever bastard, Adler thought. It made such good sense, too. All the soldiers there could now vote, and the move would look just ducky to international observers. The Deputy Secretary of State nodded as though surprised, then made a note on his pad. Across the table, the Ambassador made a mental note that he'd just scored a point of his own. It had taken long enough.

"It's real simple," the National Security Advisor said. "Will you help us?"

The rules of the meeting were not calculated to make anyone happy. It had begun with an explanation from a Justice Department lawyer of how the Espionage Act, Title 18 United States Code, Section 793E, applied to all American citizens, and how the freedoms of speech and the press did not extend to violation of that statute.

"You're asking us to help you lie," one of the senior journalists said.

"Exactly right," Ryan responded.

"We have a professional obligation — "

"You're American citizens," Jack reminded them. "So are the people on those islands. My job is not to exercise the rights you're thinking about now. My job is to *guarantee* those rights to you and everyone else in this country. Either you help us or you don't. If you do, then we can do our job more easily, cheaply, and with less bloodshed. If you don't, then some additional people are probably going to get hurt."

"I doubt that Madison and the rest ever intended the American press to help an enemy in time of war," the lady from Justice said.

"We would never do that," the man from NBC protested. "But to take action in the other direction — "

"Ladies and gentlemen, I do not have time for a discourse on constitutional law. This is quite literally a matter of life and death. Your government is asking for your help. If you do not give that help, you will sooner or later have to explain to the American people why you did not." Jack wondered if anyone had ever threatened them in this way. Turnabout, he supposed, was fair play, though he didn't expect they would see things quite the same way. It was time for the olive branch. "I will take the heat on this. If you help us out, no one will ever hear it from me."

"Don't give me that. It'll get out," CNN protested.

"Then you will have to explain to the American people that you acted as patriotic citizens."

"I didn't mean it that way, Dr. Ryan!"

"I did," Jack said with a smile. "Think about it. How will it hurt you? Besides, how will it get out? Who else is going to report it?"

The journalists were cynical enough — it was almost a professional requirement — to see the humor, but it was Ryan's earlier statement that had scored. They were in a profound professional quandary, and the natural result was to evade it by thinking in other terms. In this case, business. Failure to act in support of their country, however much they might proclaim principle and professional ethics — well, the people who watched their TV were not as impressed with those high-flying standards as they ought to be. And besides, Ryan wasn't asking all that much. Just one thing, and if they were clever about it, maybe nobody really would notice.

The news executives would have preferred to leave the room and discuss the request in privacy, but no one offered that opportunity, and none of them had the nerve to ask. So they looked at one another, and all five nodded.

You'll pay for this one someday, their eyes told Ryan. It was something he was willing to deal with, he thought.

"Thank you." When they made their way out, Ryan walked toward the Oval Office.

"We got it," he told the President.

873

"I'm sorry I couldn't back you up on that."

"It's an election year," Jack acknowledged. The Iowa caucuses were two weeks away, then New Hampshire, and though Durling had no opposition in his party, he would on the whole have preferred to be elsewhere. He could also not afford offending the media. But that's why he had a National Security Advisor. Appointed officials were always expendable.

"When this is all over . . ."

"Back to golfing? I need the practice."

That was another thing he liked about him, Durling told himself. Ryan didn't mind telling a joke once in a while, though the circles under his eyes duplicated his own. It was one more reason to thank Bob Fowler for his contrarian advice, and perhaps a reason to lament Ryan's choice of political affiliation.

"He wants to help," Kimura said.

"The best way for him to do that," Clark replied, "is to act normally. He's an honorable man. Your country needs a voice of moderation." It wasn't exactly the instructions he'd expected, and he found himself hoping that Washington knew what the hell it was doing. The orders were coming through Ryan's office, which was some consolation but not all that much. At least his agent-in-place was relieved.

"Thank you. I do not wish to put his life at risk."

"He's too valuable for that. Perhaps America and Japan can reach a diplomatic solution." Clark didn't believe it, but saying such things always made diplomats happy. "In that case, Goto's government will fall, and perhaps Koga-san will regain his former place."

"But from what I hear, Goto will not back down."

"It is also what I hear, but things can change. In any case, that is our request for Koga. Further contact between us is dangerous," "Klerk" went on. "Thank you for your assistance. If we need you again, we will contact you through normal channels."

In gratitude, Kimura paid the bill before leaving.

"That's all, eh?" Ding asked.

"Somebody thinks it's enough, and we have other things to do."

Back in the saddle again, Chavez thought to himself. But at least they had orders, incomprehensible though they might be. It was ten in the morning, local time, and they split up after hitting the street, and spent the next several hours buying cellular phones, three each of a new digital model, before meeting again. The units were compact and fit into a shirt pocket. Even the packing boxes were small, and neither officer had the least problem concealing them.

Chet Nomuri had already done the same, giving his address as an apartment in Hanamatsu, a pre-selected cover complete with credit cards and driver's license. Whatever was going on, he had less than thirty days in-country to accomplish it. His next job was to return to the bathhouse one last time before disappearing from the face of the earth.

"One question," Ryan said quietly. The look in his eyes made Trent and Fellows uneasy.

"Are you going to make us wait for it?" Sam asked.

"You know the limitations we face in the Pacific."

Trent stirred in his seat. "If you mean that we don't have the horses to — "

"It depends on which horses we use," Jack said. Both insiders considered that for a moment.

"Gloves off?" Al Trent asked.

Ryan nodded. "All the way off. Will you hassle us about it?"

"Depends on what you mean by that. Tell us," Fellows ordered. Ryan did.

"You're really willing to stick it out that far?" Trent asked.

"We don't have a choice. I suppose it would be nice to fight it out with cavalry charges on the field of honor and all that stuff, but we don't have the horses, remember? The President needs to know if Congress will back him up. Only you people will know the black part. If you support us, then the rest of the people on the Hill will fall in line."

"If it doesn't work?" Fellows wondered.

"Then there's a hanging party for all hands. Including you," Ryan added.

"We'll keep the committee in line," Trent promised. "You're playing a high-risk game, my friend."

"True enough," Jack agreed, thinking of the lives at risk. He knew that Al Trent was talking about the political side, too, but Ryan had commanded himself to set those thoughts aside. He couldn't say so, of course. Trent would have considered it a weakness. It was remarkable how many things they could disagree on. But the important thing was that Trent's word was good.

"Keep us informed?"

"In accordance with the law," the National Security Advisor replied with a smile. The law required that Congress be notified *after* "black" operations were carried out.

"What about the Executive Order?" An Order dating back to the Ford administration prohibited the country's intelligence agencies from conducting assassinations.

"We have a Finding," Ryan replied. "It doesn't apply in time of hostilities." A Finding was essentially a Presidential decree that the law meant what the President thought it meant. In short, everything that Ryan had proposed was now, technically speaking, legal, so long as Congress agreed. It was a hell of a way to run a railroad, but democracies were like that.

"Then the *i*'s are dotted," Trent observed. Fellows

concurred with a nod: "And the *t*'s are crossed." Both congressmen watched their host lift a phone and punch a speed-dial button.

"This is Ryan. Get things moving."

The first move was electronic. Over the outraged protests of CINCPAC, three TV crews set up their cameras on the edge of the side-by-side dry docks now containing *Enterprise* and *John Stennis*.

"We're not allowed to show you the damage to the ships' sterns, but informed sources tell us that it's even worse than it appears to be," the reporters all said, with only minor changes. When the live reports were done, the cameras were moved and more shots made of the carriers, then still more from the other side of the harbor. They were just backgrounders, like file footage, and showed the ships and the yards without any reporters standing in the way. These tapes were turned over to someone else and digitalized for further use.

"Those are two sick ships," Oreza observed tersely. Each one represented more than the aggregate tonnage of the entire U.S. Coast Guard, and the Navy, clever people that they were, had let both of them take a shot in the ass. The retired master chief felt his blood pressure increase.

"How long to get them well?" Burroughs asked.

"Months. Long time. Six months . . . puts us into typhoon season," Portagee realized to his further discomfort. It got worse with additional consideration. He didn't exactly relish the idea of being on an island assaulted by Marines, either. Here he was, on high ground, within sight of a surface-to-air missile battery that was sure to draw fire. Maybe selling out for a million bucks wasn't so bad an idea after all. With that sort of money he could buy another boat, another house, and do his fishing out of the Florida Keys.

"You know, you can fly out of here if you want."

"Oh, what's the hurry?"

Election posters were already being printed and posted. The public-access channel on the island's cable system updated notices every few hours about the plans for Saipan. If anything, the island was even more relaxed now. Japanese tourists were unusually polite, and for the most part the soldiers were unarmed now. Military vehicles were being used for roadwork. Soldiers were visiting schools for friendly introductions. Two new baseball fields had been created, virtually overnight, and a new league started up. There was talk that a couple of Japanese major-league teams would commence spring training on Saipan, for which a stadium would have to be constructed, and maybe, it was whispered now, Saipan would have its own team. Which made sense, Oreza supposed. The island was closer to Tokyo than Kansas City was to New York. It wasn't that the residents were happy with the occupation. It was just that they did not see any salvation, and so like most people in such a spot they learned to live with it. The Japanese were going far out of their way to make it as comfortable a process as possible.

For the first week there had been daily protests. But the Japanese commander, General Arima, had come out to meet every such group, TV cameras all around, and invited the leaders into his office for a chat, often televised live. Then came the more sophisticated responses. Government civilians and businessmen held a lengthy press conference, documenting how much money they had invested in the island, showing in graphic form the difference they'd made for the local economy, and promising to do more. It wasn't so much that they had eliminated resentment as shown tolerance of it, promising at every turn to abide by the results of the elections soon to be held. *We live here, too,* they kept say-

878

ing. *We live here, too.*

There had to be hope. Two weeks tomorrow, Oreza thought, and all they heard were reports on goddamned negotiations. Since when had America ever negotiated something like this? Maybe that was it. Maybe it was just his country's obvious sign of weakness that gave him a sense of hopelessness. Nobody was fighting back. Tell us that the government is *doing* something, he wanted to say to the Admiral at the other end of the satellite phone. . . .

"Well, what the hell." Oreza walked into the living room, put the batteries back in the phone, slid the antenna into the bottom of the mixing bowl, and dialed the number.

"Admiral Jackson," he heard.

"Oreza here."

"Anything new to report?"

"Yeah, Admiral. How the elections are going to go."

"I don't understand, Master Chief."

"I see CNN telling us we got two carriers with their legs cut off and people saying we can't do shit, sir. Jesus, Admiral, even when the Argentineans took the goddamned Falklands the Brits said they were coming back. I ain't hearing that. What the hell are we supposed to think?"

Jackson weighed his reply for a few seconds. "I don't need to tell you the rules on talking about operational stuff. Your job's to give me information, remember?"

"All we keep hearing is how they're going to hold elections, okay? The missile site east of us is camouflaged now — "

"I know that. And the search radar on top of Mount Takpochao is operating, and there's about forty fighter aircraft based at the airport and Kobler. We count sixty more at Andersen on Guam. There are eight 'cans cruising east of you, and an oiler group

879

approaching them for an unrep. Anything else you want to know?" Even if Oreza was "compromised," a polite term for being under arrest, which Jackson doubted, this was nothing secret. Everyone knew America had reconnaissance satellites. On the other hand, Oreza needed to know that Jackson was up-to-date and, more importantly, interested. He was slightly ashamed of what he had to say next. "Master Chief, I expected better from a guy like you." The reply made him feel better, though.

"That's what I needed to hear, Admiral."

"Anything new happens, you tell us about it."

"Aye aye, sir."

Jackson broke the connection and lifted a recently arrived report on *Johnnie Reb*.

"Soon, Master Chief," he whispered. Then it was time to meet with the people from MacDill Air Force Base, who were, perversely, all wearing Army green. He didn't know that they would remind him of something he'd seen a few months earlier.

The men all had to be Spanish speakers, and look Spanish. Fortunately that wasn't hard. A documents expert flew from Langley to Fort Stewart, Georgia, complete with all the gear he needed, including ten blank passports. For purposes of simplicity, they'd use their real names. First Sergeant Julio Vega sat down in front of the camera, wearing his best suit.

"Don't smile," the CIA technician told him. "Europeans don't smile for passports."

"Yes, sir." His service nickname was *Oso*, "bear," but only his peers called him that now. To the rest of the Rangers in Foxtrot Company, Second Battalion, 175th Ranger Regiment, his only name was "First Sergeant," and they knew him as an experienced NCO who would back up his captain on the mission for which he'd just volunteered.

"You need better clothes, too."

"Who's buyin'?" Vega asked, grinning now, though the picture would show the dour face he usually reserved for soldiers who failed to meet his standards of behavior. That would not be the case here, he thought. Eight men, all jump-qualified (as all Rangers were), all people who'd seen combat action in one place or another — and unusually for members of the 175th, all men who hadn't shaved their heads down to stubbly Mohawks. Vega remembered another group like this one, and his grin stopped. Not all of them had come out of Colombia alive.

Spanish speakers, he thought as he left the room. Spanish was probably the language in the Marianas. Like most senior Army noncommissioned officers, he had gotten his bachelor's degree in night school, having majored in military history — it had just seemed the right thing to do for one of his profession, and besides, the Army had paid for it. If Spanish were the language on those rocks, then it gave him an additional reason to think in positive terms about the mission. The name of the operation, which he'd overheard in a brief conversation with Captain Diego Checa, also seemed auspicious. It was called Operation ZORRO, which had amused the Captain enough to allow him to confide in his first sergeant. The "real" Zorro had been named Don Diego, hadn't he? He had forgotten the bandit's surname, but his senior NCO had not. *With a name like Vega, how can I turn down a mission like this?* Oso asked himself.

It was a good thing he was in shape, Nomuri thought. Just breathing here was hard enough. Most Western visitors to Japan stayed in the major cities and never realized that the country was every bit as mountainous as Colorado. Tochimoto was a small hill settlement that languished in the winter and expanded in summer as local citizens who grew tired of the crowded sameness of the cities moved into the country to explore. The hamlet, at the end of National Route 140, had essentially pulled in its sidewalks, but Chet was able to find a place to rent a small four-wheel all-terrain cycle, and had told the owner that he just needed a few hours to get away. In return for his money and a set of keys he'd received a stern warning, albeit polite, about following the trail and being careful, for which he'd graciously thanked the man and gone on his way, following the River Taki — more a nice brook than a river — up into the mountains. After the first hour, and about seven miles, he reckoned, he'd switched off the motor, pulled out his earplugs, and just listened.

Nothing. He hadn't seen a track in the mud and gravel path alongside the cascading stream, nor any sign of occupancy in the handful of rustic summer homes he'd passed along the way, and now, listening, he heard nothing at all but for the wind. There was a ford on his map, two more miles up, and sure enough it was both marked and usable, and allowed him to go east toward Shiraishi-*san*. Like most mountains, it had sides sculpted by time and water into numerous dead-end valleys, and Mount Shiraishi had a particularly nice valley, as yet unmarred by house or cabin. Perhaps Boy Scouts came here in summer to camp and commune with the nature the rest of their country had worked so hard to extinguish. More likely it was just a spot with no minerals valuable enough to justify a road or rail line. It was also one hundred air miles from Tokyo, and for all practical purposes might as easily have been in Antarctica.

Nomuri turned south, and climbed a smooth part of the slope to the crest of the southern ridge. He wanted a further look and listen, and, while he spotted a single half-built dwelling a few miles below, he saw no column of smoke from a wood fire, nor the rising steam from someone's hot tub, and he heard nothing at all that was not of nature. Nomuri spent thirty minutes scanning the area with a pair of compact binoculars, taking his time and making sure, then turned to look north and west, finding the same remarkable absence of human presence. Finally satisfied, he headed back down to the Taki, following the path back to the town.

"We never see anyone now," the rental agent said when Nomuri finally got back, just after sunset. "May I offer you some tea?"

"*Dozo*," the CIA officer said. He took his tea with a friendly nod. "It's wonderful here."

"You were wise to come this time of year." The man wanted conversation more than anything else. "In the summer the trees are full and beautiful, but the noise from these things" — he gestured at the ranks of cycles — "well, it ruins the peace of the mountain. But it supports me well," the man allowed.

"I must come back again. Things are so hectic at my office. To come here and feel the silence."

"Perhaps you will tell some friends," the man suggested. Clearly he needed the money to sustain him in the off-season.

"Yes, I will certainly do that," Nomuri assured him. A friendly bow sent him on his way, and the CIA officer started his car for the three-hour drive back to Tokyo, still wondering why the Agency had given him an assignment calculated to make him feel better about his mission.

"Are you guys really comfortable with this?" Jackson asked the people from SOCOM.

"Funny time for second thoughts, Robby," the senior officer observed. "If they're dumb enough to let American civilians roam around their country, well, let's take advantage of it."

"The insertion still worries me," the Air Force representative noted, looking by turns at the air-navigation charts and the satellite photos. "We have a good IP — hell, the navigational references are pretty good — but somebody's gotta take care of those AWACS birds for this to work."

"It's covered," the colonel from Air Combat Command assured him. "We're going to light up the sky for them, and you do have that gap to use." He tapped his pointer on the third chart.

"The helo crews?" Robby asked next.

"They're working on their sims now. If they're lucky they'll get to sleep on the flight over."

The mission-planning simulator was real enough to fool Sandy Richter's inner ears. The device was halfway between his youngest son's new Nintendo VR System and a full-up aircraft simulator, the over-sized helmet he wore identical with the one he used in his Comanche, but infinitely more sophisticated. What had begun with a monocle display on the AH-64 Apache was now like an I-MAX-theater view of the world that you wore on your head. It needed to be more sophisticated yet, but it did give him a view of the computer-generated terrain along with all his flight information, and his hands were on the stick and throttle of another virtual-helicopter as he navigated across the water toward approaching bluffs.

"Coming right for the notch," he told his back-seater, who was actually sitting beside him, because the simulator didn't require that sort of fidelity. In this artificial world, they saw what they saw regardless of where they were, though the backseater sitting next to him had two additional instruments.

What they saw was the product of six hours of supercomputer time. A set of satellite photographs taken over the last three days had been analyzed, folded, spindled, and mutilated into a three-dimensional display that looked like a somewhat grainy video.

"Population center to the left."

"Roger, I see it." What he saw was a patch of fluorescent blue which in reality would have been yellow-orange quartz lighting, and out of deference to it he increased altitude from the fifty feet he'd followed for the past two hours. He eased the sidestick over, and the others in the darkened room, who were observing the flight crew, were struck by the way both bodies tilted to deal with the g-forces of a turn that existed only in the computer running the simulation. They might have laughed except that Sandy Richter was not somebody you laughed at.

From the moment he crossed the virtual coast, he climbed up to a crest and ran along it. That was Richter's idea. There were roads and houses in the river valleys that ended at the Sea of Japan. Better, the pilot thought, to stay acoustically covert as much as possible and take his chances with the lookdown capability. In a just world he'd be able to deal with that threat on the inbound leg, but this was not exactly a just world.

"Fighters overhead," a female voice warned, just as it would on the real mission.

"Coming down some," Richter replied to the computer voice, slipping down below the ridgeline to the right. "If you can find me fifty feet off the ground, then I lose, honey."

"I hope this stealth shit really works." The initial intelligence reports were very concerned with the radar in the Japanese F-15s. Somehow it had taken down one B-1 and crippled another, and nobody was quite sure how it had happened.

"We're gonna find that one out." What else could the pilot say? In this case the computer decided that the stealth shit really did work. The last hour of the virtual flight was routine terrain-dodging, but strenuous enough that when he landed his Comanche, Richter needed a shower which, he was sure, would not be available where they were going. Though a pair of skis might be useful.

"What if the other guys — "

"Then I suppose we learn to like rice." You couldn't worry about everything. The lights came on, the helmets came off, and Richter found himself sitting in a medium-sized room.

"Successful insertion," the major grading the exercise decided. "You gents ready for a little trip?"

Richter picked up a glass of ice water from the table in the back of the room. "You know, I never really thought I'd drive a snake that far."

"What about the rest of the stuff?" his weapons-operator wanted to know.

"It'll be uploaded when you get there."

"And the way out?" Richter asked. It would have been better had they briefed him in on that one.

"You have a choice of two. Maybe three. We haven't decided that one yet. It's being looked at," the SOCOM officer assured them.

The good news was that they all seemed to have penthouse apartments. That was to be expected, Chavez thought. Rich dudes like these bastards would have the whole top floor of whatever building they picked. It made people like that feel big, he supposed, to be able to look down on everyone else, like people in the L.A. high-rises had looked down on the barrios of his youth. None of them had ever been soldiers, though. You never wanted to skyline yourself that way. Better to be down in the weeds with the mice and the peons. Well, everybody had their limitations, Ding told himself.

It was just a matter, then, of finding a tall spot. That proved easy. Again the pacific nature of the city worked in their favor. They merely picked the proper building, walked in, took the elevator to the top floor, and from there walked to the roof. Chavez set up his camera on a tripod, selected his longest lens, and started shooting. Even doing it all in daylight was no hardship, the instructions had told them, and the weather gods cooperated, giving them a gray, overcast afternoon. He shot ten frames of each building, rewinding and ejecting the film cassettes, which went back into their boxes for labeling. The entire operation took half an hour.

"You get used to trusting the guy?" Chavez asked after they made the pass.

"Ding, I just got used to trusting you," Clark replied quietly, easing the tension of the moment.

38

The River Rubicon

"So?"

Ryan took his time considering the answer. Adler deserved to know something. There was supposed to be honor in negotiations. You never really told the whole truth, but you weren't supposed to lie either.

"So continue as before," the National Security Advisor said.

"We're doing something." It was not a question.

"We're not sitting on our hands, Scott. They're not going to cave in, are they?"

Adler shook his head. "Probably not."

"Encourage them to rethink their position," Jack suggested. It wasn't very helpful, but it was something to say.

"Cook thinks there are political forces working over there to moderate matters. His counterpart on the other side is giving him encouraging information."

"Scott, we have a couple of CIA officers working over there, covered as Russian journalists. They've been in contact with Koga. He's not very happy with developments. We've told him to act normally. There's no sense in harming the guy, but if . . . best move, have Cook feel the guy out on what the opposition elements in their government really are, and what power they might have. He must *not* reveal who we're in contact with."

"Okay, I'll pass that one along. Otherwise keep the same line?" Adler asked.

"Don't give them anything of substance. Can you dance some?"

"I think so." Adler checked his watch. "It's at our place today. I have to sit down with Brett before it starts."

"Keep me posted."

"Will do," Adler promised.

It was still before dawn at Groom Lake. A pair of C-5B transports taxied to the end of the runway and lifted off. The load was light, only three helicopters each and other equipment, not much for aircraft designed to carry two tanks. But it would be a long flight for one of them, over five thousand miles, and adverse winds would require two midair refuelings, in turn necessitating a full relief crew for each transport. The additional flight crewmen relegated the passengers to the space aft of the wing box, where the seats were less comfortable.

Richter removed the dividers from the three-seat set and put his earplugs in. As soon as the aircraft lifted off, his hand moved automatically for the pocket of his flight suit where he kept his cigarettes — or had until he'd quit a few months earlier. Damn. How could you go into combat without a smoke? he asked himself, then leaned against a pillow and faded off to sleep. He didn't even feel the buffet of the aircraft as it climbed into the jetstream over the Nevada mountains.

Forward, the flight crew turned north. The sky was dark and would remain so for almost all of the flight. Their most important task would be to stay alert and awake. Automated equipment would handle the navigation, and the hour was such that the red-eye commercial flights were already out of the way and the regular day's business hops had hardly begun. The sky was theirs, such as it was, with broken clouds and bitterly cold air outside the aluminum skin of the aircraft, on their way to the goddamnedest destination the reserve crew had ever considered. The second Galaxy's crew was luckier. It turned southwest, and in less than an hour was over the Pacific Ocean for their shorter flight to Hickam Air Force Base.

USS *Tennessee* entered Pearl Harbor an hour early and proceeded under her own power to an outlying berth, dispensing with the harbor pilot and depending on a single Navy tugboat to bring her alongside. There were no lights, and the evolution was accomplished by the glow of the other lit-up piers of the harbor. The one surprising thing was the presence of a large fuel truck on the quay. The official car and the admiral standing next to it were to be expected, Commander Claggett thought. The gangway was rigged quickly, and ComSubPac hustled across even before the ensign was rigged on the after part of the sail. He saluted that way anyway.

"Welcome aboard, Admiral," the CO called from his control station, then headed down the ladder to meet Admiral Mancuso in his own cabin.

"Dutch, I'm glad you managed to get her under way," Mancuso said with a smile tempered by the situation.

"Glad I finally got to dance with the girl," Claggett allowed. "I have all the diesel I need, sir," he added.

"We have to pump out one of your tanks." Large as she was, *Tennessee* had more than one fuel bunker for her auxiliary diesel.

"What for, sir?"

"Some JP-5." Mancuso opened his briefcase and pulled out the mission orders. The ink was hardly dry on them. "You're going to start off in the special-ops business." The automatic tendency was for Claggett to ask *Why me?* but he restrained himself. Instead he flipped over the cover page of the orders and started checking his programmed position.

"I might get a little business there, sir," the Captain observed.

"The idea is to stay covert, but the usual rule applies." The usual rule meant that Claggett would always be free to exercise his command judgment.

"Now hear this," the 1-MC announcing system told everyone. "The smoking lamp is out throughout the ship. The smoking lamp is out throughout the ship."

"You let people smoke aboard?" ComSubPac asked. Quite a few of his skippers did not.

"Command judgment, remember?"

Thirty feet away, Ron Jones was in the sonar room, pulling a computer disk out of his pocket.

"We've had the upgrade," the chief told him.

"This one's brand-new." The contractor slipped it into the slot on the backup computer. "I got a hit on you first night out when you ran over the Oregon SOSUS array. Something loose aft?"

"Toolbox. It's gone now. We ran over two more later," the chief pointed out.

"How fast?" Jones asked.

"The second one was just under flank, and we curlicued overtop the thing."

"I got a twitch, nothing more, and that one had the same software I just uploaded for you. You got a quiet boat here, Chief. Walk down?"

"Yeah, the Cap'n tore a few strips off, but there ain't no loose gear aboard now." He paused. "Less'n you count the ends on the toilet-paper rolls."

Jones settled into one of the chairs, and looked around the crowded working space. This was his place. He'd only had a hint of the ship's mission orders — Mancuso had asked his opinion of water conditions and worried if the Japanese might have taken the U.S. Navy's SOSUS station on Honshu intact, and that had been enough, really. She was sure as hell going in harm's way, perhaps the first PacFlt sub to do so. *God, and a boomer, too,* he thought. *Big and slow.* One hand reached out and touched the workstation.

"I know who you are, Dr. Jones," the chief said, reading the man's thoughts. "I know my job, too, okay?"

"The other guy's boats, when they snort — "

"The thousand-hertz line. We have the dash-five tail and all the upgrades. Including yours, I guess." The chief reached for his coffee, and on reflection, poured a mug for his visitor.

"Thank you."

"*Asheville* and *Charlotte?*"

Jones nodded, looking down at his coffee. "You know Frenchy Laval?"

"He was one of the instructors in my A-School, long time back."

"Frenchy was my chief on *Dallas,* working for Admiral Mancuso. His son was aboard *Asheville.* I knew him. It's personal."

"Gotcha." It was all the chief had to say.

"The United States of America does *not* accept the current situation, Mr. Ambassador. I thought that I'd made that clear," Adler said two hours into the current session. In fact he'd made it clear at least eight times every day since the negotiations had begun.

"Mr. Adler, unless your country wishes to continue this war, which will profit no one at all, all you need do is abide by the elections which we plan to stage — with full international supervision."

Somewhere in California, Adler remembered, was a radio station that for weeks had played every known recorded version of "Louie Louie." Perhaps the State

Department could pipe that into the building instead of Muzak. It would have been superb training for this. The Japanese Ambassador was waiting for an American response to his country's gracious offer of returning Guam — as though it had not been taken by force in the first place — and was now showing exasperation that Adler wasn't conceding anything in return for the friendly gesture. Did he have another card to play? If so, he wouldn't set it down until Adler showed him something.

"We are gratified, of course, that your country will agree to international scrutiny of the elections, and pleased also at your pledge to abide by the results, but that does not change the fact that we are talking about sovereign national territory with a population which has *already* freely chosen political association with the United States. Unfortunately, our ability to accept that pledge at face value is degraded by the situation which prompts it."

The Ambassador raised his hands, distressed at the diplomatic version of being called a liar. "How could we make it more clear?"

"By evacuating the islands now, of course," Adler responded. But he'd already made a concession of sorts. By saying that America was not entirely displeased by Japan's promise of elections, he'd given the Ambassador something back. Not much, certainly not as much as he'd wanted — acceptance of the idea of elections to determine the fate of the islands — but something. Mutual positions were restated one more time each before the morning recess allowed a chance for everyone to stretch.

The terrace was cold and windy, and as before, Adler and the Ambassador withdrew to opposite sides of the top-floor deck which in summer was an outdoor dining area, while their staff members mingled to explore options with which the respective chief negotiators could not appear to be directly involved.

"Not much of a concession," Nagumo observed, sipping his tea.

"You're lucky to get that much, but then, we know that not everyone in your government supports the action you've taken."

"Yes," Seiji replied. "I told you that."

Chris Cook fought the urge to look around for eavesdroppers. It would have been far too theatrical. Instead he sipped at his cup, looking southwest towards the Kennedy Center. "There have been informal contacts."

"With whom?"

"Koga," Cook said quietly. If Adler couldn't play the game properly, then at least he could.

"Ah. Yes, that is the logical person to speak with."

"Seiji, if we play this right, we can both come out of this heroes." Which would be the ideal solution for everyone, wouldn't it?

"What sort of contacts?" Nagumo asked.

"All I know is that it's very irregular. Now, I need to ask you, is Koga leading the opposition you're reporting to?"

"He is one of them, of course," Nagumo replied. It really was the perfect bit of information. The Americans were conceding very little, and now the reason was clear: they hoped that Goto's fragile parliamentary coalition would collapse in the combination of time and uncertainty. And all he had to do was to break the Americans' spirits and thus win his country's position . . . yes, that was elegant. And Chris's prediction on the heroic end-game would be half-right, wouldn't it?

"Are there others?" Cook asked. The reply was predictable and automatic.

"Of course there are, but I don't dare to reveal their names to you." Nagumo was thinking the scenario through now. If the Americans were banking on the political subversion of his country, then it had

894

to mean that their military options were weak. What splendid news that was.

The first KC-10 tanker staged out of Elmendorf, linking up with the C-5 just east of Nome. It required a few minutes to find air smooth enough for the evolution, and even then it was tricky performing what had to be the most unnatural act known to man, a pair of multi-hundred-ton aircraft linking in midair like mayflies. It was all the more dangerous in that the C-5 pilot couldn't actually see much more than the nose of the tanker and had to fly in close formation for twenty-five minutes. Worst of all, the tail-mounted engine of the three-engine KC-10 threw its jet exhaust directly on the T-shaped tail of the Galaxy, creating a strong and continuous buffet that required constant control corrections. That, the pilot thought, sweating inside his flight suit, is why they pay us so much. Finally the tanks were topped off and the planes broke free, the Galaxy taking a shallow dive while the tanker turned right. Aboard the transport, stomachs settled back down as the flight path took them west across the Bering Strait. Another tanker would soon lift off from Shemya and would also enter Russian air space. Unknown to them, another American aircraft had already done so, leading the secret procession to a place marked on American air-navigation charts as Verino, a town on the Trans-Siberian Railroad that dated back to the turn of the century.

The new tailshaft was finally in place after what seemed to the skipper the longest and most tedious mechanical repair job he'd ever experienced. Inside the ship's hull, bearings were reseated and seals reinstalled throughout the shaft alley. A hundred men and women were working on that detail. The engineering crew had been working on twenty-hour days, scarcely longer than the shifts that had been demanded and gotten from the civilian yard workers who manned the heavy equipment around the enormous concrete box. The last task would soon be under way. Already the immense traveling gantry started to move a shiny new screw back toward the far end of the shaft. Thirty feet across and precisely balanced, in another two hours it would be fully attached to what would soon be the world's most expensive twin-screw ship.

The CNN report coincided with the local dawn. The shot, Ryan saw, was from across the harbor, with the female reporter holding up her microphone, and a "Live" caption in the lower-right corner of the screen. There was nothing new to report in Pearl Harbor, she said.

"As you can see behind me, USS *Enterprise* and *John Stennis* remain in dry dock. Two of the most expensive warships ever made now depend on an army of workers to make them whole again, an effort that will require . . ."

"Months," Ryan said, completing the statement. "Keep telling them that."

The other network news shows would soon give out the same information, but it was CNN that he was depending on. The source of record for the whole world.

Tennessee was just diving, having passed the sea buoy a few minutes earlier. Two ASW helicopters had followed her out, and a Spruance-class destroyer was also in view, conducting hurried workups and requesting by blinker light that the submarine pass her close aboard for a quick tracking exercise.

Five U.S. Army personnel had come aboard just before sailing. They were assigned space according to rank. The officer, a first lieutenant, got a berth that would have belonged to a missile officer, had the boomer carried any of those. The senior NCO, being an E-7, was titularly a chief petty officer and was given a space in the goat locker. The rest were berthed with the enlisted crewmen. The first order of business was to give them all new shoes with rubber soles along with a briefing on the importance of being quiet.

"Why? What's the big deal?" the senior NCO asked, looking at his bunk in the chiefs' spaces and wondering if a coffin would be any more comfortable if he lived long enough for one.

Ba-Wah!

"That's why," a chief electrician's mate replied. He didn't quite shiver, but added, "I never have gotten used to that sound."

"Jesus! What the hell was that?"

"That's an SQS-53 sonar on a tin can. And if you hear it that loud, it means that they know we're here. The Japs have 'em, too, Sarge."

"Just ignore it," the sonar chief said, forward at his duty station. He stood behind a new sonarman, looking at the display. Sure enough, the new software upgrade made Prairie/Masker a lot easier to pick up, especially if you knew there was a blue sky overhead and no reason to suspect a rainstorm pelting the surface.

"He's got us cold, Chief."

"Only 'cause the Cap'n said it was okay for him to track us for a little while. An' we ain't giving out any more freebies."

Verino was just one more former MiG base in an area with scores of them. Exactly whom the Russians had been worried about was up for grabs. From this place they could have struck at Japan or China, or defended against attacks from either place, depending on who was paranoid and who was pissed at any particular political moment, the pilot thought. He'd never been anywhere close to here before, and even with the changes in relations between the two countries hadn't expected to do much more than maybe make a friendly visit to European Russia, as the U.S. Air Force did periodically. Now there was a Sukhoi-27 interceptor a thousand yards to his two o'clock, with real missiles hanging on the airframe, and probably a whimsical thought or two in the mind of the driver. *My, what a huge target.* The two disparate aircraft had linked up an hour before because there hadn't been time to get a Russian-speaking officer on the mission, and they didn't want to risk English chatter on the air-control frequency. So the transport followed the fighter rather like a sheepdog obediently trailing a terrier.

"Runway in view," the copilot said tiredly. There was the usual low-altitude buffet, increased as the flaps and gear went down, spoiling the airflow. For all that the landing was routine, until just before touchdown the pilot noticed a pair of C–17s on the ramp. So he wasn't the first American aircraft to visit this place. Maybe the two other crews could tell him where to go for some crew-rest.

The JAL 747 lifted off with all its seats full, heading west into the prevailing winds over the Pacific and leaving Canada behind. Captain Sato wasn't quite sure how to feel about everything. He was pleased, as always, to bring so many of his countrymen back home, but he also felt that in a way they were running away from America, and he wasn't so sure he liked that. His son had gotten word to him of the B–1 kills, and if his country could cripple two American aircraft carriers, destroy two of their supposedly invincible submarines, and then also take out one or two of their vaunted strategic bombers, well, then, what did they have to fear from these people? It was just a matter of waiting them out now, he thought. To his right he saw the shape of another 747, this one in the livery of Northwest/KLM, inbound from Japan, doubtless full of American businessmen who *were* running away. It wasn't that they had anything to fear. Perhaps it was shame, he thought. The idea pleased him, and Sato smiled. The rest of the routing was easy. Four thousand six hundred nautical miles, a flight time of nine and a half hours if he'd read the weather predictions correctly, and his load of three hundred sixty-six passengers would be home to a reborn country, guarded by his son and his brother. They'd come back to North America in due course, standing a little straighter and looking a little prouder, as would befit people representing his nation, Sato told himself. He regretted that he was no longer part of the military that would cause that renewed pride of place, but he'd made his mistake too long ago to correct it now. So he'd do his small part in the great change in history's shape, driving his bus as skillfully as he could.

The word got to Yamata early in the morning of the day he'd planned to return to Saipan to begin his campaign for the island's governorship. He and his colleagues had gotten the word out through the government agencies. Everything that went to Goto and the Foreign Minister now came directly to them, too. It wasn't all that hard. The country was changing, and it was time for the people who exercised the real power to be treated in accordance with their true worth. In due course it would be clearer to the common people, and by that time they would recognize who really mattered in their country, as the bureaucrats were even now acknowledging somewhat belatedly.

Koga, you traitor, the industrialist thought. It wasn't entirely unexpected. The former Prime Minister had such foolish ideas about the purity of the governmental process, and how you had to seek the approval of common working people, how typical of his outlook that he would feel some foolish nostalgia for something that had never really existed in the first place. *Of course* political figures needed guidance and support from people such as himself. *Of course* it was normal for them to display proper, and dignified, obeisance to their masters. What did they do, really, but work to preserve the prosperity that others, like Yamata and his peers, had worked so hard to achieve for their country? If Japan had depended on her government to provide for the ordinary people, then where would the country have been? But all people like Koga had were ideals that went nowhere. The common people — what did *they* know? What did they *do?* They *knew* and *did* what their betters told them, and in doing that, in acknowledging their state in life and working in their assigned tasks, they had brought a better life to themselves and their country. Wasn't that simple enough?

It wasn't as though it were the classical period, when the country had been run by a hereditary nobility. That system of rule had sufficed for two millennia, but was not suited to the industrial age. Noble bloodlines ran thin with accumulated arrogance. No, his group of peers consisted of men who had earned their place and their power, first by serving others in lowly positions, then by industry and intelligence — and luck, he admitted to himself — risen to exercise power won on merit. It was they who had made Japan into what she was. They who had led a small island nation from ashes and ruin to industrial preeminence. They, who had humbled one of the world's "great" powers, would soon humble another, and in the process raise their country to the top of the world order, achieving everything that the military boneheads like Tojo had failed to do.

Clearly Koga had no proper function except to get out of the way, or to acquiesce, as Goto had learned to do. But he did neither. And now he was plotting to deny his country the historic opportunity to achieve true greatness. Why? Because it didn't fit his foolish aesthetic of right and wrong — or because it was dangerous, as though true achievement ever came without some danger.

Well, he could not allow that to happen, Yamata told himself, reaching for his phone to call Kaneda. Even Goto might shrink from this. Better to handle this one in-house. He might as well get used to the exercise of personal power.

At the Northrop plant the aircraft had been nick-named the armadillo. Though its airframe was so smooth that nature might have given its shape to a wandering seabird, the B-2A was not everything it appeared to be. The slate-gray composites that made up its visible surface were only part of the stealth technology built into the aircraft. The inside metal structure was angular and segmented like the eye of an insect, the better to reflect radar energy in a direction away from that of the transmitter it hoped to defeat. The graceful exterior shell was designed mainly to reduce drag, and thus increase range and fuel efficiency. And it all worked.

At Whiteman Air Force Base in Missouri, the 509th Bomb Group had led a quiet existence for years, going off and doing its training missions with little fanfare. The bombers originally designed for penetrating Soviet air defenses and tracking down mobile intercontinental missiles for selective destruction — never a realistic tasking, as its crewmen knew — *did* have the ability to pass invisibly through almost any defense. Or so people had thought until recently.

"It's big, and it's powerful, and it snuffed a B-1," an officer told the Group operations officer. "We finally figured it out. It's a phased array. It's frequency-agile, and it can operate in a fire-control mode. The one that limped back to Shemya" — it was still there, decorating the island's single runway while technicians worked to repair it enough to return to the Alaskan mainland — "the missile came in from one direction, but the radar pulses came from another."

"Cute," observed Colonel Mike Zacharias. It was instantly clear: the Japanese had taken a Russian idea one technological step further. Whereas the Soviets had designed fighter aircraft that were effectively controlled from ground stations, Japan had developed a technique by which the fighters would remain totally covert even when launching their missiles. That was a problem even for the B-2, whose stealthing was designed to defeat longwave search radars and high-frequency airborne tracking- and targeting radars. Stealth was technology; it was not quite magic. An airborne radar of such great power and frequency-agility just might get enough of a return off the -2 to make the proposed mission suicidal. Sleek and agile as it was, the B-2 was a bomber, not a fighter, and a huge target for any modern fighter aircraft. "So what's the good news?" Zacharias asked.

"We're going to play some more games with them and try to get a better feel for their capabilities."

"My dad used to do that with SAMs. He ended up getting a lengthy stay in North Vietnam."

"Well, they're working on a Plan B, too," the intelligence officer offered.

"Oh, that's nice," Chavez said.

"Aren't you the one who doesn't like being a spook?" Clark asked, closing his laptop after erasing the mission orders. "I thought you wanted back in to the paramilitary business."

"Me and my big mouth." Ding moved his backside on the park bench.

"Excuse me," a third voice said. Both CIA officers looked up to see a uniformed police officer, a pistol sitting in its holster on his Sam Browne belt.

"Hello," John said with a smile. "A pleasant morning, isn't it?"

"Yes, it is," the policeman replied. "Is Tokyo very different from America?"

"It is also very different from Moscow this time of year."

"Moscow?"

Clark reached into his coat and pulled out his passport. "We are Russian journalists."

The cop examined the booklet and handed it back. "Much colder in Moscow this time of year?"

"Much," Clark confirmed with a nod. The officer moved off, having handled his curiosity attack for the day.

"Not so sure, Ivan Sergeyevich," Ding observed when he'd gone. "It can get pretty cold here, too."

"I suppose you can always get another job."

"And miss all this fun?" Both men rose and walked toward their parked car. There was a map in the glove box.

The Russian Air Force personnel at Verino had a natural curiosity of their own, but the Americans weren't helping matters. There were now over a hundred American personnel on their base, barracked in the best accommodations. The three helicopters and two vehicular trailers had been rolled into hangars originally built for MiG-25 fighters. The transport aircraft were too large for that, but had been rolled inside as much as their dimensions allowed, with the tails sticking out in the open, but they could as easily have been mistaken for IL-86s, which occasionally stopped off here. The Russian ground crewmen established a secure perimeter, which denied contact of any sort between the two sets of air-force personnel, a disappointment for the Russians.

The two trailers inside the easternmost hangar were electronically linked with a thick black coaxial cable. Another cable ran outside to a portable satellite link that was similarly guarded.

"Okay, let's rotate it," a sergeant said. A Russian officer was watching — protocol demanded that the Americans let someone in; this one was surely an intelligence officer — as the birdcage image on the computer screen turned about as though on a phonograph. Next the image moved through a vertical axis, as if it were flying over the stick image. "That's got it," the sergeant observed, closing the window on the computer screen and punching UPLOAD to transmit it to the three idle helicopters.

"What did you just do? May I ask?" the Russian inquired.

"Sir, we just taught the computers what to look for." The answer made no sense to the Russian, true though it was.

The activity in the second van was easier to understand. High-quality photos of several tall buildings were scanned and digitalized, their locations programmed in to a tolerance of only a few meters, then compared with other photos taken from a very high angle that had to denote satellite cameras. The officer leaned in close to get a better feel for the sharpness of the imagery, somewhat to the discomfort of the senior American officer — who, however, was under orders to take no action that might offend the Russians in any way.

"It looks like an apartment building, yes?" the Russian asked in genuine curiosity.

"Yes, it does," the American officer replied, his skin crawling despite the hospitality they had all experienced here. Orders or not, it was a major federal felony to show this kind of thing to anyone who lacked the proper clearances, even an American.

"Who lives there?"

"I don't know." *Why can't this guy just go away?*

By evening the rest of the Americans were up and moving. Incomprehensibly with shaggy hair, not like soldiers at all, they started jogging around the perimeter of the main runway. A few Russians joined in, and a race of sorts started, with both groups running in formation. What started off friendly soon became grim. It was soon clear that the Americans were elite troops unaccustomed to being bested in anything, against which the Russians had pride of place and better acclimatization. *Spetznaz,* the Russians were soon gasping to one another, and because it was a dull base with a tough-minded commander, they were in good enough shape that after ten kilometers they managed to hold their own. Afterward, both groups mingled long enough to realize that language barriers prevented much in the way of conversation, though the tension in the visitors was clear enough without words.

"Weird-looking things," Chavez said.

"Just lucky for us that they picked this place." It was security again, John thought, just like the fighters and bombers at Pearl Harbor had all been bunched together to protect against sabotage or some such nonsense because of a bad intelligence estimate. Another factor might have been the convenience of maintenance at a single location, but they hadn't been assigned to this base originally, and so the hangars weren't large enough. As a result, six E-767s were sitting right there in the open, two miles away and easily distinguished by their odd shape. Better yet, the country was just too crowded for the base to be very isolated. The same factors that placed cities in the flat spots also placed airfields there, but the cities had grown up first. There were light-industrial buildings all around, and the mainly rectangular air base

905

had highways down every side. The next obvious move was to check the trees for wind direction. Northwesterly wind. Landing aircraft would come in from the southeast. Knowing that, they had to find a perch.

Everything was being used now. Low-orbit electronic-intelligence satellites were also gathering signals, fixing the patrol locations of the AEW aircraft, not as well as the ELINT aircraft could, but far more safely. The next step would be to enlist submarines in the job, but that could take time, someone had told them. Not all that many submarines to go around, and those that were left had a job to do. Hardly a revelation. The electronic order of battle was firming up, and though not everything the ELINT techs discovered was good news, at least they did have the data from which the operations people might formulate some sort of plan or other. For the moment, the locations of the racetrack patterns used by three orbiting E-767s were firmly plotted. They seemed to stay fairly stationary from day to day. The minor daily variations might have had as much to do with local winds as anything else, which made it necessary to downlink information to their ground-control centers. And that was good news, too.

The medium-price hotel was more than they could ordinarily afford, but for all that it lay right under the approach to runway three-two-left of the nearby air base. Perhaps the noise was just so normal to the country that people filtered it out, Chavez thought, remembering the incessant street racket from their hostelry in Tokyo. The back was better, the clerk assured them, but the best he could offer was a corner room. The really offensive noise was at the front of the hotel: the runway terminated only half a kilometer from the front door. It was the takeoffs that really

906

shook things up. Landings were far easier to sleep through.

"I'm not sure I like this," Ding observed when he got to the room.

"Who said we were supposed to?" John moved a chair to the window and took the first watch.

"It's like murder, John."

"Yeah, I suppose it is." The hell of it was, Ding was right, but somebody else had said it wasn't and that's what counted. Sort of.

"No other options?" President Durling asked.

"No, sir, none that I see." It was a first for Ryan. He'd managed to stop a war, after a fashion. He'd terminated a "black" operation that would probably have caused great political harm to his country. Now he was about to initiate one — well, not exactly, he told himself. Somebody else had started this war, but just though it might be, he didn't exactly relish what he was about to do. "They're not going to back off."

"We never saw it coming," Durling said quietly, knowing that it was too late for such thoughts.

"And maybe that's my fault," Ryan replied, feeling that it was his duty to take the blame. After all, national security was his bailiwick. People would die because of what he'd done wrong, and die from whatever things he might do right. For all the power exercised from this room, there really were no choices, were there?

"Will it all work?"

"Sir, that is something we'll just have to see."

It turned out to be easier than expected. Three of the ungainly twin-engine aircraft taxied in a line to the end of the runway, where each took its turn to face into the northwest winds, stopping, advancing its engines to full power, backing off to see if the engines would flame out, and when they didn't, going again to full power, but this time slipping the brakes and accelerating into its takeoff roll. Clark checked his watch and unfolded a road map of Honshu.

All that was required was a phone call. The Boeing Company's Commercial Airplane Group issued an Emergency Airworthiness Directive, called an E-AD, concerning the auto-landing system on its 767 commercial aircraft. A fault of unknown origin had affected the final approach of a TWA airliner on final into St. Louis, and until determination of the nature of the fault, operators were strongly advised to deactivate that feature of the flight-control systems until further notice. The directive went out by electronic mail, telex, and registered mail to all operators of the 767.

39

Eyes First

It came as no particular surprise that the Japanese consulates in Honolulu, San Francisco, New York, and Seattle were closed. FBI agents showed up at all of them simultaneously and explained that they had to be vacated forthwith. After perfunctory protests, which received polite but impassive attention, the diplomatic personnel locked up their buildings and walked off under guard — mainly to protect them against ragtag protesters, in every case watched by local police — into buses that would conduct them to the nearest airport for a flight to Vancouver, B.C. In the case of Honolulu, the bus went close enough to the Pearl Harbor naval base that officials got a last look at the two carriers in their graving docks, and photos were shot from the bus to record the fact. It never occurred to the consulate official who shot the pictures that the FBI personnel at the front of the bus did not interfere with his action. After all, the American media were advertising everything, as they'd been expected to do. The operation, they saw, was handled professionally in every detail. Their bags were X-rayed for weapons and explosives — there was none of that nonsense, of course — but not opened, since these were diplomatic personnel with treaty-guaranteed immunity. America had chartered an airliner for them, a United 737, which lifted off and, again, managed to fly directly over the naval base, allowing the official to shoot another five photos through the double windows from an altitude of five thousand feet. He congratulated himself on his foresight in keeping his camera handy. Then he slept through most of the five-hour flight to Vancouver.

"One and four are good as new, Skipper," the ChEng assured *Johnnie Reb*'s CO. "We'll give you thirty, maybe thirty-two knots, whenever you ask."

Two and three, the inboard shafts, were closed off, the hull openings into the skegs welded shut, and with them the top fifteen or so knots of *John Stennis*'s real top speed, but the removal of the propellers also cut down on drag, allowing a quite respectable max speed that would have to do. The most ticklish procedure had been resetting the number-four drivetrain, which had to be more finely balanced than the wheel of a racing car, lest it destroy itself at max revolutions. The testing had been accomplished the same way, by turning the screw and checking every bearing along the lengthy shaft. Now it was done, and the dry dock could be flooded tonight. The commanding officer walked tiredly up the concrete steps to the top of the immense man-made canyon, and from there the brow. It was quite a climb all the way to his at-sea cabin aft of the bridge, from which he made a telephone call.

It was just about time. Clark looked southeast out the back window of their room. The cold air was clear and dry, with a few light clouds in the distance, still white in the direct sunlight while the ground was beginning to darken with twilight.

"Ready?" he asked.

"You say so, man." Ding's large metal camera case was open on the floor. The contents had cleared customs weeks before, and appeared unremarkable, typical of what a news photographer might take with him, if a somewhat lighter load than most carried. The foam-filled interior included cutout spaces for three camera bodies and a variety of lenses, plus other cavities for photographic lights that also appeared entirely ordinary but were not. The only weapons with them did not appear to be weapons at all, a fact that had also worked well for them in East Africa. Chavez lifted one of them, checking the power meter on the battery pack and deciding not to plug it into the wall. He flipped the switch to standby and heard the thin electronic whistle of the charging capacitors.

"There it is," John said quietly when he saw the incoming lights, not relishing the job any more than his partner. But you weren't supposed to, were you?

The inbound E-767 had turned on its inboard recognition lights while descending through ten thousand feet, and now lowered its landing gear. The outboard landing lights came on next. Five miles out and two thousand feet over the industrial area surrounding the air base, the pilot saw the runway lights and told himself not to relax after the long, boring patrol flight.

"Flaps twenty-five," he said.

"Flaps twenty-five," the copilot acknowledged, reaching for the control lever that deployed the landing flaps off the rear of the wing surfaces and the slats at the front, which gave the wing needed extra lift and control at the diminishing speed.

"Kami-Three on final, runway in sight," the pilot said, this time over the radio to the approach-control officer who had guided him unnecessarily to this point. The tower responded properly and the pilot tightened his grip slightly on the controls, more thinking the slight control movements than actually moving, adjusting to the low-altitude winds and scanning for possible unnoticed aircraft in the restricted airspace. Most aircraft accidents, he knew, occurred on landing, and that was why the flight crew had to be especially alert at this time.

"I got it," Chavez said, no emotion at all in his voice as he told his conscience to be still. His country was at war. The people in the airplane wore uniforms, were fair game because of it, and that was that. It was just too damned easy, though he remembered the first time he had killed, which, in retrospect, had also been so easy as to constitute murder. He'd actually felt elation at the time, Chavez remembered with passing shame.

"I want a hot tub and a massage," the copilot said, allowing himself a personal thought as his eyes checked around, two miles out. "All clear to the right. Runway is clear."

The pilot nodded and reached for the throttles with his right hand, easing them back and allowing air friction to slow the aircraft further for its programmed touchdown speed of 145 knots, high because of the extra fuel reserves the Kami aircraft carried. They always flew heavy.

"Two kilometers, everything is normal," the copilot said.

"Now," Chavez whispered. The barrel-like extension of the light was on his shoulder, aimed almost like a rifle, or more properly like an antitank rocket launcher, at the nose of the approaching aircraft. Then his finger came down on the button.

The "magic" they had used in Africa was conceptually nothing more than a souped-up flashlight, but this one had a xenon-arc bulb and put out three million candlepower. The most expensive part of the assembly was the reflector, a finely machined piece of steel alloy that confined the beam to a diameter of about forty feet at a distance of one mile. One could easily read a newspaper by the illumination provided at that distance, but to look directly into the light, even at that distance, was quite blinding. Designed and issued as a nonlethal weapon, the bulb was shielded for ultraviolet light, which could do permanent damage to the human retina. The thought passed through Ding's mind when he triggered the light. *Nonlethal. Sure.*

The intensity of the blue-white light seared the pilot's eyes. It was like looking directly at the sun, but worse, and the pain made his hands come off the controls to his face, and he screamed into the intercom phones. The copilot had been looking off-axis to the flash, but the human eye is drawn to light, especially in darkness, and his mind didn't have time to warn him off from the entirely normal reaction. Both airmen were blinded and in pain, with their aircraft eight hundred feet off the ground and a mile from the landing threshold. Both were highly trained men, and highly skilled as well. His eyes still shut from the pain, the pilot's hands reached down to find the yoke and tried to steady it. The copilot did exactly the same thing, but their control movements were not quite the same, and in an instant they were fighting each other rather than the aircraft. They were both also entirely without visual references, and the viciously instant disorientation caused vertigo in both men that was necessarily different. One airman thought their aircraft was veering in one direction, and the other tried to yank the controls to correct a different movement, and with only eight hundred feet of air under them, there wasn't time to decide who was right and the fighting on the yoke only meant that when the stronger of the two got control, his efforts doomed them all. The E-767 rolled ninety degrees to the right, veering north toward empty manufacturing buildings, falling rapidly as it did so. The tower controllers shouted into the radio, but the aviators didn't even hear the warnings. The pilot's last action was to reach for the go-around button on the throttle in a despairing attempt to get his bird safely back in the sky. His hand had hardly found it when his senses told him, a second early, that his life was over. His last thought was that a nuclear bomb had gone off over his country again.

"Jesucristo," Chavez whispered. Just a second, not even that. The nose of the aircraft flared in the dusky sky as though from some sort of explosion, and then the thing had just veered off to the north like a dying bird. He forced himself to look away from the impact area. He just didn't want to see or know where it hit. Not that it mattered. The towering fireball lit up the area as though from a lightning strike. It hit Ding like a punch in the stomach to realize what he'd done, and there came the sudden urge to vomit.

Kami-Five saw it, ten miles out, the sickening flare of yellow on the ground short and right of the airfield that could only mean one thing. Aviators are disciplined people. For the pilot and copilot of the next E-767 there also came a sudden emptiness in the stomach, a tightening of muscles. They wondered which of their squadron mates had just smeared themselves into the ground, which families would receive unwanted visitors, which faces they would no longer see, which voices they would no longer hear, and punished themselves for not paying closer attention to the radio, as though it would have mattered. Instinctively both men checked their cockpit for irregularities. Engines okay. Electronics okay. Hydraulics okay. Whatever had happened to the other one, their aircraft was fine.

"Tower, Five, what happened, over?"

"Five, Tower, Three just went in. We do not know why. Runway is clear."

"Five, roger, continuing approach, runway in sight." He took his hand off the radio button before he could say something else. The two aviators traded a look. Kami-Three. Good friends. Gone. Enemy action would have been easier to accept than the ignominy of something as pedestrian as a landing crash, whatever the cause. But for now their heads turned back to the flight path. They had a mission to finish, and twenty-five fellow crewmen aft to deliver safely home despite their sorrow.

"Want me to take it?" John asked.

"My job, man." Ding checked the capacitor charge again, then wiped his face. He clenched his fists to stop the slight trembling he noticed, both ashamed and relieved that he had it. The widely spaced landing lights told him that this was another target, and he was in the service of his country, as they were in the service of theirs, and that was that. But better to do it with a proper weapon, he thought. Perhaps, his mind wandered, the guys who preferred swords had thought the same thing when faced with the advent of muskets. Chavez shook his head one last time to clear it, and aimed his light through the open window, working his way back from the opening as he lined up on the approaching aircraft. There was a shroud on the front to prevent people outside the room from seeing the flash, but he didn't want to take any more chances than he had to . . .

. . . right about . . .

. . . now . . .

He punched the button again, and again the silvery aluminum skin around the aircraft's cockpit flared brightly, for just a second or so. Off to the left he could hear the warbling shriek of fire engines, doubtless heading to the site of the first crash. *Not like the fire sirens at home,* he thought irrelevantly. The E-767 didn't do anything at first, and he wondered for a second if he'd done it right. Then the angle of the nose light changed downward, but the airplane didn't turn at all. It just increased its rate of descent. Maybe it would hit them in the hotel room, Chavez thought. It was too late to run away, and maybe God would punish him for killing fifty people. He shook his head and dismantled the light, waiting, finding comfort in concentrating on a mechanical task.

Clark saw it, too, and also knew that there was no purpose in darting from the room. The airplane should be flaring now . . . perhaps the pilot thought so, too. The nose came up, and the Boeing product roared perhaps thirty feet over the roof of the building. John moved to the side windows and saw the wingtip pass over, rotating as it did so. The aircraft started to climb, or attempt to, probably for a go-around, but without enough power, and it stalled halfway down the runway, perhaps five hundred feet in the air, falling off on the port wing and spiraling in for yet another fireball. Neither he nor Ding thanked God for a deliverance that they might not have deserved in any case.

"Pack the light and get your camera," Clark ordered.

"Why?"

"We're reporters, remember?" he said, this time in Russian.

Ding's hands were shaking enough that he had trouble disassembling the light, but John didn't move to help him. Everyone needed time to deal with feelings like this. They hadn't killed bad men deserving of death, after all. They had erased the lives of people not unlike themselves, doomed by their oaths of service to someone who didn't merit their loyalty. Chavez finally got a camera out, selected a hundred-millimeter lens for the Nikon F5 body, and followed

916

his boss out the door. The hotel's small lobby was already filled with people, almost all of them Japanese. "Klerk" and "Chekov" walked right through them, running across the highway to the airport's perimeter fence, where the latter started taking pictures. Things were sufficiently confused that it was ten minutes before a policeman came over.

"What are you doing!" Not so much a question as an accusation.

"We are reporters," "Klerk" replied, handing over his credentials.

"Stop what you are doing!" the cop ordered next.

"Have we broken a law? We were in the hotel across the road when this happened." Ivan Sergeyevich turned, looking down at the policeman. He paused. "Oh! Have the Americans attacked you? Do you want our film?"

"Yes!" the officer said with a sudden realization. He held out his hand, gratified at their instant co-operative response to his official authority.

"Yevgeniy, give the man your film right now."

"Chekov" rewound the roll and ejected it, handing it over.

"Please return to the hotel. We will come for you if we need you."

I bet you will. "Room four-sixteen," Clark told him. "This is a terrible thing. Did anyone survive?"

"I don't know. Please go now," the policeman said, waving them across the road.

"God have mercy on them," Chavez said in English, meaning it.

Two hours later a KH-11 overflew the area, its infrared cameras scanning the entire Tokyo area, among others. The photorecon experts at the National Reconnaissance Office took immediate note of the two smoldering fires and the aircraft parts that littered the area around them. Two E-767s had bitten the dust, they saw with no small degree of satisfaction. They were mainly Air Force personnel and, distant from the human carnage of the scene, all they saw was two dead targets. The imagery was real-timed to several destinations. In the J-3 area of the Pentagon, it was decided that Operation ZORRO's first act had gone about as they had planned. They would have said as *hoped*, but that might have spoiled the luck. Well, they thought, CIA wasn't quite entirely useless.

It was dark at Pearl Harbor. Flooding the dry dock had required ten hours, which had rushed the time up to and a little beyond what was really safe, but war had different rules on safety. With the gate out of the way, and with the help of two large harbor tugs, *John Stennis* drove out of the dock and, turning, left *Enterprise* behind. The harbor pilot nervously got the ship out in record time, then to be ferried back to shore by helicopter, and before midnight, *Johnnie Reb* was in deep water and away from normal shipping channels, heading west.

The accident-investigation team showed up almost at once from their headquarters in Tokyo. A mixed group consisting of military and civilian personnel, it was the latter element that owned the greater expertise because this was really a civil aircraft modified for military use. The "black box" (actually painted Day-Glo orange) flight recorder from Kami-Five was recovered within a few lucky minutes, though the one from Kami-Three proved harder to find. It was taken back to the Tokyo lab for analysis. The problem for the Japanese military was rather more difficult. Two of their precious ten E-767s were now gone, and another was in its service hangar for overhaul and upgrade of its radar systems. That left seven, and keeping three on constant duty would be impossible. It was simple arithmetic. Each aircraft had to be serviced, and the crews had to rest. Even with nine operational aircraft, keeping three up all the time, with three more down and the other three in standby, was murderously destructive to the men and equipment. There was also the question of aircraft safety. A member of the investigation team discovered the Airworthiness Directive on the 767 and determined that it applied to the model the Japanese had converted to AEW use. Immediately, the auto-landing systems were deactivated, and the natural first conclusion from the civilian investigators was that the flight crews, perhaps weary from their long patrol flights, had engaged it for their approaches. The senior uniformed officer was tempted to accept it, except for one thing: few airmen liked automatic-landing systems, and military airmen were the least likely of all to turn their aircraft over to something which operated on microchips and software to safeguard their lives. And yet the body of -Three's pilot had been found with his hand on the throttle controls. It made little sense, but the evidence pointed that way. A software conflict, perhaps, somewhere in system — a foolish and enraging reason for the loss of two priceless aircraft, even though it was not without precedent in the age of computer-controlled flight. For the moment, the reality of the situation was that they could only maintain a two-aircraft constant patrol, albeit with a third always ready to lift off at an instant's notice.

Overflying ELINT satellites noted the continued patrol of three E-767s for the moment, and nervous technicians at Air Force Intelligence and the National Security Agency wondered if the Japanese Air Force would try to defy the rules of aircraft operation. They checked their clocks and realized that another six hours would tell the tale, while satellite passes continued to record and plot the electronic emissions.

Jackson now concerned himself with other satellite information. There were forty-eight fighters believed based on Saipan, and another sixty-four at Guam's former Andersen Air Force Base, whose two wide runways and huge underground fuel-storage tanks had accommodated the arriving aircraft very comfortably indeed. The two islands were about one hundred twenty miles apart. He also had to consider the dispersal facilities that SAC had constructed in the islands during the Cold War. The closed Northwest Guam airfield had two parallel runways, both usable, and there was Agana International in the middle of the island. There was also a commercial airfield on Rota, another abandoned base on Tinian, and Kobler on Saipan in addition to the operating airport. Strangely, the Japanese had ignored all of the secondary facilities except for Kobler Field. In fact, satellite information showed that Tinian was not occupied at all — at least the overhead photos showed no heavy military vehicles. There had to be some light forces there, he reasoned, probably supported by helicopter from Saipan — the islands were separated by only a narrow channel.

One hundred twelve fighters was Admiral Jackson's main consideration. There would be support from E-2 AEW aircraft, plus the usual helicopters that armies took wherever they went. F-15s and F-3s, supported further by SAMs and triple-A. It was a big job for one carrier, even with Bud Sanchez's idea for making the carrier more formidable. The key to it, however, wasn't fighting the enemy's arms. It was to attack his mind, a constant fact of war that people alternately perceived and forgot over the centuries. He hoped he was getting it right. Even then, something else came first.

★ ★ ★

The police never came back, somewhat to Clark's surprise. Perhaps they'd found the photos useful, but more probably not. In any case, they didn't hang around to find out. Back in their rental car, they took a last look at the charred spot beyond the end of the runway just as the first of three AEW aircraft landed at the base, quite normally to everyone's relief. An hour earlier, he'd noted, two rather than the regular three E-767s had taken off, indicating, he hoped, that their grisly mission had borne fruit of a sort. That fact had already been confirmed by satellite, giving the green light for yet another mission about which neither CIA officer knew anything.

The hard part still was believing it all. The English-language paper they'd bought in the hotel lobby at breakfast had news on its front page not terribly different than they'd read on their first day in Japan. There were two stories from the Marianas and two items from Washington, but the rest of the front page was mainly economic news, along with an editorial about how the restoration of normal relations with America was to be desired, even at the price of reasonable concessions at the negotiations table. Perhaps the reality of the situation was just too bizarre for people to accept, though a large part of it was the close control of the news. There was still no word, for example, of the nuclear missiles squirreled away somewhere. Somebody was being either very clever or very foolish — or possibly both, depending on how things turned out. John and Ding both came back to the proposition that none of this made the least bit of sense, but that observation would be of little consolation for the families of the people killed on both sides. Even in the madly passionate war over the Falkland Islands, there had been inflammatory rhetoric to excite the masses, but in this case it was as though Clausewitz had been rewritten to say that war was an extension of economics rather than politics, and business, while cutthroat in its way, was still a more civilized form of activity than that engaged in on the political stage. But the truth of the madness was before him. The roads were crowded with people doing their daily routine, albeit with a few stares at the wreckage on the air base, and in the face of a world that seemed to be turning upside down, the ordinary citizen clung to what reality he knew, relegating the part he didn't understand to others, who in turn wondered why nobody else noticed.

Here he was, Clark told himself, a foreign spy, covered with an identity from yet a third country, doing things in contravention of the Geneva protocols of civilized war — *that* was an arcane concept in and of itself. He'd helped kill fifty people not twelve hours before, and yet he was driving a rental car back into the enemy capital, and his only immediate worry was to remember to drive on the left side of the road and avoid collision with all the commuters who thought anything more than a ten-foot space with the car ahead meant that you weren't keeping up with the flow.

All that changed three blocks from their hotel, when Ding spotted a car parked the wrong way with the passenger-side visor turned down. It was a sign that Kimura needed an urgent meet. The emergency nature of the signal came as something of a reassurance that it wasn't all some perverted dream. There was danger in their lives again. At least something was real.

Flight operations had commenced just after dawn. Four complete squadrons of F-14 Tomcats and four more of F/A-18 Hornets were now aboard, along with four E-3C Hawkeyes. The normal support aircraft were for the moment based on Midway, and the one-carrier task force would for the moment use Pacific

Islands as auxiliary support facilities for the cruise west. The first order of business was to practice mid-air refueling from Air Force tankers that would follow the fleet west as well. As soon as they had passed Midway, a standing combat air patrol of four aircraft was established, though without the usual Hawkeye support. The E-2C made a lot of electronic noise, and the main task of the depleted battle force was to remain stealthy, though in the case of *Johnnie Reb*, that entailed making something invisible that was the size of the side of an island.

Sanchez was down in air-operations. His task was to take what appeared to be a very even battle and make it one-sided. The idea of a fair fight was as foreign to him as to any other person in uniform. One only had to look around to see why. He *knew* the people in this working space. He did not know the airmen on the islands, and that was all he cared about. They might be human beings. They might have wives and kids and houses and cars and every other ordinary thing the men in Navy khaki had, but that didn't matter to the CAG. Sanchez would not order or condone such movie fantasies as wasting ammunition on men in parachutes — people in that condition were too hard to target in any case — but he had to kill their airplanes, and in an age of missiles that most often meant that the driver would probably not get the opportunity to eject. Fortunately, it was hard enough in the modern age to see your target as anything more than a dot that had to be circled by the head-up display of the fire-control system. It made things a lot easier, and if a parachute emerged from the wreckage, well, he didn't mind making a SAR call for a fellow aviator, once the man was incapable of harming one of his own.

"Koga has disappeared," Kimura told them, his voice urgent and his face pale.

"Arrested?" Clark asked.

"I don't know. Do we have anyone inside your organization?"

John turned very grim. "Do you know what we do to traitors?" Everyone knew. "My country depends on this man, too. We will get to work on it. Now, go."

Chavez watched him walk away before speaking. "A leak?"

"Possibly. Also possible that the guys running the show don't want any extraneous opposition leaders screwing things up for the moment." *Now I'm a political analyst,* John told himself. Well, he was also a fully accredited reporter from the Interfax News Agency. "What do you say we visit our embassy, Yevgeniy?"

Scherenko was on his way out to a meet of his own when the two people showed up at his office door. Wasn't this an unusual occurrence, he thought for a brief moment, two CIA officers entering the Russian Embassy for a business meeting with the RVS. Then he wondered what would make them do it.

"What's the matter?" he asked, and John Clark handled the answer:

"Koga's vanished." Major Scherenko sat down, waving his visitors to seats in his office. They didn't need to be told to close the door. "Is it something that might have happened all on its own," Clark asked, "or did somebody leak it?"

"I don't think PSID would have done it. Even on orders from Goto. It's too political without real evidence. The political situation here is — how well do you know it?"

"Brief us in," Clark said.

"The government is very confused. Goto has control, but he is not sharing information with many people. His coalition is still thin. Koga is very respected, too much so to be publicly arrested." *I think,* Scherenko didn't add. What might have been said with confidence two weeks earlier was a lot more speculative now.

It actually made sense to the Americans. Clark thought for a second before speaking. "You'd better shake the tree, Boris Il'ych. We both need that man."

"Did you compromise him?" the Russian asked.

"No, not at all. We told him to act as he normally would — and besides, he thinks we're Russians. I had no instructions other than to check him out, and trying to direct a guy like that is too risky. He's just as liable to turn superpatriot on us and tell us to shove it. People like that, you just let them do the right thing all by themselves." Scherenko reflected again that the file in Moscow Center on this man was correct. Clark had all the right instincts for field-intelligence work. He nodded and waited for Clark to go on. "If you have PSID under your control, we need to find out immediately if they have the man."

"And if they do?"

Clark shrugged. "Then you have to decide if you can get him out. That part of the operation is yours. I can't make that call for you. But if it's somebody else who bagged him, then maybe we can do something."

"I need to talk to Moscow."

"We figured that. Just remember, Koga's our best chance for a political solution to this mess. Next, get the word to Washington."

"It will be done," Scherenko promised. "I need to ask a question — the two aircraft that crashed last night?"

Clark and Chavez were already on the way out the door. It was the younger man who spoke without turning. "A terrible accident, wasn't it?"

925

"You're insane," Mogataru Koga said.

"I am a patriot," Raizo Yamata replied. "I will make our country truly independent. I will make Japan great again." Their eyes met from opposite ends of the table in Yamata's penthouse apartment. The executive's security people were outside the door. These words were for two men alone.

"You have cast away our most important ally and trading partner. You are bringing economic ruin to us. You've killed people. You've suborned our country's government and our military."

Yamata nodded as though acknowledging a property acquisition. "*Hai*, I have done all these things, and it was not difficult. Tell me, Koga, how hard is it to get a politician to do anything?"

"And your friends, Matsuda and the rest?"

"Everyone needs guidance from time to time." *Almost everyone*, Yamata didn't say. "At the end of this, we will have a fully integrated economy, two firm and powerful allies, and in time we will again have our trade because the rest of the world needs us." Didn't this politician see that? Didn't he understand?

"Do you understand America as poorly as that? Our current difficulties began because a single family was burned alive. They are not the same as us. They think differently. Their religion is different. They have the most violent culture in the world, yet they worship justice. They venerate making money, but their roots are found in ideals. Can't you grasp that? *They will not tolerate* what you have done!" Koga paused. "And your plan for Russia — do you really think that — "

"With China helping us?" Yamata smiled. "The two of us can handle Russia."

"And China will remain our ally?" Koga asked. "We killed twenty million Chinese in the Second World War, and their political leadership has not forgotten."

"They need us, and they know they need us. And together — "

"Yamata-san," Koga said quietly, politely, because it was his nature, "you do not understand politics as well as you understand business. It will be your downfall."

Yamata replied in kind. "And treason will be yours. I know you have contacts with the Americans."

"Not so. I have not spoken with an American citizen in weeks." An indignant reply would not have carried the power of the matter-of-fact tone.

"Well, in any case, you will be my guest here for the time being," Raizo told him. "We will see how ignorant of political matters I am. In two years I will be Prime Minister, Koga-san. In two years we will be a superpower." Yamata stood. His apartment covered the entire top floor of the forty-story building, and the Olympian view pleased him. The industrialist stood and walked toward the floor-to-ceiling windows, surveying the city which would soon be *his* capital. What a pity that Koga didn't understand how things really worked. But for the moment he had to fly back to Saipan, to begin his political ascendancy. He turned back.

"You will see. You are my guest for the moment. Behave yourself and you will be treated well. Attempt to escape, and your body will be found in pieces on some railroad tracks along with a note apologizing for your political failures."

"You will not have that satisfaction," the former Prime Minister replied coldly.

40

Foxes and Hounds

Scherenko had planned to do the meet himself, but urgent business had prevented him from doing so. It turned out to be just as well. The message, delivered via computer disk, was from his top agent-in-place, the Deputy Director of the PSID. Whatever the man's personal habits, he was a canny political observer, if somewhat verbose in his reports and evaluations. The Japanese military, he said, was not the least displeased by their immediate prospects. Frustrated by years of having been labeled as a "self-defense force" and relegated in the public's mind to getting in the way of Godzilla and other unlikely monsters (usually to their misfortune), they deemed themselves custodians of a proud warrior tradition, and now, finally, with political leadership worthy of their mettle, their command leadership relished the chance to show what they could do. Mainly products of American training and professional education, the senior officers had made their estimate of the situation and announced to everyone who would listen that they could and would win this limited contest — and, the PSID director went on, they thought the chances of conquering Siberia were excellent.

This evaluation and the report from the two CIA officers were relayed to Moscow at once. So there was dissension in the Japanese government, and at least one of its professional departments had a slight grasp on reality. It was gratifying to the Russian, but he also remembered how a German intelligence chief named Canaris had done much the same thing in 1939, and had completely failed to accomplish anything. It was an historical model that he intended to break. The trick with wars was to prevent them from growing large. Scherenko didn't hold with the theory that diplomacy could keep them from starting, but he did believe that good intelligence and decisive action could keep them from going too far — if you had the political will to take the proper action. It worried him, however, that it was Americans who had to show that will.

"It's called Operation ZORRO, Mr. President," Robby Jackson said, flipping the cover off the first chart. The Secretaries of State and Defense were there in the Situation Room, along with Ryan and Arnie van Damm. The two cabinet secretaries were ill at ease right now, but then so was the Deputy J-3. Ryan nodded for him to go on.

"The mission is to dislocate the command leadership of the other side by precisely targeting those individuals who — "

"You mean murder them?" Brett Hanson asked. He looked over at SecDef, who didn't react at all.

"Mr. Secretary, we don't want to engage their civilian population. That means we cannot attack their economy. We can't drop bridges in their cities. Their military is too decentralized in location to — "

"We can't do this," Hanson interrupted again.

"Mr. Secretary," Ryan said coolly, "can we at least hear what the plan is before we decide what we should and should not do?"

Hanson nodded gruffly, and Jackson continued his brief. "The pieces," he concluded, "are largely in place now. We've eliminated two of their air-surveillance assets — "

"When did that happen? How did we do it?"

"It happened last night," Ryan answered. "How we did it is not your concern, sir."

"Who ordered it?" This question came from President Durling.

"I did, sir. It was well covered, and the operation went off without a hitch." Durling replied with his eyes that Ryan was pushing his limits again.

"How many people did that kill?" the Secretary of State demanded.

"About fifty, and that's two hundred or so *less* than the number of our people whom they killed, Mr. Secretary."

"Look, we can talk them out of the islands if we just take the time," SecState said, and now the argument was bilateral, with all the others watching.

"That's not what Adler says."

"Chris Cook thinks so, and he's got a guy inside their delegation."

Durling watched impassively, again letting his staff people — that's how he thought of them — handle the debate. For him there were other questions. Politics would again raise its ugly head. If he failed to respond to the crisis effectively, then he was *out*. Someone else would be President then, and that someone else would be faced in the following year at the latest with a wider crisis. Even worse, if the Russian intelligence estimate were correct and if Japan and China made their move on Siberia in the coming autumn, then another, larger crisis would strike during an American election cycle, seriously impeding his country's ability to deal with it, making everything a political debate, with an economy still trying to recover from a hundred-billion-dollar trade shortfall.

"If we fail to act now, Mr. Secretary, there's no

telling how far this thing might go," Ryan was saying now.

"We can work this out diplomatically," Hanson insisted.

"And if not?" Durling asked.

"Then in due course we can consider a measured military response." SecState's confidence was not reflected in SecDef's expression.

"You have something to add?" the President asked him.

"It will be some time — years — before we can assemble the forces necessary to — "

"We don't *have* years," Ryan snapped.

"No, I don't think that we do," Durling observed. "Admiral, will it work?"

"I think it can, sir. We need a few breaks to come our way, but we got the biggest one last night."

"We don't have the necessary forces to assure success," SecDef said. "The Task Force commander just sent in his estimate and — "

"I've seen it," Jackson said, not quite able to conceal his uneasiness at the truth of the report. "But I know the CAG, Captain Bud Sanchez. Known him for years, and he says he can do it, and I believe him. Mr. President, don't be overly affected by the numbers. It isn't about numbers. It's about fighting a war, and we have more experience in that than they do. It's about psychology, and playing to our strengths rather than theirs. War isn't what it used to be. Used to be you needed huge forces to destroy the enemy's capacity to fight and his ability to coordinate and command his forces. Okay, fifty years ago you needed a lot to do that, but the targets you want to hit are actually very small, and if you can hit those small targets, you accomplish the same thing now as you used to need a million men to do before."

"It's cold-blooded murder," Hanson snarled. "That's what it is."

931

Jackson turned from his place at the lectern. "Yes, sir, that's exactly what war is, but this way we're not killing some poor nineteen-year-old son of a bitch who joined up because he liked the uniform. We're going to kill the bastard who sent him out to die and doesn't even know his name. With all due respect, sir, I have killed people, and I know exactly what it feels like. Just once, just one time, I'd like a crack at the people who give the orders instead of the poor dumb bastards who're stuck with carrying them out."

Durling almost smiled at that, remembering all the fantasies, and even a TV commercial once, about how different it might be if the president and prime ministers and other senior officials who ordered men off to the field of battle instead met and slugged it out personally.

"You're still going to have to kill a lot of kids," the President said. Admiral Jackson drew back from his angry demeanor before answering.

"I know that, sir, but with luck, a lot less."

"When do you have to know?"

"The pieces are largely in place now. We can initiate the operation in less than five hours. After that, we're daylight limited. Twenty-four-hour intervals after that."

"Thank you, Admiral Jackson. Could you all excuse me for a few minutes?" The men filed out until Durling had another thought. "Jack? Could you stay a minute?" Ryan turned and sat back down.

"It had to be done, sir. One way or another, if we're going to take those nukes out — "

"I know." The President looked down at his desk. All the briefing papers and maps and charts were spread out. All the order-of-battle documents. At least he'd been spared the casualty estimates, probably at Ryan's direction. After a second they heard the door close.

Ryan spoke first. "Sir, there's one other thing. Former Prime Minister Koga has been arrested — excuse me, we only know that he's kinda disappeared."

"What does that mean? Why didn't you bring that up before?"

"The arrest happened less than twenty-four hours after I told Scott Adler that Koga had been contacted. I didn't even tell him whom he'd been in contact with. Now, that could be a coincidence. Goto and his master just might not want him making political noise while they carry out their operation. It could also mean that there's a leak somewhere."

"Who on our side knows?"

"Ed and Mary Pat at CIA. Me. You. Scott Adler and whomever Scott told."

"But we don't know for sure that there's a leak."

"No, sir, we don't. But it is extremely likely."

"Set it aside for now. What if we don't do anything?"

"Sir, we have to. If we don't, then sometime in the future you can expect a war between Russia on one hand and Japan and China on the other, with us doing God knows what. CIA is still trying to do its estimate, but I don't see how the war can fail to go nuclear. ZORRO may not be the prettiest thing we've ever tried to do, but it's the best chance we have. The diplomatic issues are not important," Ryan went on. "We're playing for much higher stakes now. But if we can kill off the guys who initiated this mess, then we can cause Goto's government to fall. And then we can get things back under some sort of control."

The odd part, Durling realized, was the trade-off concerning which side was pitching which sort of moderation. Hanson and SecDef took the classical diplomatic line — they wanted to take the time to be sure there was no other option to resolve the crisis through peaceful means, but if diplomacy failed, then the door was opened for a much wider and bloodier conflict. Ryan and Jackson wanted to apply violence at once in the hope of avoiding a wider war later. The hell of it was, either side could be right or wrong, and the only way to know for sure was to read the history books twenty years from now.

"If the plan doesn't work . . ."

"Then we've killed some of our people for nothing," Jack said honestly. "You will pay a fairly high price yourself, sir."

"What about the fleet commander — I mean the guy commanding the carrier group. What about him?"

"If he chokes, the whole thing comes apart."

"Replace him," the President said. "The mission is approved." There was one other item to be discussed. Ryan walked the President through that one, too, before leaving the room and making his phone calls.

The perfect Air Force mission, people in blue uniforms liked to say, was run by a mere captain. This one was commanded locally by a special-operations colonel, but at least he was a man who'd been recently passed over for general's rank, a fact that endeared him to his subordinates, who knew why he'd failed to screen for flag rank. People in spec-ops just didn't fit in with the button-down ideal of senior leadership. They were too . . . eccentric for that.

The final mission brief evolved from data sent by real-time link from Fort Meade, Maryland, to Verino, and the Americans still cringed at the knowledge that Russians were learning all sorts of things about America's ability to gather and analyze electronic data via satellite and other means — after all, the capability had been developed for use against *them*. The exact positions of two operating E-767s were precisely plotted. Visual satellite data had counted fighter aircraft — at least those not in protective shelters — and the orbiting KH-12's last pass had counted airborne aircraft and their positions. The colonel commanding the detachment went over the penetration course that he had personally worked out with the flight crew, and while there were worries, the two young captains who would fly the C-17A transport chewed their gum and nodded final approval. One of them even joked about how it was time a "trash-hauler" got a little respect.

The Russians had their part to play, too. From Vuzhno-Sakalinsk South on the Kamchatka Peninsula, eight MiG-31 interceptors lifted off for an air-defense exercise, accompanied by an IL-86 Mainstay airborne-early-warning aircraft. Four Sukhoi fighters took off ten minutes later from Sokol to act as aggressors. The Sukhois with long-range fuel tanks headed southeast, remaining well outside Japanese airspace. The controllers in both Japanese E-767s recognized it for what it was: a fairly typical and stylized Russian training exercise. Nevertheless, it *did* involve warplanes, and merited their close attention, all the more so that it was astride the most logical approach route for American aircraft like the B-1s that had so recently "tickled" their air defenses. It had the effect of drawing the E-767s both north and east somewhat, and with them their fighter escorts. The reserve AWACS aircraft was almost ordered aloft, but the ground-based air-defense commander decided sensibly merely to increase his alert state a bit.

The C-17A Globemaster-III was the newest and most expensive air-transport aircraft ever to force its way through the Pentagon's procurement system. Anyone familiar with that procedural nightmare would have preferred flak, because at least bombing missions were designed to succeed, whereas the procurement system seemed most often designed to fail.

That it didn't was a tribute of sorts to the ingenuity of the people dedicated to confounding it. No expense had been spared, and a few new ones located for use, but what had resulted was a "trash-hauler" (the term most often used by fighter pilots) with pretensions of the wild life.

This one took off just after local midnight, heading south-southwest as though it were a civil flight to Vladivostok. Just short of that city it took fuel from a KC-135 tanker — the Russian midair refueling system was not compatible with American arrangements — and departed the Asian mainland, now heading due south exactly on the 132nd Meridian.

The Globemaster was the first-ever cargo aircraft designed with special-operations in mind. The normal flight crew of only two was supplemented with two "observer" positions for which modular instrument packages were provided. In this case, both were electronics-warfare officers now keeping tabs on the numerous air-defense radar sites that littered the Russian, Chinese, Korean, and Japanese coasts, and directing the flight crew to thread their way through as many null areas as was possible. That soon required a rapid descent and a turn east.

"Don't you just love this?" First Sergeant Vega asked his commander. The Rangers were sitting on fold-down seats in the cargo area, dressed in combat gear that had made them waddle like ducks aboard the aircraft an hour earlier under the watchful eyes of the loadmaster. It was widely believed within the Army's airborne community that the Air Force awarded points to its flight crews for making their passengers barf, but in this case there would be no complaints. The most dangerous part of the mission was right now, despite their parachutes, something the Air Force crewmen, significantly, didn't bother with. They would be of little use in any case should a stray fighter happen upon their transport at almost any time up to the programmed jump.

Captain Checa just nodded, mainly wishing he were on the ground, where an infantryman belonged, instead of sitting as helpless as an unborn child in the womb of a woman addicted to disco dancing.

Forward, the EWO displays were coloring up. The rectangular TV-type tube displayed a computer memory of every known radar installation on Japan's western coast. It hadn't been hard to input the information, as most of them had been established a generation or two earlier by Americans, back when Japan had been a massive island base for use against the Soviet Union and liable to Russian attack for that reason. The radars had been upgraded along the way, but any picket line had its imperfections, and these had been mostly known to the Americans beforehand, and then reevaluated by ELINT satellites in the last week. The aircraft was heading southeast now, leveling out two hundred feet over the water and tooling along at its maximum low-level speed of three hundred fifty knots. It made for a very bumpy ride, which the flight crew didn't notice, though everyone else did. The pilot wore low-light goggles, and swept his head around the sky while the copilot concentrated on the instruments. The latter crewman was also provided with a head-up display just like that on a fighter. It displayed compass heading, altitude, airspeed, and also gave him a thin green line to indicate the horizon, which he could sometimes see depending on the state of the moon and clouds.

"I have strobes very high at ten o'clock," the pilot reported. Those would be airliners on a standard commercial routing. "Nothing else."

The copilot gave her screen another look. The radar plot was exactly as programmed, with their flight path following a very narrow corridor of black amid radial spikes of red and yellow, which indicated areas covered by defense and air-control radars. The lower they flew, the wider was the black-safe zone, but they were already as low as they could safely fly.

"Fifty miles off the coast."

"Roger," the pilot acknowledged. "How're you doing?" he asked a second later. Low-level penetrations were stressful on everyone, even with a computer-controlled autopilot handling the stick work.

"No prob," she replied. It wasn't exactly true, but it was the thing she was supposed to say. The most dangerous part was right here, passing the elevated radar site at Aikawa. The weakest part of Japan's low-level defense perimeter, it was a gap between a peninsula and an island. Radars on both beams almost covered the seventy-mile gap, but they were old ones, dating back to the 1970s, and had not been upgraded with the demise of the Communist regime in North Korea. "Easing down," she said next, adjusting the altitude control on the autopilot to seventy feet. Theoretically they could fly safely at fifty over a flat surface, but their aircraft was riding heavy, and now her hand was on the sidestick control, itself another illusion that this was actually a fighter plane. If she saw so much as a fishing boat, she'd have to yank the aircraft to higher altitude for fear of a collision with somebody's masthead.

"Coast in five," one of the electronic-warfare officers announced. "Recommend come right to one-six-five."

"Coming right." The aircraft banked slightly.

There were only a few windows in the cargo area. First Sergeant Vega had one and looked out to see the wingtip of the aircraft dip toward a barely perceived black surface dotted with the occasional whitecap. The sight made him turn back in. He couldn't help things anyway, and if they hit and cartwheeled in, he'd have no time at all to comprehend it. Or so he'd been told once.

"I got the coast," the pilot said, catching the glow of lights first through his goggles. It was time to switch them off and help fly the aircraft. "My airplane."

"Pilot's airplane," the copilot acknowledged, flexing her hand and allowing herself a deep breath.

They crossed the coast between Omi and Ichifuri. As soon as land was visible, the pilot started climbing the aircraft. The automated terrain-avoidance system had three settings. He selected the one labeled *Hard*, which was rough on the airplane and rougher on the passengers, but ultimately safer for all concerned. "What about their AWACS?" he asked the EWOs.

"I've got emissions on one, nine o'clock, very weak. If you keep us in the weeds, we'll be okay."

"Get out the barf bags, guys." To the loadmaster: "Ten minutes."

"Ten minutes," the Air Force sergeant announced in the back. Just then the aircraft lurched up and to the right, dodging around the first coastal mountain. Then it dropped down rapidly again, like a particularly unpleasant amusement-park ride, and Julio Vega remembered once swearing that he'd never subject himself to anything like this again. It was a promise that had been broken many times, but this time, again, there were people on the ground with guns. And they weren't Colombian druggies this time, but a trained professional army.

"Jesus, I hope they give us two minutes of easy ride to walk to the door," he said between gulps.

"Don't count on it," Captain Checa said, just before he used his barf bag. It started a series of such events among the other Rangers.

The trick was to keep mountaintops between them and the radar transmitters. That meant flying in valleys. The Globemaster was slower now, barely two hundred thirty knots of indicated airspeed, and even with flaps and slats extended, and even with

939

a computer-aided flight-control system, it made for a ride that wallowed on one hand and jerked on the other, something that changed from one second to the next. The head-up display now showed the mountainous corridor they were flying, with red warning messages appearing before the eyes of the pilots that the autopilot handled quite well, thank you, but not without leading the two drivers in their front seats to genuine fear. Aviators never really trusted the things, and now two hands were on their stick controllers, almost flinching and taking control away from the computer, but not quite, in what was almost a highly sophisticated game of chicken, with the computer trying in its way to outgut the trained aviators who had to trust the microchips to do things their own reflexes were unable to match. They watched green jagged lines that represented real mountains, ranks of them, fuzzy on the edges from the trees that grew to the tops of most, and for the most part the lines were well above the flight level of their aircraft until the last second, when the nose would jerk upwards and their stomachs would struggle to catch up, and then the aircraft would dive again.

"There's the IP. Five minutes," the pilot called aft.

"*Stand up!*" the loadmaster yelled at his passengers. The aircraft was going down again, and one of the Rangers almost came off the floor of the aircraft when he stood. They moved aft toward the portside passenger door, which was now opened. As they hooked up their static lines, the rear cargo hatch dropped down, and two Air Force enlisted men removed the safety hooks from the palletized cargo that occupied the middle of the sixty-five-foot cargo bay. The Globemaster leveled out one last time, and out the door, Checa and Vega could see the shadowy valley below their aircraft, and a towering mountain to the left of them.

"Five hundred feet," the pilot said over intercom. "Let's get it done."

"Winds look good," the copilot announced, checking the computer that controlled drops. "One minute."

The green light by the passenger door turned on. The loadmaster had a safety belt attached to his waist, standing by the door, blocking the way of the Rangers. He gave them a sideways look.

"You guys be careful down there, y'hear?"

"Sorry about the mess," Captain Checa said. The loadmaster grinned.

"I've cleaned up worse." Besides, he had a private to do that. He gave the area a final check. The Rangers were safely in their places, and nobody was in the way of the cargo's roller-path. The first drop would be done from the front office. "All clear aft," he said over his intercom circuit. The loadmaster stepped away from the door, allowing Checa to take his place, one hand on either side, and his left foot just over the edge.

"Ten seconds," the copilot said forward.

"Roger, ten seconds." The pilot reached for the release switch, flipping off the safety cover and resting his thumb on the toggle.

"Five."

"Five."

"Three — two — one — *now!*"

"Cargo away." The pilot had already flipped it at the proper moment.

Aft, the Rangers saw the pallets slide out through the cavernous door. The aircraft took a major dip at the tail, then snapped back level. A second after that, the green light at the door started blinking.

"Go go go!" the loadmaster screamed over the noise.

Captain Diego Checa, U.S. Army Rangers, became the first American to invade the Japanese mainland

941

when he took his step out the door and fell into the darkness. A second later the static line yanked his chute open, and the black nylon umbrella came to full blossom a bare three hundred feet from the ground. The stiff and often hurtful opening shock came as a considerable relief. Jumping at five hundred feet made the use of a backup chute a useless extravagance. He first looked up and to his right to see that the others were all out, their chutes opening as his had just done. The next order of business was to look down and around. There was the clearing, and he was sure he'd hit it, though he pulled on one riser to spill air from his parachute in the hope of hitting the middle of it and increasing the safety margin that was as much theoretical as real for a night drop. Last of all he released his pack, which fell fifteen feet to the end of a safety line. Its sixty pounds of gear would hit the ground first, lessening his landing shock so long as he didn't land right on the damned thing and break something in the process. Aside from that he barely had time to think before the barely visible valley raced up to greet him. Feet together, knees bent, back straight, roll when you hit, the sudden lung-emptying shock of striking the ground, and then he was on his face, trying to decide if all his bones were intact or not. Seconds later he heard the muted thuds and *oof*s of the rest of the detail as they also made it to earth. Checa allowed himself a full three seconds to decide that he was more or less in one piece before standing, unclipping his back, and racing to collapse his chute. That task done, he came back, donned his low-light goggles, and assembled his people.

"Everybody okay?"

"Good drop, sir." Vega showed up first with two others in tow. The rest were heading in, all carrying their black chutes.

"Let's get to work, Rangers."

942

The Globemaster continued almost due south, going "feet-wet" just west of Nomazu, and again hugging the water, kept a mountainous peninsula between itself and the distant E-767s for as long as possible, then turned southwest to distance itself further still from them until, two hundred miles off the coast of Japan, it was safe to climb back to a safe cruising altitude into commercial airline routing G223. The only remaining question was whether the KC-10 tanker that was supposed to meet them would show up and allow them to complete their flight to Kwajalein. Only then could they break radio silence.

The Rangers were able to do it first. The communications sergeant broke out a satellite transmitter, oriented it toward the proper azimuth, and transmitted a five-letter group, waiting for an acknowledgment.

"They're down okay," an Army major told Jackson at his desk in the National Military Command Center.

The real trick is going to be getting them out, the Admiral thought. *But one thing at a time.* He lifted his phone to call the White House.

"Jack, the Rangers are in."

"Good one, Rob. I need you over here," Ryan told him.

"What for? It's busy here and — "

"Now, Robby." The line clicked off.

The next order of business was to get the cargo moved. It had landed within two hundred meters of the nominal location, and the plan had allowed for quite a bit more than that. One by one, pairs of Rangers struggled with empty fuel bladders, carrying them uphill to the treeline that bordered what seemed to be a highlands meadow. With that done, a hose was strung, and twenty thousand pounds of JP-5 pumped from one large rubber bladder into six other, smaller ones arranged in pairs at preselected spots. That operation took an hour, while four of their number patrolled the immediate area for signs of human presence, but finding nothing but the tracks of a four-wheel cycle, which they'd been told to expect. When the pumping operation was finished, the original fuel bladder was folded and dumped into a hole, then carefully covered up with sod. Next, the solid cargo had to be manhandled into place and covered with camouflage netting. That required another two hours, straining the Rangers to the limit of their conditioning with the combination of heavy work and building stress. Soon the sun would be up, and the area could not look as though there were people here. First Sergeant Vega supervised the cover-up operation. When all was done, the Rangers still outside the treeline walked in single file toward it, with the last man in line working on the grass to reduce the signs of their passage. It wasn't perfect, but it would have to do. By dawn, at the end of what had been for them a twenty-hour day as unpleasant as anyone could have contrived to make, they were in place, unwelcome guests on the soil of a foreign land, mainly shivering in the cold, unable to light a fire for warmth, eating cold MRE rations.

"Jack, I got work to do over there, damn it," Robby said on his way through the door.

"Not anymore. The President and I talked it over last night."

"What do you mean?"

"Get packed. You're taking over the *Stennis* battle group." Ryan wanted to grin at his friend, but couldn't quite bring himself to that. Not when he was sending his friend into danger. The news stopped Jackson in his tracks.

"You sure?"

"It's decided. The President has signed off on it. CINCPAC knows. Admiral Seaton — "

Robby nodded. "Yeah, I've worked for him before."

"You have two hours. There's a Gulfstream waiting for you at Andrews. We need somebody," the National Security Advisor explained, "who knows the political limits on the mission. Take it right to the edge, Rob, but no further. We have to smart our way through this."

"I understand."

Ryan stood and walked to his friend. "I'm not sure I like doing this . . ."

"It's my job, Jack."

Tennessee arrived at her station off the Japanese coast and finally slowed to her normal patrol speed of five knots. Commander Claggett took a required moment to get a position fix on a rocky outcropping known to sailors as Lot's Wife, then dived his boat below the layer to a depth of six hundred feet. The sonar showed nothing at the moment, odd for the normally busy shipping lanes, but after four and a half days of dangerously high-speed running, it came as a considerable relief to everyone aboard. The Army personnel had adapted well enough and joined sailors for their jogs in the missile room. For the moment, the mission orders were little different from those the boomer had been designed to do: remain undetected, with the additional assignment of gathering whatever information on enemy movements that came her way. It wasn't exactly exciting, but only Claggett knew at the moment how important it was.

The satellite link told Sandy Richter and his colleagues that the mission was a probable "go." It meant more simulator time for all of them while ground crews prepped their Comanches for business. Unfortunately, that meant affixing decidedly unstealthy wing fittings to the side of each aircraft, along with long-range ferry tanks, but he'd known that from the beginning, and nobody had bothered asking how much he liked the idea. There were three scenarios on the sim now, and one by one the flight crews went through them, their bodies gyrating, quite unaware of what they were doing in the real world while their minds and bodies played in the virtual one.

"How the hell do we do that?" Chavez demanded.

Russians would not have questioned the orders in quite that way, Scherenko thought. "I only relay orders from your own agency," he told them. "I also know that Koga's disappearance was not caused by any official agency."

"Yamata, you suppose?" Clark asked. That piece of information narrowed the possibilities somewhat. It also made the impossible merely dangerous.

"A good guess. You know where he lives, yes?"

"We've seen it from a distance," Chavez confirmed.

"Ah, yes — your photos." The Major would have loved to know what those had been about, but it would have been foolish to ask the question, and it was not certain that these two Americans knew the answer in any case. "If you have other assets in-country, I suggest you make use of them. We are making use of ours as well. Koga is probably the political solution to this crisis."

"If there is one," Ding noted.

"Good to fly with you again, Captain Sato," Yamata said pleasantly. The invitation to the flight deck pleased him. The pilot, he saw, was a patriot, a man of both pride and skill who really understood what was happening. What a pity he'd chosen such a lowly path for his life.

Sato took off his headset and relaxed in his command seat. "This is a pleasant change from the Canadian flights."

"How does that go?"

"I've spoken with a few executives on the way home. They say the Americans are more confused than anything else."

"Yes." Yamata smiled. "They confuse easily."

"Can we hope for a diplomatic settlement to this business, Yamata-san?"

"I think so. They lack the ability to attack us effectively."

"My father commanded a destroyer in the war. My brother — "

"Yes, I know him well, Captain." That remark, he saw, lit up the pilot's eyes with pride.

"And my son is a fighter pilot. He flies the Eagle."

"Well, they have done well so far. They recently killed two American bombers, you know. The Americans tested our air defenses," the industrialist said. "It was they who failed."

41

CTF-77

"You're back!" the rental agent said with some pleasure.

Nomuri smiled and nodded. "Yes. I had a particularly good day at the office yesterday. I do not need to tell you how stressful such a 'good' day can be, do I?"

The man grunted agreement. "In the summer my best days are those when I get no sleep. Please excuse how I appear," he added. He'd been working on some of his machines all morning, which for him had begun just after five. The same was true of Nomuri, but for a different reason.

"I understand. I own my own business, too, and who works harder than a man who works for himself, eh?"

"Do you suppose the zaibatsu understand that?"

"Not the ones I've met. Even so, you are fortunate to live in so peaceful an area."

"Not always peaceful. The Air Force must have been playing games last night. A jet flew close by and very low. It woke me up, and I never really got back to sleep afterward." He wiped his hands and poured two cups of tea, offering one to his guest.

"*Dozo,*" Nomuri said graciously. "They are playing very dangerous games now," he went on, wondering what response he'd get.

"It's madness, but who cares what I think? Not the government, surely. All they listen to are the 'great' ones." The equipment owner sipped at his tea and looked around his shop.

"Yes, I am concerned, too. I hope Goto can find a way out of this before things spin completely out of control." Nomuri looked outside. The weather was turning gray and threatening. He heard a decidedly angry grunt.

"Goto? Just one more like all the rest. Others lead him by the nose — or some other part if the rumors about him are correct."

Nomuri chuckled. "Yes, I have heard the stories, too. Still, a man of some vigor, eh?" He paused. "So can I rent another of your cycles today?"

"Take number six." The man pointed. "I just finished servicing it. Pay attention to the weather," he warned. "Snow tonight."

Nomuri held up his backpack. "I want to take some pictures of cloudy mountains for my collection. The peace here is wonderful, and fine for thinking."

"Only in the winter," the dealer said, returning to his work.

Nomuri knew the way now, and followed the Taki uphill over a trail crusty from cold and frost. He would have felt a little better about it if the damned four-wheeled cycle had a better muffler. At least the heavy air would help attenuate the sound, or so he hoped, as he headed up the same path he'd taken a few days earlier. In due course he was looking down at the high meadow, seeing nothing out of the ordinary and wondering if — wondering a lot of things. What if the soldiers had run into an ambush? *In that case,* Nomuri told himself, *I'm toast.* But there was no turning back. He settled back into the seat and steered his way down the hillside, stopping as he was supposed to in the middle of the clearing and taking the hood down off his red parka. On closer examination, he saw that some sod had been disturbed, and he saw what might have been a trail of sorts into the woodline. That was when a single figure appeared, waving him up. The CIA officer restarted the cycle and headed that way.

The two soldiers who confronted him didn't point weapons. They didn't have to. Their faces were painted and their camouflage uniforms told him everything he needed to know.

"I'm Nomuri," he said. "The password is Foxtrot."

"Captain Checa," the officer replied, extending his hand. "We've worked with the Agency before. Are you the guy who picked this spot?"

"No, but I checked it out a couple days ago."

"Nice place to build a cabin," Checa thought. "We even saw a few deer, little ones. I hope it isn't hunting season." The remark caught Nomuri short. He hadn't considered that possibility, and didn't know anything about hunting in Japan. "So what do you have for me?"

"These." Nomuri took off his backpack and pulled out the cellular phones.

"Are you kiddin' me?"

"The Japanese military has good stuff for monitoring military communications. Hell, they invented a lot of the technology our people use. But these" — Nomuri grinned — "everybody has 'em, and they're digitally encrypted, and they cover the whole country. Even here. There's a repeater tower down on that mountain. Anyway, it's safer than using your regular comms. The bill's paid to the end of the month," he added.

"Be nice to call home and tell my wife that everything's going fine," Checa thought aloud.

"I'd be careful about that. Here are the numbers you can call." Nomuri handed over a sheet. "That one's mine. That one's a guy named Clark. That one's another officer named Chavez — "

"Ding's over here?" First Sergeant Vega asked. "You know 'em?"

"We did a job in Africa last fall," Checa replied. "We get a lot of 'special' work. You sure you can tell us their names, man?"

"They have covers. You're probably better off speaking in Spanish. Not as many people here speak that language. I don't need to tell you to keep your transmissions short," Nomuri added. He didn't. Checa nodded and asked the most important question.

"And getting out?"

Nomuri turned to point, but the terrain feature in question was covered in clouds. "There's a pass there. Head for it, then downhill to a town called Hirose. I pick you up there, put you on a train to Nagoya, and you fly off to either Taiwan or Korea."

"Just like that." The comment wasn't posed as a question, but the dubious nature of the response was clear anyway.

"There are a couple of hundred thousand foreign businesspeople here. You're eleven guys from Spain trying to sell wine, remember?"

"I could use some sangria right now, too." Checa was relieved to see that his CIA contact had been briefed in on the same mission. It didn't always work out that way. "Now what?"

"You wait for the rest of the mission force to arrive. If something goes wrong, you call me and head out. If I drop out of the net, you call the others. If everything goes to hell, you find another way out. You should have passports, clothes, and — "

"We do."

"Good." Nomuri took his camera out of his backpack and started shooting photos of the cloud-shrouded mountains.

★ ★ ★

"This is CNN, live from Pearl Harbor," the reporter ended, and a commercial cut in. The intelligence analyst rewound the tape to examine it again. It was both amazing and entirely ordinary that he'd be able to get such vital information so easily. The American media really ran the country, he'd learned over the years, and perhaps more was the pity. The way they'd played up the unfortunate incident in Tennessee had inflamed the entire country into precipitous action, then driven his country into the same, and the only good news was what he saw on the TV screen: two fleet carriers still in their dry docks, with two more still in the Indian Ocean, according to the latest reports from that part of the world, and Pacific Fleet's other two in Long Beach, also dry-docked and unable to enter service — and that, really, was that, so far as the Marianas were concerned. He had to formalize his intelligence estimate with a few pages of analytical prose, but what it came down to was that America could sting his country, but her ability to project real power was now a thing of the past. The realization of that meant that there was little likelihood of a serious contest for the immediate future.

Jackson didn't mind being the only passenger in the VC-20B. A man could get used to this sort of treatment, and he had to admit that the Air Force's executive birds were better than the Navy's — in fact the Navy didn't have many, and those were mainly modified P-3 Orions whose turboprop engines provided barely more than half the speed of the twin-engine executive jet. With only a brief refueling stop at Travis Air Force Base, outside San Francisco, he'd made the hop to Hawaii in under nine hours, and it was something to feel good about until on final approach to Hickam he got a good look at the naval base and saw that *Enterprise* was still in the graving dock. The first nuclear-powered carrier and bearer of the U.S. Navy's proudest name would be out of this one. The aesthetic aspect of it was bad enough. More to the point, it would have been far better to have two decks to use instead of one.

"You have your task force, boy," Robby whispered to himself. And it was the one every naval aviator wanted. Task Force 77, titularly the main air arm of Pacific Fleet, and, one carrier or not, it was his, and about to sail in harm's way. Perhaps fifty years earlier there had been an excitement to it. Perhaps when PacFlt's main striking arm had sailed under Bill Halsey or Ray Spruance, the people in command had looked forward to it. The wartime movies said so, and so did the official logs, but how much of that had been mere posturing, Jackson wondered now, contemplating his own command. Did Halsey and Spruance lose sleep with the knowledge that they were sending young men to death, or was the world simply a different place then, where war was considered as natural an event as a polio epidemic — another scourge that was now a thing of the past. To be Commander Task Force 77 was a life's ambition, but he'd never really wanted to fight a war — oh, sure, he admitted to himself, as a new ensign, or even as far as lieutenant's rank, he'd relished the idea of air combat, knowing that as a U.S. naval aviator he was the best in the world, highly trained and exquisitely equipped, and wanting to prove it someday. But over time he'd seen too many friends die in accidents. He'd gotten a kill in the Persian Gulf War, and four more over the Med one clear and starry night, but those last four had been an accident. He'd killed men for no good reason at all, and though he never spoke of it to others, not even his wife, it gnawed at him that he had in effect been tricked into killing other human beings. Not his fault, just some sort of enforced mistake. But that's what war was for the warriors most of the time, just a huge mistake, and now he had to play his part in another such mistake instead of using TF-77 the way it was supposed to be used, just *to be*, and, merely by being, to prevent wars from happening. The only consolation of the moment was that, again, the mistake, the accident, wasn't of his making.

If wishes were horses, he told himself as the aircraft taxied to a stop. The flight attendant opened the door and tossed Jackson's one bag out to another Air Force sergeant, who walked the Admiral to a helicopter for his next flight, this one to CINCPAC, Admiral Dave Seaton. It was time to don his professional personality. Misused or not, Robby Jackson was a warrior about to assume command of others. He'd examined his doubts and questions, and now it was time to put them away.

"We're going to owe them big-time for this," Durling noted, flipping off the TV with his remote.

The technology had been developed for advertising during baseball games, of all things. An adaptation of the blue-screen systems used in the production of movies, advanced computer systems allowed it to be used in real-time, and thus the background behind the batter at the plate could be made to appear to be an advertisement for a local bank or car dealer when in fact it was just the usual green used at ballparks. In this case, a reporter could make his or her live feed from Pearl Harbor — outside the naval base, of course — and the background was that of two carrier profiles, with birds flying past and the antlike shapes of yard workers moving in the distance, and it looked as real as anything else on the TV screen which, after all, was just a collection of multicolored dots.

"They're Americans," Jack said. And besides, he was the one who'd bullied them into it, again insulating the President from the politically dangerous task. "They're supposed to be on our side. We just had to remind them of that."

"Will it work?" That was the harder question.

"Not for long, but maybe for long enough. It's a good plan we have in place. We need a few breaks, but we've gotten two in the bag already. The important thing is, we're showing them what they expect to see. They expect both carriers to be there, and they expect the media to tell the whole world about it. Intelligence people are no different from anybody else, sir. They have preconceptions, and when they see them in real life, it just reinforces how brilliant they think they are."

"How many people do we have to kill?" the President wanted to know next.

"Enough. We don't know how big the number is, and we're going to try an' keep it as low as possible — but, sir, the mission is — "

"I know. I know about missions, remember?" Durling closed his eyes, remembering Infantry School at Fort Benning, Georgia, half a lifetime before. *The mission comes first.* It was the only way a lieutenant could think, and now for the first time he realized that a president had to think the same way. It hardly seemed fair.

They didn't see much sun this far north at this time of year, and that suited Colonel Zacharias. The flight from Whiteman to Elmendorf had taken a mere five hours, all of it in darkness because the B-2A flew only in daylight to show itself to people, which was not something for which the aircraft had been conceived. It flew very well indeed, belated proof that Jack Northrop's idea dating back to the 1930s had been correct: an aircraft consisting exclusively of wing surfaces was the most efficient possible aerodynamic shape. It was just that the flight-control systems required for such an aircraft needed computerized flight controls for proper stability, something that had not been available until just before the engineer's death. At least he'd seen the model, if not the actual aircraft itself.

Almost everything about it was efficient. Its shape allowed easy storage — three could fit in a hangar designed for one conventional aircraft. It climbed rather like an elevator, and, able to cruise at high altitude, it drank its fuel in cups rather than gallons, or so the wing commander liked to say.

The shot-up B-1B was about ready to fly back to Elmendorf. It would do so on three engines, not a major problem as the aircraft would be carrying nothing more than fuel and its crew as a payload. There were other aircraft based at Shemya now. Two E-3B AWACS birds dispatched from Tinker Air Force Base in Oklahoma maintained a partial airborne-alert patrol, though this island had power radars of its own, the largest of which was the powerful Cobra Dane missile-detection system built in the 1970s. There was the theoretical possibility that the Japanese could, using tankers, manage a strike against the island, duplicating in length an Israeli mission against the PLO headquarters in North Africa, and though the possibility was remote, it did have to be considered. Defending against that were the Air Force's only four F-22A Rapier fighters, the world's first true stealth fighter aircraft, taken from advanced testing at Nellis Air Force Base and dispatched with four senior pilots and their support crews to this base at the edge of the known universe. But the Rapier — known to the pilots by the name the manufacturer, Lockheed, had initially preferred, "Lightning-II" — hadn't been designed for defense, and now, with the sun back down after its brief and fitful appearance, it was time for the original purpose. As always the tanker lifted off first, even before the fighter pilots walked from the briefing hut to their aircraft shelters for the start of the night's work.

"If he flew out yesterday, why are there lights on?" Chavez asked, looking up at the penthouse apartment.

"Timer on the lights to scare burglars away?" John wondered lightly.

"This ain't L.A., man."

"Then I suppose there's people there, Yevgeniy Pavlovich." He turned the car onto another street.

Okay, we know that Koga wasn't arrested by the local police. We know that Yamata is running this whole show. We know that his security chief, Kaneda, probably killed Kimberly Norton. We know that Yamata is out of town. And we know that his apartment has lights on. . . .

Clark found a place to park the car. Then he and Chavez went walking, first of all circling the block, looking around for patterns and opportunities in a process called reconnaissance that started at the ground level and seemed more patient than it really was.

"A lot we don't know, man," Chavez breathed.

"I thought you wanted to see somebody's eyes, Domingo," John reminded his partner.

He had singularly lifeless eyes, Koga thought, not like a human at all. They were dark and large, but seemingly dry, and they just looked at him — or perhaps they just pointed in his direction and lingered there, the former Prime Minister wondered. Whatever they were, they gave no clue as to what lay behind them. He'd heard about Kiyoshi Kaneda, and the term most often used to describe him was *ronin,* a historical reference to samurai warriors who'd lost their master and couldn't find another, which was deemed a great disgrace in the culture of the time.

957

Such men had turned into bandits, or worse, after they'd lost contact with the *bushido* code that had for a thousand years sustained the elements of the Japanese population entitled to carry and use weapons. Such men, once they found a new master to serve, became fanatics, Koga remembered, so fearful of returning to their former status that they would do nearly anything to avoid that fate.

It was a foolish reverie, he knew, looking at the man's back as he watched TV. The age of the samurai was past, and along with it the feudal lords who had ruled them, but there the man was, watching a samurai drama on NHK, sipping his tea and taking in every scene. He didn't react at all, as though hypnotized by the highly stylized tale, which was really the Japanese version of American Westerns from the 1950s, highly simplified melodramas of good and evil, except that the heroic figure, always laconic, always invincible, always mysterious, used a sword instead of a six-gun. And this fool Kaneda was devoted to such stories, he'd learned over the past day and a half.

Koga stood and started moving back to the bookcase, and that was all he had to do for the man's head to turn and look. *Watchdog*, Koga thought without looking back as he selected another book to read. And a formidable one, especially with four others about, two sleeping now, one in the kitchen, and one outside the door. He hadn't a chance of escaping, the politician knew. Perhaps a fool, but the sort that a careful man feared.

Who was Kaneda, really? he wondered. A former Yakuza, probably. He didn't show any of the grotesque tattoos that people in that subculture affected, deliberately making themselves different in a culture that demanded conformity — but at the same time demonstrating conformity in a society of outcasts. On the other hand, he just sat there wearing a business suit whose only concession to comfort was the un-buttoned jacket. Even the ronin's posture was rigid as he sat there erect, Koga saw, himself sitting back down with a book but looking over it at his captor. He knew he couldn't fight the man and win — Koga had never troubled himself to learn any of the martial arts that his country had helped develop, and the man was physically formidable. And he was not alone.

He *was* a watchdog. Seemingly impassive, seem-ingly at rest, he was in fact more like a coiled spring, ready to leap and strike, and civilized only so long as those around him acted in such a way as not to arouse him, and so obvious about it that you just knew that it was madness to offend him. It shamed the politician that he was so easily cowed, but cowed he was, because he was a bright and thoughtful man, unwilling to squander his one chance, if he had that much, in a foolish gesture.

Many of the industrialists had men like this one. Some of them even carried handguns, which was al-most unthinkable in Japan, but the right person could make the right sort of approach to the right official, and a very special permit could be issued, and that possibility didn't so much frighten Koga as revolt him. The sword of a ronin was bad enough, and in this context would merely have been theatrical, but a gun for Koga was pure evil, something that didn't belong in his culture, a coward's weapon. That was what he was dealing with, really. Kaneda was undoubtedly a coward, unable to master his own life, able even to break the law only on orders from others, but with those orders he could do anything. What a dreadful commentary on his country. People like this were used by their masters to strong-arm unions and busi-ness competitors. People like Kaneda had assaulted demonstrators, sometimes even in the open, and got-ten away with it because the police had looked the other way or managed not to be present, even though

959

reporters and photographers had come to find the scene of the day's interest. People like this and their masters held his country back from true democracy, and the realization was all the more bitter for Koga because he'd known it for years, dedicated his life to changing it, and failed; and so here he was in Yamata's penthouse apartment, under guard, probably to be released someday as the political irrelevance he already was or would soon become, then to watch his country fall totally under the control of a new kind of master — or an old one, he told himself. And not a thing he could do about it, which was why he sat with a book in his hands while Kaneda sat in front of a TV watching some actor perform in a drama whose beginning, middle, and end were all foretold a thousand times, pretending that it was both real and new, when it was neither.

Battles like this one had been fought only in simulation, or perhaps in the Roman arenas of a different age. At both ends were the AEW aircraft, E-767s on the Japanese side and E-3Bs on the American, so far apart that neither really "saw" the other even on the numerous radar screens that both carried, though both monitored the signals of the other on different instruments. In between were the gladiators, because for the third time the Americans were testing the air defenses of Japan, and, again, failing.

The American AWACS aircraft were six hundred miles off Hokkaido, with the F-22A fighters a hundred miles in front of them, "trolling," as the flight leader put it, and the Japanese F-15s were coming out as well, entering the radar coverage of the American surveillance aircraft but not leaving the coverage of their own.

On command, the American fighters split into two elements of two aircraft each. The lead element darted due south, using their ability to supercruise at over

960

nine hundred miles per hour, closing obliquely with the Japanese picket line.

"They're fast," a Japanese controller observed. It was hard to hold the contact. The American aircraft was somewhat stealthy, but the size and power of the Kami aircraft's antenna defeated the low-observable technology again, and the controller started vectoring his Eagles south to cover the probe. Just to make sure that the Americans knew they were being tracked, he selected the appropriate blips with his electronic pointer and ordered the radar to steer its beams on them every few seconds and hold them there. They had to know that they were being followed through every move, that their supposedly radar-defeating technology was not good enough for something new and radical. Just to make it a little more interesting, he switched the frequency of his transmitter to fire-control mode. They were much too far away actually to guide a missile at this range, but even so, it would be one more proof to them that they could be lit up brightly enough for a kill, and that would teach them a lesson of its own. The signal faded a bit at first, almost dropping off entirely, but then the software picked them out of the clutter and firmed up the blip as he jacked up the power down the two azimuths to the American fighters, as fighters they had to be. The B-1, though fast, was not so agile. Yes, this was the best card the Americans had to play, and it was not good enough, and maybe if they learned that, diplomacy would change things once and for all, and the North Pacific Ocean would again be at peace.

"See how their Eagles move to cover," the senior American controller observed at his supervisory screen.

"Like they're tied to the 7s with a string," his companion noted. He was a fighter pilot just arrived from Langley Air Force Base, headquarters of Air Combat Command, where his job was to develop fighter tactics.

Another plotting board showed that three of the E-767s were up. Two were on advanced picket duty while the third was orbiting in close, just off the coast of Honshu. That was not unexpected. It was, in fact, the predictable thing to do because it was also the smart thing to do, and all three surveillance aircraft had their instruments dialed up to what had to be maximum power, as they had to do to detect stealthy aircraft.

"Now we know why they hit both the Lancers," the man from Virginia observed. "They can jump to high freqs and illuminate for the Eagles. Our guys never thought they were being shot at. Cute," he thought.

"Would be nice to have some of those radars," the senior controller agreed.

"But we know how to beat it now." The officer from Langley thought he saw it. The controller wasn't so sure.

"We'll know that in another few hours."

Sandy Richter was even lower than the C-17 had dared to go. He was also slower, at a mere one hundred fifty knots, and already tired from the curious mixture of tension and boredom on the overwater flight. The previous night he and the other two aircraft in his flight had staged to Petrovka West, yet another mothballed MiG base near Vladivostok. There they'd gotten what would surely be their last decent sleep for the next few days, and lifted off at 2200 hours to begin their part in Operation ZORRO. Each aircraft now had wing sponsons attached, and on each were two extra fuel tanks, and while they were needed for the range of this flight, they were

decidedly unstealthy even though the tanks themselves had been made out of radar-transparent fiber-
glass in an effort to improve things a little bit. The
pilot was wearing his normal flight gear plus an in-
flatable life jacket. It was a concession to regulations
about flying over water rather than as anything really
useful. The water fifty feet below was too cold for
long survival. He put the thought aside as best he
could, settled into his seat, and concentrated on the
flying while the gunner in back handled the instruments.

"Still okay, Sandy." The threat screen was still more
black than anything else as they turned east toward
Honshu.

"Rog." Behind them at ten-mile intervals, two
more Comanches were heading in.

Though small and a mere helicopter, the RAH-66A
was in some ways the most sophisticated aircraft in
the world. It carried in its composite airframe the
two most powerful computers ever taken aloft, and
one of them was merely a backup in case the first
should break. Their principal task for the moment
was to plot the radar coverage that they had to penetrate to compute the relative radar cross-section of
their airframe against the known or estimated capabilities of the electronic eyes now sweeping the area.
The closer they got to the Japanese mainland, the
larger grew the yellow areas of maybe-detect and the
red areas of definite-detect.

"Phase Two," the man from Air Combat Command
said quietly aboard the AWACS.

The F-22 fighters all carried jamming gear, the better to accentuate their stealth capabilities, and on command these were switched on.

"Not smart," the Japanese controller thought.
Good. They must know that we can track them. His

screen was suddenly littered with spots and spokes and flashes as the electronic noise generated by the American fighters muddled his picture. He had two ways of dealing with that. First he increased his power further; that would burn through much of what the Americans were attempting. Next he told the radar to start flipping through frequencies at random. The first measure was more effective than the second, he saw, since the American jammers were also frequency-agile. It was an imperfect measure, but still a troublesome one. The computer software that was doing the actual tracking was based on assumptions. It started with known or estimate positions of the American aircraft, and, knowing their speed range, sought returns that matched their base courses and speeds, just as had happened with the bombers that had once probed his defense line. The problem was that at this power output, he was again detecting birds and air currents, and picking the actual contacts out was becoming increasingly difficult until he punched yet another button that tracked the jamming emissions that were more powerful than the actual returning signals. With that additional check, he reestablished a firm track on both pairs of targets. It had required only ten seconds, and that was fast enough. Just to show the Americans he hadn't been fooled, he maxed-out his power, flipped briefly to fire-control mode, and zapped all four of the American fighters hard enough that if their electronic systems were not properly shielded, the incoming radar signals would burn some of them out. That would be an interesting kill, he thought, and he remembered how a pair of German Tornado fighters had once been destroyed by flying too close to an FM radio tower. To his disappointment, the Americans simply turned away.

"Somebody just set off some mongo jammers to the northeast."

"Good, right on time," Richter replied. A quick look at the threat screen showed that he was within minutes of entering a yellow area. He felt the need to rub his face, but both his hands were busy now. A check of the fuel gauges showed that his pylon-mounted tanks were about empty. "Punching off the wings."

"Roger — that'll help."

Richter flipped the safety cover off the jettison switch. It was a late addition to the Comanche design, but it had finally occurred to someone that if the chopper was supposed to be stealthy, then it might be a good idea to be able to eliminate the unstealthy features in flight. Richter slowed the aircraft briefly and flipped the toggle that ignited explosive bolts, dumping the wings and their tanks into the Sea of Japan.

"Good separation," the backseater confirmed. The threat screen changed as soon as the items were gone. The computer kept careful track of how stealthy the aircraft was. The Comanche's nose dipped again, and the aircraft accelerated back to its cruising speed.

"They're predictable, aren't they?" the Japanese controller observed to his chief subordinate.

"I think you just proved that. Even better, you just proved to them what we can do." The two officers traded a look. Both had been worried about the capabilities of the American Rapier fighter, and now both thought they could relax about it. A formidable aircraft, and one their Eagle drivers needed to treat with respect, but not invisible.

"Predictable response," the American controller said. "And they just showed us something. Call it ten seconds?"

"Thin, but long enough. It'll work," the colonel from Langley said, reaching for a coffee. "Now, let's reinforce that idea." On the main screen, the F-22s turned back north, and at the edge of the AWACS detection radius, the F-15Js did the same, covering the American maneuver like sailboats in a tacking duel, striving to stay between the American fighters and their priceless E-767s, which the dreadful accidents of a few days before had made even more precious.

Landfall was very welcome indeed. Far more agile than the transport had been the previous night, the Comanche selected a spot completely devoid of human habitation and then started flying down cracks in the mountainous ground, shielded from the distant air-surveillance aircraft by solid rock that even their powerful systems could not penetrate.

"Feet dry," Richter's backseater said gratefully. "Forty minutes of fuel remaining."

"You good at flapping your arms?" the pilot inquired, also relaxed, just a little, to be over dry land. If something went wrong, well, eating rice wasn't all that bad, was it? His helmet display showed the ground in green shadows, and there were no lights about from streetlights or cars or houses, and the worst part of the flight in was over. The actual mission was something he'd managed to set aside. He preferred to worry about only one thing at a time. You lived longer that way.

The final ridgeline appeared just as programmed. Richter slowed the aircraft, circling to figure out the winds as he looked down for the people he'd been briefed to expect. There. Somebody tossed out a green chem-light, and in his low-light vision systems it looked as bright as a full moon.

"ZORRO Lead calling ZORRO Base, over."

"Lead, this is Base. Authentication Golf Mike Zulu, over," the voice replied, giving the okay-code he'd been briefed to expect. Richter hoped the voice didn't have a gun to its head.

"Copy. Out." He spiraled down quickly, flaring his Comanche and settling on what appeared to be an almost-flat spot close to the treeline. As soon as the aircraft touched down, three men appeared from the trees. They were dressed like U.S. Army soldiers, and Richter allowed himself a chance to breathe as he cooled off the engines prior to shutdown. The rotor had not yet completed its final revolution before a hose came out to the aircraft's fuel connection.

"Welcome to Japan. I'm Captain Checa."

"Sandy Richter," the pilot said, climbing out.

"Any problems coming in?"

"Not anymore." *Hell, I got here, didn't I?* he wanted to say, still tense from the three-hour marathon to invade the country. Invade? Eleven Rangers and six aviators. *Hey,* he thought, *you're all under arrest!*

"There's number two . . ." Checa observed. "Quiet babies, aren't they?"

"We don't want to advertise, sir." It was perhaps the most surprising aspect of the Comanche. The Sikorsky engineers had long known that most of the noise generated by a helicopter came from the tail rotor's conflict with the main. The one on the RAH-66 was shrouded, and the main rotor had five fairly thick composite blades, resulting in a helicopter with less than a third of the acoustical signature of any other rotary-wing aircraft yet built. And the area wouldn't hurt, Richter thought, looking around. All the trees, the thin mountain air. Not a bad place for the mission, he concluded as the second Comanche settled down on its landing pad, fifty meters away. The men who had fueled his aircraft were already stringing camouflage netting over it, using poles cut from the pine forest.

"Come on, let's get some food in you."

"Real food or MREs?" the chief warrant officer asked.

"You can't have everything, Mr. Richter," Checa told him.

The aviator remembered when Army C-Rations had also included cigarettes. No longer, what with the new healthy Army, and there wasn't much sense in asking a Ranger for a smoke. Damned athletes.

The Rapiers turned away an hour later, convinced, the Japanese air-defense people were sure, that they could not penetrate the Kami-Eagle line that guarded the northeast approaches to the home islands. Even the best American aircraft and best systems could not defeat what they had to face, and that was good. On their screens they watched the contacts fade off, and soon the emissions from the E-3Bs faded as well, heading back to Shemya to report their failure to their masters.

The Americans were realists. Courageous warriors, to be sure — the officers in the E-767s would not make the mistake as their forebears had of thinking that Americans lacked the ardor for real combat operations. That error had been a costly one. But war was a technical exercise, and they had allowed their strength to fall below a line from which recovery was not technically possible. And that was too bad for them.

The Rapiers had to tank on the way back, and didn't use their supercruise ability, because wasting fuel was not purposeful. The weather was again crummy at Shemya, and the fighters rode down under positive ground-control to their safe landings, then taxied off to their hangars, which were more crowded now with the arrival of four F-15E Strike Eagles from Mountain Home Air Force Base in Idaho. They also regarded the mission as a success.

42

Lightning Strikes

"Are you mad?" Scherenko asked.

"Think about it," Clark said, again back in the Russian Embassy. "We want a political solution to this, don't we? Then Koga's our best chance. You told us the government didn't put him in the bag. Who does that leave? He's probably right there." You could even see the building out Scherenko's window, as luck would have it.

"Is it possible?" the Russian asked, worried that the Americans would ask for assistance that he was quite unsuited to provide.

"There's a risk, but it's unlikely he has an army up there. He wouldn't be keeping the guy there unless he wanted to be covert about it. Figure five or six people, max."

"And two of you!" Scherenko insisted.

"Like the man said," Ding offered with a very showy smile, "no big deal."

So the old KGB file was true. Clark was not a real intelligence officer, but a paramilitary type, and the same was true of his arrogant young partner who mostly just sat there, looking out the window.

"I can offer you nothing by way of assistance."

"How about weapons?" Clark asked. "You going to tell me you don't have anything here we can use?

What kind of *rezidentura* is this?" Clark knew that the Russian would have to temporize. Too bad that these people weren't trained to take much initiative.

"I need permission before I can do any of that."

Clark nodded, congratulating himself on making a good guess. He opened his laptop computer. "So do we. You get yours. I'll get mine."

Jones stubbed out his cigarette in the Navy-style aluminum ashtray. The pack had been stuck away in a desk drawer, perhaps in anticipation of just such an occasion as this. When a war started, the peacetime rules went out the window. Old habits, especially bad ones, were easy to fall back into — but then that's what war was, too, wasn't it? He could also see that Admiral Mancuso was wavering on the edge of bumming one, and so he made sure the butt was all the way out.

"What do you have, Ron?"

"You take the time to work this gear and you get results. Boomer and me have been tweaking the data all week. We started on the surface ships." Jones walked to the wall chart. "We've been plotting the position of the 'cans — "

"All the way from — " Captain Chambers interrupted, only to be cut off.

"Yes, sir, all the way from mid-Pac. I've been playing broadband and narrow-band, and checking weather, and I've plotted them." Jones pointed at the silhouettes pinned to the map.

"That's fine, Ron, but we have satellite overheads for that," ComSubPac pointed out.

"So am I right?" the civilian asked.

"Pretty close," Mancuso admitted. Then he pointed to the other shapes pinned to the wall.

"Yeah, that's right, Bart. Once I figured how to track the 'cans, then we started working on the submarines. And guess what? I can still bag the fuckers when they snort. Here's your picket line. We get them about a third of the time by my reckoning, and the bearings are fairly constant."

The wall chart showed six firm contacts. Those silhouettes were within circles between twenty and thirty miles in diameter. Two more were overlaid with question marks.

"That still leaves a few unaccounted for," Chambers noted.

Jones nodded. "True. But I got six for sure, maybe eight. We can't get good cuts off the Japanese coast. Just too far. I'm plotting merchantmen shuttling back and forth to the islands, but that's all," he admitted. "I'm also tracking a big two-screw contact heading west toward the Marshalls, and I kinda noticed that there's an empty dry dock across the way this morning."

"That's secret," Mancuso pointed out with a quiet smile.

"Well, if I were you guys, I'd tell *Stennis* to watch out for this line of SSKs, gentlemen. You might want to let the subs head into the briarpatch first, to clean things out, like."

"We can do that, but I'm worried about the others," Chambers admitted.

"Conn, sonar."

"Conn, aye." Lieutenant Ken Shaw had the midwatch.

"Possible sonar contact bearing zero-six-zero . . . probably a submerged contact . . . very faint, sir," the sonar chief reported.

The drill was automatic after all the practice they'd undergone on the trips from Bremerton and Pearl. The fire-control-tracking party immediately started a plot. A tech on the ray-path analyzer took data directly from the sonar instruments and from that tried to determine the probable range to the target.

971

The computer required only a second.

"That's a direct-path signal, sir. Range is under twenty thousand yards."

Dutch Claggett hadn't really been asleep. In the way of captains, he'd been lying in his bunk, eyes closed, even dreaming something meaningless and confusing about a day fishing on the beach with the fish behind him on the sand and creeping closer to his back, when the call had gone out from sonar. Somehow he'd come completely awake, and was now in the attack center, standing barefoot in his underwear. He checked the room to determine depth, course, and speed, then headed into sonar to get his own look at the instruments.

"Talk to me, Chief."

"Right here on the sixty-hertz line." The chief tapped the screen with his grease pencil. It came and went and came and went, but kept coming back, just a series of dots trickling down the screen, all on the same frequency line. The bearing was changing slowly right to left.

"They've been at sea for more than three weeks . . ." Claggett thought aloud.

"Long time for a diesel boat," the chief agreed. "Maybe heading back in for refueling?"

Claggett leaned in closer, as though proximity to the screen would make a difference. "Could be. Or maybe he's just changing position. Makes sense that they'd have a patrol line offshore. Keep me posted."

"Aye, Cap'n."

"Well?" Claggett asked the tracking party.

"First cut on range is fourteen thousand yards, base course is westerly, speed about six knots."

The contact was easily within range of his ADCAP torpedoes, Claggett saw. But the mission didn't allow him to do anything about it. Wasn't that just great?

"Let's get two weapons warmed up," the Captain said. "When we have a good track on our friend,

972

we evade to the south. If he closes on us, we try to keep out of his way, and we can shoot only if there's no choice." He didn't even have to look around to know what his crewmen thought of that. He could hear the change in how they breathed.

"What do you think?" Mary Pat Foley asked.

"Interesting," Jack said after a moment's contemplation of the fax from Langley.

"It's a long-ball opportunity." This was the voice of Ed Foley. "But it's one hell of a gamble."

"They're not even sure he's there," Ryan said, rereading the signal. It bore all the marks of something from John Clark. Honest. Decisive. Positive. The man knew how to think on his feet, and though often a guy at the bottom of the food chain, he tended to see the big picture very clearly from down there. "I have to go upstairs with this one, guys."

"Don't trip on the way," MP advised with a smile he could almost hear. She was still a cowgirl on field operations. "I recommend a *Go-Mission* on this one."

"And you, Ed?" Jack asked.

"It's a risk, but sometimes you go with what the guy in the field says. If we want a political resolution for this situation, well, then we have to have a tame political figure to lean on. We need the guy, and this might be our only way to get him out alive." The National Security Advisor could hear the gritted teeth on the other end of the STU-6 circuit. Both the Foleys were true to form. More importantly, they were in agreement.

"I'll be back to you in twenty minutes." Ryan switched over to his regular phone. "I need to see the Boss right now," he told the President's executive secretary.

The sun was rising for yet another hot, windless day. Admiral Dubro realized that he was losing weight. The waistband on his khaki trousers was looser than usual, and he had to reef in his belt a little more. His two carriers were now in regular contact with the Indians. Sometimes they came close enough for a visual, though more often some Harrier's look-down radar just took a snapshot from fifty or so miles away. Worse, his orders were to let them see his ships. Why the *hell* wasn't he heading east for the Straits of Malacca? There was a real war to fight. He'd come to regard the possible Indian invasion of Sri Lanka as a personal insult, but Sri Lanka wasn't U.S. territory, and the Marianas were, and his were the only carriers Dave Seaton had.

Okay, so the approach wouldn't exactly be covert. He had to pass through one of several straits to reenter the Pacific Ocean, all of them about as busy as Times Square at noon. There was even the off-chance of a sub there, but he had ASW ships, and he could pounce on any submarine that tried to hinder his passage. But his orders were to remain in the IO, and to be *seen* doing so.

The word was out among the crew, of course. He hadn't made even a token effort to keep things quiet. It would never have worked in any case, and his people had a right to know what was going on, in anticipation of entering the fray. They needed to know, to get their backs up, to generate an extra determination before shifting from a peacetime mentality to that of a shooting war — but once you were ready, you had to *do* it. And they weren't.

The result was the same for him as for every other man or woman in the battle force: searing frustration, short temper, and a building rage. The day before, one of his Tomcat drivers had blown *between* two Indian Harriers, with perhaps ten feet of separation, just to show them who knew how to fly and who didn't, and while that had probably put the fear of God into the visitors, it wasn't terribly professional

. . . even though Mike Dubro could remember what it was like to be a lieutenant, junior grade, and could also imagine himself doing the same thing. That hadn't made the personal dressing-down any easier. He'd had to do it, and had also known afterward that the flight crew in question would go back to their quarters muttering about the dumb old fart on the flag bridge who didn't know what it was like to drive fighter planes, 'cause the Spads he'd grown up with had probably used windup keys to get off the boat . . .

"If they take the first shot, we're going to get hurt," Commander Harrison observed after announcing that *their* dawn patrol had shown up right on schedule.

"If they put an Exocet into us, we'll pipe 'Sweepers, man your brooms,' Ed." It was a lame attempt at humor, but Dubro didn't feel very humorous at the moment.

"Not if they get lucky and catch a JP bunker." Now his operations officer was turning pessimistic. *Not good,* the battle-force commander thought.

"Show 'em we care," Dubro ordered.

A few moments later the screening ships lit off their fire-control radars and locked on to the Indian intruders. Through his binoculars Dubro could see that the nearest Aegis cruiser had white missiles sitting in her launch rails, and then they trained out, as did the target-illumination radars. The message was clear: *Keep away.*

He could have ordered another wrathful dispatch to Pearl Harbor, but Dave Seaton had enough on his plate, and the real decisions were being made in Washington by people who didn't understand the problem.

"Is it worth doing?"

"Yes, sir," Ryan replied, having come to his own conclusion on the walk to the President's office. It meant putting two friends at additional risk, but that was their job, and making the decision was his — partly anyway. It was easy to say such things, even knowing that because of them he'd sleep badly if at all. "The reasons are obvious."

"And if it fails?"

"Two of our people are in grave danger, but — "

"But that's what they're for?" Durling asked, not entirely kindly.

"They're both friends of mine, Mr. President. If you think I like the idea of — "

"Settle down," the President said. "We have a lot of people at risk, and you know what? *Not* knowing who they are makes it harder instead of easier. I've learned that one the hard way." Roger Durling looked down at his desk, at all the administrative briefing papers and other matters that didn't have the first connection to the crisis in the Pacific but had to be handled nonetheless. The government of the United States of America was a huge business, and he couldn't ignore any of it, no matter how important some area might have suddenly become. Did Ryan understand that?

Jack saw the papers, too. He didn't have to know what they were, exactly. None had classified cover sheets on them. They were the ordinary day-to-day crap that the man had to deal with. The Boss had to time-share his brain with so many tasks. It hardly seemed fair, especially for someone who hadn't exactly gone looking for the job. But that was destiny at work, and Durling had voluntarily undertaken the Vice President's office because his character required service to others, as, indeed, did Ryan's. They really were two of a kind, Jack thought.

"Mr. President, I'm sorry I said that. Yes, sir, I have considered the risks, but also, yes, that is their job. Moreover, it's John's recommendation. His idea, I mean. He's a good field officer, and he knows both

976

the risks and the potential rewards. Mary Pat and Ed agree, and also recommend a Go on this one. The decision necessarily is yours to make, but those are the recommendations."

"Are we grasping at straws?" Durling wanted to know.

"Not a straw, sir. Potentially a very strong branch."

"I hope they're careful about it."

"Oh, this is just great," Chavez observed. The Russian PSM automatic pistol was of .215 caliber, smaller in diameter even than the .22 rimfire that American kids — at least the politically incorrect ones — learned to shoot at Boy Scout camps. It was also the standard sidearm of the Russian military and police forces, which perhaps explained why the Russian criminal element had such contempt for the local cops.

"Well, we do have our secret weapon out in the car," Clark said, hefting the gun in his hand. At least the silencer improved its balance somewhat. It was renewed proof of something he'd thought for years. Europeans didn't know beans about handguns.

"We're going to need it, too." The Russian Embassy did have a pistol range for its security officers. Chavez clipped a target to the rack and cranked it downrange.

"Take the suppressor off," John said.

"Why?" Ding asked.

"Look at it." Chavez did, and saw that the Russian version was filled with steel wool. "It's only good for five or six shots."

The range did have ear protectors, at least. Clark filled a magazine with eight of the bottle-necked rounds, pointed downrange, and fired off three shots. The gun was quite noisy, its high-powered cartridge driving a tiny bullet at warp speed. He longed for a suppressed .22 automatic. Well, at least it was accurate.

977

Scherenko watched in silence, angered at the Americans' distaste for his country's weapons and embarrassed because they might well be right. He'd learned to shoot years before, and hadn't shown much aptitude for it. It was a skill rarely used by an intelligence officer, Hollywood movies notwithstanding. But it was clearly not true of the Americans, both of whom were hitting the bull's-eye, five meters away, firing pairs of shots called "double-taps" in the business. Finished, Clark cleared his weapon, reloaded a magazine, and took another, which he filled and slid into a back pocket. Chavez did the same.

"If you ever come to Washington," Ding observed, "we'll show you what we use."

"And the 'secret weapon' you mentioned?" Scherenko asked the senior man.

"It's a secret." Clark headed for the door, with Chavez in his wake. They had all day to wait for their chance, if that was what it was, and get their nerves even more frayed.

It was a characteristically stormy day at Shemya. Sleet driven by a fifty-knot gale pelted the base's single runway and the noise threatened to disturb the sleep of the fighter pilots. Inside the hangars, the eight fighter aircraft were crammed together to protect them from the elements. It was especially necessary for the F-22s, as no one had yet fully determined what damage the elements could do to their smooth surfaces, and thus the radar cross section. This was not the time to find out. The storm's precipitation should pass in a few hours, the weather weenies said, though the gale-force winds could well last another month. Outside, the ground crews worried about the tie-downs on the tanker and AWACS birds, and struggled around in bulky cold-weather gear to make certain everything was secure.

The other aspects of base-security were handled

978

at the Cobra Dane array. Though it looked like the screen from an old drive-in theater, it was in fact a massive version of the solid-state radar array used by the Japanese E-767s, or for that matter the Aegis cruisers and destroyers in both contending navies. Originally emplaced to monitor Soviet missile tests and later to do SDI research, it was powerful enough to scan thousands of miles into space, and hundreds in the atmosphere. Its electronic probes swept constantly now, searching for intruders, but so far finding only commercial airliners — but those were watched very closely indeed. An F-15E Strike Eagle loaded with air-to-air missiles could be sent aloft in ten minutes if one of them looked the least bit dangerous.

The dreary routine continued through the day. For a brief few hours there was enough gray illumination through the clouds to suggest that the sun might be up, in a theoretical sense, but by the time the pilots were roused, the view out the windows of their quarters might as well have been painted black, for even the runway lights were out, lest they give some unwelcome visitor a visual aid in finding the base through the gloom.

"Questions?"

The operation had been planned rapidly but carefully, and the four lead pilots had taken a hand in it, then tested it the night before, and while there were risks, well, hell, there always were.

"You Eagle jocks think you can handle this?" the most senior Rapier driver asked. He was a lieutenant colonel, which didn't protect him from the reply.

"Don't worry, sir," a major said. "It's such a *nice* ass to look at." Then she blew a kiss.

The Colonel, actually an engineering test pilot pulled away from developmental work under way on the F-22 with the 57th Weapons Wing at Nellis Air Force Base, knew the "old" Air Force only from the movies and stories he'd heard when he'd been a youngster coming up the line, but he took the insult in the spirit in which it had been offered. The Strike Eagles might not be stealthy, but they were pretty damned mean. They were about to engage in a combat mission, and rank didn't matter as much as competence and confidence.

"Okay, people" — once he would have just said *men* — "we're time-critical on this one. Let's get it on."

The tanker crews chuckled to themselves about the fighter-jock mentality, and how the women in the Air Force had really bought into it. The Major was a dish, one of them thought. Maybe when she grew up she could come and fly United, he observed to the captain who'd be right-seating for him.

"A man could do worse," the Southwest Airlines first officer noted. The tankers got off twenty minutes later, followed by one of the E-3Bs.

The fighters, typically, went off last. The crews all wore their cold-weather nomex flight-suits and made the proper gestures about survival gear, which was really a joke over the North Pacific this time of year, but rules were rules. G-suits went on last of all, uncomfortable and restrictive as they were. One by one, the Rapier drivers walked to their birds, the Eagle crews two-by-two. The colonel who'd lead the mission ostentatiously tore off the Velcro RAPIER patch and replaced it with the counterculture one Lockheed employees had made up, the silhouette of the original P-38 Lightning overlaid with the graceful profile of the company's newest steed, and further decorated with a white-yellow thunderbolt. Tradition, after all, the Colonel thought, even though he hadn't been born until the last of the twin-boom -38s had been sold to the strippers. He did remember building models of the first American long-range fighter, used only one time for their actual designed purpose, for which a driver named Tex Lamphier had won a little immortality. This one would not be terribly different from that day over the northern Solomons.

The fighters had to be towed out into the open, and even before they started engines, every crew member could feel the wind buffeting the fighters. It was the time when the fingers tingle on the controls and the pilots shift around a little in the seats to make everything just so. Then, one by one, the fighters lit off and taxied down to the runway's edge. The lights came back on, blue parallel lines stretching off into the gloom, and the fighters lifted off singly, a minute apart, because paired takeoffs in these weather conditions were too dangerous, and this wasn't a night for unnecessary mistakes. Three minutes later, the two flights of four formed up over the top of the clouds, where the weather was clear, with bright stars and the multicolored aurora to their right, curtains of changing colors, greens and purples as the stellar wind affected charged particles in the upper atmosphere. The curtain effect was both lovely and symbolic to the Lightning pilots.

The first hour was routine, the two quartets of aircraft cruising southwest, their anticollision lights blinking away to give visual warning of the close proximity. Systems checks were performed, instruments monitored, and stomachs settled as they approached the tanker aircraft.

The tanker crews, all reservists who flew airliners in civilian life, had taken care to locate smooth-weather areas, which the fighter drivers appreciated even though they deemed everyone else second best. It took more than forty minutes to top off everyone's fuel tanks, and then the tankers resumed their orbit, probably so that their crews could catch up on their *Wall Street Journal*s, the fighter pilots all thought, heading southwest again.

Things changed now. It was time for business. Their kind.

Sandy Richter drew the mission, of course, because it had been his idea from the start, months before at Nellis Air Force Base. It had worked there, and all he had to figure out was whether it would work here as well. On that he was probably betting his life.

Richter had been in that business since he was seventeen — when he'd lied about his age and gotten away with it, being large and tough. Along the way, he'd corrected his official package, but he was still in his twenty-ninth year of service and soon to retire to a quieter life. All that time, Richter had driven snakes and only snakes. If a helicopter didn't carry weapons, then he wasn't interested. Starting with the AH-1 Huey Cobra, he had in time graduated to the AH-64 Apache and driven it into his second, briefer war in the skies over the Arabian Peninsula. Now with the last bird he would ever fly, he started the engines on the Comanche and began his 6,751st hour of flight, according to the log book.

The twin turboshaft engines spun up normally and the rotor began its rotation. The ersatz ground crew of Rangers were hamming it up with the one fire extinguisher they had. It was about large enough to put out a cigarette, Richter thought crossly as he increased power and lifted off. The thin mountain air had a negative effect on performance, but not that much, and he'd soon be down at sea level anyway. The pilot gave his head the usual shake to make sure the helmet was securely in place and headed eastward, tracing up the wooded slopes of Shiraishi-*san*.

"There they are," the lead -22 pilot said to himself. The first sign was chirping in his headset, immediately followed by information on his threat receiver: AIR

982

DEFENSE RADAR, AIRBORNE, TYPE J, BEARING 213. Next came data linked over from the E-3B, which had been in place long enough to plot its location. The Sentry wasn't using its radar at all tonight. After all, the Japanese had taught the Americans a lesson the night before, and they needed time to absorb such lessons . . . RANGE TO TARGET 1 456 MILES. Still well under the horizon from the Japanese aircraft, he gave his first vocal command of the mission.

"Lightning Lead to Flight. Split into elements, now!"

Instantly, the two sets of four aircraft divided into pairs, separated by two thousand yards. In both cases the F-22s held the lead, and in both cases the trailing F-15Es tucked in dangerously close to create a radar overlap. The colonel in command flew as straight and level as his practiced skills allowed, and he smiled to himself at the memory of the major's remark. Nice ass, eh? She was the first woman to fly with the Thunderbirds. Strobe lights went off, and he hoped that the low-light gear she was wearing was working properly. The northern E-767 was now four hundred miles away. The fighters cruised in at five hundred knots, altitude thirty-five thousand feet for fuel economy.

The work schedule typical of Japanese executives made the entry less obvious than would have been the case in America. A man was in the lobby, but he was watching TV, and Clark and Chavez walked through as though they knew where they were going, and crime was not a problem in Tokyo anyway. Breathing a little rapidly, they got into an elevator and punched a button, trading a relieved look that soon changed to renewed apprehension. Ding was carrying his briefcase. Clark was not, and both were dressed in their best suits and ties and white shirts, looking for all the world like businesspeople coming in for a late night's conference on something or other.

The elevator stopped five floors from the top, a level selected because of the lack of lights in the windows. Clark stuck his head out, knowing that it looked vaguely criminal to do so, but the corridor was empty.

They moved quickly and quietly around the central bearing core of the building, found the fire stairs, and started to climb. They looked for security cameras, and again, thankfully, there were none on this level. Clark checked up and down. No one else was in the stairwell. He continued to head up, looking and listening before every movement.

"Our friends are back," one of the airborne controllers announced over the intercom. "Bearing zero-three-three, range four-two-zero kilometers. One — no, two contacts, close formation, military aircraft inbound, speed five hundred knots," he concluded the announcement rapidly.

"Very well," the senior controller responded evenly, selecting the display for his screen as he switched channels on his command phones. "Any radar activity to the northeast?"

"None," the electronic-countermeasures officer replied at once. "He could be out there monitoring us, of course."

"*Wakarémas.*"

The next order of business was to release the two fighters orbiting east of the Kami aircraft. Both F-15Js had recently arrived on station, and had nearly full fuel tanks. An additional call ordered two more up from Chitose Air Base. They would need about fifteen minutes to get on station, but that was fine, the senior controller thought. He had the time.

"Lock on to them," he ordered the operator.

"Got us already, do you?" the Colonel asked himself. "Good." He held course and speed, wanting them to get a good feel for his location and activities. The rest was mainly a matter of arithmetic. *Figure the Ea-gles were now about two hundred miles away, closing speed about a thousand. Six minutes to separation.* He checked his clock and commanded his eyes to sweep the skies for something a little too bright to be a star.

There was a camera on the top level of the stairs. So Yamata was a little paranoid. But even paranoids had enemies, Clark thought, noticing that the body of the camera appeared to be pointed at the next land-ing. Ten steps to the landing, and ten more to the next, where the door was. He decided to take a mo-ment to think about that. Chavez turned the knob on the door to his right. It didn't appear to be locked. Probably fire codes, Clark thought, acknowledging the information with a nod but getting out his burglar tools anyway.

"Well, what d'ya think?"

"I think I'd rather be somewhere else." Ding had his light in his hand as John took his pistol out and screwed the suppressor in place. "Fast or slow?"

That was the only remaining choice, really. A slow approach, like people on regular business, lost, per-haps . . . no, not this time. Clark held up one finger, took a deep breath and bounded upwards. Four sec-onds later he twisted the knob at the top landing and flung the door open. John dove to the floor, his pistol out and training in on the target. Ding jumped past him, stood, and aimed his own weapon.

The guard outside the door had been looking the other way when the stairway entrance swung open. He turned in automatic alarm and saw a large man lying sideways on the floor and possibly aiming a gun at him. That caused him to reach for his own as his eyes locked on the potential targets. There was a sec-ond man, holding something else that —

At this range the light had almost a physical force. The three million candles of energy turned the entire

985

world into the face of the sun, and then the energy overload invaded the man's central nervous system along the trigeminal nerve, which runs from the back of the eye along the base of the brain, branching out through the neural network that controls the voluntary muscles. The effect, as in Africa, was to overload the guard's nervous system. He fell to the floor like a rag doll, his twitching right hand still grasping a pistol. The light was sufficiently bright that reflection from the white-painted walls dazzled Chavez slightly, but Clark had remembered to shut his eyes and raced for the double doors, which he drove apart with his shoulder.

One man was in view, just getting up from a chair in front of the TV, his face surprised and alarmed at the unannounced entry. There wasn't time for mercy. Clark brought the gun up in both hands and squeezed twice, both shots entering the man's forehead. John felt Ding's hand on his shoulder, which allowed him to move right, almost running now, down a hallway, looking into each room. *Kitchen,* he thought. *You always found people in the —*

He did. This man was almost his height, and his gun was already out as he moved for the hallway that led to the foyer, calling out a name and a question, but he, too, was a little slow, and his gun was still down, and he met a man with his pistol up and ready. It was the last thing he would ever see. Clark needed another half a minute to check out the rest of the luxury apartment, but found only empty rooms.

"Yevgeniy Pavlovich?" he called.

"Vanya, this way!"

Clark moved back left, taking a quick look at both of the men he'd killed as he did so, just to make sure, really. He knew that he'd remember these bodies, as he did all the others, knew that they'd come back to him, and he'd try to explain away their deaths, as he always did.

Koga was sitting there, remarkably pale as Chavez/ Chekov finished checking out the room. The guy in front of the TV hadn't managed to clear the pistol from his shoulder holster — probably an idea he'd gotten from a movie, Clark thought. The things were damned near useless if you needed your weapon in a hurry.

"Clear left," Chavez said, remembering to speak in Russian.

"Clear right." Clark commanded himself to calm down, looking at the guy by the TV, wondering which of the people they'd killed had been responsible for the death of Kim Norton. Well, probably not the one outside.

"Who are you?" Koga demanded with a mixture of shock and anger, not quite remembering that they had met before. Clark took a breath before answering.

"Koga-san, we are the people who are rescuing you."

"You killed them!" The man pointed with a shaking hand.

"We can speak about that later, perhaps. Will you come with us, please? You are not in danger from us, sir."

Koga wasn't inhuman. Clark admired his concern for the dead men, even though they had clearly not been friends. But it was time to get him the hell out of here.

"Which one was Kaneda?" Chavez asked. The former Prime Minister pointed to the one in the room. Ding walked over for a last look and managed not to say anything before directing his eyes to Clark, his expression one that only the two could possibly understand.

"Vanya, time to leave."

His threat receiver was going slightly nuts. The

screen was all reds and yellows, and the female voice was telling him that he'd been detected, but in this case he knew better than the computer did, Richter thought, and it was nice to know that the goddamned things didn't quite get everything right.

Just the flying part was hard enough, and though the Apache might have had the agility for the mission, it was better to be in the RAH-66. His body displayed no obvious tension. Years of practice allowed him to sit comfortably in the armored seat, his right forearm resting on the space provided while his hand worked the sidestick controller. His head traced regularly around the sky, and his eyes automatically compared the real horizon with the one generated by the sensing gear located in the aircraft's nose. The Tokyo skyline was just perfect for what he was doing. The various buildings had to be generating all manner of confusing signals for the radar aircraft he was closing on, and the best of computer systems could not defeat this sort of clutter. Better yet, he had the time to do it right.

The river Tone would take him most of the way he needed to go, and on the south side of the river was a rail line, and on the rail line was a train that would go all the way to Choshi. The train was cruising at over a hundred knots, and he took position right over it, one eye on the train below while another kept track of a moving indicator on his threat-receiver display. He held one hundred feet over the tops of the catenary towers, pacing the train exactly, just over the last car in the "consist."

"That's funny." The operator on Kami-Two noticed a blip, enhanced by the computer systems, closing in on the position of his aircraft. He keyed the intercom for the senior controller. "Possible low-level inbound," he reported, highlighting the contact and crossloading it for the crew commander.

988

"It's a train," the man replied at once, comparing the location with a map overlay. The problem with flying these damned things too close to land. The standard discrimination software, originally purchased from the Americans, had been modified, but not in all details. The airborne radar could track anything that moved, but there wasn't enough computer power in all the world to classify and display all the contacts that would develop from cars and trucks moving on the highways under the aircraft. To declutter the screens, nothing going slower than one hundred fifty kilometers per hour was passed through the computer-filtering system, but over land even that was not good enough, not over the country with the world's finest trains. Just to be sure, the senior officer watched the blip for a few seconds. Yes, it was following the mainline from Tokyo to Choshi. It couldn't possibly be a jet aircraft. A helicopter, theoretically, could do something like this, but from the weak character of the signal, it was probably just scatter off the metal roof of the train, and probably reflection off the catenary towers.

"Adjust your MTI-discriminator to two hundred," he ordered his people. It took three seconds for all of them to do that, and sure enough, that moving blip by the Tone and two other more obvious ground contacts disappeared. They had more interesting things to do, since -Two was crossloading the "take" from Kamis Four and Six and then downloading it to the Air Defense HQ just outside Tokyo. The Americans were probing their defenses again, and probably, again, with their advanced F-22s, trying to see if they could defeat the Kamis. Well, this time the reception wouldn't be quite so friendly. Eight F-15 Eagle interceptors were now up, four under the control of each E-767. If the American fighters came closer, they'd be made to pay for it.

He had to risk one open transmission, and even over an encrypted burst-channel it made the Colonel nervous, but the business entailed risks under the best of circumstances.

"Lightning Lead to flight. Separate in five — four — three — two — one — *Separate!*"

He pulled back on the stick, jerking his fighter up and away from the Strike Eagle that had spent the last half hour in his jetwash. At the same instant his right hand flipped off the radar transponder that he'd had on to boost the return signal the Japanese AEW aircraft had been taking off his aircraft. Behind and below, the F-15E and its female flight crew would be diving slightly and turning left. The Lightning climbed rapidly, in the process losing almost all of its forward velocity. The Colonel punched burners for rapid acceleration and used the thrust-vector capability of the aircraft to initiate a radical maneuver in the opposite direction, greatly speeding the separation.

The Japanese radar might or might not have gotten some sort of return off his fighter, the Colonel knew, but he knew how the radar system was working now: It was operating at high power and getting all sorts of spurious returns as a result, which the computer system had to classify before presenting them to the system controllers. In essence it did a job no different from that of human operator, albeit more quickly and efficiently, but it was not perfect, as he and the other three Lightnings were about to prove.

"Turning south," the controller reported — unnecessarily, as four separate people were now monitoring the progress of the inbounds. Neither he nor his fellows could know that the computer had noted a few ghostly returns turning north, but these had been weaker than other returns that were not moving rapidly enough to be classified as aircraft. Nor did they mimic the probable flight paths of aircraft. Then things got harder.

"Getting jamming from the inbounds."

The lead Lightning was now in a nearly vertical climb. There was danger in this, since the flight profile offered the E-767 the least stealthy aspect of the aircraft, but it was also offered no lateral motion to speak of, and so could well appear to be a ghost return, especially in the electronic clutter being generated by the powerful jammers on the Strike Eagles. In less than thirty seconds, the Lightnings tipped over to level flight at an altitude of fifty-five thousand feet. The Colonel was paying very close attention to his threat systems now. If the Japanese had him, they would show it by using their electronic scanning to hammer his fighter with radar energy . . . but they weren't. The stealthy nature of his fighter was enough that he was lost amid the trash-returns. The system caught side lobes now. The E-767 had shifted to its high-frequency fire-control mode, and was *not* targeted on him. Okay. He boosted power to supercruise, and his Lightning accelerated to a thousand miles per hour as the pilot selected fire-control mode for his HUD system.

"One o'clock high. I have him, Sandy," the backseater reported. "He even has his a/c lights on."

The train had stopped at a suburban station, and the Comanche had left it behind, cruising now at one hundred twenty knots toward the coastal town. Richter flexed his fingers one last time, looked up, and saw the aircraft's strobe lights far overhead. He was almost under it now, and good as its radar might be, it wouldn't be able to look straight down through the body of the airframe itself . . . yes, the center of his threat screen was black now.

"Here we go," he said over the intercom. He jammed his throttles to the firewall, deliberately over-spooling the engines as he pulled back sharply in the sidestick. The Comanche leaped upwards in a spiraling climb. The only real worry here was his engine temperature. They were designed to take abuse, but this would take it to the very limit. A warning indicator appeared in his helmet display, a vertical bar that started growing in height and changing color almost as rapidly as the numbers changed on the altitude display.

"Whoa," the backseater breathed, then he looked down and selected the weapons display for his screens, the better to utilize his time before going back to scanning outside. "Negative traffic."

Which figured, Richter thought. They wouldn't want people cluttering up the air around something as valuable as this target. That was fine. He could see it now, as his helicopter shot through ten thousand feet, climbing like the fighter plane it really was, rotor-driven or not.

He could see it in his targeting display now, still too far away to shoot, but there, a blip in a little box in the center of the head-up display. Time for a check. He activated his missile illumination systems. The F-22 had an LPI radar, meaning that there was a low probability of interception at the other end. That proved optimistic.

"We just took a hit," the countermeasures officer said. "We just took a high-frequency hit, bearing unknown," he went on, looking at his instruments for additional data.

"Probably a scatter from us," the senior controller said, busy now with vectoring his fighters onto the still-inbound contacts.

"No, no, frequency wasn't right for that." The officer ran another instrument check, but there was nothing else to support the odd feeling that had just turned his arms cold.

"Engine-heat warning. Engine-heat warning," the voice was telling him because he'd ignored the visual display rather blatantly, the onboard computer thought.

"I know, honey," Richter replied.

Over the Nevada desert, he'd managed a zoom-climb to twenty-one thousand feet, so far beyond the normal flight envelope of a helicopter that it had actually frightened him, Richter remembered, but that had been in relatively warm air, and it was colder here. He blazed through twenty thousand feet, still with a respectable climb rate, just as the target changed course, turning away from him. It seemed to be orbiting at about three hundred knots, probably using one engine for propulsion and the other to generate power for its radar. He hadn't been briefed on it, but it seemed reasonable enough. What mattered was that he had seconds to get within range, but the huge turbofan engines on the converted airliner were inviting targets for his Stingers.

"Just in range, Sandy."

"Roger." His left hand selected missiles from his weapons panel. The side doors on the aircraft snapped open. Attached to each of them were three Stinger missiles. With his last vestige of control, he slued the aircraft around, flipped the cover off the trigger switch, and squeezed six times. All of the missiles blazed off their rails, arcing upwards toward the aircraft two miles away. With that, Richter eased way back on the throttles and nosed over, diving and cooling his abused engines, watching the ground while his backseater followed the progress of the missiles.

The first Stinger burned out and fell short. The remaining five did better, and though two of them lost power before reaching the target, four of them found it, three to the right engine and one to the left.

"Hits, multiple hits."

The E-767, at low speed, didn't have much of a chance. The Stingers had small warheads, but the civilian-spec engines on the aircraft were poorly designed to deal with damage. Both immediately lost power, and the one that had actually been powering the aircraft came apart first. Fragments of turbine blades exploded through the safety casing and ripped into the right wing, severing the flight controls and destroying aerodynamic performance. The converted airliner rolled immediately right, and did not recover, its flight crew surprised at the unannounced disaster and quite unable to deal with it. Half of the starboard wing separated from the aircraft almost at once, and on the ground, radar operators saw the alphanumeric display marking the position of Kami-Two flip to the emergency setting of 7711 and then simply disappear.

"That's a hard kill, Sandy."

"Roger." The Comanche was falling rapidly now, heading toward the clutter of the coast. Engine temps were back to normal, and Richter hoped he hadn't done them permanent harm. As for the rest, he'd killed people before.

"Kami-Two just dropped off the air," the communications officer reported.

"What?" the senior controller asked, distracted by his intercept mission.

"Garbled call, explosion, something like that, then the data links just dropped off."

"Stand by, I have to vector my Eagles in."

It had to be getting twitchy for the 15-Echoes, the Colonel knew. Their job for the moment was to be

994

bait, to draw the Japanese Eagles out farther over the water while the Lightnings went in behind them to chop down their AEW support and spring the trap. The good news for the moment was that the third E-767 had just gone off the air. So the other side of the mission had happened as planned. That was nice for a change. And so, for the rest . . .

"Two, this is lead, executing, now!" The Colonel flipped his illumination radars on, twenty miles from the orbiting AEW aircraft. Next he opened the weapons-bay doors to give the AMRAAM missiles a chance to see their quarry. Both One and Two had acquisition, and he triggered both off. "Fox-Two, Fox-Two on the North Guy with two Slammers!"

The opening of the weapons bay instantly made the Lightnings about as stealthy as a tall building. Blips appeared on five different screens, along with additional warnings as to the speed and heading of the newly discovered aircraft. The additional word from the countermeasures officer was the final voice of doom.

"We're being illuminated at very close range, bearing zero-two-seven!"

"What? Who is that?" He had problems of his own, with his Eagles about to launch missiles at the incoming Americans. Kami-Six had just switched to fire-control mode, to allow the interceptors to fire in the blind-launch mode, as they'd done with the B-1 bombers. He couldn't stop that now, the senior officer told himself.

The last warning was far too late for counteraction. Just five miles out, the two missiles switched on their own homing radars. They were coming in at Mach-3+, driven by solid-fuel rocket motors toward a huge radar target, and the AIM-120 AMRAAM, known to its users as the Slammer, was one of the new generation of brilliant weapons. The pilot finally got the word, listening in to the countermeasures channel. He rolled his aircraft left, attempting a nearly impossible split-S dive that he knew was a waste of effort because at the last second he saw the yellow glow of rocket exhaust.

"Kill," Lightning Lead whispered to himself. "Lightning Flight, this is lead. North Guy is down."

"Lead, this is Three, South Guy is down," he heard next.

And now, the Colonel thought, using a particularly cruel Air Force euphemism, it was time to kill some baby seals. The four Lightnings were between the Japanese coast and eight F-15J Eagle interceptors. To seaward of them, the F-15E Strike Eagles would be turning back in, lighting off their own radars and loosing their own AMRAAMs. Some would make kills, and the Japanese fighters that survived them would run for home, right into his flight of four.

The ground-control radars couldn't see the aerial combat taking place. It was too far out and below the radar horizon. They did see one aircraft racing for their coast, one of theirs by the transponder code. Then it stopped cold in the air, and the transponder went off. In the air-defense headquarters, data downloaded from the three dead AEW aircraft gave no clues, except for one fact — the war their country had started was now very real and had taken an unexpected turn.

43

Dancing to the Tune

"I know you're not Russians," Koga said, sitting in the back of the car with Chavez while Clark did the driving.

"Why would you think that?" John asked innocently.

"Because Yamata thinks that I have been in contact with Americans. You two are the only gaijin with whom I have spoken since this madness began. What is going on here?" the politician demanded.

"Sir, what is going on right now is that we rescued you from people who wanted you dead."

"Yamata would not be so foolish as that," Koga retorted, not yet recovered from the shock of seeing violence uncontained by the borders of a TV cabinet.

"He has started a war, Koga-san. What is your death against that?" the man in the driver's seat inquired delicately.

"So you are Americans," he persisted.

Oh, what the hell, Clark thought. "Yes, sir, we are."

"Spies?"

"Intelligence officers," Chavez preferred. "The man who was in the room with you — "

"The one *you* killed, you mean? Kaneda?"

"Yes, sir. He murdered an American citizen, a girl named Kimberly Norton, and I am actually rather happy that I took him down."

"Who was she?"

"She was Goto's mistress," Clark explained. "And when she became a political threat to your new Prime Minister, Raizo Yamata decided to have her eliminated. We came to your country just to get her home. That was all," Clark went on, telling what was partially a lie.

"None of this is necessary," Koga said discordantly. "If your Congress had just given me a chance to — "

"Sir, maybe that's right. I don't know if it is or not, but maybe it is," Chavez said. "That doesn't much matter now, does it?"

"Tell me, then, what does matter?"

"Ending this goddamned thing before too many people get hurt," Clark suggested. "I've fought in wars and they are not fun. Lots of young kids get to die before they have the chance to get married and have kids of their own, and that's bad, okay?" Clark paused before going on. "It's bad for my country, and for damned sure it's going to be worse for yours."

"Yamata thinks — "

"Yamata is a businessman," Chavez said. "Sir, you'd better understand this. He doesn't know what he's started."

"Yes, you Americans are very good at killing. I saw that myself fifteen minutes ago."

"In that case, Mr. Koga, you also saw that we left one man alive."

Clark's angry reply stopped conversation cold for several seconds. Koga was slow to realize that it was true. The one outside the door had been alive when they'd walked over his body, moaning and shuddering as though from electric shocks, but definitely alive.

"Why didn't you . . . ?"

"There was no reason to kill him," Chavez said. "I'm not going to apologize for that Kaneda bastard. He had it coming, and when I came into the room, he was reaching for a weapon, and that's tough cookies, sir. But this isn't a movie. We don't kill people for amusement, and we came in to rescue you because somebody has to end this goddamned war — okay?"

"Even then — even then, what your Congress did . . . how can my country survive economically — "

"Will it be better for anybody if the war goes on?" Clark asked. "If Japan and China kick off against Russia, what happens to you then? Who do you suppose will really pay the price for that mistake? China? I don't think so."

The first word in Washington came via satellite. One of NSA's orbiting "hitchhiker" ELINT birds happened to be overhead to record the termination of signal — that was the NSA term for it — from three AEW aircraft. Other NSA listening posts recorded radio chatter that lasted for several minutes before ending. Analysts were trying to make sense of it now, the report in Ryan's hands told him.

Only one kill, the Colonel told himself. Well, he'd have to be content with that. His wingman had bagged the last of the -15Js. The southern element had gotten three, and the Strike Eagles had gotten the other four when their support had been cut off, leaving them suddenly and unexpectedly vulnerable. Presumably the ZORRO team had gotten the third E-767. On the whole, not a bad night's work, but a long one, he thought, forming his flight of four back up for the rendezvous with the tanker and the three hours back to Shemya. The hardest part was the enforced radio silence. Some of his people had to be counting coup in a big way, full of themselves in the way of

999

fighter pilots who had done the job and lived to tell the tale, and wanting to talk through it. That would change shortly, he thought, the enforced silence forcing him to think about his first-ever air-to-air kill. Thirty people on the aircraft. Damn, he was supposed to feel *good* about a kill, wasn't he? So why didn't he?

Something interesting had just happened, Dutch Claggett thought. They were still catching bits and pieces of the SSK in their area, but whoever it was, it had turned north and away from them, allowing *Tennessee* to remain on station. In the way of submarines on patrol, he'd come close enough to the surface to put up his ESM antenna and track the Japanese radar aircraft for the past day or so, learning what he could for possible forwarding to others. Electronic-intelligence gathering had been a submarine mission since before his application to Annapolis, and his crew included two electronics techs who showed a real aptitude for it. But they'd had two on the monitoring systems that had just gone — poof! Then they'd caught some radio chatter, excited by the sound of it, and one by one those voices had gone off the air, somewhere to his north.

"You suppose we just got up on the scoreboard, Cap'n?" Lieutenant Shaw asked, expecting the Captain to know, because captains were supposed to know everything, even though they didn't.

"Seems that way."

"Conn, sonar."

"Conn, aye."

"Our friend is snorting again, bearing zero-zero-nine, probable CZ contact," the sonar chief thought.

"I'll start the track," Shaw said, heading aft for the plotting table.

"So what happened?" Durling asked.

"We killed three of their radar aircraft, and the strike force annihilated their fighter patrol." This was not a time, however, for gloating.

"This is the twitchiest part?"

Ryan nodded. "Yes, sir. We need them confused for a while longer, but for now they know something is happening. They know — "

"They know it might be a real war after all. Any word on Koga?"

"Not yet."

It was four in the morning and all three men were showing it. Koga was over the stress period, for the moment, trying to use his head instead of his emotions while his two hosts — that was how he thought of them, rather to his surprise — drove him around and wondered how smart it was to have left the one guard alive outside Yamata's condo. He would be up and moving by now? Would he call the police? Someone else? What would result from the night's adventure?

"How do I know that I can trust you?" Koga asked after a lengthy silence.

Clark's hands squeezed the wheel hard enough to leave fingerprints in the plastic. It was the movies and TV that caused dumbass questions like that. In those media, spies did all manner of complicated things in the hope of outsmarting the equally brilliant adversaries against whom they were pitted. Reality was different. You kept operations as simple as you could because even the simplest things could blow up on you, and if the other guy was so goddamned brilliant, you wouldn't even know who the hell he was; and tricking people into doing the things you wanted them to do was something that only worked if you arranged a single option for the other guy, and even then he'd often as not do something unexpected anyway.

"Sir, we just put our lives at risk for you, but,

1001

okay, don't trust us at all. I'm not dumb enough to tell you what to do. I don't know your politics well enough for that. What I'm telling you is very simple. We will be doing things — what all of them are, I do not know anyway, so I can't tell you. We want to end this war with a minimum of violence, but there will be violence. You also want the war to end, right?"

"Of course I want it to end," Koga said, his manners not helped by his fatigue.

"Well, sir, you do whatever you think is best, okay? You see, Mr. Koga, you don't have to trust us, but we sure as hell have to trust you to do what's best for your country and for ours." Clark's comment, exasperated as it was, turned out to be the best thing he could have said.

"Oh." The politician thought that one over. "Yes. That's right, isn't it?"

"Where can we drop you off?"

"Kimura's home," Koga said at once.

"Fine." Clark dredged up the location and turned the car onto Route 122 to head for it. Then he reminded himself that he'd learned one highly important thing this night, and that after getting this guy to a place of relative safety, his top priority was getting *that* information to Washington. The empty streets helped, and though he wished for coffee to keep himself alert, it was a mere forty minutes to the crowded neighborhood of diminutive tract homes where the MITI official lived. The lights were already on when they pulled up to the house, and they just let Koga out to walk to the door. Isamu Kimura answered the door and took his guest inside with a mouth almost as wide as the entrance to his home.

Who ever said these people didn't show emotion? Clark asked himself.

"Who do you suppose the leaker is?" Ding asked, still in the backseat.

"Good boy — you caught that, too."

1002

"Hey, I'm the only college graduate in the car, Mr. C." Ding opened the computer to draft the dispatch to Langley, again via Moscow.

"They did *what?*" Yamata snarled into the phone.

"This is serious." It was General Arima, and he'd just gotten the word from Tokyo himself. "They smashed our air defenses and just went away afterwards."

"How?" the industrialist demanded. Hadn't they told him that the Kami aircraft were invincible?

"They don't know how yet, but I'm telling you this is very serious. They have the ability to raid the Home Islands now."

Think, Yamata told himself, shaking his head to clear the cobwebs. "General, they still cannot invade our islands, can they? They can sting us, but they cannot really hurt us, and as long as we have nuclear weapons . . ."

"Unless they try something else. The Americans are not acting as we have been given to expect."

That remark stung the next Governor of Saipan. Today was supposed to have been the day on which he'd begin his campaign. Well, yes, he'd overestimated the effect his action would have on the American financial markets, but they *had* crippled the American fleet, and they *had* occupied the islands, and America did *not* have the ability to storm even one of the Marianas, and America did not have the political will to launch a nuclear attack on his country. Therefore they were still ahead of the game. Was it to be expected that America would not fight back somewhat? Of course not. Yamata lifted his TV controller and switched it on, catching the beginning of a CNN Headline News broadcast, and there was the American correspondent, standing right on the edge of some dock or other, and there behind her were two American carriers, still in their docks, still unable to do anything.

"What does intelligence tell us about the Indian Ocean?" he asked the General.

"The two American carriers are still there," Arima assured him. "They were seen both visually and on radar yesterday, within four hundred kilometers of Sri Lanka."

"Then they cannot really hurt us, can they?"

"Well, no, really they cannot," the General admitted. "But we must make other arrangements."

"Then I suggest you make them, Arima-san," Yamata replied in a voice so polite as to constitute a stinging insult.

The worst part was not knowing what had happened. The data links from the three dead Kami aircraft had ended with the elimination of -Two. All the rest of their information was inferred rather than actually known. Ground-based monitoring stations had copied the emissions of -Four and -Six and then seen those emissions stop within the same minute. There had been no obvious alarm for any of the three radar aircraft. They'd just stopped transmitting, leaving nothing more behind than floating debris on the rolling ocean. The fighters — well, they did have tapes of the radio conversations. It had taken less than four minutes for that. First the confident, professionally laconic comments of fighter pilots closing on targets, then a series of *What?*s, followed by hurried calls to go active with their radars, more calls that they'd been illuminated. One pilot had reported a hit, then immediately gone off the air — but a hit from *what?* How could the same aircraft that killed the Kamis have gotten the fighters, too? The Americans had only four of their expensive new F-22s. And the Kamis had been tracking those. What evil magic had . . . ? But that was the problem. They didn't know.

The air-defense specialists, and the engineers who had developed the world's finest airborne radar systems, shook their heads, looking down, feeling immense personal disgrace and not knowing why. Of the ten such aircraft built, five were destroyed, and only four others available for service, and all they knew for sure was that they couldn't risk them over water anymore. Orders were also issued to deploy the standby E-2C aircraft that the E-767s had replaced, but those were less capable American designs, and the officers had to accept the fact that somehow the air defenses of their country had been severely compromised.

It was seven in the evening, and Ryan was about to leave for home when the secure fax machine started buzzing. His phone started ringing even before paper appeared.

"Can't you people ever keep secrets?" an accented voice demanded angrily.

"Sergey? What's the problem?"

"Koga is our best chance for terminating hostilities, and someone on your side told the Japanese that he's in contact with you!" Golovko nearly shouted from his home, where it was three in the morning. "Do you want to kill the man?"

"Sergey Nikolay'ch, will you for Christ's sake settle the hell down?" Jack sat back down in his chair, and by this time he had the page to read. It had come directly from the U.S. Embassy communications people in Moscow, doubtless on orders of a sort from the RVS. "Oh, shit." Pause. "Okay, we got him out of trouble, didn't we?"

"You're penetrated at a high level, Ivan Emmetovich."

"Well, you should know how easy it is to do that."

"We're working to find out who it is, I assure you." The voice was still angry.

Wouldn't that be great? Jack thought behind painfully closed eyes. *The Russian Foreign Intelligence Service testifies in Federal District Court.*

"Not many people know this. I'll get back to you."

"I am so pleased to hear that you restrict sensitive information to such trustworthy people, Jack." The line went dead. Ryan depressed the switch and punched up another number from memory.

"Murray."

"Ryan. Dan, I need you here in a hurry." Jack's next call was to Scott Adler. Then he walked off again toward the President's office. The positive news he had to report, Ryan supposed, was that the other side had used important information clumsily. Yamata again, he was sure, acting like a businessman rather than a professional spook. He hadn't even troubled himself to disguise the information he had, not caring that it would also reveal its source. The man didn't know his limitations. Sooner or later he'd pay dearly for that weakness.

Jackson's last set of orders before heading off to the Pacific had involved ordering twelve B-1B bombers of the 384th Bomb Wing to fly east from their base in southern Kansas, first to Lajes in the Azores, staging on from there toward Diego Garcia in the Indian Ocean. The flight of ten thousand miles took more than a day, and when the aircraft arrived at the base farthest from America of any, the crews were thoroughly exhausted. The three KC-10s that brought along ground crewmen and support equipment landed soon thereafter, and the entire assembly of people was soon asleep.

"What do you mean?" Yamata demanded. It was a chilling thought. His own home had been invaded. By whom?

"I mean Koga has disappeared and Kaneda is dead.

1006

One of your security people is still alive, but all he saw was two or three *gaijin*. They disabled him and he doesn't even know how."

"What is being done?"

"It's being handled as a police matter," Kazuo Taoka told his boss. "Of course I didn't tell them about Koga."

"He must be found, and quickly." Yamata looked out the window. Luck was still with him. The call, after all, had caught him at home.

"I don't know — "

"I do. Thank you for the information." Yamata killed the line, then placed another call.

Murray hurried through White House security, having left his service pistol in his official car. His month had not been any better than the rest of the government's. He'd blown the Linders case with a rookie mistake. Brandy plus a cold medication, he said to himself yet again, wondering just what Ryan and the President would have to say to him about that. The criminal case had come apart, and his only satisfaction was that at least he had not brought a possibly innocent man to trial and further embarrassed the Bureau. Whether or not Ed Kealty was really guilty of anything was a side issue for the FBI executive. If you couldn't prove it to a jury, then the defendant was innocent, and that was that. And the man would soon be leaving government service for good. That was something, Murray told himself as a Secret Service agent conducted him not to Ryan's office, but to the one at the opposite corner of the West Wing.

"Hi, Dan," Jack said, standing when he came in.

"Mr. President," Murray said first. He didn't know the other man in the room.

"Hi, I'm Scott Adler."

"Hello, sir." Murray took his hand. Oh, that was

the guy running the negotiations with the Japs, he realized.

Some work had already been accomplished. Ryan could not believe that Adler was the leak. The only others who knew were himself, the President, Brett Hanson, Ed and Mary Pat, and perhaps a few secretaries. And Christopher Cook.

"How close are we keeping tabs on Japanese diplomats?" Ryan asked.

"They don't move around without somebody keeping an eye on them," Murray assured them. "We're talking espionage?"

"Probably. Something very important leaked out."

"It has to be Cook," Adler said. "It just has to be."

"Okay, there are some things you need to know," the National Security Advisor said. "Less than three hours ago we slam-dunked their air defenses. We think we killed ten or eleven aircraft." He could have gone further, but did not. It was still possible that Adler was the leak, after all, and the next step of Operation ZORRO had to come as a surprise.

"That's going to make them nervous, and they still have nuclear weapons. A bad combination, Jack," the Deputy Secretary of State pointed out.

Nukes? Murray thought. *Jesus.*

"Any changes in their negotiating position?" the President asked.

Adler shook his head. "None, sir. They will offer us Guam back, but they want the rest of the Marianas for themselves. They're not backing off a dot from that, and nothing I've said has shaken them loose."

"Okay." Ryan turned. "Dan, we've been in contact with Mogataru Koga — "

"He's the ex–Prime Minister, right?" Dan asked, wanting to make sure he was up to speed on this. Jack nodded.

"Correct. We have two CIA officers in Japan covered as Russians, and they met with Koga under that cover. But Koga got himself kidnapped by the guy who we think is running the whole show. He told Koga that he knew about contacts with *Americans.*"

"It has to be Cook," Adler said again. "Nobody else on the delegation knows, and Chris does my informal contacts with their number-two, Seiji Nagumo." The diplomat paused, then let his anger show. "It's just perfect, isn't it?"

"Espionage investigation?" Murray asked. Significantly, he saw, the President let Ryan handle the answer.

"Fast and quiet, Dan."

"And then?" Adler wanted to know.

"If it's him, we flip the bastard right over." Murray nodded at once on hearing the FBI euphemism.

"What do you mean, Jack?" Durling asked.

"It's a real opportunity. They think they have a good intel source, and they've shown the willingness to use the information from it. Okay," Jack said, "we can use that to our advantage. We give them some juicy information and then we stick it right up their ass."

The most immediate need was to buttress the air defenses for the Home Islands. That realization caused no small amount of thinking at Japanese defense headquarters, and most uncomfortably, it was based on partial information, not the precise sort of data that had been used to prepare the overall operational plan that the military high command was trying to stick with. The best radar warning systems their country owned were seaborne on the four Kongo-class Aegis destroyers patrolling off the northern Marianas. They were formidable ships with self-contained air-defense systems. Not quite as mobile as the E-767s, they were more powerful, however, and able to take care of themselves. Before dawn, therefore, an order was flashed out for the four-ship squadron to race north to establish a radar-picket line east of the Home Islands. After all, the U.S. Navy wasn't doing anything, and if their country's defenses came back together, there was yet a good chance for a diplomatic solution.

On *Mutsu*, Admiral Sato saw the logic of it when he receipted the signal and gave orders for his ships to go to their maximum sustained speed. Nonetheless, he was concerned. He knew that his SPY radar systems *could* detect stealthy aircraft, something the Americans had demonstrated in tests against their own, and his ships were sufficiently powerful that American aircraft would not lightly engage them. What worried him was that for the first time his country was not acting but *re*acting to American moves. That, he hoped, was temporary.

"That's interesting," Jones observed at once. The traces were only a few minutes old, but there were two of them, probably representing more than two ships in a tight formation, making noise and with a slight northerly bearing change.

"Surface ships, sure as hell," OT2/c Boomer observed. "This looks like pounding — " He stopped when Jones circled another trace in red.

"And that's a blade-rate. Thirty-plus knots, and that means warships in one big hurry." Jones walked over to the phone and called ComSubPac. "Bart? Ron. We have something here. That 'can squadron that's been operating around Pagan."

"What about it?" Mancuso asked.

"They seem to be doing a speed-run north. We have anybody up waiting for them?" Then Jones remembered several inquiries about the waters around Honshu. Mancuso wasn't telling him everything, as was to be expected for operational matters. The way he evaded the question would be the real answer, the civilian thought.

"Can you plot me a course?"

Bingo. "Give us a little while, an hour maybe? The data is still a little fuzzy, Skipper."

The voice was not overly disappointed at the answer, Jones noted. "Aye, sir. We'll keep you posted."

"Good work, Ron."

Jones replaced the phone and looked around. "Senior Chief? Let's start doing a plot on these traces." Somewhere north, he thought, somebody was waiting. He wondered who it might be, and came up with one answer.

Time was working in the opposite direction now. Hiroshi Goto opened his cabinet meeting at ten in the morning, local time, which was midnight in Washington, where his negotiators were. It was clear that the Americans were making a contest of it, though some in the room thought that it could just be a negotiating ploy, that they had to make some show of force in order to be taken seriously at the negotiating table. Yes, they had stung the air-defense people badly, but that was all. America could not and would not launch systematic attacks against Japan. The risks were too great. Japan had nuclear-tipped missiles, for one thing. For another, Japan had sophisticated air defenses despite the events of the previous night, and then there was simple arithmetic. How many bombers did America have? How many could strike at their country even if there were nothing to stop them? How long would such a bombing campaign take? Did America have the political will for it? The answers to all of these questions were favorable to their country, the cabinet members thought, their eyes still fixed on the ultimate goal, whose shining prize glittered before them, and besides, each man in this room had a patron of sorts to make sure that they took the proper spin on things. Except Goto, they knew, whose patron was elsewhere at the moment.

For the moment, the Ambassador in Washington would object strongly to the American attack on Japan, and note that it was not a helpful act, and that there would be no further concessions until they were stopped. It would be further noted that any attack on the Japanese mainland would be considered an exceedingly grave matter; after all, Japan had not attacked vital American interests directly . . . yet. That threat, behind the thinnest of veils, would surely bring some rationality to the situation.

Goto nodded agreement to the suggestions, wishing that his own patron were about to support him and knowing that Yamata had already bypassed him and spoken with defense officials directly. He'd have to talk to Raizo about that.

"And if they come back?" he asked.

"We'll have our defenses at maximum alert tonight, and when the destroyers arrive on station, they will be as formidable as before. Yes, they have made their show of force, but they have not as yet so much as flown over our territory."

"We must do more than that," Goto said, recalling his instructions. "We can put more pressure on the Americans by making our ultimate weapons public."

"No!" a minister said at once. "That will cause chaos *here!*"

"It will also cause chaos there," Goto replied, somewhat weakly, the rest of the cabinet thought. Again, they saw, he was voicing the thoughts and orders of someone else. They knew who that was. "It will force them to alter the tone of their negotiations."

"It could easily force them to consider a grave attack on us."

"They have too much to lose," Goto insisted.

"And we do not?" the Minister shot back, wondering just where his loyalty to his patron ended and his loyalty to his countrymen began. "What if they decide to preempt?"

"They cannot. They don't have the weapons to do it. Our missiles have been very carefully located."

"Yes, and our air-defense systems are invincible, too," another minister snorted.

"Perhaps the best thing to do is for our ambassador to suggest that we might reveal that we have the atomic weapons. Perhaps that would be enough," a third minister suggested. There were some nods around the table, and Goto, despite his instructions, agreed to that.

The hardest part was keeping warm, despite all the cold-weather gear they had brought along. Richter snuggled himself into the sleeping bag, and allowed himself to be vaguely guilty for the fact that the Rangers had to maintain listening outposts around the rump airfield they'd established on this frigid mountainside. His principal worry was a system failure in one of the three aircraft. Despite all the redundancies built into them, there were several items which, if they broke, could not be fixed. The Rangers knew how to fuel the birds, and how to load weapons, but that was about it. Richter had already decided to let them worry about ground security. If so much as a platoon showed up in this high meadow, they were doomed. The Rangers could kill every intruder, but one radio call could have a battalion here in hours, and there was no surviving that. Special-operations, he thought. They were good so long as they worked, just like everything else you did in uniform, but the current situation had a safety margin so thin that you could see through it. Then there was the issue of getting out, the pilot reminded himself. He might as well have joined the Navy.

"Nice house."

The rules were different in time of war, Murray

told himself. Computers made it easier, a fact that the Bureau had been slow to learn. Assembling his team of young agents, the first task had been to run nothing more sophisticated than a credit check, which gave an address. The house was somewhat upscale, but within the reach, barely, of a supergrade federal employee if he'd saved his pennies over the years. That was something Cook had not done, he saw. The man did all his banking at First Virginia, and the FBI had a man able to break into the bank records, far enough to see that, like most people, Christopher Cook had lived largely from one biweekly paycheck to the next, saving a mere fourteen thousand dollars along the way, probably for the college education of his kids, and that, Murray knew, was on the dumb side of optimistic, what with the cost of American higher education. More to the point, when he'd settled ŏn the new house, the savings had gone untouched. He had a mortgage, but the amount was less than two hundred thousand dollars, and with the hundred-eighty realized from the sale of his previous home, that left a sizable gap that bank records could not explain. Where had the other money come from? A call to a contact at the IRS, proposing a possible case of tax evasion, had turned up other computerized records, enough to show that there was no additional family income to explain it; a check of antecedents showed that the parents of both the Cooks, all deceased, had not left either husband or wife with a windfall. Their cars, a further check showed, were paid for, and while one of them was four years old, another was a Buick that probably had the original smell still inside, and that also had been purchased with cash. What they had was a man living beyond his means, and while the government had often enough failed to make note of that in espionage cases, it had learned a little of late.

"Well?" Murray asked his people.

"It's not a case yet, but it sure as hell smells like one," the next-senior agent thought. "We need to visit some banks and get a look at more records." For which a court order was required, but they already knew which judge to go to for that. The FBI always knew which judges were tame and which were not.

Similar checks, of course, had been run on Scott Adler, who, they found, was divorced, living alone in a Georgetown flat, paying alimony and child support, driving a nice car, but otherwise very normal. Secretary Hanson was quite wealthy from years of practicing law, and a poor subject for attempted bribery. The extensive background checks run on all the subjects for their government offices and security clearances were reexamined and found to be normal, except for Cook's recent auto and home purchases. Somewhere along the line they'd find a canceled check drawn on some bank or other to explain the easy house settlement. That was one nice thing about banks. They had records on everything, and it was always on some sort of paper, and it always left a trail.

"Okay, we will proceed on the assumption that he's our boy." The Deputy Assistant Director looked around at the bright group of agents who, like him, had neglected to consider the possibility that Barbara Linders had been on a prescription medication that had acted with the brandy Ed Kealty had once kept close at all times. Their collective embarrassment was as great as his own. Not an entirely bad thing, Dan thought. You worked hard to restore your credibility after a goof.

Jackson felt the hard thump of the carrier landing, then the snapping deceleration of the arrestor wire as he was pressed hard into the back-facing passenger seat of the COD. Another odious experience over, he thought. He much preferred to land on a carrier with his own hands on the controls, uncomfortable with trusting his life to some teenage lieutenant, or so they now all looked to the Admiral. He felt the aircraft turn to the right, heading off to an unoccupied portion of the flight deck, and presently a door opened and he hustled out. A deck crewman saluted, pointing him to an open door in the carrier's island structure. The ship's bell was there, and as soon as he got under cover, a Marine saluted, and a bosun's mate worked the striker on the bell, announcing into the 1-MC system, "Task Force Seventy-Seven, arriving."

"Welcome aboard, sir," Bud Sanchez said with a grin, looking very natty in his flight suit. "Captain's on the bridge, sir."

"Then let's get to work."

"How's the leg, Robby?" the CAG asked halfway up the third ladder.

"Stiff as hell after all the sitting." It had taken time. The briefing at Pearl Harbor, the Air Force flight to Eniwetok, then waiting for the C-2A to show up to bring him to his command. Jackson was beyond jet lag, but for all that, eager now, about noon, he thought, according to where the sun was.

"Is the cover story holding?" Sanchez asked next.

"No telling, Bud. Until we get there." Jackson allowed a Marine to open the door to the wheelhouse. His leg really was stiff, just one more reminder that flight operations were over for him.

"Welcome aboard, sir," the CO said, looking up from a sheaf of dispatches.

The roar of afterburners told Jackson that *Johnnie Reb* was conducting flight operations, and he looked quickly forward to see a Tomcat leap off the port-forward cat. The carrier was about halfway between the Carolines and Wake. The latter island was somewhat closer to the Marianas, and for that reason was not being used for anything. Wake had a fine airfield, still supported by the Air Force. Eniwetok was just a recovery field, known to be such, and therefore made a more covert base for staging aircraft, if a far less convenient one for maintaining them.

"Okay, what's been happening since I left Pearl?" Jackson asked.

"Some good news." The CO handed over one of the dispatches.

"It's definite as hell," Jones said, leaning over the sonar traces.

"They sure are in a hurry," Mancuso agreed, his eyes plotting speed and distance and not liking what they saw, further confirming what Jones suspected.

"Who's waiting for them?"

"Ron, we can't — "

"Sir, I can't be much help to you if I don't know," Jones observed reasonably. "You think I'm a security risk or something?"

Mancuso thought for a few seconds before answering. "*Tennessee*'s lying right overtop the Eshunadaoki Seamount, supporting a special operation that goes off in the next twenty-four hours."

"And the rest of the Ohios?"

"Just off Ulithi Atoll, heading north a little slower now. The SSN force will lead the carrier in. The Ohios are tasked to get inside early." Which all made sense, Jones thought. The boomers were too slow to operate effectively with a carrier task force, which he'd also been tracking on SOSUS, but they were ideal for getting inside a patrol line of SSKs . . . so long as the skippers were smart about it. There was always that consideration.

"The Jap 'cans will be about on top of *Tennessee* right about — "

"I know."

"What else do you have for me?" ComSubPac asked briskly.

1017

Jones led him over to the wall chart. There were now seven SSK-silhouettes circled on the display, with only one "?"- marked. That one, they saw, was in the passage between the northernmost of the Marianas, called Moug, and the Bonins, the most famous of which was Iwo Jima.

"We've been trying to concentrate on this passage," Jones said. "I've gotten a few twitches, but nothing firm enough to plot. If I were them, though, I'd cover that area."

"So would I," Chambers confirmed. One likely move for the Americans would be to put a submarine patrol line astride the Luzon Strait, to attempt to interdict oil traffic to the Japanese mainland. That was a political decision, however. Pacific Fleet did not yet have authorization to attack Japanese merchantmen, and intelligence reported that at the moment most of the tanker traffic in and out was composed of flag-of-convenience shipping, attacks on which had all sorts of political ramifications. *We couldn't risk offending Liberia,* Mancuso told himself with a grimace. *Could we?*

"Why the speed-run for the 'cans back home?" Jones asked. It was not something that appeared very sensible.

"We hammered their air defenses last night."

"Okay, so they'll scoot west of the Bonins . . . that means I'll lose them soon. Anyway, their speed of advance is thirty-two, and their course is still a little fuzzy, but homeward bound, sure as hell." Jones paused. "We're starting to play with their heads, eh?"

Mancuso allowed himself a smile for once. "Always."

44

"Does it have to be this way?" Durling asked.

"We've run the simulation twenty times," Ryan said, flipping through the data yet again. "It's a matter of certainty. Sir, we have to take them all the way out."

The President looked at the satellite overheads again. "We're still not one hundred percent sure, are we?"

Jack shook his head. "Nothing is ever that sure, no. Our data looks pretty good — the overheads, I mean. The Russians have developed data, too, and they have as much reason to want to be right as we do. There are ten birds here. They're dug in deep, and the site seems to have been selected deliberately for relative immunity from attack. Those are all positive indicators. This is not a deception operation. The next question is making sure that we can hit them all. And we have to do it quickly."

"Why?"

"Because they're moving ships back toward the coast that are marginally capable of detecting the aircraft."

"No other way?"

"No, Mr. President. If this is going to work, it has to be tonight." And the night, Ryan saw, checking his watch, had already started on the far side of the world.

"We protest in the strongest terms the American attack on our country," the Ambassador began. "We have refrained at all times from doing such things, and we expected a similar courtesy from the United States."

"Mr. Ambassador, I am not consulted on military operations. Have American forces struck your mainland?" Adler asked by way of reply.

"You know quite well what they have done, and you must also know that it is a precursor move to a full attack. It is important that you understand," the diplomat went on, "that such an attack could result in the gravest possible consequences." He let that phrase hang in the air like a cloud of lethal gas. Adler took a moment before responding.

"I would remind you first of all that we did not begin this conflict. I would further remind you that your country made a deliberate attack to cripple our economy — "

"As you have done!" the Ambassador shot back, showing real anger that might have been a cover for something else.

"Excuse me, sir, but I believe it is my turn to speak." Adler waited patiently for the Ambassador to calm down; it was plain that neither one had gotten a full night's sleep. "I would further remind you that your country has killed American servicemen, and if you expected us to refrain from corresponding moves, then you were possibly mistaken in that expectation."

"We have never attacked vital American interests."

"The freedom and security of American citizens is ultimately my country's *only* vital interest, sir."

The acrimonious change in atmosphere could hardly have been more obvious, as was the reason for it. America was making a move of some sort, and the move would clearly not be a subtle one. The people on both sides of the table, again on the top floor of the State Department, might well have been carved from stone. No one wanted to concede anything, not even a blink, at the formal sessions. Heads might have turned fractionally when the leaders of the respective delegations took their turns to speak, but no more than that. The absence of facial expressions would have done professional gamblers proud — but that was precisely the game being played, even without cards or dice. The discussions never got as far before the first recess as a return to the possession of the Marianas.

"Christ, Scott," Cook said, walking through the doors to the terrace. From the circles under his eyes, the chief negotiator, he saw, had been up most of the night, probably at the White House. The primary season would be driving this mess now. The media were harping on the crippled ships at Pearl Harbor, and TV coverage was also coming from Saipan and Guam now, people speaking with obscured faces and disguised voices — on one hand about how they wanted to be American citizens, and on the other how much they feared being on those islands if a real counterattack developed. The ambivalence was exactly the sort of thing to confuse the public, and opinion polls were divided, though with a majority expressing outrage at what had been done, and a slightly smaller majority expressing the wish for a diplomatic solution. If possible. A plurality of 46 percent, the *Washington Post*/ABC poll had stated this morning, didn't see much hope of that. The wild card, however, was the Japanese possession of nuclear arms, which had been announced by neither country, in both cases for fear of panicking the respective populations. Everyone in these sessions had really hoped for a peaceful settlement, but much of that hope had just evaporated, and in a period of a mere two hours.

"It's being politically driven now," Adler explained, looking away to let out his own tension with a long breath. "It had to happen, Chris."

"What about their nukes?"

The Deputy Secretary of State shrugged uneasily. "We don't think they're that crazy."

"We don't *think* they are? What genius came up with that assessment?" Cook demanded.

"Ryan, who else?" Adler paused. "He's running this. He thinks the next smart move is to blockade — well, declare a maritime exclusion zone, like the Brits did down at the Falklands. Cut off their oil," Adler explained.

"Nineteen forty-one all over again? I thought that bonehead was a historian! That's what *started* a world war, in case anybody forgot!"

"The threat of it — well, if Koga has the guts to speak out, we think their government'll come apart. So," Scott went on, "find out what the other side — I mean, what sort of strength the opposition really has."

"It's a dangerous game we're playing, man."

"Sure enough," Adler agreed, looking right in the man's eyes.

Cook turned and walked to the other side of the terrace. Before, it had seemed a normal part of the proceedings to Adler, part of the rubric of serious negotiations, and how stupid that had been, for the real proceedings to be handled over coffee and tea and cookies because the real negotiators didn't want to risk making statements that . . . well, those *were* the rules, he reminded himself. And the other side had made very skillful use of them. He watched the two men talk. The Japanese Ambassador looked far more uneasy than his principal subordinate. *What are you really thinking?* Adler would have killed to know that. It was too easy to think of the man as a personal enemy now, which would be a mistake. He was a professional, serving his country as he was paid and sworn to do. Their eyes met briefly, both of them deliberately looking away from Nagumo and Cook, and the professional impassivity broke for a moment, just an instant really, as both men realized that it was war they were talking about, life and death, issues imposed on them by others. It was a strange moment of comradeship as both men wondered how things had broken down so badly and how grossly their professional skills were being misused by others.

"That would be a very foolish move," Nagumo said pleasantly, forcing a smile.

"If you have a pipeline to Koga, you better start using it."

"I have, but it's too soon for that, Christopher. We need *something back.* Don't your people understand that?"

"Durling can't get reelected if he trades away thirty-some-thousand U.S. citizens." It really was that simple. "If it means killing a few thousand of your people, he'll do that. And he probably thinks that threatening your economy directly is a cheap way out."

"That would change if your people knew — "

"And how will your citizens react when they find it out?" Cook knew Japan well enough to understand that the ordinary men and women on the street regarded nuclear arms with revulsion. Interestingly, Americans had come to the same view. Maybe sense was breaking out, the diplomat thought, but not quickly enough, and not in this context.

"They will understand that those weapons are vital to our new interests," Nagumo answered quickly, surprising the American. "But you are right, it is also vital that they never be used, and we must forestall your efforts to strangle our economy. People will die if that happens."

"People are dying now, Seiji, from what your boss said earlier." With that, the two men headed back to their respective leaders.

"Well?" Adler asked

"He says he's been in contact with Koga."

That part of it was so obvious that the FBI hadn't thought of it, and then nearly had had kittens when he'd suggested it, but Adler knew Cook. He was enjoying his part in this diplomatic effort, enjoying it just a little too much, enjoying the importance he'd acquired. Even now Cook did not know what he had blurted out, just like that. Not quite definite evidence of wrongdoing, but enough to persuade Adler that Cook was almost certainly the leak, and now Cook had probably just leaked something else, though it was something Ryan had thought up. Adler reminded himself that years ago, when Ryan had just been part of an outside group brought in to review CIA procedures, he'd come to high-level attention from his invention of the Canary Trap. Well, it had been sprung again.

The weather this morning was cold enough that the delegations headed back inside a little early for the next set of talks. This one might actually go somewhere, Adler told himself.

Colonel Michael Zacharias handled the mission briefing. It was routine despite the fact that the B-2s had never fired a shot in anger — actually *dropped* a shot, but the principle held. The 509th Bomb Group dated back to 1944, formed under the command of one Colonel Paul Tibbets, U.S. Army Air Force, fittingly, the Colonel thought, at a base in Utah, his own family home. The wing commander, a brigadier, would fly the lead aircraft. The wing XO would fly number two. As deputy commander operations, he would take in number three. His was the most distasteful part of the job, but it was sufficiently important that he'd considered the rules on ethics in war and decided that the mission parameters fell within the confines that lawyers and philosophers had placed upon warriors.

It was bitterly cold at Elmendorf, and vans conveyed the flight crews to the waiting bombers. That night they would fly with crews of three. The B-2 had been designed for a pilot and copilot only, with provision for a third crewman to work defensive systems which, the contractor had promised, the copilot could do, really. But real combat operations always required a safety margin, and even before the Spirits had left Missouri, the additional three hundred pounds of gear had been added along with the additional two hundred or so pounds of electronic-warfare officer.

There was so much that was odd about the aircraft. Traditionally U.S. Air Force birds had tail numbers, but the B-2 didn't *have* a tail, and so it was painted on the door for the nose gear. A penetrating bomber, it flew at high altitude rather than low — though the contract had been altered in mid-design to allow for a low-flight profile — like an airliner for good fuel economy. One of the most expensive aircraft ever built, it combined the wingspan of a DC-10 with near-total invisibility. Painted slate gray for hiding in the night sky, it was now the shining hope for ending a war. A bomber, it was hoped that its mission would go as peacefully as possible. Strapping in, it was easier for Zacharias to think of it as a bombing mission.

The four GE engines lit off in turn, the ribbon gauges moving to full idle, already drinking fuel at the same rate as if it were at full power at cruising altitude, while the copilot and EWO checked out their onboard systems and found them good. Then, one at a time, the trio of bombers taxied off the ramp and into the runway.

"They're making it easy," Jackson thought aloud, now in the carrier's Combat Information Center, below the flight deck. His overall operational plan had allowed for the possibility, but he hadn't allowed himself to expect it. His most dangerous adversary was the four Aegis destroyers the Japanese had dispatched to guard the Marianas. The Navy had not yet learned to defeat the radar-missile combination, and he expected the job to cost him aircraft and crews, but sure enough, America now had the initiative of sorts. The other side was moving to meet his possible actions, and that was always a losing game.

Robby could feel it now. *John Stennis* was moving at full power, heading northwest at thirty knots or so. He checked his watch and wondered if the rest of the operations he'd planned in the Pentagon were going off.

This was a little different. Richter powered up his Comanche as he had the night before, wondering how often he could get away with this, and reminding himself of the axiom in military operations that the same thing rarely worked more than once. A pity that the guy who'd thought this idea up had not known that fact. His last mental lapse was to wonder whether it had been that Navy fighter jock he'd met at Nellis all those months before. Probably not, he judged. That guy was too much of a pro.

Again the Rangers stood by with their dinky little extinguishers, and again they proved unnecessary, and again Richter lifted off without incident, climbing immediately up the slopes of Shuraishi-*san*, east for Tokyo, but this time with two other aircraft behind him.

"He wants to see Durling personally," Adler said. "He said that at the end of the morning session."

1026

"What else?" Ryan asked. Typically, the diplomat had covered his business first.

"Cook's our boy. He told me that his contact has been working with Koga."

"Did you — "

"Yes, I told him what you wanted. What about the Ambassador?"

Ryan checked his watch. The timing had to be so close, and he didn't need this complication, but neither had he expected the other side to cooperate. "Give it ninety minutes. I'll clear it with the Boss."

The electronic-warfare officer also drew the duty of checking out the weapons systems. Able to carry eighty 500-pound bombs, the bomb bays were large enough for only eight of the two-thousand-pound penetrators, and 8 times 3 made 24. It was another exercise in arithmetic that made the final part of the mission necessary, which the carriage of nuclear weapons would have made entirely unnecessary, but the orders didn't contemplate that, and Colonel Zacharias didn't object. He had a conscience to live with.

"Everything's green, sir," the EWO said. Not too surprising, as every weapon had been checked out personally by a senior weapons officer, a chief master sergeant, and an engineer from the contractor, individually run through a dozen simulations, and then handled like fresh fruit all the way into the bomb bay. They had to be if they wanted to maintain the manufacturer's guaranteed P_k of 95%, though even that wasn't enough for certainty. They needed more aircraft for the mission, but there were no more aircraft to be had, and working three Spirits together was tricky enough.

"Starting to get some fuzz, bearing two-two-five. Looks like an E-2 for starters," the EWO reported. Ten minutes later it was clear that every ground-based radar in the country was lit up to full power. Well, that's why they'd built the thing, all three members of the crew thought.

"Okay, give me a course," Zacharias ordered, checking his own screen.

"One-nine-zero looks good for the moment." The instruments identified every radar by type, and the smartest move was to exploit the oldest of them, happily enough an American design whose characteristics they knew quite well.

Forward of the B-2s, the Lightnings were working again, this time alone and covertly, approaching Hokkaido from the east while the bombers behind took a more southerly course. The exercise was more mental than physical now. One of the E-767s was up, this time well back over land, and probably with fighters in close attendance while the less capable E-2Cs patrolled just offshore. They'd be working the fighter pilots hard now, and sure enough, his threat receiver showed that some Eagles were searchlighting their APG-70 radars around the sky. *Well, time to make them pay for that.* His two-plane element turned slightly right and headed for the two nearest Eagles.

Two were still on the ground, one of them with a scaffolding around the radome. Maybe that was the one undergoing overhaul, Richter thought, approaching cautiously from the west. There were still hills to hide behind, though one of them had a radar on it, a big, powerful air-defense system. His onboard computer plotted a null-area for him, and he flew lower to follow that in. He ended up three miles from the radar site, but below it, and then it was time to do what the Comanche was designed for.

Richter lifted up over the final hilltop, and his Longbow radar swept the area before him. Its computerized memory selected the two E-767s from its library of hostile shapes and lit them up on the weapons display. The touch screen at Richter's left knee showed them as icons numbered 1 and 2 and identified as what they were. The pilot selected Hellfire from his short list of weapons options, the weapons-bay doors opened, and he fired twice. The Hellfire missiles roared off the rails, heading downhill toward the air base, five miles away.

Target Four was an apartment building, happily the top floor. ZORRO-Three had taken a southerly route into the city, and now its pilot slewed his helicopter sideways, worried about being spotted from the ground but wanting to find a window with a light on. There. Not a light, the pilot thought. More like a TV. Good enough in any case. He used the manual-guidance mode to lock on the spot of blue light.

Kozo Matsuda now wondered how he'd gotten into this mess in the first place, but the answer always came up the same. He'd overextended his business, and then been forced to ally himself with Yamata — but where was his friend now? Saipan? Why? They needed him here. The Cabinet was getting nervous, and though Matsuda had his man in that room to do what he was told to do, he'd learned a few hours earlier that the ministers were thinking on their own now, and that wasn't good — but neither were recent developments. The Americans had breached his country's defenses to some extent, a most unwelcome surprise. Didn't they understand that the war had to be ended, the Marianas secured once and for all, and America forced to accept the changes? It seemed that power was the only thing they understood, but while Matsuda and his colleagues had thought that they had the ability to employ power, the Americans weren't intimidated the way they were supposed to be.

What if they . . . what if they don't *cave in?* Yamata-san had assured them all that they had to, but he'd assured them also that he could wreak chaos in their financial system, and somehow the bastards had reversed that more adroitly than one of Mushashi's swordfights, such as he was now watching on late-night TV. There was no way out now. They had to see it through or they would all face a ruin worse than what his . . . faulty judgment had almost inflicted on his conglomerate. Faulty judgment? Matsuda asked himself. Well, yes, but he'd weathered that by allying himself with Yamata, and if his colleague would only return to Tokyo and help them all keep the government in line, then maybe —

The channel on the TV changed. Odd. Matsuda picked up the controller and changed it back. Then it changed again.

Fifteen seconds out, the pilot of ZORRO-Three activated the infrared laser used to guide the antitank missile in for terminal flight. His Comanche was in autohover now, allowing him essentially to hand-fly the weapon. It never occurred to him that the infrared beam of the laser was on the same frequency as the simple device his kids used at home to switch from Nickelodeon to the Disney Channel.

Damn the thing! Matsuda flipped the channel back a third time, and still it reverted back to a news broadcast. He hadn't seen this movie in years, and what was wrong with the damned TV? It was even one of his own large-screen models. The industrialist got out of bed and walked over to it, aiming the channel-controller right at the receptor on the front of the TV. And it changed again.

"Bakayaro!" he growled, kneeling down in front of it and changing the channel manually, and yet once more it flipped back to the news. The lights were out in his bedroom, and at the last second Matsuda saw a yellow glow on the screen of the TV. A reflection? Of what? He turned to see a yellow semicircle of flame approaching his window, a second or so before the Hellfire missile struck the steel I-beam just next to his bed.

ZORRO-Three noted the explosion on the top floor of the apartment building, turned abruptly left, and tracked in on the next target. This was really something, the pilot thought, better even than his minor part in Task Force NORMANDY, six years before. He'd never really wanted to be a snake-eater, but here he was, doing their work. The next shot was similar to the first. He had to blink his eyes clear, but he was sure that anyone within twenty meters of the missile hit would not have lived to tell the tale.

The first Hellfire took the plane with crewmen around it. Mercifully it hit the E-767 right on the nose, and the explosion may have spared some of them, Richter thought. The second missile, like the first guided exclusively by the computer, blew the tail off the other one. Japan was down to two of the things now, both probably aloft somewhere, and he couldn't do anything about that. They wouldn't even come back here, but to make sure of it, Richter turned, selected his cannon, and strafed the air-defense radar site on the way out.

Binichi Murakami was just leaving the building after a lengthy chat with Tanzan Itagake. He would meet with his friends in the Cabinet tomorrow and counsel them to stop this madness before it grew too late. Yes, his country had nuclear missiles, but they had been built in the expectation that their mere existence would be sufficient to prevent their use. Even the thought of revealing their presence on his country's soil — rock, as it turned out — threatened to destroy the political coalition that Goto had in place, and he understood now that you could order political figures only so far before they realized that they did have power of a sort.

A beggar in the street was the thought that kept coming back. But for that, he might not have been swayed by Yamata's arguments. But for that, he tried to tell himself. Then the sky turned white over his head. Murakami's bodyguard was next to him and flung him to the ground next to the car while glass rained on them. The sound of the event had hardly passed before he heard the echoes of another several kilometers away.

"What is this?" he tried to ask, but when he moved, he felt liquid on his face, and it was blood from his employee's arm, slashed open from glass. The man bit his lip and kept his dignity, but he was badly hurt. Murakami helped him into the car and ordered his driver to head for the nearest hospital. As the man nodded at the order, yet another flash appeared in the sky.

"Two more baby seals," the Colonel said quietly to himself. He'd gotten within five miles before launching his Slammers from behind them, and only one of the Eagles had even attempted to evade, that one too late, though the pilot punched out and was now floating to the ground. That was enough for now. He turned his Lightning northeast and headed out at Mach 1.5. His flight of four had slashed a hole in the Hokkaido defenses, and behind them the Japanese Air Force would move aircraft to plug the gap, fulfilling his mission for the night. For years the Colonel had told everyone who would listen that combat wasn't about fairness, and he'd laughed at the cruel euphemism for a stealthy aircraft in combat against a conventional plane. Killing baby seals. But they weren't seals, and it was the next thing to murder, and the officer raged at the necessity for what he was doing.

The EWO had steered them between two air-defense radars, and within a hundred miles of an orbiting E-2C. There was all manner of radio chatter, terse and excited, from ground stations to fighters, all to their north now. Landfall was over a town named Arai. The B-2A was at forty-three thousand feet, cruising smoothly at just under six hundred knots. Under the first layer of the fabric-based skin, a copper mesh absorbed much of the electronic energy now sweeping over their aircraft. It was part of the stealth design to be found in any high-school physics book. The copper filaments gathered in much of the energy, much like a simple radio antenna, converting it to heat that dissipated in the cold night air. The rest of the signals hit the inner structure, to be deflected elsewhere, or so everyone hoped.

Ryan met the Ambassador and escorted him into the West Wing, further surrounded by five Secret Service agents. The atmosphere was what diplomats called "frank." There was no overt impoliteness, but the atmosphere was tense and minus the usual pleasantries that marked such meetings. No words were exchanged beyond those required, and by the time they entered the Oval Office Jack was mainly worried about what threat, if any, would be delivered at this most inopportune of moments.

"Mr. Ambassador, won't you please take a seat," Durling said.

"Thank you, Mr. President."

Ryan picked one between the visiting diplomat and Roger Durling. It was an automatic action to protect his president, but unnecessary. Two of the agents had come in and would not leave the room. One stood at the door. The other stood directly behind the Ambassador.

"I understand you have something you wish to tell me," Durling observed.

The diplomat's delivery was matter-of-fact. "My government wishes me to inform you that we will soon make public our possession of strategic weapons. We wish to give you fair warning of that."

"That will be seen as an overt threat to our country, Mr. Ambassador," Ryan said, performing his task of shielding the President from the necessity of speaking directly.

"It is only a threat if you make it so."

"You are aware," Jack noted next, "that we too have nuclear arms which can be delivered to your country."

"As you have already done," the Ambassador replied at once. Ryan nodded.

"Yes, in the case of another war begun by your country."

"We keep telling you, this is only a war if you make it so."

"Sir, when you attack American territory and kill American servicemen, that is what makes it a war."

Durling watched the exchange with no more reaction than a tilted head, playing his part as his National Security Advisor played his own. He knew his subordinate well enough now to recognize the tension in him, the way his feet crossed at the bottom of his chair while his hands clasped lightly in his lap, his voice soft and pleasant-sounding despite the nature of the conversation. Bob Fowler had been right all along, more so than either the former President or the current one had realized. *Good man in a storm*, Roger Durling thought yet again, a saying that dated as far back as men had gone to sea. Headstrong and hot-tempered though he sometimes was, in a crisis Ryan settled down rather like a doctor in an operating room. Something he'd learned from his wife? the President wondered, or perhaps something he'd learned because it had been forced upon him in the past ten or twelve years, in and out of government service. Good brains, good instinct, and a cool head when needed. What a shame the man had avoided politics. That thought almost made Durling smile, but this wasn't the place for it. No, Ryan would not be good at politics. He was the sort who sought to handle problems directly. Even his subtlety had a sharp point to it, and he lacked the crucial ability to lie effectively, but for all that, a good man for dealing with a crisis.

"We seek a peaceful conclusion to this episode," the Ambassador was saying now. "We are willing to concede much."

"We require nothing more than a return to status quo ante," Ryan replied, taking a chance that made his shoes turn under him. He hated this, hated taking the point, but now he had to float the ideas that he and the President had discussed, and if something went wrong, it would merely be remembered that it was Ryan who misspoke and not Roger Durling. "And the elimination of your nuclear arms under international inspection."

"You force us to play a very dangerous game."

"The game is of your making, sir." Ryan commanded himself to relax. His right hand was over his left wrist now. He could feel his watch, but didn't dare to look down at it for fear of giving an indication that something time-related was now under way. "You are already in violation of the Non-Proliferation Treaty. You have violated the U.N. Charter, which your government has also signed. You are in violation of several treaty relationships with the United States of America, and you have launched a war of aggression. Do you expect us to accept all of this, *and* your enslavement of American citizens? Tell me, how will your citizens react when they learn all of this?" The events of the previous night over Northern Japan had not become public yet. They had controlled their media far more thoroughly than Ryan's own play with the American TV networks, but there was a problem with that sort of thing. The truth always got out. Not a bad thing if the truth worked for you, it could be a terrible thing if it did not.

"You must offer us something!" the Ambassador insisted, visibly losing his diplomatic composure. Behind him, the Secret Service agent's hands flexed a little.

"What we offer you is the chance to restore the peace honorably."

"That is nothing!"

"This is more properly a subject for Deputy Secretary Adler and his delegation. You are aware of our position," Ryan said. "If you choose to go public with your nuclear weapons, we cannot stop you from doing so. But I caution you that it would be a grave psychological escalation which neither your country nor ours needs."

The Ambassador looked at Durling now, hoping for a reaction of some sort. Iowa and New Hampshire would be happening soon, and this man had to start off well . . . was that the reason for the hard line? the diplomat wondered. His orders from Tokyo commanded him to get some maneuvering room for his country, but the Americans weren't playing, and the culprit for that had to be Ryan.

"Does Dr. Ryan speak for the United States?" His heart skipped a beat when he saw the President shake his head slightly.

"No, Mr. Ambassador. Actually, I speak for the United States." Durling paused for a cruel instant before adding, "But Dr. Ryan speaks for me in this case. Do you have anything else for us?"

"No, Mr. President."

"In that case we will not detain you further. We hope that your government will see that the most profitable way out of this situation is what we propose. The other alternatives do not bear inspection. Good day, sir." Durling didn't stand, though Ryan did, to walk the man out. He was back in two minutes.

"When?" the President asked.

"Anytime."

"This had better work."

The sky was clear below them, though there were some wisps of cirrus clouds at fifty thousand feet. Even so, the Initial Point, called the IP, was too difficult for the unaided human eye to see. Worse, the other aircraft in the flight of three were quite invisible, though they were programmed to be only four and eight miles ahead, respectively. Mike Zacharias thought of his father, all the missions he'd flown into the most sophisticated defenses of his time, and how he'd lost his professional gamble, just once, and miraculously survived a camp supposed to be a final resting place. This was easier, after a fashion, but also harder, since the B-2 could not maneuver at all except to adjust its position slightly for winds.

"Patriot battery around here, off at two o'clock," the captain on the electronic-warfare board warned. "It just lit off."

Then Zacharias saw why. There were the first flashes on the ground, a few miles ahead. *So the intelligence reports were right,* the colonel thought. The Japanese didn't have many Patriots, and they wouldn't put them out here for the fun of it. Just then, looking down, he saw the moving lights of a train just outside the valley they were about to attack.

"Interrogate-one," the pilot ordered. Now it got dangerous.

The LPI radar under the nose of his bomber aimed itself at the piece of ground the satellite-navigation system told it to, instantly fixing the bomber's position with respect to a known ground reference. The aircraft then swept into a right turn and two minutes later it repeated the procedure —

"Missile-launch warning! Patriot is flying now — make that two," the EWO warned.

"That's -Two," Zacharias thought. *Must have caught him with the doors open.* The bomber wasn't stealthy with its bomb bay open, but that only took a few seconds before —

There. He saw the Patriots coming up from behind a hill, far faster than the SA-2s that his father had dodged, not like rockets at all, more like some sort of directed-energy beams, so fast the eye could hardly follow them, so fast he didn't have much chance to think. But the two missiles, only a few hundred meters apart, didn't alter their path at all, blazing toward a fixed point in space, and streaking past his bomber's altitude, exploding like fireworks at about sixty thousand feet. *Okay, this stealth stuff really does work against Patriot, as all the tests said it did.* The operators on the ground must be going crazy, he thought.

"Starting the first run," the pilot announced.

There were ten target points — missile silos, the intelligence data said, and it pleased the Colonel to be eliminating the hateful things, even though the price of that was the lives of other men. There were only three of them, and his bomber, like the others, carried only eight weapons. The total number of weapons carried for the mission was only twenty-four, with two designated for each silo, and Zacharias's last four for the last target. Two bombs each. Every bomb had a 95 percent probability of hitting within four meters of the aim point, pretty good numbers really, except that this sort of mission had precisely no margin for error. Even the paper probability was less than half a percent chance of a double miss, but that number times ten targets meant a five percent chance that one missile would survive, and that could not be tolerated.

The aircraft was under computer control now, which the pilot could override but would not unless something went badly wrong. The Colonel pulled his hands back from the controls, not touching them lest he interfere with the process that required better control than he could deliver.

"Systems?" he asked over the intercom.

"Nominal," the EWO replied tensely. His eyes were on the GPS navigation system, which was taking its signals from four orbiting nuclear clocks and fixing the aircraft's exact position in three dimensions, along with course and groundspeed and wind-drift figure generated by the bomber's own systems. The information was crossloaded to the bombs, already programmed to know the exact location of their targets. The first bomber had covered targets 1 through 8. The second bomber had covered 3 through 10. His third bomber would take the second shots at 1, 2, 9, and 10. This would theoretically ensure that since no single aircraft handled both shots at one target, an electronic fault would not guarantee the survival of one of the missiles on the ground.

"That Patriot battery is still looking. It seems to be at the entrance to the valley."

Too bad for them, Zacharias thought.

"Bomb doors coming open — now!" the copilot said. The resulting news from the third crewman was instant.

"He's got us — the SAM site has us now," the EWO said as the first weapon fell free. "Lock-on, he has lock-on . . . launch launch launch!"

"It takes a while, remember," Zacharias said, far more coolly than he felt. The second bomb was now out. Then came a new thought — how smart was that battery commander? Had he learned something from his last chance at a bomber? *God, the mission could still fail if he —*

Two seconds later the fourth weapon dropped free, and the bomb doors closed, returning the B-2 Spirit to electronic invisibility.

"It's a stealth bomber, it has to be," the intercept controller said. "Look!"

The large, inviting contact that had suddenly appeared just over their heads was gone. The big phased-array acquisition radar had announced the target's presence visually and with a tone, and now the screen was blank, but not completely. Now there were four objects descending, just as there had been eight only a minute before. Bombs. The battery commander had felt and heard the impact up-valley from his launch vehicles. The last time, he'd gone for the bombers, wasting two precious missiles; and the two he'd just fired would also go wild . . . but . . .

"Reengage now!" the battery commander shouted at his people.

"They're not guiding on us," the EWO said with more hope than conviction. The tracking radar was searchlighting now, then it steadied down, but not on them.

To make it even less likely, Zacharias turned the aircraft, which was necessary for the second part of the mission anyway. It would take him off track for the programmed path of the missiles and avoid the chance possibility of a skin-skin contact.

"Talk to me!" the pilot ordered.

"They're past us by now — " A thought confirmed by one, then another bright flash of light that lit up the clouds over their heads. Though the three crewmen cringed at the light, there wasn't a sound or even a buffet from the explosions, they must have been so far behind them.

Okay, that's that . . . I hope.

"He's still — lock-on-signal!" the EWO shouted. "But — "

"On us?"

"No, something else — I don't know — "

"The bombs. Damn it," Zacharias swore. "He's tracking the bombs!"

There were four of them, the smartest of smart bombs, falling rapidly now, but not so fast as a diving tactical aircraft. Each one knew where it was in space and time and knew where it was supposed to go. Data from the B-2s' onboard navigation systems had told them where they were — the map coordinates, the altitude, the speed and direction of the aircraft, and against that the computers in the bombs themselves had compared the location of their programmed targets. Now, falling, they were connecting the invisible dots in three-dimensional space, and they were most unlikely to miss. But the bombs were not stealthy, because it hadn't occurred to anyone to make them so, and they were also large enough to track.

The Patriot battery still had missiles to shoot, and a site to defend, and though the bomber had disappeared, there *were* four objects on the screen, and the radar could see them. Automatically, the guidance systems tracked in on them as the battery commander swore at himself for not thinking of this sooner. His operator nodded at the command and turned the key that "enabled" the missile systems to operate autonomously, and the computer didn't know or care that the inbound targets were not aircraft. They were moving through the air, they were within its hemisphere of responsibility, and the human operators said, *kill.*

The first of four missiles exploded out of its boxlike container, converting its solid-rocket fuel into a white streak in the night sky. The guidance system was one that tracked targets via the missile itself, and though complex, it was also difficult to jam and exceedingly accurate. The first homed in on its target, relaying its own signals to the ground and receiving tracking instructions from the battery's computers. Had the missile a brain, it would have felt satisfaction as it led the falling target, selecting a point in space and time where both would meet . . .

"Kill!" the operator said, and night turned to day as the second SAM tracked in on the next bomb.

The light on the ground told the tale. Zacharias could see the strobelike flashes reflected off the rocky hillsides, too soon for bomb hits on the ground. So whoever had drawn up the mission parameters hadn't been paranoid after all.

"There's IP Two," the copilot said, recalling the aircraft commander back to the mission.

"Good ground-fix," the EWO said.

Zacharias could see it clearly this time, the wide flat path of deep blue, different from the broken, darker ground of this hill country, and the pale wall that held it back. There were even lights there for the powerhouse.

"Doors coming open now."

The aircraft jumped upwards a few feet when the six weapons fell free. The flight controls adjusted for that, and the bomber turned right again for an easterly course, while the pilot felt better about what he'd been ordered to do.

The battery commander slammed his hand down on his instrument panel with a hoot of satisfaction. He'd gotten three of the four, and the last explosion, though it had been a miss, might well have knocked the bomb off-target, though he felt the ground shake with its impact on the ground. He lifted his field phone for the missile command bunker.

"Are you all right?" he asked urgently.

"What the hell hit us?" the distant officer demanded. The Patriot commander ignored that foolish question.

"Your missiles?"

"Eight of them are gone — but I think I have two left. I have to call Tokyo for instructions." It was amazing to the officer at the other end, and his immediate thought was to credit the site selection. His silos were drilled into solid rock, which had made a fine armor for his ICBMs after all. What orders would he receive now that the Americans had tried to disarm him and his nation?

I hope they tell you to launch, the SAM officer didn't quite have the courage to say aloud.

The last four bombs from the third B-2 tracked in on the hydroelectric dam at the head of the valley. They were programmed to strike from bottom to top in the reinforced-concrete face of the structure, the timing and placement of the target points no less crucial than those of the weapons that had tracked in on the missile silos. Unseen and unheard by anyone, they came down in a line, barely a hundred feet separating one from another.

The dam was a hundred thirty meters high and almost exactly that thick at its base, the structure narrowing as it rose to a spillway width of only ten meters. Strong, both to withstand the weight of the reservoir it held back and also to withstand the earthquakes that plague Japan, it had generated electricity for more than thirty years.

The first bomb hit seventy meters below the spillway. A heavy weapon with a thick case of hardened steel, it burrowed fifteen meters into the structure before exploding, first ripping a miniature cavern in the concrete, the shock of the event rippling through the immense wall as the second weapon struck, about five meters over the first.

A watchman was there, awakened from a nap by the noise from downvalley, but he'd missed the light show and was wondering what it had been when he saw the first muted flash that seemed to come from inside his dam. He heard the second weapon hit, then the delay of a second or so before the shock almost lifted him off his feet.

"Jesus, did we get them all?" Ryan asked. Contrary to popular belief, and contrary now to his own fervent wishes, the National Reconnaissance Office had never extended real-time capability to the White House. He had to depend on someone else, watching a television in a room at the Pentagon.

"Not sure, sir. They were all close hits — well, I mean, some were, but some of the bombs appeared too premature — "

"What does that mean?"

"They seem to have exploded in midair — three of them, that is, all from the last bomber. We're trying to isolate in on the individual silos now and — "

"Are there any left intact, damn it?" Ryan demanded. Had the gamble failed?

"One, maybe two, we're not sure. Stand by, okay?" the analyst asked rather plaintively. "We have another bird overhead in a few minutes."

The dam might have survived two, but the third hit, twenty meters from the spillway, opened a gap — really, it dislodged a chunk of concrete triangular in shape. The section jerked forward, then stopped, held in place by the immense friction of the man-made rock, and for a second the watchman wondered if the dam might hold. The fourth hit struck in the center of that section and fragmented it. By the time the dust cleared, it had been replaced with fog and vapor as the water started pouring through the thirty-meter gap carved in the dam's face. That gap grew before the watchman's eyes, and only then did it occur to him to race for his shack and lift a phone to warn the people downstream. By that time, a river reborn after three decades of enforced sleep was racing down a valley it had carved over hundreds of millennia.

"Well?" the man in Tokyo demanded.

"One missile seems to be fully intact. That's number nine. Number two — well, there may be some minor damage. I have my people checking them all now. What are my orders?"

"Prepare for a possible launch and stand by."

"Hai." The line clicked off.

Now what do I do? the watch officer wondered. He was new at this, new at the entire idea of managing nuclear weapons, a job he'd never wanted, but nobody had ever asked him about that. His remembered protocol of orders came quickly to him, and he lifted a phone — just an ordinary black instrument; there hadn't been time for the theatrics the Americans had affected — for the Prime Minister.

"Yes, what is this?"

"Goto-san, this is the Ministry. There has been an attack on our missiles!"

"What? When?" the Prime Minister demanded. "How bad?"

"One, possibly two missiles are operational. The rest may be destroyed. We're checking them all now." The senior watch officer could hear the rage at the other end of the line.

"How quickly can you get them ready for launch?"

"Several minutes. I have already given the order to bring them to launch status." The officer flipped an order book open to determine the procedures to actually launch the things. He'd been briefed in on it, of course, but now, in the heat of the moment, he felt the need to have it in writing before him as the others in the watch center turned and looked at him in an eerie silence.

"I'm calling my cabinet now!" And the line went dead.

The officer looked around. There was anger in the room, but even more, there was fear. It had happened again, a systematic attack, and now they knew the import of the earlier American actions. Somehow they had learned the location of the camouflaged missiles, and then they had used timed attacks on the Japanese air-defense system to cover what they really wanted to do. So what would they themselves be ordered to do now? Launch a nuclear attack? That was madness. The General thought so, and he could see that the cooler heads in his command center felt the same way.

It was a miracle of sorts. Missile Number Nine's silo was nearly intact. One bomb had exploded a mere six meters away, but the rock around the — no, the officer saw, the bomb hadn't exploded at all. There was a hole in the rocky floor of the valley, but in the light of his flashlight he could see right there, amid the broken rock, the afterpart of something — a fin, perhaps. A dud, he realized, a smart bomb with a faulty fuse. Wasn't that amusing? He raced off next to see Number Two. Running down the valley, he heard some sort of alarm horn and wondered what that was all about. It was a frightening trip, and he marveled at the fact that the Americans hadn't attempted to attack the control bunker. Of the ten missiles in the collection, eight were certainly destroyed. He choked with the fumes of the remaining propellants, but most of that had fireballed into the sky already, leaving behind only noxious gas that the night winds were sweeping away. On reflection he donned a gas mask that covered his face, and, fatally, his ears.

Silo two had taken a single bomb hit — near miss, he corrected himself. This bomb had missed the center target by perhaps twelve meters, and though it had thrown tons of rock about and cracked the concrete liner, all they had to do was sweep off the debris from the access hatch, then go down to see if the missile was intact.

Damn the Americans for this! he raged, lifting his portable radio and calling the control bunker. Strangely, there was no reply. Then he noticed that the ground was shaking, but halfway wondered if it might be his own trembling. Commanding himself to be still, he took a deep breath, but the rumbling didn't stop. An earthquake . . . and what was that howling outside his gas mask? Then he saw it, and there wasn't time to race for the valley walls.

The Patriot crew heard it also, but ignored it. It was the reload crew who got the only warning. Set in the wye of the railroad tracks, they were rigging a launch canister of four more missiles when the white wall exploded out the entrance to the valley. Their shouts went unheard, though one of their number managed to scramble to safety before the hundred-foot wave engulfed the site.

Two hundred miles over his head, an orbiting camera overflew the valley from southwest to northeast, all nine of its cameras following the same rush of water.

45

Line of Battle

"There they go," Jones said. The shuttling pencils on the fan-fold paper showed nearly identical marks, the thin traces on the 1000hz line indicated that Prairie-Masker systems were in use, and similarly faint lower-frequency marks denoted the use of marine diesel engines. There were seven of them, and though the bearings were not showing much change as yet, they soon would. The Japanese submarines were all now at snorting depth, and the time was wrong. They snorted on the hour, usually, typically one hour into a watch cycle, which allowed the officers and men on duty time to get used to the ship after a rest period, and also to do a sonar check before entering their most vulnerable evolution. But it was twenty-five after the hour now, and they'd all started snorting within the same five-minute period, and that meant movement orders. Jones lifted the phone and punched the button for SubPac.

"Jones here."

"What's happening, Ron?"

"Whatever bait you just dropped in the water, sir, they just took after it. I have seven tracks," he reported. "Who's waiting for them?"

"Not on the phone, Ron," Mancuso said. "How are things over there?"

"Pretty much under control," Jones replied, looking around at the chiefs. Good men and women already, and his additional training had put them fully on-line.

"Why don't you bring your data over here, then? You've earned it."

"See you in ten," the contractor said.

"We got 'em," Ryan said.

"How sure are you?" Durling asked.

"Here, sir." Jack put three photos on the President's desk, just couriered over from NRO. "This is what it looked like yesterday." There was nothing to see, really, except for the Patriot missile battery. The second photo showed more, and though it was a radar photo in black and white, it had been computer-blended with another visual overhead to give a more precise picture of the missile field. "Okay, this is seventy minutes old," Ryan said, setting the third one down.

"It's a lake." He looked up, surprised even though he'd been briefed.

"The place is under about a hundred feet of water, will be for another few hours," Jack explained. "Those missiles are dead — "

"Along with how many people?" Durling asked.

"Over a hundred," the National Security Advisor reported, his enthusiasm for the event instantly gone. "Sir — there wasn't any way around that."

The President nodded. "I know. How sure are we that the missiles . . . ?"

"Pre-flood shots showed seven of the holes definitely hit and destroyed. One more probably wrecked, and two unknowns, but definitely with shock damage of some sort. The weather seals on the holes won't withstand that much water pressure, and ICBMs are too delicate for that sort of treatment. Toss in debris carried downstream from the flooding. The missiles are as dead as we can make them without a nuclear strike of our own, and we managed to do the mission without it." Jack paused. "It was all Robby Jackson's plan. Thanks for letting me reward him for it."

"He's with the carrier now?"

"Yes, sir."

"Well, it would seem that he's the man for the job, wouldn't it?" the President asked rhetorically, clearly relieved at the evening's news. "And now?"

"And now, Mr. President, we try to settle this one down once and for all."

The phone rang just then. Durling lifted it. "Oh. Yes, Tish?"

"There's an announcement from the Japanese government that they have nuclear weapons and they hope — "

"Not anymore, they don't," Durling said, cutting off his communications director. "We'd better make an announcement of our own."

"Oh, yeah," Jones said, looking at the wall chart. "You did that one in a big hurry, Bart."

The line was west of the Marianas. *Nevada* was the northernmost boat. Thirty miles south of her was *West Virginia.* Another thirty and there was *Pennsylvania. Maryland* was the southernmost former missile submarine. The line was ninety miles across, and really extended a theoretical thirty more, fifteen to the north and south of the end-boats, and they were two hundred miles west of the westward-moving line of Japanese SSKs. They had just arrived in place after the warning from Washington that the word had been leaked somehow or other to the Japanese.

"Something like this happened once before, didn't it?" Jones asked, remembering that these were all battleship names, and more than that, the names of battlewagons caught alongside the quays one morning in December, long before his birth. The original hold-

1050

ers of the names had been resurrected from the mud and sent off to take islands back, supporting soldiers and Marines under the command of Jesse Oldendorf, and one dark night in Surigao Strait . . . but it wasn't a time for history lessons.

"What about the 'cans?" Chambers asked.

"We lost them when they went behind the Bonins, sir. Speed and course were fairly constant. They ought to pass over *Tennessee* around midnight, local time, but by that time our carrier — "

"You have the operation all figured out," Mancuso observed.

"Sir, I've been tracking the whole ocean for you. What d'ya expect?"

"Ladies and gentlemen," the President said in the White House Press Room. He was winging it, Ryan saw, just working off some scribbled notes, never something to make the Chief Executive comfortable. "You've just this evening heard an announcement by the Japanese government that they have fabricated and deployed nuclear-tipped intercontinental missiles.

"That fact has been known to your government for several weeks now, and the existence of those weapons is the reason for the careful and circumspect way in which the Administration has dealt with the Pacific Crisis. As you can well imagine, that development has weighed heavily on us, and has affected our response to Japanese aggression against U.S. soil and citizens in the Marianas.

"I can now tell you that those missiles have been destroyed. They no longer exist," Durling said in a forceful voice.

"The current situation is this: the Japanese military still hold the Marianas Islands. That is not acceptable to the United States of America. The people living on those islands are American citizens, and

1051

American forces will do anything necessary to redeem their freedom and human rights. I repeat: we will do anything necessary to restore those islands to U.S. rule.

"We call tonight on Prime Minister Goto to announce his willingness to evacuate Japanese forces from the Marianas forthwith. Failure to do so will compel us to use whatever force is necessary to remove them.

"That is all I have to say right now. For whatever questions you have on the events of this evening, I turn you over to my National Security Advisor, Dr. John Ryan." The President walked toward the door, ignoring a riot of shouted questions, while a few easels were set up for visual displays. Ryan stood at the lectern, making everyone wait as he told himself to speak slowly and clearly.

"Ladies and gentlemen, this was called Operation TIBBETS. First of all let me show you what the targets were." The cover came off the first photo, and for the first time the American people saw just what the nation's reconnaissance satellites were capable of. Ryan lifted his pointer and started identifying the scene for everyone, giving the cameras time to close in on them.

"Holy shit," Manuel Oreza observed. "That's why."

"Looks like a pretty good reason to me," Pete Burroughs observed. Then the screen went blank.

"We're sorry, but a technical problem has temporarily interrupted the CNN satellite feed," a voice told them.

"My ass!" Portagee snarled back.

"They'll come here next, won't they?"

"About fuckin' time, too," Oreza thought.

"Manny, what about that missile thing on the next hill?" his wife wanted to know.

"We're preparing copies of all these photos for you. They should be ready in about an hour or so. Sorry for the delay," Jack told them. "It's been rather a busy time for us.

"Now, the mission was carried out by B-2 bombers based at Whiteman Air Force Base in Missouri — "

"Staging out of where?" a reporter asked.

"You know we're not going to discuss that," Jack said in reply.

"That's a nuclear-weapons platform," another voice said. "Did we — "

"No. The strike was carried out with precision-guided conventional munitions. Next card, please," Ryan said to the man at the easel. "As you can see here, the valley is largely intact . . ." It was easier than he'd expected, and perhaps better that he'd not had much time to worry about it, and Ryan remembered his first time delivering a briefing in the White House. It had been harder than this one, despite the blaze of TV lights now in his face.

"You destroyed a dam?"

"Yes, we did. It was necessary to be completely certain that these weapons were destroyed and — "

"What about casualties?"

"All of our aircraft are on their way back — might already be there, but I haven't — "

"What about Japanese deaths?" the reporter insisted.

"I don't know about that," Jack replied evenly.

"Do you care?" she demanded, wondering what sort of answer she'd get.

"The mission, ma'am, was to eliminate nuclear arms targeted on the United States by a country that has already attacked U.S. forces. Did we kill Japanese citizens in this attack? Yes, we did. How many? I do not know. Our concern in this case was American lives at risk. I wish you would keep in mind that we didn't start this war. Japan did. When you start a war you take risks. This is one risk they undertook — and in this case they lost. I am the President's National Security Advisor, and my job description is to help President Durling safeguard this country first of all. Is that clear?" Ryan asked. He'd allowed just a little anger to enter his reply, and the indignant look on the reporter's face didn't prevent a few nods from her colleagues.

"What about asking the press to lie in order to — "

"Stop!" Ryan commanded, his face reddening. "Do you wish to place the lives of American servicemen at risk? Why do that? Why the hell would you want to do that?"

"You bullied the networks into — "

"This feed is going worldwide. You do know that, don't you?" Ryan paused to take a breath. "Ladies and gentlemen, I would remind you that most of the people in this room are American citizens. Speaking for myself now" — he was afraid to look to where the President was standing — "you do realize that the President is responsible to the mothers and fathers and wives and children of the people who wear our country's uniform for their safety. Real people are at risk today, and I wish you folks in the press would bear that in mind from time to time."

"Jesus," Tish Brown whispered behind Durling. "Mr. President, it might be a good idea to — "

"No." He shook his head. "Let him go on."

The Press Room became silent. Someone whispered something sharp to the standing journalist, who managed to take her seat, flushing as she did so.

"Dr. Ryan, Bob Holtzman of the *Washington Post*," he said unnecessarily. "What are the chances of ending this conflict without further violence?"

"Sir, that is entirely up to the Japanese government. The citizens of the Marianas are, as the President said, *American* citizens, and this country does not allow other nations to change such things. If Japan is willing to withdraw her forces, they may do so in peace. If not, then other operations will take place."

"Thank you, Dr. Ryan," Holtzman said loudly, effectively ending the press conference. Jack hustled toward the door, ignoring the additional questions.

"Nice job," Durling said. "Why don't you go home for some sleep?"

"And what is this?" the customs officer asked.

"My photographic equipment," Chekov replied. He opened the case without an order to do so. It was warm in the terminal, the noon tropical sun beating through the wall of windows and overpowering the air conditioning for the moment. Their newest orders had been easily implemented. The Japanese wanted journalists in the islands, both to check up on the election campaign and to safeguard against American attack by their mere presence in the islands.

The customs officer looked at the cameras, gratified to see that it was all Japanese. "And this?"

"My lighting equipment is Russian," Ding explained in slow English. "We make very fine lights. Perhaps one day we will sell them in your country," he added with a smile.

"Yes, perhaps so," the official said, closing the case and marking it with chalk. "Where will you be staying?"

"We weren't able to make hotel arrangements," "Klerk" replied. "We'll check the local hotels."

Good luck, the official didn't say. This idea had come off half-baked, and every hotel room on Saipan, he was sure, was already filled. Well, that wasn't his problem.

"Can we rent a car?"

"Yes, over that way." The man pointed. The older Russian looked nervous, he thought.

"You're late."

"Well, sorry about that," Oreza replied tersely. "There's nothing new happening at all. Well, maybe the fighters are a little more active, but not much, and they've been pretty busy anyw— "

"You're going to get some company soon," the National Military Command Center told him.

"Who?"

"Two reporters. They have some questions for you," was the answer because of the renewed concern for Oreza's secure status.

"When?"

"Anytime, probably today. Everything okay with you, Chief?"

Master Chief, you turkey, Portagee didn't say. "Just great. We saw part of the President's speech, and we're a little worried because that missile site is so close to us and — "

"You'll have enough warning. Does your house have a basement?" the voice asked.

"No, it doesn't."

"Well, that's okay. We'll let you know, okay?"

"Sure, sir. Out." *Does your house have a basement? No. Well, that's okay.* If it's okay, why did you ask, goddamn it? Oreza deactivated the phone after taking it out of the mixing bowl and walked to the window. Two Eagles were taking off. Such a mechanical thing to watch. Something was happening. He didn't know what. Perhaps their pilots didn't either, but you couldn't tell what they were thinking from looking at their aircraft.

Shiro Sato reefed his F-15J into a right turn to clear the civilian air traffic. If the Americans attacked, they would do it as the attacks on the Home Islands had come, off island bases, supported by tankers, from a long way off. Wake was a possibility, and so were a few other islands. He'd face aircraft not unlike his own. They would have airborne radar support, and so would he. It would be a fair fight unless the bastards brought down their stealth aircraft. Damn the things. Damn their ability to defeat the Kamis! But the Americans had only a few of them, and if they flew in daylight, he'd take his chances. At least there would be no real surprises. There was a huge air-defense radar on Saipan's highest point, and with the squadrons based on Guam, this would be a real fight, he told himself, climbing up to patrol altitude.

"So what's the big deal?" Chavez asked, playing with the map.

"You wouldn't believe it if I told you."

"Well, take the next left, I think, by Lizama's Mobil." Chavez looked up from the map. There were soldiers everywhere, and they were digging in, something they ought to have done sooner, he thought. "Is that a Patriot battery?"

"Sure looks like one to me." *How the hell am I going to handle this?* Clark asked himself, finding the last turn and heading into the cul-de-sac. The house number was the one he'd memorized. He pulled into the driveway and got out, heading for the front door.

Oreza had been in the bathroom, finishing a needed shower while Burroughs handled the running count on the aircraft in and out of Kobler when the doorbell rang.

"Who are you?"

"Didn't they tell you?" Clark asked, looking around. Who the hell was this guy?

"Reporters, right?"

"Yeah, that's it."

"Okay." Burroughs opened the door with a look up and down the street.

"Who are you, anyway? I thought this was the house of — "

"*You're dead!*" Oreza was standing in the hall, wearing just khaki shorts, his chest a mass of hair as thick as the remaining jungle on the island. The hair looked especially dark now, with the rest of the man's skin turning rapidly to the color of milk. "You're fuckin' dead!"

"Hi, Portagee," Klerk/Clark/Kelly said with a smile. "Long time."

He couldn't make himself move. "I saw you die. I went to the goddamned memorial service. I was *there!*"

"Hey, I know you," Chavez said. "You were on the boat our chopper landed on. What the hell is this? You Agency?"

It was almost too much for Oreza. He didn't remember the little one at all, but the big one, the old one, his age, about, was — couldn't be — was. It wasn't possible. Was it?

"John?" he asked after a few seconds of further incredulity.

It was too much for the man who used to be known as John Kelly. He set his bag down and came over to embrace the man, surprised by the tears in his eyes. "Yeah, Portagee — it's me. How you doin', man?"

"But how — "

"At the memorial service, did they use the line about 'sure and certain hope that the sea will give up its dead'?" He paused, then he had to grin. "Well, it did."

Oreza closed his eyes, thinking back over twenty years. "Those two admirals, right?"

"You got it."

"So — what the hell have you been — "

"CIA, man. They decided they needed somebody who could, well — "

"I remember that part." He really hadn't changed all that much. Older, but the same hair, and the same eyes, warm and open to him as they had always been, Portagee thought, but underneath always the hint of something else, like an animal in a cage, but an animal who knew how to pick the lock whenever he wanted.

"I hear you've been doing okay for a retired coastie."

"Command Master Chief." The man shook his head. The past could wait. "What's going on?"

"Well, we've been out of the loop for a few hours. Anything new that you know?"

"The President was on. They cut him off, but — "

"Did they really have nukes?" Burroughs asked.

" 'Did'?" Ding asked. "We got 'em?"

"That what he said. Who the hell are you, by the way?" Oreza wanted to know.

"Domingo Chavez." The young man extended his hand. "I see you and Mr. C know each other."

"I go by 'Clark' now," John explained. It was odd how good it felt to talk with a man who knew his real name.

"Does he know?"

John shook his head. "Not many people know. Most of them are dead. Admiral Maxwell and Admiral Greer both. Too bad, they saved my ass."

Oreza turned to his other new guest. "Tough luck, kid. It's some fuckin' sea story. You still drink beer, John?"

"Especially if it's free," Chavez confirmed.

"Don't you see? It's finished now!"

"Who else did they get?" Yamata asked.

"Matsuda, Itagake — they got every patron of every minister, all except you and me," Murakami said, not adding that they had nearly gotten him. "Raizo, it is time to put an end to this. Call Goto and tell him to negotiate a peace."

"I will not!" Yamata snarled back.

"Don't you see? Our missiles are destroyed and — "

"And we can make new ones. We have the ability to make more warheads, and we *have* more missiles at Yoshinobu."

"If we attempt that, you know what the Americans will do, you fool!"

"They wouldn't dare."

"You told us that they could not repair the damage you did to their financial systems. You told us that our air defenses were invincible. You told us that they could never strike back at us effectively." Murakami paused for a breath. "You told us all these things — and you were wrong. Now I am the last one to whom you may speak, and I am not listening. *You* tell Goto to make peace!"

"They'll never take these islands back. Never! They do not have the ability."

"Say what you please, Raizo-chan. For my part it is over."

"Find a good place to hide then!" Yamata would have slammed the phone down, but a portable didn't offer that option. "Murderers," he muttered. It had taken most of the morning to assemble the necessary information. Somehow the Americans had struck at his own council of zaibatsu. How? Nobody knew. Somehow they'd penetrated the defenses that every consultant had told him were invincible, even to the point of destroying the intercontinental missiles. "How?" he asked.

"It would seem that we underestimated the quality of their remaining air forces," General Arima replied with a shrug. "It is not the end. We still have options."

"Oh?" *Not everyone was giving up, then?*

"They will not wish to invade these islands. Their ability to perform a proper invasion is severely compromised by their lack of amphibious-assault ships, and even if they managed to put people on the island

— to fight amidst so many of their own citizens? No."
Arima shook his head. "They will not risk it. They
will seek a negotiated peace. There is still a chance
— if not for complete success, then for a negotiated
peace that leaves our forces largely intact."

Yamata accepted that for what it was, looking out
the windows at the island that he wanted to be his.
The elections, he thought, could still be won. It was
the political will of the Americans that needed attacking, and he still had the ability to do that.

It didn't take long to turn the 747 around, but the
surprise to Captain Sato was that the aircraft was half
full for the flight back to Narita. Thirty minutes after
lift-off, a stewardess reported to him by phone that
of the eleven people she'd asked, all but two had said
that they had pressing business that required their
presence at home. *What pressing business might that
be?* he wondered, with his country's international
trade for the most part reduced to ships traveling
between Japan and China.

"This is not turning out well," his copilot observed
an hour out. "Look down there."

It was easy to spot ships from thirty thousand feet,
and of late they'd taken to carrying binoculars to identify surface ships. Sato lifted his pair and spotted the
distinctive shapes of Aegis destroyers still heading
north. On a whim he reached down to flip his radio
to a different guard frequency.

"JAL 747 calling *Mutsu*, over."

"Who is this?" a voice instantly replied. "Clear this
frequency at once!"

"This is Captain Torajiro Sato. Call your fleet commander!" he ordered with his own command voice.
It took a minute.

"Brother, you shouldn't be doing this," Yusuo
chided. Radio silence was as much a formality as a

real military necessity. He knew that the Americans had reconnaissance satellites, and besides, his group's SPY radars were all up and radiating. If American snooper aircraft were about, they'd know where his squadron was. It was something he would have considered with confidence a week before, but not now.

"I merely wanted to express our confidence in you and your men. Use us for a practice target," he added.

In *Mutsu*'s CIC, the missile techs were already doing exactly that, but it wouldn't do to say so, the Admiral knew. "Good to hear your voice again. Now you must excuse me. I have work to do here."

"Understood, Yusuo. Out." Sato took his finger off the radio switch. "See," he said over the intercom. "They're doing their job and we have to do ours."

The copilot wasn't so sure, but Sato was the captain of the 747, and he kept his peace, concentrating on navigational tasks. Like most Japanese he'd been raised to think of war as something to be avoided as assiduously as plague. The overnight development of a conflict with America, well, it had felt good for a day or so to teach the arrogant gaijin a lesson, but that was fantasy talking, and this was increasingly real. Then the double-barreled notification that his country had fielded nuclear arms — that was madness enough — only immediately to be followed by the American claim that the weapons had been destroyed. This *was* an American aircraft, after all, a Boeing 747-400PIP, five years old but state-of-the-art in every respect, reliable and steady. There was little America had to learn about the building of aircraft, and if this one was as good as he knew it to be, then how much more formidable still were their military aircraft? The aircraft his country's Air Force flew were copies of American designs — except for the AEW 767s he'd heard so much about, first about how invincible they were, and more recently about how there were only a few left. This madness had to stop. Didn't everyone see that? Some must, he thought, else why was his airliner half full of people who didn't want to be on Saipan despite their earlier enthusiasm?

But his captain did not see that at all, did he? the copilot asked himself. Torajiro Sato was sitting there, fixed as stone in the left seat, as though all were normal when plainly it was not.

All he had to do was look down in the afternoon sunlight to see those destroyers — doing what? They were guarding their country's coast against the possibility of attack. Was that normal?

"Conn, Sonar."

"Conn, aye." Claggett had the conn for the afternoon watch. He wanted the crew to see him at work, and more than that, wanted to keep the feel for conning his boat.

"Possible multiple contacts to the south," the sonar chief reported. "Bearing one-seven-one. Look like surface ships at high speed, sir, getting pounding and a very high blade rate."

That was about right, the CO thought, heading for the sonar room again. He was about to order a track to be plotted, but when he turned to do so, he saw two quartermasters already setting it up, and the ray-path analyzer printing its first cut on the range. His crew was fully drilled in now, and things just happened automatically, but better. They were thinking as well as acting.

"Best guess, they're a ways off, but look at all this," the chief said. It was clearly a real contact. Data was appearing on four different frequency lines. Then the chief held up his phones. "Sounds like a whole bunch of screws turning — a lot of racing and cavitation, has to be multiple ships, traveling in column."

"And our other friend?" Claggett asked.

"The sub? He's gone quiet again, probably just

tooling along on batteries at five or less." That contact was a good twenty miles off, just beyond the usual detection range.

"Sir, initial range cut on the new contacts is a hundred-plus-thousand yards, CZ contact," another tech reported.

"Bearing is constant. Not a wiggle. They heading straight for us or close to it. They pounding hard. What are surface conditions like, sir?"

"Waves eight to ten feet, Chief." A hundred thousand yards plus. More than fifty nautical miles, Claggett thought. Those ships were driving hard. Right to him, but he wasn't supposed to shoot. Damn. He took the required three steps back into control. "Right ten-degrees rudder, come to new course two-seven-zero."

Tennessee came about to a westerly heading, the better to give her sonar operators a range for the approaching destroyers. His last piece of operational intelligence had predicted this, and the timing of the information was as accurate as it was unwelcome.

In a more dramatic setting, in front of cameras, the atmosphere might have been different, but although the setting was dramatic in a distant sense, right now it was merely cold and miserable. Though these men were the most elite of troops, it was far easier to rouse yourself for combat against a person than against unremitting environmental discomfort. The Rangers, in their mainly white camouflage over-clothing, moved about as little as possible, and the lack of physical activity merely made them more vulnerable to the cold and to boredom, the soldier's deadliest enemy. And yet that was good, Captain Checa thought. For a single squad of soldiers four thousand miles from the nearest U.S. Army base — and *that* base was Fort Wainwright in Alaska — it was a hell of a lot safer to be bored than to be excited by the stimulus of a combat action without any hope of support. Or something like that. Checa faced the problem common to officers: subject to the same discomfort and misery as his men, he was not allowed to bitch. There was no other officer to bitch to in any case, and to do so in front of the men was bad for morale, even though the men probably would have understood.

"Be nice to get back to Fort Stewart, sir," First Sergeant Vega observed. "Spread on that sunblock and catch some rays on the beach."

"And miss all this beautiful snow and sleet, Oso?" At least the sky was clear now.

"Roge-o, Captain. But I got my fill o' this shit when I was a kid in Chicago." He paused, looking and listening around again. The noise-discipline of the other Rangers was excellent, and you had to look very closely indeed to see where the lookouts were standing.

"Ready for the walk out tonight?"

"Just so's our friend is waiting on the far side of that hill."

"I'm sure he will be," Checa lied.

"Yes, sir. I am, too." *If one could do it, why not two?* Vega thought. "Did all this stuff work?"

The killers in their midst were sleeping in their bags, in holes lined with pine branches and covered with more branches for additional warmth. In addition to guarding the pilots, the Rangers had to keep them healthy, like watching over infants, an odd mission for elite troops, but troops of that sort generally drew the oddest.

"So they say." Checa looked at his watch. "We shake them loose in another two hours."

Vega nodded, hoping that his legs weren't too stiff for the trek south.

The patrol pattern had been set in the mission briefing. The four boomers had thirty-mile sectors, and

1065

each sector was divided into three ten-mile segments. Each boat could patrol in the center slot, leaving the north and south slots empty for everything but weapons. The patrol patterns were left to the judgment of individual skippers, but they worked out the same way. *Pennsylvania* was on a northerly course, trolling along at a mere five knots, just as she'd done for her now-ended deterrence patrols carrying Trident missiles. She was making so little noise that a whale might have come close to a collision, if it were the right time for whales in this part of the Pacific, which it wasn't. Behind her, at the end of a lengthy cable, was her towed-array sonar, and the two-hour north-south cycle allowed it to trail straight out in a line, with about ten minutes or so required for the turns at the end of the cycles to get it straight again for maximum performance.

Pennsylvania was at six hundred feet, the ideal sonar depth given today's water conditions. It was just sunset up on the roof when the first trace appeared on her sonar screens. It started as a series of dots, yellow on the video screen, trickling down slowly with time, and shifting a little to the south in bearing, but not much. Probably, the lead sonarman thought, the target had been running on battery for the past few hours, else he would have caught the louder signals of the diesels used to charge them, but there the contact was, on the expected 60hz line. He reported the contact data to the fire-control tracking party.

Wasn't this something, the sonarman thought. He'd spent his entire career in missile boats, so often tracking contacts which his submarine would maneuver to avoid, even though the boomer fleet prided itself on having the best torpedomen in the fleet. *Pennsylvania* carried only fifteen weapons aboard — there was a shortage of the newest version of the ADCAP torpedo, and it had been decided not to bother carrying anything less capable under the circumstances.

It also had three other torpedolike units, called LEMOSSs, for Long-Endurance Mobile Submarine Simulator. The skipper, another lifelong boomer sailor, had briefed the crew on his intended method of attack, and everyone aboard approved. The mission, in fact, was just about ideal. The Japanese had to move through their line. Their operational pattern was such that for them to pass undetected through the Line of Battle, as the skipper had taken to calling it, was most unlikely.

"Now hear this," the Captain said over the 1-MC announcing system — every speaker had been turned down, so that the announcement came as a whisper that the men strained to hear. "We have a probable submerged contact in our kill zone. I am going to conduct the attack just as we briefed it. Battle stations," he concluded in the voice of a man ordering breakfast at HoJo's.

There came sounds so faint that only one experienced sonarman could hear them, and that mostly because he was just forward of the attack center. The watch had changed there so that only the most experienced men — and one woman, now — would occupy the weapons consoles. Those people too junior for a place on the sub's varsity assembled throughout the boat in damage-control parties. Voices announced to the attack-center talker that each space was fully manned and ready, and then the ship grew as silent as a graveyard on Halloween.

"Contact is firming up nicely," the sonarman said over his phones. "Bearing is changing westerly, bearing to target now zero-seven-five. Getting a faint blade-rate on the contact, estimate contact speed is ten knots."

That made it a definite submarine, not that there was much doubt. The diesel sub had her own towed-array sonar and was doing a sprint-and-drift of her own, alternately going at her top speed, then slowing to detect anything that she might miss with the increased flow noise.

"Tubes one, three, and four are ADCAPs," a weapons technician announced. "Tube two is a LEMOSS."

"Spin 'em all up," the Captain said. Most COs liked to say *warm 'em up*, but otherwise this one was by-the-book.

"Current range estimate is twenty-two thousand yards," the tracking party chief announced.

The sonarman saw something new on his screen, then adjusted his headphones.

"Transient, transient, sounds like hull-popping on Sierra-Ten. Contact is changing depth."

"Going up, I bet," the Captain said a few feet away. *That's about right*, the sonarman thought with a nod of his own. "Let's get the MOSS in the water. Set its course at zero-zero-zero. Keep it quiet for the first ten thousand yards, then up to normal radiating levels."

"Aye, sir." The tech dialed in the proper settings on her programming board, and then the weapons officer checked the instructions and pronounced them correct.

"Ready on two."

"Contact Sierra-Ten is fading somewhat, sir. Probably above the layer now."

"Definite direct-path to Sierra-Ten," the ray-path technician said next. "Definitely not a CZ contact, sir."

"Ready on tube two," the weapons tech reported again.

"Fire two," the CO ordered at once. "Reload another MOSS," he said next.

Pennsylvania shuddered ever so slightly as the LEMOSS was ejected into the sea. The sonar picked it up at once as it angled left, then reversed course, heading north at a mere ten knots. Based on an old Mark 48 torpedo body, the LEMOSS was essentially a huge tank of the OTTO fuel American "fish" used, plus a small propulsion system and a large sound-transducer that gave out the noise of an engine plant. The noise was the same frequencies as those of a nuclear power plant, but quite a bit louder than those on an Ohio-class. It never seemed to matter to people that the thing was too loud. Attack submarines almost always went for it, even American ones who should have known better. The new model with the new name could move along for over fifteen hours, and it was a shame it had been developed only a few months before the boomers had been fully and finally disarmed.

Now came the time for patience. The Japanese submarine actually slowed a little more, doubtless doing its own final sonar sweep before they lit off the diesels for their speedy passage west. The sonarman tracked the LEMOSS north. The signal was just about to fade out completely before the sound systems turned on, five miles away. Two miles after that, it jumped over the thermocline layer of cold and warm water and the game began in earnest.

"Conn, Sonar, Sierra-Ten just changed speed, change in the blade-rate, slowing down, sir."

"He has good sonar," the Captain said, just behind the sonarman. *Pennsylvania* had risen somewhat, floating her sonar tail over the layer for a better look at the contact while the body of the submarine stayed below. He turned and spoke more loudly. "Weapons?"

"One, three, and four are ready for launch, solutions on all of them."

"Set four for a stalking profile, initial course zero-two-zero."

"Done. Set as ordered, sir. Tube four ready in all respects."

"Match bearings and shoot," the Captain ordered from the door of the sonar room, adding, "Reload another ADCAP."

Pennsylvania shuddered again as the newest version of the venerable Mark 48 torpedo entered the sea, turning northeast and controlled by an insulated wire that streamed out from its tailfin.

This was like an exercise, the sonarman thought, but easier.

"Additional contacts?" the skipper asked, behind him again.

"Not a thing, sir." The enlisted man waved at his scopes. Only random noise showed, and an additional scope was running diagnostic checks every ten minutes to show that the systems were all functioning properly. It was quite a payoff: after nearly forty years of missile-boat operations, and close to fifty of nuclear-sub ops, the first American sub kill since World War II would come from a boomer supposedly on her way to the scrapyard.

Traveling far more rapidly, the ADCAP torpedo popped over the layer somewhat aft of the contact. It immediately started radiating from its own ultrasonic sonar and fed the picture back along the wire to *Pennsylvania.*

"Hard contact, range three thousand and close to the surface. Lookin' good," sonar said. The same diagnosis came from the weapons petty officer with her identical readout.

"Eat shit and die," the male member of the team whispered, watching the two contact lines close on the display. Sierra-Ten went instantly to full speed, diving at first below the layer, but his batteries were probably a little low, and he didn't make more than fifteen knots, while the ADCAP was doing over sixty. The one-sided chase lasted a total of three and a half minutes and ended with a bright splotch on the screen and a noise in the headphones that stung his ears. The rest was epilogue, concluding with a ripping screech of steel being crushed by water pressure.

"That's a kill, sir. I copy a definite kill." Two minutes later, a distant low-frequency to the north suggested that *West Virginia* had achieved the same goal.

"Christopher Cook?" Murray asked.

"That's right."

It *was* a very nice house, the Deputy Assistant Director thought as he pulled out his identification folder. "FBI. We'd like to talk to you about your conversations with Seiji Nagumo. Could you get a coat?"

The sun had a few more hours to go when the Lancers taxied out. Angered by the loss of one of their number not so long before, the crews deemed themselves to be in the wrong place, doing the wrong thing, but nobody had troubled himself to ask their opinion, and their job was written down. Their bomb bays taken up with fuel tanks, one by one the bombers raced down the runway and lifted off, turning and climbing to their assembly altitude of twenty thousand feet for the cruise northeast.

It was another goddamned demonstration, Dubro thought, and he wondered how the hell somebody like Robby Jackson could have thought it up, but he, too, had orders, and each of his carriers turned into the wind, fifty miles apart to launch forty aircraft each, and though these were all armed, they were not to take action unless provoked.

46

Detachment

"We're almost empty," the copilot said in a neutral voice, checking the manifest as part of the preflight ritual.

"What is the matter with these people?" Captain Sato growled, looking over the flight plan and checking the weather. That was a short task. It would be cool and clear all the way down, with a huge high-pressure area taking charge of the Western Pacific. Except for some high winds in the vicinity of the Home Islands, it would make for a glassy-smooth ride all the way to Saipan, for the thirty-four passengers on the flight. *Thirty-four!* he raged. *In an aircraft built for over three hundred!*

"Captain, we will be leaving those islands soon. You know that." It was clear enough, wasn't it? The people, the average men and women on the street, were no longer so much confused as frightened — or maybe even that wasn't the proper word. He hadn't seen anything like it. They felt — betrayed? The first newspaper editorials had come out to question the course their country had taken, and though the questions asked were mild, the import of them was not. It had all been an illusion. His country had not been prepared for war in a psychological sense any more than a physical one, and the people were suddenly realizing what was actually going on. The whispered reports of the murder — what else could one call it? — of some prominent zaibatsu had left the government in a turmoil. Prime Minister Goto was doing little, not even giving speeches, not even making appearances, lest he have to face questions for which he had no answers. But the faith of his captain, the copilot saw, had not yet been shaken.

"No, we will not! How can you say that? Those islands are ours."

"Time will tell," the copilot observed, returning to his work and letting it go at that. He did have his job to do, rechecking fuel and winds and other technical data necessary for the successful flight of a commercial airliner, all the things the passengers never saw, assuming that the flight crew just showed up and turned it on as though it were a taxicab.

"Enjoy your sleep?"

"You bet, Captain. I dreamed of a hot day and a hot woman." Richter stood up, and his movements belied his supposed comfort. *I really am too old for this shit,* the chief warrant officer thought. It was just fate and luck — if you could call it that — that had put him on the mission. No one else had as much time on the Comanche as he and his fellow warrants did, and somebody had decided that they had the brains to do it, without some goddamned colonel around to screw things up. And now he could boogie on out of here. He looked up to see a clear sky. Well, could be better. For getting in and getting out, better to have clouds.

"Tanks are topped off."

"Some coffee would be nice," he thought aloud.

"Here you go, Mr. Richter." It was Vega, the first sergeant. "Nice iced coffee, like they serve in the best Florida hotels."

"Oh, thanks loads, man." Richter took the metal

cup with a chuckle. "Anything new on the way out?"

This was not good, Claggett thought. The Aegis line had broken up, and now he had one of the god-damned things ten miles away. Worse still, there had been a helicopter in the air not long before, according to his ESM mast, which he'd briefly risked despite the presence of the world's best surveillance radar. But three Army helicopters were depending on him to be here, and that was that. Nobody had ever told him that harm's way was a safe place. Not for him. Not for them, either.

"And our other friend?" he asked his sonar chief. The substantive reply was a shake of the head. The words merely confirmed it.

"Off the scope again."

There were thirty knots of surface wind, which was whipping up the waves somewhat and interfering with sonar performance. Even holding the destroyer was becoming difficult now that it was slowed to a patrol speed of no more than fifteen knots. The submarine off to the north was gone again. Maybe really gone, but it was dangerous to bank on that. Claggett checked his watch. He'd have to decide what to do in less than an hour.

They would be going in blind, but that was an awkward necessity. Ordinarily they'd gather information with snooper aircraft, but the real effort here was to achieve surprise, and they couldn't compromise that. The carrier task force had avoided commercial air lanes, hidden under clouds, and generally worked very hard to make itself scarce for several days. Jackson felt confident that his presence was a secret, but maintaining it meant depending on spotty submarine reports of electronic activity on the islands, and all these did was to confirm that the enemy had several E-2C aircraft operating, plus a monster air-defense radar. It would be an encounter battle aloft. Well, they'd been training for that over the past two weeks.

"Okay, last check," Oreza heard over the phone. "Kobler is exclusively military aircraft?"

"That is correct, sir. Since the first couple of days, we haven't seen any commercial birds on that runway." He really wanted to ask what the questions were all about, but knew it was a waste of time. Well, maybe an oblique question: "You want us to stay awake tonight?"

"Up to you, Master Chief. Now, can I talk to your guests?"

"John? Phone," Portagee announced, then was struck nearly dumb by the normality of what he'd just said.

"Clark," Kelly said, taking it. "Yes, sir . . . Yes, sir. Will do. Anything else? Okay, out." He hit the kill button. "Whose idea was this friggin' umbrella?"

"Mine," Burroughs said, looking up from the card table. "It works, doesn't it?"

"Sure as hell," John said, returning to the table and tossing a quarter in the pot. "Call."

"Three ladies," the engineer announced.

"Lucky son of a gun, too," Clark said, tossing his in.

"Lucky hell! These sunzabitches ruined the best fishing trip I ever had."

"John, you want I should make some coffee for tonight?"

"He makes the best damned coffee, too." Burroughs collected the pot. He was six dollars ahead.

"Portagee, it has been a while. Sure, go ahead. It's called black-gang coffee, Pete. Old seaman's tradition," Clark explained, also enjoying the pleasant inactivity.

"John?" Ding asked.

"Later, my boy." He picked up the deck and started

shuffling adeptly. It would wait.

"Sure you have enough fuel?" Checa asked. The supplies that had been dropped in included auxiliary tanks and wings, but Richter shook his head.

"No prob. Only two hours to the refueling point."

"Where's that?" The signal over the satcomm had said nothing more than PROCEED TO PRIMARY, whatever that meant.

"About two hours away," the warrant officer said. "Security, Captain, security."

"You realize we've made a little history here."

"Just so I live to tell somebody about it." Richter zipped up his flight suit, tucked in his scarf, and climbed aboard. "Clear!"

The Rangers stood by one last time. They knew the extinguishers were worthless, but somebody had insisted on packing them along. One by one the choppers lifted off, their green bodies soon disappearing into the darkness. With that, the Rangers started dumping the remaining equipment into holes dug during the day. That required an hour, and all that remained was their walk to Hirose. Checa lifted his cellular phone and dialed the number he'd memorized.

"Hello?" a voice said in English.

"See you in the morning, I hope?" The question was in Spanish.

"I'll be there, Señor."

"Montoya, lead off," the Captain ordered. They'd keep to the treeline as far as they could. The Rangers clasped weapons so far unused, hoping to keep it that way.

"I recommend two weapons," Lieutenant Shaw said. "Spread the bearings about ten degrees, converge them in from under the layer, and nail him fore and aft."

"I like it." Claggett walked over to the plot for a final examination of the tactical situation. "Set it up."

"So what gives?" one of the Army sergeants asked at the entrance to the attack center. The trouble with these damned submarines was that you couldn't just hang around and watch stuff.

"Before we can refuel those helos of yours, we have to make that 'can go away," a petty officer explained as lightly as he could.

"Is it hard?"

"I guess we'd prefer he was someplace else. It puts us on the surface with — well, somebody's gonna know there's somebody around."

"Worried?"

"Nah," the sailor lied. Then both men heard the Captain speak.

"Mr. Shaw, let's go to battle stations torpedo. Firing-point procedures."

The Tomcats went off first, one every thirty seconds or so until a full squadron of twelve was aloft. Next went four EA-6B jammers, led by Commander Roberta Peach. Her flight of four broke up into elements of two, one to accompany each of the two probing Tomcat squadrons.

Captain Bud Sanchez had the lead division of four, unwilling to entrust the attack of his air group to anyone else. They were five hundred miles out, heading southwest. In many ways the attack was a repeat of another action in the early days of 1991, but with a few nasty additions occasioned by the few airfields available to the enemy and weeks of careful analysis of operational patterns. The Japanese were very regular in their patrols. It was a natural consequence of the orderliness of military life and for that reason a dangerous trap to fall into. He gave one look back at the formation's sparkling wakes and then focused his mind on the mission.

"Set on one and three."

"Match generated bearings and shoot," Claggett said calmly.

The weapons technician turned his handle all to the left, then back to the right, repeating the exercise for the second tube.

"One and three away, sir."

"One and three running normal," sonar reported an instant later.

"Very well," Claggett acknowledged. He *had* been aboard a submarine and heard those words before, and that shot had missed, to which fact he owed his life. This was tougher. They didn't have as good a feel for the location of the destroyer as they would have liked, but neither did he have much choice in the matter. The two ADCAPs would run slow under the layer for the first six miles before shifting to their highest speed setting, which was seventy-one knots. With luck the target wouldn't have much chance to figure where the fish had come from. "Reload one and three with ADCAPs."

Timing, as always, was crucial. Jackson left the flag bridge after the fighters got off, and headed below to the combat information center, the better to co-ordinate an operation already figured out down to the minute. The next part was for his two Spruance destroyers, now thirty miles south of the carrier group. That made him nervous. The Spruances were his best ASW ships, and though SubPac reported that the enemy sub screen was withdrawing west, hope-fully into a trap, he worried about the one SSK that might be left behind to cripple Pacific Fleet's last carrier deck. So many things to worry about, he thought, looking at the sweep hand on the bulkhead-mounted clock.

Precisely at 11:45:00 local time, destroyers *Cushing* and *Ingersoll* turned broadside to the wind and began launching their Tomahawk missiles, signaling this fact by a five-element satellite transmission. A total of forty cruise missiles angled up into the sky, shed their solid-fuel boosters, then angled down for the surface. After the six-minute launch exercise, the destroyers increased speed to rejoin the battle group, wondering what their Tomahawks would accomplish.

"I wonder which one it is?" Sato murmured. They'd passed two already, the Aegis destroyers visible only from their wakes now, the barely visible arrowhead at the front of the spreading V of white foam.

"Call them up again?"

"It will anger my brother, but it must be lonely down there." Again Sato switched his radio setting, then depressed the switch on the wheel. "JAL 747 Flight calling *Mutsu*."

Admiral Sato wanted to grumble, but it was a friendly voice. He took the headset from the junior communications officer and closed his thumb on the switch. "Torajiro, if you were an enemy I would have you now."

He checked the radar display — only commercial targets were on the two-meter-square tactical-display screen. The SPY-1D radar showed everything within a hundred-plus miles, and most things out to nearly three hundred. The ship's SH-60J helicopter had just refueled for another antisub sweep, and though he was still at sea in time of war, he could allow himself a joke with his brother, flying up there in the big aluminum tub, doubtless filled with his countrymen.

"Time, sir," Shaw said, checking his electronic stopwatch. Commander Claggett nodded.

"Weps, bring them up and go active."

The proper command went to the torpedoes, now nearly two miles apart on either side of the target. The ADCAP — "additional capability" — version of the Mark 48 had a huge solid-state sonar system built into its twenty-one-inch nose. The unit launched from tube one was slightly closer, and its advanced imaging system acquired the destroyer's hull on the second sweep. Immediately, the torpedo turned right to home in, relaying its display to the launch point as it did so.

"Hydrophone effects, bearing two-three-zero! Enemy torpedo bearing two-three-zero!" a sonar officer shouted. "Its seeker is active!"

Sato's head turned sharply toward the sonar room, and instantly a new item appeared on the tactical display. Damn, he thought, and *Kurushio* said the area was safe. The SSK was only a few miles off.

"Countermeasures!" *Mutsu*'s captain ordered at once. In seconds the destroyer streamed an American-designed Nixie decoy off her fantail. "Launch the helicopter at once!"

"Brother, I am somewhat busy now. Have a good flight. Good-bye for now." The radio circuit went dead.

Captain Sato first wrote off the end of the conversation to the fact that his brother *did* have duties to perform, then before his eyes he saw the destroyer five miles below him turn sharply to the left, with more boiling foam at her stern to indicate a sudden increase in speed.

"Something's wrong here," he breathed over the intercom.

"We got him, sir. One or both," the fire-controlman announced.

"Target is increasing speed and turning to starboard," sonar reported. "Both units are in acquisition and closing. Target isn't pinging anything yet."

"Unit one range to target is now two thousand yards. Unit three is twenty-two hundred out. Both units are tracking nicely, sir." The petty officer's eyes were locked on the weapons display, ready to override a possible mistake made by the automated homing systems. The ADCAP was at this point not unlike a miniature submarine with its own very precise sonar picture, enabling the weapons tech to play vicarious kamikaze, in this case two at once, a skill that nicely complemented his skill on the boat's Nintendo system. The really good news for Claggett was that he wasn't trying a counterdetection, but rather trying to save his ship first. Well, that was a judgment call, wasn't it?

"There's another one forward of us, bearing one-four-zero!"

"They have us," the Captain said, looking at the display and thinking that probably two submarines had shot at him. Still, he had to try, and ordered a crash turn to port. Top-heavy like her American Aegis cousins, *Mutsu* heeled violently to the right. As soon as the turn was made, the CO ordered full astern, hoping that the torpedo might miss forward.

It couldn't be anything else. Sato was losing sight of the battle, and overrode the autopilot, turning his aircraft into a tight left bank, leaving it to his right-seater to hit the seat belt signs for the passengers. He could see it all in the clear light of a quarter moon. *Mutsu* had executed one radical turn and then twisted into another. There were flashing lights on her stern as the ship's antisub helicopter started turning its rotor, struggling to get off and hunt whatever — yes, it had to be a submarine, Captain Sato thought, a sneaking, cowardly submarine attacking his brother's proud and beautiful destroyer. He was surprised to see the ship slow — to stop almost dead with the astern thrust of her reversible propeller — and wondered why *that* maneuver had been attempted. Wasn't it the same as for aircraft, whose rule was the simple axiom: Speed Is Life . . .

"Major cavitation sounds, maybe a crash-stop, sir," the sonar chief said. The weapons tech didn't give Claggett a chance to react.

"Don't matter. I have him cold on both, sir. Setting three for contact explosion, getting some magnetic interference from — they must use our Nixie, eh?"

"Correct, sailor."

"Well, we know how that puppy works. Unit one is five hundred out, closing fast." The technician cut one of the wires, letting unit one go on its own now, rising to thirty feet and fully autonomous, activating its onboard magnetic field and seeking the metal signature of the target, then finding it, letting it grow and grow . . .

The helicopter just got off, its strobe lights looping away from the now-stationary destroyer. The moment seemed fixed in time when the ship started turning again, or seemed to, then a violent green flash appeared in the water on both sides of the ship, just forward of the bridge under the vertical launch magazine for her surface-to-air missiles. The knifelike shape of the hull was backlit in an eerie, lethal way. The image fixed in Sato's mind for the quarter second it lasted, and then one or more of the destroyer's SAMs exploded, followed by forty others, and *Mutsu*'s forward half disintegrated. Three seconds later, another explosion took place, and when the white water returned back to the surface, there was little more to be seen than a patch of burning oil. Just like her namesake in Nagasaki harbor in 1943 . . .

"Captain!" The copilot had to wrench the control-wheel level away from the Captain before the Boeing went into a stall. "Captain, we have passengers aboard!"

"That was my brother . . ."

"We have *passengers* aboard, damn you!" Without resistance now, he brought the 747 back to level flight, looking at his gyrocompass for the proper heading. *"Captain!"*

Sato turned his head back into the cockpit, losing sight of his brother's grave as the airliner changed its heading back to the south.

"I am sorry, Captain Sato, but we also have a job we must do." He engaged the autopilot before reaching out to the man. "Are you all right now?"

Sato looked forward into the empty sky. Then he nodded and composed himself. "Yes, I am quite all right. Thank you. Yes. I am quite all right now," he repeated more firmly, required by the rules of his culture to set his personal emotions aside for now. Their father had survived his destroyer command, had moved on to captain a cruiser on which he had died off Samar, the victim of American destroyers and their torpedoes . . . and now again . . .

"What the hell was that?" Commander Ugaki demanded of his sonar officers.

"Torpedoes, two of them, from the south," the junior lieutenant replied. "They've killed *Mutsu.*"

"What from?" was the next angry shout.

"Something undetected, Captain," was the weak reply.

"Come south, turns for eight knots."

"That will take us right through the disturbance from — "

"Yes, I know that."

★ ★ ★

"Definite kill," sonar told him. The signature on the sonar screen was definite. "No engine sounds from target bearing, but breakup noises, and this here was one big secondary explosion. We got him, sir."

Richter crossed over the same town the C-17 had overflown a few days earlier, and though somebody might have heard him, that was less of a concern now. Besides, at night a chopper was a chopper, and there were plenty of them here. He settled his Comanche to a cruising altitude of fifty feet and headed due south, telling himself that, sure, the Navy would be there, and sure, he could land on a ship, and sure, everything was going to go just fine. He was grateful for the tailwind until he saw the waves it was whipping up. Oh, shit . . .

"Mr. Ambassador, the situation has changed, as you know," Adler said gently. The room had never heard the sound of more than one voice, but somehow it seemed far quieter now.

Seiji Nagumo, sitting next to his senior, noted that the chair next to Adler was occupied by someone else, another Japanese specialist from the fourth floor. Where was Chris Cook? he asked himself as the American negotiator went on. Why was he not here — and what did it mean?

"As we speak, American aircraft are attacking the Marianas. As we speak, American fleet units are engaging your fleet units. I must tell you that we have every reason to believe that our operations will be successful and that we will be able to isolate the Marianas from the rest of the world. The next part of the operation, if it becomes necessary, will be to declare a maritime exclusion zone around your Home Islands. We have no wish to attack your country directly, but it is within our capabilities to cut off your maritime trade in a matter of days.

"Mr. Ambassador, it is time to put an end to this . . ."

"As you see," the CNN reporter said from her perch next to USS *Enterprise*. Then the camera panned to her right, showing an empty box. "USS *John Stennis* has left her dry dock. We are informed that the carrier is even now launching a strike against the Japanese-held Marianas. We were asked to cooperate with government deception operations, and after careful consideration, it was decided that CNN is, after all, an *American* news service . . ."

"Bastards!" General Arima breathed, looking at the empty concrete structure, occupied only by puddles and wooden blocks now. Then his phone rang.

When it was certain that the Japanese E-2Cs had them, two Air Force AWACS aircraft flipped their radars on, having staged in from Hawaii, via Dyess on Kwajalein Atoll. In electronic terms it would be an even fight, but the Americans had more aircraft up to make sure it was fair in no other way. Four Japanese Eagles were aloft, and their first instinctive action was to turn northeast toward the intruders, the better to give their comrades standing ground alert time to get aloft and join the air battle before the incoming attack got close enough to catch their comrades on the ground. Simultaneously the ground defenses were warned to expect inbound hostile aircraft.

Sanchez lit off his own targeting radar as he saw the Japanese fighters just over a hundred miles away, heading in to launch their missiles. But they were armed with AMRAAMs, and he was armed with Phoenix, which had about double the range. He and three other aircraft launched two each for a max-range engagement. The eight missiles went into ballistic arcs, heading up to a hundred thousand feet before tipping over at Mach-5 and heading back down, their height giving them the largest possible radar cross section to home on. The Eagles detected the attack and tried to maneuver clear, but seconds later two of the F-15Js were blotted from the sky. The remaining pair kept driving in. The second wave of Phoenixes took care of that.

"What the hell?" Oreza wondered.

The sound of many jet engines starting up interrupted the card game, and all four men in the room went to the windows. Clark remembered to turn all the lights out, and stole the only set of binoculars in the house. The first pair of aircraft blazed off Kobler Field just as he brought them to his eyes. They were single-engine aircraft judging by their afterburner flames.

"What's happening, John?"

"Nobody told me, really, but it shouldn't be too hard to figure out."

Lights were on all over the field. What mattered was getting the fighters off as rapidly as possible. The same thing would be happening on Guam, probably, but Guam was a good ways off, and the two fighter groups would be engaging the Americans separately, negating the Japanese numerical advantage.

"What are those?"

Commander Peach and her jammers were also at work now. The search radar was powerful, but like all of its type it also transmitted low-frequency waves, and those were easily jammed. The massive collection of false dots both confused their understanding of the developing air action and knocked back their ability to detect the small but unstealthy cruise missiles. Fighters that might have tried to engage them had in fact overrun the inbound targets, giving them a free advance to the island's targets. The search radar atop Mount Takpochao picked them up barely thirty miles out instead of the hoped-for hundred, and was also trying to get a count on the inbound fighters. That gave the three operators on the set a complex task, but they were trained men, and they bent to the demands of the moment, one of their number sounding the alarm to get the island's Patriot missile batteries alerted.

The first part of the operation was going well. The standing Combat Air Patrol had been eliminated without loss, Sanchez saw, wondering if it had been one of his missiles that scored. No one would ever know about that. The next task was to take out the Japanese radar aircraft before the rest of their fighters arrived. To accomplish that, a division of four Tomcats went to burner and rocketed straight for them, rippling off all their missiles for the task.

They were just too brave for their own good, Sanchez saw. The Japanese Hawkeyes should have pulled back, and the defending Eagles should have done the same, but true to the fighter pilot's ethos they'd come out to engage the first wave of raiders instead of waiting. Probably because they thought this was a genuine raid instead of a mere fighter-sweep. The flanking division of four, called *Blinder Flight*, fulfilled its limited mission of killing the airborne-radar birds, then turned back to *John Stennis* to refuel and rearm. Now the only airborne radar was American. The Japanese came on, trying to blunt the attack that really did not exist, seeking to engage targets whose only goal had been the attention of the outbound interceptors.

It was obvious to the radar operators that the majority of the missiles were headed for them instead of the airfield. They didn't trade remarks about that. There wasn't time. They watched as the E-2s fell from the sky, too far away for them to guess exactly why, but the remaining AEW aircraft was still on the runway at Kobler as the fighters were racing to get off, and the first of them were approaching the distant American aircraft, which were, surprisingly, not headed in as expected. Guam was on the radio now, requesting information at the same time it announced that its fighters were scrambling off the ground to deal with the attack.

"Two minutes on the cruise missiles," one of the operators said over the interphones.

"Tell Kobler to get its E-2 up immediately," the senior officer in the control van said when he saw that the two already up were gone. Their van was a hundred yards from the radar transmitter, but it hadn't been dug in yet. It had been planned for the coming week.

"Wow!" Chavez observed. They were outside now. Some clever soul had killed the electrical power for their part of the island, which allowed them to step out of the house for a better view of the light show. Half a mile to their east, the first Patriot blew out of its box-launcher. The missile streaked only a few hundred meters up before its thrust-vector controls turned it as sharply as a billiard ball off a rail, aiming it down below the visible horizon. Three more followed a few seconds later.

"Cruise missiles coming in." This remark came from Burroughs. "Over to the north, looks like."

"Going for the radar on that hilltop, I bet," Clark thought. There followed a series of flashes that outlined the high ground to their east. The thunder of the explosions they represented took a few seconds more. Additional Patriots went off, and the civilians watched as the battery crew erected another box-launcher on its truck-transporter. They could also see that the process was taking too long.

* * *

The first wave of twenty Tomahawks was climbing now. They'd streaked in a bare three meters over the wave tops toward the sheer cliffs of Saipan's eastern coast. Automated weapons, they did not have the ability to avoid or even to detect fire directed at them, and the first ripple of Patriot SAMs did well, with twelve shots generating ten kills, but the remaining ten were climbing now, all targeted on the same spot. Four more of the cruise missiles fell to SAMs, and a fifth lost power and slammed into the cliff face at Laolao Kattan. The SAM radars lost them at that point, and the battery commanders called a warning to the radar people, but it was far too late to be helpful, and, one by one, five thousand-pound warheads exploded over the top of Mount Takpochao.

"That takes care of that," Clark said when the sound passed. Then he paused to listen. Others were out in the open now, standing around the cul-de-sac neighborhood. Individual hoots joined into a chorus of cheers that drowned out the shouts of the missile crew on the hilltop to the east.

Fighters were still rocketing off Kobler Field below them, generally taking off in pairs, with some singles. The blue flames of their afterburners turned in the sky before blinking off, as the Japanese fighters turned to form up and meet the inbound raid. Last of all, Clark and the others heard the electric-fan sound of the last remaining Hawkeye, heading off last of all despite the advice of the now-dead radar crew.

The island grew silent for a few moments, a strange emptiness to the air as people caught their breath and waited for the second act of the midnight drama.

Only fifty miles offshore, USS *Pasadena* and three other SSNs came to antenna depth and launched six missiles each. Some of them were aimed at Saipan.

Four went to Tinian. Two to Rota. The rest skimmed the wave tops for Andersen Air Force Base on Guam.

"Up scope!" Claggett ordered. The search periscope hissed up on hydraulic power. "Hold!" he called as the top of the instrument cleared the water. He turned slowly, looking for lights in the sky. None.

"Okay, the antenna next." Another hiss announced the raising of the UHF whip antenna. The Captain kept his eyes on the scope, still looking around. His right hand waved. There were some fuzzy radar signals from distant transmitters, but nothing able to detect the submarine.

"INDY CARS, this is PIT CREW, over," the communications officer said into a microphone.

"Thank God," Richter said aloud, keying his microphone. "PIT CREW, this is INDY LEAD, authenticate, over."

"Foxtrot Whiskey."

"Charlie Tango," Richter replied, checking the radio codes on his knee pad. "We are five out, and we sure could use a drink, over."

"Stand by," he heard back.

"Surface the ship," Claggett ordered, lifting the 1-MC. "Now hear this, we're surfacing the ship, maintain battle stations. Army crews, stand by."

The proper gear was sitting next to the midships escape trunk and the larger capsule hatch designed to handle the guidance packages for ballistic missiles. One of *Tennessee*'s damage-control parties stood by to pass the gear, and a chief would work the fueling-hose connector hidden in the casing over the missile room.

"What's that?" INDY-TWO asked over the radio circuit. "Lead, this is Three, chopper to the north.

1090

Say again, chopper to the north, big one."

"Take him out!" Richter ordered at once. There could be no friendly choppers about. He turned and increased altitude for a look of his own. The guy even had his strobes on. "PIT CREW, this is INDY LEAD, there's chopper traffic up here to the north. What gives, over?"

Claggett didn't hear that. *Tennessee*'s sail had just broken the surface, and he was standing by the ladder to the top of the sail. Shaw took the microphone.

"That's probably an ASW helo from the destroyer we just sunk — splash him, splash him *now!*"

"Aerial radar to the north!" an ESM tech called a second later. "Helicopter radar close aboard!"

"Two, take him out now!" Richter relayed the order.

"On the way, Lead," the second Comanche responded, turning and dipping his nose to increase speed. Whoever it was, that was just too bad. The pilot selected guns. Under his aircraft the 20-millimeter cannon emerged from its canoelike enclosure and turned forward. The target was five miles out and didn't see the inbound attack chopper.

It was another Sikorsky, Two's pilot saw, possibly assembled in the same Connecticut plant as his Comanch', the Navy version of the UH-60, a big target. His chopper blazed directly at it, hoping to get his kill before it could get a radio call out. Not much chance of that, and the pilot cursed himself for not engaging with a Stinger, but it was too late for that now. His helmet pipper locked on to the target and he triggered off fifty rounds, most of which found the nose of the approaching gray helicopter. The results were instant.

"Kill," he announced. "I got him, Lead."

"Roger, what your fuel state?"

"Thirty minutes," Two replied.

"Circle and keep your eyes open," Lead commanded.

"Roger, Leader." As soon as he got to three hundred feet came another unwelcome surprise. "Lead, Two, radar to the north, system says it's a Navy billboard one."

"Great," Richter snarled, circling the submarine. It was large enough to land on, but it would have been easier if the goddamned thing wasn't rolling around like the beer barrel at an Irish wake. Richter brought his chopper into hover, approaching from straight aft, and lowered his wheels for landing.

"Come left into the wind," Claggett told Lieutenant Shaw. "We have to cut the rolls down for 'em."

"Gotcha, Skipper." Shaw made the necessary orders, and *Tennessee* steadied up on a northwesterly heading.

"Stand by the escape and capsule hatches!" the CO ordered next. As he watched, the helo came down slowly, carefully, and as usual, landing a helicopter aboard a ship reminded him of two porcupines making love. It wasn't lack of willingness; it was just that you couldn't afford any mistakes.

They were lined up like an army of mounted knights now, Sanchez thought, with the Japanese two hundred miles off Saipan's northeast tip, and the Americans a hundred miles beyond. This game had been played out many times by both sides, and often enough in the same war game centers. Both sides had their tracking radars on and searching. Both sides could now see and count the strength of the other. It was just a question of who would make the first move. The Japanese were at the disadvantage and knew it. Their remaining E-2C was not yet in position, and worse than that, they could not be entirely sure who the opposition was. On Sanchez's command, the Tomcats moved off first, going to afterburner and climbing high to volley off their remaining Phoenix missiles. They fired at a range of fifty miles, and over a hundred of the sophisticated weapons turned into a wave of yellow flames climbing higher still before tipping over while their launch aircraft turned and retreated.

That was the signal for a general melee. The tactical situation had been clear, and then became less so as the Japanese fighters also went to maximum speed to close the Americans, hoping to duck under the Phoenix launch to launch their own fire-and-forget missiles. It was a move that required exquisite timing, which was hard to do without expert quarterbacking from a command-and-control aircraft, for which they had not waited.

It hadn't been possible to train Navy personnel to do it quickly enough, though a party of sailors did hold the wings up as the trained Army ground crewmen attached them to hardpoints on the side of the first Comanche. Then the fuel hoses were snaked to the openings, and the ship's pumps were switched on, filling all the tanks as rapidly as possible. Another Navy crewman tossed Richter a phone on the end of an ordinary wire.

"How did it go, Army?" Dutch Claggett asked.

"Kinda exciting. Y'all got some coffee, like hot maybe?"

"On the way, soldier." Claggett made the necessary call to the galley.

"Who was that chopper from?" Richter asked, looking back at the fueling operations.

"We had to take out a 'can about an hour ago. He was in the way. I guess the helo was from him. Ready to copy your destination?"

"Not Wake?"

"Negative. There's a carrier waiting for you at twenty-five north, one-fifty east. Say again, two-five north, one-five-zero east."

The warrant officer repeated the coordinates back twice, getting an additional confirmation. *A whole carrier to land on? Damn,* Richter thought. "Roger that, and thank you, sir."

"Thanks for splashing the helo, INDY."

A Navy crewman stepped up and banged on the side of the aircraft, giving a thumbs-up sign. He also handed over a *Tennessee* ball cap. Then Richter saw that the breast pocket on his shirt had a bulge in it. Most impolitely, he reached down and plucked out the half-pack of cigarettes. The sailor laughed over the noise and tossed a lighter to go along with it.

"Stand clear!" Richter shouted. The deck crewmen retreated, but then another man jumped out of the hatch with a thermos bottle, which was passed up. With that, the canopy came down and Richter started his engines back up. Barely a minute later, the Comanche lifted off, making room for -Two as his lead aircraft took an orbit position over the sub. Thirty seconds after that, the pilot was sipping coffee. It was different from the Army brew, far more civilized. A little Hennessey, he thought, and it would be about perfect.

"Sandy, look north!" his backseater said as -Two came down on the deck of the submarine.

Six Eagles fell to the first volley of missiles, with two more damaged and withdrawing, the AWACS controllers said. Sanchez couldn't see, as he was heading away from the advancing enemy fighters, the Tomcats making room now for the Hornets. It was working. The Japanese were pursuing, coming away from their island at high-power settings, driving the Americans away, or so they thought. His threat receiver said that there were enemy missiles in the air now, but they were American-designed missiles, and he knew what they could do.

"What's that?" Oreza wondered.

Just a shadow at first. The airfield lights were still on for some reason or other, and they saw a single white streak crossing the end of Kobler's runway. It banked sharply over the threshold and tracked down the center of the single strip. Then it changed shape, the nose blowing off, and small objects sprinkling down on the concrete. A few exploded. The rest just disappeared, too small to see unless they were moving. Then came another, and another, all doing the same thing, except for one that headed straight for the tower, and blew the top right off of it, and along with it, the fighter wing's radios.

Farther south, the commercial airfield was also lit up still, four 747s sitting at the terminal or elsewhere on the ramp. Nothing seemed to approach the airport. To their east, several more missile launches lit up the Patriot battery, but they'd shot off their first load of missiles, and the crews now had to erect additional box launchers, then connect them to the command van, and that took time. They were getting kills, but not enough.

"Not going for the SAMs," Chavez noted, thinking that they really ought to be under cover for all this, but . . . but nobody else was, as though this were some sort of glorious Fourth of July display.

"Avoiding civilian areas, Ding," Clark replied.

"Nice trick. By the way, what's this Kelly stuff?"

"My real name," the senior officer observed.

"John, how many of the bastards did you kill?" Oreza wanted to know.

"Huh?" Chavez asked.

"Back when we were both children, your boss here did a little private hunting, drug dealers, as I recall."

"It never happened, Portagee. Honest." John shook his head and grinned. "Well, not that anybody can prove," he added. "I really am dead, you know?"

"In that case you got the right set of initials for the new name, man." Oreza paused. "Now what?"

"Beats me, pal." Oreza wasn't cleared for his new orders, and he didn't know that they were possible anyway. A few seconds later it occurred to someone to switch off the remaining electrical power on the south end of the island.

Mutsu's helicopter had announced the presence of a submarine on the surface, but nothing more. That had caused *Kongo* to launch her Seahawk, now coming south. Two P-3C Orion antisub aircraft were approaching as well, but the helicopter would get in first, carrying two torpedoes. That aircraft was coming in at two hundred feet, without its look-down radar on, but with flashing strobes that looked very bright in Richter's headset.

"Sure is busy here," Richter said. He was at five hundred feet, with a new target just on the horizon. "PIT CREW, this is INDY LEAD, we have another chopper in the neighborhood."

"Splash him!"

"Copy that." Richter increased speed for his intercept. The Navy didn't have any problems making decisions. The closure speed guaranteed a rapid intercept. Richter selected STINGER and fired at five miles. Whoever it was, he didn't expect hostile aircraft in the area, and the cold water under him made a fine contrast background for the heat-seeking missile. The Seahawk spun in, leaving Richter to wonder if there might be survivors. But he didn't have the ability to perform a rescue, and didn't close in to see.

-Two was up now, and took the protective orbit position, allowing the leader to turn for the rendezvous. He gave the submarine a low saluting pass and headed off. He had neither the fuel nor the time to linger.

"You realize we're an aircraft carrier?" Ken Shaw asked, watching the deck crew finishing up refueling for the third and last visitor. "We scored kills and everything."

"Just so we live long enough to be a submarine again," Claggett replied tensely. As he watched, the canopy came down and the crewmen started securing topside. Two minutes later his deck was nearly clear. One of his chiefs tossed extraneous gear over the side, waved to the sail, and disappeared down the capsule hatch.

"Clear the bridge!" Claggett ordered. He took one last look around before keying the microphone one last time. "Take her down."

"We don't have a straight board yet," the Chief of the Boat objected in the attack center.

"You heard the man," the officer of the deck snapped back. With that command the vents were opened and the main ballast tanks flooded. The topside bridge hatch changed a second later from a circle to a dash, and Claggett appeared a moment later, closing the bottom-end hatch to the bridge, making a straight board.

"Rigged for dive. Get us out of here!"

"That's a submarine," the Lieutenant said. "Diving — venting his tanks."

"Range?"

"I have to go active for that," the sonar officer warned.

"Then do it!" Ugaki hissed.

"What are those flashes?" the copilot wondered. They were just over the horizon to the left of their flight path, no telling the distance, but however far away they were, they were bright, and one turned into a streak that cometed down into the sea. More streaks erupted in the darkness, lines of yellow-white going mainly right-to-left. That made it clear. "Oh."

"Saipan Approach, this is JAL Seven-Oh-Two, two hundred miles out. What is happening, over?" There was no reply.

"Return to Narita?" the copilot asked.

"No! No, we will not do that!" Torajiro Sato replied.

It was a tribute to his professionalism that rage didn't quite overcome his training. He'd already dodged two missiles to this point, and Major Shiro Sato did not panic despite the ill-luck that had befallen his wingman. His radar showed more than twenty targets, just out of missile range, and though some others of his squadron mates had fired their AMRAAMs, he wouldn't until he had a better chance. He also showed multiple radars tracking his aircraft, but there was no helping that. He jerked his Eagle around the sky, taking hard turns and heavy gees as he closed on burner. What had begun as an organized battle was now a wild melee, with individual fighters entirely on their own, like samurai in the darkness. He turned north now, selecting the nearest blips. The IFF systems automatically interrogated them, and the answer was not what he expected. With that Sato triggered off his fire-and-forget missiles, then turned back sharply to the south. It wasn't at all what he'd hoped for, not a fair fight, skill against skill in a clear sky. This had been a chaotic encounter in darkness, and he simply didn't know who had won or lost. He had to turn and run now. Courage was one thing, but the Americans had drawn them out so that he scarcely had the fuel remaining for his home field. He'd never know if his missiles had scored. Damn.

1098

He increased power one last time, going to burner to disengage, angling right to keep clear of the fighters advancing in from the south. Those were the planes from Guam, probably. He wished them luck.

"TURKEY, this is TURKEY LEAD. Disengage now. I say again, disengage now!" Sanchez was well behind the action now, wishing that he were in his Hornet instead of the larger Tomcat. Acknowledgments came in, and though he'd lost a few aircraft, and though the battle had not been entirely to his liking, he knew that it had been a success. He headed north to clear the area, checking his fuel state. Then he saw strobe lights at his ten o'clock and turned further to investigate.

"Jesus, Bud, it's an airliner," his radar-intercept officer said. "JAL markings." That was obvious from the stylized red crane on the high tailfin.

"Better warn him off." Sanchez turned on his own strobes and closed from the portside. "JAL 747, JAL 747, this is U.S. Navy aircraft to your portside."

"Who are you?" the voice asked over the guard frequency.

"We are a U.S. Navy aircraft. Be advised there is a battle going on here. I suggest you reverse course and head back home. Over."

"I don't have the fuel for that."

"Then you can bingo to Iwo Jima. There's a field there, but watch out for the radio tower southwest of the strip, over."

"Thank you," was the terse reply. "I will continue on my flight plan. Out."

"Dumbass." Sanchez didn't put on the air, though his backseater fully agreed. In a real war they would have just shot him down, but this wasn't a real war, or so some people had decided. Sanchez would never know the magnitude of his error.

"Captain, that is very dangerous!"

"Iwo Jima is not lighted. We'll approach from the west and stay clear," Captain Sato said, unmoved by all that he'd heard. He altered course to the west, and the copilot kept his peace on the matter.

"Active sonar to starboard, bearing zero-one-zero, low-frequency, probably a sub." And that was not good news.

"Snapshot!" Claggett ordered at once. He'd drilled his crew mercilessly on this scenario, and the boomers did have the best torpedomen in the fleet.

"Setting up on tube four," the weapons petty officer answered. On command, the torpedo was activated. "Flooding four. Tube four is flooded. Weapon is hot."

"Initial course zero-one-zero," the weapons officer said, checking the plot, which didn't reveal much. "Cut the wires, set to go active at one thousand!"

"Set!"

"Match and shoot!" Claggett ordered.

"Fire four, four away!" The sailor nearly broke the firing handle.

"Range four thousand meters," the sonar officer reported. "Large submerged target, beam aspect. Transient — he's launched!"

"So can we. Fire one, fire two!" Ugaki shouted. "Left full rudder," he added the moment the second tube was clear. "Ahead flank!"

"Torpedo in the water. *Two* torpedoes in the water, bearing zero-one-zero. Ping-and-listen, the torpedoes are in search mode!" sonar reported.

"Oh, shit. We've been here before," Shaw noted, recalling an awful experience on USS *Maine*. The Army officer aboard and his senior sergeant had just come into the attack center to thank the Captain for his part in the helicopter mission. They stopped cold on the portside, looking around and seeing the tension in the compartment.

"Six-inch room, launch decoy, now!"

"Launching now." There was slight noise a second later, just a jolt of compressed air.

"We have a MOSS set up?" Claggett asked, even though he'd given orders for exactly that.

"Tube two, sir," the weapons tech replied.

"Warm it up."

"Done, sir."

"Okay." Commander Claggett allowed himself a deep breath and time to think. He didn't have much, but he had some. How smart was that Japanese fish? *Tennessee* was doing ten knots, not having had rudder or speed orders after submerging, and was at three hundred feet of keel depth. Okay.

"Six-inch room, set up a spread of three canisters to launch on my command."

"Standing by, sir."

"Weps, set the MOSS for three hundred feet, circling as tight as you can at this depth. Make it active as soon as it clears the tube."

"Stand by . . . set. Tube is flooded."

"Launch."

"MOSS away, sir."

"Six-inch room, launch now!"

Tennessee shuddered again, with three decoys ejected into the sea along with the torpedo-based lure. The approaching torpedo now had a very attractive false target to track.

"Surface the ship! Emergency surface!"

"Emergency surface, aye," the chief of the boat replied, reaching himself for the air manifold. "Full rise on the planes!"

"Full rise, aye!" the helmsman repeated, pulling back on his control yoke.

"Conn, sonar, the inbound torpedoes are still in

ping-and-listen. Our outbound unit is now on continuous pinging. It has a sniff."

"Their fish is like an early -48, troops," Claggett said calmly. His demeanor was a lie, and he knew that, but the crew might not. "Remember the three rules of a -48. It has to be a valid target, it has to be over eight hundred yards, and it has to have a bearing rate. Helm, all stop."

"All stop, aye. Sir, engine room answers all stop."

"Very well, we'll let her coast up now," the Captain said, out of things to say now. He looked over at the Army people and winked. They looked rather pale. Well, that was one advantage of being black, wasn't it? Claggett thought.

Tennessee took a thirty-degree up-angle, killing a lot of her forward speed as she rose and tumbling several people to the deck, it came so abruptly. Claggett held on to the red-and-white periscope-control wheel to steady himself.

"Depth?"

"Breaking the surface now, sir!" the COB reported. A second later came a rush of exterior noise, and then the submarine crashed sickeningly back down.

"Rig for ultraquiet."

The shaft was stopped now. *Tennessee* wallowed on the surface while three hundred feet down and half a mile aft, the MOSS was circling in and out of the decoy bubbles. He'd done all that he could do. A crewman reached into his pocket for a smoke, then realized that he'd lost his pack topside.

"Our unit is in acquisition!" sonar reported.

"Come right!" Ugaki said, trying to be calm and succeeding, but the American torpedo had run straight through the decoy field . . . just as his had done, he remembered. He looked around his control room. The faces were on him, just as they had been the other time, but this time the other boat had shot first despite his advantage, and he only needed a look at the plot to see that he'd never know if his second submarine attack had succeeded or not.

"I'm sorry," he said to his crew, and a few heads had time to nod at his final, sincere apology to them.

"Hit!" sonar called next.

"Thank you, Sonar," Claggett acknowledged.

"The enemy fish are circling below us, sir . . . they seem to be . . . yeah, they're chasing into the decoy . . . we're getting some pings, but . . ."

"But the early -48s didn't track stationary surface targets, Chief," Claggett said quietly. The two men might have been the only people breathing aboard. Well, maybe Ken Shaw, who was standing at the weapons panel. It only made things worse that you couldn't hear the ultrasonic noise of a torpedo sonar.

"The damned things run forever."

"Yep." Claggett nodded. "Raise the ESM," he added as an afterthought. The sensor mast went up at once, and people cringed at the noise.

"Uh, Captain, there's an airborne radar bearing three-five-one."

"Strength?"

"Low but increasing. Probably a P-3, sir."

"Very well."

It was too much for the Army officer. "We just sit still?"

"That's right."

Sato brought the 747 in largely from memory. There were no runway lights, but he had enough from the moon to see what he was doing, and once again his copilot marveled at the man's skill as the aircraft's landing lights caught reflections from lights on the ground. The landing was slightly to the right of the centerline, but Sato managed a straight run to the end, this time without his usual look over at the junior officer. He was bringing the aircraft right onto the taxiway when there was a flash in the distance.

Major Sato's was the first Eagle back to Kobler, actually having passed two damaged aircraft on his way in. There was activity on the ground, but the only radio chatter was incoherent. He had little choice in any case. His fighter was running on vapors and memory now, all the fuel gauges showing almost nothing. Also without lights, the aviator chose the proper glide-slope and touched down in exactly the right spot. He didn't see the softball-size submunition that his nosegear hit. The fighter's nose collapsed, and the Eagle slid, pinwheeling off the end of the runway. There was just enough vapor in the tanks to start a fire, then an explosion to scatter parts over the Kobler runway. A second Eagle, half a mile behind Sato's, found another bomblet and exploded. The twenty remaining fighters angled away, calling on their radios for instructions. Six of them turned for the commercial field. The rest looked for and approached the large twin runways on Tinian, not knowing that they, too, had been sprinkled with cluster munitions from a series of Tomahawk missiles. Roughly half survived the landing without hitting anything.

Admiral Chandraskatta was in his control room, watching the radar display. He'd have to recall his fighters soon. He didn't like risking his pilots in night operations, but the Americans were up in strength, doing another of their shows of force. And surely they could attack and destroy his fleet if they wished, but now? With a war against Japan under way, would America choose to initiate another combat action? No. His amphibious force was now at sea, and in two days, at sunset, the time would come.

★ ★ ★

The B-1s were lower than the flight crews had ever driven them. These were reservists, mostly airline pilots, assigned by a particularly beneficent Pentagon (with the advice of a few senior members of Congress) to a real combat aircraft for the first time in years. For practice bombing missions over land, they had a standard penetration altitude of no less than two hundred feet, more usually three hundred, because even Kansas farms had windmills and people erected radio towers in the damnedest places — but not at sea. Here they were down to fifty feet, and smokin', one pilot observed, nervously entrusting his aircraft to the terrain-avoidance system. His group of eight was heading due south, having turned over Dondra Head. The other four were heading northwest after using a different navigational marker. There was lots of electronic activity ahead, enough to make him nervous, though none of it was on him yet, and he allowed himself the sheer exhilaration of the moment, flying over Mach-1, and doing it so low that his bomber was trailing a different sort of vapor trail, more like an unlimited-class racing boat, and maybe cooking some fish along the way . . .

There.

"Low-level contacts from the north!"

"What?" The Admiral looked up. "Range?"

"Less than twenty kilometers, coming in very fast!"

"Are they missiles?"

"Unknown, Admiral!"

Chandraskatta looked down at his plot. There they were, the opposite direction from the American carrier aircraft. His fighters were not in a position to —

"Inbound aircraft!" a lookout called next.

"Engage?" Captain Mehta asked.

"Shoot first without orders?" Chandraskatta ran for

the door, emerging onto the flight deck just in time to see the white lines in the water even before the aircraft causing them.

"Coming up now," the pilot said, aiming himself just at the carrier's bridge. He pulled back on the stick, and when it vanished under his nose, checked his altitude indicator.

"Pull up!" the voice-warning system told him in the usual sexy voice.

"I already did, Marilyn." It sounded like a Marilyn to the TWA pilot. Next he checked his speed. Just under nine hundred knots. Wow. The noise this big mother would make . . .

The sonic boom generated by the huge aircraft was more like a bomb blast, knocking the Admiral off his feet and shattering glass on the wheelhouse well over his head and wrecking other topside gear. Another followed seconds later, and then he heard more still as the massive aircraft buzzed over his fleet. He was slightly disoriented as he stood, and there were glass fragments on the flight deck as he made his way back under cover. Somehow he knew his place was on the bridge.

"Two radars are out," he heard a petty officer say. "*Rajput* reports her SAMs are down."

"Admiral," a communications lieutenant called, holding up a growler phone.

"Who is this?" Chandraskatta asked.

"This is Mike Dubro. The next time we won't be playing. I am authorized to tell you that the U.S. Ambassador is now meeting with your Prime Minister . . ."

"It is in everyone's best interest that your fleet should terminate its operations," the former Governor of Pennsylvania said after the usual introductory pleasantries.

"You may not order us about, you know."

"That was not an order, Madame Prime Minister. It was an observation. I am also authorized to tell you that my government has requested an emergency session of the U.N. Security Council to discuss your apparent intentions to invade Sri Lanka. We will offer to the Security Council the service of the U.S. Navy to safeguard the sovereignty of that country. Please forgive me for speaking bluntly, but my country does not intend to see the sovereignty of that country violated by anyone. As I said, it is in everyone's interest to prevent a clash of arms."

"We have no such intentions," the Prime Minister insisted, taken very aback by the directness of this message after the earlier one she'd ignored.

"Then we are agreed," Ambassador Williams said pleasantly. "I will communicate that to my government at once."

It took nearly forever, in this case just over half an hour, before the first, then the second torpedo stopped circling, then stopped pinging. Neither found the MOSS a large-enough target to engage, but neither found anything else, either.

"Strength on that P-3 radar?" Claggett asked.

"Approaching detection values, sir."

"Take her down, Mr. Shaw. Let's get below the layer and tool on out of here."

"Aye, Cap'n." Shaw gave the necessary orders. Two minutes later, USS *Tennessee* was underwater, and five minutes after that at six hundred feet, turning southeast at a speed of ten knots. Soon thereafter they heard splashes aft, probably sonobuoys, but it took a long time for a P-3 to generate enough data to launch an attack, and *Tennessee* wasn't going to linger about.

47

Brooms

"Not with a bang but a whimper?" the President asked.

"That's the idea," Ryan said, setting the phone down. Satellite imagery showed that whatever the losses had been in the air battle, the Japanese had lost another fourteen aircraft due to cluster munitions on their airfields. Their principal search radars were gone, and they'd shot off a lot of SAMs. The next obvious step was to isolate the islands entirely from air and sea traffic, and that could be done before the end of the week. The press release was already being prepared if the necessity presented itself.

"We've won," the National Security Advisor said. "It's just a matter of convincing the other side."

"You've done well, Jack," Durling said.

"Sir, if I'd managed to get the job done properly, it never would have started in the first place," Ryan replied after a second's pause. He remembered getting things started along those lines . . . about a week too late to matter. Damn.

"Well, we seem to have done that with India, according to what Dave Williams just cabled in." The President paused. "And what about this?"

"First we worry about concluding hostilities."

"And then?"

"We offer them an honorable way out." Upon elaboration, Jack was pleased to see that the Boss agreed with him.

There would be one more thing, Durling didn't say, but he needed just a little more thinking about it. For the moment it was enough that America looked to be winning this war, and with it he'd won reelection for saving the economy and safeguarding the rights of American citizens. It had been quite an interesting month, the President thought, looking at the other man in the room and wondering what might have come to pass without him. After Ryan left, he placed a telephone call to the Hill.

One other advantage of airborne-radar aircraft was that they made counting coup a lot easier. They could not always show which missile killed which aircraft, but they did show them dropping off the screen.

"*Port Royal* reports recovery complete," a talker said.

"Thank you," Jackson said. He hoped the Army aviators weren't too disappointed to have landed on a cruiser instead of *Johnnie Reb*, but he needed his deck space.

"I count twenty-seven kills," Sanchez said. Three of his own fighters had fallen, with only one of the pilots rescued. The casualties were lighter than expected, though that fact didn't make the letter-writing any easier for the CAG.

"Well, it's not exactly like the Turkey Shoot, but it wasn't bad. Tack on fourteen more from the Tomahawks. That's about half their fighter strength — most of their F-15s — and they only have the one Hummer left. They're on the short end from now on." The battle-force commander went over the other data. A destroyer gone and the rest of their Aegis ships in the wrong place to interfere with the combat action. Eight submarines definitely destroyed. The overall operational concept had been to detach the arms from the body first, just as had been done in the Persian Gulf, and it had proved to be even easier over water than over land. "Bud, if you were commanding the other side, what would you try next?"

"We still can't invade." Sanchez paused. "It's a losing game any way you cut it, but the last time we had to come this way . . ." He looked at his commander.

"There is that. Bud, get a Tom ready for a flight with me in the back."

"Aye aye, sir." Sanchez made his way off.

"You thinking what I — " Stennis's captain asked with a raised eyebrow.

"What do we got to lose, Phil?"

"A pretty good admiral, Rob," he replied quietly.

"Where do you keep your radios in this barge?" Jackson asked with a wink.

"Where have you been?" Goto asked in surprise.

"In hiding, after your patron kidnapped me." Koga walked in without so much as an announcement, took a seat without being bidden, and generally displayed the total lack of manners that proclaimed his renewed power. "What do you have to say for yourself?" the former Prime Minister demanded of his successor.

"You cannot talk to me that way." But even these words were weak.

"How marvelous. You lead our nation to ruin, but you insist on deference from someone whom your master almost killed. With your knowledge?" Koga asked lightly.

"Certainly not — and who murdered the — "

"Who murdered the criminals? Not I," Koga assured him. "There is a more important question: what are you going to do?"

"Why, I haven't decided that yet." This attempt at a strong statement fell short on several counts.

"You haven't spoken to Yamata yet, you mean."

"I decide things for myself!"

"Excellent. Do so now."

"You cannot order me about."

"And why not? I will soon be back in that seat. You have a choice. Either you will resign your position this morning or this afternoon I will speak in the Diet and request a vote of no-confidence. It is a vote you will not survive. In either case you are finished." Koga stood and started to leave. "I suggest you do so honorably."

People were lined up in the terminal, standing in line at the counters to get tickets home, Captain Sato saw, as he walked past with a military escort. He was only a young lieutenant, a paratrooper still apparently eager to fight, which was more than could be said for the others in the building. The waiting jeep raced away, heading for the military airfield. The natives were out now, unlike before, carrying signs urging the "Japs" to leave. Some of them ought to be shot for their insolence, Sato thought, still coming to terms with his grief. Ten minutes later, he entered one of Kobler's hangars. Fighters were circling overhead, probably afraid to stray offshore, he thought.

"In here, please," the Lieutenant said.

He walked into the building with consummate dignity, his uniform cap tucked inside his left arm, his back erect, hardly looking at anything, his eyes fixed on the distant wall of the building until the Lieutenant stopped and pulled the rubber sheet off the body.

"Yes, that is my son." He tried not to look, and blessedly the face was not grossly disfigured, possibly protected by the flight helmet while the rest of the body had burned as he sat trapped in his wrecked fighter. But when he closed his eyes he could see his only child writhing in the cockpit, less than an hour after his brother had drowned. Could destiny be so cruel as this? And how was it that those who had served his country had to die, while a mere transporter of civilians was allowed to pass through the American fighters with contempt?

"The squadron command believes that he shot down an American fighter before coming back," the Lieutenant offered. He'd just made that up, but he had to say something, didn't he?

"Thank you, Lieutenant. I have to return to my aircraft now." No more words were passed on the way back to the airport. The army officer left the man with his grief and his dignity.

Sato was on his flight deck twenty minutes later, the 747 already preflighted, and, he was sure, completely filled with people returning home under the promise of safe passage by the Americans. The ground tractor pushed the Boeing away from the jetway. It was driven by a native, and the gesture he flashed to the cockpit on decoupling from their aircraft was not exactly a friendly one. But the final insult came as he waited for clearance to take off. A fighter came in to land, not a blue Eagle, it was a haze-gray aircraft with NAVY painted on the engine nacelles.

"Nice touch, Bud. Grease job," Jackson said as the canopy came up.

"We aim to please, sir," Sanchez replied nervously. As he taxied off to the right, the welcoming committee, such as it was, all wore green fatigues and carried rifles. When the aircraft stopped, an aluminum extension ladder was laid alongside the aircraft. Jackson climbed out first, and at the bottom of the ladder a field-grade officer saluted him correctly.

"That's a Tomcat," Oreza said, handing over the binoculars. "And that officer ain't no Jap."

"Sure as hell," Clark confirmed, watching the black officer get into a jeep. What effect would this have on his tentative orders? Attractive as it might be to put the arm on Raizo Yamata, even getting close enough to evaluate the possibility — his current instructions — was not a promising undertaking. He had also reported on conditions on Saipan, and that word, he thought, was good. The Japanese troops he'd seen earlier in the day were not the least bit jaunty, though some officers, especially the junior ones, seemed very enthusiastic about their mission, whatever that was right now. It was about what you expected of lieutenants in any army.

The Governor's house, set on the local Capitol Hill next to the convention center, seemed a pleasant enough structure. Jackson was sweating now. The tropical sun was hot enough, and his nomex flight suit was just too good an insulator. Here a colonel saluted him and led him inside.

Robby knew General Arima on sight, remembering the intelligence file he'd seen in the Pentagon. They were of about the same height and build, he saw. The General saluted. Jackson, bareheaded and under cover, was not allowed to do so under naval regulations. It seemed the proper response not to, anyway. He nodded his head politely, and left it at that.

"General, can we speak in private?"

Arima nodded and led Jackson into what looked like a combination den/office. Robby took a seat, and his host was kind enough to hand over a glass of ice water.

"Your position is . . . ?"

"I am Commander Task Force Seventy-Seven. I gather you are the commander of Japanese forces on Saipan." Robby drank the water down. It annoyed him greatly to be sweating, but there was no helping that.

"Correct."

"In that case, sir, I am here to request your surrender." He hoped the General knew the semantic difference between "request" and "demand," the customary verb for the occasion.

"I am not authorized to do that."

"General, what I'm about to say to you is the position of my government. You may leave the islands in peace. You may take your light weapons with you. Your heavy equipment and aircraft will remain behind for later determination of status. For the moment we require that all Japanese citizens leave the island, pending the restoration of normal relations between our countries."

"I am not authorized to — "

"I'll be saying the same thing on Guam in two hours, and the American Ambassador in Tokyo is now requesting a meeting with your government."

"You do not have the ability to take this one island back, much less all of them."

"That is true," Jackson conceded. "It is also true that we can easily stop all ships from entering or leaving Japanese ports for the indefinite future. We can similarly cut off this island from air and sea traffic."

"That is a threat," Arima pointed out.

"Yes, sir, it is. In due course your country will starve. Its economy will come to a complete halt. That serves no one's purposes." Jackson paused. "Up until this point only military people have suffered. They pay us to take chances. If it goes any further, then everyone suffers more, but your country most of all. It will also generate additional bad feelings on both sides, when our actions should be to restore normal relations as rapidly as circumstances allow."

"I am not authorized to — "

"General, fifty years ago you could have said that, and it was the custom of your armed forces to fight to the last man. It was also the custom of your armed forces to deal with people in the lands you occupied in a way that even you must find barbaric — I say that because you have behaved honorably in all respects — or so all my information tells me. For that I thank you, sir," Jackson went on, speaking evenly and politely. "This is not the nineteen-forties. I wasn't born before the end of that war, and you were a toddler then. That sort of behavior is a thing of the past. There is no place for it in the world today."

"My troops have behaved properly," Arima confirmed, not knowing what else to say under the circumstances.

"Human life is a precious commodity, General Arima, far too precious to be wasted unnecessarily. We have limited our combat actions to militarily important targets. We have not as yet inflicted harm on the innocent, as you have not. But if this war continues, that will change, and the consequences will be harder on you than on us. There is no honor in that for either side. In any case, I must now fly to Guam. You know how to reach me by radio." Jackson stood.

"I must await orders from my government."

"I understand," Robby replied, thankful that Arima meant that he would follow those orders — from his *government*.

Usually when Al Trent came to the White House it was in the company of Sam Fellows, the ranking minority member of the Select Committee, but not this time, because Sam was in the other party. A member of his party's Senate leadership was there also. The hour made this a political meeting, with most of the White House staffers gone for the day, and a President allowing himself a release from the stress of his office.

"Mr. President, I gather that things have gone well?"

Durling nodded cautiously. "Prime Minister Goto is not yet able to meet with the Ambassador. We're not sure why, but Ambassador Whiting says not to worry. The public mood over there is shifting our way rapidly."

Trent took a drink from the Navy steward who served in the Oval Office. That part of the White House staff must have kept a list of the favored drinks for the important. In Al's case it was vodka and tonic, Finnish Absolut vodka, a habit begun while a student at Tufts University, forty years earlier.

"Jack said all along that they didn't know what they were getting into."

"Bright boy, Ryan," the senior Senator agreed. "He's done you quite a few favors, Roger." Trent noted with annoyance that this stalwart member of what he liked to call "the upper house" felt the right to first-name the President in private. Typical senator, the House member thought.

"Bob Fowler gave you some good advice," Trent allowed.

The President nodded agreement. "True, and you're the one who put the bug in his ear, Al, aren't you?"

"Guilty." The word was delivered with a laugh.

"Well, I have an idea I want to float on the both of you," Durling said.

Captain Checa's squad of Rangers made the last treeline just after noon, local time, concluding a thoroughly murderous trek through snow and mud. There was a single-lane road below. This part of town must have been some sort of summer resort, the Captain thought. The hotel parking lots were almost entirely empty, though one had a minibus in it. The Captain pulled the cellular phone from his pocket and speed-dialed the proper number.

"Hello?"

"Señor Nomuri?"

"Ah, Diego! I've been waiting for hours. How was

your nature hike?" the voice asked with a laugh.

Checa was formulating his answer when the lights on the minibus flashed twice. Ten minutes later all the men were inside, where they found some hot drinks and room to change their clothing. On the drive down the mountain, the CIA officer listened to the radio, and the soldiers could see his demeanor relax as he did so. It would be a while longer before the Rangers did the same.

Captain Sato performed another perfect landing at Narita International Airport, entirely without thinking about it, not even hearing the congratulatory comment of his copilot as he completed the run-out. Outwardly calm, inside the pilot was a vacuum, performing his customary job robotically. The copilot did not interfere, thinking that the mechanics of handling the aircraft would itself be some solace to his captain, and so he watched Sato taxi the 747 right up to the jetway, stopping again with the usual millimetric precision. In less than a minute the doors were opened and passengers clambered off. Through the windows of the terminal they could see a crowd of people waiting at the gate, mainly the wives and children of people who had flown so recently to Saipan in order to establish themselves as . . . citizens, able to vote in the newest Home Island. But not now. Now they were coming home, and families welcomed them as those who might have been lost, now safe again where they belonged. The copilot shook his head at the absurdity of it all, not noticing that Sato's face still hadn't changed at all. Ten minutes later the flight crew left the aircraft. A relief crew would take it back to Saipan in a few hours to continue the exodus of special flights.

Out in the terminal, they saw others waiting at other gates, outwardly nervous from their expressions, though many were devouring afternoon papers just delivered to the airport's many gift shops.

Goto Falls was the headline: *Koga to Form New Government.*

The international gates were rather less full than was the norm. Caucasian businessmen stood about, clearly leaving the country, but now looking about in curiosity, so many of them with little smiles as they scanned the terminal, looking mainly at the flights inbound from Saipan. Their thoughts could hardly have been more obvious, especially the people waiting to board flights eastward.

Sato saw it too. He stopped and looked at a paper dispenser but only needed to see the headline to understand. Then he looked at the foreigners at their gates and muttered, *"Gaijin . . ."* It was the only unnecessary word he'd spoken in two hours, and he said nothing else on the way to his car. Perhaps some sleep would help him, the copilot thought, heading off to his own.

"Aren't we supposed to go back out and — "

"And do what, Ding?" Clark asked, pocketing the car keys after a thirty-minute spin around the southern half of the island. "Sometimes you just let things be. I think this is one of those times, son."

"You saying it's over?" Pete Burroughs asked.

"Well, take a look around."

Fighters were still orbiting overhead. Cleanup crews had just about cleared the debris from the periphery of Kobler Field, but the fighters had not moved over to the international airport, whose runways were busy with civilian airliners. To the east of the housing tract the Patriot crews were also standing alert, but those not in the control vans were standing together in small knots, talking among themselves instead of doing the usual soldierly make-work. Local citizens were demonstrating now, in some cases loudly, at various sites around the island, and nobody was arresting them. In some cases officers backed up by armed soldiers asked, politely, for the demonstrators to stay away from the troops, and the local people prudently heeded the warnings. On their drive, Clark and Chavez had seen half a dozen such incidents, and in all cases it was the same: the soldiers not angered so much as embarrassed by it all. It wasn't the sign of an army ready to fight a battle, John thought, and more importantly, the officers were keeping their men under tight control. That meant orders from above to keep things cool.

"You think it's over?" Oreza asked.

"If we're lucky, Portagee."

Prime Minister Koga's first official act after forming a cabinet was to summon Ambassador Charles Whiting. A political appointee whose last four weeks in the country had been very tense and frightening indeed, Whiting noted first of all that the guard detail around the embassy was cut by half. His official car had a police escort to the Diet Building. There were cameras to record his arrival at the VIP entrance, but they were kept well back, and two brand-new ministers conducted him inside.

"Thank you for coming so quickly, Mr. Whiting."

"Mr. Prime Minister, speaking for myself, I am very pleased to answer your invitation." The two men shook hands, and really that was it, both of them knew, though their conversation had to cover numerous issues.

"You are aware that I had nothing at all to do — "

Whiting just raised his hand. "Excuse me, sir. Yes, I know that, and I assure you that my government knows that. Please, we do not need to establish your goodwill. This meeting," the Ambassador said generously, "is proof positive of that."

"And the position of your government?"

★ ★ ★

At exactly nine in the morning, Vice President Edward Kealty's car pulled into the underground parking garage of the State Department. Secret Service agents conducted him to the VIP elevator that took him to the seventh floor, where one of Brett Hanson's personal assistants led him to the double doors of the office of the Secretary of State.

"Hello, Ed," Hanson said, standing and coming to meet the man he'd known in and out of public life for two decades.

"Hi, Brett." Kealty was not downcast. In the past few weeks he'd come to terms with many things. Later today he would make his public statement, apologizing to Barbara Linders and several other people by name. But before that he had to do what the Constitution required. Kealty reached into his coat pocket and handed over an envelope to the Secretary of State. Hanson took it and read the two brief paragraphs that announced Kealty's resignation from his office. There were no further words. The two old friends shook hands and Kealty made his way back out of the building. He would return to the White House, where his personal staff was already collecting his belongings. By evening the office would be ready for a new occupant.

"Jack, Chuck Whiting is delivering our terms, and they're pretty much what you suggested last night."

"You might catch some political heat from that," Ryan observed, inwardly relieved that President Durling was willing to run the risk.

The man behind the ornate desk shook his head. "I don't think so, but if it happens, I can take it. I want orders to go out for our forces to stand down, defensive action only."

"Good."

1120

"It's going to be a long while before things return to normal."

Jack nodded. "Yes, sir, but we can still manage things in as civilized a way as possible. Their citizens were never behind this. Most of the people responsible for it are already dead. We have to make that clear. Want me to handle it?"

"Good idea. Let's talk about that tonight. How about you bring your wife in for dinner? Just a private one for a change," the President suggested with a smile.

"I think Cathy would like that."

Professor Caroline Ryan was just finishing up a procedure. The atmosphere in the operating room was more akin to something in an electronics factory. She didn't even have to wear surgical gloves, and the scrub rules here were nothing like those for conventional surgery. The patient was only mildly sedated while the surgeon hovered over the gunsightlike controls of her laser, searching around for the last bad vessel on the surface of the elderly man's retina. She lined up the crosshairs as carefully as a man taking down a Rocky Mountain sheep from half a mile, and thumbed the control. There was a brief flash of green light and the vein was "welded" shut.

"Mr. Redding, that's it," she said quietly, touching his hand.

"Thank you, doctor," the man said somewhat sleepily.

Cathy Ryan flipped off the power switch on the laser system and got off her stool, stretching as she did so. In the corner of the room, Special Agent Andrea Price, still disguised as a Hopkins faculty member, had watched the entire procedure. The two women went outside to find Professor Bernard Katz, his eyes beaming over his Bismarck mustache.

"Yeah, Bernie?" Cathy said, making her notes for

1121

Mr. Redding's chart.

"You have room on the mantel, Cath?" *That* brought her eyes up. Katz handed over a telegram, still the traditional way of delivering such news. "You just bagged a Lasker Award, honey." Katz then delivered a hug that almost made Andrea Price reach for her gun.

"Oh, Bernie!"

"You earned it, doctor. Who knows, maybe you'll get a free trip to Sweden, too. Ten years of work. It's one hell of a clinical breakthrough, Cathy."

Other faculty members came up then, applauding and shaking her hand, and for Caroline Muller Ryan, M.D., F.A.C.S., it was a moment to match the arrival of a baby. *Well,* she thought, *almost. . . .*

Special Agent Price heard her beeper go off and headed to the nearest phone, taking the message down and returning to her principal.

"Is it really that good?" she finally asked.

"Well, it's about the top American award in medicine," Katz said while Cathy basked in the glow of respect from her colleagues. "You get a nice little copy of a Greek statue, the Winged Victory of Samothrace, I think, the Goddess Nike. Some money, too. But mainly what you get is the knowledge that you really made a difference. She's a great doc."

"Well, the timing is pretty good. I have to get her home and changed," Price confided.

"What for?"

"Dinner in the White House," the agent replied with a wink. "Her husband did a pretty good job, too." Just how good was a secret from nearly everyone, but not from the Service, from whom nothing was secret.

"Ambassador Whiting, I wish to apologize to you, to your government, and to your people for what has happened. I pledge to you that it will not happen again. I also pledge to you that the people responsible will answer to our law," Koga said with great if somewhat stiff dignity.

"Prime Minister, your word is sufficient to me and to my government. We will do the utmost to restore our relationship," the Ambassador promised, deeply moved by the sincerity of his host, and wishing, as many had, that America had not cut his legs out only six weeks earlier. "I will communicate your wishes to my government immediately. I believe that you will find our response to your position is highly favorable."

"I need your help," Yamata said urgently.

"What help is that?" Tracking down Zhang Han San had taken most of the day, and now the man's voice was as cold as his name.

"I can get my jet here, and from here I can fly directly to — "

"That could be viewed as an unfriendly act against two countries. No, I regret that my government cannot allow that." *Fool,* he didn't add. *Don't you know the price for this sort of failure?*

"But you — we are allies!"

"Allies in what?" Zhang inquired. "You are a businessman. I am a government official."

The conversation might have gone on with little point, but then the door to Yamata's office opened and General Tokikichi Arima came in, accompanied by two other officers. They hadn't troubled themselves to talk with the secretary in the anteroom.

"I need to speak with you, Yamata-san," the General said formally.

"I'll get back to you," the industrialist said into the phone. He hung up. He couldn't know that at the other end the official instructed his staff not to put the calls through. It would not have mattered in any case.

"Yes — what is it?" Yamata demanded. The reply was equally cold.

"I am ordered to place you under arrest."

"By whom?"

"By Prime Minister Koga himself."

"The charge?"

"Treason."

Yamata blinked hard. He looked around the room at the other men, now flanking the General. There was no sympathy in their eyes. So there it was. These mindless automatons had orders, but not the wit to understand them. But perhaps they still had honor.

"With your permission, I would like a few moments alone." The meaning of the request was clear.

"My orders," Arima said, "are to return you to Tokyo alive."

"But — "

"I am sorry, Yamata-san, but you are not to avail yourself of that form of escape." With that the General motioned to the junior officer, who took three steps and handcuffed the businessman. The coldness of the steel startled the industrialist.

"Tokikichi, you can't — "

"I must." It pained the General not to allow his . . . friend? No, they'd not been friends, not really. Even so it pained him not to allow Yamata to end his life by way of atonement, but the orders from the Prime Minister had been explicit on that score, and with that, he led the man from the building, off to the police station adjacent to his soon-to-be-vacated official quarters, where two men would keep an eye on him to prevent any attempt at suicide.

When the phone rang, it surprised everyone that it was *the* phone, and not Burroughs' satellite instrument. Isabel Oreza got it, expecting a call from work or something. Then she turned and called, "Mr. Clark?"

"Thank you." He took it. "Yes?"

"John, Mary Pat. Your mission is over. Come on home."

"Maintain cover?"

"Affirmative. Good job, John. Tell Ding the same thing." The line went dead. The DDO had already violated security in a major way, but the call had taken only a few seconds, and using the civilian line made it even more official than the covert sort could.

"What gives?" Portagee asked.

"We've just been ordered home."

"No shit?" Ding asked. Clark handed the phone over.

"Call the airport. Tell them that we're accredited newsies and we might just get a priority." Clark turned. "Portagee, could you do me a favor and forget you ever saw me?"

The signal was welcome though surprising. *Tennessee* immediately turned due east and increased speed to fifteen knots for the moment, staying deep. In the wardroom, the gathered officers were still joshing their Army guest, as was also happening with the enlisted men.

"We need a broom," the engineering officer said after some deep thought.

"Do we have one aboard?" Lieutenant Shaw asked.

"Every submarine is issued a broom, Mr. Shaw. You've been around long enough to know that," Commander Claggett observed with a wink.

"What are you guys talking about?" the Army officer asked. Were they jerking him around again?

"We took two shots and both were kills," the engineer explained. "That's a clean sweep, and that means when we enter Pearl, we have a broom tied to the number-one periscope. Tradition."

"You squids do the weirdest things," the lone man in green fatigues observed.

"Do we claim the helos?" Shaw asked his CO.

"We shot them down," the ground-pounder objected.

"But they flew off our deck!" the Lieutenant pointed out.

"Jesus!" All this over breakfast. What would the squids do for lunch?

The dinner was informal, up on the bedroom level of the White House, with what passed for a light buffet, albeit one cooked by a staff good enough to upgrade the rating of any restaurant in America.

"I understand congratulations are in order," Roger Durling said.

"Huh?" The National Security Advisor hadn't heard yet.

"Jack, I, uh, got the Lasker," Cathy said from her seat across the table.

"Well, that's two in your family who're the best around," Al Trent observed, saluting with his wineglass.

"And this one's for you, Jack," the President said, lifting his glass. "After all the grief I've gotten on foreign affairs, you've saved me, and you've saved a lot of other things. Well done, *Mister* Dr. Ryan."

Jack nodded at the toast, but this time he knew. He'd been around Washington long enough, finally, to hear the falling sandbag. The trouble was that he didn't know exactly why it was falling toward his head.

"Mr. President, the satisfaction comes from — well, from service, I guess. Thanks for trusting me, and thanks for putting up with me when I — "

"Jack, people like you, well, where would our country be?" Durling turned. "Cathy, do you know everything Jack has done over the years?"

"Jack? Tell me secrets?" She had a good laugh at that.

"Al?"

"Well, Cathy, it's time you learned," Trent observed, much to Jack's discomfort.

"There is one thing I've always wondered about," she said at once. "I mean, you two are so friendly, but the first time you two met several years ago, I — "

"The dinner, the one before Jack flew off to Moscow?" Trent took a sip of the California chardonnay. "That was when he set up the defection of the head of the old KGB."

"What?"

"Tell the story, Al, we have lots of time," Durling urged. His wife, Anne, leaned in to hear this one, too. Trent ended up speaking for twenty minutes, telling more than one old tale in the process despite the look on Jack's face.

"That's the sort of husband you have, Dr. Ryan," the President said when the stories were ended.

Jack looked over at Trent now, a rather intense stare. What was at the end of this?

"Jack, your country needs you for one last thing, and then we'll let you go," the Congressman said.

"What's that?" *Please, not an ambassadorship,* he thought, the usual kiss-off for a senior official.

Durling set his glass down. "Jack, my main job for the next nine months is to get reelected. It might be a tough campaign, and it's going to absorb a lot of my time under the best of circumstances. I need you on the team."

"Sir, I already am — "

"I want you to be my Vice President," Durling said calmly. The room got very quiet then. "The post is vacant as of today, as you know. I'm not sure yet who I want for my second term, and I am not suggesting that you fill the post for more than — what? Not even eleven months. Like Rockefeller did for Gerry Ford. I want somebody whom the public respects, somebody who can run the shop for me when

I'm away. I need somebody heavy in foreign affairs. I need somebody who can help me put my foreign-policy team together. And," he added, "I know you want out. You've done enough. And so, after this, you *can't* be called back for a permanent post."

"Wait a minute. I'm not even in your party," Jack managed to say.

"As the Constitution was originally drafted, the Vice President was supposed to be the loser in the general election. James Madison and the others assumed that patriotism would triumph over partisanship. Well, they were wrong," Durling allowed. "But in this case — Jack, I know you. I will not use you in a political sense. No speeches and baby-kissing."

"Never pick up a baby to kiss it," Trent said. "They always puke on you, and somebody always gets a picture. Always kiss the baby in the mom's arms." The good political advice was sufficient to lighten the atmosphere a little.

"Your job will be to get the White House organized, to manage national-security affairs, really to help me strengthen my foreign-policy team. And then I'll let you go and nobody will ever call you back. You'll be a free man, Jack," Durling promised. "Once and for all."

"My God," Cathy said.

"It's what you wanted, too, isn't it?"

Caroline nodded. "Yes, it is. But — but, I don't know anything about politics. I — "

"Lucky you," Anne Durling observed. "You won't have to get stuck with it."

"I have my work and — "

"And you'll still do it. A nice house comes along with the job," the President went on. "And it's temporary." He turned his head. "Well, Jack?"

"What makes you think that I can be confirmed — "

"Leave that to us," Trent said in a way that announced quite clearly that it had already been settled.

"You won't ask me to — "

"My word on it," the President promised. "Your obligation ends next January."

"What about — I mean, that makes me President of the Senate, and in the event of a close vote — "

"I suppose I ought to say that I'll tell you how I want you to vote, and I will, and I hope you'll listen, but I know you'll vote your conscience. I can live with that. As a matter of fact, if you were any other way, I wouldn't be making this offer."

"Besides, nothing on the schedule will be that close," Trent assured him. They'd talked that one over, too, the night before.

"I think we should pay more attention to the military," Jack said.

"If you make your recommendations, I'll incorporate them in the budget. You've taught me a lesson on that, and I may need you to help me hammer it through Congress. Maybe that will be your valedictory."

"They'll listen to you, Jack," Trent assured him.

Jesus, Ryan thought, wishing that he'd gone easier on the wine. Predictably he looked over to his wife. Their eyes met, and she nodded. *You sure?* his eyes asked. She nodded again.

"Mr. President, under the terms of your offer, and just to the end of your term, yes, I will do it."

Roger Durling motioned to a Secret Service agent, letting her know that Tish Brown could make the press release in time for the morning papers.

Oreza allowed himself to board his boat for the first time since Burroughs had landed his albacore. They left the pier at dawn, and by nightfall the engineer was able to conclude his fishing vacation with another sizable game fish before catching a Continental flight to Honolulu. His return to work would include more than a fish story, but he wouldn't mention the gear that the boat's skipper had dumped over the side as soon as they were out of sight of land. It was a shame to dump the cameras and the expensive lights, but he supposed there was some reason for it.

Clark and Chavez, still covered as Russians, managed to bully their way onto a JAL flight to Narita. On the way aboard they saw a well-dressed man in handcuffs with a military escort, and from twenty feet away, as they moved the man into the first-class cabin, Ding Chavez looked into the eyes of the man who had ordered the death of Kimberly Norton. He briefly wished for his light or a gun, or maybe even a knife, but that was not in the cards. The flight to Japan took just over two boring hours, and both men walked their carry-ons across the international terminal. They had first-class reservations on another JAL flight to Vancouver, and from there they would fly to Washington on an American carrier.

"Good evening," the Captain said first in Japanese, then in English. "This is Captain Sato. We expect this to be a smooth flight, and the winds are good for us. With luck we should be in Vancouver at about seven in the morning, local time." The voice sounded even more mechanical than the cheap ceiling speakers, but pilots liked talking like robots.

"Thank God," Chavez observed quietly in English. He did the mental arithmetic and decided that they'd be in Virginia around nine or ten in the evening.

"About right," Clark thought.

"I want to marry your daughter, Mr. C. I'm going to pop the question when I get back." There, he'd finally said it. The look his offhand remark generated made him cringe.

"Someday you'll know what words like that do to a man, Ding." *My little baby?* he thought, as vulnerable to the moment as any man, perhaps more so.

"Don't want a greaser in the family?"

"No, not that at all. It's more — oh, what the hell, Ding. Easier to spell Chavez than Wojohowitz. If it's okay with her, then I suppose it's okay with me."

That easy? "I expected you to bite my head off."

Clark allowed himself a chuckle. "No, I prefer guns for that sort of thing. I thought you knew that."

"The President could not have made a better selection," Sam Fellows said on "Good Morning, America." "I've known Jack Ryan for nearly eight years. He's one of the brightest people in government service. I can tell you now that he is one of the men most responsible for the rapid conclusion of hostilities with Japan, and was also instrumental in the recovery of the financial markets."

"There have been reports that his work at CIA — "

"You know that I am not free to reveal classified information." Those leaks would be handled by others, and the proper senators on both sides of the aisle were being briefed in this morning as well. "I can say that Dr. Ryan has served our country with the utmost personal honor. I cannot think of another intelligence official who has earned the trust and respect that Jack Ryan has."

"But ten years ago — the incident with the terrorists. Have we ever had a Vice President who actually — "

"Killed people?" Fellows shook his head at the reporter. "A lot of Presidents and Vice Presidents have been soldiers. Jack defended his family against a vicious and direct attack, like any American would. I can tell you that out where I live in Arizona, nobody would fault the man for that."

"Thanks, Sam," Ryan said, watching his office TV. The first wave of reporters was scheduled to assault him in thirty minutes, and he had to read over briefing materials, plus a sheet of instructions from Tish

Brown. Don't speak too fast. Don't give a direct answer to any substantive political question.

"I'm just glad to be here," Ryan said to himself. "I just play them one game at a time. Isn't that what they tell rookie ballplayers to say?" he wondered aloud.

The 747 touched down even earlier than the pilot had promised, which was fine but wouldn't help on the connecting flight. The good news for the moment was that the first-class passengers got off first, and better still, a U.S. consular official met Clark and Chavez at the gate, whisking them through customs. Both men had slept on the flight, but their bodies were still out of synch with the local time. An aging Delta L-1011 lifted off two hours later, bound for Dulles International.

Captain Sato remained in his command seat. One problem with international air travel was the sameness of it all. This terminal could have been almost anywhere, except that all of the faces were gaijin. There would be a day-long layover before he flew back, doubtless full again of Japanese executives running away.

And this was the remainder of his life, ferrying people he didn't know to places he didn't care about. If only he'd stayed in the Self-Defense Forces — maybe he would have done better, maybe it would have made a difference. He was the best pilot in one of the world's best airlines, and those skills might have . . . but he'd never know, would he, and he'd never make a difference, just one more captain of one more aircraft, flying people to and from a nation that had forfeited its honor. *Well.* He climbed out of his seat, collected his flight charts and other necessary papers, tucked them in his carry-bag and headed out of the aircraft. The gate was empty now, and he was able to walk down the bustling but anonymous terminal. He saw a copy of *USA Today* at a shop and picked it up, scanning the front page, seeing the pictures there. Tonight at nine o'clock? It all came together at that moment, really just an equation of speed and distance.

Sato looked around once more, then headed off to the airport administrative office. He needed a weather map. He already knew the timing.

"One thing I'd like to fix," Jack said, more at ease than ever in the Oval Office.

"What's that?"

"A CIA officer. He needs a pardon."

"What for?" Durling asked, wondering if a sandbag was descending toward his own head.

"Murder," Ryan replied honestly. "As luck would have it, my father worked the case back when I was in college. The people he killed had it coming — "

"Not a good way to look at things. Even if they did."

"They did." The Vice President–designate explained for two or three minutes. The magic word was "drugs," and soon enough the President nodded.

"And since then?"

"One of the best field officers we've ever had. He's the guy who bagged Qati and Ghosn in Mexico City."

"That's the guy?"

"Yes, sir. He deserves to get his name back."

"Okay. I'll call the Attorney General and see if we can do it quietly. Any other favors that you need taken care of?" the President asked. "You know, you're picking this political stuff up pretty fast for an amateur. Nice job with the media this morning, by the way."

Ryan nodded at the compliment. "Admiral Jackson. He did a nice job, too, but I suppose the Navy will take good care of him."

"A little presidential attention never hurt any

1133

officer's career. I want to meet him anyway. You're right, though. Flying into the islands to meet with them was a very astute move."

"No losses," Chambers said, and a lot of kills. Why didn't he feel good about that?
"The subs that killed *Charlotte* and *Asheville*?" Jones asked.
"We'll ask when the time comes, but probably at least one of them." The judgment was statistical but likely.
"Ron, good job," Mancuso said.
Jones stubbed out his cigarette. Now he'd have to break the habit again. And now, also, he understood what war was, and thanked God that he'd never really had to fight in one. Perhaps it was just something for kids to do. But he'd done his part, and now he knew, and with luck he'd never have to see one happen again. There were always whales to track.
"Thanks, Skipper."

"One of our 747s has mechanical'd rather badly," Sato explained. "It will be out of service for three days. I have to fly to Heathrow to replace the aircraft. Another 747 will replace mine on the Pacific run." With that he turned over the flight plan.
The Canadian air-traffic official scanned it. "Pax?"
"No passengers, no, but I'll need a full load of fuel."
"I expect your airline will pay for that, Captain," the official observed with a smile. He scribbled his approval on the flight plan, keeping one copy for his records, and gave the other back to the pilot. He gave the form a last look. "Southern routing? It's five hundred miles longer."
"I don't like the wind forecast," Sato lied. It wasn't much of a lie. People like this rarely second-guessed pilots on weather calls. This one didn't either.

"Thank you." The bureaucrat went back to his paperwork.

An hour later, Sato was standing under his aircraft. It was at an Air Canada service hangar — the space at the terminal was occupied again by another international carrier. He took his time preflighting the airliner, checking visually for fluid leaks, loose rivets, bad tires, any manner of irregularity — called "hangar rash" — but there was none to be seen. His copilot was already aboard, annoyed at the unscheduled flight they had to make, even though it meant three or four days in London, a city popular with international aircrew. Sato finished his walk-around and climbed aboard, stopping first at the forward galley.

"All ready?" he asked.

"Preflight checklist complete, standing by for before-start checklist," the man said just before the steak knife entered his chest. His eyes were wide with shock and surprise rather than pain.

"I'm very sorry to do this," Sato told him in a gentle voice. With that he strapped into the left seat and commenced the engine-start sequence. The ground crew was too far away to see into the cockpit, and couldn't know that only one man was alive on the flight deck.

"Vancouver tower, this is JAL ferry flight five-zero-zero, requesting clearance to taxi."

"Five-Zero-Zero Heavy, roger, you are cleared to taxi runway Two-Seven-Left. Winds are two-eight-zero at fifteen."

"Thank you, Vancouver, Five-Zero-Zero Heavy cleared for Two-Seven Left." With that the aircraft started rolling. It took ten minutes to reach the end of the departure runway. Sato had to wait an extra minute because the aircraft ahead of his was another 747, and they generated dangerous wake turbulence. He was about to violate the first rule of flight, the one about keeping your number of takeoffs equal to

1135

that for landings, but it was something his countrymen had done before. On clearance from the tower, Sato advanced the throttles to the takeoff power, and the Boeing, empty of everything but fuel, accelerated rapidly down the runway, rotating off before reaching six thousand feet, and immediately turning north to clear the controlled air space around the airport. The lightly loaded airliner positively rocketed to its cruising altitude of thirty-nine thousand feet, at which point fuel efficiency was optimum. His flight plan would take him along the Canadian-U.S. border, departing land just north of the fishing town of Hopedale. Soon after that, he'd be beyond ground-based radar coverage. Four hours, Sato thought, sipping tea while the autopilot flew the aircraft. He said a prayer for the man in the right seat, hoping that the copilot's soul would be at peace, as his now was.

The Delta flight landed at Dulles only a minute late. Clark and Chavez found that there was a car waiting for them. They took the official Ford and headed down to Interstate-64, while the driver who'd brought it caught a cab.

"What do you suppose will happen to him?"

"Yamata? Prison, maybe worse. Did you get a paper?" Clark asked.

"Yeah." Chavez unfolded it and scanned the front page. "Holy shit!"

"Huh?"

"Looks like Dr. Ryan's getting kicked upstairs." But Chavez had other things to think about for the drive down toward the Virginia Tidewater, like how he was going to ask Patsy the Big Question. What if she said no?

A joint session of Congress is always held in the House chamber due to its larger size, and also, members of the "lower" house noted, because in the Senate seats were reserved, and those bastards didn't let anyone else sit in *their* place. Security was usually good here. The Capitol building had its own police force, which was used to working with the Secret Service. Corridors were closed off with velvet ropes, and the uniformed officers were rather more alert than usual, but it wasn't that big a deal.

The President would travel to the Hill in his official car, which was heavily armored, accompanied by several Chevy Suburbans that were even more heavily protected, and loaded with Secret Service agents carrying enough weapons to fight off a company of Marines. It was rather like a traveling circus, really, and like people in the circus, they were always setting up and taking down. Four agents, for example, humped their Stinger missile containers to the roof, going to the customary spots, scanning the area to see if the trees had grown a little too much — they were trimmed periodically for better visibility. The Secret Service's Counter-Sniper Team took similar perches atop the Capitol and other nearby buildings. The best marksmen in the country, they lifted their custom-crafted 7mm Magnum rifles from foam-lined containers and used binoculars to scan the rooftops they didn't occupy. There were few enough of those, as other members of "the detail" took elevators and stairs to the top of every building close to the one JUMPER would be visiting tonight. When darkness fell, light-amplification equipment came out, and the agents drank hot liquids in order to keep alert.

Sato thanked Providence for the timing of the event, and for the TCAS System. Though the transatlantic air routes were never empty, travel between Europe and America was timed to coincide with human sleep patterns, and this time of day was slack for westbound flights. The TCAS sent out interrogation signals, and would alert him to the presence of nearby aircraft.

At the moment there was nothing close — his display said CLEAR OF CONFLICT, meaning that there was no traffic within eighty miles. That enabled him to slip into a west-bound routing quite easily, tracking down the coast, three hundred miles out. The pilot checked his time against his memorized flight plan. Again he'd figured the winds exactly right in both directions. His timing had to be exact, because the Americans could be very punctual. At 2030 hours, he turned west. He was tired now, having spent most of the last twenty-four hours in the air. There was rain on the American East Coast, and while that would make for a bumpy ride lower down, he was a pilot and hardly noticed such things. The only real annoyance was all the tea he'd drunk. He really needed to go to the head, but he couldn't leave the flight deck unattended, and there was less than an hour to endure the discomfort.

"Daddy, what does this mean? Do we still go to the same school?" Sally asked from the rear-facing seat in the limousine. Cathy handled the answer. It was a mommy-question.

"Yes, and you'll even have your own driver."

"Neat!" little Jack thought.

Their father was having second thoughts, as he usually did after making an important decision, even though he knew it was too late for that. Cathy looked at his face, read his mind, and smiled at him.

"Jack, it's only a few months, and then . . . ."

"Yeah." Her husband nodded. "I can always work on my golf game."

"And you can finally teach. That's what I want you to do. That's what you need to do."

"Not back to the banking business?"

"I'm surprised you lasted as long as you did in that."

"You're an eye-cutter, not a pshrink."

"We'll talk about it," Professor Ryan said, adjusting Katie Ryan's dress. It was the eleven-months part that appealed to her. After this post, he'd never come back to government service again. What a fine gift President Durling had given them both.

The official car stopped outside the Longworth House Office Building. There were no crowds there, though some congressional staffers were heading out of the building. Ten Secret Service agents kept an eye on them and everything else, while four more escorted the Ryans into the building. Al Trent was at the corner entrance.

"You want to come with me?"

"Why — "

"After you're confirmed, we walk you in to be sworn, and then you take your seat behind the President, next to the Speaker," Sam Fellows explained. "It was Tish Brown's idea. It'll look good."

"Election-year theatrics," Jack observed coolly.

"What about us?" Cathy asked.

"It's a nice family picture," Al thought.

"I don't know why I'm so darned excited about this," Fellows grumbled in his most good-natured way. "This is going to make November hard for us. I suppose that never occurred to you?"

"Sorry, Sam, no, it didn't," Jack replied with a sheepish grin.

"This hovel was my first office," Trent said, opening the door on the bottom floor to the suite of offices he'd used for ten terms. "I keep it for luck. Please — sit down and relax a little. One of his staffers came in with soft drinks and ice, under the watchful eyes of Ryan's protective detail. Andrea Price started playing with the Ryan kids again. It looked unprofessional but was not. The kids had to be comfortable around her, and she'd already made a good start at that.

President Durling's car arrived without incident.

Escorts conveyed him to the Speaker's official office adjacent to the chamber, where he went over his speech again. JASMINE, Mrs. Durling, with her own escorts, took an elevator to the official gallery. By this time the chamber was half-filled. It wasn't accepted for people to be fashionably late, perhaps the only such occasion for members of the Congress. They assembled in little knots of friends for the most part, and walked in by party, the seats divided by a very real if invisible line. The rest of the government would come in later. All nine justices of the Supreme Court, all members of the Cabinet who happened to be in town (two were not), and the Joint Chiefs of Staff in their beribboned uniforms were led to the front row. Then the heads of independent agencies. Bill Shaw of the FBI. The Chairman of the Federal Reserve. Finally, under the nervous eyes of security people and the usual gaggle of advance personnel, it was ready, on time, as it always seemed to happen.

The seven networks interrupted their various programming. Anchorpersons appeared to announce that the Presidential Address was about to begin, giving the viewers enough information that they could head off to the kitchen and make their sandwiches without really missing anything.

The Doorkeeper of the House, holder of one of the choicest patronage jobs in the country — a fine salary and no real duties — walked halfway down the aisle and performed his one public function with his customary booming voice:

"Mr. Speaker, the President of the United States."

Roger Durling entered the chamber, striding down the aisle with brief stops to shake hands, his red-leather folder tucked under his arm. It held a paper copy of his speech in the event that the Tele-PrompTers broke. The applause was deafening and sincere. Even those in the opposition party recognized that Durling had kept his promise to preserve, protect, and defend the Constitution of the United States, and as powerful a force as politics was, there was also still honor and patriotism in the room, especially at times like this. Durling reached the well, then climbed up to his place on the podium, and it was time for the Speaker of the House to do his ceremonial duty:

"Members of the Congress, I have the distinct privilege, and high honor, to introduce the President of the United States." And the applause began afresh. This time there was the usual contest between the parties to see who could clap and cheer the loudest and the longest.

"Okay, remember what happens — "

"Okay, Al! I go in, the Chief Justice swears me in, and I take my seat. All I have to do is repeat it all back." Ryan sipped a glass of Coke and wiped sweaty hands on his trousers. A Secret Service agent fetched him a towel.

"Washington Center, this is KLM Six-Five-Niner. We have an onboard emergency, sir." The voice was in clipped aviatorese, the sort of speech that people used when everything was going to hell.

The air-traffic controller outside Washington noted the alpha-numeric icon had just tripled in size on his scope and keyed his own microphone. The display gave course, speed, and altitude. His first impression was that the aircraft was making a rapid descent.

"Six-Five-Niner, this is Washington Center. State your intentions, sir."

"Center, Six-Five-Niner, number-one engine has exploded, engines one and two lost. Structural integrity in doubt. So is controllability. Request radar vector direct Baltimore."

The controller waved sharply to his supervisor, who came over at once.

1141

"Wait a minute. Who is this?" He interrogated the computer and found no "strip" information for KLM-659.

The controller keyed his radio. "Six-Five-Niner, please identify, over." This reply was more urgent.

"Washington Center, this is KLM-Six-Five-Niner, we are 747 charter inbound Orlando, three hundred pax," the voice replied. "Repeating: we have two engines out and structural damage to port wing and fuselage. I am descending one-zero thousand now. Request immediate radar vector direct Baltimore, over!"

"We can't dick around with this," the supervisor thought. "Take him. Get him down."

"Very well, sir. Six-Five-Niner Heavy. Radar contact. I read you one-four thousand descending and three hundred knots. Recommend left turn two-niner-zero and continue descent and maintain one-zero-thousand."

"Six-Five-Niner, descending one-zero thousand, turning left two-niner-zero," Sato said in reply. English was the language on international air travel, and his was excellent. So far so good. He had more than half of his fuel still aboard, and was barely a hundred miles out, according to his satellite-navigation system.

At Baltimore-Washington International Airport, the fire station located near the main terminal was immediately alerted. Airport employees who ordinarily had other jobs ran or drove to the building, while controllers decided quickly which aircraft they could continue to land before the wounded 747 got close and which they would have to stack. The emergency plan was already written here, as for every major airport. Police and other services were alerted, and literally hundreds of people were snatched away from TV sets.

★ ★ ★

"I want to tell you the story of an American citizen, the son of a police officer, a former Marine officer crippled in a training accident, a teacher of history, a member of America's financial community, a husband and father, a patriot and public servant, and a genuine American hero," the President said on the TV. Ryan cringed to hear it all, especially when followed by applause. The cameras panned over Secretary of the Treasury Fiedler, who had leaked Jack's role in the Wall Street recovery to a group of financial reporters. Even Brett Hanson was clapping, and rather graciously.

"It's always embarrassing, Jack," Trent said with a laugh.

"Many of you know him, many of you have worked with him. I have spoken today with the members of the Senate." Durling motioned to the Majority and Minority leaders, both of whom smiled and nodded for the C-SPAN cameras. "And with your approval, I wish now to submit the name of John Patrick Ryan to fill the post of Vice President of the United States. I further request the members of the Senate to approve this nomination tonight by voice vote."

"That's pretty irregular," a commentator observed while the two senators stood to walk down to the well.

"President Durling has done his homework well on this," the political expert replied. "Jack Ryan is about as noncontroversial as people can be in this town, and the bipartisan — "

"Mr. President, Mr. Speaker, members of the Senate, and our friends and colleagues of the House," the Majority Leader began. "It is with great satisfaction that the Minority Leader and I . . ."

1143

★ ★ ★

"Are we sure this is legal?" Jack wondered aloud.

"The Constitution says that the Senate has to approve you. It doesn't say how," Sam Fellows said.

"Baltimore Approach, this is Six-Five-Niner. I have a problem here."

"Six-Five-Niner Heavy, what is the problem, sir?" the tower controller asked. He could already see part of it on his scope. The inbound 747 hadn't turned to his most recent command as sharply as he had ordered a minute earlier. The controller wiped his hands together and wondered if they'd be able to get this one down.

"My controls are not responding well . . . not sure I can . . . Baltimore, I see runway lights at my one o'clock . . . I don't know this area well . . . busy here . . . losing power . . ."

The controller checked the direction vector on his scope, extending it to —

"Six-Five-Niner Heavy, that is Andrews Air Force Base. They have two nice runways. Can you make the turn for Andrews?"

"Six-Five-Niner, I think so, I think so."

"Stand by." The controller had a hot line to the Air Force base. "Andrews, do you — "

"We've been following it," the senior officer in that tower said. "Washington Center clued us in. Do you need help?"

"Can you take him?"

"Affirmative."

"Six-Five-Niner Heavy, Baltimore. I am going to hand you off to Andrews Approach. Recommend turn right three-five-zero . . . can you do that, sir?" the controller asked.

"I think I can, I think I can. The fire's out, I think, but hydraulics are bottoming out on me, I think the engine must have . . ."

"KLM-Six-Five-Niner Heavy, this is Andrews Approach Control. Radar Contact. Two-five miles out, heading three-four-zero at four thousand feet descending. Runway Zero-One-Left is clear, and our fire trucks are already moving," the Air Force captain said. He'd already punched the base panic button, and his trained people were moving out smartly. "Recommend turn right zero-one-zero and continue descent."

"Six-Five-Niner," was the only acknowledgment.

The irony of the situation was something Sato would never learn. Though there were numerous fighter aircraft based at Andrews, at Langley Air Force Base, at Patuxent River Naval Air Test Center, and at Oceana NAS, all within a hundred miles of Washington, it had never occurred to anyone to have fighter aircraft aloft over the capital on any other night like this one. His elaborate lies and maneuvers were hardly necessary at all. Sato brought his aircraft around at a painfully slow rate to simulate a crippled jumbo, coached every degree of the way by a very concerned and professional American controller. And that, he thought, was too bad.

"Aye!"

"Opposed?" There was silence after that, followed a moment later by applause. Then the Speaker stood.

"The Doorkeeper of the House will escort the Vice President into the chamber so that he can be properly sworn."

"That's your cue. Break a leg," Trent said, standing and heading for the door. The Secret Service agents fanned out along the corridor, leading the procession to the tunnel connecting this building with the Capitol. Entering it, Ryan looked along the curving structure, painted an awful off-yellow and lined, oddly enough, mostly with pictures done by schoolchildren.

"I don't see any obvious problem, no smoke or fire." The tower controller had his binoculars on the incoming aircraft. It was only a mile out now. "No gear, no gear!"

"Six-Five-Niner, your gear is up, say again your gear is up!"

Sato could have replied, but chose not to. It was really all decided now. He advanced his throttles, accelerating his aircraft up from approach speed of one-hundred-sixty knots, holding to his altitude of one thousand feet for the moment. The target was in view now, and all he had to do was turn forty degrees left. On reflection, he lit up his aircraft, displaying the red crane on the rudder fin.

"What the hell is he doing?"

"That's not KLM! Look!" the junior officer pointed. Directly over the field, the 747 banked left, clearly under precise control, all four engines whining with increased power. Then the two looked at each other, knowing exactly what was going to happen, and knowing that there was literally nothing that could be done. Calling the base commander was just a formality that would not affect events at all. They did that anyway, then alerted the First Helicopter Squadron as well. With that, they ran out of options, and turned to watch the drama whose conclusion they'd already guessed. It would take a little over a minute to conclude.

Sato had been to Washington often and done all the usual tourist things, including visiting the Capitol Building more than once. It was a grotesque piece of architecture, he thought again, as it grew larger and larger, and he adjusted his flight path so that he was now roaring right up Pennsylvania Avenue, crossing the Anacostia River.

The sight was sufficiently stunning that it momentarily paralyzed the Secret Service agent standing atop the House Chamber, but it was only a moment, and ultimately meaningless. The man dropped to his knees and flipped the cover off the large plastic box.

"Get JUMPER moving! Now!" the man screamed, taking out the Stinger.

"Let's go!" an agent shouted into his microphone, loudly enough to hurt the ears of the protective detail inside. A simple phrase, for the Secret Service it meant to get the President away from wherever he was. Instantly, agents as finely trained as any NFL backfield started moving even though they had no idea what the danger was. In the gallery over the chamber, the First Lady's detail had a shorter distance to go, and though one of the agents tripped on the step, she was able to grab Anne Durling's arm and start dragging her away.

"What?" Andrea Price was the only one to speak in the tunnel. The rest of the agents around the Ryan family instantly drew their weapons, pistols for the most part, though two of their number pulled out submachine guns. All of them brought their weapons up and scanned the yellow-white corridor for danger, but there was none to be seen.

"Clear!"

"Clear!"

"Clear!"

On the floor of the chamber, six men raced to the podium, also scanning about with drawn weapons in a moment that millions of television viewers would fix in their minds forever. President Durling looked at his chief agent in genuine puzzlement, only to hear a screamed entreaty to move at once.

The Stinger agent atop the building had his weapon shouldered in record time, and the beeping from the missile tracker told him that he had acquisition. Not a second later he loosed his shot, knowing even then that it didn't matter a damn.

Ding Chavez was sitting on the couch, holding Patsy's hand — the one with the ring now on it — until he saw the people with guns. The soldier he would always be leaned into the TV to look for danger, but seeing none, he knew that it was there even so.

The streak of light startled Sato, and he flinched somewhat from surprise rather than fear, then saw the missile heading for his left-inboard engine. The explosion was surprisingly loud, and alarms told him that the engine was totally destroyed, but he was a mere thousand meters away from the white building. The aircraft dipped and yawed slightly to the left. Sato compensated for it without a thought, adjusting trim and nosing down for the south side of the American house of government. They would all be there. The President, the parliamentarians, all of them. He selected his point of impact just as finely as any routine landing, and his last thought was that if they could kill his family and disgrace his country, then they would pay a very special price for that. His last voluntary act was to select the point of impact, two thirds of the way up the stone steps. That would be just about perfect, he knew . . .

Nearly three hundred tons of aircraft and fuel struck the east face of the building at a speed of three hundred knots. The aircraft disintegrated on impact. No less fragile than a bird, its speed and mass had already fragmented the columns outside the walls. Next came the building itself. As soon as the wings broke up, the engines, the only really solid objects on the aircraft, shot forward, one of them actually smashing into and beyond the House Chamber. The Capitol has no structural steel within its stone walls, having been built in an age when stone piled on stone was deemed the most long-lasting form of construction. The entire east face of the building's southern half was smashed to gravel, which shot westward — but the real damage took a second or two more, barely time for the roof to start falling down on the nine hundred people in the chamber: one hundred tons of jet fuel erupted from shredded fuel tanks, vaporizing from the passage through the stone blocks. A second later it ignited from some spark or other, and an immense fireball engulfed everything inside and outside of the building. The volcanic flames reached out, seeking air and corridors that held it, forcing a pressure wave throughout the building, even into the basement.

The initial impact was enough to drop them all to their knees, and now the Secret Service agents were on the edge of real panic. Ryan's first instinctive move was to grab his youngest daughter, then to push the rest of the family to the floor and cover them with his body. He was barely down when something made him look back, north up the tunnel. The noise came from there, and a second later there was an advancing orange wall of flame. There was not even time to speak. He pushed his wife's head down, and then two more bodies fell on top to cover them. There wasn't time for anything else but to look back at the advancing flames —

— over their heads, the fireball had already exhausted the supply of oxygen. The mushrooming cloud leaped upwards, creating its own ministorm and sucking air and gas out of the building whose occupants it had already killed —

— it stopped, not a hundred feet away, then pulled away as rapidly as it had advanced, and there was an instant hurricane in the tunnel, going the other way. A door was wrenched off its hinges, sliding toward them but missing. His little Katie screamed with terror and pain at all the weight on her. Cathy's eyes were wide, looking at her husband.

"Let's go!" Andrea Price screamed before anyone else, and with that, the agents lifted every member of the family, carrying-dragging them back to the Longworth Building, leaving the two House members to catch up on their own. That required less than a minute, and then Special Agent Price was the first again:

"Mr. President, are you okay?"

"What the hell . . ." Ryan looked around, moving to his kids. Their clothing was disheveled but they seemed otherwise intact. "Cathy?"

"I'm okay, Jack." She checked the children next, as she had once done for him in London. "They're okay, Jack. You?" There was a thundering crash that made the ground shake, and again Katie Ryan screamed.

"Price to Walker," the female agent said into her microphone. "Price to Walker — anybody, check in now!"

"Price, this is LONG RIFLE THREE, it's all gone, man, the dome just went down, too. Is SWORDSMAN okay?"

"What the hell was that?" Sam Fellows gasped from his knees. Price didn't have time even to hear the question.

"Affirmative, affirmative, SWORDSMAN, SURGEON, and — shit, we don't have names for them yet. The kids are — everybody's okay here." Even she knew that was an exaggeration. Air was still racing past them into the tunnel to feed the flames in the Capitol building.

The agents were recovering their composure somewhat now. Their guns were still out, and had so much as a janitor appeared in the corridor right then, his life might have been forfeit, but one by one they breathed deeply and relaxed just a little, at the same time trying to focus in on what they had been trained to do.

"This way!" Price said, leading with her pistol in both hands. "RIFLE THREE, get a car to the southeast corner of Longworth — and do it now!"

"Roger."

"Billy, Frank, take point!" Price commanded next. Jack hadn't thought she was the senior agent on the detail, but the two male agents weren't arguing. They sprinted ahead to the end of the corridor. Trent and Fellows just watched, waving the others on their way.

"Clear!" the one with the Uzi said at the far end of the corridor.

"Are you okay, Mr. President?"

"Wait a minute, what about — "

"JUMPER is dead," Price said simply. The other agents had heard the same radio chatter and had formed a very tight ring around their principal. Ryan had not and was still disoriented and trying to catch up.

"We have a Suburban outside!" Frank called. "Let's go!"

"Okay, sir, the drill is to get you the hell away from here. Please follow me," Andrea Price said, lowering her weapon just a little.

"Wait, now wait a minute, what are you saying? The President, Helen — "

"RIFLE THREE, this is Price. Anybody get out?"

"No chance, Price. No chance," the sniper replied.

"Mr. President, we have to get you to a place of safety. Follow me, please."

It turned out that there were two of the oversized vehicles. Jack was forcibly separated from his family and pushed into the first one.

"What about my family?" he demanded, now seeing the orange pyre that had been the centerpiece of America's government only four minutes earlier.

"Oh, my God . . ."

"We'll take them to — to — "

"Take them to the Marine Barracks at Eighth and I streets. I want Marines around them now, okay?" Later, Ryan would remember that his first presidential order was something from his own past.

"Yes, sir." Price keyed her mike. "SURGEON and kids go to Eighth and I. Tell the Marines they're coming!"

His vehicle just headed down New Jersey Avenue, away from the Hill, Ryan saw, and for all their sophisticated training the Secret Service people were mainly trying to clear the area.

"Come around north," Jack told them.

"Sir, the White House — "

"A place with TVs, and right now. I think we need a judge, too." That idea didn't come from reason or analysis, Jack realized. It just came.

The Chevy Suburban headed well west before turning north and looping back toward Union Station. The streets were alive now with police and fire vehicles. Air Force helicopters from Andrews were circling overhead, probably to keep news choppers away. Ryan got out of the car under his own power and walked within his protective ring to the entrance of the building where CNN operated. It was just the closest. More agents were arriving now, enough that Ryan actually felt safe, knowing how foolish that feeling was. He was taken upstairs to a holding room until another agent arrived with someone else a few minutes later.

"This is Judge Peter Johnson, D.C. Federal Court," an agent told Jack.

"Is this what I think?" the judge asked.

"I'm afraid so, sir. I'm not a lawyer. Is this legal?" the President asked.

Again it was Agent Price: "President Coolidge was sworn by his father, a county justice of the peace.

1152

It's legal," she assured both men.

A camera came close. Ryan put his hand on the Bible, and the judge went from memory.

"I — state your name, please."

"I, John Patrick Ryan — "

"Do solemnly swear that I will faithfully execute the office of President of the United States."

"Do solemnly swear that I will faithfully execute the office of President of the United States . . . and will to the best of my ability, preserve, protect, and defend the Constitution of the United States, so help me God." Jack completed the oath from memory. It was little different, really, from the one he had sworn as a Marine officer, and it meant the same thing.

"You hardly needed me at all," Johnson said quietly. "Congratulations, Mr. President." To both men it seemed an odd thing to say, but Ryan took his hand anyway. "God bless you."

Jack looked around the room. Out the windows he could see the fires on the Hill. Then he turned back to the camera, for beyond it were millions, and like it or not, they were looking back at him, and to him. Ryan took a breath, not knowing that his tie was crooked in his collar.

"Ladies and gentlemen, what happened tonight was an attempt by someone to destroy the government of the United States. They killed President Durling, and I guess they killed most of the Congress — it's too soon, I'm afraid, to be sure of much.

"But I am sure of this: America is much harder to destroy than people are. My dad was a cop, as you heard. He and my mom were killed in a plane crash, but there are still cops. A lot of fine people were killed only a few minutes ago, but America is still here. We've fought another war and won it. We've survived an attack on our economy and we'll survive this too.

"I'm afraid I'm too new at this to say it properly, but what I learned in school is that America is a dream, it's — it's the ideas we all share, it's the things we all believe in, most of all it's things we all do, and how we do them. You can't destroy things like that. Nobody can, no matter how hard they might try, because we are who and what we choose to be. We invented that idea here, and nobody can destroy that either.

"I'm not really sure what I'm going to do right now, except to make sure my wife and children are really safe first, but now I have this job, and I just promised God that I'd do it the best way I can. For now, I ask you all for your prayers and your help. I'll talk to you again when I know a little more. You can turn the camera off now," he concluded. When the light went off, he turned to Special Agent Price.

"Let's get to work."